The Black Pearl is one ~~...~~ fascinating accounts of one man's 'secret' erotic life ever to emerge from the late-Victorian and Edwardian age of public morality (or, at any rate, public moralizing) and private sexual excess. The title indicates that the anonymous author was influenced by that classical journal of 19th century erotica, *The Pearl*, and there is much of *The Pearl's* flavour of outspoken rebellion against the official prudery of the time in these uninhibited memoirs.

But there are intriguing additional dimensions to the writings of 'Horby' (the pseudonym adopted by the author of *The Black Pearl* to disguise – very effectively so – his true identity). It is clear that the financial freedom that his independent income gave him, together with his aristocratic status, allowed him access to the inner circles of the artistic and occult world of his time.

The Black Pearl Anthology II: The Memoirs of a Victorian Sex-Magician

Anonymous

NEW ENGLISH LIBRARY
Hodder & Stoughton

Black Pearl Volume Three Copyright © 1995 by Hodder and Stoughton
Black Pearl Volume Four Copyright © 1999 by Hodder and Stoughton

This collected volume published in paperback in 2001
by Hodder and Stoughton
A division of Hodder Headline

A NEL Paperback

10 9 8 7 6 5 4 3 2 1

A CIP catalogue record for this title
is available from the British Library.

ISBN 0 340 73333 0

Printed and bound in Great Britain by
Mackays of Chatham PLC, Chatham, Kent

Hodder and Stoughton
A division of Hodder Headline
338 Euston Road
London NW1 3BH

The Black Pearl Volume Three

PUBLISHER'S FOREWORD

The Black Pearl: The Memoirs of a Victorian Sex-Magician is a legendary classic of Victorian underground writing. Although the identity of the author presently remains unknown, it is clear from the text that he was a member of the aristocracy who knew all the leading figures of his age, both male and female. This eminently respectable figure obviously enjoyed the hidden and lascivious side of high life in his time: and he was also drawn to low-life. As such, we have a unique portrayal of the undertones of life in the 1890s and after.

His title obviously indicates that he was influenced by that classic journal of Victorian erotica, THE PEARL. The date of composition cannot be ascribed with exactitude though the text indicates that the author was recalling events some years after their happenstance. The edition discovered by Dr Geraldine Lamb, the editor, indicates on the publishers' notes opposite the title page that this work was privately printed in an edition of 156 copies by Van den Haagen of Amsterdam, 1925. It was set in 12pt Bembo, 1 pt leaded, printed on Japanese paper, crown quarto in size, bound in black buckram, with gold-stamped lettering which has led some bibliophiles to identify the latter work as that of Spalding & Hodge of London.

This book is of value to the sociologist, the psychologist,

1

the historian, those fascinated by literary anecdotes and political tales by a man who knew personally all those of whom he speaks; and above all to those who find in the study of human sexuality, a key to human nature.

EDITOR'S PREFACE
TO VOLUME I

It is not often that one comes upon a classic of Victorian erotica whose very existence is a matter of speculation and rumour. Much Victorian erotica was written by debauched aristocrats in their leisure hours, then privately printed for presentation to friends. Some of these works were issued during the 1890s by the drug-addicted publisher, Leonard Smithers, who also published works of genuine literature by Oscar Wilde and works of art by Aubrey Beardsley. Others were not set, bound, printed and presented until many years later in order to protect both the name of the author and the reputations of those he mentioned.

Such is the case with *The Black Pearl: The Memoirs of a Victorian Sex-Magician*. If the publisher's notation can be trusted, it was not issued until 1925 and then only in a strictly limited edition. I came upon it in a curious way.

Following on from my B.A. at Cambridge, I went on to pursue M.A. studies at Harvard and it was there that I found myself debating issues of sexuality with distinguished men and women such as Norman Mailer and Dr Camille Paglia. Although both of them appeared to venerate the penis, they both seemed to see it as a tool of vengeance. Both, however, in their separate ways, seemed to be committed to the idea that human evolution could be advanced by sexuality. I was discerning a similar ideal in the poetry of England's Fiona Pitt-Kethley.

My essay *The Penis: Tool of Vengeance or Tool of Love? An Exploration of Socio-Phallicism* was eventually printed (1992) in *The New Rationalist*, published out of Harvard. I received a number of letters on account of it, some of them dismally predictable, but one, at least, was extraordinarily interesting. This was from an English baronet who has insisted that he remain anonymous. After a lengthy correspondence, he invited me to his castle, where he was a kind, courteous and considerate host.

It was during my stay that he showed me a copy of THE BLACK PEARL. I was absolutely astonished by this work. Most pieces of Victorian erotic writing show us simply the sleazy tenderloin of the repressed sexuality of that time. We get certain insights and there is entertaining rebellion against prevailing official mores but precious little more, even when the descriptions of the sexual encounters themselves are very well-written. Yet here was a rake who came to perceive sexuality as the holiest truth between man and woman – and as a way of advancing human consciousness.

In the text, he was at first simply a man of late middle-age recalling his youthful sexual exploits. He was reminiscing too about his encounters with celebrities such as Oscar Wilde, Lillie Langtry, Bernard Shaw, Ellen Terry, Frank Harris and Mrs Bram Stoker, among so many others. Yet he was also searching for something more and ventured into the many esoteric orders of his time such as the Hermetic Order of the Golden Dawn, the German Ordo Templi Orientis, the American Female Flagellants of New York, the Temple of the Smokers of the Sacred and numerous others. It was clear to me that in the course of his curious quest, he had become learned in many arcane techniques of expanding consciousness, which he refers to in the text as both 'Magick' and 'Mysticism'. There was much too about the use of plants and minerals to achieve a state he calls 'ecstasy'.

Who was he? My host refused to tell me, other than to state that he was the friend of a distant elderly cousin. In the text he makes it clear that he was an independently rich Viscount with access to both the rich and the poor – and the middle classes. The memories he records of his contemporaries have the ring of truth and yet it is so far impossible to identify him. My host showed me a stack of papers which had passed into the hands of the family. From these it is obvious that he chose to operate under the pseudonym of 'Horby'.

'I see that boys and "feasting with panthers" are not to your taste, Horby,' reads a scribbled card from Oscar Wilde, adding: 'but hock and seltzer should be. Do delight me at the Cadogan, 1.00, Tuesday.' The following telegram is obvious: 'LUNCHEON STOP TWO CAFE ROYAL STOP BE THERE HORBY STOP FRANK HARRIS'. Harris was then Editor of *The Saturday Review* and one of the most influential literary figures in London. Another telegram: 'SORRY CANT AND WONT STOP GBS' is obviously (and typically) from Bernard Shaw. 'Glad you appreciate poetry, Horby, but there's more to it than that,' is the inscription in the author's handwriting on Aleister Crowley's WHITE STAINS, which was privately printed (1898) and which has subsequently been criticised for its scandalous obscenity. A copy of the 1895 John Lane, The Bodley Head edition of *The Great God Pan* contains the following message by its author, Arthur Machen: 'Come to wine on Wednesday rather than to whine. And then you too, Horby, can sample the Jar of Avallaunius.' 'Absinthe any time, so get in touch, Horby, be pleased to hear from you, John Davidson,' are the drunkenly scrawled words on another bespattered postcard. 'Horby' must have stayed in touch with some of his old friends from the Nineties, for in this collection I discovered a 1921 edition, published in New York, of *Oscar Wilde: His Life and Confessions* by Frank Harris with the inscription: 'Horby, you old rogue! Don't forget your old friends! And don't you miss those glad, erect days!? – Frank Harris.'

Unfortunately for the researcher, there are no compromising documents from identifiable women. One assumes that either Horby or his family destroyed any letters of this nature. However, there are some perfectly proper signed photographs of beautiful and fully-dressed celebrities of the Nineties, such as Lillie Langtry, Ellen Terry, Florence Farr and Florence Balcombe. Lillie Langtry was, of course, the leading courtesan of her age and was for a time the mistress of the Prince of Wales. Ellen Terry was the leading actress of her era and was celebrated most in her role of Lady Macbeth. Florence Farr, a leading actress and dramatist, was also the lover of men such as Bernard Shaw, William Butler Yeats and Aleister Crowley. Oscar Wilde wanted to marry Florence Balcombe on account of her exceptional physical beauty but she spurned him in favour of Bram Stoker, author of *Dracula*. On the back of each one of these photographs, erasures have been made.

There is no doubt whatsoever in my mind that *The Black Pearl* should be published in the 1990s, giving us a quite unique insight into the 1890s. For my own part, I am still tracking down clues which will lend insight into this remarkable author. He has given us a document of great human interest which spans the academic disciplines of sociology, psychology, history, literature and sexology. It will surprise and possibly shock those who have a clichéd view of Victorian attitudes. It certainly lifts the manhole cover off a steaming underworld. The author explores every facet of his own sexuality and that of those he encounters. At times his interests are simply those of dissipation and debauchery. At other moments he relates the strange kinks of those he meets, which embroider the rich tapestry of human sexuality. For me, however, the most remarkable feature of this book is that its aristocratic Victorian author, outwardly a veritable pillar of the Establishment, comes to look upon sex as the holiest sacramental act in the known Universe.

Geraldine Lamb PhD.,
University of North Texas.

EDITOR'S PREFACE
TO VOLUME II

For those who have not had the good fortune to study Volume I of *The Black Pearl*: the *Memoirs of a Victorian Sex-Magician*, a few words of explanation are assuredly in order for the approach to Volume II.

In Volume I, Horby reveals that he has inherited a Viscouncy, lands, possessions, an income from the funds of £100,000 a year 'on which a man can just about jog along these days' and letters of introduction to some of the most famous and infamous men and women of his time. He is initiated into sex by his extraordinary governess, Rosemary Radcliffe, who tutors him towards a place at Trinity College, Cambridge 1895–98. Rosemary is about ten years older and plays a prominent part in the *Memoirs*. So does the Hon. Claire Woodrough, a distant cousin he seduces when they are both in their teens and with whom he cultivates a lasting relationship. Both Rosemary and Claire, the true identity of whom diligent enquiry has hitherto failed to discover, continue to write Horby astonishingly frank letters about their manifold adventures and sexual experiences.

Horby encounters literary London, wining and dining at the Café Royale in the company of Frank Harris, Oscar Wilde, Bernard Shaw, Aubrey Beardsley, Whistler, Dégas, beautiful women and variously assorted rich drunkards. At Cambridge University he meets fellow undergraduate Aleister Crowley, poet, mountaineer and seeker after the spirit, later to be reviled in the tabloid press as 'the wickedest man in the world.' On coming down from Cambridge, he leads the life of a London man-about-town, purchasing his pornography from Leonard Smithers and discussing sex with Arthur Machen, Aleister Crowley, Ellen Terry, Mr & Mrs Bram Stoker, Bob Fitzsimmons (the Heavyweight Boxing Champion of the World), the Marquis of Queensberry, Lillie Langtry, Florence Farr and H.G. Wells, among others.

During this time, Horby proceeds to enjoy a bewildering variety of sexual experiences, both as practitioner and as voyeur. The text shows that his primary taste is for straight heterosexuality, though he clearly enjoys cunnilingus and fellatio and, on occasion, sodomy with a female and the spanking of her buttocks. On two occasions, he is bound by rapacious females wholly unexpectedly, and although the experiences excite him, he does not volunteer for them again. Indeed, when he is caned against his wish, he exacts a rapacious revenge upon the two lady perpetrators of this outrage to his manhood. Even so, he enjoys the sight of the birch being applied by women to the blushing bottoms of both males and females.

The features which distinguish this work from other pieces of Victorian erotica include an obvious love of women, however absurd some of Horby's attitudes may strike the contemporary reader as being. He loves the sight or the description of two beautiful women enraptured in the act of lesbian lust. He regards his journeys through salons, restaurants, music halls, clubs, pubs, cafés, brothels and strictly private houses as being not just a spelunking in debauchery but as a quest for the Holy Grail. He equates this Holy Grail with an ecstasy to be found within the vagina of a woman.

All the while, his perception that sex can be the holiest and most sacred ecstatic religious sacrament in the Universe is being augmented and refined by the letters he receives from Rosemary and Claire. He confesses that these do more for him than the secret magical society which he has joined, The Hermetic Order of the Golden Dawn. Rosemary, whose health appears to be erratic, enjoys erotic episodes in Brighton, Wales and Whitby, where she meets the mysterious and cadaverous 'Black Douglas', an international banker and an expert on vampirism: this intrigues Rosemary, who is a West Country hereditary witch, and she becomes his mistress. Claire, meanwhile, experiences the delights of both satanism and Rosicrucianism in Paris, then continues to Vienna for psycho-analysis with Dr Sigmund Freud and an intriguing affair with the Arch-Duke of the Austro-Hungarian Empire, Francis-Ferdinand.

Horby becomes friends with one Sir Richard Bellingham, Bart. Although to all outward appearances Bellingham is a buffoon, he has a good heart and welcomes every manner and mode of sexual and culinary experience, rejoicing in rhy.ne and bawdry. Horby has obviously thoroughly disguised the identity of this unashamedly scandalous gentleman since close enquiry has been unable to identify him.

After enjoying a wide variety of women, including 'the World's most beautiful woman', Lillie Langtry, mistress of the Prince of Wales – done for a bet with the aid of a phial of love potion made according to Rosemary's instructions – Horby takes the heiress and daughter of a senior clergyman, Emily Ward-Bishop, to a croquet contest with Rosemary and the enigmatic Douglas at £10,000 a side. Horby loses, Emily is spanked and stood in a corner for poor play, Rosemary relates her tale of performing fellatio upon the future King Edward VII beneath his dining table, Horby wins back his money on a bet concerning the true meaning of the word 'SNOB', sex is relished by the two couples and Douglas invites Horby and Emily to his castle near Vienna to witness a Sex Magick ritual.

Joined by Sir Richard Bellingham and a former mistress of Crowley, Horby and Emily embark on the Golden Arrow from London to Paris on a train chartered by Douglas and Rosemary. It's then Wagons-Lit carriages on a train to Vienna, chartered by Douglas, as these three couples fornicate their way across Europe. The *Memoirs* imply that this is well worth their while for they witness a solemn low mass of Sex Magick, wherein Douglas is the Priest, Rosemary the High Priestess, and Claire and Arch-Duke Francis Ferdinand are their Assistants. Horby is possessed by a trance of ecstasy but calls this 'only the end of the beginning of my sexual education.'

One can only exhort the keen student of Psychology, History, Literature and Sociology to turn to Volume I* in order fully to comprehend the sensibility with which he commences the second volume, which must surely be numbered among the most interesting documents of the period.

Geraldine Lamb PhD.,
University of California San Diego.

---

* Published in paperback by the New English Library.

EDITOR'S PREFACE TO VOLUME III

Some words of explanation are in order for those unfortunate enough not to have read Volumes I and II of *The
Black Pearl: Memoirs of a Victorian Sex-Magician*.[*]

In Volume II, Horby continues to enjoy London life,
seducing a suffragette he meets at a party hosted by
Sydney and Beatrice Webb; attending the Rhymers' Club
of Johnson, Davidson and Dowson; visiting brothels and
exploring all sorts of occult societies. As a member of the
Hermetic Order of the Golden Dawn, he supplies us with
his own unique perspective on the quarrels between its
leader, 'MacGregor' Mathers, William Butler Yeats and
his curious friend, Aleister Crowley. With John Davidson,
he visits the East End, smokes opium with The Smokers
of the Sacred then returns to the West End to pass the
evening at a strictly private club of flagellation confined to
the nobility, the aristocracy, the gentry and all others who
can pay its extortionate sums. He eats and drinks with
Shaw, Wells, Chesterton, Belloc and Arthur Machen,
recording their views on sex and society.

He visits New York twice. On the first occasion it is to
witness the World Heavyweight Boxing Championship
followed by a night with a secret society known as The
Beautiful Female Flagellants of New York. On the

[*] Published in paperback by New English Library.

second, his adventures include an evening with Butch Cassidy and the Sundance Kid, along with their 'Wild Bunch.' He continues to fornicate relentlessly. On his ocean crossing, he learns much about gambling from Arnold Rothstein, future banker to the New York Underworld.

Horby enjoys a wide variety of acquaintanceship. There is Robert Ross in Paris, Frank Harris in Monaco, James McNeill Whistler in Venice; and Prime Minister Lord Salisbury with his nephew and successor, Arthur Balfour, at an English country weekend where the issues of the day are decided. He becomes involved in espionage, epitomising the English ideal of the gentleman amateur, and in Berlin encounters the intriguing international spy 'Maria', whom he will later meet in both London and Paris. He is also initiated by German sex-magicians into the Ordo Templi Orientis (OTO) which practises sex for the enhancement of consciousness though the narrator already knows this from previous experience. Back in London, he sees the humiliation of a woman by a man; then hears of the humiliation of a man by a woman. He crosses to Paris for the wedding of his old friend, Sir Richard Bellingham, and finds the links of that occasion with secret societies which enshrine the act of sex to be quite astonishing.

Bellingham plays a prominent part in these *Memoirs*, though further research has still not elicited his true identity. Nor has diligent enquiry managed to discover the name of his bride, given in the text as Mrs Davina Price-Hughes, a wealthy widow apparently worth between one and ten million pounds sterling. Nor does the text make it clear whether Bellingham is merely a fortunately-born buffoon or a holy and divine Fool in an obscure English medieval tradition, as portrayed in Tudor times by Shakespeare when writing of Falstaff.

Other prominent characters continue to elude close scrutiny of their true identities. Horby's former governess, Rosemary, High Priestess of this secret cult, continues to write him explicit letters from Istanbul, Vienna, Venice and Paris, making love with him whenever there is an opportunity to meet independently; though some of her liaisons are outrageous. The same can be said of the Hon. Claire Woodrough, another pupil of Rosemary and Horby's first young love. She journeys to New York, New Orleans and San Francisco, encountering characters as diverse as Scott Joplin, Harry Houdini, William Randolph Hearst, Ambrose Bierce and Buffalo Bill, and learns more of the mysteries of Voodoo. She is a Priestess of this secret cult and joins Rosemary and Horby in Paris for Bellingham's astounding Wedding Reception.

The names of those who appear to witness Sir Richard Bellingham's Wedding Reception in a Paris Temple have obviously been put in a code understood only by the select few to which *The Black Pearl* would be distributed privately. An especially mysterious figure is the man Horby calls 'the Black Douglas', a fabulously wealthy international banker who has Rosemary as his mistress, among many other women; who dines with the Prime Minister of England to discuss international affairs; and who is also the High Priest of the cult of enlightenment via sexuality.

There are three more men of mystery: Ram Singh, a Priest at Bellingham's wedding, has invited Claire to his ashram. 'Pierre', a very strange figure who has witnessed the lesbian activities of Rosemary and Claire, plays the peculiar role of The Monk at Bellingham's reception-come-orgy. The unpleasant Viscount Maulerby arouses a repulsion that is justified fully in the foregoing.

The intriguing Mrs Joan Smythe continues to intrude upon the narrative as the Queen of flagellation and female domination, managing a variety of sado-masochistic schemes such as The Female Flagellants of New York, The Smythe Reform Academy and the Society for the Promulgation of Petticoat Government. One Miss Emily Ward-Bishop is enthused by these pursuits; although she also relishes the pleasures of receiving chastisement from a man and to judge by the text, would like to marry Horby, a fact angrily deplored by Claire Woodrough.

'The Black Douglas' is somewhat sadistic in his treatment of women, though they do not appear to object, and, from the text, he appears to be on excellent terms with four beautiful and unusual young ladies: Lady Alison Utley and Lady Jane Fortescue, mistresses to the wealthy and powerful who enjoy their own peculiar perversities: and Lady Candida Lauderdale and Miss Amelia Edwards, an actress, friends of Bellingham's bride, the former Mrs Davina Price-Hughes, former mistresses of Aleister Crowley – in common with their friend – and both of them ensnared by a desire for the decadent.

All these questions and issues are explored honestly, behind certain necessary 'blinds,' in the third volume of the *Memoirs*, which take the reader around the world in a bizarre travelogue of sexual adventure, education and experience. In common with its predecessors, this volume is hardly 'politically correct.' The narrator was possessed of many of the prejudices of his time, although he repudiates the vice of racism including anti-semitism and continually advocates an unrestricted love of women, coming all the while closer in his obsessive quest for the Holy Grail.

Some may see merely obscenity within this document, to which one can only retort that those who dwell within a conceptual sewer tend to notice very little other than their immediate surrounds. The more educated, however, may obtain invaluable insights into the sociology, history and psychology of the period, including perceptions deriving from world-wide travel, within these pages – pages of unique literary interest.

Geraldine Lamb PhD.,
University of California at Berkeley.

AUTHOR'S INTRODUCTION
TO VOLUME I

As I take up my pen to write of my life, I remain convinced that fighting and fucking are when two people come closest. You can grow close to a man either by fighting against him or by fighting with him on the same side as one slogs along through various battles. However, I am of the opinion that it is not possible to grow close to a woman unless one fucks her.

My personal view is that when fucking a woman, one should jolly well roger her brains out and give it some arse. I'm well aware that this view is thought unfashionable in our degenerate modern times. Female emancipation has indeed proceeded apace and I have never opposed it but the results have not been precisely what I wanted nor, one suspects, exactly the results desired by the fairer sex. It is indeed a delight to regard our modern young girls in their slim, short skirts but they lack the mystery and romanticism of the long, rustling white petticoats of yesteryear. These days, they all wear rosy red-leaf lip-stick and they all smoke and they pout sexily but despite all that delicious expanse of white thigh and ankle, they lack the eroticism of the women of my youth. These days one takes a girl for morning cocktails at 'The Apple Tree', goes on to luncheon at 'Pietro Le Fueno', proceeds to an afternoon session at 'Dolly's', where one's ears are deafened with jazz, takes afternoon tea at The

Connaught, goes on to cocktails at the Ritz, sees the latest play at the Theatre Royal, the Haymarket, has drinks and then dinner at The Savoy, and all the thanks you receive is 'Cheerio.'

Ah! It wasn't like that in the days of my golden, gilded youth! Women really were women in those spacious times! They certainly weren't boys with short bobs for hair, flat chests and thin skin and bone where the buttocks should have been. It is said that times have become increasingly sexually free. It is so and I welcome the development yet some inscrutable element has been lost. How is the matter best put? I am reminded of Lady Charlotte X, who always used to defend the institution of marriage on the grounds that it lent so much spice to the pleasures of adultery. Forbidden fruit does indeed taste so much sweeter. In a similar vein, one could advance the proposition that the very restrictions of my youth gave each forbidden encounter an exquisite charm that is wholly lacking in these present days that are so permissive and yet so cold.

Nevertheless, it is impossible for me to complain about a life indefatigably blessed by good fortune. I am hardly a rich man but even in these inflationary times it is just about possible to jog along on £100,000 a year. The only duties incumbent upon me are maintaining the lands, a job done most capably by the family stewards; and turning up at the House of Lords occasionally whenever there is a vital vote. My quiet position has enabled me to meet some of the most interesting men and women in the land and also to travel abroad to meet more.

Throughout my life, I have been a lover of Woman, in all her intriguing shapes and guises. Although I have enjoyed the good fortune of meeting with some of the strongest, most powerful and most intelligent men of my era, and although I have assuredly learned wisdom from their lips, I have received yet greater education from the labia of ladies. This may be thought a peculiar view but I shall demonstrate my case.

Too many men of my acquaintanceship, however illustrious, have informed me that they regard the sexual act as being merely the prodding of a stiff rod between soft thighs into a soft and welcoming female orifice. Although their joy in this glorious matter can hardly be denied and although I take a deep share in their joy, knowing of it to my own good, I nevertheless insist that there is something more to the matter.

The sexual act, properly understood, is more than merely the delights of animal gratification, splendid though these are. It is more than the doing of a deed alleged to be 'dirty' and therefore somehow sinful, in consequence of which its execution imparts a sinister thrill, an added *frisson* of forbidden pleasure. It can be the holiest, most religious act in the World when a man and a woman come together and create energy between one another as a sacrament. It can elevate one's consciousness and enable one, if one dares say so, to evolve beyond the level of the apes who originally sired us.

During my life, I have been able to acquaint myself with a number of occult groups, from some of whom I learned much and from others of whom I learned nothing at all. Most of them have taught me techniques, nevertheless, which I have found to be useful. It is my willed intention to put down here all I know before I die so that possibly some others may benefit from the recounting of my experiences.

In the beginning, I knew nothing other than my rampant rod and of its lust for a slick, juicy cunt. By the end, I had discovered the Holy Grail. I shall begin, then, amidst the mist of ignorance, continue through a hard middle and, one trusts, finish with a flourish at the end.

AUTHOR'S INTRODUCTION TO VOLUME II

As I commence dictation to my charming and beautiful secretary, whose name discretion forbids me to mention, and set forth the second volume of my *Memoirs*, a few more words of explanation are required if this work is not to receive more severe censure than that which it doubtless deserves.

'The proper study of mankind is Man,' wrote Alexander Pope and one trusts that his use of the generic term was inclusive of Woman. From an early age I have discerned the holy truth that the highest grace is conferred by the union of the male and the female in sexual congress. This perception was fully confirmed by my experience of a low mass at the castle of 'the Black Douglas', as I have referred to him, near Vienna. It is the purpose of this volume to explore my memory and retrieve from it the words and images of all encounters which have granted me understanding and wisdom, especially in terms of the practical application of my apperception.

O! how I sigh some mornings for those spacious days of the *fin de siècle* . . .! We were all so young then and burning with lust for the World. If that be Decadence, then I loved every moment of it! Today (1925) it strikes me that so much Romance has gone out of the World. Take the recent postcard, for example, which I received this morning from my old friend, Frank Harris.

Hope you're still keeping it up, Horby! Why not come and visit me in Nice? Know the latest rhyme about the girls today?

If the skirts get any shorter
Said the Flapper with a sob;
I'll have two more cheeks to powder
And a lot more hair to bob.
All the grimmest
Frank.

I remain fond of the former lion of literary London, though he has been savaged by critics for the first volume of his autobiography, *My Life and Loves*, which I, for one, thoroughly enjoyed, both for its literary, political and social reminiscences and for its unabashed sexual candour. One gathers that he is presently subject to a wave of puritanical persecution. His mistake, in my view, was to cast pearls before swine in this increasingly narrow, moralistic climate of opinion, where even the United States of America, once boasting itself to be the 'home of the brave and the land of the free,' has had the stupid temerity to ban the imbibing of alcoholic beverages. Ah! how I savour the memory of those spacious days of my youth! I shall describe my visits to America in the course of this volume.

The mistake of Harris was to place his private life before the profane eyes of the riff-raff and one assumes that only the pressures of financial need persuaded him to embark on so inadvisable a course of action. I shall make no such error. This work is only for the eyes of my cultivated friends.

My morning post also brought a greetings card from H.G. Wells, thanking me for the dinner I gave him the other day. Wells has of course deservedly acquired world fame – and his amorous activities continue unabated. He is too sensible, though, to soil his reputation among the respectable by publishing publicly his reminiscences of his many encounters. 'If you don't like your life, you can change it,' he always used to say and the man was certainly a living example of practising what one preaches. In my case, however, I was too fortunate to have much desire to change my life and I do not regret anything that I have done. I regret only that which I *haven't* done.

It will readily be discerned by the reader that I received much benefit from my visit to Vienna and my witnessing of a 'low mass' of Sex-Magick. Allow me, then, to essay a narrative of my further exploration in my quest for the Holy Grail.

AUTHOR'S INTRODUCTION
TO VOLUME III

As I dictate these words of my Memoirs to my exquisitely efficient and charmingly pretty secretary, one cannot help remarking that some savour of the spacious days of my youth has gone out of the world. Personally, I blame the brutality of the Great War. Everything I knew seems to have become rather insane ever since the Armistice. I served my country in the Great War and I fought for freedom, justice and a better world for one and all, especially Great Britain. Where is it?

I don't enjoy seeing unemployed and disabled ex-soldiers on the streets, homeless and starving, especially since Lloyd George promised them 'homes fit for heroes.' I don't think it's right for the wages of the workers to be reduced by Government legislation. I freely admit that I am one of the lucky ones and that shrewd investments made by my assistants have made me richer now than I have ever been before. If I wanted to, even in this time of inflation, I could have a thirteen-year-old girl for the same price as in 1901: they're all out there whoring for their disabled fathers. It's just that unripe apples have never been of much sexual interest to me.

Take other aspects of modern life, for instance. Poetry? None of it rhymes or has scansion, rhythm or metre. Painting and sculpture? These 'Dada' chaps paint moustaches on a postcard of the Mona Lisa or else put their toe-nail clippings in a jam jar and have the nerve to call it Art! And some people are stupid enough to pay for it! Architecture? I see buildings being erected that look just like the Corn-Flakes packages of Dr Kellogg – and some poor people actually have to live in them. There's no grace any more and where will it all end?

Sex? These short dresses which expose lovely legs certainly arouse my carnal lusts – but why do the girls these days have to look as straight and flat in their figures as these new 'A' roads that our wretched Government is plastering everywhere across the landscape of our once beautiful countryside? The motor-car, although it has its undeniable uses, farts forth fumes that poison our lungs. They'll be abolishing the railways next! Sometimes I really do feel like those old retired Colonels who write letters to *The Morning Post* signed 'Disgusted, Tunbridge Wells', for whilst I am certainly no Socialist, I'm damned if I know which aspects of the national heritage the Conservative Party is conserving.

Ah! It was rather different in the days of my youth when it seemed as though the world was my oyster and I travelled around the globe in search of its elusive black pearl. I invite you, gentle reader – as authors used to state a century ago – to join me in my exploration of the sacred mystery of Sex.

I had thought, after the adventures I described in my second volume, that there was precious little more for me to learn. How wrong I was! And I don't mind admitting it. There was still so much for me to discover as I journeyed around the world, witnessing all manners and mores and sexual customs, in my own singular quest for the Holy Grail.

CHAPTER ONE

One thing is for certain: it was a damn good fuck that night in Paris, New Year's Day 1901. I was tumbling Emily Ward-Bishop in a four-poster bed in one of the many houses that her family owned, just off the Rue de Rivoli. Sir Richard Bellingham and his newly wed wife Davina had departed for their honeymoon and one understood that after Paris, it would proceed to Cannes and Nice, after which their voyaging would be a secret for the ensuing three months. Rosemary was with the mysterious Douglas and Claire with the mystifying Pierre. It had been a most unusual and delightful Wedding Reception and, certainly, I had no cause for complaint as Emily sucked my cock with the utmost skill and rapture.

With her mouth full of my glistening shaft, she squeezed my balls as a stream of creamy spunk hurtled out of my cock into her eager, warm, moist mouth. Gamely, she swallowed my entire gushing emission, draining my shaft of its salty flow whilst a wonderful orgasmic wave swept over me. Then she opened her lips to release my fast-deflating tadger and panted: 'Oh, your sperm has such an invigorating taste. I can hardly wait till you fuck the arse off me again, yes!'

I responded by kissing her crimson nipples as I cupped her chubby, firm buttocks in my hands, squeezing them lecherously whilst I slid all the way down until my lips were only inches away from her soft strands of pussy hair and she parted her thighs to make her moist, swollen cunny lips more accessible to me. Emily let out a delighted gasp as my tongue moved over every inch of her juicy, damp crack; and she breathed a long sigh whilst my eager tongue delved everywhere in the folds of her vagina, probing and sliding from her slit to her bum-hole, licking and lapping up the odoriferous love juices which her cunt now exuded.

I stiffened the tip of my tongue and started to lick the soft, puffed inner lips and inhaled her unique feminine aroma as she moaned again with unslaked desire. Then, suddenly, I thrust my tongue between her cunt lips, pushing within the warm, wet cunny channel. Her hips gyrated madly as I tongue-fucked this luscious girl, licking her cunt up and down and feeling her clitty grow harder each time my tongue flicked across it.

Now it was time to concentrate on this swollen bud and I nibbled at the jerking love button whilst I moved my hand upwards and slid first one and then two fingers into her wetness. Her voracious cunt was hot and tight and she bucked as I twisted my fingers inside her, arching her body with joy when I tickled her clit with the tip of my tongue.

Again and again I drove my tongue inside her, feeling her vaginal walls clutch it as my lips paid homage to her clitty, kissing and sucking the erectile flesh as Emily writhed under my erotic ministrations. The throbbing vibrations of her body excited me further and my rampant prick rubbed sinuously against her legs as my own hips worked to and fro. I continued to tongue-fuck Emily towards the ultimate peak of pleasure. She reached her climax with a throaty shriek as the orgasm burst inside her cunt in a mighty explosion and my face was flooded by a fierce, fresh outpouring of cuntal juice which I gulped down as if I were devouring oysters; while Emily now shivered all over with the force of her climactic spend.

I gave her no respite and promptly mounted her, gasping my joy aloud as my stiff, throbbing rod prodded right into her warm, juicy and welcoming cunt. My thrusts began slowly and deeply, so that the tip of my knob touched the entrance of her womb and made her quiver all over.

'Let's try a new position, Horby!' Emily gasped. 'Move in deeply – yes, that's it; now throw your left leg up over my loins, and put your right under my left leg, fork fashion . . . isn't it awfully nice? Your cock goes into the exact angle of my quim and its tip touches the very entrance to my womb! Ah! ah! Ohhh . . .! You do make me spend . . . I can't help it. Go on quicker, you darling! Ah, it drives me mad! You make me melt all over . . .'

For my own part, I was in ecstasy and my delighted prick was so sensitive to the clinging grip of her lascivious cunt that I was compelled to cry out that I could not bear it any longer as my hot spunk spurted into her quim.

Good heavens! This prim and proper – to all outward appearances – little bitch was once again quite insatiable. After a rest of only a couple of minutes or so, she once more took possession of my prick and lovingly kissed, sucked and tongued my balls, her busy fingers doing their best by teasing my increasingly impetuous shaft, causing it to re-enter her foaming vagina which was overflowing with our creamy emissions. I kept myself back before another spend and so drew out the length of that glorious fuck as she fixed her pearly white teeth in my shoulders until her lips were crimsoned by my blood. At the climax, we rolled around together in a perfect fury of amorous frenzy.

I had thought that I could do no more and so we took cognac and talked. I smoked a Turkish cigarette while she told me a joke.

'A chap went up in a balloon the other day here in Paris, didn't you know?' Emily told me. 'He went higher, it is reliably reported, than any man before him, but he came down in a shocking state. Just before he passed out and had to be rushed to hospital, he declared: "I saw God." Well,' she continued animatedly, 'the doctors and nurses saved his life, but when he recovered consciousness, his hospital bed was surrounded by journalists asking: "Did you see God?" He nodded dazedly. "And what was God like?" He refused to tell them. Finally, the room was cleared and the President of the French Republic himself came to see the gallant captain. "*Courage, mon brave!*" he exclaimed, "*mon cher monsieur*, you say that you saw God?" The captain nodded. "And," the President enquired, "what was God like?" The captain gasped a few words before slumping into a coma which would last a year, but those words were: "Yes, I saw God. And *she was black!*" '

I laughed and could not resist kissing Emily passionately, our lips glued together. My forefinger felt that her clit was trembling and tingling with reaffirmed desire. My sturdy shaft once more pressed hard against her belly as she covered my neck and shoulders with playful little love-bites. She wrapped her thighs around my hips, knowing that I was strong enough to hold her in this position, and soon enough she was once more spitted on my stiffly swollen cock. Our mouths met hungrily, again and again; then, abruptly, I bent my head down and started to suck on her titties, which so electrified her that she rocked violently from side to side, overbalanced and toppled over out of the bed.

Scrambling to our feet and shouting with laughter, we flung ourselves back upon the bed. I chose to spear her from behind with my rampant rod, easing it into her squelchy cunt: and then my belly slammed hard against her bum cheeks. I fucked her with delight as she groaned with joy.

'Oh!' she shrieked out. 'I just love it when your prick pistons in and out of my sopping cunny whilst your firm, manly hands squeeze and knead my breasts!' My tongue brushed her neck and shoulders lightly and she sighed with the pleasure of true sensuality. She pushed out her delectable bottom to meet my powerful thrusts and my balls slapped against the backs of her thighs. As I worked my thick tadger backwards and forwards, I murmured: 'Goddess! What a delicious cunt you have, Emily . . . there's no other cunny which clasps my cock so beautifully! That's it, my darling, work your arse!' My hot, wet, stiff shaft slewed to and fro, faster and faster.

'Aah . . .!' she cried out. 'Shoot your spunk, my love! Empty your balls, you gorgeous man!' And with my face buried in her neck and with my heated breath blowing upon her shoulder, I ejaculated a fountain of frothy jism inside her throbbing cunt: and her own spend arrived seconds later so that her quim was once more awash with our combined love juices. We writhed around in an undignified heap of entwined limbs as we enveloped ourselves in the delights of this simultaneous spend, and then we stretched ourselves out on the four-poster bed and enjoyed a peace which passeth all understanding.

Emily left Paris on the following morning after a delightful breakfast of exquisitely brewed dark coffee and the most crisp and buttery croissants I have ever tasted, accompanied by the conserves of the peach and the apricot. As always, she had relatives to see in England. Naturally I had hired a carriage for her transport to the Gare du Nord and she looked rather splendid as her gloved hand waved goodbye, encumbered by far too many hat-boxes and cases; the horses drew away with an appropriate jingling of bells.

I could now address my undivided attention to a further matter which had to engage my finest faculties during my visit to Paris. The reader of my second volume may recall my revelation that I have on occasion undertaken missions of espionage on behalf of the British Intelligence services. This had brought me into contact with the delectably lecherous Maria, apparently an agent for every Great Power in Europe, not to mention America. This time my mission had been given to me by both Sir Richard Bellingham and my cousin at our Berlin Embassy. It was to investigate Satanism in Paris.

It was believed in high circles, apparently, that there might be a global grouping of men and women devoted to the Devil and all the evidence pointed to Paris as being the international headquarters of this nefarious organization. Prior to my arrival, and Bellingham's wedding, I had acquired information enabling me to write and propose meetings to various personages. I had also milked Claire and Maria for further information.

'What is truth?' asked Pontius Pilate. I'm still waiting for an answer. The stories of Satanism were many and multifarious and complicated by the fact that it was difficult to tell whether one was receiving accurate information or not. For instance, it had been alleged that one Albert Pike had established Satanism in America and had sent 'the Devil's Daughter', Diana Vaughan, to strengthen its cause in Paris and in Western Europe generally. Published books had been written to this effect,

34

especially *The Devil in the Nineteenth Century* by Dr Bataille (1892). This detailed the devil-worship of Albert Pike and his 'Palladian Order' in Charleston, South Carolina, USA, and linked it to Freemasonry in a manner expounded by Lee Taxil in *The Mysteries of Freemasonry* and *Are There Women in Freemasonry*: followed by *Confessions of an Ex-Free Thinker* by Gabrièle Jogand-Pages. *Là-Bas*, the literary novel by the celebrated author J.K. Huysmans, gave a detailed description of a Black Mass in Paris. All these works were best-sellers and set forth the notion of an international Satanic conspiracy.

At the time, this notion was plausible; and a plethora of books detailing sinister conspiracies had poured out of Paris. Now, I was hardly a stranger to secret societies, being a member, *inter alia*, of the Golden Dawn, the Order Templi Orientis, the Smokers of the Sacred, the Female Flagellants of New York (admittedly, only as an associate), various groupings of the British Intelligence services (doing my bit for Queen and Country as a gentleman amateur) and the mysterious cluster comprising Douglas, the international banker, Rosemary, Claire and other curious figures such as Pierre and Ram Singh. The difficulty lay in working out the actual significance which lay behind these sundry groupings.

Matters were not made any easier by the way in which espionage is conducted. One is given both information and disinformation and it is rather hard to tell which is which. For instance, Rosemary had written me letters from Whitby in Yorkshire concerning Douglas, only later to state that these had been fiction. Was she telling the truth or not? All I knew for certain was that she was the High Priestess of an international Order of which Douglas was the High Priest, that this Order regarded sex as being sacred, that I had witnessed its activities in a castle in

Vienna and at Bellingham's wedding at a house in Paris; and that my association with Rosemary and with this Order had brought me nothing but good. I could discern no evidence of Satanism in the rites I had witnessed; yet an atheistic bourgeois might well call these 'disgusting' and a Christian clergyman might well interpret them as being 'Satanic'.

Maria had informed me that there was 'certainly' an international Satanic conspiracy but then she might have been feeding me the disinformation she was paid to give to so many others. Claire had written me a letter from Paris in which she had given me all the lubricious details of a Satanic initiation at the hands, eager and willing, of her cousin Charlotte and her friend Jean-Charles. She had insisted upon its veracity: yet even though my loving involvement with Claire had done me so much good, and even though she had served as a Priestess at Sir Richard's extraordinary wedding, there was still the possibility that she might have been telling me an amusing piece of fiction.

At the time, I found it rather hard to make sense of it all. I was equipped with every possible advantage, having my own private agents, the full co-operation of the British Embassy in Paris and its attached intelligence services, and the names and addresses of the alleged Satanists as willingly supplied by Claire. This trail of enquiry led nowhere. Jean-Charles, who sometimes added extra confusion to the matter by calling himself Jean-Pierre, had apparently vanished off the face of the Earth, accompanied by Claire's alleged cousin Charlotte. Yes, a man and a woman answering to the descriptions Claire had given me had indeed resided at the address to which their residence was ascribed: yet their neighbours spoke of them as 'a quiet couple' who, having paid their rent, had vanished into thin air, leaving no traces behind them. I bombarded Claire with telegrams at every address at which she might be residing and of which she had informed me but received no reply.

She had left Paris, I knew, with Pierre, another mysterious one whom I desired to interview, but all endeavours to trace him were proving to be equally useless. Rosemary and Douglas, who could have helped me at that point, had vanished too. Therefore I had no alternative other than to follow the leads I possessed at that point and meet Viscount Maulerby, who did some work for the Foreign Office, and his companion, Father Armand Binoire (Society of Jesus, no less) at a café on the Rue de Rivoli over pernod.

My dislike of Lord Maulerby, with his piggy eyes and all too evident folds of bulging flesh has already been made only too clear. Father Armand Binoire was a thin, pale and skeletal individual, with hard, cold eyes and a mean, tight mouth which immediately led me to detest him even more. Maulerby was aware of the nature of my mission. I wondered how he managed to reconcile his investigation of Satanism and his acquaintanceship with a Roman Catholic priest with his lecherous behaviour at Sir Richard Bellingham's wedding.

'My advice, Horby,' Lord Maulerby pontificated, 'is that you listen to Father Binoire here. Now, he knows *the facts!*'

'What are they?' I enquired. 'I'll listen gladly.'

'Essentially,' said Father Binoire, who spoke English perfectly with only the slightest of foreign accents, 'we are speaking of a conspiracy between various groupings to destroy Christian culture and Christian civilization.'

'Down with it!' Maulerby exclaimed.

'Quite so,' I murmured.

'The threat comes,' said Father Binoire, 'from the Satanists in alliance with the Freemasons . . .'

This struck me as being absurd on one level; yet perfectly understandable on another. I happen to be a Freemason as recognized by United Grand Lodge of England, which I have found to be an innocuous, fraternal and charitable organization, enacting in ceremony various alleged 'truths' of 'The Grand Architect of the Universe.' My friend Aleister Crowley had been initiated both into this and into the Ancient And Accepted Scottish Rite and in certain conversations, conducted within the rules of all Oaths duly sworn and therefore spoken obliquely, the basic principles of Liberty, Equality and Fraternity – as enunciated in the French Revolution – appeared to be the same. A difficulty arose in discussing the French Grand Orient Lodge. English United Grand Lodge demands as a condition of initiation the acceptance of some form of God or Higher Power. French Grand Orient Lodge insists upon atheism. Ancient And Accepted Scottish Rite Freemasonry preserves 'the auld alliance' with France and admits atheists on the grounds that the human can be divine.

Moreover, many of the seniors of the Golden Dawn and the Ordo Templi Orientis were Freemasons. These Orders not only practised ceremonies but actually taught Ceremonial Magic: and what was one to make of *that*? I had discerned no Satanism at all; nor could I see how the atheists of the French Grand Orient Lodge could be Satanists either: since how the devil can you believe in the Devil if you don't believe in God?

'An alliance, Father Binoire?' I therefore queried as I sipped some more good pernod. 'An alliance with whom?'

'The Jews . . .' Father Binoire stated solemnly.

'God damn 'em!' Maulerby expostulated.

'Oh . . .?' I had always thought of the Jews as being the victims of persecution rather than the instigators of same. 'And who else?'

'The machinations of International Finance,' said Father Binoire. 'But essentially it's manipulated by the Rothschilds.' I scratched my head in puzzlement. Obviously the Jews were making money in international finance whenever and wherever they could: but so was everyone else involved. I found it rather hard to picture a group of Jews giving Satanism more than one minute of their time, still less taking part in rites of Devil Worship when they could be sitting comfortably in their offices or enjoying chicken soup with their wives at home.

The level on which I could understand the point of view of Father Binoire was simple. As far as he was concerned, *every* religion not controlled by the Roman Catholic Church had to be inspired by the work of the Devil. This was especially true of Freemasonry, which had been anathematized by the Pope well over a century ago and to which no Roman Catholic could belong. In other words, everyone who wasn't a Christian was a Satanist. This made his 'information' worthless, but I nodded patiently as he passed me a Vatican document for my attention, nodded further as he expounded his theory that the United States of America had been founded by a Satanic conspiracy of Jews, Satanists and Freemasons and nearly nodded off to sleep when he deplored women as being secondary creatures, created by the Devil in order to tempt men from the paths of righteousness.

If I were an atheist, I thought, *I'd say 'Thank God for it!'* after listening to this ridiculous fool. Even so, 'Manners Makyth Man', as they so rightly say, so I shook the hands of both my companions and departed on my way in search of sex.

I spent my evening fucking Maria. As I later learned, Maulerby spent his paying a tart to sit on his face and Father Armand Binoire S.J. enjoyed *his* whipping a thirteen-year-old choir-boy with a martinet before buggering him. I was starting to wonder just where the real Satanists were.

CHAPTER TWO

My *Memorandum 813* informs me that on the following day, I enjoyed a solitary luncheon at the Café de la Paix in the charming Opera Quarter. I have never had better *Moules Marinière*, roasted *gigot* of lamb, dripping with blood and accompanied by a portion of buttered spinach, and *tarte tatin* – all washed down by a jolly good bottle of vintage Chambertin. There is a world of difference between *eating* on one's own, whereby one suffers the pangs of loneliness, and *dining* on one's own, whereby one relishes the pleasures of solitude. One doesn't need to talk; one can simply enjoy the food and wine as one calmly surveys the world. It is said that, if you sit for long enough in the Café de la Paix, everyone you have ever known will be encountered, which makes it sound rather like the Afterlife, whether in Heaven or in Hell. Fortunately, this did not happen in the three hours I passed there, relishing my repast and the pleasures of quiet contemplation.

Lord Maulerby and Father Binoire had disturbed my mental processes with their bloody, wretched nonsense. Maria, delectable fuck though she was, had exacerbated further my perturbation of the brain by giving me more confusing information. To compound this confounded matter, there was in my pocket a letter from Claire which had been hand delivered to my hotel by private messenger service.

My darling Horby,

Surprise! Again it's me – but, as has been said before, truth is stranger than fiction.

Unfortunately, I am in a state of requiring solace since my grandmother died so unexpectedly. What a matriarch she was! It was necessary that I attend her funeral at Highgate Cemetery, the first time I have ever been an attendant at a burial. It was a solemn occasion as the grim-faced pall-bearers carried my grandmother's coffin to the grave next to that of my grandfather, who had died the year before. (I have to admit that their relationship had been volatile and sometimes even vitriolic.) It was gratifying to witness that hundreds came to pay their respects to my late grandmother, and of course we were all garbed in severe and sober black. Why do women always look so beautiful at funerals? My own hair had been styled in a petite chignon *and was graced by a black hat which sported a white ostrich plume. When the coffin of Grandmama was laid to rest, I wiped away my tears yet found it necessary that I should temporarily retire from this solemn occasion of grief.*

I meandered around the cemetery to look upon the graves of those who had died before. There was Hovis, the inventor of cheap, mass-produced brown bread. And there was Karl Marx, whom everyone within my immediate acquaintanceship appears to hate but whose books I had studied with pleasure and profit under the tutelage of Rosemary. He seemed to think that there are inevitable laws of history, that the owners of land are having power stripped from them by the owners of manufacturing industry – which may well be true – and that the industrial workers will arise, have a bloody revolution and install a dictatorship, after which the State will 'wither away', which sounds most unlikely. You know, my darling, that Politics doesn't interest me that much.

Why is it that one always feels so sentimental at funerals? And why is it also that there is usually a macabre tendency to laugh? At that moment, however, there were inexplicable palpitations within my heart. Suddenly, there was a tap upon my left shoulder. I had read and heard that this was the Sign of Death: and I dissolved into tears of grief, turning around to stare into the black eyes of Douglas, that man of mystery, secrecy and enigma.

'At last you acknowledge my presence,' he said softly.

'Douglas,' I replied, 'initially I did not see you.' I sobbed once. 'I was preoccupied with my own thoughts.'

'Let me kiss away your tears,' he replied as they dribbled gently down my cheeks.

'Did you know my grandmother?'

'Oh, very well,' he replied.

'How well?'

'You will find out soon,' was his response. We walked throughout the cemetery, arm in arm, observing the gargoyles, the angels, the seraphim and cherubim and the statues of the Spirits of the Four Elements: Michael, Gabriel, Raphael and Uriel – Air, Water, Fire and Earth.

'I am so sad that my grandmother is dead,' I said, upon reaching the garden of tranquillity and appreciating the momentary peace of our silence, where not even the doves made their presence known, staying as silent and invisible as the earthworms at their grim feasting six feet beneath us. I felt sequestered from the rest of the world. Abruptly, Douglas took me into his arms and kissed me passionately upon the lips; and I could not resist his charms. He understood the stress and tension in my life yet, beneath it all, I felt his throbbing, pulsating with a wild desire to be released.

'*Madam,*' he said, '*I desire desperately to fuck you.*'

'*Do you think that this is the most appropriate time?*' I responded, adding a sarcastic, '*Sir . . .?*'

'*I assure you that it is.*'

'*But there might be an intruder!*'

'*Only mine,*' he replied.

I lifted up my skirt hem, rolled down my silken stockings and removed my suspenders. Off came my thigh garter, too; this was of scarlet with engraved gilt buckles and frills of taffeta.

I am so ashamed to say that we fucked upon a tombstone. How he did prod his rod into me and how stiff it was! Yes! A mighty ram-rod with the power of a steam-engine piston, pumping and pumping as my thighs trembled. How my clit twitched! And how my toes did tingle as my breasts heaved beneath my tight corset and my nipples stood erect like two little guardsmen.

To my stunned stupefaction, he produced a wicked, gleaming knife from his trouser pocket and proceeded to slit my corset in two down its middle! Then he took my left teat into his mouth and proceeded to suck upon it.

'*This is rather like the Matterhorn,*' he murmured.

'*But now you must enjoy the pleasure of my other mammary,*' I sighed, '*for you might find it to be like Mont Blanc.*' He nuzzled his head between my breasts before ascending the next mountain. I delighted in his kisses as he gently bit upon my right bosom, finally to reach my right areola.

'*Mont Blanc . . .?*' he growled. '*This, my dear, is what I would call Mount Everest!*' His voice became gentler. '*How many men have conquered this mountain before?*' Too many, I thought. '*What a sublime elevation!*' I felt the same way as his mighty member thrust within my cunt to shake me with its rhythm, prior to its *spurting of his love juices into me – but abruptly we were rudely interrupted in our final copulation. How could anybody behave so discourteously at my grandmother's funeral?*

Whack! whack! whack! *That was the sound of a parasol beaten upon the naked and twitching slim buttocks of Douglas.* Whack! whack! whack! *again – and how his prick and his sperm did penetrate me! It was as if the barriers of a dam had been burst wide open and his secretion of juices entered my vagina as if I were the sole recipient of the indundation of some fearsome deluge. How he did emit his sperm from here to eternity! He shot his juices inside me as if he were a mighty fountain – or perhaps a volcano such as Mount Etna might be a more accurate analogy.*

At that moment, I looked into the eyes of my former tutor, Rosemary. They were sparkling blue, bright and alive as she thrashed Douglas upon his bare bottom as he recovered swiftly to fuck me once more in the quiet of the garden of remembrance, city of the dead and valley of dry bones.

'Rosemary!' I exclaimed, in between gasps of pleasure, 'what is the connection between you and my grandmother?'

'I have known that great matriarch for many a year,' she replied coolly, then carried on calmly whipping Douglas's bottom with her unfurled parasol. 'In my youth, I attended her finishing school in Switzerland and was one of her star pupils. I learned . . .' whack! *'. . . ah, so very much from her, including . . .'* whack! *'. . .the finest disciplines in life.'* Whack! whack! whack! *she went; and Douglas groaned and gasped in a curious admixture of agony and ecstasy as my cunt unambiguously enjoyed the jerking thrustings of his*

prick. 'Also matters such as riding a horse, cooking a dinner fit for a gourmet, figure skating, needlepoint and making a bed with proper hospital corners.' Whack! *'Oh, and she also taught me the craft of embroidery.'* She lifted up her black skirt of satin to reveal the finest pair of white silk knickers that I have ever seen. They came down to the backs of her knees and were adorned with frills of lace.

Douglas turned his head and was visibly amazed by her finery, her fal-de-lal, her frills and furbelows, her crimson suspender belt and her black, silken stockings. The tight lacing of her corset made her breasts thrust forward as if they desired to be eaten and her bottom thrust backwards as though it desired to be kissed. Suddenly I realized the nature of the situation between them. It was so obvious that they now wanted to be together that I gracefully retired from my recumbent posture atop the tombstone, taking up a new position behind an old yew tree with red berries in full bloom. It was a joy to be a voyeur as they made an exhibition of their mutual ribaldry, hedonism and debauchery. Douglas licked her cunt, sodomised her bottom and rejoiced as Rosemary sucked his prick before he thrust within her and they both screamed out their shared joy as they came together.

Afterwards, Douglas lit a Turkish cigarette and produced a silver flask of brandy and we sat merrily upon the tombstone, reminiscing about the life of my grandmother, Dorothea. They spoke of her acquaintanceship with that great American poet, Walt Whitman, for she had enjoyed her travels throughout the world. She had been a good friend of Pierre and Marie Curie, only now receiving their just share of recognition after years of neglect. Amidst tales of adventures among the Russian aristocracy, I was not expecting Rosemary to lift up her frock.

'Would you not say . . .' she murmured languorously, 'that my cunny is not unlike the shape of a Russian samovar? Douglas, would you not like to drink of my hot tea?' His head darted forth eagerly to suck greedily upon her quim.

I realized that I should leave them to their own devices and so wandered on to the wake in Hampstead, the cries of lascivious lovers ringing in my ears. What strange obsequies! I departed to the house of a relative, there to utter my condolences before those festivities which customarily follow a funeral.

I believe that my grandmother has left me certain properties in her will, one of them being in Rajasthan, India, the city of the Holy Men, where I believe that the intriguing Dr Ram Singh has his ashram. One gathers that the most sacred of Temples are there.

My darling, I must conclude this letter now. The past few days have just been so exhausting for me. But one cannot complain too much about necessary matters of grave concern. I miss you.

All my love,
Claire

My whirling mind was put into further fevers of perturbation that evening when I saw Maria.

'That Douglas,' she said, 'do you know who he really is?'

'Who is anyone *really?*' I enquired as I poured cognac for both of us in my hotel suite.

'He is the Count of Saint Germain!' Maria exclaimed fiercely. 'Do you not know of him?'

'Of course I do,' I replied. 'He was a mysterious

eighteenth century gentleman heavily involved in the esoteric arts and in international espionage, working both for Louis XV of France and Frederick the Great of Prussia. He claimed to have discovered the Elixir of Life via his practice of Alchemy, stating seriously that in common with his pupil, Cagliostro, he had walked and talked with Nefertiti and Cleopatra in the days of Ancient Egypt. A fascinating man, indeed, Maria, with a charming gift of implausible phrase, but I cannot see how or why you identify him with Douglas, since Saint Germain is dead and buried.'

'No, he isn't,' she answered. 'After his death I am reliably informed that he was seen twice in India by travellers from both France and England. Moreover, your Lord Edward Bulwer-Lytton, that politician, novelist and magician, friend of your Dickens and Disraeli, met him in London and made him the inspirer of that most notable novella: *The Haunted and the Haunters: or The House and the Brain*.'

'That's a wonderful story,' I said, 'but surely you are joking?'

'No,' she returned coolly, 'I am not. Nobody ever really knew how the Count of Saint Germain managed to appear so carelessly wealthy. The same is true of Douglas.'

'Maria,' I responded, 'I find it easy enough to believe that mysterious people make much money in mysterious ways and become involved in secret societies. What I don't believe is that the Count of Saint Germain as an old man faked his own death and burial and then returned rejuvenated in our time as Douglas.'

'Then all the more fool you,' Maria retorted with a classically Parisian shrug of her nubile shoulders. By this time, I had had enough of trying to make sense of all these matters and so seized her unresisting hand and, fired by the stare of her deep, dark eyes, I placed it upon my trousered prick and was at once rewarded by the gentle pressure of her slender fingers, which assured me that she quite understood my need for delicate attention. Adroitly unfastening my buttons, she grasped the stiff and naked truth, which twitched under her delicious fingering in such a way that a very few motions of her delicate hand brought on a throbbing state of bliss.

Instinctively our lips met in a long, impassioned kiss. Tongue to tongue, we revelled in a gorgeous osculation. It was ecstatic having this lascivious girl close by my side, with my right arm around her waist, whilst my left hand found no resistance in its voyage of discovery underneath her petticoats. What mossy treasures my fingers searched out! Whilst for her part, one arm was draped around my neck and the warming touches of her right hand amply repaid my investigations into her regions of passion. My fiery kisses roved from her lips all over her face and neck, until I took possession of the heaving globes of her bosom. How she shuddered with ecstasy as my lips drew in one of her nipples and gently sucked the delicious morsel. A very few moments of this exciting dalliance was too much for her. She sank back on the bed.

Then followed delicious kissings and toyings; no part of Maria's person was neglected, and when, as a finale, she surrendered the moist dewy lips of the grotto of love itself to my warm tonguings, the excess of voluptuous emotion so overcame her that she screamed out her delight, when the crisis came again and again in rapid succession.

I still didn't know much about Satanism, or the similarities between the Count of Saint Germain and Douglas; but I cried out my joy in orgasm when I prodded my rod deep inside this perplexing bitch and this latest act of love became an accomplished fact.

CHAPTER THREE

It was on the ensuing afternoon that, as previously arranged, I met Joris-Karl Huysmans at a *Salon de Thé* on the Rue de Rivoli. Any Englishman who protests that one cannot enjoy a good pot of tea in France has obviously not been there. My own preference that day was for Darjeeling with milk and sugar; Huysmans took Lapsang Souchong without any accoutrements though we both agreed that that delicate little piece of *patisserie*, the *japainais*, would be a suitable accompaniment.

Huysmans was a tall, lean man with a gaunt face and haunted dark eyes, dressed in sober, clerical black. There was an element of the cadaverous about him. If anyone had overheard the first half hour of our conversation, it would have been assumed that Huysmans was a civil servant relaxing after a relatively easy day at the Ministry, a man who led a life both conventional and conservative. This was perfectly true: yet his imagination had caused him to create two of the most remarkable novels that I have ever read.

A Rebours or *Against Nature* had caused a sensation on its publication over ten years before and had inspired both the Aesthetic and the Decadent Movements: it was the 'book that corrupted Dorian Gray' in Oscar Wilde's memorable novel. Its hero, Des Esseintes, is a decadent aristocrat of independent means who chooses to live largely within his own imagination, influenced in his life-style and interior decoration by Edgar Allan Poe's *The Fall of the House of Usher*: and also by the bejewelled paintings of Gustav Moreau, most notably *Salomé*. In one chapter, he orders his servants to pack his bags for a trip to London, where he has never before been. Then he sits and imagines what London might be like, using the words of Dickens to paint a mental picture of beefsteak and oyster pie enjoyed in a roistering tavern as a thick yellow fog swirls about the window panes. Having explored this vision fully, as if in trance, he tells his servants to unpack his bags, for there is no longer any point in going to London.

His later novel, *Là-Bas* or *Down There* had also caused a sensation, especially upsetting all those who knew of it only by evil repute. Here, a rather cold writer called Durtal researches the life of the alleged Satanist, pervert and child-murderer Gilles de Rais, also a brave warrior, a friend of Joan of Arc and Marshal of France, who was eventually burned at the stake. In the course of Durtal's research, he discovers that Satanism is alive and well in the Paris of his time: and the closing chapter consists of a detailed description of our hero witnessing the Black Mass.

This was why I was keen to see Huysmans, quite aside from my genuine admiration for his writings. I asked him to what extent there might be Black Magic and Satanism in Paris and whether he had actually witnessed the matter which he described so well in his fiction.

'Lord Horby,' he said, 'I can only tell you of my own experience.' He sipped his tea thoughtfully. 'Have you heard of a half-mad prophet called Vintras?' I shook my head. 'He claimed to have been visited by the Archangel Michael who apparently informed him that his task was to inaugurate the coming "Age of the Holy Ghost". He travelled around the country, preaching his doctrines of redemption, declaring that even Satan would be ultimately redeemed, and soon built up a considerable following. He was a powerful preacher – he could never remember afterwards what he had said so one presumes that he spoke while in a state of trance – and his disciples included not only unlettered men such as himself but priests and aristocrats. He founded the Church of Carmel and, clad in vestments decorated with an inverted cross, proclaimed that "the reign of the suffering Christ is over and the reign of the Holy Ghost has begun."

'This Vintras has had quite an influence,' Huysmans continued coolly. 'He used to celebrate *The Provictimal Sacrifice of Mary*, a mass of his own devising, and during these masses his followers became totally hysterical. They declared that they saw empty chalices suddenly brim over with blood, smelled wondrous perfumes, beheld the consecrated host bleeding and even witnessed the Holy Ghost, in the form of a dove, perching on Vintras's shoulder. It was hardly surprising,' Huysmans smiled wryly, 'that the Roman Catholic Church quickly condemned Vintras for heresy or that, in 1842, after an unfair trial, he was sentenced to seven years of imprisonment on a charge of fraud. On his release in 1848, he passed some time in London then returned to his native land of France to die in 1875. You may be wondering about the relevance of this matter, *mon cher monsieur*, but allow me to explain.

'Vintras had influence upon Eliphas Lévi, author of *The Ritual and Dogma of Transcendental Magic* and *The Key of the Mysteries*.' I nodded. I had read both books and had been rather impressed by Lévi's insistence that the mysterious pack of cards called the Tarot is a pictorial exposition of the data contained in the Jewish Qabalah. The

Hermetic Order of the Golden Dawn had always praised Lévi as a master of esoteric wisdom; and so had Aleister Crowley, who would later translate Lévi's *The Key of the Mysteries* for Rider Books, adding his own sardonic footnotes. Moreover, I knew that Lévi had visited Lord Edward Bulwer-Lytton in England, which latter was stunned by the former's knowledge of esoterica. I shook my head bemusedly, for Maria had mentioned Bulwer-Lytton in connection with the Count of Saint Germain on the previous night. 'Vintras,' Huysmans continued, 'also attracted sexual deviants into his sect, for unorthodox mysticism frequently goes hand-in-hand with unorthodox sex. One ex-disciple, a priest named Gozzoli, accused Vintras of being homosexual, conducting secret masses at which both priests and people were naked, indulging in group sexual activities and masturbating at the foot of the altar. *Moi?*' Huysmans shrugged. 'Gozzoli was a most unpleasant character who was inclined to charge other people with vices to which he himself was inclined. Yet Vintras did exert an influence upon that most peculiar character, the Abbé Boullan, who had been unfrocked and who had previously been imprisoned in France for fraud and in Rome for heresy. In 1859, he had founded The Society for the Reparation of Souls whereby he cured and exorcised demon-possessed nuns by feeding them a mixture of consecrated communion wafers and human excrement.' Huysmans's thin voice dripped with acid sarcasm. 'I have evidence that on 8th January 1860, Boullan conducted a Black Mass at which he ritually sacrificed his own bastard child born to one Adèle Chevalier. After meeting Vintras, he declared himself a convert to the teachings of the Church of Carmel and after Vintras's death, he proclaimed himself to be a reincarnation of John the Baptist and the new Supreme Pontiff.

'His doctrines were curious,' said Huysmans, 'teaching as they did a form of sexual magic. He held that the Fall of Man had been caused by an act of love on the part of Adam and Eve and that, as he said to me "it is through acts of love accomplished in a religious spirit that the Redemption of Humanity can be achieved." He claimed that the evolutionary ladder could be climbed more speedily by humanity if we partook of sexual intercourse with celestial beings. One might think, Lord Horby, "Yes, and lead me to them" but he held also that mankind could accelerate the evolution of brute creation by copulating with animals. He moreover urged his disciples to enjoy sexual relations with incubi and succubi, the male and female spirits one arouses in the act of onanism. Some of his disciples thought that they were enjoying lascivious relations with archangels, angels and the spirits of Alexander the Great and Cleopatra. He also taught his female disciples a method of having sex with his astral body.'

'He sounds rather intriguing,' I remarked. 'Can you introduce me to him?'

'*Non*,' said Huysmans, 'for he is dead. It was as a result of a magical duel, part of which I witnessed. In the course of my own research into Satanism, I came across Boullan and his reputation. It was when I was breaking away from the influence of Emile Zola. Are you familiar with his work?'

'Yes,' I replied, 'and I agree with Oscar Wilde. He finds life crude and leaves it raw.'

'*Eh bien*,' Huysmans finished his tea and looked unconcerned, 'I wrote to Boullan, thinking it likely that he was either a Satanist or else could put me in touch with them, asking for reliable information on the subject of devil-worship and offering to depict him in my forthcoming novel as "the Superman, the Satanist, the only one in

existence, far removed from the spiritism of the occultists." Boullan replied in a friendly fashion, assuring me
that he was "an Adept who has declared war on all
demoniacal cults." He also offered to loan me documents
"which will enable you to prove that Satanism is active in
our time and in what form and in what circumstances."
Subsequently I received a great mass of material from
Boullan's home in Lyons, a hot-bed of Freemasonry
which has enjoyed a reputation for unorthodoxy ever
since the Middle Ages. It all gave me a somewhat
favourable impression of Boullan and inspired me to
portray him as the saintly Dr Johannes, enemy of all
Satanism and respected theologian in my novel *Là-Bas*.
Unfortunately, I was reckoning without the influence of
his enemies, the *Kabbalistic Order of the Rose-Croix* of
Stanislas de Guiata, Sâr Peládan and their associates. I
became involved in a magical war . . .' he arose.
'*Excusez-moi, monsieur, je vais au pissoir*,' he remarked
with eloquent French simplicity.

I remained to ponder both his words and the extraordinary scene in which I had eagerly participated on the
preceding night.

After our fuck, Maria had informed me that, unless I
objected, a friend of hers called Dominique would be
arriving shortly. This was a proposition to which I had
assented gladly and the eventual appearance of Dominique fully justified my anticipation. Dominique was possessed of a beautiful pale face surmounted by rich dark
brown hair. Her delectable figure had been accentuated in
the fashionable 'S' curse in a manner which would have
been preposterous, were it not so erotic. After a good
round of stiff brandies, Maria lost no time in stripping
Dominique of her evening dress and unlacing her tight

basque, enabling her to breathe freely once more. My penis was still flaccid but Maria's response was to pluck a pink India-rubber dildo from her bag and she giggled wickedly as she addressed the other ravishing young girl.

'They call this The Ladies' Comforter,' she informed Dominique. 'And I'm truly looking forward to fucking you with it.'

'It's very lifelike, isn't it?' Dominique giggled as she made herself comfortable on the bed next to me, lying back with her soft thighs spread open, her long, lissom legs stretched out and her exquisitely well-manicured finger-nails diddling her pussy.

'Yes, this is one of the best-made dildoes I have ever seen,' Maria remarked as she smoothed the imitation rubber cock over Dominique's hardening nipples. Dominique and I laughed lightly as Maria took a firm grasp upon the superbly fashioned instrument and pressed its bulbous knob between the pouting cunny lips of Dominique. It slipped in easily and I found it quite thrilling to see Maria's busy fingers nipping and pinching Dominique's finely developed clitty, which stood out so proudly as Maria manipulated the dildo with a truly feminine subtlety.

Dominique started to moan, twisting and turning as Maria plunged the dildo in and out of her gaping honeypot; and then they changed positions, with the young girl now brandishing the rubber prick. This new tableau made even my sated shaft twitch and, slowly but surely, it began to swell up. Dominique noticed this happy state of affairs and, with a little cry of joy, she swooped her head down to my cock and started to suck noisily on my knob until my tool was standing up hard and stiff as she swirled her wet tongue around my uncapped helmet.

Maria was now writhing from side to side with a blissful smile of satisfaction on her face as Dominique continued to wield the dildo in and out of her tingling passion-pit; and both girls were frigging their own cunnies as I hauled myself up and positioned myself behind Dominique. I parted her legs: I could see the love juice dripping down her inner thighs from her quim, and I licked my lips as I regarded that rosebud of an arse-hole which winked at me from within her cheeky bum-globes. It was in my mind to bugger this delectable young girl and so I eased my rampant shaft towards her tiny, puckered rosette.

'No! Ah, *non!*' Dominique cried out as she felt the tip of my prick nudging her sweet sphincter. Yet she did not miss a beat of her rhythmic dildo-fucking of Maria's cunny. 'I would far rather you fucked my dear little cunt instead.'

'By all means,' I whispered as Maria rubbed my cock until it was at its fullest length. Then I made Dominique bend forward and stick her deliciously rounded backside high into the air. 'But I really must insist first on paying your delightful *derrière* the merest token of a compliment.' So saying, I grasped her hips firmly and returned my rock-hard knob-end to her shy nether entrance. She must have realized by now that further protest was useless for, apart from an involuntary gasp of shock, Dominique made no further sound as I gently but firmly eased the head of my rigid cock through the wonderfully tight flesh-ring of her secret hole before sinking its whole stiff length on into the warm depths beyond. Having, I felt, made my point about who was in charge here, I then allowed chivalrous impulse to overrule carnal instinct and decided to withdraw – albeit with some reluctance – after this one marvellous deep stroke.

I slid my engorged shaft out of Dominique's arse and

without further ado plunged it below the voluptuous curve of her soft white bum cheeks. We both purred with pleasure as I at last embedded my throbbing rod inside her clinging cunt.

'Go on, you two!' Maria gasped, fully discerning the nature of what was transpiring as she wrested the dildo from Dominique's hand. 'Have a wonderful fuck! And do not worry, Dominique, my sweetheart, I can easily bring myself off.'

Thanks to this generous gesture, Dominique was able to concentrate fully on enjoying the delicious sensations of my cock see-sawing a squelchy passage into her welcoming quim and of my balls bouncing against her pubic fleece. She jerked her hips forwards and backwards in time with my pistoning strokes in and out of her juicy love-sheath and she gasped: 'Aaah! Aargh! How scrumptious! Push your prick in harder, Horby, further in, that is the way!' Her rounded backside responded to every shove as I drove home, excited to fresh, raging peaks of pleasure; and I almost fainted away as the sweet friction of her cunny lips against my stiff shaft made every nerve tingle with that exquisite, unique, amatory delight until the thrusts from my lusty prick coupled with the electric contractions of her cunt finally sucked out a frothy emission of spermy jism from my cock.

At this point, I wanted to relax but these young ladies appeared to be quite insatiable. Maria stretched Dominique across her knees, stroking her bare buttocks as I lay upon the bed and gazed at them with gradually renewed erotic interest. I could hardly refrain from gloating over the tight little bum cheeks which were so rudely exposed to my lascivious gaze.

'Go on, my love,' Dominique said to Maria as the latter stroked her bare white buttocks and she grinned cheekily.

'Give me a nice little spanking – not too hard, though.'
Maria was not unwilling to oblige her and commenced
gently to smack Dominique's firm flesh until a pink blush
showed on her superbly rounded bum cheeks. Maria
paused and Dominique murmured: 'Go on, my mistress,
give me a neat spanking for my naughtiness.' Maria began
to spank her hard, transforming the pink blush to one of
crimson. 'Oooh! Oh la la!' the girl squealed. 'My arse is
really tingling.'

Maria responded by slapping Dominique's beautiful
bottom more lightly yet with increasing rapidity until her
jiggling bum cheeks changed colour from crimson to
burning scarlet: and my cock was once more rock-hard as
the victim winced and wiggled under the spanking.

'Ouch! Ouch! That's enough, quite enough . . .!'
Dominique gasped and Maria relented as the girl turned
her head to me. I seized her within my arms and as I took
one of her protruding nipples within my mouth, her
slender fingers caressed the other one whilst my hold upon
her clitoris aroused her amorous flame in all its intensity.
My lips imprinted hot kisses upon her face, the cheeks of
which were burning with a fire as strong as that which
warmed her bottom.

Higher and higher crept my insinuating hand, till I had
got fair possession of her chink, all moistened as it was
with warm, creamy emission. Dominique sobbed slightly
on my shoulder, owing to the spanking, as her legs parted
slightly and a perceptible shudder of suppressed emotion
informed me surely enough that my success would soon be
complete. As I withdrew my hand from that burning spot,
she lifted her naked foot so that it rested upon my
rampant tool, stiff and hard as iron; and my prick
throbbed beneath the heel of that caressing foot as it
gently frigged me.

From her face, my lips found their way to Dominique's bosom once more and her sighs too plainly uttered her feelings. My tremendous truncheon was stiff against her belly. Now Maria placed her cool hand upon it and directed it into Dominique's cunt. We commenced a delightful side-fuck, our lips again glued together, 'tipping' one another with the ends of our tongues. I kept up the strokes until she spent in an agony of delight. Resting for a few moments, I went on again, with her legs entwined over my waist as she heaved and writhed in all the voluptuous ecstasy of her lecherous nature, to the intense delight of my prick, which revelled in the joyful moisture, becoming firmer and more excited moment by moment.

'Ah!' Dominique shrieked, barely able to catch her breath. My bounding strokes were making the bed creak as Maria laughed with a deep, throaty chuckle. 'Drive on, push it in, balls and all – oh – fuck me, fuck me! Oh! I'm coming again! . . . so do you . . . what a spend yours is! . . . how to you shoot it into me, you grand fellow! . . .'

I was aroused from my reverie by the return to the Salon de Thé of Monsieur J.K. Huysmans, my estimable companion.

'*Eh bien, monsieur*,' he remarked with severely clerical sobriety. 'Now, where was I?' I dragged my mind back from my memory of a memorable encounter with the daughter of one of the most influential men in France. What had *he* thought about in the *pissoir?*

'I was wondering . . .' I said.

CHAPTER FOUR

'Let us refresh ourselves with Chinese Green Gunpowder Tea,' J.K. Huysmans suggested courteously, 'as I proceed to tell you my tale of Black Magic. Ten years before, I might have offered you absinthe, but as I have seen, it is the drink which drives men mad.' I stared at the two looking-glasses, full-length mirrors between which our table was positioned and which reflected our images forever unto Infinity, and was glad that we were not having absinthe. 'Green is a curious colour,' he continued meditatively. 'Why, green tea can make a man mad. You are assuredly acquainted with the story of that name by that exquisite Irish writer, Sheridan Le Fanu?'

I nodded an uneasy assent. In this tale, a devout clergyman drinks copious quantities of green tea which leads to his being haunted by a monkey-like figure whom no one else can perceive and which destroys his sanity.

'My mood is a little green today,' Huysmans announced, coolly regarding the small emerald embedded in a gold ring which adorned the little finger of his left hand. 'So let us enjoy pernod, the legal equivalent of absinthe. It is green: and to accompany this, let us enjoy a portion of green plums, which you in England call green-gages. However, *mon cher monsieur*, let us restrain ourselves from the debauchery of green *sauce menthe* with which your countrymen choose to ruin roasted lamb; *je n'aime pas ça.* It reminds me that green is also the colour of slime. A man must be sparing in his choice of green.' The refreshments he ordered came swiftly and proved to be delicious as this intriguing man continued with his tale.

'Have you heard,' he asked me, 'of Stanislas de Guaita, Gerard Encausse and – or – Sâr Peládan?'

'Yes,' I responded as I stiffened involuntarily, for I recalled Claire's epistolary description of her initiation into an allegedly Rosicrucian Order in Paris, done in terms of Sex Magick.

'Permit me to explain,' said Huysmans. 'Stanislas de Guaita was a Marquis and a poet of great promise with a wide literary acquaintanceship. Around 1884, he became friendly with another poet, editor and novelist, Catulle Mendés, son-in-law of the immortal Théophile Gautier, whose novels were brilliant, most notably *Mademoiselle de Maupin*. The novels of Mendés were less distinguished, using the themes of incest and other sexual peculiarities, but this man urged de Guaita to read the works of the great French magus, Eliphas Lévi. The Marquis did so and was immediately subjected to what he himself termed the *coup de foudre occulte* – the "occult thunderstroke".

'As a result, he changed his way of life completely,' Huysmans continued calmly. 'He read magical and alchemical works rather than poetry, attempted to contact the spirits by Magic in his scarlet-draped study converted into a magical Temple and took hashish and cocaine to assist his communion with deities and demons. In 1885, on making the acquaintanceship of Encausse and Peládan, he founded the Kabalistic Order of the Rose-Croix with the objectives of studying and practising magic, spreading a knowledge of occult principles among the French public and revivifying the artistic life of Western Europe. Leading members included that extraordinary composer and pianist, Erik Satie; and Oswald Wirth, an expert on the Tarot cards, who designed his own remarkable pack, clarifying the wisdom contained in the *Tarot de Marseilles.*'

'So far, this sounds rather laudable,' I remarked.

'If only it had been so,' Huysmans replied. 'These men found it increasingly difficult to work together. Joséphin "Sâr Peládan was a wizard, novelist, fanatical Wagnerian and an unorthodox Catholic, finding it difficult to resolve these contradictions within himself. Oswald Wirth always desired to fight "occult battles" against those whom he considered to be "black magicians": he should have looked more closely at his own associates.

'When Guiata wasn't taking drugs, his principal interest lay in traditional occult practices as drawn, *n'est-ce pas?*, from *The Key of Solomon* and *The Grimoire of Pope Honorius*. These sinister works evoke demons. Encausse became a practising physician, an expert hypnotist and a writer on occultism under the pseudonym "Papus". Perhaps you have read his *The Tarot of the Bohemians*?' I had, finding it utterly incomprehensible. (I note from my vantage point of 1925 that "Papus" became charlatan-in-chief to Tsar Nicholas II of Russia, a position from which he was eventually displaced by that mad monk, Rasputin.)

'As for Peládan . . .' Huysmans shrugged his shoulders helplessly, 'he affirmed that he was a reincarnation of an ancient Assryian king, Sâr Merodach, whom he might translate as King Marduk, the principal deity of the Mesopotamian religion in ancient time: yet he managed to reconcile this with an ardent adherence to Roman Catholicism. *L'homme, c'est fou!*' Huysmans exclaimed indignantly. 'He quarrelled with de Guiata and founded his own Order of the Rose-Croix of the Temple and the Grail or the Catholic Rose-Croix in 1890, with a membership list as brief as its title was long.'

'But didn't he manage to do something for the arts?' I queried.

' "Something"?' Huysmans sipped tea, arched his eyebrows disdainfully and smiled archly. 'He wrote inept novels such as *The Supreme Vice* and maladroit works of magical instruction such as *How to Become a Fairy*. His writing? Bah! *C'est terrible!* But you are correct, Lord Horby, in your surmise that he essayed good work on behalf of the visual arts. There were six exhibitions of the *Salons de Rose-Croix*, organized between 1892 and 1897 and showing magnificent painters such as Gustave Moreau, Félicien Rops, Georges Rouault and the Comte de Larmandie. The magical artistic theory was summed up by Peládan in a manifesto issued by his Order:

Artist! You are a priest: Art is the great Mystery . . .
Artist! You are a king: Art is the true Empire . . .
Artist! You are a magician: Art is the great miracle . . .

'What's wrong with that?' I asked.

'What became of it,' he replied. 'As I mentioned earlier, I became friends with Boullan, portraying him favourably in my *Là-Bas*. *Maintenant*, de Guiata had infiltrated Boullan's Lodge in Lyons, posing as a would-be convert, as had the Marquis' disciple, Oswald Wirth. De Guiata and Wirth later wrote a book about Boullan, *The Temple of Satan*, calling him "a pontiff of infamy, a base idol of the mystical Sodom, a magician of the worst type, a wretched criminal, an evil sorcerer, and the founder of an infamous sect." They made a declaration of war upon Boullan, sending him a letter in which they affirmed that he was a condemned man.'

'Sorry, Monsieur Huysmans,' I murmured, 'I'm not quite sure just who are the evil Satanists here.'

'An interesting question.' Huysmans gave me a dry smile. 'According to Boullan, spells and curses were exchanged between Lyons and Paris with great spiritual struggles taking place on "the astral plane": yet de Guiata and Wirth claimed that these "astral" struggles existed only in Boullan's imagination. However, Boullan died three years after I met him. Partly I blame myself.'

'How so?' I really did need my green pernod, never mind my green tea.

'Boullan believed our friendship had drawn me into his struggles,' Huysmans answered. 'He was anxious to protect me, and twice in the summer of 1890 he performed magical operations designed to protect us from our enemies. They proved insufficient.' The man spoke as if he were describing a visit to the dentist. 'I suffered from bouts of fluidic fisticuffs.'

'Sorry . . .?'

'My cat and I were struck blows by an invisible antagonist.' He finished his tea in one gulp. 'I took Boullan's instructions, isolated myself and burned a pastille of Boullan's Paste of Exorcism, a mixture of camphor, cloves, frankincense and myrrh, and then, brandishing a miraculous host of the Prophet Vintras within my right hand, I clasped the blessed scapular of Carmel close to my body and recited conjurations which dissolved the astral fluids and paralysed the power of the sorcerers.'

'I see,' I said. I didn't see at all.

'During the summer of 1891,' Huysmans continued, 'I spent several weeks in Lyons where more elaborate ceremonies were performed for our protection. The battles of Black and White Magic had begun again. Boullan was jumping about like a tiger whenever he held one of his hosts. He invoked the aid of St Michael and the eternal justicaries and standing before the altar, he cried out:

"Strike down Peládan! Strike down Peládan!" Unfortunately, the powers of Satan prevailed and it was Boullan who was struck down. The day before he was due to go to Paris to lecture of Mysticism, he collapsed and died suddenly, on 3rd January 1893, the victim of Satanism and black magic!'

'Was he previously in good health?' I enquired.

'Ah, Lord Horby, I see that you don't believe me.' Huysmans looked mildly disappointed. 'Yes, there was the matter of heart trouble and a problem with his liver . . . but I assure you that it was Black Magic of the deepest dye. Why, my learned acquaintance Jules Bois, a journalist and former member of the Church of Carmel of Vintras and Boullan, why, he shares my opinion. In an article published in *Gil-Blas*, Jules Bois, a severely rational man, accused de Guiata and Peládan of astral murder. It is indisputable that de Guiata and Peládan practised Black Magic every day. Poor Boullan was perpetually in conflict with the evil spirits they sent him from Paris. My poor friend Boullan succumbed to a supremely powerful spell: and on the evening that he died, my cat and I were subjected to a particularly severe infliction of what the Americans would term "fluidic fisticuffs".'

'But you're still alive,' I said.

'For reasons I shall explain,' Huysmans replied. He glanced briefly at our empty glasses. 'Let us take green Chartreuse now.' I agreed. 'De Guiata was still determined to kill me. He publicly denied that he was a diabolist and murderer and challenged both Jules Bois and myself to a duel. I will not fight a man who has black magic in his gunpowder and so thought it prudent to apologize via my seconds, stating that I was not responsible for the statements of Jules Bois. But Jules Bois has always been a stubborn one and he publicly repeated his allegations, this time also implicating Dr Gerard Encausse in his accusation of astral homicide. Two duels took place. You look sceptical, Lord Horby, but allow me to tell you the truth.' I sipped my chartreuse and nodded.

'When Bois left his home for the duel with de Guiata,' Huysmans informed me, 'some very singular things occurred on both sides. On both sides our allies were praying for us and practising conjurations. And on the road to Versailles, for I heard this from Bois's second, Paul Foucher, one of the horses pulling Bois's carriage stopped suddenly and began to tremble, then it staggered, *as though it had seen the Devil in person*. It was impossible to proceed. The trembling lasted for twenty minutes. The duel took place eventually and two bullets were exchanged without result.'

'Honour was satisfied . . .' I murmured.

'But there is a curious fact or two.' Huysmans smiled wryly. 'My words can be verified by Paul Foucher, Bois's second, and by Gastine-Renette, the leading gunsmith of Paris, to whom the pistols were taken for examination later in the day. "What happened?" the famous gunsmith demanded. "The bullet of one of the duellists didn't leave the barrel." Paul Foucher said: "I was sure that the pistol of Jules Bois had not missed fire. As for the pistol used by the Marquis De Guiata, it is quite unbelievable that neither he nor his seconds, one of whom was an officer and the other Laurent Tailhade, should not have noticed that the pistol did not fire." The occultists could therefore pride themselves on having terrified the horse of one of the opponents and having prevented the bullet from leaving the pistol of Monsieur de Guaita.'

'There was a second duel,' Huysmans informed my

bemused ears in between sips of his green chartreuse, 'between Jules Bois and Dr Gerard Encausse, this time to be fought with rapiers, and it took place three days later. *Encore*, horses were involved. The horse drawing the carriage of Bois to the duelling field collapsed. Bois engaged a second carriage but *encore*, the horse collapsed, this time throwing Bois violently to the ground. Even so, a bruised, cut and bleeding Bois insisted upon keeping his appointment with a formidable antagonist. "I remember Papus taking off his coat," Bois told me, "I remember the words, the gypsy eye of my adversary, the impatient wrinkle in his forehead, his beard and jovial lips, his heavy build. He was a bull among these improvised evangelists." '

'What happened?' I asked, not being a bad swordsman myself.

'Both antagonists were wounded in the encounter but neither seriously,' Huysmans replied. 'As Paul Foucher told me, although the swords were magical, the wounds they inflicted were slight and have long since healed. Shortly afterwards, they were reconciled as friends . . . but Stanislas de Guiata died in 1897 from an overdose of drugs.'

'And you . . .?' I queried.

'Some time ago, a very learned Jesuit priest told me that at some moment in my life, I would have to choose between the point of a pistol or the foot of the Cross. I have chosen the foot of the Cross.' I could now understand why that although I had relished *A Rebours* and *Là-Bas*, I had found his *En Route* to be a monumentally tedious account of the follies of the Christian Mysticism he had misguidedly chosen to embrace. 'Have you had the good fortune to meet Father Binoire S.J.?'

'I have encountered him, yes,' I replied, 'but you

obviously know him rather better than I do. And since it is a green evening, allow me to confess that I feel quite green with envy.'

'Lord Horby, do I detect a slight trace of sarcasm in your attitude? It is the lowest form of wit.' He sipped the last of his green chartreuse and shrugged his shoulders dismissively. 'Satanism or Catholicism, that is the only choice for those of mystical persuasion.'

'Is it?' I queried innocently. (Today, in 1925, I recall Aleister Crowley's saying: "J.-K. Huysmans tried to betray the Secrets to the Roman Catholic Church and died of cancer of the tongue", which he did a few years after our meeting.)

'It is,' Huysmans retorted with dogmatic defiance. 'Now drink up your green chartreuse, *mon cher monsieur*, and if it be your wish, kindly accompany me to a sanctuary of The Church, therein to witness the punishment of a female penitent convicted of the crime of Witchcraft.'

CHAPTER FIVE

J.K. Huysmans swore me to secrecy concerning the precise location of what we proceeded to witness, though I am permitted to say that the event to be described took place in the Jardin des Plantes Quartier at a Convent School for young ladies. We journeyed there by cabriolet and he led me into a grim and forbidding building just as the moon was rising. A nun admitted us through a bare hall into a luxuriously furnished anteroom. I wondered if I were at last to witness Satanism but instead saw Lord Maulerby and Father Binoire sipping *fino* sherry. We greeted one another and they were obviously well acquainted with Huysmans. The nun filled and replenished our glasses as we conversed inconsequentially about nothing in particular. Eventually, the Mother Superior was ushered in by two more nuns and we greeted her.

It was difficult to discern her figure beneath her habit though she possessed a plump and pretty face, marred only by the tightness of her mouth and the hardness of her eyes. I was introduced to her as an English *milord* who was contemplating the taking of Instruction in the Roman Catholic faith and saw no cause, at that instant, to disillusion her, so intrigued was I by the proceedings. She had the nuns usher us into another antechamber, where she left us. I followed the example of my companions in taking a white, hooded robe as indicated by the nuns, who promptly departed. All four of us changed our clothes and we looked as if we were inspectors from the Spanish Inquisition when Father Binoire knocked once upon the door. A nun re-entered to admit us into a central hall.

The air was thick with the smoke of frankincense and myrrh. A hidden organist was playing some of Bach's more gloomy compositions. We were given sofas at the back of the hall, upon a raised platform, which gave us a perfect view. Before us, there were rows of empty chairs and, beyond them, a stage. The hall was illuminated throughout by tall white candles. At the back of the stage, nailed up high on the oak-panelled wall, was a statue of Jesus Christ upon the Cross and, directly below that, a white marble statue of the Virgin Mary. There were two cages on either side of this statue and each one contained a young girl, certainly no younger than eighteen and no older than twenty. One girl was slim and blonde, the other one was pleasantly plump and brunette and the hair of both had obviously been elegantly styled for this auspicious occasion. Both wore yellow ribbons in their hair and their heads had been crowned with the white dunces' caps; they had also the adornment of white frilly blouses; knee-length skirts, pleated and in grey; white socks which reached to just below the knee; and shiny black shoes with silver buckles. The cages were labelled: CATHERINE for the blonde and JEANNE for the brunette.

Both girls stood with their heads bowed and their hands tied behind their backs. Each girl had had a placard hung around her neck and the slogan, immaculately lettered, on each was: I AM A WITCH. I AM A WHORE. I AM TO BE BIRCHED. I AM GRATEFUL FOR MY JUST PUNISHMENT. As the organ music continued to play, around fifty girls dressed in white blouses and long black skirts entered backstage, filed past the penitents, then stepped down the stage steps to take their seats, though not before taunting the girls in their cages. I heard comments such as: 'You thought you were so important, didn't you?', 'You've always been such a snooty bitch', 'Look at you now' and 'That'll teach you to be cheeky.'

The nuns filed in silently and took their seats in the front row. I could hear much rustling of petticoats among the seated convent schoolgirls. The Mother Superior mounted the stage and led us in a hymn to the Mercy of Christ. After that, we knelt and prayed for the souls of the sinners. On arising, I saw an eager, flushed anticipation upon the cheeks of the schoolgirls. The Mother Superior proceeded to make a speech. She informed one and all of the crimes with which Catherine and Jeanne had been charged and found guilty. The principal crime was Witchcraft but it was compounded by sexual immorality: Catherine and Jeanne had been found in bed together. There was a slight gasp from the girls, instantly suppressed as the nuns turned their heads. Their private belongings had been searched in consequence and two nuns now entered upon the stage, bearing the grisly exhibits.

The evidence, in terms of the Convent, seemed to be incontrovertible. Both had hidden photographs of a Parisian music hall star called Le Pétomaine, whose speciality consisted of farting musical tunes out of his arse. Both had scrawled obscene words in their Bibles: Catherine had scrawled FUCK THIS over the passage in which Jesus Christ declares: 'I am the Way, the Truth and the Life.' Jeanne had written BUGGER THIS over the verse: 'Suffer little children to come unto me.' They had not denied that these words had been lettered in their handwriting. Moreover, in addition to holding up the disfigured pages of the Bible for our inspection the Mother Superior asked if anyone would deny that the scripts had indeed issued forth from the pens of the culprits: no one did. Finally, she held up a wax figurine of a woman with obscenely gross breasts and buttocks, bearing an observable resemblance of the Mother Superior. The word BITCH had been painted in what could have been blood across the thighs and belly of this figurine and two pins had been inserted into the vagina.

'What is your verdict, my children?' the Mother Superior asked earnestly.

'Birch them,' the girls chanted in unison. 'Birch them! *Birch* them! BIRCH THEM!!!' The girls writhed in semi-hysteria.

'Thank you, my children, but we must consider the case for the defence. After all, the good God is merciful and just.'

'NO!!!' the girls screamed.

'I insist upon hearing the case for the defence,' the Mother Superior insisted calmly. 'Sister Agnes,' she turned to the nun upon her right, 'kindly conduct it.'

' "Father forgive them for they know not what they do," ' the slim Sister Agnes quoted from the Bible as she raised her eyes to heaven. 'Looking at their confessions made to you and me, Mother Superior,' she consulted a sheaf of papers, 'Catherine and Jeanne claim that they were the innocent victims of demonic possession. This must be true, for only the demonically possessed could possibly be guilty of such disgraceful acts of blasphemy. I therefore beseech you, on their behalf, to show them the greatest possible mercy by increasing the strokes from the customary six to a round dozen in order to ensure a gracious exorcism of these penitents.'

'Nobly spoken, Sister,' the Mother Superior declared, 'and your plea for mercy is granted.' The whole school cheered at the justice of the decision. 'Sister Elizabeth, kindly bring me the penitent Catherine.' Sister Elizabeth gladly obliged, unlocking the cage and bringing the girl to the front of the stage. Sister Agnes pushed an altar on wheels to the centre of it, then lovingly covered it with a white linen cloth, on the front of which was emblazoned a red cross. 'Catherine!' the Mother Superior commanded sharply, causing the girl's bottom to quiver visibly within her pleated skirt, 'you have heard the verdict of the School. Fetch the rod, which you have spent the morning making.' The trembling girl briefly left the stage to return with a pliant birch, neatly trimmed and adorned by a yellow ribbon. She then knelt at the feet of the Mother Superior, offered the rod for approval and begged softly and tearfully for a good whipping.

The Mother Superior graciously granted her request and Catherine was led to the altar by the two Sisters, Agnes and Elizabeth, who bent her over and secured all her four limbs with leather straps. Her skirt and petticoat were lifted and her drawers pulled down to her well-turned ankles, revealing one of the loveliest curvaceous pouting rears that I have ever seen. Her bare flesh was displayed to the entire girls' school and the masked male 'inquisitors' in what must surely have been a supreme humiliation. Her bottom appeared to be blushing with shame before the birch even reached it.

The Mother Superior tapped the birch across the buttocks of Catherine. Instantly they tensed and clenched.

'Present your bottom properly for punishment, Catherine,' her mentor commanded sharply. The girl raised her trembling fesses into the air. After an almost audible silence, the Mother Superior swished the birch down hard and smartly across the centre of her victim's bottom. It made a soft, smacking sound but it left no mark, although

Catherine sucked in her breath and nervously jerked, perhaps more from the torturing suspense than from the first stroke itself. I feasted my vision to the utmost, for it was extraordinarily, mouth-wateringly tasty, this sight of a young girl's twitching, punished buttocks.

The second stroke descended with a hiss, landing just below the centre but well above the slender thighs and I enjoyed the sight of the birch thwacking across those tender hemispheres. Catherine gasped a little more loudly this time, nervously tried to shift from foot to foot and visibly dragged on her bound wrists. From the way her sides were trembling – and I could see the lovely ribcage plainly outlined against her taut white skin – I knew that she was lamenting the long duration of her atonement. The third lash whistled through the air to land about an inch below the place which the second had punished.

Catherine's hips gave an involuntary swerve to the side and her head tilted back a little as she sighed softly. At this moment when the makings of stripes and weals could be discerned, the Mother Superior commanded Sisters Agnes and Elizabeth to wheel a large looking-glass upon the stage and to place in it before the penitent as a gasp of pleasure from the girls in the audience ascended up to heaven, no doubt.

'You see, my darling child, Catherine, what the practices of witchcraft and immorality have brought you to?' the Mother Superior demanded. I could see that Catherine's eyes were full of tears and her nostrils were beginning to dilate rather rapidly. She was not kept waiting for the fourth swish which was applied almost instantly thereafter, yet exactly over the last place attacked. A reiterative stroke on bare flesh which has already been sensitised produces much more than a double effect of irksome heat, which radiates throughout the entire feminine nervous system and thus aggrandises the punishment and, also, the voluptuous titilations which a whipping always produces in a female in any sensitivity whatsoever, as any connoisseur of flagellation can tell you from experience.

The fifth swish took a little longer and Catherine nervously glanced back for a second, then again bowed her head and stiffened herself. It cut directly across the plumpest curves of both her naked arse-globes, producing a faint sob and a convulsive squirming which I found maddeningly stimulating to my roused and savagely excited cock. The Mother Superior made her wait almost a minute for the sixth lash, which wrapped the pliant birch around the base of that wonderfully contoured backside of the girl, and a twig may possibly have darted in toward her furry gap, for she lunged to the left, sticking her bottom out in straining fashion with a plaintive groan of entreaty.

The Mother Superior paid no attention to the penitent's sighs and cries. She promptly applied several more strokes, placing them straight across the jounciest region of the summits of Catherine's naked, striped behind. I was enraptured by my contemplation of this spectacle. For all I knew, Catherine might be a most delightful and charming girl, albeit a naughty one; but I could feel no pity. I was fascinated by the sight of her scarlet glowing bottom as it twisted and turned.

As the final stroke was applied, tears poured out of her eyes. She groaned and sobbed, writhed and jerked, but in the main I had to admit that she had borne her dozen strokes with relatively good grace, far better than many an English girl would have done if bent over a desk to receive chastisement for poor lessons or inattentiveness or rudeness to a schoolmistress.

The punishment completed, the girl who had been so well whipped was released from her bondage and the

Sisters restored the state of her drawers and brushed down her petticoat and skirt. She then had to kneel once more, kiss the rod – by now bearing all the markings of its contact with her tender flesh – thank the Mother Superior for her just chastisement and implore forgiveness and permission to retire.

'You are forgiven, my child,' the Mother Superior replied gently. The whole school applauded in a frenzy of excitement. 'Arise.' Catherine obeyed. 'Curtsey.' She did so graciously as she sobbed. 'You will now go and stand in the corner for an hour and quietly contemplate both your sins and your way of being forgiven.'

Catherine was led to the back of the hall by Sisters Agnes and Elizabeth, who placed her in a bleak white corner, face to the wall, with her hands behind her back. Sister Agnes drew her white, lacy drawers down to her ankles and Sister Elizabeth pinned up her skirt and petticoat once more to reveal her scarlet, punished buttocks. It struck me that one could spent a delightful hour watching her bottom change colour as it trembled and shivered, and the other schoolgirls seemed to be of the same opinion; but after a few minutes, the drawers were raised and the skirt and petticoat lowered. A card was hung upon her back declaring: I HAVE BEEN RIGHTLY BIRCHED FOR MY INSOLENCE. Her bottom continued to twitch, causing the pleats of her skirt to quiver quite enticingly.

Jeanne was then released from her cage and a similar performance ensued. There was one noticeable difference, though: her buttocks were much more round and plump and took longer to redden. When that happened, however, and it would have been at about the sixth stroke that they blazed with a fiery glow, one was amazed both by the thrusting and writhing of her hips and sighs and gasps of her fellow schoolgirls. I noted also that the facial cheeks of the Mother Superior and her fellow Sisters were almost as red as the bum cheeks of their penitents. Nor could one avoid noticing that the schoolgirls who had not surreptitiously placed their hands actually within their skirts were rubbing their palms hard against their covered pubic mounds or else were squeezing their thighs so tightly together that I feared they might shriek out as loud as Jeanne at the end of her birching.

I shan't forget my disrobing in the antechamber with the men, once Jeanne had been placed in her corner to be teased with Catherine by the schoolgirls after a hymn and final prayers, when I couldn't help spotting that the white underpants of Lord Maulerby, J.-K. Huysmans and Father Binoire S.J. were soaked in semen.

'I trust,' said Huysmans, as Maulerby and Binoire gazed approvingly at a rampaging erection which I could not hide, 'that you are beginning to discern the joys of penitence and Christianity.'

'Oh, indeed,' I replied. 'But I'm bloody well damned if I know the differences between a brothel, Satanism and this.'

CHAPTER SIX

The following morning brought a letter from Claire, postmarked southwest London. Why the hell hadn't the bitch answered my telegrams? I needed to communicate with her now more than ever and so I ripped the envelope open with some irritation.

My darling,

I have met an interesting elderly gentleman recently and, according to my estimation, he is of the same age as my father. I do not think that I have ever suffered from an Electra 'complex' as Dr Freud would have it, that feeling of sexual attraction to the father with hostility towards the mother, yet this gentleman had great magnetism; and my father is renowned for his own charm.

Upon this auspicious occasion, I was attending a dinner party at the home of a friend. A total of ten guests had assembled in Knightsbridge to enjoy the banquet thoughtfully prepared for us. Six of the guests were married couples and sometimes I wonder if I will ever marry. Most of my friends have accepted a proposal, have been led to the altar as lambs to the slaughter and have become living embodiments of the old proverb: 'Marry in haste, repent at leisure.'

I hope that wedlock will never be forced upon me but

such was the case with the hostess, Maud, a dear friend from my schooldays, who had stood at the altar when eight months pregnant to join her life to that of a gross but wealthy country squire, Sir Toby Downshire. On their honeymoon in Ireland, she gave birth to twins and a cousin who was present swore that she saw the leprechauns present in the room, the little people, those mischievous spirits. The twins were both born with cauls upon their heads, which is a good omen as they will develop the inner sight and powers of perception.

My dinner companion to my right was Pyotr Alexeyvich Kropotkin, known in London Society as Prince Peter Kropotkin. I could not take my eyes away from him. He spoke with such a strong Russian accent, even though it emerged that he had lived in England as a political exile since 1886. He talked in a fascinating fashion about his life and about his passion for Geography and Geology, in which he had achieved a respected reputation, though he did not at that point mention that he was also a notorious anarchist. I had fondly imagined that all anarchists wore black, broad-brimmed hats with black cloaks and carried incendiary devices bearing the label BOMB.

I had never met a Geologist before, let alone an anarchist, yet I knew that they have a desire to penetrate the crust of the Earth, to prod into the layers of granite and basalt and ultimately to penetrate our planet's burning core. He spoke of his travels in the Siberian tundra and of the savage cold of the winter weather.

'I wish I had been there to keep you warm,' I remarked over the sixth course (of beef and Burgundy) as I allowed my hand to rest upon his knee. 'It must have been terrible for you. Did you suffer from frostbite at all?'

'My toes turned blue.' He looked into my eyes and his

piercing gaze burned me within. My hand crept up his thigh.

'How miserable it must have been,' I responded sympathetically.

'Yes, my dear, it was, but if I had had the pleasure of the company of a beautiful and intelligent woman such as yourself, it would have been much more tolerable . . .' My hand reached his scrotum, appreciating the feel of his bulging testicles through the cloth of his trousers. My thumb stroked his pulsating ram-rod and I knew then just how much his throbbing member wanted to penetrate my pussy. 'We must fornicate!' he roared in the voice of a mad Russian.

There were shock and amazement upon the faces of one couple at the dinner-table and I'm afraid that I forget their names. Poor dears, they were so dismally middle-class and simply didn't know how to behave. They stared aghast at our hostess who knows my nature intimately well and who carried on eating as if nothing untoward had occurred. The hideous nature of their social faux pas slowly dawned upon them as they turned their heads to stare at Squire Toby, who was tucking away wine, as usual.

'Bloody good idea!' he bellowed in a voice like thunder. 'The trouble with this country is that there's not enough fucking!'

'Quite agree,' his wife returned icily. I looked coy.

'Let us drink some more!' Prince Kropotkin declared, accepting another glass of La Tache. 'And then a good rogering, as they say in England. A splendid expression!' He glared at the middle-class couple who were shrinking into their seats. Pulling a revolver from his pocket, he glanced for permission at our hostess, who nodded once. The hapless couple dived beneath the table as Prince

Kropotkin promptly shot a crystal off the overhanging chandelier.

'Damn good shot, sir!' Squire Toby exclaimed approvingly. 'Never seen it hit so accurately yet. Damnit, sir, you and me must go tiger hunting some time.'

As the bourgeois couple crawled miserably back into their seats, perpetually to be a laughing-stock in London Society, Prince Kropotkin replaced his smoking gun, the other guests carried on chatting about the theatre and the servants continued to pour more wine as if this sort of thing happened every evening. What insolence, arrogance, haughtiness, cockiness, brashness, bumptiousness he had, and with such a flagrantly self-assured manner!

The atmosphere relaxed over treacle pudding with whipped cream, followed by a compote *that seemed to consist mainly of cherries. I am sure that some specks of dried* cantharides, *popularly known as Spanish Fly, had been sprinkled over the top, and there was the royal jelly of the bees and flowers. This sweet, viscous, yellow fluid had been applied liberally to soak into the mellow fruit. As the ladies left the table to withdraw for coffee and liqueurs, leaving the men to their port and nuts, I heard Squire Toby say:*

'Think you're a damn fine fellow, Kropotkin, damn fine fellow. But I don't hold with any of this anarchist nonsense of yours. Isn't it all about a bloody revolution or some such rubbish like that?'

'A revolution, certainly, Sir Toby,' Kropotkin replied, 'but it need not be a bloody one provided that we all see sense in terms of the next step of Mankind in terms of evolution.'

'Humph!' Squire Toby snorted. 'Intellectual balderdash. Still, you shoot straight, I'll give you that. But look

here, Prince, don't take it too far. Why, you'll be wanting to abolish the House of Lords next . . .'

The ladies left the gentlemen to sort out the world, which on the whole they do very badly, and concentrated instead in our conversation on local, practical matters, which on the whole we do very well. I enjoyed my mocha coffee topped by dollops of Guernsey cream sprinkled with flakes of chocolate and a pinch of cinnamon, and the glass of Drambuie was a welcome addition. It was a joy to sit around the roaring open fire of wood and the men appeared genial when they joined us. Squire Toby kept seizing the poker and prodding it into the coals beneath the wood to encourage the flames further, just as my father was wont to do. For a nightcap, we were served brandy, kindled by a flame of lambent blue. Some guests left, including 'les nouveaux riches' who were now 'les misérables.' Others had been invited to stay the night and I was ushered to my chamber, whereupon I discarded my clothing, attired myself in my silken night-gown and covered myself with the eiderdown.

I lit the oil lantern beside my bed, enjoying the strange optical illusions it created upon the ceiling and on the walls. Suddenly there was a knock upon my door as I was settling down to read some short stories by Arthur Machen.

'Who is it?' I queried gently.

'It is I, the Prince Peter Kropotkin and I have been requested to deliver you a deoch an doris, a stirrup cup,' his strong Russian voice boomed, 'so that you might have a peaceful sleep tonight.' I removed my nightcap and quickly combed my hair, then opened the door.

'Do come in.' Within seconds he had seized me in his arms.

'You do not know how long I have been waiting for this moment!' he sang out passionately and, he held me close and tightly to him, my belly was pressed against his rigid member. His shoe shot back to slam the door shut. *'You have nothing to fear, my dear,'* he sighed within my ear. *'In Russia, we men love to treat a lady well.'* Thereupon, he lifted me up and tossed me onto the bed. I bounced upon the springs as he quickly removed his clothing and then he tore off my silken nightie with one mighty rip! He sprang to suck my bosoms eagerly then took his tongue down to my quivering thighs. Gooseflesh trembled up and down my legs in a deliciously tickling sensation.

Suddenly he entered me. As he penetrated further into the deep heart within my labia, I entered into a world of fantasy, ecstasy and wondrous imagination as his empowering hands closed tightly upon my wrists to hold them down, spread upon the bed.

'Give it the rhythm, bitch,' he growled, *'yes, definitely give it the rhythm . . .'* I did so and he swived me as I have rarely been swived before. His rhythm was that of a piston and the shot of his juices, that of a pistol. Afterwards he gratified my tender sensibilities in that my essences had trickled down my thighs and he slurped noisily upon my fine nectar as if he were a bear devouring the wild honey of Siberian bees.

Afterwards he offered me an Imperial Russian cigarette, a long, thin object, half of which consists of the filter; and then he produced a flask of polished silver.

'This is what we like to drink in Russia after our sacred act of love,' he rumbled. It was as if mingled fire and water were passing down my throat and yet I recognised the aphrodisiacal qualities immediately. We sat upon the bed and discussed sundry matters. He told me that he

had joined the Russian Anarchist Movement during the 1870s.

'Doesn't that imply a radical evolution?' I enquired.

'Yes,' he responded simply. 'You cannot believe the oppression that I suffered in consequence of advocating the proposition that Man is essentially good and that governments are instruments of repression, not evolution and hence I advocate revolution. My autobiography will be entitled Memoirs of a Revolutionist.'

'Perhaps one day I shall write my autobiography,' I answered. 'Possibly I shall call it Memoirs of an Aristocratic Whore.' He gave me a wicked grin and a deeply rich chuckle. 'May I include you?'

'If you so desire.'

'I desire you,' I replied. He graciously accepted my invitation and this time we made love with laughter and tomfoolery. Afterwards he produced a balalaika from a deep inside pocket of his evening tail-coat and sang me Russian songs. I asked him to translate them and they all seemed to be about sex and violence. As the early morning sun arose, we fell asleep in one another's arms and I awoke in the afternoon to find that my anarchist, geological, geographical and royal lover had silently left: leaving his balalaika behind.

All my love,
Claire

This was all very well: but why the devil wasn't she assisting me in my search for the truth about Satanism? I was glad when Maria visited early that evening.

'Still engaged in the pursuit of Satanism, Horby?' She shrugged her shoulders and laughed mockingly over our *bocks*. 'Well, I have ensured that Gabriele Jogand will indeed be present at Le Chat Blanc in Montmartre tomorrow at luncheon to inform you of the unvarnished truth. Meanwhile we have more pressing matters at hand. Do you have your pistol?'

'I always do,' I replied.

That said, I sprang upon her, pushing her down upon the bed and kissing the inviting globes of her firm breasts with their pert, upstanding nipples, having roughly pulled her low-cut blouse down to her slender waist. Maria responded by moaning sweet endearing words, as if she was being caressed by one for whom she genuinely cared! My right hand pushed her coyly protective arm aside and took possession of her tender muff-cleft, squeezing it through the thin material of her skirt. Then I gently placed one leg over hers, pressing my rigid penis – by now almost tearing its own way out of the constraining trousers that held it back from its goal of Maria's tantalizing cunt – close to her delectable and voluptuous body. We looked into one another's eyes, nodded and proceeded instantly to divest ourselves of our outer clothes.

I noticed at once that Maria wore a red silk basque that she could untie from the front and very brief white lace panties that hugged her cunt so tightly that her pouting vaginal lips and dark-haired pubic mound were clearly outlined. Sheer black silk stockings, held up by a red-and-black lace suspender belt, sheathed her long, shapely legs high up her smooth thighs, leaving a breathtakingly enticing span of naked flesh between stocking-top and pantie-edge. The whole ensemble was clearly designed to focus the male gaze with burning intensity on the magic triangle of Maria's wondrous quim.

What thrills of delightful expectation shot through my whole frame! With my rod stiffly erect, I quivered from head to foot, for this luscious temptation and the intensity of lustful feeling it inspired produced an urge to ravish that would stand no further delay. So I glued my lips to Maria's in a long, lecherous kiss, holding the whole length of her marvellous lithe body tightly against mine. I ran my hands down her back, over her slender waist and on down to cup the firm flesh-globes of her superbly shapely buttocks. I squeezed them hard through the lace of her panties, pressing Maria's barely-covered cuntal mound roughly against my own bulging crotch at the same time as I rasped the hairs of my chest across her stiffening nipples. Breaking off our kiss, she arched her head back and moaned softly. I continued to squeeze her delectable arse hard, and forced both hands beneath the tight lower edge of the panties until I had two handfuls of smooth, warm, naked bumflesh in my grasp. Kneading them savagely, I insinuated the middle finger of my right hand into the fleshy groove between them until it reached the puckered portal of Maria's anus. After a preliminary circular stroking that caused her to shiver all over, I stuck the questing digit up to the second joint into her arse, relishing the sensation of the tight grip of her sphincter. 'Horby, you devil,' Maria breathed as I withdrew my finger from her bumhole, 'whatever next?'

My answer was not verbal but was certainly direct. Gripping Maria's tight, brief panties in both hands – one hand holding the flimsy item by its front, the other grasping it at the rear – I wrenched hard and ripped them off her in one quick movement, flinging the torn white lace aside. Maria shrieked in outraged surprise and instinctively tried to cover her suddenly revealed dark-haired muff with her hands. Gently but firmly, I forced her hands away from her pubic mound and held both of them easily behind her back in one of mine, using the other to fondle her now defenceless quim, preparing the way for my raging cock's assault upon her honeypot.

Maria gasped, struggling and trying to twitch her cunt, by now well lubricated, away from my clutching hand. I recognized the signs: Maria liked, on occasion, to pretend that she was a reluctant victim of her male partner's lustful desires. She gained extra excitement from the fantasy that she was helpless and at the mercy of a heartless rapist. I was more than happy to play along with her in this charade of the flesh.

I pulled Maria close against me and leant forward to speak softly in her ear. 'Maria,' I murmured, 'you beautiful, cockteasing bitch. It's me, Horby. You should know that you can't lead me on like you have been and expect to get away with just a friendly hug. And you *certainly* can't flaunt your wonderful body in that provocative underwear in front of me – or any man worthy of the name – without getting what you're asking for and getting it hot and hard. Just *looking* at your cunt lips bulging through those tight panties (before I ripped them off you), framed by your smooth thighs in those stockings and suspenders, nearly made me come on the spot. Which would have been a real waste of the flood of spunk I'm going to drench the depths of your jellybox with in a few minutes' time. My pork sword is going to teach your teasing twat a lesson it won't forget in a hurry. Whether you want me to or not, I'm going to fuck you senseless right now.'

Maria breathed in deeply and opened her mouth wide. I thought she was going to scream in mock terror so I sealed her lips with another soul-sucking kiss which seemed fairly to shut her up. When our lips disengaged, she muttered tearfully. 'The fancy underwear isn't for *your* benefit, please believe me. I only wear it for my *real* lover. You were never supposed to see me in it: I never intended to excite you or any other man apart from him. How can I help it if you assault me, undress me forcibly and like what you find so much that you want to rape me? Oh, show some pity and let me go, please. Oh, *please*.'

Maria was certainly getting into the spirit of the charade and no mistake. Her *ad lib* (or was it?) dialogue was a nice twist to the proceedings. But if I was going to be as good as my word about fucking her senseless, it was now time for action rather than dialogue. Otherwise there was likely to be an embarrassing case of premature ejaculation on stage, so to speak.

'Too late for pity, I'm afraid, Maria,' I said. 'If I don't get up you in the next five minutes, my balls will explode. I don't imagine that's the kind of interior decoration you want for this place, eh?' I pushed Maria back down onto the bed and knelt over her, my massively engorged member swinging stiffly from side to side above her breasts, before lowering myself onto her quivering form. She did not speak this time but appeared awfully discomposed nonetheless: long drawn-out sighs came from deep within her bosom as her breasts trembled (actually with excitement) and her hands feebly and increasingly unconvincingly tried to push away my intrusive fingers as they tweaked her nipples and pubic bush, kneaded her bum cheeks and thrust urgently between her cunt lips and into the depths of her quim. Desire eventually overcame her entirely false modesty; her return of my passionate kisses became more ardent and her straining, wonderfully firm and smooth thighs gradually gave in to my efforts to penetrate between them and parted with only a token reluctance. Instead of playing at repulsing my advances, her arms were now entwined around my body.

But, once again, Maria recollected the fantasy of rape in which she was engaged. She suddenly abandoned her embracing of me, beating at my chest – albeit weakly – with clenched fists and clamping her slender legs so tightly together that her cunt lips were hidden from view and only her dark pubic bush could be seen, framed enticingly by her trembling suspendered and stockinged thighs.

Obviously the citadel of Maria's pretended chastity had been stormed successfully many a time before yet she certainly acted as though it hadn't. Reaching the limits of my own self-control, I thrust my hands between her thighs and forced her legs apart, pushing them up and back, brutally exposing her quim to the battering ram of my lust – which still had to be vigorously applied to supposedly reluctant pussy-portals before a breach was made sufficient to effect a deep lodgement. Although Maria's cunt lips were actually sopping with love-juice, her amazingly developed vaginal muscles were able to keep the entrance to her joxy clenched tight. Not that she had the ghost of a chance by now of keeping me out. The sight of her plump pink honeypot lips and damply glistening pubic hair laid defenceless at last between her splayed, shapely thighs, and this whole fantastic target area so arousingly framed by suspender belt and stocking-tops, raised my surging desire to boiling point.

I grasped Maria's firm, beautifully rounded buttocks with both hands in a kneading grasp of iron, slipping a middle finger deep into the rosebud of her arse. Next, I leant the weight of my upper torso on the backs of her raised, frantically thrashing thighs, stilling them and forcing them yet further apart and back, so that her silk-sheathed knees now almost pressed against her shoulders. I manoeuvred my groin into position and placed the swollen tip of my poker-hard prick against the outer lips of Maria's damp cooze, relishing briefly the delightful sensation of the grip of the flesh-ring of her cuntal entrance around my bulging glans. Then, unable to delay a second longer, I savagely thrust the whole length of my rigid, engorged cock into the inner reaches of her warm, moist quim. I shouted in triumph – and Maria screamed a horrified 'No!'

So now, what anguished pleas for mercy and sighs of submissive despair!' What involuntary murmurs of real erotic joy, mingled with moans of pretended protest! As for me, I kept a tight hold of Maria's wonderful arse-globes, pulling her crotch tightly against my thrusting rod-root as my hips proceeded to move with a driving, pounding rhythm of their own, plunging my stiff dick to its hilt into Maria's vanquished, stockings-and-suspenders-adorned cunt time and time again. Soon enough I felt the familiar welcome rush of tingling, electric sensation from the depths of my balls through my pistoning shaft and out through the tip of my prick as I came explosively in a spurting tidal wave of jism, pulse after pulse after pulse. As my tadger shot its liquid load, Maria tossed her head from side to side and gasped an incoherent mix of grateful endearments alternating with tearful cries of outrage at the successful climax of my 'violation' of her innermost fleshy depths.

'That was *most* enjoyable, my darling Horby,' Maria said over the customary cognac which we both liked to take after a fuck, 'but it was not *quite* what I meant when I referred to your pistol, you hateful rapist, you.'

'Oh, if you mean something with which one shoots men rather than women, yes, I think I have a useful revolver somewhere,' I responded.

'You will need it,' Maria returned, 'for I have informa-tion that may shock you. You are, I believe, acquainted with a Viscount Maulerby, yes?'

'I have that particular misfortune,' I sighed.

'Are you aware,' she enquired, arching a thinly-pencilled eyebrow, 'that he is a double-agent, working in the interests of the German Empire?'

'Surely not! I mean, I know the man's a complete shit,' I expostulated, 'but a traitor . . . impossible!'

'Then look at this.' She extracted a sheaf of documents from her bag and passed them to me. I leafed through them with growing amazement though, thanks to my cousin at the Embassy in Berlin, I was not entirely unfamiliar with their contents. Here were detailed plans in the event of war with France, which had nearly come about due to the Fashoda clash in Africa 1898.

'How did you obtain them?' I queried.

'Simple.' Maria shrugged. 'I slept with Maulerby and took them from the ridiculous fool as he slumbered. And here is a letter to him,' she passed it over to me, 'from the deputy chief of the Prussian Secret Service congratulating Maulerby on subverting British interests in German East Africa.' I looked and there was no denying this most disturbing matter. 'I am endeavouring,' Maria said, 'to bring about peace through a maintenance of the balance of power on the Continent of Europe. This can best be done via closer relations between the British and the French. To this end I have been sleeping with two leading British Generals: John French and Douglas Haig. Both of them are obstinate, unimaginative fools. French thinks that any war in Europe can be won by a cavalry charge by the British dressed in red coats; Haig thinks that repeated assaults by massed infantry can do the trick. Neither of them appear to have heard of railway trains, minefields, barbed wire, poison gas or machine guns, such as I have heard about from my German lovers. Also they are both useless in bed. Even so, if the English idiots speak with the French idiots, then perhaps there can be an *Entente Cordiale* to block German Imperial expansionist ambitions peaceably.'

'This makes sense, Maria,' I said. (By God, it did! With the hindsight of 1925. There *were* 'informal military discussions' between the General Staffs of England and France; there *was* the *Entente Cordiale* of 1902; and when the Great War unfortunately came, Sir John French and Douglas Haig proved themselves to be even more useless than Maria had declared them to be.) 'But what are you proposing with regard to Maulerby?'

'Expose him as the traitor that he is,' Maria replied, 'one who is trying to spoil plans for peace between Great Britain and France by working for Germany and who is harming British Empire interests in Africa. Now, he thinks tonight that I will be walking into his trap; but given your co-operation, he will be walking into mine . . .' I listened to her proposal and smiled, fondly fingering my Harris tweed jacket.

'Let's go,' I said, smiling sadistically.

CHAPTER SEVEN

The British Secret Service can be damned good in action: it's its intelligence gathering that's the problem. I don't suppose that the relevant chap at its French HQ, obviously in the British Embassy in Paris, would have given me the time of day had it not been for my various social connections. The instant that some possibility of action was discerned, however, there was a definite stirring and plans were made.

Later in the evening, Maria entered the apartment block where Maulerby had rented a flat in Montparnasse. As she informed me later, he ushered her through the hallway and into the drawing-room where he produced a revolver, fondly imagining that as a British agent he was in one of our many 'safe houses'. Five minutes later, I came through the door with the key I had been given in my left hand and a revolver in my right to find Maria bound over a block, stripped naked, and Maulerby grinning gleefully as he poised and switched a martinet in his hand.

'The game's up, Maulerby,' I said. 'You and Maria will be changing places. Drop the martinet and untie the lady.'

'Stay out of this, Horby,' he snarled back. 'This woman is a spy and I'm working for British Intelligence. Just don't get involved in matters which don't concern you.'

'Oh, a spy, eh? Just as you are?' I responded. 'British Intelligence services will be here soon enough: how do you think that I have the key?' I waved it in the light of the oil-lamps. 'Unfasten the lady or I shall shoot you in the balls, with my gun going off by unfortunate accident.' Maulerby dropped the martinet and untied Maria, whose bottom was still a lustrous pearly white, owing to my arrival in the nick of time. 'Over to you, Maria,' I said as I picked up Maulerby's martinet and revolver, handing them to Maria as I kept him covered.

'You'll be hearing from High Command!' he spluttered. 'I warn you!'

'Dear me,' I retorted, 'and poor you.' My left hand slipped the keys into my jacket pocket then pulled out a Cuban panatella. I lit the cigar from an oil lamp as I continued to keep Maulerby covered with my pistol. 'Over to you, Maria.'

Maulerby stood there and looked foolish as Maria put her clothes back on. Eventually she rustled her skirts angrily and in return he quivered more than her petticoats.

'Take down your trousers, you traitor!' she snapped, her eyes ablaze. Lord Maulerby looked so foolish as his trousers tumbled to his ankles. 'Now pull down your drawers. Bend over that block where you intended to flog me. O! you were so sneeringly sadistic, weren't you? Now it is my turn.' She smiled gleefully as she clicked the handlocks and footlocks upon his wrists and feet, leaving his white behind perfectly positioned for punishment. She twirled the martinet in the air.

'This is an implement of French design,' she declared, 'invented by the French Major Martinet for use on the bare bottoms of negligent officer cadets at St Cyr. It closely resembles a cat o' nine tails, does it not?' She flicked it against his buttocks and he shuddered, his small, piggy eyes bulging at the unexpected and alarming reversal of roles. I took a glass of the champagne he had intended to sip as he flogged Maria and offered one to her, which she graciously accepted. 'It is a curious implement,' Maria continued as she suddenly lashed his bottom. The six thongs went *tsuck!* and Maulerby squealed. 'I suppose that the French simply have to be different,' she observed airily as she flicked him again and his hips twitched in response. 'You chose the martinet to punish me, you foolish boy, and now *I* shall use it to punish *you*.' She brought it down with a solid *thwack* in a stroke reminiscent of those ladies who have recently chosen to play tennis, raising two blue welts upon Maulerby's bottom and extracting a squawk that came from the depths of his throat. 'Painful, is it?' she laughed.

'Now look here . . .' Maulerby gasped. 'Don't. The consequences will be dreadful. I am highly connected, I warn you . . .' Maria responded with a further fierce lash and I watched with detached interest as the six thongs of the martinet raised marks all over his twitching buttocks. He shrieked and writhed as Maria giggled and I puffed upon my cigar. 'Highly connected, indeed,' Maria observed.

'And you had no compunction about doing this to me, did you, Lord Maulerby?' She whipped him again and he shouted out his pain as his florid face turned puce. 'On the whole,' Maria remarked casually, 'I find the martinet to be less useful than the birch, and considerably more inaccurate. In common with all whips, even the properly tapered varieties, it has an unfortunate lashing effect . . .'

'Ow!' Maulerby shrieked as the thongs lashed him.

'I find,' said Maria, 'that the tips of the thongs curl around the far flank and inflict the greatest punishment, not on the bottom, but in the region of the hip.' A further stroke which indeed landed on the side of Maulerby's hip made the man squirm. 'The answer,' Maria continued evenly, 'is to stand a little. Further. Back.' That enunciated, she extracted a phial of lipstick from her bag and wrote in scarlet upon his buttocks: 'I AM A TRAITOR TO GREAT BRITAIN. PLEASE WHIP ME.' There was a mirror in front of the flogging block in which Maulerby was confronted by his wretched and perspiring face. Maria now took a hand mirror from the bathroom and held it up so that the traitor could see her words scrawled in scarlet upon his whaled, twitching bottom. The next stroke landed on his upper thighs and he shrieked. 'It is a different instrument to control,' said Maria, thoughtfully surveying the damage, 'but the night is yet young.'

These deliberations were interrupted by an expected knock upon the door of the apartment and I admitted our operatives. The British Secret Service was among the first to employ female agents and Agnes, Maud and Beatrice, who entered, certainly did credit to the process of selection. Agnes bore a camera, Maud had the tripod and Beatrice carried the photographic plates. Maulerby writhed in pain and shame as the infernal device was swiftly set up in order to portray his disgrace.

'I believe, Lord Maulerby,' Maria sneered, 'that you are financially embarrassed and are proposing to solve this particular difficulty by being a traitor to Great Britain; and also via your engagement to Lady Sarah Hogg. Lady Sarah,' she commented acidly, 'who is an heiress, might change her mind were she to see the ensuing photography.' That said, she draped a pair of her own drawers around his sweating neck. 'It suits you, this dog collar!' she laughed merrily. Agnes, Maud and Beatrice took a dozen photographs of Maulerby in his somewhat undignified condition. 'If ever you betray British interests again,

Lady Sarah Hogg will be seeing these photographs, so you had better be a good boy and behave yourself, hadn't you? *Hadn't* you??' She whipped him again with her martinet; he gasped and squirmed as the girls giggled then proposed to depart as swiftly as they had arrived, declining my proffered refreshments on the grounds that they were on duty.

'Oh, my dear girls, do stay for the *finale*,' Maria insisted. They looked at each other and smiled briefly as Maria released Maulerby from the flogging-block, though she kept his wrists handcuffed. 'Now dance before us.'

The girls hooted with laughter as Maulerby proceeded to dance with all the grace of a clumsy bear. Every time he made a false step, which was uncomfortably often, Maria lashed him on his legs, thighs, arms or bottom, causing him to shriek volubly as the ladies chuckled appreciatively. 'By using my whip on limbs that go astray,' Maria observed, 'I ensure that not too many mistakes are made.' Maulerby danced obediently, ladies' knickers around his neck and flinching from the flick of Maria's martinet as further photographs were taken. Then he had to lie down upon his back and, in turn, each woman lowered her drawers and proceeded to sit upon his face for five minutes; and he had to lick each separate arse-hole and kiss their bottom-cheeks. Now it was the women's turn to writhe and squirm, but with pleasure rather than pain.

When every woman had come upon his florid face, Maulerby was led back to the flogging block he had intended for Maria and chained down there once more. A dog-bowl, lipsticked with the words 'FIDO', was put in front of him and Maria proceeded to pee in it. 'You might be needing some water,' she remarked. Taking a feather from her hat, she proceeded to tickle his prick until he screamed with a curious mixture of agony and ecstasy. As his rod spurted forth, his face plunged involuntarily into the dog-bowl of women's piss and another memorable photograph was taken. 'Wouldn't your family just like to see this?' Maria taunted him as the magnesium-powder lights flashed. 'It could persuade your father to change his will. So just be an obedient one in future.'

We then departed, leaving him bound and helpless, to be rescued, no doubt, from this awkwardly humiliating position by the maid of the apartment block on the following morning.

Maria had once again kept her word in arranging my luncheon on the following day with Gabriele Jogand at Le Chat Blanc in Montmartre. This was a café for artists and, to employ a slang expression that has recently come into vogue, 'piss-artists'. Monsieur Jogand turned out to be a man with a charming manner, dressed in immaculate clerical black though sporting a floppy bow tie in mauve and yellow. His figure was short and tubby and he radiated pleasantness until one looked into his very hard blue eyes, which nevertheless twinkled as though the irises were gemstones. A thin, waxed moustache adorned his smiling mouth with its full lips. We agreed to drink St Emilion, accompanied by a variety of nuts.

I was interested in Jogand because he had for a time been hailed as Europe's leading master Satanist who had repented and turned to Roman Catholicism, exposing in his many best-selling books the evils of Satanism and its twin, Freemasonry. His views had furthermore received confirmation from the authors Leo Taxil and Dr Bataille.

After our elementary pleasantaries, I broached the matter and I have rarely heard a man laugh so hard, wiping tears away from his eyes in between in copious quaffing of wine.

'*Mon cher monsieur* . . .' he grinned broadly as he dried his eyes with a napkin, 'do not please say that a man of your intelligence has also been fooled by my ridiculous tricks?' He chuckled and lit a slim panatella, which he proceeded to smoke with evident enjoyment. 'My books are a complete fraud,' he said. 'Leo Taxil is simply a pseudonym I use and Dr Bataille is an old friend of mine, a former ship's surgeon whose name is Charles Hacks and to whom I offered the opportunity of making money on my idea. Why, do you not know the full story?' I shook my head. 'I can tell you the truth,' he chortled, 'now that it is over.'

'I wish someone would,' I responded.

'*Eh bien*,' Jogand puffed out a perfect smoke-ring, 'I was educated in the Roman Catholic faith and I grew to hate it beyond belief. When I saw the attacks of the Church upon Freemasonry and its scattering of the accusation of Satanism too freely and loosely upon all who dissented, I saw my opportunity both to make money and to exact revenge. After a course of reading, I invented an international, world-wide conspiracy of Freemasons and Satanists.'

'Why not bring the Jews in too?' I asked.

'I may need them in a future volume,' he replied. 'In any event, I then confessed my sins to the Church and they welcomed back their prodigal son, especially since I was giving them what they thought to be 'top secret' information about Satanism and Freemasonry. How I do pity poor Albert Pike of New Orleans! By every account, he is a quiet and pleasant scholar, sincerely dedicated to the ideals and ceremonies of Freemasonry. I accused this innocent fellow of being the International Head of the global Satanic conspiracy.'

'Bit dirty, isn't it?' I murmured, 'to accuse an innocent man?'

'Not at all,' Jogand retorted. 'He had about three members in his grouping before I accused him in my books. Now he receives hundreds of applications to join his allegedly notorious society and, in consequence, thousands of dollars. So he is happy. I made a small fortune through the books of mine which accused him: so *I* am happy and my publishers are happy. My readers are happy for they bought my second volume. And the Church is happy because at last it has discerned the man who is the Devil's representative on Earth. Of course, in order to complete the happiness of the Church, I had to produce the Devil's female representative, the Whore Babylon from *The Book of Revelations*; so I invented Diana Vaughan, who was in fact my charming and delightful secretary.

'I gave this beautiful, rampaging and rampant bitch a post as High Priestess and 'Daughter of the Devil' at Albert Pike's allegedly infamous Lodge, which idea excited many. Then I announced that she was repenting and was desirous of joining the Roman Catholic Church, therein to pour out all the secrets of her sins, her fornication and her iniquity. The Church became itself quite frantic with lascivious desire for me to produce Diana Vaughan. They ached for my confirmation of their false beliefs and I wanted their money: so it was so far an eminently satisfactory transaction.

'Did you not read about it in the papers? Dear me, the Church must have exercised all its influence to suppress the story. *Non*, on April 19th, 1897, at the lecture hall of the Paris Geographical Society on the

Boulevard Saint-Germain, it was announced that Diana Vaughan would be present in person. The matter had been primed well by the *Memoirs* of Diana, published the previous February. The hall was packed; there was not even standing-room at the back. It made me smile to see that the audience was evenly divided between the Catholic and Masonic camps, with Bishops sitting in uncomfortable social promiscuity with Masonic Grand Masters – there was also, unsurprisingly, a large journalistic contingent present.'

'What happened?' I asked.

'Why, I told them the truth, of course!' Jogand roared with laughter. 'I blew the entire *gaffe*. I explained to the Church precisely how I had managed to take their money and fool them for twelve years and to the Masons precisely why I had done so.

'Then I removed my gold pince-nez, bowed politely to the astounded gathering and walked away from the platform. I left the building by a side-door, walked across the Boulevard Saint-Germain to a café opposite, ordered a cup of coffee and a glass of cognac; and awaited developments.

'The instant that I left the hall, pandemonium broke out, the booing and whistling of the embarrassed Catholic party mixing with the jubilant jeers and catcalls of the Masonic supporters. Shame soon turned to fury and blows were traded. Cleric and Grand Master brawled with total loss of dignity and only my prompt summoning of the police prevented a full-scale riot. In consequence, it is nowadays impossible for anybody in France to take Satanism seriously as a threat. For let it be stated definitely,' Jogand smiled wryly, '*Satanism as an organized conspiracy has never, and does not now, exist*. Those who claim to have attended Black Masses are either deluded, liars or the victims of fraud.'

'What about white Masses?' I enquired, 'which celebrate the sex act as holy and which some say are celebrated by international orders such as the Rosicrucians?'

'*Mon dieu* . . .' he groaned wearily, 'you have obviously been mixing with the occultists of Paris. I know them well, Lord Horby, and to which one do you refer? The late Stanislas de Guiata? Why, he was simply a drug addict making endeavours to realize his fantasies, the same as that crazy Jesuit priest, Father Binoire. Huysmans is these days a Catholic penitent looking for an evil enabling him to expiate his guilt. Peládan is mad and Encausse is boring, even more so whenever he writes under the name of "Papus". Believe me, sir, these occultists are fools. I know. I've made my money out of them so this atheist says thank God for their folly! And you English are no better. Have you heard of a Doctor W. Wynn Westcott?' I nodded in acknowledgement of his mention of a senior Founder Member of the Golden Dawn.

'Nice but naive.' Jogand leered at me. 'I persuaded him to give me a specimen of his signature for "spiritual" purposes. I then forged it on a Charter for an Order which I sold to a gullible American for thousands of dollars. Ha! ha! no fool like an occult fool!'

'So you don't think that anyone can harm anyone else by Black Magic?'

'Ha! ha! ha!' His ample sides heaved with mirth and merriment. 'I have received so many curses in my life that I could paper my walls with them: that is all they are fit for. Please, some common sense, monsieur. You *can't* be magically attacked unless you *want* to be magically attacked, and then it is your own mind that does the tricks.'

Jogand was a charming companion over luncheon though I never saw him afterwards. One gathers that he retired to a life of comparative luxury in Provence and died there in 1907. I shan't forget his words of departure:

'Forget Sin and Satanism, Lord Horby. Life is merely made up of fleeting moments of joyous sex and raucous laughter.'

CHAPTER EIGHT

'And this is the thing, to run away from a lady?!' the Countess of Salzburg exclaimed. 'I shall now take great liberties with you, young sir.' Helena proceeded to take possession of my manly jewel as it now sprang forth in all its grandeur when she opened the front of my dressing-gown. I had tired of Satanism and Paris and, needing a change, had taken the night express to Munich. In the dining-car I had discerned a delightfully voluptuous brunette, styled at the height of fashion, and evidently her motives for travel had not been entirely dissimilar to mine.

'The love!' she shrieked out and a button burst upon her blouse. 'Now it's mine! What a beauty!' The Countess Helena leaned over me and implanted hot, wanton kisses on the head of the rampant prisoner within her kid-gloved fingers. I fairly sighed and heaved with excitement under such skilful osculation. I had rarely felt such an ecstatic thrill before it was altogether a new sensation. The tonguing and pressures of her sucking lips and the tickling tips of the gloved hands of this wanton woman opened up such a new source of delight that I almost fainted under her caresses. She did not even blush as she withdrew her scarlet lips from my glistening knob, drew me to the side of the bed and, as the Wagons-Lit carriage clattered on into the European night, raised her skirt-hem and petticoats to expose her lovely cleft to my amorous gaze.

'My fanny always expects a little kiss first,' she whispered to me as at last her face flushed slightly, which added considerably to her beauty. I was kneeling in a moment, paying my devotions to that divinely delicate-looking pink slit. She turned her body and I adored her vagina, shaded by golden hair, as soft as the finest silk. My tongue divided its juicy lips, searching out her pretty clitoris, which at once stiffened under my lascivious probing. My tongue-tip flicked across its rosy head as I gently licked it, sucking at the same time. A perfect shudder of emotion thrilled throughout her body.

'Oh! *oh!!* Fuck me quick! Your kisses have set me on fire!' Suiting the action to the words, she threw herself backwards across the bed and I rose to the charge in a moment, hurling myself over her, gluing my lips to hers as my stiff sex-weapon forced its way between the moist but yielding lips of her tight little quim.

A quiver of delight enlivened her face as I gained complete insertion. Her lovely legs, encased in drawn-down, delicate, white and silken knickerbocker drawers, fringed with lace, and sheathed to her firm thighs in rose-coloured silk stockings, spread wide and she cried out as she threw her high-heeled Parisian boots amorously around my waist.

'O, your fine, manly buttocks!' she shouted. My own hands were clasped around her lovely rump as it rose in agitated heaves in response to my vigorous thrusts.

It was a wonderful night of sex and I had no occasion to escort the lady into her own bedchamber. Early on, she swooned with joy: my own hands beneath her bottom were bathed by her copious flow of love-juices. Ah! how we profited by our intercourse! I went on my knees between her legs and made her stretch her white satin thighs wide apart. Just before I entered, she took my vigorous fleshy firebrand within a hand still kid-gloved in fawn. The flicks of her fingers made it harder than ever. She squeezed and stroked it for some seconds, then pushed it gradually into herself while I savoured slowly the delightful pleasure. When the arrow had completely disappeared within its quiver, I leant over her and, lifting her two legs over my arms, forced the Countess backwards, upturning her arse, and thence went to work so lustily that soon a second ejaculation became added to the first.

I do not intend to retrace moment by moment all our delicious passages. I will limit myself to a description of the most striking facts of this adorable *liaison* which I wished could last all eternity. My lover knew how to vary our pleasures without ever reaching satiety, she felt a singular pleasure in the arts of enjoyment and emission and she found in me a keen and eager student. Sometimes a woman in her mid-forties can be the ripest fruit of all.

The Countess taught me all the obscene European names for genitalia, sometimes making me say them, but only in the whirl of passion. She used them herself in supreme moments of bliss, pretending, and rightly, too, that such a high spice should never be too much hackneyed, else 'twould lose its flavour. As I write on, I forget myself in these sweet recollections . . .

What cunning caresses! What lecherous postures did she not teach me! What innocent play and prolonging of pleasure on both sides! And what *refinements* of pleasure did we not realize as soon as thought of! I made such progress under such a good mistress that at moments I surpassed her.

We kept changing the way of doing it. For instance,

when she was plugged from behind, one of my favourite positions, she would mischievously unhorse her cavalier, turn around quickly, give a kiss to her rosy conqueror, wet with her spendings, and escape to the other end of the railway chamber, lit only by a dim blue light. She would place herself upon the *cabinet* which concealed the wash-basin, her legs upraised and her pussy quite open, giving it provocative, twitching movements. I was hardly in her again when by a fresh whim, she would draw my prong out, turn her bottom upon me and then, seizing my courser, lead it to plunge within her body up to the very hilt until my burning jet completed that part of our sweet operation.

During that unique night, as the train rattled onwards, her cunt, this splendid vessel of my joy, became my abiding passion, the object of true worship. Helena responded by admiring and delighting at the thickness of my rod, its strength and its length. '*Formidable . . .*' she sighed dreamily as she handled it, dandled it, sucked it, licked it as if it were a sugared lollipop, caressed it in a thousand different ways, rubbed it between her titties, holding it there between them by pressing hard with her gloved hands. When my prick was held captive within this voluptuous cleft, it threw forth all its dew.

My lover returned all my caresses and with added interest. Her pussy became my goddess and idol; I assured her that no woman had ever possessed a more perfect one. I loved to open it, like the petals of a flower, and frig her clitty and fuck her cunt in every conceivable way. As my prick finally began to weary of the sport, it was neverthe-less still a supreme delight to apply my lips to her quim and extract, so to speak, the quintessence of voluptuous-ness by titillations of the tongue which led her to exclaim: '*Moi! Je suis fou!*'

Was she mad? I have only a dim and hazy memory of the last hour before which the train steamed into the Bahnhofstrasse station at Munich; and that is unfortunate in view of the ensuing consequences. I have led, on the whole, a quiet and retiring life, remote from the fields of front-line adventure, and remain unused to the unusual. I have to tell now of one of the strangest things that has ever happened to me.

I suppose that in my usual fashion, I would have escorted Helena, Countess of Salzburg, to her compartment, enabling her to prepare herself for our arrival. After all, we had been drinking vintage champagne and the finest cognac all night. Naturally I would have ordered porters for the lady's luggage at the station but I have no memory of the fact, if fact it be. All I know for certain is that I have a visiting card before me, here, now, as I write, with a Hapsburg crest announcing the Countess Helena of Salzburg at some castle near Munich: the lengthy German name of this castle is beyond the wit of any sane Englishman to pronounce soberly. On the back of this visiting card, a spidery feminine hand was written in hard but delicate pencil an invitation to dinner at an address overleaf for the night following my arrival in Munich.

I imagine that I escorted my fair lady to a carriage and bade her a sweet *au revoir* until the evening. Certainly I went directly to a good hotel opposite Munich's grotesquely baroque yet massively impressive Palace of Justice. Once settled, I was determined not to be late for this enchanting lady and so resolved to ascertain the swiftest method of transportation to her for the magical moment when dusk would fall, for I had been invited to arrive at 8:00 pm. Unfortunately, absolutely nobody in Munich had ever heard either of the castle in question or of Helena, Countess of Salzburg. Finally I tried the

British Consulate, the staff of which proved to be courteous and efficient. According to my description and their information, I had been mildly duped by an international confidence trickster known to the police as Helena Zuttendorf.

The expressions of the helpful consular officials became progressively more fixed as they studied some newspapers. Eventually I was ushered into the presence of the Consul, a Major Bull, officer and gentleman of the old school, who gave me a stiff whisky.

'Do you realise, Lord Horby, that the corpse of Helena Zuttendorf, alias the Countess of Strasbourg – who is not called Helena, incidentally – was found by the railway line at the precise spot reached by the Paris-Munich night express one hour before it gets into Munich?'

I could not quite believe that I was hearing this.

'I have it here.' Major Bull tapped the newspaper before him with a questioning index finger. 'The lady you intended to see tonight at a non-existent castle . . . this confidence trickster and lady impostor died at 7:00 a.m.'

'Oh . . .' I turned pale.

'So far,' Major Bull said it calmly, 'it appears that her death was a suicide. All the evidence points to her flinging herself from the door of the moving train. Probably couldn't take her life of crime and espionage any more, poor girl.' I froze with horror, to furiously deny within myself the possibility that I might have had anything to do with the death of this wondrously enchanting woman. 'But don't worry about it, old chap, you did the right thing and nobody will ever be able to pin this one on you,' Major Bull continued blithely. 'You're in the clear. Every document, including relevant newspapers, concurs with the fact that Helena Zuttendorf died at 7:00 *two days* ago. So the woman you were with was probably pretending to be

Helena Zuttendorf, who was herself pretending to be Helena, Countess of Salzburg.' His fingers flicked to a photograph upon his desk and he held it up before me. 'Recognize her?'

'Yes,' I said. 'That was the woman I was with last night and this morning on the Paris-Munich express.' I dug my railway ticket out of my pocket for impartial verification.

'Can't be, old boy,' the Major responded. 'As I've told you, she died two days ago.'

'And you're asking me to believe that I slept with the impersonator of an impostor?'

'Possibly . . .' Bull murmured thoughtfully. 'Although we old Munich hands do have a curious legend among us. It's that there's a ghostly lover on the Paris-Munich night express, that she gives a man a quite incredible fuck and that she is compounded of all the ghosts of adventurous women, disillusioned and despoiled in love, who have committed suicide on that particular journey.' He coughed. 'More whisky?'

'A ghost could not give me a visiting card.'

'It was a false one, though, wasn't it?' Major Bull said.

As Christopher Marlowe has it:

Thou hast committed
Fornication: but that was in another country
And besides, the wench is dead.

CHAPTER NINE

I had a further motive in going to Munich in early 1901 as my *Memorandum 993* informs me. My cousin in Berlin wanted me to meet and report on two gentlemen going by the names of Guido von List and Lanz von Liebenfels, based in Vienna, and my membership of the OTO of Karl Kellner and Theodor Reuss, as described in the second volume of *The Black Pearl*, made the matter readily easy to secure in terms of channels of communication. There was some sort of international convention of European occultists taking place in Munich, enabling me to encounter the gentlemen in question.

I had arranged to meet them for 'a light supper' at the *Höfbrähaus*, a celebrated beer hall which can seat between two and three thousand people. The atmosphere was jovial as lusty Bavarian wenches smilingly served steins of excellent beer, though I confess that I had my doubts about my companions. This was not on account of the fact that the 'light supper' they had proposed consisted of mountains of sauerkraut topped by bockwurst, bierwurst, bratwurst, weisswurst, knockwurst and frankfurters, which were delicious. I was perplexed both by their demeanour and by their attitudes.

List looked like a grey-bearded magus in his flowing black robes. In 1875, he informed me, he had celebrated the Summer Solstice by burying a number of empty wine bottles on the summit of a hill overlooking Vienna. These wine bottles had been placed in the form of a sign which had not been seen in the land before: it was Tibetan in origin; it was a symbol exclusive to the Aryan peoples; I had learned of it in the Golden Dawn as The Hermetic Cross and the Hammer of Thor; and it was the Swastika.

Liebenfels looked like an elementary schoolteacher in his ill-fitting light grey suit of cheap cloth, the crumpled jacket of which came half-way up his arse, yet he concurred fully with List in venerating the sign of the Swastika. This, they agreed, stood for Light, as I had learned in the Golden Dawn, and also, they argued, for abandoning Christianity, an embracing of neo-paganism, an affirmation of Aryan racial superiority; and a desire to become or create something called 'the Superman.' Both deplored Satanism as 'a childish excrescence' and affirmed that they were 'fighting for the Light, the future and *der fuehrer*, a leader for whom they were waiting – rather like the Orthodox Jews who wait for their Messiah. Obviously the *von* was false: they weren't Barons *von* anywhere, merely lower-middle-class autodidacts fond of high-sounding titles. Still, the beer provoked them into talking.

'I renounced the Catholic faith at the age of fourteen in 1862, and vowed to build a Temple to Wotan,' List told me. 'And I have done so. Furthermore, there is now a flourishing Guido von List Society. Lord Horby, you may be interested, with your credentials and connections, in joining the Inner Order of Armanen Initiates.' I looked enquiring and earnest. 'I have been clairvoyantly inspired,' List declared proudly. 'I have been given true visions of the ancient race of German Supermen called the Armanen and I am the last surviving member.'

'Kindly excuse my ignorance,' I queried innocently, 'but how can this be so when by your own account, you were born in 1848 . . .' and added, 'if you would be so kind as to answer me, Baron von List.' At the mention of this title, List shuffled his robes and preened himself.

'That was in a previous incarnation,' he replied, 'but now I have returned to fulfil the mission I swore to Wotan. WOTAN!' he shouted. 'We must study the runes and you know what the runes tell us?' I shook my head. 'They tell us that the Jews are the sworn enemy of the Aryan race and that this scum can only be extirpated from the face of the Earth when the German Empire includes also Austria. We must study, to this end, the sagas of the Teutonic tribes and the occult folklore of our people.

'I am presently working,' List continued relentlessly, 'upon my masterpiece, *Laws of the Aryan Germans*. (*Editor's Note: This was finally published in Vienna in 1908, the year Adolf Hitler took up residence in that city*.) If the German people are to be saved from their enemy, the hydra-headed international Jewish conspiracy, which enslaves them with capitalism on the one hand and communism on the other, then we must construct a racial state in which inferior peoples become the slaves of the Aryans. This new *Reich* must be divided into units called *Gaue*, each one with its *Gauleiter*.' He drank deeply of his beer as his eyes blazed with fanaticism. 'The Leader will be a self-chosen *Fuehrer* to whom each German willingly submits but bound to his followers by a sacred oath. Their will be special, racial laws exalting the Aryans and degrading their inferiors, including stringent marriage laws to prevent mongrelization. The symbols of the new Reich will be the Swastika: and also the double '*Sig*' rune to be adopted by its warrior élite, whom I would like to see called: *The SS*. WOTAN!

'The Reich,' List declared feverishly, 'will then be ready to annihilate the enemy . . . all military preparations must be made in the most complete detail in order to fight this inevitable war to build a Greater Germany, which will come because it *must* come. Then there will be established a racially pure community that will destroy both Democracy and Jewry. *Mit Armanengruss und Heil!*' he screamed, raising his right arm in a rigid salute.

(*Editor's Note: The U.S. Library of Congress contains a book taken from Adolf Hitler's private library, the flyleaf of which is signed by List: 'To Adolf Hitler, my dear brother in Armanen.'*)

'Very interesting,' I said. An Englishman, after all, always says that he is interested whenever he is bored. 'And do you agree, Baron Lanz von Liebenfels?' I asked the little fellow in the crumpled suit.

'*Jawohl*,' he replied firmly. 'I have the utmost respect for my brother and colleague.' List looked pleased as Liebenfels ordered more beer. 'I am a proud member of his Armanen Order and I hope that he is proud to be a member of my Order of New Templars.' List inclined his head. 'The Aryans are responsible for all creativity in history. This is what makes racial purity a necessity.' He spoke in harsh, cold, clipped tones. 'I advocate forced labour and a starvation diet for any and all who indulge in inter-racial sexual relationships. In addition, citizenship should be denied to non-Aryans for we are opposed in all we do by the Dark Forces of Jews, Slavs and Negroes. The best remedy against race pollution is the castration of male offenders: and give the females a clitorectomy.' He drank more beer, ate another sausage, rubbed his hands with joy and appeared to relish the prospect.

'Why this obsessive need for racial purity?' I queried.

'Because the coming race of Supermen can be *bred*,'

Liebenfels replied firmly as List nodded agreement, 'and bred only from pure Aryan stock. Why, I openly propose the establishment of special breeding colonies.' (*Editor's Note: The Book of German Psalms: the Prayerbook of Arios Racial Mystics and Anti-Semites by Adolf Lanz as 'Lanz von Liebenfels' became part of Hitler's private collection, preserved in the U.S. Library of Congress*). 'You are English, Lord Horby. Ponder upon the significance of future Anglo-Saxon racial supremacy. *Natürlich*, the British Empire and the German Empire can rule the world together.'

'And you have rites, ceremonies and rituals of Magick to attain this goal?' I enquired.

'JA!' they both affirmed. 'Come and join us in the present for our creation of the past and our celebration of the future.'

'Plenty of good-looking German girls, I hope?' I responded cheerfully with a wicked grin, for actually I felt that I could do with a fuck. They glanced uneasily at one another.

'Lord Horby,' List explained patiently, 'we do not admit women to our sacred rites and ceremonies. A woman should be a tender, cuddly thing, soft, sweet and stupid. We call it KKK: *Kinder, Kirche, Küche*: the children, the church and the kitchen – that is where women belong.' The pair of them looked as though they hadn't enjoyed a good swiving in ten years and I had had enough of their bloody nonsense. It was expounded recently, of course, by one Corporal Adolf Hitler who recently endeavoured to take over Bavaria by occupying one Munich beer hall but this ridiculous idiot is now in prison after which he will vanish into a richly deserved obscurity.

'Gentlemen,' I said as I drained my mug and arose,

'thank you. I shall ever afterwards think of you as Biffo and Boffo.' They both looked exceptionally puzzled.

'*Vas ist das?*' List asked.

'It's an Old English saying,' I replied.

'And what does it mean?' Liebenfels queried.

'It might be unkind to tell you.' I smiled. 'Have a good time, as the Jews would say; and *Auf Wiedersehen*.' I walked out into a refreshing blast of cold, crisp air.

I took a carriage to the Schwabing, an area of the city peopled mainly by artists and poets and students and general riff-raff. I had been told that by walking through its twisted cobbled streets, I could enjoy a much more interesting encounter than if I went to a respectable brothel. This turned out to be the case, for in a bar I encountered two delightful girls, Astrid and Heidi, who were more than happy to be bought drinks and dinner and to listen to my proposals.

'Are your intentions honourable?' Astrid asked over her mountain of sausages and sauerkraut, which is all they ever seem to eat in these places, not that it tastes badly. She was an artist's model who aspired to be an artist and who, having run away from her no doubt stiflingly petit-bourgeois home in Hanover, was also waiting at tables and tending bars with her friend Heidi, an angular brunette from Hamburg.

'Extremely *dis*honourable,' I said genially and ordered the best wine which the house had to offer. How I enjoy a really good hock! The upshot of the matter is that the three of us returned to my hotel. These charming German girls needed precious little encouragement, I can tell you! In no time at all, Heidi was sitting naked on the sofa, sipping fiery German brandy as she watched me tumble Astrid.

I threw my arms about this strapping wench and,

drawing her to me, pressed her to my heart, our lips joined so that there was a long and audible kiss.

'My delightful, darling Astrid!' I exclaimed. 'Allow me to embrace you again . . . Give me your beautiful eyes, your lovely teeth, your divine white neck! O! how I could eat them!' Astrid gave herself up to me, returning kiss for kiss and caress for caress as her colour heightened and her eyes sparkled.

'I am all yours . . .' she sighed gently. One may judge the effect that such gentle verbal and physical caresses had upon me. My temperament ignited as if struck by an electric spark, for I could sense the nature of the joys to come. What charms I had exposed! Under Astrid's fine cambric chemise were legs worthy of Venus, encased in the silk stockings I had now removed, secured above the knee by garters of the colour of fire; then two adorable thighs, white, round and firm, surmounted by a fleece of black and lustrous curls.

'How I love it!' I declared. 'How young, beautiful and fresh it is! Open yourself a little, my angel, that I may kiss those adorable lips!' Astrid did as I demanded. Her thighs opened to display her rosy slit to its fullest advantage. I glued my lips upon it and Astrid writhed in ecstasy, shutting her eyes and speaking broken words, then thrusting up her hips in response to my kissing and licking which had transported her so.

'*Auf!*' she shrieked. '*Wieder!!! . . . ich schön . . .*' she gasped. 'Go on! . . . *er macht . . .* It's coming! . . . *Ai! . . .* I . . . *ich . . . I'm coming! . . . ICH KOMMT!!! . . .* Aargh!!' Good God! How she writhed and rocked and rolled upon the bed!

Now Astrid turned over and proudly presented two voluptuous globes of dazzling white for my delectation. By now, my instrument was enormous and I had no hesitation in my introduction of its tip between the two crimson lips my eyes had already perceived. Astrid did not flinch and opened as much as possible the part which she presented, which seemed without the aid of her willing hands to open itself and at length absorb my long and mean machine tool, which penetrated so well that it disappeared entirely.

'Ah!' Astrid shrieked as my happy belly became glued to her luscious bottom. There was then a conjunction of combined movements followed by broken words. 'I feel you . . . push it all well into me . . . softly . . . let me come first AH! . . . I feel it . . . I'm coming! . . . Quicker! I come . . . stop . . . there you are! I die . . . I . . . I . . . Ahhhh!' With my eyes half-closed and my hands holding her hips, I felt inexpressibly happy.

'Hold . . .' I sighed. 'My angel, my all, ah! How fine it is! Push well! Do come again . . . there; it's coming, is it not!? Go on . . . I feel you're coming . . . push well, my darling!' We both stopped for a moment. Astrid appeared momentarily exhausted but she did not change her position, lightly turning her head at length to give me a lover's kiss.

'Now both together!' she shouted out, adding: 'You let me know when you are ready.' Thence she thrust upwards quite wickedly.

'AH! . . .' I cried out in return. 'I feel it coming . . . you are ready, my love? Yes . . . yes . . . there I am . . . push, again . . . go on . . . I spend . . . I am yours. I . . . I . . . Ah! What a pleasure . . . I . . . sp- . . . *spend!*'

A long silence followed. Eventually I recovered my senses to find myself lying upon the ample bosom of Astrid. Turning my head, I saw that Heidi had just come over the slim forefinger she had employed to pleasure her cunt.

Now Heidi joined me upon the bed as Astrid took her seat and helped herself to copious quantities of brandy.

As Astrid sipped, there was Heidi naked before my delighted eyes. No one could dream of a finer sight! Her nipples, firm and high, stuck out boldly in bright rose-pink; the line of her back and her backside were both admirable. At the base of her white and polished belly, her luxuriant dark fleece could be plainly seen. Suddenly she knelt before me and almost reverently imprinted two or three ardent kisses on the object of her desires. My hands parted her willing thighs, yielding another delicious view of her dark, bushy mount, with just a discernible vermilion slit beneath the slim belly.

My ramrod, refreshingly renewed, was thrusting between those slender thighs quicker than it takes to say so and, throwing my body over hers, I proceeded to kiss her face and neck in the most impassioned manner, being too well within her body to lick her heaving bosom, though I caressed and moulded her right breast with my left hand. The girl seemed instinctively to open her thighs wider. She gasped as I withdrew abruptly, then sighed as I put forth the swelling head of my tremendous cock, opening her quim lips until the throbbing head had re-entered about an inch.

Her hands pressed my buttocks downwards – and both of us quivered with joy and spent at this moment. We lay motionless for a few moments as Astrid stroked herself noisily; but there was to be no peace for the wicked.

'Horby! Milord!' Heidi gave my bottom two slaps with her hand. 'Again, my love . . .' she whispered. 'You did make me feel nice as you spurted into me just then. I shan't be so tight now. Go on – go on – oh!' My abruptly renewed ramrod plunged within her cunny to its full depth. She shrieked out her joy as if in agony and I withdrew to give it another hard push, and thrust again and again, clasping her fainting body as she uttered a piercing scream and lost consciousness.

This sound and the sight of my still throbbing instrument aroused Astrid to action for, in response, she heaved up her rump and writhed in a perfect state of erotic frenzy, inviting me to fuck her on the sofa, to fuck her well, to shove it all – balls and all – into her cunt as she used every international bawdy expression of which she was plentifully capable. She was a demon at the game now and to judge by her languid sighs and alternating screams of rapacious delight at my thrusting, she was coming continuously.

She appeared to gain in strength as I weakened. Without warning, her flanks thrust me away, then she rushed me to the bed, pinned me on my back and in rampant triumph and beside her lascivious girl-friend, straddled and bestrode my still stiff penis. I roared like a lion as I came.

Ah, yes! They can keep the men of Munich! I'll fuck their women any day!

CHAPTER TEN

It was a very good idea of mine to answer the sudden telegram received from Douglas in Cairo and to join him on a river cruise along the Nile. Sometimes a man really does need to get away from it all: This was the case with both of us, and it was a pleasure to enjoy his company on a river yacht he had chartered. He had also hired two beautiful whores, Nina of England and Leila of Turkey, for our pleasure. Abdul, the Turkish chef, proved to be excellent, fulfilling his proud boast that the cuisine of his country is equal to that of the French and has influenced the cooking of the entire Eastern Mediterranean.

'*Réculez pour mieux sauter*, my dear fellow,' Douglas said on our first evening aboard. 'Really, the French have it right: step back so as to jump forward better.'

'Quite agree,' I murmured as I watched the silvery crescent moon and its exquisite reflection upon the waters. 'I'm finding it rather hard,' I continued, puffing on an excellent Hoyo de Monterey cigar, 'to make sense of Satanism.'

'That's because there is no sense there, only non-sense,' Douglas replied. We drank our Armagnac thoughtfully. 'If there *is* any Satanism out there, it's done either by perverted Christians or else by some bunch of wealthy perverts who delight in ritual and want salt with their sex and pepper with their perversions.

The genuine Rosicrucians know that sex is the holiest act in the Universe if done with love under will but we have no time at all for occult fools. Look!' he suddenly exclaimed. 'Crocodiles.'

I looked to see that these reptiles infested this particular section of the river.

'The Ancient Egyptians venerated this prehistoric creature,' Douglas continued. 'They seemed to realize that the crocodile had been around during the age of the dinosaurs and so personified its spirit as Sebek, crocodile God and God of Time.' Douglas gazed fondly upon these creatures, some of which lay like rocks in the waters of the Nile, looking as though they had lain still for one hundred million years and were ready to do so for a further aeon of time. Others lazed upon the river bank, their jaws open as little birds popped inside to peck at their teeth and eat all insects and decay within their gaping cruel mouths.

'When they wish to move, they can be so swift,' Douglas resumed his discourse and grinned at me wickedly. 'But soon enough now, we'll be coming into hippo country. These mammals hate the crocs and that's why they divide the river between them and the reptiles. A hippo has little to fear from a crocodile, whose teeth will make little impact on a hippo's thick skin. As for the deadly whack of a crocodile's tail, this will make little impact upon a mammal that weighs well over two tons. The crocodile cannot harm a full-grown hippo in the water and once on land the hippo simply stomps the croc to death with its hooves. However, the crocodiles do occasionally try and poach a baby hippo and that is why the hippos hate them. There's not a croc that won't turn tail when faced with an angry adult hippo.

'I'd love to be a hippo,' Douglas sighed wearily, but added: 'Sometimes. Just think on it, Horby, for if you were a hippo, you wouldn't need to think at all. What creature attacks a hippo? Hippos can sprint at up to thirty miles per hour and they can bite a man in half – and a crocodile too, for that matter. Even men leave 'em alone. Hippo meat is totally disgusting to eat. And would you want to give your mistress a purse or bag made of hippo skin? They're quite useless for the purposes of humanity. All they do is laze around in muddy water. They eat vegetables and weeds and occasionally surface to capsize a boat unintentionally. What a life!' The boat cruised past a mother hippo coming to the surface with a smiling baby hippo upon her back.

'Nature . . .!' Douglas breathed enthusiastically; and I must record that I am appreciative of the matters he showed me during our cruise. I saw a deer come to drink by the river. Instantly, what looked like a rock moved with the speed of a crocodile and sank its teeth into the deer's belly. A hippo that had been drinking some hundred yards away instantly charged in a gesture of mammalian solidarity and stomped upon the crocodile, driving away one sorely battered reptile. The deer sagged to the ground, bleeding badly from its belly. The hippo tried to cure the wound with huge, sympathetic licks but the damage was done and the deer died. As the sun set, I saw a dead deer and by it, a hippo hanging its head in mourning and grief.

'The rhino is a much maligned creature,' Douglas said to me on another occasion in the course of our cruise. 'It simply eats vegetation and, apart from man and wild dogs, no other creature dares to trespass on its territory. They can be very bad-tempered beasts and I certainly wouldn't want a two-ton rhino coming at me at twenty miles an hour. But they're extremely stupid and forgetful. Sometimes they charge in a rage, then they stop that charge and trot away because they can't remember what it was that they were becoming so angry about. Sounds rather like some human beings, doesn't it?'

'Wild dogs?' I queried.

'Oh, yes,' said Douglas, giving orders for the boat to anchor. 'Look at that.' I looked and saw a female rhino protecting her baby from the attack of ten wild dogs. 'Dogs are so nice and cuddly when domesticated,' said Douglas, 'but in the wild, they're truly vicious.' I saw them jumping nimbly between the slashing horn and pounding hooves of the mother rhino as they chewed bits out of the baby. Mother rhino managed to spear one dog with her horn and to scrunch two more with her hooves but meanwhile her baby bled to death from the wounds inflicted. The mother appeared to go mad and charged at the dogs, who used their superior agility to avoid her clumsy lunges. She settled down to watch over the corpse of her child and the dogs settled down around fifty yards away, knowing that she could not transport it. Behind them, a pack of hyenas had gathered, one could discern a few jackals and since it was merely a matter of time before the meal, vultures already wheeled in the sky.

'As Oscar Wilde said,' Douglas remarked, 'the only tyranny that ever lasts is that of the weak over the strong.' On a succeeding evening, we cruised into lion country. 'Extraordinary, isn't it?' my host commented, 'if you're a lion, all you have to do is marry for an easy life. A lion usually has three lionesses in his pride. They go out and do the hunting whilst he lazes about all day and, I suppose, cuffs the cubs occasionally. His wives drag the kill back to his kingdom and the lion gets the first bite of the best. What a lazy brute the lion is! He normally sleeps for eighteen hours a day. That's probably why lions don't mind life in a circus: they perform and they get fed and after that they can go back to sleep. Have you ever heard of a lioness tamer?' I shook my head because the idea was too ridiculous. 'So how come the lionesses put up with this?' Douglas demanded. 'Simple. In the mating season, the lion can do it twenty-six times in twenty-four hours. There's a moral in there some-where, Horby, wouldn't you say?'

I agreed with him and still do; and I cannot forget the sight of a lion and a lioness crossing a shallow stream together. Suddenly the lioness looked at the lion and with one swish of her massive paw, sprayed him with water. He looked at her as if to say: 'You lovely, silly bitch,' and they walked on contentedly together. I am sure that the higher mammals have a sense of humour.

When I wasn't chatting to Douglas or fucking Leila or Nina, or eating and drinking, I sat on deck with a drink, a pipe of hashish and a good book. 'A good book is the precious life-blood of a master spirit,' said Lord Macau-ley. They can be even better than friends: you can put them down when you are bored and they will not take offence. I also perused my correspondence and arched an eyebrow as I read the following letter from Emily, pres-ently in Tunbridge Wells. After opening with greetings and expressed affection, it read:

The last time that we met, my darling, I seem to recall that you enquired after the progress of the Society for the Promulgation of Petticoat Government. Allow me to assure you, my dear boy, that it is flourishing.

Do you recall my tale of young Jeremy, scion of one of the noblest families in the land, who was petticoated in a fashionable ladies' department store in Bournemouth on account of his sexual misbehaviour? Young Lady Charlotte had complained of his unwelcome importun-ings, impolite behaviour and lustful glances: and they were both pupils at Mrs Joan Smythe's Academy. Well, after this purchase of his female attire, Jeremy was put back into a red tartan kilt, with silken knickers and a petticoat beneath and, carrying the shopping bags, had to follow Joan Smythe and I along the sea-front. She had strictly instructed him to walk ten paces behind us with his head submissively lowered and his eyes gazing in homage upon our hips. Both Joan and I found it to be such a spiteful joy to tease him by switching our bottoms in ladylike triumph. Jeremy blushed positively crimson as he endeavoured to conceal his erection and also his shamefully petticoated condition from the ladies who passed by. The wind blowing off the sea made his kilt flutter prettily, causing him to catch its hem continuously, though at one moment it blew upwards and his frilly white petticoat was exposed to the enquiring eyes of two dear old friends of ours whom you know, Lady Alison Utterley and Lady Jane Fortescue. Joan and I made Jeremy curtsey to them on the sea-front as the waves splashed in.

Jane and Alison, with whom I believe you are intimately acquainted, are of course notable ex-pupils of Mrs Smythe's Academy in Tunbridge Wells and I gladly accepted the invitation to visit that institution. This took place a few days later. It's about five miles from the town itself and set in rolling meadows flanked by thick woods. It is inaccessible unless one has a horse and carriage. To all outward appearances, it is a rather grim neo-Gothic building, surmounted by mysterious domes and turrets. One also notices beautiful flower-gardens, an immaculate croquet lawn, a fine court for lawn tennis and the cheerful faces of most of the pupils in their smart navy blue uniforms.

I was greeted at the front door by Jeremy and instantly

noticed the contrast in his uniform. The boys wear white shirts with ties, knee-length navy blue shorts, white socks to just below the knee and shiny black shoes with silver buckles. The girls wear the same, except that the heels of their shoes are elevated by an inch and, in place of trousers, they wear knee-length, knife-pleated skirts beneath which the lace of a white petticoat was peeping. Jeremy was wearing the girls' uniform.

He curtsied to me most politely, then obeyed my request to conduct me to the Headmistress. Joan Smythe was enjoying dry sherry with Alison and Jane, all of whom welcomed me as if I were one of their own, which I suppose I am. After some more sherry, I was taken on a tour of the school, founded, I was informed, 'to cure the recalcitrant habits of incorrigible boys and girls.' The conditions of the pupils were certainly comfortable and I sampled their luncheon and found it delicious; moreover, what I saw of the teaching was thorough, caring and altogether excellent, done well by smartly-dressed, well-educated women. However, discipline was very strict.

Any girl who misbehaved would be stood in the corner or spanked privately, strapped in front of the class or birched in front of the whole school. Boys received the cane instead of the strap; and for them there was a worse punishment. If there was any insult to a girl, the boy would be deprived of his trousers, put into girls' uniform and assigned to fag for the Girls' Prefects Common Room, which was given permission to spank him should he prove to be sullen or unwilling at his servile duties.

'Jeremy, of course,' Mrs Smythe beamed smugly, 'is rather a special case. He is being punished for his unwelcome sexual advances to Charlotte, our Head Prefect, and so is under petticoat discipline and must fag for her, gratifying her loftiest whim in the minutest

particular. This will fit him for marriage, which tonight he will be proposing to her before our senior gels and,' she smiled graciously, *'our most distinguished graduates and visitors to the Academy.'*

After devouring an exquisitely tender goose with bottles of vintage claret, we filed in with our liqueurs – yellow chartreuse, as I recall – to a hall with a platform and a grand piano. This piano stood to the right and in the centre there was a throne with two grand oaken chairs at either side of it. The walls had been painted in shocking pink: so now I know what goes on in these peculiar turrets!

Jeremy, still dressed as a schoolgirl, was standing obediently in the corner, face to the wall, his hands holding up his skirt and petticoat to reveal a crimson bottom that glowed from a previous spanking; girls' frilly bloomers encumbered his ankles.

Now Mrs Joan Smythe took her throne at the centre of the stage, placing her voluptuous rear upon the cushion as though it were the face of a grateful male lover. She was followed by the Junoesque Jane and the willowy Alison: together they plucked a golden crown out of a potted thicket of thorns and placed behind the throne. Alison laid the pot of thorns at the feet of Joan as Jane placed the crown of gold upon her head. The Headmistress responded by plucking two silver coronets from beneath the purple velvet drapes which adorned the sides of her throne. Each lady knelt before her and was graced by a coronet.

The ladies took their seats. A clock chimed 8:00. Eight schoolmistresses entered. They all wore tight, white, fussy blouses and severe black, ankle-length skirts, the cloth of which appeared to have fallen in love with their hips. A gong resounded. Eight young female Prefects entered, immaculately dressed in school uniform. They were bare-headed whereas the schoolmistresses were wearing elegant straw boaters adorned with flowers. Your friend Sir Richard once said to me: 'Any man who likes women's hats is either a fashion designer or a pervert. Hats are things women wear to impress other women.' Possibly so; but being a woman, I love the sight of other women's hats.

We all stood as Jane and Alison rang bells and Joan stepped forward to speak to us. As always, her voice was high, clear and hard, with every vowel and consonant strictly enunciated.

'A very happy event has transpired,' she declared. 'There was a time when this boy here,' she gestured at the penitent in the corner, 'was ever so badly behaved. Now that he has been brought under petticoat rule,' she preened herself proudly, 'he will never misbehave himself again. For the yoke of marriage is about to be put upon him and after that,' she laughed lightly, 'he will always be governed by his wife's petticoat.'

A gong was struck by someone unseen. A beautiful young lady entered to mount the platform, whom I correctly surmised to be Lady Charlotte. She wore a vivid dress of shining black silk which accentuated her perfectly proportioned figure. Upon her feet were high-heeled, laced boots of shining leather. Her face was quaint, piquant and sexy rather than conventionally beautiful but one could not help noticing her shining hazel eyes and her slightly spiteful mouth, nor the taunting way in which she switched her taut bottom.

Oh! what a darling Jeremy was! He had to hoist his knickers at Charlotte's command, approach her and curtsey as Joan Smythe sat down at the grand piano and began to play airs and graces from the Piano Concerto

No. 2 in G Minor *by Saint-Saens. Then he had to kneel on the floor before Charlotte, kiss her shining black leather boots, lick them and promise evermore to be faithful and obedient to her if only she would condescend to marry him.*

Charlotte responded by flicking out her fan as he lay at her feet and Alison and Jane swept forward to bring her red and white petticoats. Charlotte commanded Jeremy to arise and step into them, which he did. Charlotte smoothed his skirt down and kissed him upon the lips. Joan Smythe ceased her skilful playing of the piano.

'Jeremy's going to be such *a good boy now that he's marrying and put into skirts.' She chuckled throatily. 'Aren't you, Jeremy?'*

'Yes, Madam.' He curtsied to her.

'Oh, what *a pretty curtsey, Jeremy!' Joan Smythe exclaimed. 'Your affianced will be* so *pleased with you.'*

'Curtsey,' Charlotte commanded and as he obeyed, his prick fairly threatening to tear through the ladies' attire that so delicately imprisoned it, she clapped her hands for joy in witnessing his subjugation. 'Now remember, my husband-to-be, you will always walk respectfully behind me.' With that, Charlotte swished and swisked her skirts, turned upon her heel and left the stage arrogantly, with Jeremy following humbly behind her.

'Oh! What a beautiful petticoating!' Jane exclaimed.

'Quite exquisite,' said Alison; and the delicate hands of all schoolmistresses, schoolgirls and visitors present came together in applause. What a hoot! Must dash. More next time. Loads of love,

Emily.

After reading Emily's letter, I really needed a stroll on deck and as our boat glided past the river banks and my ears were enlivened by the night-time sounds of the jungle all around us, I was pleased to see the silhouette of Douglas, smoking a Burmese cheroot.

'Oh, glad to see you, Horby,' he said. 'Sometimes a man can do with a spot of good company. Just been thinking about women.'

'So have I,' I said.

'Know old puce-faced Belloc?' Douglas queried sharply and I nodded acknowledgement. 'Women are like hippos in one way and in one way only.' He threw back his brandy in one gulp. 'Allow me to alter one word of Belloc, my dear fellow, and this verse of his will reveal the secret of my success with women:

I shoot the hippopotamus
With bullets made of platinum,
'Cos if I use leaden ones
Her hide is sure to flatten 'em.

'Ha! ha!' he laughed cruelly and raucously. 'Now let's go and have another brandy below decks. The old serpent of the Nile can be quite chilly at night.'

CHAPTER ELEVEN

On the first night that I entered Leila's cabin as we cruised along the Nile, I was delighted by the sight that greeted my eyes. She stood there, the olive skin of her beautiful thighs set off to perfection by the black silk stockings high along them, with flouncy rosette garters holding them up on her lovely long legs. Otherwise, she was magnificently naked; and the sheen of her bare flesh, the deep chiseled hollow of her supple back seemed all the more alluring and libidinously enticing against the contrast with her nudity which those silken stockings made.

And now that she was naked, I could feast my eyes unimpeded upon her charms and compare her with Nina, my second choice, who had been preferred by Douglas, though we had both fucked the pair of them. Nina's legs were a trifle too short for her but this very defect added to the fascination of her figure. Her plump and rounded thighs tapered to the neatest of calves and ankles and tiny patrician feet. Her waist was dainty but not too small and she had fine rounded arms with small well-shaped hands. Nina's magnificent curves of hips and haunches, the graciously swelling belly with its deep navel and the full, fat, fleshy and prominent mound of love together with her rather full, firm and outstanding breasts had made her wholly mouthwatering.

Yet Leila was visibly more mature and slightly taller,

which added further to her seductiveness. She turned around to display the jouncy, full ovals of her naked bottom which fairly invited pinches and slaps; and the beautifully pronounced curve of her back and the dimple at her chinkbone which marked that beginning of the sinuous shadowy groove separating her superb buttocks set my cock to aching all over again. I seized her, tumbled her upon the bed and fucked her swiftly.

I wanted the second fuck to be done in a more leisurely and thorough way. When a man initially takes a beautiful and spirited girl, the excitement of the procedure very often defeats him and he cannot withhold himself to make the conquest as complete as he would like. This had been the case with me, for the ecstatic feeling of my rigid prick inside Leila's choice warm cunt had overcome even my own excellent staying powers, and I had spurted a veritable come-flood into the juicy flesh-depths of this gorgeous, exotic young female. But now that the first furious libation to Venus had been poured out, I knew that I would be able easily to prolong my pleasure with this brown-haired beauty.

Leila's coiffure added an ambiguity: along the top of her high forehead was a little fringe of frilly curls which suggested a saucy, rather coy girlishness, an almost juvenile ingenuousness. Yet at the back of her stately head, the mass of her glossy brown hair was fixed into an exaggeratedly large oval-shaped bun, which resembled a kind of crown. That portion of her coiffure indicated her innate and insolent wish to dominate and to 'lord it over' even her betters. And that was why I reached up with both hands and began to unknot that arrogant crown.

Once again I had hit home directly. Leila started and uttered a husky sobbing after perceiving my action in the mirror before her, then tried to turn her head. I gave her hair a little yank.

'Hold still unless you want to feel pain,' I commanded. This momentarily quelled her and when she saw me loosen her hair and rumple it out with my fingers until it fell in a rich dark cascade to her shoulderblades, she caught her breath again and closed her eyes and bowed her head in resignation. Decidedly I had attacked her vulnerability. Now there was a wonderful femininity and grace to her which she had not had before. Now she was much more softly alluring.

I lay there for a long moment behind her with my cock in full erection as if pondering her fate. Actually, I had long since decided on it but this pause was purposely chosen to tantalize her, to heighten her suspense, to weaken her nervous whore's resistance to the point where she would be frantically willing to grant me what I yearned for from her lusciously olive-tinted, vibrant flesh.

I now passed my hands round and in front of her, grasping her beautiful bubbies and squeezing them lingeringly as I moved up close behind her so that the tip of my aching cock just brushed the base of her behind and suggestively prodded the warm, slightly humid furrow that divided that magnificent posterior. Once again, Leila caught her breath and stiffened, uttering a long, heartrending sigh. She also closed her eyes so that she would not have to be shamed by watching my sinewy strong fingers close like tentacles over her swelling, glorious breasts. Whores have their pride.

'Are you feeling a little more humble now, my dear?' I demanded sarcastically. I felt her bottom twitch and contract against my gently, slyly prodding cocktip and I stared over her right shoulder to follow her reactions in the huge mirror placed before her. A wave of scarlet suffused her lovely, haughty face and her chin was trembling as she bit her own full lips, unable to answer. Her breasts rose and fell with violent turbulence now. She drew a long, shuddering breath, lifted her head and bowed it and then, while my cockhead lightly nuzzled at the shadowy groove between her luscious bare bottom cheeks, falteringly responded with a sigh.

Turning Leila around, I gripped the backs of her stockinged thighs and, lowering my head, put my tongue to the warm twitching and palpitating olive skin of her left thigh, just above the rosette garter. How warm and tasty it was to savour! Not only was there the subtle perfume of musk with which she had evidently sprayed herself; there was also the stronger and more exciting compound of perspiration and the tang of her feminine scent from her delicious Venus-vent.

In an involuntary reflex, Leila dashed her bottom backwards. But my fingers rose up to grip the base of those olive-sheened nether ovals and I forced her back to me as my tongue rasped upwards again until it attained the sensitive, soft twitching flesh of the groin as I made my way towards the sweet fig of her voluptuous cunt.

My instrument stood up proudly for the fray, rearing its haughty head and boasting of its uncommon length and thickness; Leila's thighs opened wider. She slid her head down slightly, hiding her face on my shoulder and gave herself up to me, fully offering herself to me.

'I desire . . .' she moaned, 'and yet I fear the entrance of such a handsome guest.' She soon enough felt the head of my penis between the lips of her grotto; and then I thrust inwards, and deeply. My lips pressed softly against hers as my prick pressed to her very vitals. 'I am beside myself . . .' Leila sighed. 'I feel that I am going mad.' The supreme moment arrived for both of us and she writhed about, uttering inarticulate sounds.

I withdrew my prick from Leila's quim with a feeling of quiet satisfaction – yet also with an awareness that I had unfinished business with her that required attention sooner rather than later. She had rolled over onto her stomach as soon as I had pulled out and the sight of her delightfully rounded buttocks above her stockinged thighs caused a fresh surge of lust to course through my groin. My cock began to swell once more. But after two climaxes in swift succession, I knew that this time its staying power would be equal to the task that lay before it.

I reached out and stroked Leila's back from the nape of her neck to her wonderful arse, where I allowed my hand to linger, cupping and squeezing the lower curve of one delectable flesh-globe. At the same time, I insinuated a finger into her cunt – she moaned softly – and gathered a quantity of love-juice from Leila's well-rogered joxy-depths onto the digit concerned. Taking it out, I trans-ferred my ministrations to her bumhole, thrusting my slippery finger past the tight flesh-ring of its entrance and on into its secret regions.

'Ah! No!' Leila gasped, seeking to clench her buttocks tight against this unexpected intruder. 'What are you doing?' She tried to turn onto her side to escape my grasp. I restrained her with my other hand, pinning her fast to the bed.

'I am endeavouring, madam, to show some small meas-ure of gentlemanly courtesy and consideration by lubricat-ing your back passage with a *soupçon* of spend from your placket before paying your delightful backside the compli-ment of a visit from Lord John Thomas,' I replied.

At this, Leila renewed her struggles, twisting desper-ately to free herself from my grip. But to no avail; if anything, her movements – the jiggling of her firm

breasts, the frantic motions of her stockinged thighs –
heightened my state of arousal. And they definitely made
my determination to penetrate her bumhole all the
stronger.

'Lord Horby, please desist, oh, please, I beg of you!'
Leila pleaded as I raised myself to straddle her lithe form.
I grasped both her wrists in one of my hands and held
them firmly. Sitting back on my heels, I surveyed the
wondrous prospect before me: Leila's beautiful if appre-
hensive face in profile against the pillow, her tousled,
lustrous hair, the smooth olive skin of her back and
buttocks and her thighs (squeezed so tightly together now
in futile resistance to the coming assault) emerging from
the enticing sheer black silk of her stockings. Desisting
was the last thing I intended.

'I don't imagine for one moment that Douglas intended
any restriction or limitation to be put upon the use of your
and Nina's sundry orifices when he signed you up for this
cruise,' I said. 'That being so – and, of course, your arse
being of such overwhelming attractiveness – I fully intend
to ensure that he gets his money's worth. By proxy, as it
were. And, by the by, a word to the wise and all that, I
wouldn't advise any unseemly screams of protest from
here on in, so to speak. Douglas won't appreciate having
his own session with Nina interrupted. And – who knows?
if he *was* to look in on us he might decide to avail himself
of your bottom-hole facility too. Then you'd be getting
two for the price of one. Not quite the kind of bargain you
might have in mind, eh?'

Leila strained against my grip on her wrists. 'Oh, no,
no, *no*. I can't . . . You mustn't . . .'

'Oh, mustn't I? I shouldn't have to remind you who's in
charge here but it seems as though there's a lesson *you*
must learn, my girl,' I responded. With my free hand, I

picked up the silken cord of Leila's negligée from the coverlet and briefly released her wrists before seizing them again and binding them together – securely but not tightly enough to cause discomfort or to restrict the flow of blood – behind her back. 'Now, you might as well attempt to put into practice the old adage about relaxing and enjoying it because nothing you can do or say will dissuade me from my course.'

That said, I proceeded to run my hands down Leila's smooth sides, sliding them around and under to knead her breasts and tweak her nipples before moving them down to her thighs, relishing the sensuous feel of the contrast between silken stocking-top and warm thigh-flesh. I thrust one hand between her thighs, forcing them apart and pressing my palm against her moist cunt-lips before moving it to her bumhole with its fresh load of lubricant. Then I took an arse-cheek in each hand and gently but firmly prised them apart sufficiently to expose Leila's shy sphincter to my gaze – and to the narrow eye of my bulging purple cockhead, surmounting by now a rigid, thick length of beef bayonet that was raring, – nay, raging – to go.

Leila still sought to escape the by now inescapable by pressing her pelvis hard down into the coverlet in a futile attempt to put as much distance as possible between her bumhole and my rampant cock. Briefly releasing her luscious bottom-globes, I reached behind me and grabbed a small cushion of Turkish (how appropriate!) design, one of several scattered about upon the bedspread. Raising Leila's hips quickly by pressing strongly upward against he cuntal mound with one hand, I stuffed the cushion between the bed and her pubic region so that, even when I had released my hold upon her Venus mount, her derrière remained raised slightly – but sufficiently – from the bed's surface.

Leila made one last desperate effort to plead with me. 'Lord Horby, oh milord, I beg you to ravish my cunt or my mouth instead of my bumhole. Your weapon is so monstrously huge that . . . aaaaaah, oh yes, yes . . .'

Seized by a sudden urge to mischief, I had indeed at this point gone along with Leila's suggestion of an alternative approach to the extent of swiftly plunging my engorged flesh-shaft to its hilt between her slick pussy lips. She sighed with relief – until she felt me withdraw completely from her cunt after the one stroke and once more grasp a bum-cheek in each hand. As I manoeuvred my hips to guide my swollen glistening pricktip into position against her private entrance, she whispered in final submission, 'Oh, cruel, cruel . . .'

'Sorry for the momentary false sense of security there. Couldn't resist the opportunity for a bit of trickery-pokery, what? Anyway, joke over, back to business. Here comes Old One-Eye!' So saying, I urged the taut glans of my ramrod into the snug entrance to Leila's sweet bottom-hole, resting it there a moment to relish the supreme sensation of its tight grip. Leila gasped and groaned but made no further movement of attempted avoidance. I pressed on in, savouring to the full the delicious constrictive feeling as the whole length of my prick became engulfed in the secret reaches of this beautiful, exotic whore's arse.

I am sure that if I had not already experienced two orgasms within the past hour I would have spent within seconds of penetrating Leila's bum, such was its grip. As it was, though, the stamina bestowed by those earlier climaxes enabled me to thrust on and on into her wonderful arse, increasing the force of my plunges steadily as I sensed her relaxing when the sensation of the fleshy intruder up her jacksie grew less unfamiliar. Keeping a strong hold on one firm, rounded arse-globe, I slipped my other hand around to Leila's cuntal mound, running my fingers through her silky pubic hair and locating the bud of her clitoris which I proceeded to frig gently as I continued thrusting into her bum-depths. This combination of sensations caused her to buck and shudder in an ecstasy of sensual delight – and to my own great satisfaction it also induced spasms in the flesh-ring of her anus which squeezed and clenched around my cock in exquisite fashion. As a result I soon felt the spunky floodtide gathering in my balls, building its pressure up to the point where no further holding back was possible. I surged down the length of my pounding prick to explode in a volcanic release of pulsating sensation in Leila's innermost secret flesh-depths – just at the moment that she herself cried out in the unmistakable tones of female orgasm.

'So, you see,' I said as Leila's no longer so shy sphincter relinquished its grip on my finally shrinking member, 'this butt-fucking business isn't necessarily such a pain in the arse. I hope you won't give the next punter who fancies a bit of your bum such a tough time. Well, I'm for a celebratory snifter – care to join me? Bottoms up!'

After a drink and some kisses and caresses, I went up on deck and gazed at the Nile for a while, graced as it was by a crescent moon. After a time, my reverie was interrupted by the clack of balls and, turning around, I discerned that Douglas was playing this new-fangled game of snooker on a billiard table which he had had the forethought to install.

'Care for a game?' he asked. I nodded and entered the cabin. 'Had a good fuck?' he enquired. We looked one another in the eyes and smiled, then Douglas potted some coloured ball. 'Glass of port?' He indicated a decanter of old tawny on a sideboard and I took my fill from one of the crystal glasses. 'Can't travel anywhere without port,' Douglas murmured as he potted another ball. 'Obvious, isn't it, why England has Portugal as its oldest ally. Ready to play?'

'Let's just talk for a while,' I said.

'All right.' He placed his cue on the rack and took another glass of port. 'Enjoying the cruise?'

'Immensely, thank you. Rather reminded me of one of my heroes, Sir Richard Burton. Didn't he discover the source of the Nile with Speke?'

'Yes,' Douglas replied, 'and he discovered many other things in addition, most notably in matters of literature.'

'Of course,' I concurred, 'there's his wonderful translation of *The Arabian Nights*, also known as *The One Thousand Nights and a Night of Sheherezade*. I tell you, I could curse that wretched widow of his for burning his private papers. What a forlorn, Presbyterian prude! Why the fuck did he marry her?'

'Fortunately she didn't burn all his works,' Douglas responded. 'There's still *The Perfumed Garden*, translated from the Arabic; and *The Kama Sutra*, which he translated from the Sanskrit. Got 'em, Horby?'

'Of course,' I replied truthfully.

'Read 'em?'

'I've glanced through them,' I answered, 'and discerned no matter worthy of close study. *The Perfumed Garden* seemed to tell me that I should eat bread and raw eggs to keep my erection thick, long and strong, also that I should try not to come too quickly; the latter I did know before. *The Kama Sutra* appeared to give me unenjoyable and anatomically uncomfortable sexual positions.'

'Then you have missed the truth and the beauty.'

'Evidently,' I said. 'Kindly explain it to me.'

'*The Perfumed Garden*,' he replied, 'refers to the vagina

and its varying emissions during a 28-day cycle of the moon. It is a manual of instruction concerning how to pleasure it, arguing also that in this way, you will increase your own pleasure. *The Kama Sutra* declares roughly the same proposition but proposes the use of advanced yoga postures so as to increase sensory enjoyment. There is a cultural difference insofar as the author of *The Perfumed Garden* discerned women as being lazy but greedy to be pleasured, the author of the Hindu *Kama Sutra* saw women as being only too willing and eager to join in. Such is the sexual difference between the male Muslim and Hindu minds, my dear sir.'

'And the Rosicrucians?' I queried. 'Where do they fit in here?'

'Depends to which Rosicrucians you refer,' he replied coolly. 'The English Masonic Societas Rosicruciana is honest and harmless and makes no false pretences. If its members happen as a rule to be pompous busy-bodies, enlarging the borders of their phylacteries and scrupulous about cleansing the outside of the cup and the platter, that is their affair. But those orders run by persons *claiming* to represent the True Ancient Fraternity are common swindles. The claims of "Papus" (Dr Encausse), Stanislas de Guaita, the late, and Sâr Peládan merit respect as serious, but lack full knowledge and authority. I have respect too for Mathers but it remains to be seen where it will all lead and the same is true of Crowley. The "Ordo Rosae Crucis", presently chartering Temples in America, is a mass of ignorance and falsehood, though this may be a deliberate device for masking itself. I can't say that we're worried, Horby. Fancy a game of billiards?'

I joined him in the billiard room and over our games, he informed me that Rosemary had gone to visit a relative in Montreal but would be writing to the pair of us and she hoped that her letters would arrive at the British Consulate on our return to Cairo. Douglas was a good player but I'm quite skilful with a cue and we were three games all when we agreed to break for more port.

'You know,' he said as he poured more velvety port for both of us, 'I'd like to tell you a story with a moral about a billiard table and a man.' I nodded acquiescence. 'This man, an acquaintance of mine, went to London's leading department store to purchase a billiard table. He was an explorer and he asked them to have it ready for him by the time he came back from the Himalayas. They did. "Your billiard table, sir."

' "What's this?" he protested. "A billiard table with six legs? Everyone knows that a billiard table has *seven* legs. Never known such tomfoolery. I'm off to the Andes. Have it ready for me next time I come back."

' "Your billiard table, sir," they said on his return. "*What?*" The Duke was outraged. "Never known such nonsense!" he expostulated: 'You have given me an oblong table and everyone knows that a billiard table is round. I'm off to the Arctic. Be sure to have it ready for me next time I come back."

' "Your billiard table, sir," they said on his next return. "*Ri-diculous!*" the Duke shouted. "You have given me round balls when all the world knows that in billiards, the balls, so-called, are square. And what're these funny long wooden things? Cues, eh? Oh, for heaven's sake, one plays billiards with proper bone clubs. And do get rid of that useless blue chalk; can't see the slightest use for it. Hah! Billiards? And I thought that this establishment knew its business. Well, I'm off to explore the outback of Australia. Have it ready for me next time I come back."

'Unfortunately,' Douglas continued evenly, 'the dear Duke was eaten alive in the Australian outback by a pack of wild dogs. So do you know anyone who wants to buy a round billiard table with seven legs, clubs of bone and square "balls" . . .?'

'No,' I said, 'but what's the moral?'

'Never deal with lunatics,' said Douglas. 'Fancy another game of billiards?' On this particular game, which we both agreed would decide the 3-3 issue, he proceeded to outplay me with greater skill. He was ahead and about to pot a perfect shot when the boat lurched and caused him to muff it completely, putting me back in the game with a winning chance. According to the crew, it was a hippo that was responsible but the accident rather upset his concentrated play and I managed to take the win and the thousand pounds that we had bet.

'Tales of the unexpected,' Douglas said as he paid the bet and poured more port for us. 'Always like that, isn't it? However well you may plan anything, there is always that random factor, infinite and unknown . . . how d'you fancy swopping girls for tonight?'

'Fine,' I answered.

CHAPTER TWELVE

After an exceedingly enjoyable cruise, Douglas and I were both pleased to receive letters from Rosemary in Montreal. Mine read:

Mon cherie, mon petit choux,

Comment allez-vous? Très bien? *Please excuse my terrible French for I am now in the most delightful city of Montreal. I gather meanwhile that you have been cruising along the Nile with Douglas and one trusts that you enjoyed the experience.*

When my godmother invited me to her mansion in Westmount, I could hardly refuse it. Her house overlooks the western slope of Mount Royal, often referred to as le petit montagne. *I believe that it was volcanic at one time. It rather reminds me of my godmother. She is getting on in age and often in the afternoon likes to have 'forty winks', or as she often says as she retires for her* siesta *'to lie in the arms of Morpheus.' Then she declares: 'Jacques, would you please bring me* le thé avec l'orange pressée? Je suis très fatiguée. *Rosemary, excuse me, my darling, I must retire for a while.'*

I am certain that the strong, handsome young Jacques is a housecarl but he does treat her well. On my first afternoon, I sat and contemplated the view before me. In 1842, Charles Dickens had visited the place with his wife and had written well of the city. Montreal is pleasantly situated on the margin of the St Lawrence and is backed by bold heights around which there are charming drives and rides. The streets are generally narrow and irregular. Yet as I sat in quiet contemplation, I was amazed by the sounds of the activities which were taking place overhead. I had always thought that sounds did not carry within a colonial building of this nature but evidently this one was an exception.

'Fuck me! Fuck me!' my prim and proper godmother was screaming at Jacques, 'but first of all, let me suck your cock.' I could not help but eavesdrop whilst the floor vibrated overhead.

'My love! My beautiful coquette!' Jacques roared. 'Let me lick upon your quim, upon your beautiful cunty, upon the lips of your marvellous labia!' Then the doorbell rang at the instant that my godmother was yelling words of orgasmic relief. I knew that guests were vaguely expected and also, obviously, that Jacques was presently in no condition to admit them; therefore I opened the door to reveal a young gentleman who was in possession of the slightest trace of a moustache and with his hair shiningly pomaded and parted down the middle. Bidding him welcome, I led him into the main drawing-room and helped him to a glass of wine, thereupon introducing myself.

'Rosemary, Rosemary . . .' he enthused, 'that evergreen, fragrant shrub, Rosemary taken as an emblem of remembrance,' and he softly blew me a kiss. How formal he was! And how he did blush!

'My name is Smith, yet you, Ma'am, can call me by my first name, which is Robert.'

'Robert, it is so apparent that you are an educated man.'

156

'*At the present time, Ma'am,*' he flushed furiously, '*I am pursuing my studies at McGill University. My desire is to achieve a degree in Philosophy; yet my greatest wish is to excel at hockey.*'

'*A hockey player . . .?*'

'*Indeed, Ma'am. I have invented the* puck *by cutting off the sides of an Indian Rubber Ball!*' he announced proudly.

'*How fascinating . . .*' I murmured as Catherine, my godmother, swanned into the room, followed by Jacques.

'*Mr Smith . . .!*' she greeted him. '*What a pleasure it is to see you again!*' She smiled at him graciously. '*You simply must introduce my god-daughter Rosemary to the delights of skating! It is,*' she remarked as Jacques served her with wine, '*such a joy to see how much you already appear to be enjoying one another's company.*'

'*Madame Vigère,*' Robert Smith replied, '*it is such a pleasure to enjoy your hospitality once again. And I am greatly looking forward to the arrival of the other guests.*'

'*Ah, yes,*' she responded, '*I am sure you will find them all as interesting as you find yourself.*' She smiled bitchily as he blushed. '*Age before beauty, I always say,*' giving him another smile to show that the shot had been executed without malice. '*Although I am a devotee of beauty.*' She glanced at Jacques, who was busy uncorking more wine. '*One fellow you must meet desires to build the most beautiful hotel in Montreal, combining the glamour of the Ritz in Paris with the splendour of the Carlton in London . . .*' her flow was interrupted since the guests suddenly arrived all at once as they are wont to do.

Eventually, eight of us were finally seated around the dining table to relish the cuisine of Jacques. His potage de pois, tortières, *molluscs simmered in cream and calvados*, le biftek *and an unusual accompaniment of* fruits de mer *were among outstanding highlights. I was reminded of an old French Canadian folk song:*

> There are some who love good food
> Beans with pork and also green peas;
> And plenty of pork also with beans.
> There are some who eat; others who don't.
> The spoiled gherkins in the salad . . .
> There are some who eat them and make themselves
>   sick!
> But to eat pea soup?
> The Canadians are always ready!
> Ah! Ah! The Canadians are always ready!

This somewhat banal nationalist anthem did not augur well for the future of Canada as a Great Power; but it certainly did not interfere with my enjoyment of Jacques's excellent pea soup; and it was a delight to sit opposite Robert. I could not take my eyes away from his. He had a double set of eyelashes which I have never seen before on a man; I think it is the sign of the second sight. Occasionally, he winked at me, an indication, one hoped, of something further to come.

After the occasion ended, I retired to my room, one that is always set aside for me, and put on my nightgown, sipping my hot chocolate and gazing into the glowing coal fireplace, both services which had been rendered by the attentive Jacques. The snow fell that evening, crystals dancing upon the ground as the moon glittered upon each ballerina falling from the sky. There was then a tap upon my door – a tale of the expected.

'Who is there?' I enquired in a voice of 'sauve qui peut'.

Of course, it was Robert and I was delighted to welcome him and to give us both a glass of apple brandy which Jacques had thoughtfully placed upon the bedside table. We talked pleasantly until he said:

'Rosemary, have you ever played the game of Smacking Bottoms?'

'I thought that only happened in Public Schools in Great Britain.'

'Possibly so,' he smiled, 'though there are their imitators throughout the Empire. Would you care to participate?'

'Yes?'

'This is a game of strength and skill . . .' We both removed our attire and squatted on the bed with our legs intertwined, each one of us holding a towel in the air. Abruptly, I shoved and twisted Robert over onto his abdomen and I slapped him viciously upon the buttocks. How they did redden and quiver! I knew that I was setting fire to his loins. Upon this cold winter's night, it was assuredly essential to raise the temperature. Droplets of steam appeared upon the window as, outside, the white flakes from heaven fell ever quicker and quicker.

As the coals glowed, we made love again, again and again. It was such a blazing inferno, this incandescence of heat between our loins. In the course of our outbursts of passion, we were both in a fever of pyrexia. My darling, I was suffering from violent ebullitions. Towards the early hours of the morning, he announced his intention of temporarily retiring from this bliss to his room.

'Mon chérie,' he said, 'I would love to teach you the art of skating when we can have the whole rink to ourselves but first of all, I must exercise in my sport.' I agreed to watch him practise his 'hockey' on the

*following afternoon at McGill and then fell asleep.
Around midday, there was a gentle knock upon my
door. I called out my assent to entrance and was
greeted by Jacques, who was bearing a tray.*

'Bonjour, Madame,' *he smiled, revealing wickedly
white teeth.* 'I come to bring you le petit déjeuner.'

'What have you brought me exactly?'

'Le café avec les crullers.'

'Come in, then' *I replied, suddenly feeling so abashed
to realize that my left breast was exposed. Before I knew
it, Jacques and I were frollicking upon the bed together.
How he did tickle my cunny! What a young stud he was!
Any farmer would hire him to breed!*

*Horby, you do not know how exhausting some activi-
ties in life can be. As you know, I am a very orgasmic
woman. The French can be such paramours . . . and
Jacques is a golden example. However, I had made an
arrangement to be with Robert later that day yet I did not
want to appear too* distinguée.

*I went to Eaton's to purchase a skirt of vermilion, the
frills of which were trimmed with ermine, that fur which
changes colour throughout the year – occasionally
marked with black spots. My outfit included a warm
vermilion pullover of wool, a little red hat, a furry brown
muff to keep my hands warm and a pair of thick, red
stockings of wool in addition to a pair of figure skates.*

*On my arrival, and on greeting Robert Smith, it was a
pleasure to see that we had the whole rink to ourselves. I
had learned figure skating at St Moritz during my
teenage years and so it was a joy to glide upon the ice
once again. It was an even greater pleasure to be served
hot mulled wine which he had made. We toasted one
another's health.*

'I hope that you become the greatest hockey player that

Canada has ever known,' I said. (Editor's Note: Robert Smith is regarded as the Founder of Canadian Ice Hockey.)

'So do I,' he replied, 'but now I must change into my costume. 'Unfortunately, it is necessary that I change in front of you.' I wondered just why it might be necessary since there was a clear sign stating CHANGING ROOMS on the EXIT door. Yet I could not help but look as Robert removed his clothing, down to his combinations. They were bright red with a flap for his bottom.

The combination of the ice upon the surface of the rink, the warmth within the room and the mulled wine put me in such a jovial mood. How we did frolic! We even sang a few chansons de geste. *As we danced upon the ice together, I began to feel the throbbing between his thighs, yes, I could feel a major protrusion under his cardinal red undergarment.*

'Turn around,' I said teasingly as we slid along the ice, 'and then bend over.' He complied and I released the flap to see his firm young buttocks, which initially I nibbled gently with playful bites. I can never have too much of a mouthful of ham, especially that of a fine, young gentleman. I did gently rim him, at the same time flicking my fingers upon his posterior, the haunches, hunkies, hindquarters of a fine young stud. I have never seen such a fine pair of hunkers in all my life, apart from yours, my darling.

Outside it was so cold in terms of temperature as Montreal froze under the intense brunal *of Winter.*

'How much longer do I have to wait before we can once more glide upon the ice together?' I asked.

'If you are going to be so attractive and alluring, it could be forever. Allow me to serve you another negus,*'*

he added as he sped away to refresh our glasses. What spices he had put into this concoction!

We then fell into one another's arms, with sparks flying and the room numinous with light. He was scintillating as he caught me on the ice, then slowly unlaced my boots and gradually removed all my attire and there and then did penetrate me with his marvellous art. What a slow fluidity there was between the two of us! He rammed it in sufficiently hard for me to forget temporarily the pleasures of skating. I was so looking forward to gliding upon the ice with an exquisite ease and yet, in another sense, this was taking place here and now as his prick throbbed within my cunt.

Douglas tells me that you have gone on a Nile cruise with him. I hope that the pair of you are misbehaving yourselves. I've made my own arrangements to meet Douglas; my advice to you, Horby, is: 'Go East, young man,' and don't be like my grandmother who always used to say: 'I don't want to try it because I might like it.'

All my love,
Rosemary.

Douglas and I finished reading our separate letters from Rosemary simultaneously. The British Consulate in Cairo provided an excellent smoking-room in those days.

'Remarkable woman, isn't she?' I said.

'Oh, indeed,' he answered firmly. 'So now let's do what she'd want us to do and pick up some good girls and fuck their brains out.'

CHAPTER THIRTEEN

It proved to be relatively easy to attain our desired objective. We were staying at a certain hotel in Cairo, the name of which, even now, discretion forbids me to mention, for it is still in being. If I mention the small golden pyramid within a glass case housed just to the left of Reception, then some of my readers may know of it. Essentially, it was – and, I believe, still is – an excellent rendezvous for wealthy and respectable gentlemen and ladies.

As was customary with him, Douglas had spared no expense for his every whim to be gratified. We had adjoining suites with a connecting door and even Tutenkhamen or Queen Nefertiti would have been gratified by the gaudy splendour. It was in Douglas's drawing-room that I smoked the *hubble-bubble* of hashish with him and also took copious quantities of gin-and-tonic. This is not, in fact, my favourite drink but the quinine in the tonic is a most advisable protection against the dangers of malaria.

When we wandered somewhat airily downstairs and into the dining-room, I had become so used to his eccentricities that I was not at all surprised by his choice of menu.

'All influenced by North Africa, Horby,' he murmured; and the fact is that in Cairo's finest establishments, they will bring you whatever you want as long as you can pay for it. We therefore took a glass or two of *arak*, a hot, white, burning spirit and commenced with a Tunisian speciality, *brikl*, thin pastry folded over a filling of vegetables and raw egg, deep-fried and served with a side salad, and observing the custom of the country, we ate it with our right hands. 'Watch that you don't end up with egg on your face,' said Douglas. I did not; though I was watching two extraordinarily attractive young women who were dining at a table across the room from ours. Douglas noticed my appreciative glances.

'Ah, that's Juanita and Alicia,' he murmured over our *chorba*, a spicy soup with lemon. 'All is easy as ABC here, as you may have discerned from the menu I have chosen, for our next course will consist of *dolmades*. We've having an alphabet dinner. Just enjoy it, old chap, this'll keep your pecker up.' I nodded my appreciation of the spiced minced meat and rice wrapped in vine leaves. With it we were drinking a young Turkish white wine which truly did taste of the grape. 'Anyway, Juanita, the *Marquesa*, and *Doña* Alicia are long-standing friends of mine from Spain and they'll be only too delighted to join with us for a good fuck later.' My sense of appetite was rising, since both ladies were exquisitely dressed in silk, Juanita in black and Alicia in white. 'And so that's my letter 'e': *e*ager.' He chuckled wickedly. 'Takes a whole alphabet of ingredients to make a good dinner and a good occasion, wouldn't you say so, Horby?'

I nodded assent since my prick was rising at the sight of these two exquisite women who were speaking together quietly yet eating voraciously. Juanita, the *Marquesa*, had long, wavy dark hair and high cheek-bones which set off to perfection her flashing eyes. Lady Alicia had masses of flaming red curls and her expression was somewhat haughty and disdainful. Juanita was beautifully buxom whilst Alicia was delectably slender. I wanted to fuck the pair of them there and then but turned back to my gaunt, cadaverous and curious host.

'*E* is also for eggs,' he smiled as a small plate of one of my favourite delicacies, plovers' eggs, appeared upon our table. This dinner was certainly memorable. For *f* there was a delicious fish stew to accompany our *g* for grain, a North African speciality called *couscous* and this was excellent. 'You may well be asking what I'll be doing for *h, i* and *j*. Why, *h* is for that delicious dish of mashed chick peas that is coming, called *hummus*, *i* is for *I* since *I* am the host and you still find me *i*nscrutable,' (which was true), and *j* is the *jambon*, for we will be enjoying a few slices of exquisite smoked ham from France. *L*,' he continued, 'is for the *l*adies present, for we'll be wanting a good fuck after dinner and meanwhile we admire the view; *m* is for meat, since we shall, one trusts, enjoy a dish of exquisite, thinly sliced raw fillet of beef in the Lebanese fashion; and chopped cashew *nuts*, as in *n* are a fitting accompaniment. After that, we shall require an *o* for orange, sliced into four quarters, to refresh ourselves for the next dish.

'This will commence,' Douglas informed me, 'with *p* for peppers spiced and roasted to accompany our *q* for quails roasted within the same dish and accompanied by a small portion of *r* for rice, plentifully flavoured with the world's rarest spice, which is *s* for saffron. There is of course a *t* for twist in this tale of our dinner *together, for it is a t*ale of the unexpec*t*ed, a *u* for the indispensable *u*tensils we employ to eat it, a *v* for our victuals generally – and let's not forget our *e*ventual *v*ictory over those *v*oluptuous women – a *w* for our wine; and I've ordered plenty of robust Moroccan red to go with it.' He drew a deep breath then smiled benevolently. '*X* is simply the factor infinite and unknown which informs every encounter, *y* is for the yogurt appropriate to so many of these dishes, and as for *z*, that's when we invite the ladies to our table to join us in partaking of that magical Italian dessert, *zabaglione*.'

'Sounds splendid, Douglas,' I returned with genuine enthusiasm. 'But as we proceed to enjoy this feast, can I ask you a couple of questions which continue to puzzle me?'

'Be my guest.'

'Is Emily Ward-Bishop really your niece?'

'If she says so, then she is,' Douglas returned with a wry, dry smile. 'I wouldn't doubt her word and heaven knows, if you were to research the matter, you might well find that we are related by marriage between a wide variety of relatives. Next question.'

'About a year ago, the Hon Claire Woodrough wrote me a letter from Paris in which she described Satanism as practised by her cousin Charlotte with her paramour Jean-Pierre. This mysterious and intriguing couple have left Paris without a trace. What is your opinion?'

'My opinion,' Douglas replied, 'is either that Claire was having you on to excite your libidinous fantasies; or else that it was not a Mass but a mess. There sometimes are these pieces of theatre staged in Paris to sort out the wheat from the chaff; and Claire is definitely among the wheat.'

'Any idea where she might be now?' I stared into his eyes, which were like cold gun-muzzles.

'Out in India with Ram Singh, I imagine,' he answered casually. 'And that's where you ought to be, as I keep telling you, my dear fellow. You keep on looking for Truth, don't you?' He laughed harshly. ' "What is truth?" asked Pontius Pilate; and you're still waiting for an answer. Why, Hasan Al Sabah, leader of the Sect of

Assassins, also called "The Hashishin", declared: "Nothing is true; everything is permitted." And I say to you now: "Truth is what you believe." Incidentally, don't believe *me*. You never know, I might be lying. Make up your own mind, Horby, and come with me tomorrow to the King's Chamber of the Great Pyramid. Meanwhile, enough of this intellectual nonsense. Let us invite Juanita and Alicia to our tables – incidentally it's rumoured that they made their fortunes by marrying and killing aged, wealthy, titled men – let's enjoy *zabaglione* and let's fuck!'

Fifteen minutes later I had no cause for complaint as I fucked the voluptuous Juanita. Her every cry was in tune with mine. Next door, I knew, Douglas was fucking Alicia. I was enjoying a very good fuck indeed. My right hand assaulted her delectable bubbies as my left advanced towards her navel, flicking all around into that delightful nook, and then with the same hand, I swept a peacock plume at the socket of her sweet and quivering left hip, tickling the shivering skin with a lingering peroration. She gasped and wriggled, bit her lips and then closed her eyes, delighting in her submission. My fingers glided down her stockinged thighs and stroked the fine black silk sheath about the knee and then on up to where that lovely column joined her hip, thence to brush against her lower abdomen where the curls of her pubis flourished. As I lowered the tip of my finger toward the top of her cunt, Juanita uttered a low sobbing groan.

Upper class ladies are so easy to seduce, provided that one has the right surroundings. As for one's behaviour, I concur with Beau Brumell: 'I treat all the chambermaids like duchesses and all the duchesses like chambermaids.' That is why I suddenly slapped her face, a quick flick to the right cheek. Her eyes blazed with anger.

'Why did you do that?' she demanded furiously.

'Because you're such an insolent, snooty bitch, aren't you?' I replied. And with this, I lowered my right hand down toward the very tip of her cunt and began to tickle her.

The bourgeoisie fail utterly to realize that the aristocracy and gentry behave like farmyard animals, which is why we usually get on so well with the working classes. If ever royalty pretends to ape middle-class behaviour, that will be the eventual doom of it. In any event, Juanita's eyes widened as she stared down at herself and all of a sudden, a fiery blush suffused her contorted, flushed cheeks. Then she gnawed her lower lip and stiffened herself but she could not help a sporadic trembling which shook her body from head to foot.

I stared greedily at the thick verdure of her crisp silky growth which so luxuriantly and protectively fleeced her slit. And I prodded my finger until its tip touched through the curls to open her outer labia, then began very slowly but deftly to rasp it up and down the lip nearest to me, so as to sensitize it. Meanwhile my left hand continued with its gliding touches all along her trembling thigh, abruptly visiting her leg with long and deliberate caresses. A tiny whimpering gasp escaped from my naked victim and lover.

Now the fingers of my right hand moved over to the top of the other fleshy outer lip which helped to form that lovely fig, that sweet miniature conch-shell which was her voluptuous vagina and I proceeded to tickle it in the same way. But now I glided the feather that I had picked up again down to the very base of her slit and then back up again along that crinkly, fleshy pink lovelet, while my left now moved to the inside of her right thigh, very near to that furry grape which I was so intent upon peeling.

'Ohh . . . oh! what are you doing, oh my Lord for I thought you were an English Gentleman. I'm only a helpless woman . . . ahhh!!! – oooh! – oh! no more, no more, in the name of mercy!'

"Between a woman's yes and a woman's no, I would not care to put the point of a pin," wrote Cervantes in *Don Quixote*: and who am I to disagree? Naturally I deplore rape: but the point of the pin is when you put your finger into a woman's cunt. If it is wet, that means an affirmative. If it is dry, that means a retreat in good order with chivalry. And let us not forget that if there is sufficient chivalry, she may yet change her mind. After all, that is assuredly a woman's prerogative.

As it happened, I continued to tickle this delectable, small, wet cunt and Juanita began to jerk and twist, swaying her hips from side to side in a coy endeavour to disengage my hands from their stealthy and relentless attack.

Now, and slyly, I moved my left hand over to her cunt and in a trice had the soft downy lips moving up and down, caressing these fleshly portals which concealed the road to paradise. Juanita uttered a shriek as I touched an acutely sensitive spot and lunged her bottom backwards to escape my dual siege of her most sensitive and sacrosanct regions. She really did excite me with her convulsive gyrations and her buckings and lungings which made her thighs and bubbies jounce and jiggle and express the luscious resilience of her naked flesh. The fingers of both my hands directed their diabolically persuasive caresses up and down the outer labia of my lady's twitching quim.

'Ah! – oh! – God in heaven – oh! – you'll drive me crazy – oh, please, sir . . . – oh! in the name of heavenly mercy . . . I beseech you . . . DON'T! . . . oh, DO . . . stop! eeeowow! – oh! Lord, oh! . . . . it's too much! I can't bear it any longer!' she gasped. 'Oh! Sir, do have mercy upon a poor helpless woman and spare me, milord!' Her soft vibrant voice was choked with sobs and gasps and groans as she twisted and arched and wriggled back and forth, her eyes now fixedly staring down at the prick aimed at her crotch, that very prick which now proceeded with its swollen head to tickle the quivering coral petals of her love-slit.

I drew my prick away so that I could have a look at the threshold of my coming attunement. Yes, the curly thicket of Juanita's pussy-hair was ruffled and here and there I could perceive the exquisite crinkly surfaces of that voluptuous membrane which was her temple of Venus, her nymph's grotto of satyr's delight. And then, with a cool little smile as I stared down at her, I thrust my cock deep into her cunt and worked it back and forth.

The effect was magical! Juanita emitted a wild, piercing shout of '*Aaaah! Ohh! nooo-o-o-o-o!!!*' as she madly jerked her glorious bottom backwards.

This was a perfect cue for me to push my mid-finger up her arse and she writhed with the pleasure of it. I cupped her glorious bottom within my palms and relished the sensation of her soft, young and tender flesh. Initially, I moved my stiff prick slowly in order to make a gentlemanly acquaintanceship with her ladylike cunt. Once gracious admission to her more inward recesses had been granted, I began to step up the pace and the rhythm.

First, I gave it to her in the long way, which is to draw your cock in and out at its full length, and on the odd inward thrust, follow the advice of *The Perfumed Garden* and try to make the tip of your cock touch the outer lips of her womb. Once she has sighed her signal to sexual surrender, slam in hard. I suddenly moved very fast, whipping my prick in and out and surprising her with my speed. Then it's *slam*. That is a sequence to the sexual dance which I find increasingly hard to repeat as I age – though it is still possible on occasion – and it consists of grinding one's rod-root against her pubic bone. One wants her to be walking around with the feel of your cock up her cunt for at least a week even though you're miles away; and certainly, that way, the lady will not forget you.

Slam can be so exciting to both man and woman that the man might well come but it is best not to do so. I returned to long, loving strokes within her warm wet cunt as Juanita writhed and twisted her swan-like neck with the pleasure of it. There was a moment when she realized that I was about to come and she made it glorious by gripping her creamy thighs around me. When I shot my load of spunkshot into her, my hips went into a spasm, my spine tingled from brain to balls and in my mind, the glory of my seed spurted forth unto the stars within her.

CHAPTER FOURTEEN

There is no doubting that the sexual act is the holiest act in the Universe. The male conjoins with the female in ecstasy, celebrating all creation. One should therefore despise anyone who opposes this noble movement of Nature as a fool, charlatan and bearer of foul mental diseases.

I am hardly an expert in scientific matters but it seems to me as though the research and discoveries of our present scientists confirm the statements of Ancient and Renaissance philosophers who declared that everything is relative, depending upon the point of view of the observer; and that everything in the Universe is somehow connected with everything else.

Philosophy, however, was not in the forefront of my mind on the following morning. After good, strong coffee with Juanita, we joined Douglas and Alicia for a light breakfast of more coffee and bread and eggs. Both of them looked as though they had enjoyed a marvellous time, which caused me to wonder increasingly about Douglas. Although I had spent weeks in his good company and he had been and was being an excellent host, I still did not know very much about him and he had pointedly declined to answer all my questions of a personal nature. Nevertheless, I acceded to his proposition for the day, which was to take camels to the Great Pyramid.

It was a curious procession. Douglas was surrounded by fierce tribesmen, all of whom seemed to be devoted to his welfare. They were the sort of chaps who might slit your throat for one bad word and think nothing of it: and if you were to touch their sisters in a disrespectful manner, they would chop your balls off and stick them in your mouth. Aside from this, they were dignified men of the utmost courtesy.

I was also baffled by the fact that they had brought two sorts of camels: the Dromedary with one hump; and the Bactrian with two. They gave the one-humped Dromedaries to Juanita and Alicia, assuring them that they would be more comfortable that way; the men rode the two-humped Bactrians. Camels really are extraordinary desert creatures. They store their food in their humps and their water in their bellies and they can go for weeks or even months without either as they plod along at a slow and steady pace. Juanita and Alicia initially found it difficult to master the knack, as I did, but since we were accustomed to horses, the matter only required a period of adjustment and the Bedouin friends of Douglas rendered us every possible assistance in the course of our learning process. After a couple of hours, I was sitting well in my saddle and so was everyone else.

'Extraordinary, isn't it, Horby,' said Douglas, 'that Mohammad was for a time an illiterate camel driver. Nothing more. Then, by his own account, while he was quietly meditating in a cave, endeavouring to seek the Truth of God, the Angel Gabriel came to him and dictated *The Qu'ran*. This Book made of him the Prophet of Islam and he restored Civilization to the West, then suffering the Dark Ages of totalitarian Christianity. Mohammad restored Art, Science and the rights of Woman.'

'Quite agree,' I replied, for I had read a translation of *The Qu'ran*. 'Isn't it a pity, though, that this holy scripture can be misinterpreted as a tool of foul oppression?'

'True,' Douglas sighed heavily. 'As Schiller has it: "With stupidity, the Gods Themselves argue in vain." '

We trekked on our way towards the Pyramids. There was nothing to see except sand. Does anything ever happen among those burning dunes or does it remain as uneventful as a cricket match upon an English village green?

Will Eternity be like this? I wondered as we continued with our bumpy ride across the endless dunes of sand. It's been said that cricket is the closest knowledge that any Englishman will ever have of Eternity. Even cricket is more interesting than this endless vision of sand. It was a joy when some pyramids came into view. There was also the Sphinx and I thought of Her Riddle of Man. The sun really does addle one's brain sometimes; and so did the conversation of Douglas.

'Have you ever considered, Horby,' he asked me, 'the fact that there might be alien creatures among us?'

'Is that a fact?' I replied. 'It sounds like something from the scientific romances of H.G. Wells.'

'I didn't say it was a *fact*. I said that it *might*, be a possibility. After all, there are billions of stars within our own galaxy, some of which may support planetary systems. For all we know, there are billions of galaxies. Some form of intelligent life might have sent alien beings to this planet in order to accelerate human evolution.' I nodded my assent to this possibility. It was conceivable that it might explain the behaviour of Douglas, not to mention Rosemary and Claire. 'Now look at the Great Pyramid coming up ahead of us.' I looked with astonished admiration at this magnificent sight. 'Did you know that if you multiply its height by a million, you get the distance from the Earth to the Moon accurately to two decimal places?' I didn't. 'The pyramid also exemplifies *pi* in its structure,' Douglas continued remorselessly. 'The fact is, my dear fellow, that it would be virtually impossible even for us, with our modern technology, to construct a building possessing such minute mathematical exactitude in the plain truths about the physical Universe of which it plainly informs us. It is not impossible that alien intelligences may have informed a primitive but hard-working people of knowledge well beyond their ken.'

'Not impossible . . .' I muttered as this magnificent structure came into full view.

What followed was one of the most extraordinary experiences of my life. The four of us spent a night in the King's Chamber of the Great Pyramid after dismissing the servants at the foot of the Great Gallery.

By the light of a single candle placed on the edge of the coffer, Douglas began to read: 'The Preliminary Invocation' of *The Goetia*. This was a fragment of a Graeco-Egyptian papyrus, discovered in the British Museum and edited for The Cambridge Antiquarian Society, with a translation, by one Charles Wycliffe Goodwin (1852), as Douglas informed me, and it was given to the Adepts of the Golden Dawn once they had entered into the Inner Order of the Rosy Cross. The original, which he kindly gave me, follows:

An address to the god drawn upon the letter.
I call thee, the headless one, that didst create earth and heaven, that didst create night and day, thee the creator of light and darkness. Thou art, Osoronnophris, whom no man hath seen at any time: thou art Iabas, thou art Iapōs, thou hast distinguished the just and the unjust, thou didst make female and male, thou didst produce seeds and fruits, thou didst make men to love one another and to hate one

another. I am Moses thy prophet, to whom thou didst commit thy mysteries, the ceremonies of Israel; thou didst produce the moist and the dry and all manner of food. Listen to me: I am an angel of Phapro Osoronnophris; this is thy true name, handed down to the prophets of Israel. Listen to me . . . .
. . . . hear me and drive away this spirit.

I call thee the terrible and invisible god residing in the empty wind, ...
thou headless one, deliver such an one from the spirit that possesses him. . . . .
. . . . strong one, headless one, deliver such an one from the spirit that possesses him . . . . .
. . . .
deliver such an one . . . .
This is the lord of the gods, this is the lord of the world, this is he whom the winds fear, this is he who made voice by his commandment, lord of all things, king, ruler, helper, save this soul . . . .
. . . . angel of God . . . . .
. . . . I am the headless spirit, having sight in my feet, strong, the immortal fire; I am the truth; I am he that hateth that ill-deeds should be done in the world; I am he that lighteneth and thundereth; I am he whose sweat is the shower that falleth upon the earth that it may teem; I am he whose mouth ever burneth; I am the begetter and the bringer forth; I am the Grace of the World; my name is the heart girt with a serpent. Come forth and follow – The celebration of the preceding ceremony – Write the names upon a piece of new paper, and having extended it over your forehead from one temple to the other, address yourself turning towards the north to the six names, saying: Make all the spirits subject to me, so that every spirit of heaven and of the air, upon the earth and under the earth, on dry land and in the water, and every spell and scourge of God, may be obedient to me – And all the spirits shall be obedient to you . . .

As he went on, I noticed that he was no longer stooping to hold the page near the light. He was standing erect, yet the manuscript from which he read was not less but more legible. Looking about me, I saw that the Kings Chamber was glowing with a soft light which I discerned as being at the violet edge of the spectrum. If I had to affix a conventional label, I should probably call it pale lilac, though the quality of the light was much more striking than that colour. Here the word 'phosphorescence' occurs to the mind. It is one of the mysteries of physics that the total light of the sky is very much greater than can be accounted for by the luminous bodies in the heavens. There are various theories, but I personally believe that the force presently called radio-activity, which we know to be possessed in some degree by every particle of matter, is responsible. Our eyes are affected with the impression of light by forces which are not in themselves recognized as luminous.

However, back to facts. The King's Chamber was aglow as if with the brightest tropical moonlight. The pitiful dirty yellow flame of the candle was like a blasphemy and Douglas rightly put it out. The light remained during the entire session of all that ensued.

Douglas had obviously ordered his servants to place couches in the chamber prior to our arrival. These were carved, ornamented and fashioned with every extreme of oriental luxuriance. I gazed at Alicia, with whom I had not yet made love. She was as beautiful as an earthly Venus, with eyes that were large, dark and dreamily voluptuous, in whose depths true love had evidently found no place. She was clothed in some sort of light, flimsy garment, showing the charming slender curves and displaying the mobile undulations of her lovely form. At my beckoning, she placed herself beside me as Douglas fixed his own attentions upon Juanita.

Ye Gods of Ancient Egypt! What a maddening sight

now met my enamoured eyes as they feasted with insatiable delight upon the supreme beauty thus given to my view. Her rounded, softly moulded chin merging into the white column of her neck, this gradually widening until it indicated two round, swelling breasts, crowned each with a delicious pink bud, and their very colour, which was a dusky brown . . . all of this added to my delight. What tides of ecstasy thrilled through my maddened spirit as my hands wandered unrestrained over the soft expanse of her breasts as they swelled to meet my gentle, kneading pressure.

The light was leaving me in a delirium, though I knew that through some mysterious power, Alicia would fully respond to my endeavours as I fastened upon her lovely mouth and sucked in her fragrant breath. As if in answer to my prayers, her face suddenly flushed and her breasts began to heave with innocent bliss. With what joy I saw her body tremble in ecstasy! Her efforts to respond to my fond pressures had somewhat disordered her dress and I now perceived that it had fallen entirely from her limbs.

If I had been excited before, this was increased threefold when I moved back to the other end of the couch and saw her most secret beauties revealed in all their maddening luxuriance: her legs had opened wide and as I gazed my eyes dwelt on each softly rounded limb, from tapered ankle to glowing thigh. Her hand, meantime, prompted perhaps by the light aroused within the Pyramid, wandered down until it rested between her quivering thighs, and almost unconsciously, played with the short, silky, curling hair that covered this delectable slot.

Excited and aroused by this unusual occupation, a pair of scarlet, pouting lips opened, whilst the soft mound above thrilled and throbbed as if longing for some unknown pleasure. I watched fascinated as she brought herself to some kind of dreamy climax. Her whole body heaved upwards as if to meet some responding pressure, whilst her breasts rose high and her nipples visibly engorged with the exquisite ecstasy of love's enjoyment. At last, unable to bear this unusual pleasure, she lay back, her cheeks flushing and her eyes half-closed in delicious languor, still disorientated by the effect of her orgasm.

Maddened by the sight in the violet light, I embraced Alicia with frantic eagerness and kissed her breasts again and again until, prompted by my unruly desires, my hand suddenly plunged through her panting mounds of pleasure and took possession. All this rendered her nearly helpless in my arms. Both her arms were now joined around my neck and she was lost in the mazes of her warm imagination. She now encouraged my hands to rove unrestrained all over her lovely neck and breasts, now and then wandering to her slender waist and softly rounded belly. Her mouth was half open like a ripe pomegranate, returning my burning kisses whilst her tongue darted between my lips.

'This is like nothing earthly!' she gasped. My desires had now reached a height entirely beyond my control; and indeed, she seemed to be in almost a like condition. We lay stretched face to face now, our bodies pressed together in frantic embraces and our limbs disordered. I threw myself upon her and clasped my arms around her waist whilst hers embraced my neck. Alicia pressed closer and closer amidst humid kisses and soft murmuring, as if she wished to incorporate our bodies into one.

Whether by accident or by remembering the movements of her own masturbation, Alicia's limbs by degrees opened to admit my pulsating prick, her legs twining convulsively about my loins. Nearly fainting with the unaccustomed ecstasy of our still raging and as yet unappeased desires, we heaved and pressed frantically against one another. She resisted so as to prolong the delicious torment but could feel my member pressing against that lovely spot between her thighs, determined to force its imperious way despite all impediments; and with longing, her cunt pouted wider at each instance of assault, longing despite itself to admit the dear invader.

All thoughts of modesty or maiden diffidence within the King's Chamber of the Great Pyramid was now completely overwhelmed and forgotten amidst the rampaging impulses of her unappeased desires. She sank down before me, her eyes half closed with love, her breasts thrusting high, as if willing to be pressed, her legs thrown apart, impatient to clasp my body. I prepared to consummate our mutual bliss. With trembling eagerness, she aided and abetted my every endeavour.

My invading weapon now entered the open gates of my longing partner and pressed onward. Her breasts heaved upwards against my chest, as each eager thrust sent a thrill of heavenly delight through her frame. Her thighs quivered and clasped around me while she seemed to dissolve in an agony of enjoyment.

Now wriggling with her hands clasped around my loins, all at once we suddenly struggled more fiercely, clasped tighter and tighter, till with one hot kiss, we came together and sank fainting into one another's arms.

When I recovered consciousness, my prick was still in the cunt of the slumbering Alicia. I looked around to see that this was the case also with the seemingly somnolent Douglas as he lay aboard the tender Juanita. The curious light, which had no natural, physical explanation and which I have since heard called 'astral light', remained; though it lessened in intensity as we composed ourselves to sleep.

In the morning, it had completely dissipated and the only sound was the flitting of bats.

CHAPTER FIFTEEN

There was a parting of the ways in Cairo after this extraordinary event. Douglas had urgent matters of business in Europe which called for his urgent attention; Juanita and Alicia had to return to Spain to administer their estates; and I had decided to take the advice of Douglas and go East. As I bade farewell to this excruciatingly enigmatic man, whom perhaps one day I would understand, I thanked him for his lavish and astonishing hospitality.

'I hope you've received a good letter from Rosemary,' were his last, jovial words to me before I boarded a French steamer, S.S. *Dupleix*, for a passage to India.

The voyage was actually atrocious; the ship stank of oil, partly from the engines, partly from the cooking and partly from the crew. But the consolation, there was indeed a letter from Rosemary:

My darling
How I miss you so much! I have never known such a long, arduous, onerous, toilsome train journey as that across Canada. I am so glad that I had brought some interesting literature with me; for instance The Ballad of Reading Goal *by the late Oscar Wilde; and other words of litterae, humaniores, a veritable chrestomathy; and belles lettres.*

I felt it so necessary that I bring my needlework with me also in order to wile away the hours. I am working upon a rich arras as a gift for you upon my return. How I do like to be so meticulous, attentive and accurate with my stitching! I so much loathed doing samplers when I was at school, especially when I did accidentally pierce my finger with my sewing needle and the blood would slowly ooze out upon my fine white linen.

The weather is so cold and the daylight hours so short . . . I thought that my railway journey across the Prairies would never end. However, I must tell you, my darling, of how spectacular the sunsets were, the most lavish and amazing display of lights in the sky that I have ever seen: hues of reds and orange, crimson, carnation, pink, even a touch of imperial purple with the transparency of garnet.

It is believed by some that the period of sunset, shading into twilight and dusk, is the declining period of life: yet I know it is not so, as the great Sun God Mithras gradually falls down unto the Earth to meet the arising Goddess of the Moon, known under a variety of names such as Luna, Phoebe and Selene; and they kiss and touch with reverence before they part until their next meeting on the following evening.

When the world stands still, the Blind Man's Holiday is the instant of the day just before the lamps are lit.

What was even more brilliant and histrionic was the sight of the Aurora Borealis, streamers of light radiating from the northern sky. Am I wrong in stating that the Aurora was named after the Roman Goddess of Dawn?

Upon my first evening within this train, I wanted to delight in the beauty of the night sky, enjoying a brandy in the observation car prior to retiring to my Pullman compartment. Admittedly, I was desirous of company,

*especially that of a gentleman and stag, such as you are.
Midnight approached. I felt so reluctant to depart, even
though I was the last customer. Suddenly, a man entered
and approached me, swaggering with bravado and with
the odour of whiskey upon his breath. However, the
sight was a delight. His hair was long, jet black and long,
and it was shining; and he wore an outfit similar to that I
have seen in picture books: that of the Native American
Indian.*

*We spoke; and he told me that he was the son of a chief
of the Blackfoot tribe in my destination, the Province of
Alberta. He expressed surprise when he learned where I
was going.*

*'I'm going to see a Great Aunt of mine,' I explained.
'Recently there has been a discovery of oil upon her
land.'*

*'Do you not think that there is more to life than mere
financial gain?' he queried.*

'Would you please explain?'

*'Yes. You people are expropriating our land and
putting us on reservations.' I could see that I was talking
to a very angry young man and I started to feel somewhat
intimidated by his audacious and impudent manner.*

'I must go now,' I said.

*'Sit!' he demanded peremptorily whilst producing a
proffered flask of whiskey. As we sat and drank, I
could not look away from his eyes that affected me so
hypnotically.*

'Really . . .' I smiled. 'Now I must retire.'

*'And so you may,' he smiled back with gracious
condescension.*

*I made sure that the door to my compartment was
safely locked. The clickety-click of the railway wheels
had a somnolent effect upon my body. Yet within my*

compartment, there was a greater resonation, such as that of tom-toms, hand-beaten drums. To my stupefaction, I came out of my sleepiness to see a young, naked man with feathers in his hair with an eagle poised atop his head.

'Do you not remember me?' he asked. Abruptly I recalled a certain Initiation.

'How could I forget you, ATOTARHO?' I replied. I stared upon his naked, bronzed, muscular, almost hairless body, possessed of a throbbing, very erect penis, which I immediately took into my mouth, sucking upon the knob before I allowed his complete member to plunge down my throat. His juices were as tasty as those of pemmican, a dried and powdered meat that is flavoured with currants.

'Now stand up,' he demanded. 'I will do you no harm; as I am the Great Shaman.' He fondled upon each breast and took each nipple gently into his mouth. Then he started to kiss me with a wild rapture that made me feel so excitable. I winced and flinched as his tongue gradually approached my cunt. When his tongue finally did enter me, it was like that of a fire-breathing dragon. How my knees did tremble as he rampantly drank my juices and I felt ablaze within! 'Your cunt is hotter than a prairie fire,' he said. 'You even arouse more heat than the dog days, the heliacal rising of Sirius, the Dog Star!' Then he added very gently: 'Please do lie down since I would really like to make love to you.'

I could not resist. I was aware of the bald eagle flapping its wings overhead with the sound of drums beating as ATOTARHO again penetrated my cunny, but this time with his penis. I could not believe the smoothness of his skin against mine as he pumped into me. His orgasm almost left me exhausted. However, he produced *a piece of* tobacca *that was inserted into a pipe and once smoked, this had the effect of a renewing aphrodisiac.*

As the sun rose, we again made love with a greater intensity that was even more fulfilling in its alacrity. I clung on to his muscular biceps and to all the other contractile fibrous bands of nerves in his body; and kissed those of his inner thighs and calves and his firm young buttocks which gently quivered like some well-set raspberry jelly; and maybe there was a spot of whipped cream and a maraschino cherry on top, just demanding to be eaten!

You cannot imagine how much I delighted in the morning light which daybreak brought! Then, after I came, weariness swept over me and he could see it in my eyes as he gently laid me down upon my bed and kissed me tenderly upon each eyelid. His powers appeared to be greater than those of the Sandman as I sank into a deep slumber. I recall dreamily his final words: 'We will meet again soon.'

I wonder if we ever will. He has left the train. Anyway, in a day's time, all being well, I shall have reached my destination and will correspond with you again as I do miss you so much.

All my love,
Rosemary.

After reading this intriguing letter, I went up on deck and gazed at the sea for a time, then retired to the bar in search of good company, though the hope seemed somewhat forlorn. To use the words of Samuel Taylor Coleridge in his *The Rime of the Ancient Mariner*: 'We were a dismal crew.' Yet to my delight there suddenly entered a chap whom I'd met in London and with whom I was vaguely acquainted, the psychologist Dr Harry

Maudesley. He seemed to be as despairing of good company as I was so we readily agreed to dine together.

Dinner was as awful as everything else on the voyage. Anyone who thinks that the French regularly eat well has not endured the misfortune of travelling to the East upon the *Dupleix*. There was a bowl of hot water with swimming vegetables, a limp and tasteless fish in powdered cheese sauce, a pork chop upon which one could break one's teeth accompanied by overcooked cabbage and 'sauce piquante' – mustard seeds with water – then Bombe Surprise – an ice-cream with chocolate made so badly that no sane man could eat it; hard cheese followed that, even though it was supposed to be camembert. The wine tasted as though it were sweat scraped away from the feet of the peasants who had pressed it.

'What are we doing here . . .?' I sighed.

'Studying humanity, I suppose,' Dr Maudesley sighed back in return. He was a tall gaunt man with hollow cheeks and a morose expression. He became slightly more cheerful when the brandy was brought, although this turned out to be only barely acceptable. I tried to cheer things up by quoting my acquaintance, Chesterton.

'If a thing is worth doing,' I said, 'then it is worth doing badly.'

'Such is the course of evolution,' he replied. I thoroughly enjoyed the conversation of this fascinating man who went on to found one of London's most celebrated psychiatric hospitals. Maudesley thought that every psychological matter could be reduced to problems of Cerebral Neurology.

'What about altered states in consciousness?' I queried.

'You remind me of a curious chap called Crowley,' he answered. 'Once went on a sea voyage and he was one of the passengers. Come across him at all?' I signified my assent, mentioning that we'd been at Cambridge together. 'Crowley thought that these altered states you mention could be a cue to propel the billiard balls of human evolution.'

'And what did you think?'

'Well,' said Maudesley, calling pointedly for more brandy and relighting his pipe, 'it was hard for a man of science such as myself to ascertain the precise nature of his terminology. How on earth does one equate the propositions of Science with those he termed "Magick"? The methods he described to me obviously stimulate the brain and therefore results in consciousness alteration are more than likely to follow. How is one to explain this curious phenomenon? I put it to him that the "demons" and "spirits" he "evoked" by his peculiar methods were merely cells of his own brain, stimulated sufficiently so as to cause him to enjoy particular hallucinations. I must admit, however,' Maudesley continued, 'that his techniques could be valuable in our understanding of the brain's functioning and he did not disagree with me.'

'What about sex, though?'

'Sorry . . .?'

'Sex in terms of furthering human evolution,' I said. 'Sex with intention. Let's face it, Dr Maudesley, no biologist knows why something which squanders energy as much as sex was ever necessary for the purposes of breeding. (Nobody still does, 1925). (*Nobody still does, 1995: Editor's Note*). 'Yet,' I continued remorselessly, 'the union of the human male and the human female, when done with appropriate ritual, seems to bring about altered states of consciousness. How do you explain that?'

'I will give you in reply the three most honest words in the English language,' said Dr Maudesley. 'These are: *I DON'T KNOW*. We have insufficient data. But believe me, sir, it is a question upon which the scientists will be working. You strike me as being quite an artistic sort of chap, Lord Horby. The trouble with Art, it strikes me, is: how do you measure it, save by like and dislike? And that's entirely subjective. Science, however, tests everything by experiment. That's how we advance.'

'So then, let us make an experiment,' I replied. 'See those two bitches there?' He looked and saw an English mother and daughter suffering a bad dinner at a table a few feet away from us. They were wearing somewhat tawdry finery and were obviously lower-middle-class 'ladies' going out to India to join some wretched subaltern. They both had dyed blonde hair and hard but sexy faces. 'Let's go for some Cerebral Neurology,' I said.

It was so easy to enter into their company. All I needed to do was send a magnum of the ship's bad champagne to their table, accompanied by my card. It's rare to see mouths gape so wide and one could sense their itching cunts as Maudesley and I crossed the room in response to their eager invitation, written on a card which declared The Larches and was somewhere in Middlesborough. Yes, Gladys Tracey (Mrs) was indeed going to India in order to join her husband Wally in Calcutta and meanwhile hoped to sell off her daughter, Victoria, to the highest bidder, in that cattle market known as marriage.

Anyone who chooses to undertake a sea voyage on the *Dupleix* is either as careless and crazy as I am; a keen student of human nature such as Harry Maudesley; or very short of money. Clichés are tiresome but true: to charm Mrs Gladys Tracey of Middlesborough was but the work of a trice. She was enchanted to be in the company of a Lord and a Doctor, and I feared that Harry Maudesley might be wearied shitless by her account of her ailments and her pleadings for his prescriptions. However, one cannot deny those sexual attractions to which we are all susceptible.

I enquired as to whether young Miss Victoria Tracey ever behaved badly and was informed by her mother, with a fluttering of eye-lashes, that to her regret, this *was* sometimes the case. I ventured my opinion that naughty girls should be punished and chastised by their mothers, doing so while young Miss Victoria was visiting the Ladies. At the same time, I made sure to slip an envelope of banknotes into the bag of Mrs Tracey. Victoria returned to be informed that her bad behaviour on the cruise was so insupportable that she would receive a sound spanking in their cabin in front of two stern gentlemen.

Victoria saw the look in her mother's eyes, pouted charmingly, wiped away a tear from her eye and obviously decided that the exposure of her buttocks for punishment before two well-established men could either make a match of the matter or else lead to suitable connections. Blushing deeply and charmingly, she curtsied graciously to us, all aflutter in a sea of skirt and petticoats, and walked away with a sexual rustle.

It really is quite amazing how so many mothers are willing to prostitute their daughters but I don't care as long as I receive sexual pleasure. Maudesley and I walked into the second class cabin to see Mrs Gladys Tracey preening herself as Miss Victoria Tracey stood obediently in a corner with her hands above her head. We took our seats and our brandy. At a stern command from her mother, Victoria turned, curtsied to us once more and confessed to the crimes of insolence, impertinence and impudence.

'And insubordination?!' Mrs Tracey snapped. Victoria confessed obediently and submitted to her chastisement. Her mother arranged her black skirt and then the daughter lay over her lap to receive maternal punishment. Mrs

Tracey crossed her thigh over her daughter's and, looking cross, whipped up the skirts and petticoats of Victoria to expose knee-length, lace-trimmed white knickers which had obviously been purchased at the best department store in Middlesborough. I overheard Dr Maudesley sigh quietly as Gladys pulled down the satin knickers to reveal a pearly white bottom of surpassing excellence.

'Now, my girl!' the mother commanded sternly. 'You will present your bottom for appropriate punishment.' Victoria edged her bottom a few inches higher, almost as if she was aching to be fucked, which, I reflected, she probably was. Mrs Tracey proceeded to don leather gloves of elbow length. 'You will receive a dozen strokes,' she said fiercely.

Maudesley and I smoked our cigars and watched the discipline of the Midlands with considered fascination. The girl writhed and jerked upon the older woman's thighs as the sound slaps came down with a heavy *smack!*

'Victoria is a high-spirited girl,' said Mrs Tracey as her leather-gloved hand came down hard to impart a faint pink hue to her daughter's white and trembling buttocks. 'On occasion, therefore, maternal chastisement is required.' *Smack! smack! SMACK!* Victoria writhed as her beautiful bottom changed its shade to a bright crimson. I heard a groan of ecstasy from Maudesley and assumed that he had creamed. Victoria started to jerk her bottom around in a wild and crazy spasm as it came to glow in bright scarlet.

I really cannot imagine a better advertisement for the marital prospects of a young and beautiful girl. When he arose from her mother's lap and executed a gracious curtsey for her deserved chastisement, her bottom glowing red beneath the frills of her white, pleated skirt, I really wanted to fuck her so badly. Her mother's forbidding look made it obvious that her daughter was a virgin on the market and as such could not be shop-soiled until the night of her marriage, probably to a subaltern as boring as her mother's Wally.

I was hardly prepared to make that particular marital commitment and therefore suggested that Victoria should be sent to bed in order to recover from her public spanking. Dr Maudesley looked in need of bed on his own. I suggested to Gladys that she might care to enjoy a coffee and a brandy in my cabin and she looked only too eager to accept my invitation. After bidding goodnight to Dr Maudesley and to the soundly spanked young teenage girl who, in truth, looked chastised indeed but only too willingly, ready and eager to masturbate, I took the mother to my cabin.

It hardly took me a moment to tip her over my knee, whip up her skirt and petticoats and pull down her drawers in order to redden her bottom as scarlet as she had made her daughter's. My hand came down time and time again upon her plump, womanly bottom, deriving a malicious pleasure from its smacking contact with her glowing flesh, a glow which contrasted so pleasantly with the creamy whiteness of her thighs. As she wriggled and writhed, I took a sadistic pleasure in smacking her harder, turning the colour of her behind from scarlet to puce. She cried out for me to stop but I would not, gaining much pleasure from the sight of that firmly rounded bum jerking around in squirming pain.

She had a good thin slit of a cunt, covered with a fair and luxuriant brush and so it was a pleasure to turn her over and ram my rod within her. This prim, prissy and pretentious bitch sighed, shouted and shrieked obscenities as I pronged her. Her cunt, which smelled delicious, oozed all the oils of womanhood. My prick rammed in up to the very hilt and she sighed and cried amidst the throes of her orgasm.

'You bossy little tart,' I growled as I shot my load deep into her. She responded by scraping my back with her long, red, manicured finger-nails.

As I held her in my arms, 'to sleep, perchance to dream,' I could not help reflecting upon the curious bond which obtains between mothers and daughters.

CHAPTER SIXTEEN

'So how d'you feel about the death of Queen Victoria, Horby?' Aleister Crowley asked me. We were drinking tea inside a bungalow at Kandy, Ceylon, and outside it was pouring with torrential rain.

'What am I supposed to feel?' I asked. I had left the ship at Colombo since I couldn't stand it any longer, much as I had enjoyed my conversations with Maudesley and my erotic experiences with Gladys and Victoria. 'I don't feel anything at all. Nothing whatsoever. How about you?' It had been a relatively easy matter to locate Crowley. Enquiries at the British Consulate had directed me to Sri Parananda, accomplished yogi and Solicitor-General of Ceylon. This gracious and kindly man confirmed that he had hosted both Crowley and Allan Bennett, giving instruction in Yoga to 'two of the most astonishing students of Yoga that I have ever encountered.'

'*I* felt joy,' said Crowley. 'And I have never forgotten the occasion.' He sipped tea calmly. 'I went mountaineering in Mexico with Oscar Eckenstein, inventor of the crampon, or climbing iron, and unquestionably the greatest rock climber and mountaineer in the world. The pair of us now hold every mountaineering record, especially those for pace uphill at high altitudes. We proved that to a sceptical journalist on Popacatapetl, lugging up this lazy bastard like the dead weight he was; but he should have seen us race up Ixtaccihuatl, which is the Aztec word for "sleeping woman". Eckenstein, provided he could get three fingers on something that could be described by a man far advanced in hashish as a ledge, would be smoking his pipe on that very ledge a few seconds later and one could not tell how he had done it. Whereas I, totally incapable of the mildest gymnastic feats, was able to get up to all sorts of places that Eckenstein could not attempt. On Ixtaccihuatl, we established a camp at 14,000 feet and remained there for three weeks, climbing this beautiful mountain from all sides and living off canned food and champagne. You don't believe me? No one does.'

'More tea?' Crowley offered and I accepted. The rain poured down outside. 'Now, when we returned to Amecameca to celebrate our triumphs, we were greeted by our charming host with a long face. He broke the sad news as gently as he could; Queen Victoria was dead. To his stupefaction, he saw us fling our hats into the air and dance for joy. Let's face it, Horby, to all artists and thinkers, Queen Victoria was sheer suffocation, a vast thick fog which has enveloped us so that we were unable either to see or to breathe. The spirit of her age had killed everything we cared for. Smug, sleek, superficial, servile, snobbish, sentimental shopkeeping has spread everywhere.'

'Quite agree,' I replied. 'So have you come out here for more mountaineering in the Himalayas?'

'Of course,' he answered. 'In due course, Eckenstein and I shall lead an expedition to climb the second highest mountain in the world: K2. The only reason that we're not attempting Everest is that access to it is presently denied by the King of Nepal. Meanwhile, as Eckenstein organises the expedition and chooses the team, I am studying Oriental Philosophy and practising Yoga.'

'Kindly explain.'

'The main idea,' he replied, 'is that the Infinite – God, the Oversoul, or whatever you may prefer to call it – is always present; but veiled or masked by the thoughts of the mind, just as one cannot hear as individual heart-beat in a noisy city . . . then to obtain knowledge of That, it is only necessary to still all thoughts.'

'That's easy enough,' I said. 'Just go to sleep.'

'True, perhaps, roughly speaking,' he answered, 'but the perceiving function is stilled also.'

'Then you wish to obtain a perfect vigilance and attention of the mind, uninterrupted by the rise of thoughts?'

'Absolutely, my dear Horby.'

'And how do you proceed?'

'Firstly, we still the body by the practice called Asana and secure its ease and the regularity of its functions by Pranayama, a process of breathing. Thus no messages from the body will disturb the mind. Secondly, by Yama and Niyama, we still the emotions and passions, and thus prevent them arising to disturb the mind. Thirdly, by Pratyahara we analyse the mind yet more deeply and begin to control and suppress thought in general of whatever nature. Fourthly, we suppress all other thoughts by a direct concentration upon a single thought. This process, which leads to the highest results, Dharana, Dhyana and Samadhi, grouped under the single term, Samyana.'

'I'm sorry,' I said, 'these technical terms baffle me and I haven't the faintest idea of what on earth you are talking about.'

'My apologies also,' Crowley responded. 'Yama means DO and Niyama means DON'T. It's a simple code of behaviour which leads to self-respect and calms the mind, emotions and passions. Dharana is concentration, utterly one-pointed and single-minded; Dhyana is the trance of stillness in contemplation; Samadhi is when you unite totally with the object of your contemplation. Samyana is the knack of putting all these three things together at once.'

'How's your progress?' I asked casually, almost as if he were practising P.T.

'Not too bad,' he replied; and promptly proceeded to sit on his hard, straight-backed chair for two hours without moving a muscle, his spine erect, his knees together and his hands laid upon them, rather like those statues of Egyptian gods that one sees in the British Museum. All endeavours to distract him, including speech, jokes and the public school trick of flicking paper pellets from an elastic band, proved to be futile. He was as immobile as a lump of finely-chiselled stone.

'That Maudesley fellow you mentioned is a fine chap,' he said after a while. 'He thinks that all problems of expanding consciousness and human evolution can be reduced to propositions of Cerebral Neurology, and he may well have something there. After all, what is Pranayama other than control by breath over the central nervous system?'

Crowley proceeded to demonstrate his point by breathing in and out via alternate nostrils and holding his breath on the climax of inhalations and exhalations, timing it all at fifteen seconds each by his stop-watch. I drank tea and watched his activities with no little fascination. I saw firstly, a peculiar kind of perspiration, that smelled very sweet. After an hour of this exercise, I discerned that his body had attained a notable rigidity of the muscles. There then occurred a most curious phenomenon. His body, whilst still absolutely rigid, was taking little hops in various directions without the slightest sign of perceptible conscious effort. It seemed as if he were somehow raised, possibly an inch from the ground, and deposited very gently a short distance away. Yet he did not seem to be at all conscious of the fact.

'Just jumping about like a frog, Horby,' he told me when he came out of his trance. 'That's what the yogis call it. Oh!' he exclaimed as he relaxed, sighed and lit his curved, briar pipe. 'Yoga, properly understood, is a simple psychological method of attaining a definite psychological state.'

'So is sex,' I replied.

'Possibly so but I wouldn't know,' he responded, 'since I haven't had any sex in three months. Never thought I'd be celibate but there we are. Had any good fucking, Horby?'

'Yes,' I responded. 'Gladys and Victoria.' I explained to Crowley how I had witnessed an exquisite spanking and enjoyed a good seduction of the mother. 'My money and position persuaded them to get off that dreadful boat and join me for a weekend in Colombo, and I paid for the next stage of their journey. Ah! how rich, how soft, how peaceful is Colombo, "the place where four winds meet," the crossroads of the civilized world. The palms, the flowers, the swooning song of the surf, the dim and delicate atmosphere heavy with sensuous scents, the idle, irresponsible people purring with placid pleasures . . .' Crowley nodded his benign agreement. 'Anyway, in the best suite of the best hotel, Mrs Gladys and Miss Victoria were true to their appointment. Mrs Tracey had decided, after all, to accept my handsome but discreet offer for her daughter's virgin cunt even though no marital commitment accompanied the purse of sovereigns that changed hands. (How could it?) As Gladys drank some good Bollinger, Victoria and I sat down on a quiet seat for a few moments and enjoyed some kissing and groping. The bed was prepared.

'I found the amorous Victoria so difficult to enter on account of the narrowness of her passage,' I continued, 'that she had to bite her lips in suppressed agony from the pain of my attempt. But courage effects everything and she was so determined to be rammed at last that I found myself most deliciously fixed in the tightest quim I had ever entered. It was simply most voluptuous and the pressures of this girl's sheath upon my delighted instrument made me come in a moment or two. Then, the lubricant applied, things went easier; and a most luscious combat ensued.

'Victoria was perfectly beside herself with erotic passion whilst her mother Gladys, instead of standing on guard, lasciviously handled my shaft and appendages in her soft hand, until the excitement was more than I could bear, making me actually shout with pleasure at the moment of orgasm. Mother and daughter repeated the game without interruption and Victoria had me place the head of John Thomas just between the lips of her pussy.

'After spending an hour or so upon this slow and delectable amusement, we all agreed to dress and visit the City Park.

'Say what you like about the British Raj – and who doesn't eh, Crowley? But from what I witnessed, it's hardly sexually repressive. There were so many unblushing games going on. Our soldiers were rogering young girls, old fellows were fumbling servant girls and there was no end of the most unblushing indecency on every side. Why, it could have been the Green Park in London! Remember that? If couples could only get into the Green Park before the gates closed at ten p.m., they might stop there all night, or could at any time go out by the turnstile at the end of Constitution Hill into Grosvenor Place.' We smiled fondly at the memory. 'The one or two bobbies who patrolled the park seemed to take no notice, or were easily squared by the girls who used the place for business.

'This stout old British tradition is maintained, I'm glad to say, in Colombo. In fact, I saw one stalwart officer of the peace doing a glorious grind on the grass until a Guardsman came up and, slapping his naked rump as hard as he could, told him jovially to set a better example, which caused great fun to several who were looking on, especially when the soldier challenged the policeman for half-a-crown to exhibit his civilian prick against his military one for the amount he had paid, the girl to be the judge. The policeman evidently decided that discretion was the better part of valour.

'These sights produced an extraordinary effect upon young Miss Victoria Tracey, y'know, Crowley. On our return to my hotel, we all separated temporarily for our ablutions, but I know what she told me subsequently. "The hand of my mother refreshed with care all the parts which had been so well worked earlier by you, Horby. All at once I saw her stop still, then a finger fixed upon a little eminence which showed itself prominently; this finger rubbed lightly at first, then with a kind of fury. At length she gave the same symptoms of pleasure which I had so often seen before. I understood it all now! My head was on fire, my bosom palpitated, and my steps tottered, but I was determined at once to play by myself the last act I had seen and which required no partner." '

'You have,' Crowley commented, 'a remarkable memory for a young lady's words.'

'Certainly,' I returned. 'They are so remarkable that they are etched upon my mind. (1925: Unforgettably so; Victoria bore me an illegitimate child in consequence of which she has enjoyed rich pickings from me ever since, precisely as her mother Gladys had accurately forecast and for which the scheming bitch had plotted.) But to continue with her words: "I arrived in my room in a state of madness, threw my hat on the floor, shut and double-locked the door to my hotel bedroom and collapsed upon the bed. I turned up my clothes to the end, recollecting in the minutest details what Gladys – my mother, my self – had done, and as she had done with her hand, so I placed mine between my legs. Some essays were at first fruitless but I found at length the point for which I searched. The rest was easy: a delicious sensation seized me. I continued with fury and soon fell into such an ecstasy that I lost consciousness. When I came to myself, I was in the same position, my hand all moistened by an unknown dew." '

'And . . .?' Crowley queried, adding: 'That's rather sweet.'

'Well, when Victoria and Gladys re-entered my chamber, I lost no time in kissing that young girl's two pure globes as she reclined backwards, shuddering beneath the caresses that seemingly caused her to shiver in every vein. Profiting from this movement, I toyed for a moment with her lovely, silky pubic hairs. Then, slightly opening the nook they were hiding, I let my finger slip upwards a little to renew the playful friction which had caused us such enjoyment. I also displayed my splendid member and neither mother nor daughter could take their eager eyes away from this sight. Victoria opened her thighs once more and therefore stretched her slit, which did not appear longer than my little finger. *How is it possible?* I asked myself, that an instrument of my size can penetrate entirely into such a little place? Yet she received this great machine with gladness and for a while we continued with a silent and joyous clicketing.

' "Ah!" she shrieked suddenly. "My darling! . . . go on . . . Ah! I am so happy! . . . How lovely you are, Horby . . . Oh! how I shall spend! . . . It's coming now! . . . Do it a little longer! . . . Ah! I die . . ." There was a long and silent pause while Victoria seemed to be quite overcome; her beautiful form thrown back, her head hidden upon my shoulder, her glorious thighs still wide apart. I gazed at her intently, ravished at the sight.'

'Great stuff!' Crowley exclaimed with a chuckle. 'And did you fuck the mother once again for good measure?'

'Yes, she was a good fuck and I'm just coming to that.'

'In a moment,' my host returned. 'As you know, I'm sharing this bungalow with Allan Bennett who is presently my guru in Yoga. Presently, he's meditating, as usual, and it's my duty to bring him his food. Incidentally, it is very rare to encounter Europeans who can sit in the attitude called Padmasana, which is that usually seen in seated images of the Buddha. Yet Allan can do it. He can knot his legs so well that, putting his hands on the ground, he can swing his body to and fro in the air between them. Anyway, enough of that; I've made him a good salad of okra. Let's go and see how he is.'

I can only record what I saw. Earlier, I had seen Crowley 'jumping about like a frog', contrary to all known Laws of Physics. When we looked into Allan Bennett's room, we found him, not seated on his meditation mat, which was in the centre of the room at the end farthest from the window, but in a distant corner ten or twelve feet off, still in his knotted position, resting on his head and right shoulder, exactly like an image overturned. Crowley set him right way up and he came out of his trance. He was quite unconscious of the fact that anything unusual might have happened. But he had evidently been thrown there by the mysterious forces generated by Pranayama.

The rain poured down outside.

CHAPTER SEVENTEEN

There was a young man who said: "God
Must find it exceedingly odd,
If he finds that this tree
Continues to be
When there's no one around in the Quad."

'Heigh ho!' said Crowley. 'And here we have the Hindus saying exactly the same thing as Bishop Berkeley in Western Philosophy, which is that something can exist only if someone perceives it.' He smiled genially over his tea and tobacco at an impassive Allan Bennett and myself. 'But of course, gentlemen, there is an answer:

"Dear Sir: your argument's odd.
I am always about in the Quad.
And that's why this tree
Will continue to be,
Since observed by Yours truly, GOD."

'What if there is no *I* and no GOD?' Allan Bennett enquired. Allan looked so much healthier since when I had last seen his asthma-attacked and drug-ravaged body in London. I supposed that he owed his continuing life either to Crowley's Ceremonial Magic or else to the money freely given by a Crowley mistress, arguably

Davina Price-Hughes, now Davina Bellingham. Crowley responded with:

Let me die in a ditch
Damnably drunk
Or lipping a punk
Or in bed with a bitch.
I was ever a whore.
Dung? I am one with it.
Let me die in a ditch . . .
Die and be done with it!

'Well, that's no good, is it?' said Allan Bennett. 'You'll only come back to reincarnate on the Wheel of Suffering and Illusion. Fancy a walk in the jungle?' His lean body hauled itself to its feet as we nodded assent, arose and followed his sandaled feet, their bareness oblivious to the thorns that tore at his bare flesh. I had no idea at the time that this was the man who, as Bikku Ananda Metteya, would bring Buddhism in its purest Theravada/Hinayana form to Great Britain. However, I shall never forget the moment that I saw a krait in the grass.

This snake was lying just beside the sandy road. I had been warned by Douglas about the krait. It is, in terms of poison, the deadliest snake in the world. It is not a case of once bitten, twice shy; no, you can die in agony within an hour. Crowley spotted that snake too and promptly drew his Webley revolver, only to have his arm stayed by Bennett.

'No, Brother,' he said. 'I know that you are skilful enough to shoot the snake's head away, even at this distance, but kindly allow me to deal with this matter in my own way.' With that said, this intriguing man walked up to the krait, stared it in the eyes and said: 'Little krait, it is not good to bite the innocent and kill them. But let me tell you all about Buddhism and of how we can all evolve and improve . . .' The serpent, so deadly, turned tail and slithered away.

As we entered the jungle, Allan Bennett motioned Crowley to put aside the machete he had drawn for the appropriate purpose of chopping a passable walkway through the dense and lush vegetation. Allan Bennett led the way through a writhing and weaving of his lean, lithe body, declining to harm even so much as a stick of forest life. Three times Crowley drew his revolver and on each occasion, he was right, for even my inexperienced eyes discerned dangerous animals: a tiger, a panther and a buffalo. Each time Bennett brushed away his gun, then snaked forward through the undergrowth to face the deadly danger. He was so far ahead of us at times that I cannot swear to what I saw, so swift were his movements; and in subsequent conversation, neither of us felt that we could swear to the matter either: but both of us *thought* we saw, through the curious quarter-light of the jungle, Allan Bennett joyfully hugging a tiger. It was only a glimpse and then the image was gone.

'Can you believe,' Crowley asked me on our ten-mile march from the jungle along the dirt track which led to his bungalow, 'that this man,' he indicated Bennett who was this time walking peaceably behind us, '*terrified* all occult circles in London with his blasting rod?' Was Bennett laughing behind me? 'Yes, Allan used to carry a *lustre* – a long glass prism with a long neck and a pointed knob such as adorns old-fashioned chandeliers. He used this as a wand. One day, a party of theosophists – you know, the sort of wets who think there's some sort of "new age" coming, but even if there is, they simply cannot face its implications – anyway, they were chatting sceptically about the power of the "blasting rod". Allan promptly produced his and blasted one of them. It took fourteen hours to restore the incredulous individual to the use of his muscles.'

'He seems to have mellowed,' I commented to Crowley.

'Yes and no,' Crowley replied. 'Remember the Golden Dawn?' I nodded. 'Personally, I find it very easy to adapt to Hinduism, since their deities equate with the Egyptian ones we worshipped in the Golden Dawn. Yet there is one thing I find to be very odd about Mathers. I had honestly thought that whatever his faults might be, he was Head of the Rosicrucians and my principal link with the Gods. Then I heard a disturbing story and Allan has confirmed its truth.'

'Oh . . .?' I murmured.

'Yes, indeed, "O!" If I may resume my tale?' Crowley returned. 'One trusts that you are familiar with the Gods who are the prime manifestation of the Infinite Brahman, which in itself is All and Nothing: Brahma the Creator; Vishnu the Preserver; Shiva the Destroyer. Now, back in the London days, Allan became a particular devotee of Shiva. Bennett said to Mathers of Shiva: "If one repeats His name often enough, He will open His eye and destroy the Universe." Mathers disagreed. The thought that his life should depend on Shiva keeping his Third Eye shut was too much for him. Allan retorted by assuming his Padmasana yoga posture and repeating the mantra: *Shiva, Shiva, Shiva, Shiva, Shiva, Shiva, Shiva, Shiva* . . . "Will you stop blaspheming?!" roared Mathers, worked into a rage by this quiet man sitting there and chanting: *Shiva, Shiva, Shiva, Shiva, Shiva, Shiva, Shiva, Shiva* . . . and let's face it, Horby, Shiva is the Great God of the Mysteries of Sex and Death.

'Well, Horby, Mathers produced a revolver and yelled:

"If you don't stop, I'll shoot you!" But Allan, totally concentrated, took no notice and merely carried on chanting: *Shiva*. Wonderful, isn't it? The man who claims to be our link with the Secret Chiefs is terrified and infuriated simultaneously by the chanting of the name of a Great God. He *wanted* to pull the trigger on Allan: what a disappointment and disgrace! Fortunately, before Mathers could cock back the hammer, Moina Mathers entered the room and may possibly have saved Allan's life . . . not that he cares.'

On our arrival back at the bungalow, we found a rain-soaked messenger with a letter for me; for I had used telegrams and my paid staff to facilitate communications wherever I ventured upon the globe.

'So what's this, then, Horby?' Bennett chuckled pleasantly. I chuckled back and proceeded to read out Rosemary's letter, written in Alberta, Canada:

'*My darling,*

'*Finally I have arrived in Calgary. It is so cold. The weather is so fierce, brumal and hiemal. A continuous wind blows across the prairies and I am now suffering from chilblains. How my hands and feet do itch!*

'*Yesterday there was a* chinook, *which is a warm, dry wind that blows east of the Rocky Mountains, raising the temperature suddenly as much as 50 degrees Fahrenheit within a couple of hours and it can evaporate a snowfall of several feet within a day. This can make the most sane person suffer from* non compos mentis, *quite deprived of one's wits; and can lead even to hysterical and psychotic behaviour.*

'*This town is so strange and is completely different from the East Coast of Canada. It is so good to see my Great Aunt Catherine again, however eccentric she might be. Her father was one of the early Scottish settlers out here and when he died, he left his property to her: the old homestead; a large cattle ranch not too far from Calgary. The reason that he chose to settle here is that it had the attraction, allurement and (to him) charm of the moors and lowlands of Scotland.*

'Upon her arrival, Great Aunt had found the life harsh and she had felt lonely and isolated. A number of beaux had courted her in London but only my Great Uncle had attracted her. A new life in the New World, after the death of her first husband, had appealed to her. Initially, she had gone with a gold prospector, who promised her life-long riches. This nuptial bond did not last long and before the promised gold came, he was killed in a gunfight. She married again: Tom is my step-Great Uncle.

'It appeared to me that her life was a series of ingerminate occurrences in continuously repeated sequence. However, I hope that this will not happen to me. She told me of how difficult life was, especially for the early homesteaders. They had to plant crops and she told me of the blazing sun and the devastating grass fires and of how the land had to be cleared, restored and ploughed using horses and oxen. Mind you, as she told me when the Donkhobors settled here, they hitched women to their ploughs in order to till the land.

'It appears that Great Aunt does love her third husband, Tom, the cattle baron, though they have to spend much of the year apart from one another. Tom does amuse me. When I arrived, he tipped his hat, bowed slightly and clicked his heels.

' "Good afternoon, Ma'am," he said with the greatest politeness when he met me at the railway station. He has such bandy legs! He also has a six-gun in his holster and

I imagine that he is fully capable of using it well. And even though he doesn't have to do it these days, he seems to enjoy spending many hours of the day in the saddle.

'Great Aunt Catherine has married well. I was amused to see her applying wax to his moustache. I enjoyed our first evening together, for the meal included venison and marinated and tenderised buffalo meat. Around the dinner table, with the log fire blazing upon the hearth, I was told wild and wonderful stories about Tom's son John.

' "He sounds rather fascinating," I remarked. "I hope that I may experience the joy of his company at some future occasion."

' "Unfortunately," Tom replied, "he's kind of a – uh – kind of what an educated lady like you would call – uh – yeah – a 'dilettante'; and I figure that he does not take life too seriously."

"Where is he?" I asked.

' "In some bar," Tom sighed, "probably brawling or else trying to engage the attentions of some beautiful young woman, even if she has committed herself to another. He likes to flirt, bill and coo; even poodlefake."

'Suddenly the door burst open and in entered one of the most attractive men that I have ever seen. He just stormed in.

' "Do not call me licentious!" he yelled. "Anybody round here been calling me licentious?" At that moment, Great Aunt and her husband decided to retire to their bedroom. "Glad they've retired for the evening," he said as he pulled out a cigar. "What does this remind you of?"

' "A cigar," I replied.

' "Yes, my dear," he returned, 'it is indeed a cylindrical object with a pointed end and yet let me tell you, *before the evening is over, you will see and experience an even larger cylindrical object." He gazed momentarily and reflectively at the six-gun in his holster. "I have a trunk, bole, column . . . that has satisfied too many women."* What insolence! *I thought. "Do you know what a Calgary Red Eye is?" he demanded.*

' *"No, not really."*

' *"Then let me make you one." He proceeded to mix a concoction of beer and tomato juice, a drink that I have never experienced before. What a brew! and it's such an erotic stimulant! The juices were soon stirring within my cunt and I could feel that my silken knickers were wet. He was a man of bravado, boldness, and bellicosity, a braggart and a swaggart. "I am a warrior and I can tame anything and anyone, including you," he boasted. It appeared to me that this was an angry young man with a giant ego and an even larger erection. It was so obvious that between the two of us, the lust of carnal knowledge had been aroused.*

'*Instinctively, we both decided to remove our clothes together in front of the fireplace, that burning inglenook. Then he stood before me wearing bright red combinations; my cowboy, cowpuncher, bronco-buster and gaucho! I opened the buttons and took his firm rod into my mouth. He penetrated so deeply within my throat that my murmurs went from:* "Oh, that's lovely," *to* "Ohugghhrrr!" *Then he shot his juices in: and how saline they were! Brackish and salsuginous.*

'*Then, gazing upon my exposed breasts, he kissed my nipples lovingly and there was such a throbbing within my inner thighs. My vagina was aching for a penetration. He kissed each nipple so gently; and then suddenly he stopped.*

' *"Please carry on," I requested.*

' *"You have a third nipple here." He pointed out my extra mamilla. As you know, Horby, it looks like a rather enlarged freckle.*

' *"Yes . . ." I sighed, "I am well aware of this."*

' *"You are a witch . . . an enchantress . . ." he gasped as I took his throbbing penis into my cool and delicate hands.*

' *"Occasionally, I have some powers of perception," I murmured; and then he was upon me in a riotous act of coitus, copulation and capitulation. The resulting heat of our fuck, yes, the tornado we engendered, was greater even than that of the* chinook.

'*I must close now, my darling. I miss and love you so much.*

Rosemary.'

Bennett was silent and smiling.

'Introduce me,' said Crowley.

'Slam! Bam! Thank you, Ma'am!' I said. 'That's Canada.'

CHAPTER EIGHTEEN

'Ah! The Romance of Lust!' Crowley declared heartily. 'And I haven't enjoyed it in what seems like ages.' He sipped more tea. 'Did you find Colombo to be as good for that as I did, Horby?'

'Yes, I did,' I replied, 'for in one brothel I saw something most erotic.' Crowley sat up attentively and Bennett looked quietly indifferent. 'I saw two slim young women, Pabloo and Naznin, lying upon a bed together. "I must have it all!" Pabloo cried out as she writhed naked upon the bed, twitching her slender buttocks this way and that. "I want it all!" she shrieked. "Come, I am on fire. I burn, Naznin, so quick, you must flood me with your bounteous liquor."

'Naznin threw off her dressing-gown,' I continued, 'and stretched herself beside Pabloo upon the bed. How beautiful she was, built like a slender Athena to her partner's Aphrodite: or perhaps I should speak of Shiva's consort, Parvati and of Lakshmi, the consort of Vishnu. Anyway, don't you find that one of the greatest mysteries of Womanhood is the clitoris? I could see that proud instrument of Naznin stiffly growing out of a wide slit and thick bush that showed it off splendidly.

'Pabloo was lying on her back, her legs parted and lifted a little. Naznin got on her knees between her thighs, and their naked forms were exposed to my gaze. For an instant, Pabloo turned her backside to her lover in a flirtatious gesture, then Naznin turned her back over and stretched herself upon her. Pabloo lifted her legs and crossed them upon Naznin's back, in such a manner that no detail escaped my vision. I could distinctly see Naznin's fingers capture Pabloo's clitoris, directing a forefinger to the centre of the little slit that opened to receive it. Naznin gave her partner a vigorous rubbing of her pudenda and Pabloo sighed lazily, jerking her hips upwards with an energetic stroke of the loins. Naznin answered her by the insertion of her forefinger into the little hole, which dilated and began to engulf it. A few more movements completed the insertion, and I saw their two growths of pubic hair mingled together. Now there was nothing but movements, sighs, inarticulate words and maddening shivers.

' "Let me have it all . . . Pabloo sighed: "Ah! How fine your clitty is . . . Go gently . . . let us spend slowly . . . hold me tight!"

' "My sweet darling," Naznin sighed back, "Lift up your thighs, so that we can be right in . . . There! Do you feel it? Ah! how delightful!"

' "I die . . .!" Pabloo squealed. "Are you ready? . . . My Naznin! I'm going to spend . . . I . . . I . . . make haste!"

' "I'm ready . . . It's coming . . . There it comes.. spend now . . ." Naznin murmured: ' "I'm spending . . . Ah! . . . I've come! Oh . . ."

'Both remained quiet for a moment. Pabloo remained longer without giving signs of life but she got up at last and after smothering Naznin with kisses, went for an instant to the lavatory. I thought that it was all over and began to arrange my retreat, but a secret presentiment made me stop. Pabloo re-entered, went to the bed again, embraced her lover in her arms and then they engaged in sweet conversation.

' "I have been so happy, dear!" Pabloo exclaimed. "It is so much better when we are at our ease and you do it so well."

' "My darling," Naznin responded, "there is not a more perfect woman than you in the whole world . . . and I want to eat you up bodily!"

And once more, tickling the breasts of Pabloo, Naznin covered with kisses the whole of her beautiful body that trembled beneath her caresses; and when she arrived at the centre of bliss, she opened it, bit it gently and kissed it passionately.

' "Stop, dear!' Pabloo cried out. "Stop! You will fatigue yourself. Rest, rest!"

' "No, darling, look!" Naznin waggled her pretty pink tongue at Pabloo. "See, she once more asks permission to go into her little companion. You won't refuse her?"

' "Let me see, my dear. So your tongue continues in its exquisite state, Naznin? Well, well, I'll let you put it in the prison of my cunt once more in good time. There, place yourself like that and don't move!"

' "What you are going to do?" Naznin demanded.

' "You know, dear, how I like a change." Pabloo picked up a thick, white dildo from beneath the mattress and brandished this erect phallus in the air. She promptly proceeded to plunge it into Naznin, up to the hilt, then she moved it gently in and out. Naznin was fairly spitted by this enormous spindle. Pabloo teased her, blew her kisses and showed Naznin her adorable titties, smiling and pouting at her all the time. ' "'Tis *I* who have *you* now," she said, "You are my little wife. See how well I do it!"

'After a few instants of this dalliance, it was easy to see that the supreme moment was being reached. Pabloo fell upon Naznin, who received her in her arms and pressed her lover's flesh to her own, as Pabloo took hold of the olive cheeks of Naznin's shapely bottom. Pleasure mounted to an ecstasy which seized them together: then Naznin left Pabloo's embrace and lazily stretched herself out at her lover's side. This was not enough for Pabloo.

' "My bosom is panting!" she cried out. "An active fire is coursing through my veins." She alternately touched each of Naznin's breasts; and the nipples swelled up. Feeling her partner's body, Pabloo reached her exquisitely delicate spot and rummaged there with great curiosity. It seemed to me as an observer that a slight change had taken place. The lips of the little nook were plumper; and Pabloo was singing. "I seek the place that is greedily swallowing this monstrous dildo!" she cried out as Naznin gasped with pleasure. "There is a little spot here which this tool cannot touch without admixture of pleasure and pain," she cooed, pushing up the dildo a little and then rubbing it in.

' "Ah!" Naznin ejaculated. "An indescribable sensation invades my entire being." Pabloo used the dildo to rub softly first, then quicker, afterwards slower, then again with more vigour as Naznin shrieked: 'I spend! . . . Ah! I come . . . I come . . . Ah!"

'At length, a nervous spasm overtook her. I felt transported with an immense pleasure which I only fully appreciate now. I wasn't expecting Pabloo to place a big cushion in front of the wardrobe and to kneel upon it, her head and arms much lower than her ravishing buttocks, which, thrown out and developed by this magnificent position, presented the path of pleasure well in view and largely open.

'Naznin placed herself behind her, commencing to stroke Pabloo with her slender fingers.

' "Oh, you can see too much of me!" said Pabloo.

' "How can I see too much of such beauty? Look in the glass!"

' "Oh, no; it's too bad! . . . Ah!" Pabloo gasped as she stared into the mirror before them. "You've taken my bloody dildo, you bitch! . . . It's going into me! Stop a little . . . Ah! What a fine girl you are!"

' "My adored one, how lovely you are!" Naznin retorted as she toyed with the dildo and her lover writhed. "What admirable hips! What an adorable – ARSE!"

' "Oh, Naznin!" Pabloo sighed. "What is that naughty word?"

' "Don't be frightened, darling," Naznin cooed back. "Lovers can say anything. These words, out of place in colder moments, add fresh relish to the sweet mystery of love. You will soon say them too and understand their charm." Whilst she spoke, she continued with her delicate movements. Pabloo, in silent enjoyment, said naught, but devoured with eager eyes the lustful endeavours of Naznin. I was somewhat stupefied to hear her say a minute later:

' "Do you love it so very much?"

' "What!" Naznin exclaimed.

' "Why . . . my."

' "You *what*?"

' "Well . . . my . . . arse!"

' "Ah, Pabloo, how sweet you are to me. Oh, yes; I love it. Your beautiful arse. I adore it!"

' "Feel it, then. It's yours – yours alone" Pabloo cried out. 'My arse . . . arse!! . . . arse!!!" ' As she concluded her broken utterances, she let herself go until she reached the rapture of complete enjoyment. Naznin, who was herself rapidly arriving at the height of sovereign pleasure, reached the desired goal with her and fell upon her completely overcome.'

'A good time,' Bennett muttered.

'Allan,' I said, 'do I detect a slight trace of sarcasm in your attitude?'

'Yes,' he answered. 'Where does all this sex get us? It just further snares us in illusion.'

'Typical!' Crowley laughed.

'*Everything* is an illusion,' Bennett responded impassively. 'And it's no use committing suicide for you'll simply come back to face the same problems in your next incarnation. The Gods and Goddesses of Hinduism and the Golden Dawn, and their attractively erotic interaction, are an illusion too. Mathers is simply dancing well amidst these veils of illusion. And so are we unless we improve ourselves.' He smiled slightly. 'And the way to do that is Yoga. Hinduism is false in stating that there is a central "I" or *atman* which is the essence of *Brahman*, or God or the Supreme. Buddhists are right in declaring that there is no Self, that there is no God and that there is no "I". Is there the same water in the repeated waves which roll in upon a sea-shore? No. No. There is only the wheel of Existence, which is Suffering or Samsara: and there is Deliverance from Suffering, which is Nirvana.'

'And what is Nirvana?' I asked.

'Ultimate cessation of Existence,' Bennett answered.

'Wishing you a speedy termination of Existence, Horby,' Crowley chuckled. 'And it'll take you quite a while.'

'Thank you very much,' I replied. 'Your kind remarks are truly appreciated,' I added sarcastically, 'but I'm quite happy here and now, thanks again.' I accepted Crowley's offer of more tea. 'Though I'm most impressed by your astonishing feat of apparent levitation, Allan.'

'Another illusion,' he murmured dismissively.

'Yet there is no doubt whatsoever about this phenomenon,' said Crowley. 'It is quite common. But the yogis claim that the lateral motion is due to lack of balance and that if one were in perfect equilibrium, one would rise directly in the air. I have never seen any case of levitation and hesitate to say that it has happened to me, though I have actually been seen by others on several occasions apparently poised in the air. Unfortunately, I can form no theory as to how the practice of Pranayama could counteract the force of gravitation, which makes of one a sceptic. Yet, after all, the stars are suspended in space. There is no *a priori* reason why the forces which prevent them rushing together should not come into operation in respect of the earth and the body.' He lit his curved meerschaum pipe and I promptly detected the aroma of latakia and perique. 'You see, I had an extraordinary experience only the other day. I was practising Dharana and concentrating on the tip of my nose.

'Well,' Crowley continued animatedly, 'I obtained a clear understanding of the unreality of that nose. This persists. An hour later whilst breathing on my arm as I was asleep, I said to myself, "What is this hot breath from?" I was forced to *think* before I could answer "my nose". Then I pinched myself and remembered at once; but again breathing, the same thing happened again. Therefore the "Dharanization" of my nose dividualizes me and my nose, affects my nose, abolishes, annihilates and expunges my nose. What do you think, Horby?'

'I think you're talking incomprehensible shit,' I said. Crowley and Bennett burst out laughing.

'Probably,' Crowley retorted. 'I often do. It's impossible to put into words that which lies beyond them. If you don't believe me, suck it and see.'

'Still on for stricter measures?' Bennett asked Crowley, adding, 'despite the sceptical remarks of our friend here?'

'Definitely,' Crowley answered.

'Good,' said Allan Bennett. 'Oh, and by the way, I've brought you this as a present.' Whipping up his robe, he smilingly produced a dead five foot cobra. 'You trod right on its neck with your heel on your midnight stroll last night and never noticed it. You should be more careful in future. But never mind. Tomorrow, let's go for *it*. That means no more tea and no more tobacco.'

'You're stopping my baccy and my tea?!' Crowley cried out in mock-horror. 'No, no, not that! Anything but that!' Bennett just smiled and nodded.

'Anyway, if you gentlemen would kindly excuse me,' he said, 'I am off to bed.'

'With him that means two further hours of strict meditation,' Crowley commented.

'Ouch!' I suddenly shrieked. This was because some mosquitoes had battened onto my bare arms and were biting.

'Oh, those . . .' Bennett sighed wearily. 'You can prevent the things from biting you by certain breathing exercises. Hold the breath in such a way that the body becomes spasmodically rigid and insects cannot pierce the skin. Here, allow me to assist.' To my absolute stupefaction, Allan offered the veins on his wrists and the mosquitoes flitted from my arms to his. As he breathed, his body became rigid. My vision blurred momentarily but when I looked again, the dratted insects were gone.

'It's one of his favourite party tricks,' Crowley observed. 'There's a pool near here and we often put our hands together into the water. His always comes out free and mine has a dozen leeches on it. Well, Allan, a coyote

222

will not eat a dead Mexican.' Bennett remained impassive. 'You see?' Crowley demanded. 'Even I can't annoy him.' His discourse was interrupted by the whining of new mosquitoes in the room.

'I wouldn't worry about them too much, Horby,' Bennett said. 'Simply love them and invite them to make a feast out of your body and blood, wishing them well all the while. The first night is hell, I assure you; but after that, they leave you alone.'

'I can vouch for that.' Crowley concurred. So can I: after one night of absolute hell. Yet mosquitoes have left me alone ever since that ghastly night of absolute torture.

'So it's no sex for you, eh, Crowley?' I jested after Allan Bennett had gone to bed. 'Most unusual.'

'That's Yoga,' he replied. 'I'm racing for results like an athlete and I don't want any impedimentia. Let's just say that I'm Off Games for the time being. Sure you don't want to join me in this honourable quest for super-consciousness?'

'Thanks but no thanks,' I responded. 'I think I prefer sex.'

CHAPTER NINETEEN

For about a month, I wallowed in the flesh-pots of Colombo, Ceylon, finding life to be lazy and pleasant, with many sensual diversions. I felt like one of Tennyson's '*The Lotus Eaters*'. In common with the people of his poem, I could not summon up the energy to tear myself away and press on with my design to visit India.

Now, I have often found that in life, it is always a case of 'either too much or too little'. There was a place of refreshment I used to attend regularly called simply Parvati, the name of the consort of Shiva. Here they served excellent cocktails in the bar, superlative curries in the restaurant, opium of the finest quality upstairs and, on the top floor, there were some of the island's most exquisite whores. I walked in one mid-day, expecting it to be just the same as every other day only to find an horribly familiar figure declaiming his verses to a group of polite but puzzled Indians. Yes: it was that deplorable poet, Wilfred Sedgewick.

Each perfectly see it is so
And yet the fool to logic go.
He only taking in as sent
Away will reason increment.
Not faith but knowledge would lead man
Did he himself but see as can.

'There's the true gold!' roared a familiar voice. 'Until the very last word you think it's going to mean something; and then – smash!'

'Bellingham!' I bellowed. 'What the devil are you doing here, old chap?!'

'Suffering same as the natives, Horby,' he replied, and we greeted one another warmly. I also greeted Sedgewick, for after all and no matter what our quarrels, Englishmen abroad must jolly well stick together. I was genuinely pleased to encounter Sir Richard.

'But what are you really doing here, Bellingham? I thought you were on honeymoon.'

'I *am* on honeymoon,' he returned indignantly. 'It's just that Davina takes all day to decide which outfit to wear for the evening and a man needs a drink and some company.'

'And how about you, Sedgewick?'

'I,' he responded primly, 'have a position here with the Colonial Service,' after which he preened his waxed, handlebar moustache.

'Oh,' said Bellingham, 'so *that's* why the natives listen to you.'

'Bellingham,' said Sedgewick, 'you have no ear for poetry.' He proceeded to order three absolutely delicious drinks, served in halves of scooped-out pineapple and consisting mainly of strong spirits and coconut milk: rather more pleasing than his verses. 'And anyway, you've only just arrived here and so you don't know the ropes. They respect my poetry here. Why, only the other day, I wanted the best table and at first the Head Waiter was most disobliging, but when I told him who I *was*, then naturally, I had a table at once.'

'And who *were* you?' Bellingham yawned.

'What do you know about life out here?' Sedgewick

sneered. 'Javed!' he shouted at the slim, dark barman. 'Do you know who I am?'

'No, sir,' came the reply, 'but I can find out for you.'

'Oh, just give us a bloody table, Mr Javed,' said Sir Richard; and we were promptly escorted politely to the best that the restaurant had to offer. The resulting meal was excellent and confirmed my view that Indian cuisine can be superb. There was a mixed grill of chicken, lamb chops and sausage in the North Indian *tandoori* style; then a prawn *biryani* in the South Indian style, accompanied by a delicious porridge of lentils with garlic which they call *tarka dhall*; there was a delectable dish of lambs' brains so hot that it made Sedgewick choke, so that he had to be brought the cooling fruit of the mango; nor shall I forget the exquisite lamb with spinach, which I believe they call *Sag gosht*. We drank plenty of good, strong beer with it too.

'Nothing like this sort of stuff,' Bellingham chortled as he spooned copious quantities of mango chutney and *raita*, yoghourt with onion and cucumber, onto the brains of the lamb. 'Oh, and Mr Javed, could I have some more of those little green chillies, please?' Mr Javed gaped at him with open-mouthed astonishment and turned so pale, I swear, that in that instant, he could have passed muster as an Englishman.

'You want, sir . . .' he faltered, '*more* green chillies . . .?'

'Well, obviously,' Bellingham returned briskly, 'since I've eaten them all. Why else should I be wanting 'em, for heaven's sake?' He quaffed more beer. 'Some people just don't see the obvious. Ah! Jolly good!' he exclaimed when the plate of chillies arrived and he proceeded to offer them around the table. Sedgewick coughed and declined; I took two which burned my mouth and throat but which otherwise caused a pleasurable sensation; and in his typical fashion, Bellingham greedily scoffed the rest and called loudly for more beer, then wiped away copious quantities of curry sweat from his brow. 'Good place, Colombo. Delicious food. Mind you, it's full of perverts. Why, there's one part of this town that's just packed jam-full of men in womens' clothing and blatant homosexualists. I mean, if you drop a rupee, you have to kick it for ten streets before you bend down to pick it up. Mind you, that doesn't worry me, chaps. I always wear a pair of stout English trousers!'

'Can we get away from these sordid matters and return to the sublime?' Sedgewick demanded.

'Oh, very well, if we must,' returned Bellingham. 'Yet more poetry, is there? I shall eat and suffer in silence.'

Sedgewick proceeded to declaim:

> Ere was condition manifest,
> The unconditioned was at rest.

'Yes, certainly,' I concurred. 'That I did know before.'

> Relations of rest with unrest
> Hence did conditions manifest.

'Um. Seems to skate over the difficulty a little,' said Bellingham. 'But go on.'

> To such relation specify
> We use the word velocity.

'Do we?' I queried.

> Velocity sole history
> Of uncondition's mystery.

'But this is only the Introduction,' said Bellingham. 'This is all mere mashie chips on the green. Let's see what he can do with a wooden club, this plus-four Wilfred Sedgewick.'

While man trains up the child in way men go,
It goes without saying that man's way
In life convention only will display.
As each one by himself can surely know;
Hence may these notes that light of rush-light throw
Where glares so-called, civilization's day.
Without night's darkness chasing once away,
Perchance as simple truth for some one glow.

'Yes . . .' Bellingham nodded cautiously. 'I think I would almost swear what these lines mean to my knowledge. Education leads to conventionality, lines 1-4, therefore these notes may glow as simple truth for some one. I'm afraid that:

Each perfectly see it is so
And yet the fool to logic go

is one on me. But all speculations are futile. Carry on, Sedgewick.'

If seen the curse, if be a curse, on man
Is taxing self to understand, amid
Environment that ever keeps its place,
What shape may take his life, if any can,
That haunting foolishness not bid
Him to endure, with pain, but for disgrace.

'Where's your subject now?' I burst out indignantly. 'Where's your principal sentence? Where's any vestige of connection with anything? I cannot imagine in my wildest moments any nexus with the last three lines of the sestet. I cannot see the merest germ of an apodosis for that majestic protasis.'

'Horby, you're just an ignorant, aristocratic, philistine,' Sedgewick retorted acidly.

'I personally find more poetry in the letter I recently received from young Miss Emily Ward-Bishop,' said Sir Richard, handing an envelope over to me. 'She asked me to pass on this enclosure whenever we met. I was happy with my letter. Go on, Horby, why don't you read yours out to us?'

'Very well.' I ripped open the envelope, read through the contents quickly and proceeded to read them aloud.

'*My darling Horby,*

'*One trusts that you are well but what with all this gallivanting all over the globe that you're currently doing, I thought it best to entrust my missive to Bellingham. Many thanks for your telegrams: but do let me know where your next port of call will be, otherwise I shall be sorely tempted on your return to these shores to take you by the ear to the Reform Academy of Mrs Joan Smythe, thence to be subjugated to Petticoat Government.*

'*The place is so popular at the present time. Mothers of the country's most distinguished families are eager to enrol their sons and daughters; and I have recently taken employment there as a teacher of French and an Assistant Housemistress. As part of my apprenticeship, Joan Smythe invited me to witness her lesson in Biology.*

'*I entered the classroom to see ten girls sitting up attentively and expectantly: one could breathe in the heady perfume of wet knickers and female excitement. Lady Jane and Lady Alison, who are Governesses of the School and Official Visitors, had taken up their places in armchairs to the left and the right of the blackboard. A bell rang: and the Headmistress entered, wheeling a push-chair. There was a young man manacled to this push-chair whose name was Clarence and I must say that I was pleased to see him chained as he was since he had behaved rather badly during my French classes and I had duly complained to the Headmistress.*

'I also sensed that Clarence had behaved badly to the girls, to judge by their behaviour. They arose promptly and obediently upon the entrance of Mrs Smythe, curtsied submissively, then, on received permission, sat down with a fluttering of skirts and a rustling of petticoats as they smiled wickedly at young Clarence and then exchanged glances of glee. Clarence had been forced to wear a frilly white blouse with a pink bow tie, a pink, knee-length pleated skirt with flouncy white petticoats, white silken stockings and shiny, black, high-heeled court shoes. His face was blushing a perfect crimson with the shame of his public humiliation. Alison and Jane took the push-chair from Joan and wheeled it into a corner, so that he faced the wall during the first part of the Biology lecture and a yellow dunce's cap was placed upon his head by Alison in order to emphasise his disgrace.

'Mrs Smythe then gave the girls a straightforward account of human reproduction with diagrams, explaining precisely what occurs in the process of generation between the male and the female. She gave wise advice on matters of contraception before proceeding to sketch expertly an immaculate diagram of the vagina, etched lovingly in glistening wax crayons. She pointed out the

clitoris and stressed its importance when it came to female pleasure.

' "There is also another spot within you which can lead to ecstasy, gels," she continued evenly, "but this can only be found by yourselves through trial and error, which is why I warmly recommend the practice of masturbation. As you should know by now, practice makes perfect. Once you have located it, you must train the male you capture to titillate it at all times." Skirts swished and petticoats crackled with excited approval among her audience. "However," she continued, "there is no denial of the fact that a stiff, thick, hot male penis within the vagina gives the greatest of pleasure to ladies."

'At this point, she nodded to Jane and Alison, who promptly wheeled the scarlet-faced Clarence to the front of the class, whipped up his skirt and petticoats and pulled down his silken, white, knee-length knickers to expose a full-blooded and pulsating erection.

' "Now regard Clarence's tool closely," the Headmistress urged the girls, who were only too willing to obey her instructions. There were audible gasps at the size of this thick, monstrous dick and I noticed that a number of pupils had slipped their fingers up their skirts and were listening to the lesson in a dreamy and, alas, rather clearly dissolute sort of way. "Unfortunately, most males are brutes," Joan Smythe continued, "and their sole desire is to prod their rod into any female they can find. The secret that I am about to teach you is that you should never be frightened of the masculine sex organ. Rather, you should learn how to manipulate it." At this instant, she touched the tip of Clarence's penis with her black, leather-clad, elbow-length-gloved hand and he sighed and shuddered.

' "Now!" Mrs Smythe snapped, dipping her hand into

a black leather bag to emerge with thirteen exquisite peacock feathers. "I want you gels to see just how easy it can be to control the penis of the male; there really is no need to be frightened. Take a feather from this desk and proceed to stroke it. As you know, Clarence has been petticoated for sexual misbehaviour and disrespect to girlhood and womanhood. It is now your turn to have power over him."

'One by one, Anita, Cynthia, Diana, Elaine, Georgina, Harriet, Lola, Nina, Suzanna and Teresa took a peacock feather from the desk and proceeded to stroke the rampaging penis of the chained and bound young man, who shuddered and writhed in the grip of his torment of agony and ecstasy. His chair shot forwards, backwards and sideways as Joan laughed spitefully. When Alison, Jane and I tickled his organ simultaneously, he emitted a hoarse cry as his rod shot a jet of ripe spunk straight into the lap of my new, navy-blue, pleated, bell-shaped skirt – aimed perfectly at my cunt! Can you not imagine my vociferous outrage?

' "My apologies for the bad behaviour of Clarence," Mrs Smythe hastened to reassure me. "I'm afraid that he is wholly lacking in sexual manners. He thoroughly deserves a sound caning from you for this singular atrocity. And he shall endure your punishment tomorrow." The schoolgirls rubbed their thighs together with gladness and glee. "Clarence may be jolly good at rugger but he still does not have the faintest idea about how to conduct himself in the presence of young ladies."

'This might well have been the case for, to my astonishment, John Thomas began to rise again, throbbing in all his glistening and pristine glory. The young ladies were thrilled by this intriguing sight and so was I.

'*Mrs Joan Smythe responded to it by producing a yellow ribbon about three yards long from her shining black-leather handbag; and she proceeded to knot it in a bow around the rampant prick of Clarence. The ends of the ribbon she thence fixed to her own slender wrist. It took just one jerk and two twirls amidst the silk before the young man shot his seed again, this time straight into the pleated skirt of Anita.*

' *"Anita," said Joan. "Do you take this male to be your lawful, wedded husband?"*

' *"I do, Madam," she replied as Clarence sighed and sagged within the chains of his bondage.*

' *"So be it," the Headmistress declared, "and never forget the importance and effect of petticoat power." With that, she snapped her fingers, Alison and Jane wheeled Clarence away to bed, thence to contemplate my caning of his bottom on the morrow; and Anita, a hale and hearty lady who shone on the hockey pitch, though hardly in the classroom, caressed her own buxom body and positively glowed with pleasure at the thought of marrying and governing one of the wealthiest landowners in England.*

'*I shall tell you more of all these doings in a subsequent letter. Meanwhile, Goddess bless; and if you can't be good, be careful.*

'*All my love,*
Emily.'

'Poetry indeed,' I murmured.

'No!' shouted Sedgewick. 'That's not poetry at all. To quote my own noble verse:

All other were mere vanity
Save, sadly, 'tis profanity.

'Thank you,' I said. 'Most grateful for your illumination.'

'Glad you see it, Horby,' Sedgewick went on remorselessly. 'For:

> For other than what is may not say 'tis
> But to impose on blind a fool's design
> As thorns about the brow of Christ define
> Not him, but those who mock, with emphasis:
> Less puncto see and pundit silent pass
> Mankind from truth will ever wander on.

'And so on, almost intelligibly,' came another familiar voice. I looked up to see Aleister Crowley descending the staircase with his arm around an exquisite whore within whose slender limbs I myself had derived great profit and enjoyment. 'With a single word, our dear Wilfred Sedgewick knocks down our castle of cards. Who or what is "puncto"?'

'Crowley! You old bastard!' Bellingham roared. 'What the fuck are you doing here?'

'I couldn't stand celibacy any longer,' said Crowley.

CHAPTER TWENTY

Naturally we invited Crowley to join our table and he told us all about his Yoga practices with Bennett, informing us that these had occupied sixteen hours each day, every day, without tobacco, alcohol, sex or even tea.

'I was very alarmed one day,' he told us, 'to find that I had completely lost the object of concentration. I could not think what I wished to find or where to find it. I naturally thought something was very wrong. Here was an occasion where Allan's experience proved invaluable. Without it, I might have been frightened into giving up the practice. But he told me the result was good, showing that I was approaching the state of what is called "neighbourhood concentration".

'Another experience,' Crowley continued excitedly, 'was this: I found myself at one and the same moment conscious of external things in the background after the object of my concentration had vanished, and also conscious that I was *not* conscious of these things. To the normal mind this is of course sheer contradiction, but Buddhist psychology mentions this peculiar state. The higher faculties of the intelligence are not subject to the same laws as the lower.' He attacked the dish of lamb brains quite greedily, as though he had not eaten meat for a month. 'I continually increased the number of hours which I devoted to my work.'

'Jolly interesting,' said Bellingham, 'but what on earth are you doing here, then?'

'Oh . . .' Crowley sighed and gulped some strong beer, 'I just need to go "on the bust", so to speak, prior to returning to this rigorous austerity.'

'Well, *I*'ve never been one for rigorous austerity,' Bellingham declared. 'Good luck, old chap. Anyway, Horby, I've not only brought you a letter from Emily; here's one from Claire, presently in Rajasthan. Why don't you read it out to us?' I proceeded to comply with his request:

>'*My darling,*
>
>'*I do apologize for the utter negligence on my behalf in replying to your missives. Sometimes one can be rather remiss and thoughtless, even insouciant in one's duties. Please do accept my tergiversation.*
>
>'*I am now in Jaipur yet took a detour upon the way to Agra in order to visit the Taj Mahal, the globe's greatest monument to love. How beautiful it is! When Shah Jahan's beloved Mumtaz Mahal died in 1631, his grief and despair were beyond belief and he wanted to create a mausoleum for her. He hired 20,000 labourers and craftsmen and it took 21 years to build. When I saw this sight, it took my breath away, what with the four rising minarets. The dome is so magnificent. That unjustly neglected painter, William Hodges, wrote in 1876 that it was "like a most perfect pearl on an azure ground."*
>
>'*Ram Singh is such a delightful host; however, I am rather baffled by such strange coincidences in Life. As you may recall, we first met by chance in a Parisian café. It was such a strange coincidence that subsequently he was a Priest at Sir Richard Bellingham's excellent wedding; and then he invited me to his* ashram. *An invitation*

of such distinction was hardly one that I could refuse.

'He recognised that I was a trifle fatigued after my railway journey but this did not impede the excellence of his hospitality. For the evening meal I was served **Khargosh Mokal**, *shredded hare sautéed with chillies, cumin and cardamon; followed by Venison in the* Nizami *style, the flesh of the deer having been marinated in papaya and then simmered in a curry. I must admit that* Gosht Achari *was my favourite dish – lamb cooked with lemon juice, curd, mustard seed, chillies and tamarind, which latter is a spice used often in medicinal beverages. I was also appreciative of the spinach and the bread, this air-light* **Methi Puri**, *enhanced with fenugreek.*

'It is necessary that one should use the right hand to eat, never the left – which is customarily used to wipe one's bottom – mixing mouthfuls of rice with meat and vegetables. I am reminded of the old Indian proverb: "Eating with a knife and fork is like making love through an interpreter."

'Upon the ensuing day, Ram Singh insisted upon a day of fasting in order to celebrate the Festival of Shivarath, a day dedicated to Shiva, the male principle, who represents bliss yet who is sometimes portrayed as the Destroyer, and his female counterpart, Shakti, the mother of the Universe.

' "Let me take you to my Temple," Ram Singh demanded of me. I could not resist his offer. Once therein, he requested: "Anoint my lingam."

' "I will, on one condition," I replied. "That you arouse, energize, stimulate and quicken the pulse within my yoni."

' "The world is bound by lust and it is only this animal desire, sexual indulgence, lasciviousness and passion that* *can release us from our trappings . . ." And so he took me into his arms and slowly removed my attire, an outfit which, he remarked, binds us too much to the material world. He then applied oil to my forehead, breasts, knees and feet, finally anointing my finely trimmed pubic hair with an unguent. A garland of jasmine encircled my neck; yes, it was the flower of the moonshine, small white flowers that are so pungently fragrant at night.*

'After that, he produced a hookah, an elaborate hubble-bubble pipe, and he filled the bowl with bhang.

'What a gradual build up it was to making love! It was a leisurely progression in andante *timing, leading up to a* crescendo. *I have never felt such soft lips upon mine; and simultaneously, he was stroking my young breasts and I could feel my nipples being aroused and becoming erect under his beautifully manicured fingertips. When he began to kiss each breast, I could feel an arousal within my loins. How I did want his male projectile to penetrate my hinterland! What a delight it was when he began to lick upon my quim!*

' "Your cunt," he sighed, "is like the flower of bougainvillea with a cerise blossom within." His tongue shot in and out; and then his palpus savoured and relished my flavoured juices, as they poured within his mouth and slid down his oesophagus. "This is better than lassi," he sighed. "There is both salt and sweetness, the true essence of your body."

'At that moment, I could sense the nature of his throbbing penis. I do not appreciate conjectures; however, I feel that this was not one. There would be a conjunction, an ultimate collision, the violent encounter of two moving bodies, male and female. The heat between the two of us was intense, zealous, torrid – and then he plunged his penis into me. Within seconds I had

my first orgasm: such a tarantism, a dancing mania.

'*He kept on penetrating deeper and deeper in order to reach the quintessence, which as you know is the purest and most perfect form and force whenever heavenly bodies meet with no perversions. Until the early hours of the morning, we made love. We embraced and cherished one another, taking pleasure in each others' bodies. Oh! What a flame of passion and bedazzlement! Mr Ram Singh had the power to ingratiate himself with the treasure he possessed.*

'*Finally he said to me: "We must go to sleep as it is necessary that we prepare for the Feast of Kali, which will begin within the next twenty-four hours." I awoke in the early afternoon to the sounds of ululation; the high-pitched screeching, piercing notes of the peacocks in the garden. The male bird has always been somewhat more extravagant than the female. He has such a brilliant plumage of lapis lazuli, sapphire and emerald whilst the female wears mere tawny brown, reminding me of my aunt, the dowager duchess. As the male courted the female, fanning his feathers, there was a knock upon the door.*

' *"It's Josephine," said Ram Singh. "Please do enter."* *A slim and attractive girl obeyed his wish.*

' *"Mr Singh," she said, "I have brought tea for you and your guest." Not only was there a salver with a silver pot of Indian tea but also there was an epergne. What a delightful ornamentation! There was a vase containing rose flowers, jasmine, yellow champa and laburnum; and a bowl of fresh fruit with limes, guavas, chickoos, kinos and petias – a large pumpkin whose flesh is cut up, pricked and cooked in syrup until it becomes white and then transparent.*

' *"We must celebrate the Festival of Holi together,"*

Ram Singh declared, leaving me a little puzzled, since I had thought he had been referring to Kali. "But until noon tomorrow, all customary social conventions are in abrogation, completely suspended."

' "Tell me more," I requested.

' "It is the rebirth of Spring," he said. "We will have a bonfire tonight to celebrate the destruction of the demon Holika by the infant Krishna."

' "Then," I queried, "will there be rockets? O! those lovely projectiles in cylindrical casings that are fired to ignite the night sky!"

' "You are right," he muttered, once Josephine had left the room, "but I would like once again to penetrate you."

' "Let me be your fizgig," I said.

' "You are much more than that," he replied swiftly. His thick, erect penis once again entered me and moved slowly and strongly in and out. Our orgasms were completely uncontrollable as our bodies tremored and twitched. We then showered each other with pink powder and water, which produced a pleasing, cleansing fizzing upon our light and dark skins. How we did dance and flirt and sing!

'He invited me to join the festivities within the ashram and upon the street and, my darling, it was so beautiful to experience the chanting and the beat of the big chang *drum.*

'I hope that all goes well with you and that you will respond to me soon enough.

'All my love,

Claire.'

'Ah, yes, a splendid gel,' Bellingham muttered as he tucked into more curry. 'Mind you, I've always been rather fond of Ram Singh.' He drank more beer. 'Splendid fellow!'

'I am not impressed,' Sedgewick replied stiffly. 'And I have summarized the matter in my poetry. My *Sonnetical Notes on Philosophy* under my pseudonym of Wm Howell Williams has now been published. And I summarize the matter well:

> Through aggregation form, as semblance place,
> Where mere sensation will substantial find
> Unseen relation force conditioned mind
> Form aggregation ever set to face
> Perception shall be as fixed for the case.
> *Example:* Huxley nihil bonum screen;
> How . . .

'Parse *screen*!' Bellingham demanded.

'And what can it mean, this Fragment of Ozymandias?' Crowley queried. 'It stands there, absolutely isolated from any reference to Huxley; as an "example", but of what, who can say? On all sides, boundless and bare, the lone and level sonnets stretch far away.'

'Did Huxley put a screen on the market called the *nihil bonum*?' I asked.

'Did he give shelter to "nothing good"?' Crowley demanded.

'Or did "nothing good" save him from exposure?' Bellingham suggested.

'Or was Huxley's screen no good?' asked Crowley.

'Or is it no good to screen Huxley?' I wondered aloud.

'You are all idiots, gentlemen,' Sedgewick retorted. 'And I leave you to your idiocy. Myself, I am going upstairs to make love with Naznin and Pabloo.'

'Well, at least you'll be doing something useful in your

life,' said Bellingham. 'Really!' he exclaimed as Sedgewick went upon his intended mission, 'that fellow is such a bore. Anyway, chaps, I've been travelling around the world with my dear lady wife, Davina. Allow me to order another round of these excellent drinks and then I'll tell you all about an extraordinary piece of flagellation, a woman's most delectable bottom being flogged from the colour of black to lobster red, yes, on a sugar cane plantation in Jamaica.' We settled back in expectation to hear his tale but we were abruptly interrupted by the sound of gunfire. We sprang to our feet and sprinted up the stairs to find Pabloo nodding us towards a bedroom. The three of us burst within to find Wilfred Sedgewick face down upon the floor – and Naznin with a smoking gun in her hand.

'Who shot this man?!' Bellingham roared.

'I did,' Naznin answered.

'Congratulations,' said Bellingham.

CHAPTER TWENTY-ONE

'Why did you do that, Naznin?' I asked.

'It was his poetry,' she replied solemnly. 'Anything he did to me I could take; but not his terrible poetry. This is too much for a young girl to endure.'

'Quite agree,' Crowley murmured in a rather bored tone of voice. 'It's just a question of what we do with all the mess and of how we'll handle the various authorities.'

'Simple,' I said; for I had discerned the true nature of the matter. 'This is just one of Bellingham's jokes. If you look at Naznin's gun, I think you'll find that it actually contains blanks and poor old Sedgewick has fallen down in a dead faint. Look! He's stirring into life again!' This was undeniable as Sedgewick hauled himself to his feet and we all started to laugh.

'Sedgewick,' said Bellingham, 'I've just heard news from the Colonial Office that you're due for a transfer, *old chap*. So why don't you just piss orf out of here . . . Jolly good!' Sir Richard bellowed as Sedgewick slunk away. 'Must say that Naznin and Pabloo did their jobs well. Utterly unsuitable for Ceylon, that man!' he snorted disgustedly. 'Best place for him is probably teaching English to Arab boys in Aden; and from what I hear of Aden, the punishment fits the crime. But allow me to continue with my tale which my own practical joke so rudely interrupted. Now look here, Horby, and you too,

Crowley . . .' He called for brandy, 'I was about to tell you of my time in Jamaica. There's a friend of mine called Geoffrey who runs a sugar plantation. Now he's not nearly as bad as his grandfather, who was an extremely cruel man. Why, when one nigger was so hungry that he nibbled at a piece of sugar cane and – poor bugger – got caught, Geoff's grandfather flogged the fellow to within an inch of his life and then forced another nigger slave at the point of a whip to drop a huge cockroach in his mouth. Disgusting! And I don't hold with it. Yet I have some sympathy with the treatment Geoffrey meted out to a black woman working in the sugar fields upon his plantation. He had made her a manager of molasses processing, the condition being that she didn't fuck with anyone apart from him. What did she go and do but – no, not give it to some raw black stud, no, far worse: she started to give away his trade secrets of molasses, treacle, golden syrup, sugar and rum in its forms of white, dark and golden to his nearest white business rival for money. Well, he felt that he had been betrayed. Now let me tell you about his revenge:

'Davina and I entered the main part of a tiled barn which stank of horses' shit and where a padded leather bench stood at the centre of the floor. Joanna, an exquisitely voluptuous female, had been stripped, made to kneel at one end of the bench and lie forward along it. Her knickers had been pulled down around her ankles. Geoffrey's servants had tied her glossy dark hair into a short pony-tail.

'Joanna's arms were strapped to the far end of the bench, her waist was buckled down and her legs were belted tightly together just above her knees.

'All this will sound so severe to you, gentlemen, that you will scarcely credit how much pleasure there might be for Joanna in her punishment. Yet some women have the sense to realize that they have done wrong, surely? And then they ought to accept the punitive measures they receive.

'Myself, I squatted down behind her and studied the area which offered itself as a target to Geoffrey. Joanna's buttocks, firmly and fully presented by her posture, were stretched hard apart. Both the rear pout of her vaginal purse and her anal cleft were in full view.

' "You've been making love, haven't you, Joanna?" Davina teased the punished girl since she was a second cousin of Geoffrey. He, meanwhile, stroked her down the length of her cleavage, between the dark-skinned sturdiness of her buttocks, tickling the rear of her vaginal pouch and finding it visibly moist. She was far away in mind by now, her eyes glazed, her mouth open a little, and her imprisoned bosom heaved.

'Now, Davina is a lover of that delight known to us as "Birching in the Boudoir". Every caning is an occasion for her pleasure. It is true, is it not, that certain girls have found a succinct pleasure under the rod? And is it not so that certain women find an exquisite pleasure in the fact of it? I could discern that Joanna's black, firm thighs, in all their stocky power, were squeezing rhythmically together. It was impossible to prevent it, except perhaps by ordering her thighs to be strapped apart. To tell you the truth, my curiosity was so great that I could not bear to request it.

' "No wonder you've been watched as you were set out on a harness display," said Geoffrey to Joanna. "You have been misbehaving most dreadfully."

Joanna, it seemed, had no shame, She continued with her thigh-squeezing and buttock-clenching as though she could not have stopped for dear life. Geoffrey promptly cut the air with a trial swish of his bamboo cane; our young black masturbatrix stopped, frozen in a moment which mingled apprehension with self-love.

'A dozen strokes across your bare bottom, Joanna,' Geoffrey growled as he began the punishment with a long and supple cane of bamboo. How the first stroke of his cane rang out across the firm, dark cheeks of Joanna's bottom! She gasped, cried out; but never ceased to squeeze her love-lips hard between her thighs. Again the cane lashed across her seat, and again. She uttered a soft cry but it was hard to say whether pain or pleasure drew it from her. Geoffrey was quite pitiless with her. Believe me, chaps, any true disciplinarian who might have watched Joanna displaying her bottom would have approved of that.

'Six times the cane raised a weal across the cheeks of Joanna's buttocks – with a gratuitous lash across the backs of her thighs. She cried out with the hurt – and with the curious pleasure of her own thigh-squeezing at the same time. The vicious bamboo was a smarting agony across the bare cheeks of her backside yet the swelling balloon of pleasure within her own loins enabled her to take it with commendable insouciance. This irritated Geoffrey.

' "Almost at the summit of your climb, Joanna?" he sneered. He waited until her thighs seemed to beat quickly together in their squeezing, like soft, black wings. Then he caned this impudent woman without compunction. I was conscious that Davina was watching with a hot flush upon her cheeks and with her eyes focused upon every nook and writhing cranny. Joanna screamed out and her dark, soulful eyes brimmed over with tears. The anger of Geoffrey brought thin ruby trickles from the renewed weals across her bottom cheeks.

'At last Joanna lay limp and gasping, her black behind

now glowing as red as that of a hot, cooked lobster and marked by swollen stripes.

' "What do we do with this punished bitch?" Geoffrey demanded as Joanna sobbed and her beautiful bottom twitched and writhed in a series of spasms.

' "Quite simple," said Davina. "D'you have any oils?"

'It turned out that he had some oils of benzoin and patchouli. Davina proceeded to amaze the pair of us as she soothed Joanna's twitching bottom with soft strokes; then, by inserting her deft fingers into the young lady's cunt, my wife brought her to orgasm. Joanna's head twitched and turned as much as her bottom.

' "She needs gentle discipline for her wrongdoing," Davina said as Joanna waved her bottom in the air and appeared to implore it. Now, I might well argue with my wife on major things but it's a foolish chap who argues with his wife on minor ones. When, therefore, Davina demanded the finest of soft, silken underwear and clothing for Joanna, I nodded to Geoffrey that I was in absolute agreement.

'The punished girl was released from the block at Davina's request and made to stand in the corner with her face pressed against the wall while we discussed her fate. She had to hold her dress and petticoats above her waist: and it was indeed a positive pleasure to sip our drinks and watch the state of her wealed and whaled bottom as the stripes slowly changed colour. Eventually, Davina put her into the softest of clothing, she had to curtsey to us and thank us for her justly deserved punishment; and then Davina put her to bed. I don't know precisely what happened at that moment but Davina was away for quite a while and I can guess.

'Anyway, gentlemen!' Bellingham threw the contents of his glass down his throat, 'that's my story. Anyone got a better one to tell?'

CHAPTER TWENTY-TWO

I caught a rather ordinary steamboat to Madras a couple of days later, though at least the cabin was moderately comfortable and the food was adequate. It was a pleasure to stroll upon deck and gaze at the Indian Ocean, all the while reflecting upon my experiences. Crowley had returned to Kandy, there to practise more Yoga under the capable tuition of Bennett.

'The trouble with you, Crowley,' Bellingham had said, 'is that presently you're too bloody austere. All this asceticism of yours does no good, you know.'

'That,' Crowley had replied, 'remains to be seen.'

'Oh, well, please yourself,' Bellingham retorted. 'Don't know if you'll be pleasing anybody else.' He had then continued on his way with Davina, sailing to Bombay.

'You seem to be enjoying the sight of the ocean,' said an unfamiliar voice. I turned to see a tall dark man with a thick moustache, who introduced himself as Amin Shah, from Persia. One always needs an interesting man to talk to on a sea voyage, I find, and I had no cause for complaint. He informed me that he was a Sufi going to visit a friend who was a Yogi.

'What exactly *is* a Sufi?' I queried. 'One's informed that the Sufis – and the word means "weavers" – are part of Islam as some sort of mystical sect.'

'Sufis adapt themselves to times and changes,' he

replied. 'Every description of our activities is at least a century out of date. Essentially, we are about learning how to learn so as to advance human evolution.'

'Most laudable. But can you give me an example?'

'Yes,' said the Sufi. 'Sir, I would like to put the light on for you. Please do not be like one of the many fish who swam to a reputedly wise old fish and said: "What's this *water* that we've heard so much about lately?" Allow me to illustrate my point regarding learning how to learn by telling you a joke. Actually, it is two jokes, and I have yet to meet a Westerner who finds the first joke to be funny. However, the condition of the telling is that however much you may deplore the first joke, you must agree to listen to the second.'

'Agreed.' At that moment, there was fuck-all else to do.

'There is a shepherd,' Amin Shah commenced, 'and among his flock, he has a sheep called Lucy, of whom he is particularly fond. Now one day he wakes up, goes to the meadow and Lucy the sheep is missing. So he goes into the village and tries the tavern. "Any of you seen Lucy the sheep?" he asks. No, nobody has. He tries the grocer. "Have you seen Lucy the sheep?" No. The confectioner. "Have you seen Lucy the sheep?" No. He tries the baker, the greengrocer and the cobbler, all the while asking: "Have you seen Lucy the sheep?" and all the while getting the same answer – No. Now, he has tried every shop in the town and nobody has seen Lucy the sheep – except the very last shop, which is the butcher's.'

'I think I know what's coming,' I murmured.

'So he goes in there,' Mr Shah continued, 'and says: "Mr Butcher, have *you* seen Lucy the sheep?" And the butcher says . . . "No".'

There was a pause.

'Please go on,' I requested, adding: 'I'm terribly interested.'

'That's the joke,' he responded. 'I didn't think that you would find it to be humorous.'

'It's not funny at all,' I said indignantly. 'In fact, I think it's the worst joke that I have ever heard.'

'No, I suppose it is not terribly good,' he smiled regretfully, 'but I assure you that the second one, to which you promised to listen, is much better. There are two men in the compartment of a railway train. One of them has a pet monkey sitting next to him. He also has a box of cigars and is greatly looking forward to smoking them. Well, he lights a good cigar but the other man says: "Excuse me, my dear sir, I suffer from bronchitis and asthma and although you are permitted by law to smoke in this compartment, I wonder if here and now you would be kind enough to refrain." Now, the first man is a little irritated but he is a gentleman and so he stubs out his cigar. Then he thinks that there is precious little to do except go to sleep. He does: and so does the other man. And while they are both asleep, the monkey takes the box of cigars and disappears. After a while, the first man wakes up to see that his monkey has vanished. That perturbs him – and his cigars have vanished, too. He wakes up the second man who declares that he was asleep throughout these events and knows nothing. The second man goes back to sleep as the first explores the train, entering every corridor and enquiring within each compartment, looking for his monkey and his box of cigars. "Have you seen my monkey and my box of cigars?" is his question to everyone he encounters but all the time he receives the same answer – No. Now, sir, the very last carriage of this train is where they have the buffet and the bar. He enters that compartment – and there, sitting at the bar, wearing his glasses, reading a newspaper, drinking beer and smoking his cigars . . . whom do you think he sees?'

'The monkey,' I answered smartly.

'No,' said the Sufi, 'Lucy the sheep.'

After that, of course I bought the fellow a brandy and invited him to dine with me, mentioning only that it could not be tonight since I was previously engaged at the Captain's table.

'So am I,' he replied, 'so we shall be dining together after all.'

I started to wonder just what sort of boat I was on that night when I sat down to dine at the Captain's table. Captain Jack Rivers was a genial, fat, florid-faced buccaneer who had been sailing the South Seas for many a year and who was also surprisingly well-read. Although there were some attractive women on the voyage, only Amin Shah and I sat with Rivers. 'I don't often get the chance to have a good men's evening of congenial and intelligent conversation,' the Captain explained.

'I'm quite interested in Sufism,' Captain Jack Rivers declared, 'having listened to Amin here on a number of previous voyages.' It was the end of a good and satisfying meal based largely around hot lamb curry, and he poured generous quantities of brandy for both of us. 'I love listening to people who talk sense or make me laugh. Why, on my last voyage, I was listening to a Chinese Zen Master. "What is Zen?" I asked him. He told me the following story: "One day Chan Tzu-lin was walking in the sunshine and was greeted warmly by Wu Pei-fu. 'Hot weather,' said the Master. 'A good day for work.' Thence Wu Pei-fu was enlightened." '

'Yes . . .' I muttered. 'Go on.'

'That's it,' said the Captain. 'That is Zen. At least,

that's what he told me. Frankly, gentlemen, I can't make the slightest sense out of it. Can you?'

'No,' I said.

'I can put the same truth to you in another way,' Amin Shah interposed gently. 'Chan Tzu-lin one day took Wu Pei-fu to a meadow in order to show him Enlightenment. This was in the form of a cow grazing. The Master pointed and the disciple looked and the sacred cow went: "MU". And thereupon absolutely nobody was enlightened. Would you like to know why?'

'Yes,' I said.

'Nobody could speak Chinese,' he retorted.

'I think I'm beginning to comprehend,' I said smilingly as the Captain roared with laughter and poured more cognac for all of us. 'Both Zen and Sufism are about different ways of perceiving the obvious.'

'Why do you think I sail the seas, sir?' Captain Jack Rivers demanded. 'I listen to all my more interesting passengers, gaze at the ocean waves and am thrilled each day at perceiving the obvious all the time. There're so many who just can't.' He lit a huge *Corona de Corona*, offering us his box of Cuban cigars, then glanced pointedly at one of three young ladies dining together. She appeared to be thrilled by his sharp glance. 'A very good night to you, gentlemen. Personally, I *love* the obvious!'

I retired to my cabin and re-read the most recent letter I had received from Claire, finding it to be as paradoxical as everything else I had heard this evening.

My darling,

I miss you so much and hope that you received my last letter. Upon the Festival of Holi, Josephine, a 'younger sister' of Ram Singh, insisted that I be properly decorated and applied henna *upon my hands in a lattice pattern,* with lines, dots and triangles forming diamond figures like those of heraldry. She applied this concoction of nut gallis, ashes, spices, all heated by fire at the point of a calema, a piece of sharpened wood. Throughout the ritual of ornamentation of my body, she chanted with such a goddess-like, transcendent voice.

'You will be the most beautiful at the Festival,' she sang softly, 'for your skin is so pale. The darkness of the henna contrasts so delicately with the pallor of your skin.'

She then produced a sari for me to wear, woven of the finest gossamer red silk and exquisitely embroidered; such fine ornamentation in gold thread, a filament so delicately fashioned . . . I had never worn a sari before with so many folds of fabric held together in such a simple and sensible style of elegant dress. Upon my forehead, Josephine applied tikka, a spot of red appropriate to a Brahmin priestess; and she dotted my chin with a siyala, a lucky charm; and finally there was a circle drawn upon the end of my nose to ward off the evil eye.

'Do you not know . . .?' Josephine asked me, 'that the Singh family have been the rulers of Jaipur since the late 16th century and that includes the father of Ram Singh. The family is highly distinguished.'

'He never told me of the history of his family,' I replied with astonishment, recalling my initial encounter in a Parisian café and our subsequent roles as Priest and Priestess at the wedding of Sir Richard to Davina in Paris.

'Mr Singh is a very modest man,' Josephine observed. 'His family is putting great pressure on him to marry diplomatically so that he can produce many fine sons. Let us not forget that his great-grandfather had 300 wives *and a harem of 5,000 concubines, occupying two-thirds of the palace.'*

'Josephine, how did he manage to satisfy them all?' I asked with bewilderment. Suddenly the door flew open and in strode a man dressed in the most magnificent oriental finery. Josephine silently left the room.

'Later on, Memsahib!' he cried out proudly, 'I shall show you how he managed to satisfy, please and content them all.'

'Please show me now,' I requested, recognizing Ram Singh.

'First of all you must catch me!' he roared.

'Oh, do stop teasing me . . .' Suddenly, and to my complete stupefaction, he proceeded to perform a series of somersaults and handstands.

'If you want me, then you must chase me,' he teased as he tempted newly excited and aroused desires of the flesh within me. 'If you can ambush and trap me, then I will be compliant, devoted and submissive to your demands: heh! heh!' Then, without warning, he dashed down the stairs and into the street. I pursued him. It was annoying, upon my entry into the street, to see so many people in festive attire blocking the way. Cows were ornamentally decorated and I had to push and thread my way through the throng. The chanting resonated throughout the air as the women hunted and stalked their men.

I was the quester, seeker and searcher after Ram Singh. I prowled and pursued his every pervading scent that permeated and saturated the air. Yet it was virtually impossible to push my way through the multitudes assembled.

Unexpectedly, there was a kiss upon my lips: it was curious; it was not rough; but it lacked the tenderness of Ram Singh.

I stared into the eyes of Douglas.

'What are you doing here?' I asked.

'Everyone has to be somewhere,' he replied lightly, 'and I would like to ask the same of you.' Again he kissed me resplendently upon the lips and vanished as swiftly as he had arrived. I turned around to face Ram Singh.

'At last I have found you!' he exclaimed warmly. 'It is the end of the chase. The hunter is the hunted and the biter bit.' Amidst the dancing and the chanting, we kissed so passionately. 'I only desire to give you even greater pleasures this evening,' he informed me. 'Let us rid ourselves of this maddening crowd.' I gladly agreed as we strolled leisurely through the winding side-streets, enjoying the various festivities. There was an intensity in our walking and a greater magnetic field that would bring us even closer together. Finally we arrived back at his ashram, and when the doors closed behind us, he took me into his arms. 'What magic power do you possess that you should find me so quickly?' he asked.

'You found me,' was my response. 'It is the Goddess within me.'

'Let us now make love,' he said, 'and we must retire to my sanctuary, the inmost recess, the shrine to penetralia.'

Within the confines of this sanctum, he embraced me again.

'You have never looked more beautiful,' he remarked, 'so now I shall show you how a man can satisfy over 5,000 women.' He lifted my sari and within seconds his penis had entered my moist cunny in a gradual, leisurely and meticulous build-up to a forthcoming climax; yet much faster than the pace of a piaffer, even developing his rhythm up to that of a canter and thence to the gallop of a stallion. How his ramrod did shoot into me! And

when his orgasm did occur, it was a total immersion, an inundation of his manly fluids, a saturation of my vulva. I have never known such a plenteous and precious spurting of semen!

These festivals appear to carry on for days – or "Daze", it might be said – for there is continuous dancing and chanting, with the accompaniment of gaily caparisoned elephants and camels; yet it was our choice to remain within our doors and to watch from the balcony and the windows. I think I began to generate more power within his phallus, a veneration such as that between Shiva and Shakti or between Vishnu and Lakshmi. Throughout the night, we made love, yet I think I want more than what he has offered to me, including a proposal of marriage.

I cannot deny that there is a powerful passion within his loins. He can make love so many times a night but I think he also wants to scatter his seed around a harem.

There is a wishing-pond in the garden. It contains so many beautiful fish. I threw my robe into the pool to watch it gradually ripple and to hope that my deepest desire comes through.

All my love,
Claire.'

After reading that, I went up on deck and was glad not to hear any further words of insight. Instead, I picked up a stupid but beautiful French tart called Jacqueline, who had gorgeous, glossy, black wavy hair; upstanding tits; a voluptuous, rounded, firm bottom; and, yes, I thrust my stiff rod within her, and as she writhed and moaned just before she came, I fucked her brains out.

CHAPTER TWENTY-THREE

I found Madras to be sleepy, sticky and provincial; yet there were compensations. I continued to dine with the intriguing Amin Shah and it had been warmly recommended to me that I visit Lady Joanna Featherstonehaugh – pronounced 'Fanshaw' for some indiscernible reason – who received me warmly and turned out to be everything that Bellingham had described: a beautiful and stylishly-dressed voluptuous redhead. Within thirty minutes of my arrival, she asked me if I liked riding, and when I assented she exclaimed: 'Then I'll ride upon you.'

Only a fool would refuse so gracious an offer from so lovely a lady: and so I undid my trousers and sat upon a chair. Joanna pulled up all her petticoats and proceeded to set herself in the saddle. She then seized my vigorous implement and commenced the physical introduction by pushing down her bottom as it slowly entered. I was so placed that I could enjoy the sight from behind and consequently could not miss the slightest detail. My enormous tool soon disappeared completely. Joanna lifted up her legs, placed her high heels on the bars of the chair and began to rise and fall with frequent gasping.

The accustomed sighs and words rose to her lips as our souls melted together in mutual enjoyment.

'Ah! how finely you do it!' said she. 'Gently, my angel . . . Uncover him well . . . Now quicker. Stop! Go on again! Ah! I feel it coming! Quicker! . . . I . . . I spend . . . I come!'

She could not help opening up her thighs wider and elevating her petticoats in a sheer transport of delight. Her hands gripped my thighs fast in her embrace, impatiently desiring the supreme moment. The lips of her womb soon enough felt the tip of the head of my instrument. I shoved it in as far as was possible and she uttered a raucous cry: 'I am spending!' So violent were her convulsions that I almost lost my senses. I stopped for a second or two, astonished at her transports, then returned to the performance of my sweet duty. What a remarkable woman! She poured out her delicious dew upon my penis at least four times! All the while she was pushing out her bottom as if she were riding a stallion. As, in a sense, she was. At last I shuddered and sighed and a fiery, flaming jet of jism inundated her flesh-depths.

After a period of silent embracing, she arose, rang a bell and summoned a slender maid called Laura, all the while smoothing her skirt.

'Laura, you've been a very naughty girl,' Joanna informed her with a severe crackling of her petticoats. 'Now be a good girl and go and fetch my birch.' She chuckled wickedly. 'You need another erection, Horby, and the tender rump of Laura will give you much satisfaction. She's such a coward and the first cut will make her wince yet we all know how nice and delightful the finish is. This will excite your cock to another great fuck.'

A timorous Laura returned, holding the birch requested by Lady Joanna.

'Would you kindly be the horse, Horby?' she asked me; and I acceded to her demand, which entailed bending over as the fanciable Laura was placed upon me with her wrists bound to mine by thongs of brown leather. There were four mirrors upon each wall of the chamber of milady, enabling me to watch the progress of the punishment from a variety of perspectives.

'I am very much obliged to you for your kindness,' Lady Joanna addressed me, 'but Laura's bottom will soon be *aglow* for your delectation once I begin to apply some of Mrs Martinet's scientific touches to it. Laura is a bonded maidservant and so she shall remain. This is a serious business,' she declared, swishing both her skirts and the birch within her hand. 'Thin ticklers are only useful just to touch up a man in the act of fucking. Laura's whipping must be *much* more severe in order to stimulate your presently languid tool and rouse it again to a state of lustful fury by the exhibition of the reddened flesh, weals, and dripping drops of the ruby, as it is distilled from the abraded skin.'

'Oh, pray don't be as bad as that, Milady,' Laura pleaded apprehensively.

'No, Miss Pert, no nonsense, no drawing back, or I really *will* make it worse for your wicked bum!' exclaimed Lady Joanna, standing up straight and looking fiercely at her helpless victim, firmly fastened over my manly back. The birching commenced: and my cock was in a state of glorious stiffness.

'Oh, it stings so!' Laura gasped. 'Ah, not so hard, Joanna, darling,' Laura sighed as the first two or three swishes made her buttocks tingle under the smart.

'Is that better, you rude girl?' Joanna retorted. 'Didn't I catch you frigging yourself in bed this morning?' she demanded with a spiteful smile upon her face.

'Ah, ah, oh, no! My God, how you cut me! I shall die of it. I never frigged myself. I should be ashamed to do such a thing,' she sobbed, the tears trickling down cheeks that were blushing more scarlet than the twitching bottom I could see in the looking-glasses. Her exposed bottom was being fairly reddened beneath the smarting cuts and this love-canter quickened into an impetuous gallop so that, when the emitting crisis came, the three of us fairly howled and shouted with excess of delighted emotion, while Laura went into a fit of hysteria, laughed, cried and stiffened herself over me, almost throwing me out of position as her teeth closed convulsively upon the flesh of my neck.

'Just listen to this hard bitch!' cried Lady Joanna. 'It's as bad as saying I'm a liar.' She let fly with two vicious cuts that made Laura squirm in agony and drew the blood up under the skin of her rump. 'Ah, you bad girl, I'll whip the frigging fancy out of you. Wouldn't it be nice to be frigged just now with your cunt rubbing against Horby's back?'

'Oh! Oh!! Oh!!! I didn't!' Laura screamed back as she squirmed. The cuts fell in rapid succession on her devoted bum, which now began to exhibit weals upon the broken skin. The victim still writhed and struggled upon my back and under Joanna's scathing cuts yet her head fell forward upon my shoulder, her face suffused with crimson flushes, and her eyes closed in a voluptuous langor.

I had decided to act on the frigging accusation and by the light pressures of my lower back on her excited clitoris, had made her close to fainting under the combination of excitements, as she spent so profusely that her thick, creamy emission trickled down my back.

'Lay her down upon the bed and let's have her later!' Lady Joanna commanded imperiously, flinging down the rod which was considerably worn by its work. 'Who'll have *me* on the horse-hair sofa? Will you, Horby?'

'I'm randy enough for anything, my love,' I exclaimed as the bonds were untied by her and a sobbing Laura was tucked into bed. 'Ah! Horse-hair throw-rug, eh? It's just how Adam and Eve must have shagged on the grass in Eden.'

'Oh, it does prick the flesh so,' Joanna exclaimed as she plumped her bottom on the horse-hair. 'But it's the finest thing to stimulate a woman that you can think of: the little prickly ends of the stiff hair are like pins and make your arse bound under every single stroke. It's simply delicious. No one but those who try it can appreciate the delights of a horse-hair sofa-fuck.'

How she bounded and writhed as I fairly and furiously pounded my prick into her swimming cunt, which seemed to be perfectly appositioned and quite insatiable. She was spending again and again, every two or three minutes, until at last, with a perfect howl of delight, she drew upon my pent-up emission, which shot up into her vitals like a stream of liquid fire.

Kissing and billing, we lay entranced within each other's arms until the soundly birched Laura remarked that it would soon be time for breakfast.

Dinner was my main concern when I met Amin Shah, who invited me to sample delicious Southern Indian vegetarian cuisine, eaten with the right hand off a huge banana leaf. The *dosa*, something made of wheat and rice which was betwixt and between a piece of crisp bread and a pancake proved to be particularly notable. The *thali*, a selection of dishes in each of which a blend of spices has made the crisp vegetables deliciously picquant, added to the memory of this meal. With it we drank something called *lassi* or *lhasi* – who knows and who cares about the minute exactitude of its spelling and translation? Anyway, it's a jolly good beverage made out of yoghurt. Amin Shah set two glasses before me, one salty and the other sweet, asking me to choose them.

'Salty first,' I think I remarked, 'and sweet later.' He burst out laughing. 'I'm glad that you are amused,' I said, 'but what's so funny?'

'You,' he replied.

'Well, if I'm such a figure of fun,' I answered, 'at least one's doing something useful with one's life. I mean, what's your function?' I burst out indignantly. 'You say you're a Sufi Master but you haven't yet made me laugh.'

'I'll tell you a Nazrudin story,' he responded. Nazrudin is, of course, the Robin Hood of the Middle East. 'Once upon a time, Nazrurdin was on hard times, down on his luck and living in straitened circumstances with his wife. A rich relative came to visit and he brought Nazrudin and his wife a freshly-slaughtered duck and suggested that it be cooked for their dinner. Very good it was, too! The rich relative departed on the following day; and two days later, there was a knock upon the door. "Hallo, Nazrudin, I am a friend of the relative who brought you the duck." "Come in!" Nazrudin the Mullah exclaimed warmly, "dinner is served!" Two days later, there was another knock upon the door. "Hallo, Nazrudin, I am a friend of the friend of the relative that brought you the duck." "Come in," said Mullah Nazrudin; "dinner is served." Two days later there was yet another knock upon the door. "Hallo, Nazrudin, I am the friend of the friend of the friend of the relative that brought you the duck." By this time, the host's wife was berating him for his feckless hospitality. "Come in," sighed Hodja Nazrudin; "dinner is served. Here is the soup of the soup of the soup of the duck that my relative brought me." '

I couldn't resist a chuckle at that one and, in order to encourage my host further in his purveying of anecdotes, I offered him a brandy 'or anything else you might like'; and he told me calmly that a glass of neat Scotch whisky would suit him best. This sounded like a jolly good idea so I decided to join him.

'Seen your Yogi friend?' I enquired.

'No,' Amin Shah replied. 'He's been delayed and won't be here for a couple of weeks or so: but I assure you, he is worth meeting. Another man you must meet is Sir Richard Bellingham.'

'Thank you.' It was hard to maintain a straight face. 'But I've known him for years.'

'I know.'

'Then why did you ask me to meet him?'

'Simply to observe your reaction to the suggestion.'

'You are a very curious creature,' I replied.

'Yes,' he said simply. 'And I hope you don't make the mistake of the vast majority of creatures, which is continually to confuse something with what it isn't. For instance, there was once a bear who was told by his father: "For hibernation, son, never forget to take plenty of *berries* or else you'll starve to death." This bear was later found in a cave by the bunnies, starved and frozen to death. Upon his head, paws and feet, he had *berets*. Most people are just like that.'

'Yes, I've had similar sufferings on account of misunderstanding,' I replied. 'I'm slightly short-sighted, and a few years ago, I was on a railway journey, sitting in the buffet car and hoping to order a spot of lunch. Unfortunately, I'd forgotten my glasses and my monocle and so I couldn't read the menu properly. I asked a pleasant-faced woman, seated opposite, to assist me in telling me what the bloody hell was on the thing. She told me and I ordered – probably just a cheese and tomato sandwich. Then she said: "You mustn't be embarrassed, you know.

There's nothing of which to be ashamed." "Not ashamed at all of anything," I retorted indignantly. "Six weeks is all it would take," she responded, "and please listen, for a new world of truth and beauty would open up before your eyes." "You sound like some sort of crusader," I remarked. "Yes!" she cried; "for I teach the noble arts of reading and writing. Come to my Adult Illiteracy Classes!" ' Shah chuckled.

'Communication, so-called, is so frequently so conditioned by preconceptions so as to be socially dysfunctional,' the Sufi remarked. 'Have you ever heard of the fabled American Western gunfighter, Wild Bill Hickock?'

'Of course.'

'It happened during the Civil War of the American States, so we're told,' said Amin Shah, 'in wide-open North Platte, Nebraska. Bill Hickock, Union scout, Indian fighter and dead shot with a lightning quick draw, hitched his horse, Black Nell, to a post and entered a saloon for supper. A waitress approached him nervously and whispered that she had *heard two men plotting to kill him*. One was going to come in the front door and the other the rear, guns blazing before Mr Hickock could whip out his Colt Dragoon .44's.

'Hickock, this gentleman pistoleer,' Amin Shah continued, 'swept a lock of golden-brown tresses off his shoulder and chucked the trembling bearer of Death's tidings under her chin. "Little girl," he said, "you get to one side. You might get hurt in the overflow." The waitress fled to the kitchen. The resulting carnage has been described by a biographer, Mr O.W. Coursey, though I quote from memory: "Wild Bill, facing the desperate character who entered the front door, had shot him with a revolver in his left hand, while with the right hand he had thrown the other gun over his left shoulder and shot the man coming in from the rear. History does not record a more daredevil act, a more astute piece of gun work".'

'Marvellous!' I exclaimed. 'What's wrong with that?'

'As a story, nothing,' said the Sufi. 'The episode fits nicely with our picture of Wild Bill Hickock as the fearless square-shootin' hero who triumphs over the damnedest odds. "*Marvellous!*" indeed, as you say, sir. The only trouble with it is that there isn't a shred of evidence that it ever happened.'

CHAPTER TWENTY-FOUR

The finest whore for the best fuck that I met in Madras was Janine, who was half English, a quarter French and a quarter Indian.

'My dear Horby,' she murmured as she licked my stiff prick, 'I am glad that you are drinking brandy.' She wriggled her soft and rounded bottom delectably as her long, dark, glossy hair cascaded over my belly. 'Gin is too depressing for men and takes all the starch out of their pricks. You know the saying: "Whisky makes the love hot but brandy makes it long." For my part,' she continued after a long, deep suck on my cock, 'give me a man who can keep his place well and go on with his fucking, getting stiffer and bigger inside my cunt, until he stirs my blood, raises all my passions to such a pitch, that when at length both come together, it is really the melting of two souls into one and leaves you to fall into that blissful ecstasy afterwards which,' she sighed languidly, 'only true and experienced fuckers really understand. Fancy a bottle of fizz?'

'Yes, fetch the fizz,' I replied, 'my impudent cheeky beauty. I hope to give you a new sensation for, despite the impending chill of the champagne, you look warm enough for anything.'

'Thank you for the compliment. I own I'm not a lump of ice but I'll be quick as I'm curious to experience your

style.' She vanished briefly to reappear with a bottle of
Veuve Cliquot, which she opened expertly, rather as
though she were bringing a penis to orgasm. She thence
pledged me 'a long life and plenty of fucking.' Slipping off
her dressing gown, which at once revealed that she had
only her corset, chemise and drawers to hide her person,
set off to best advantage by pink silk stockings, pretty
gold-buckled blue garters and elegant high-heeled French
slippers, she lay over the end of the sofa and bared her
exquisite backside. 'As hard as you like, darling, but make
it long and slow before the finish.'

'I'll be all there when my pounding makes you spend,
Janine,' I answered as my prick penetrated her delicate
labia and I commenced my thrusting. 'And afterwards I
wouldn't mind sucking up every drop.' My belly slammed
against her truly magnificent olive rump and her vaginal
squeezing of my stiff cock possessed all the stock-in-trade
of as handsome and pretty a young whore as any man
could wish to experience. 'And I'll begin as I mean to go
on.'

My deep penetration, with the tip of my penis touching
the outer lips of her womb, made her writhe with exceptional joys of sensation. Her face flushed as the blood
tingled in her veins. She shivered with emotion and
voluptuous desire.

After about five minutes of fucking in depth, slowly
and rhythmically, Janine gave most evident signs of the
impending crisis. She closed her eyes and hung her head
over the end of the sofa, her bottom and thighs fairly
quivering with the excess of her emotions; and I rushed
upon my victim with all the energy of a lustful satyr,
thence turning the girl over on her back and burying my
face between her thighs to lick and suck up every drop
of spendings from her quivering quim. I kissed her

sweetly-scented cunt and said: 'I must fuck you again.'

She fell upon her knees and seized my cock between her lips, engulfed it within her mouth and sucked it with raging delirium.

'Oh!' she gasped. 'I just can't resist that beautiful, rubicund head!' Turning over and lying upon a Persian rug, she exposed her irresistible buttocks. In a twinkling, I had penetrated her rosebud of an anus, filling it up with my instrument which on this night appeared to know no rest. Ah! How she helped me by opening and shutting the cheeks of her backside, by writhing, twisting and swooning with joy.

I roared like a lion when I came. We lay closely together for a while and then I ordered more champagne, more brandy, lobster and prawns, requesting that she dress for a little supper. Janine responded by donning a black gown of shining silk with a wide belt of gleaming black leather and a silver buckle. Her thrusting breasts threatened to split the fabric at the front and her small, tight bottom looked fit imminently to burst out of the erotic fabric in which it was so tightly wrapped, making it quite visually devastating. Her white petticoats of satin rustled each time she moved her slim legs. After our meal, I could not bear it any longer.

I crushed out my cigar in the ash-tray and rose from my chair. Janine sucked in her breath, her dark eyes widening supremely, and in mock horror, tried to fling herself backward at my approach. I put my hands out to those splendid naked globes of her bosom and lovingly squeezed and stroked them, feeling her nipples stiffen and tingle as my palms lingeringly grazed those crinkly tit-bits. Then I lowered my hands under her skirt and suddenly yanked it up.

'Oh, sir!' she shrieked. 'Don't do that! Why, and I

thought that you were such a gentleman!' In moves of intoxicating tantalization, she lunged this way and that, whilst her beautiful breasts jiggled and danced in a most delicious choreography.

Her skirt, although it squeezed her hips, was exceptionally full around her peeping ankles and there was also the matter of her petticoats. When I had grasped all this fabric in my left hand and lifted it up to her waist, I found to my rising excitement that she had surreptitiously sheathed the vulnerable targets of her loins and bottom in dainty, lace-trimmed pink silk drawers, whose legs reached nearly to mid-thigh and whose snugness defined the shape of the plump prominence of her mound of Venus. Through the transparency of the thin material, I could see the thick bush of black silky curls which crowned her luscious cunt.

'Madam,' I said, 'kindly lie down upon the couch like a goddess who disposes herself to receive adoration from her followers. You have a lovely warm cunt so tender it to my warm, sweet mouth. And thus we will give one another the true kiss of peace!' Blushingly, she took her position and I slipped my hands beneath her bottom and put my mouth to the raven thicket of her mound of Venus, applying a long, sweet, sucking kiss.

'Oooh! Ohh, Horby, what're you doing?' she squealed. When I perceived that Janine's hips and loins had begun once more to wriggle and lunge and when I heard her inarticulate sighs and groans and knew her to be further along the pathway to paradise, I seized her by the waist and pressing her down upon her back, inserted my near-bursting cock into her moist slit and with a single mighty lunge, thrust myself home to the hilt.

Janine uttered a strident cry, flung her arms round my shoulders and, nimbly wrapping her legs over my sinewy and jerking behind, arched up to meet me in the frenetic gymnastics by which we both attained our climax. Happily, considering that I had poured forth such a deluge of essence into Janine's cunt, I discovered that my cock retained its rigidity even after it had spurted forth to acclaim the heated reception this lady's quaking love-canal had bestowed upon it.

I was resting after our embrace and watching with rapt fascination as Janine moaned feverishly, one slim hand now slyly frigging herself as she posed with heels planted upon the couch, knees up and yawningly straddled, her skirt and petticoats all in disarray. I chided her teasingly:

'I will give that little hand something better to play with. Reach out and I'll be there!'

'Ohh, *yes*, Horby dearest,' she sighed, opening her moist eyes and uttering a joyous gasp. 'Oh! that'll be ever so much better!' Janine grasped my ramrod and guided it into her twitching, damp, pink crevice. And once again, with a single, mighty lunge, I impaled her to my very balls and then commenced to fuck her with long, hard digs, as she was clutching me with her arms and stockinged legs, moaning and kissing me feverishly until she poured down her furious tribute.

Gallantly, I then retired, for I had left double the money which she had expected and I feel that delightful ladies of the night are entitled to a period of rest. I shall always recall her fondly as a damn fine fuck, with grace to match it, and I fully intended to visit her again but my plans were to be changed without my knowledge prior to the event upon this very night.

The mysterious Sufi, Amin Shah, had invited me to take some refreshment with him at midnight at a house he was renting in the centre of Madras so as to meet his friend the Yogi who had finally arrived. A huge Sikh proceeded to usher me into a bare room consisting solely of a large round table and ten straight-backed chairs of teak where Amin Shah was drinking fine old malt whisky with Aleister Crowley. We greeted one another warmly and Shah's malt whisky was of surpassing excellence.

'This is a very pleasant surprise,' I said, 'but where is your friend, Amin, the Adept of Yoga?'

'Here,' said Shah, indicating Crowley. 'I have been waiting for him.' I looked more closely and discerned that Crowley was positively glowing with good health and high spirits.

'Got there in the end, Horby,' he told me, 'thanks to the teaching of Allan Bennett. After I saw you in that brothel bar, I went back to Allan and positively raced for results. Twenty hours a day,' he said calmly and with sincere conviction. 'Eventually I achieved the exalted trance of *Dhyana*.'

'Sorry . . .?' I enquired.

'Contemplation,' he replied. 'In analysing the nature of this work of controlling the mind, two things are involved: the person seeing and the thing seen; and the person knowing and the thing known; and one normally regards this as the necessary condition of all consciousness. But what happened to me is that this consciousness of the Ego and the non-Ego, the seer and the thing seen, the knower and the thing known, was blotted out. There was an intense light, an intense sound and a feeling of such overwhelming bliss that the resources of language have been exhausted again and again in the attempt to describe it. *It is an absolute knock-out blow to the mind*. By its light, all other events of life are as darkness.'

'Quite agree,' Amin Shah responded. 'And thank heavens, Mr Crowley, that you are a strong and genuine poet whose use of language may eventually give your readers some intimations of this experience. I don't think that you'll be one of those semi-educated stutterers wallowing in oceans of gush.'

'Too kind, sir.' Crowley smiled. 'And incidentally, Horby, it might greatly interest you to know that the practice of Yoga has greatly improved my sexual performance. These days I can go four hours of rod-ramming without coming. Take up Yoga for that reason, Horby, if for nothing else.'

'So what are your future plans?' I asked.

'Tonight I'm going to have a good dinner and a good fuck,' Crowley responded. 'Then I'm going to escort my dear guru Allan Bennett through the swamps and jungles to Burma, where he wishes to take the Yellow Robe as a Buddhist monk. That is his vocation in life and I respect it immensely but it is not mine. I'll be off after that for some big-game hunting in the jungles with a good chap called Edward Thornton. Now I *would* go tiger-hunting with him.'

'And then?' I queried.

'You sound just like my father,' he answered with a smile. 'Various Rajahs and Maharajahs have kindly invited me to their palaces. I also have appointments with a variety of holy men such as the estimable Mr Shah here.'

'I'm not "holy",' Shah demurred, 'whatever that word may mean. 'I simply endeavour to apply my intelligence.'

'I hope the other ones do, too,' Crowley retorted. 'Then it'll be time to link up again with my dear friend Oskar Eckenstein and climb K2, the second highest mountain in the world.'

'Good luck,' I said.

'You may need it,' Shah added. 'And what of your studies?'

'I shall pursue my studies in Cerebral Neurology;

Psychology, both Western and Eastern; and Philosophical Metaphysics, hoping by reason to persuade men of Science to investigate extra-ordinary states of consciousness as being the next step in human evolution.'

'Good luck,' said Shah, 'for you will need it. And if you come up with a genuine discovery, you will be lucky to escape the prison bars and financial ruin. I predict, though, that at some point in your life, within the next five years, you will encounter an Intelligence way beyond your own which will make of you a true Prophet yet ruin your reputation, which will survive for some generations solely as a classic of infamy. Such is the lot of those who seek too openly to improve the condition of this planet.'

'It may be so, sir,' Crowley answered, 'but I'm always on for a good adventure.' He rose and shook hands warmly. 'Excuse me, gentlemen, but I'm just dying for a fuck. Look after yourself, Horby,' were his last words to me, 'and don't do anything that I wouldn't do. If you can't be good, be careful.'

Today (1925), contemplating my *Memorandum 1023*, I recall the prophetic words of Mr Amin Shah. Allan Bennett did indeed take the Yellow Robe as a Buddhist monk and thence brought Theravada/Hinayana Buddhism to Great Britain. Crowley did indeed win a formidable reputation as a hunter of big game, stalking and shooting the tiger, the leopard, the crocodile and that most dangerous of all creatures, the water buffalo. The Eckenstein-Crowley expedition to K2 smashed more world records and even though they did not succeed in reaching the summit, no one else has either; and the height reached at 22,000 feet has only recently been surpassed. 'An Intelligence way beyond your ken?' Well, Crowley claimed to have encountered this in Cairo in 1904, where it dictated to him an intensely beautiful prose poem called *The Book of the Law*. As a result of endeavouring to preach its doctrines and put them into practice, I gather that Mussolini has expelled Crowley from his 'Abbey of Thelema' in Cefalu, Sicily and he is regularly excoriated in the gutter press. Personally, I cannot believe that he is any worse than I am and for all I know, he may well be a damn' sight better. Certainly I don't believe the salacious tales about him manufactured by 'journalists' unfit to be the smegma in his foreskin. Peace be with thee, friend, where e'er thou be.

Now, I was about to take my leave of Amin Shah when his Sikh butler and bodyguard ushered a familiar figure into the room. Shah greeted him with a few ceremonial formalities.

'Douglas, you old bugger!' I exclaimed. 'It's always a pleasure to see you but what the fuck are you doing here? I thought that after our charming Nile cruise, you had to attend to your business and political interests.'

'I have,' he replied. 'And I am a Master of the art of delegation. First-rate people hire first-rate people. Second-rate people hire third-rate people.'

'You sound just like an adviser to our present Prime Minister,' I replied, 'whose advice has been ignored.'

'Quite right, Horby,' he responded smartly, 'my political and economic advice on Tariff Reform and Imperial Preference *has* been ignored and the Cabinet is merely a menagerie of mediocrities. I have handled my financial interests accordingly. They can all get on as best they like without me for the time being. Anyway,' he took a crystal glass of malt whisky from Amin Shah, 'you chaps simply must come with me on a sea voyage. It's aboard one of my ships going back to England.'

And that was how I came on board the S.S. *Albion* with Douglas and Amin to see an astonishing sight in the bar.

My dear Rosemary was there and so was my darling Claire! And Bellingham and Davina were quaffing champers too! It was a joy to see Emily Ward-Bishop again. The willowy Lady Alison Utterley and the voluptuous Lady Jane Fortescue were there too as well as the strange Mr Ram Singh and the ship's Captain, good old Jack Rivers. The finest of French vintage champagne was flowing freely.

'Welcome to Albion,' said Douglas.

'Rule Britannia!' Emily exclaimed.

'Britannia rules the waves!' sang Davina.

'Britons never, never, never shall be slaves!' bellowed Bellingham.

'Aboard the Good Ship Venus, perhaps . . .?' Ram Singh murmured.

'Or possibly the Ship of Fools?' Amin Shah suggested.

'Land of Hope and Glory!' Captain Jack Rivers roared.

'Mother of the free . . .' sang Rosemary at strong alto.

'How shall we extol thee?' Claire sang in exquisite soprano. We all paused to recharge our glasses.

'Wider still and wider!' sand Lady Jane.

'Shall thy bounds be set,' Lady Alison chimed in delicately.

'God who made thee mighty,' I sang.

'MAKE THEE MIGHTIER YET!' they all responded; and then we all joined in the rousing chorus of:

God, who made thee mighty,
Make thee mightier yet.

'Speech! Speech!' Sir Richard Bellingham shouted.

'Ladies and gentlemen,' said Douglas. 'It is my pleasure and privilege to welcome you on board. By staying on board, you will enable me to realize a dream which I have for long cherished. I don't know just how many of you have read that wondrous and miraculous book, *Gargantua and Pantagruel* by Rabelais.'

'Who the fuck has, Douglas?' Sir Richard cried out. 'Just tell us your point, old chap, and please, no sermonizing.'

'I was expecting you to say something along those lines, Sir Richard,' Douglas retorted coolly. 'My point is simply that in this book, there is an Abbey of Thelema, the Ancient Greek word for Will, in which the only commandment is: "Do what thou wilt." That is the rule on this voyage from Madras to the Port of London. I trust that you will all find your cabins to be comfortable. There is a double four-poster bed in each one of them. For those of you who might be in the mood for calmer pleasures, there is a good library. Others of you may prefer billiards, cards or quoits and, naturally, there is provision for all of these activities. Deep-sea swimming in the Indian Ocean is a delightful activity; though when we come into colder waters, there is a heated pool in which we can swim or paddle. I trust, furthermore, that my chefs, Abdul of Turkey, Marcel of France and Chang Ku-Wei of China will be able to delight your palates in addition to improving the condition of your stomachs. Then there's Mario, our Italian barman, who will give you any drink you want in whatever quantities you order; and Dr Aziz, the ship's medical officer, who will treat your ailments and also give you as much opium and hashish as anyone could conceivably desire. Absolutely everything upon this ship is voluntary, although one hopes that you might choose to be sociable. If, however, you prefer to stare at life on the ocean wave, read pornography and frig yourself, that is your right too. Any questions?'

'Yes,' said Davina Bellingham. 'Why are you doing this?'

'Oh, I've done so much harm to some people in my life,' Douglas responded, 'that I felt it was about time that I did something good. Horby, will you be joining us for the journey?'

'Yes,' I said. 'Yes.'

CHAPTER TWENTY-FIVE

The arrangements on the S.S. *Albion* proved to be admirable in every respect. One could hardly call my luxurious suite 'a cabin': I delighted in the sight of a huge four-poster bed and noted that there was a crystal chandelier firmly affixed to the ceiling should the rocking and rolling of the ship inspire me to essay experimental sexual positioning. I had thought that my desire to join the boat might be impeded by delays occasioned by the difficulties in transporting my possessions but the Ship's Purser, a Mr Clarke, dealt with my query in a trice, proved to be a model of efficiency and organized the matter immaculately.

Clearly, he was doing the same thing for Bellingham for I saw a steward carrying baskets of birches and canes to his cabin, which adjoined that of Davina.

'Got to have all supplies on board, y'know, Horby,' he chortled, having padded up silently behind me, a brandy in his hand and a cigar in his mouth. 'It'll be a long voyage and so the wife and I may be wanting a good bit of flagellation to pass the time. Anyway, they grow good bamboo out in these parts. After all, we don't want our voyage to be all rhubarb and custody.'

'Ah, Horby!' Douglas exclaimed, joining our company with a glass of champagne in his right hand and a black Russian cigarette tipped with gold reposing within a cigarette holder of ebony he was cradling in his left. 'Everything going all right? We're weighing anchor and casting off at dawn – and let it be a golden dawn – but there'll be scrambled eggs on toast with champers and brandy at the Captain's table for anyone who wants the stuff at 4:00 a.m.'

In fact, all the passengers joined the Captain's table at that hour for refreshment that was absolutely delicious. There I gathered the information regarding the various adventures that had brought us all together, here and now, at this moment. Ram Singh and Claire had travelled together at the former's instigation from Rajasthan to Madras upon the Indian railway built by the British after word had been received from Douglas, who had encountered Claire earlier. Douglas himself had travelled with Emily, Jane and Alison, linking up with Mr and Mrs Bellingham in Bombay and then proceeding by rail to Madras in order to meet Rosemary, who had come by sea from North America.

I felt in the mood for a fuck but I wanted to make sure who was going for whom. Rosemary clearly wanted Douglas and he clearly wanted her. Claire and Emily both competed for my attention. I had wondered whether Claire might be engaged to Ram Singh but he did not seem to be at all put out by her flirtatious behaviour towards me and instead flirted with the blonde and buxom Lady Jane. Amin Shah appeared to have taken quite a shine to Lady Alison. Sir Richard Bellingham appeared to be enjoying his honeymoon with Davina so much that suddenly they slipped beneath the table and commenced a noisy fuck. Nobody batted an eyelid.

'Have you gone below decks and looked out of the portholes?' the willowy Lady Alison asked in her, high, clear, slightly lisping, lilting voice. 'They're absolutely *wonderful!* You can see all these brilliant tropical fish swimming around, eating one another and having what passes for sex.'

'What *passes* for sex?' Douglas queried, as Bellingham humped Davina amidst grunts and groans beneath the round table. 'I think that human beings enjoy it more than fish. But do they? Rosemary, my dear, you've just joined us from the Yukon so perhaps you can tell us all about it?'

'Certainly,' said Rosemary. 'And I might add that I am rather pleased to be heard'. She drank some champagne. 'My sea journey from Anchorage, Alaska to Madras, India was a long and arduous one, as the actress said to the bishop.' She laughed merrily. 'Douglas, you're such an enigma, a dark horse, yet I would not exactly classify you as being a skeleton in the cupboard; even though,' she smiled at us, 'he is still to me a man of mystery.' Douglas remained impassive.

'What can I say about my journey?' Rosemary continued. 'I saw some Pacific grey whales. They are such beautiful creatures. Do you not remember that line from Shakespeare's *Hamlet*: "Very like a whale"; an assent to an absurd statement. At this time I can only reminisce in a retrospection, a rather self-indulgent survey of the recent past, of the Arctic Circle, where the weather is always so bitterly cold. Semi-nomadic peoples do actually live in igloos, relying upon the trapping and trading that will provide them with essentials such as guns, provisions . . . sustenance; the general contents of the larder.

'Sometimes I gazed at the ocean and reflected upon my time in the Yukon. I recall coming across a strange saloon: *Diamond Tooth Gertie's Gambling Hall*, with can-can dancers, beautiful women moving with the tinkling of the piano player's ivories: high kicks with a display of long legs, exposing frilly petticoats. One of the dancers came over and introduced herself, sitting beside me.

' "Hi! My name is Bessie. If you are looking for Wyatt Earp," – which I was, and how did she know? – "he has come and gone." I felt rather disappointed. I did so much want to meet that infamous gunman, the most feared lawman in the West! "But you may never know when he might show up," Bessie told me, adding: "His brother Virgil is sometimes an effective double."

' "What do you mean by that?" I queried.

' "He walks in his brother's boots."

' "How well do you know Wyatt Earp?" I asked.

' "For a while I was employed in his gambling parlour." I could understand why. She had such fine chiseled cheekbones, deep, dark, brown eyes and hair as jet-black as a tar-barrel. "Would you like a drink on the house?" she offered; and I accepted. "I must treat you to the speciality of the house: a Sourtoe Cocktail!"

' "I have never heard of a Sourtoe Cocktail."

' "Not many people have," she responded, "but let me tell you how this drink came into existence. Our winters are extremely cold and you can often suffer from severe frostbite. During an exceptionally cold winter, a miner had his big toe frozen off and so he pickled it in a jar of rum. After the drink is consumed, the toe is returned."

' "I think a glass of rum straight without the big toe will satisfy me," I said.

' "You British are all alike!" she laughed. "You know, at one time I was courted by an Englishman, a poet, the Bard of the Yukon?"

' "Robert Service?" I asked.

' "One of the best – yet I had many other lovers. Shookum Jim, Tagish Charlie and George Washington Carmack."

' "These were the founding fathers of the gold rush,

weren't they? Were they all, in your opinion, rather lusty men?"

' "Yes."

'Darlings,' said Rosemary to us, 'I loved her joviality so much and the way in which she conducted herself with such dignity, elegance and grace without any sign of vulgarity. Unexpectedly, she kissed me upon the lips and I was sensitive to the fact that my cheeks were blushing. "You suffer from *mauvaise honte*," she declared in Quebec French. "Why is it that you British always pretend to be so modest, elusive and oblique?" 'She pronounced it '*oh* blique.'

' "*U*blique," I replied.

' "Like a herring?" she pressed.

' "The *herring* is a way of ascending a slope with one's skis pointed outward."

' "Yes," she replied. "However, the descent is easier than the ascent and I would love to reach your muff."

' "I am not wearing a muff," I responded, even though everyone else in the bar was wearing this fur to keep their hands warm.

' "It is the *other* muff that I want to reach," Bessie retorted, "the soft, fine hair that enhances and adorns the bedizenment of my desires." Escorting me to her apartment, she then gradually and slowly unloosened the stays of my basque, so painfully stiffened by whalebone. Kissing me gently upon the breasts, she gently caressed my papilla to arousal: and how my nipples did stand up! She took each one in turn between lips so soft; and she playfully nibbled upon each, dallying with temptation, incitement and an attraction which plucked upon my very heartstrings. Bait to entrance? I was overwhelmed by her presence, an omnipresence, diffusion with a desire to permeate, pervade, saturate and, in her way, penetrate into my body.

'How she did activate and stimulate my yoni! Ladies, do you not know that exquisite feeling? As her finger entered my vagina, I could feel an uncontrollable tremor between my thighs, a pulsation throbbing to build up a climax to the ultimate orgasm.

' "Let me lick your cunny," she requested softly.

' "On one condition," I replied, "that I can do justice to yours." My tongue slowly penetrated her labia, the colour of incarnadine, brilliant crimson. While I nibbled, she stroked me so gently upon my head, fondling my hair. Suddenly, she took my hands in hers, grasping each in a moment of frenzy.

'I drank her orgasmic fluid with such voracity, possessed by an insatiable, inordinate desire, a thirst that may never be quenched. We then kissed each other upon the lips, savouring the flavour of our exchanged juices and relishing its swallowing with great gusto. Before we fell asleep, I gave her a butterfly kiss upon the cheek.

'She wanted to appear so tough; yet I could discern the tenderness within her heart. In the morning I had to leave and she prepared me coffee in a tin-can kettle. However, I saw a sadness within her eyes.

' "I will miss you," she said. "I have slept with several hundred men, including the most notorious and infamous outlaws; yet I would love to come and visit you in London to attend one of your tea parties."

'I would be pleased to invite her,' said Rosemary, 'but, as I had to inform her, I will not be in London for quite a while. So much for my sojourn within the Arctic Circle: now I wonder how unending another sea journey can be. I am so grateful that I do not suffer from sea-sickness! Anyway, isn't my tale enough for today?'

We all agreed that Rosemary had told us an excellent tale but now there was the question of bed. Despite all the enticing advances of Emily, I could not resist the temptations of Claire. I must confess to a twitching of my private parts, a trustworthy and never-failing indication that she had already begun to arouse the basest carnal desires of which my bachelor nature was capable.

Her body, five feet nine inches in height roughly, was magnificently proportioned for that stature. Her hair was worn then in a popular style of that time: a delicious little fringe of affectatious curls all along the top of her high, arching forehead and a prim, huge oval-shaped bun at the back of her head, which suggested somewhat the semblance of a crown. Perhaps it was symbolic, for surely she would be my Queen of Lust for these hours until we cast off. I vowed to myself that I would have her hair unbound and falling in a glossy sheath against her naked skin before she would be allowed to dress and return to her own cabin.

I noticed that her nose was a trifle snub, which gave her an aspect of disdain, quite in keeping with what I already knew about her. Her nostrils were widely flaring, quite sensuous, as was her mouth, somewhat small with a pronouncedly ripe upper lip that completed the delineation of insolence. Her eyes were a dark, imperious blue, very widely set apart from the bridge of her exquisite nose and surmounted by exaggeratedly thin-plucked eyebrows and extremely short but thick lashes.

During this period, to be sure, it may fairly be said that women wore far too many clothes for the immediate savouring pleasure of one of today's rakes. Myself, I cannot concur. I must admit that it was always delightful to prolong the moment of my conquest by having to remove the many garments turn by turn. This paradox heightened my pleasure a good deal as there was always the element of suspense in wondering just what treasures I should at last espy naked when all the outer conventional costume should be removed and the bare flesh come into ardent view. And from the lady's viewpoint, it was far more thrilling, as her suspense was being constantly augmented until the supreme moment of finding herself Eve-naked in my presence whilst I remained fully clothed.

Seeing Claire dressed at the height of fashion gave extra impulse to my own lust as I recalled her physical charms and delightful curves. I fondly remembered that she had had a somewhat slender waist from which – if her bustle's contours could be faithfully believed – there flared impudently rounded, full and ample hips. Perhaps she did not have so curvaceous a form as Emily Ward-Bishop but she nonetheless gave in every way the prospect of being an absolutely breathtaking morsel of pulchritude when she should finally be stripped down to the indisputable state of helpless nakedness that I meant to exact from her.

'I'm going to be cruel to you,' I told her.

'Oh, simply *soopah!*' she responded. '*When?*'

We excused ourselves from the Captain's table. Jack Rivers beamed benevolently, for he had been casting his eager eyes upon Emily for the past two hours. Sir Richard and Davina continued to hump away beneath the table, blithely oblivious to everything other than the act of fucking. The moment we entered our venue, which was my cabin, I flung Claire down upon the bed and stripped her naked. I unbuttoned my fly to release my stiff cock and simply pranged it into her.

'Oh, Horby . . .' she sighed as we both came together,

'sometimes you can be so crude . . . but it's been such a long time, hasn't it?' She touched my balls and kissed me on the lips. '*Bon voyage*,' she said.

The ship's siren sounded and our boat weighed anchor in the golden dawn as we enjoyed our orgasms.

CHAPTER TWENTY-SIX

'Jolly good show, the British Army!' Sir Richard Bellingham declared. He relaxed in his chair and regarded the glass of fine old Burgundy he was cradling in his hand. We were all now cruising pleasantly in the Indian Ocean and had enjoyed an excellent Lebanese *meze*, a selection of all sorts of tasty dishes prepared well by Abdul. 'And I'm all for the *British* traditions,' Bellingham continued. 'Oh, yes, the public school is a damn fine thing. Those people who didn't go there strike me as being a pretty grisly set of oicks. No manners and what-not.' He dug his fork into a dish of thinly sliced raw beef and crammed it into his mouth, biting on it so hard and with such satisfaction that blood flowed down his chin and had to be wiped away by Davina.

'I gather that your English public schools are very strict,' Amin Shah commented mildly, helping himself to more bread and *tahini*, a delicious dish made out of sesame seeds.

'Oh, yes, Amin, and quite right too,' Bellingham retorted. 'Lots of beating. Why, when I was at school, we used to get six of the best every day. Made me what I am.'

'And what *are* you?' Rosemary enquired.

'Oh, just a bloody fool, Madam, same as all the other men here.' Bellingham seized a plate of prawns and devoured five of them in one mouthful. 'The nature of Man is to penetrate and the nature of Woman is to enclose. This is why we men, although we sometimes make the odd discovery that advances human evolution, usually just carry on making ruddy pricks of ourselves. Let's face it, men are stupid sods and women are silly bitches and if we only were to realize that basic truth, we'd all get along a jolly sight better.'

'Slightly pessimistic, perhaps . . .?' lisped Alison.

'Not at all, my dear.' Bellingham seized a spoon and dug greedily into a bowl of *hummus* – mashed chick peas with yoghurt and spices – and then popped three *falafels* – compressed and fried chick-peas – into his mouth.

'There's only one way to stop Bellingham declaring his opinions,' Douglas observed drily as Bellingham chewed. 'Keep feeding the bloody man!' He helped himself to one of the delicate little pastries which enclouded spiced minced meat with onion. 'But continue with your military theme. One hopes that it might lead to something profitable.'

'Yes,' Ram Singh muttered, 'sales of armaments to under-developed countries.'

'All right,' said Bellingham, 'here's a joke. The Commanding Officer calls in the Regimental Sergeant-Major as the men are on parade. "It's bad news for Private Smith," says the C.O. "His father's just died. Break the news to him, Sergeant Major". So the Sergeant Major goes out onto the Parade Ground and bellows: "Private Smiff!" "Sah!" "Your faver's just died!" Private Smith keels over, has a breakdown and time in hospital but after three months he's back on parade again. The C.O. calls in the Sergeant Major and says: "More bad news for Private Smith, I'm afraid. His mother's just died. Break the news to him, Sergeant Major." So the Sergeant Major goes out onto the Parade Ground and roars: "Private Smiff!" "Sah!" "Yer muvver's just died!" Private Smith keels over, has another breakdown and it's time in hospital for him again. After six months he's finally back on parade. The C.O. calls in the Sergeant Major and says: "Poor old Private Smith doesn't seem to be having too much luck lately. His wife has just died. Break the news to him, Sergeant Major . . . oh, and Sergeant Major . . . *Sergeant Major* . . . I understand there's been a spot of upset in the past. Now, gently does it, Sergeant Major, gently does it. Tact and diplomacy, that's what's required heah." So the Sergeant Major goes out onto the Parade Ground and yells: "All those wiv a wife take one pace for-ward . . . *Smiff*! you 'orrible bleeder, where you fink you're going?'

The women hooted with laughter as the men looked slightly unhappy.

'What is the point of this story?' Ram Singh enquired.

'It's a cruel, hard world,' said Bellingham.

'And you approve of the British Army?' Ram Singh pressed the matter. Bellingham took more Burgundy.

'As the Iron Duke of Wellington said,' he answered, ' "I don't know what they'll do to the enemy but, by God, they frighten me." As he also said "The battle of Waterloo was won on the playing fields of Eton".'

'I see. Officers and men,' Ram Singh responded. 'Somewhat class-ridden, wouldn't you say, Sir Richard?'

'Not at all!' Bellingham snorted dismissively. 'As Wellington said when some upstart tried to embarrass him at a ball with "Good evening, sir. Mr Smith, I believe", he replied: "If you believe that, you will believe anything." '

'Thank you, Sir Richard,' Ram Singh replied. 'You have just shown me precisely why the British Empire has won and now covers one-fifth of the entire globe's land surface.' Bellingham quaffed his wine and nodded approvingly. 'You have also shown me,' Ram Singh continued, 'precisely why it will in due course be lost: in the end, the whole remaining territories will not amount to a greater size than one of your smallest English counties.'

'Oh?' Bellingham raised a quizzical eyebrow. 'And why's that?'

'I think it would be unkind to tell you,' Ram Singh retorted.

'Well, it's no disgrace to be honestly mistaken,' Bellingham replied. 'And you are.'

'Quite right, Sir Richard,' Ram Singh responded with a gentle grin. 'Only time will tell.'

'I suppose that fighting and fucking are the activities in which two people come closest,' Rosemary observed. 'And fighting is all very well, though I find it to be a game for boys. Enough of fighting, Sir Richard! Tell us about some fucking.'

'Gladly, my dear lady,' Bellingham replied. 'Oh, how I lust after a grand fuck!' I noticed that his wife Davina was gazing at him approvingly. 'There can be no male who cannot find the opposite sex fascinating and provocative, who cannot tremble with hardly suppressed excitement at the anticipation of fulfilling all his most lustful whims. I dare say that in each of us, an incipient sadism lingers, product of earlier, less gentle ages when women were slaves and men their lawful masters. Who, for heaven's sake, has not chafed under the scorn of some haughty girl, baffled and raging at the knowledge that no retaliatory move is possible under the code of society that treats the female as being an helpless, weak creature that must be shielded at all costs from villainy and violence? Therefore, I unashamedly admit before you tonight, that in the days before my marriage to my darling lady wife here,' Davina smiled at him, 'a bitch made a fool out of me and I resolved upon revenge.'

'I adore revenge,' Jane murmured dreamily, 'for cruelty is rarely dull.'

'It can be,' said Alison, 'if it is executed without appropriate imagination.'

'I am merely erotically excited,' Emily declared, 'by tales of dominance and submission.' She was sitting at the right hand of Captain Jack Rivers, who looked at her with appreciation and approval.

'The facts are,' said Sir Richard, 'that at one point in my earlier days, I was engaged to the beautiful and charming . . . let's call her Lady Arabella. I had a jolly good chum called . . . well, Lord Horace Somebody, and he was engaged to . . . shall we say Lady Henrietta? Now, a woman I shall call Patricia was a close friend of both of these ladies and Horace and I found her to be exceedingly attractive. Patricia proceeded to seduce me away from my lady love, an heiress, charmed me and after our fuck, swore undying love to me; though I must confess that I wasn't on particularly good sexual form that night. However, I departed feeling utterly infatuated.

'Horace,' Bellingham continued, 'had always sworn to me that he would never make a pass at any woman with whom I was involved. He congratulated me on my success: yet the next thing I knew, and at least he told me to my face, was that *he'd* deserted his affianced for her alleged best friend, Patricia, who had declared her undying love for *him*, and had departed utterly infatuated. I was really rather offended. It all rather spoiled the relationship between Horace and myself; but there was worse to come.

'Patricia, who was called with some truth "the best lay in London" at the time, now endeavoured to blackmail Horace and myself with the indiscreet letters of infatuation we had foolishly written to her. Well, I emulated the

Duke of Wellington in saying: "Publish and be damned." So did Lord Horace; but the consequences were unfortunate. Patricia exacted her vengeance by sending copies of our letters, which revealed sexual acts which our respective affiances would not countenance, to Arabella and Henrietta. I think that probably the most embarrassing moment of my life was when Horace and I were confronted by our intended partners in holy matrimony – heiresses both, I might add – waving these bits of paper in our faces and spitting self-righteous scorn all over our heads. Patricia had furthermore told everyone in London that Horace and I were utterly useless in bed. She nicked-named me "Woody Woodpecker" and she called him "Droopy".' And we had enjoyed a reputation as rake-hells! She had just spun us around her little finger and made of us a pair of clots.

' "I can forgive you for an affair," each lady said to us separately, "but I cannot forgive you for making such an idiot of yourself in public." And so ended two intended marriages which could have been most fortunate.'

'Good,' said Davina Bellingham. 'It would never have worked anyway.'

'Glad that's your attitude, my dear,' Sir Richard responded, 'but I was determined to exact my revenge for this appalling humiliation. I invited Patricia to one of my houses, swearing my own undying love for her, no matter what she had done. It was an invitation to afternoon tea, as I recall, and I had it set before her, all the while behaving with the utmost deference and gentlemanly courtesy. For if you have never had in your home an arrogant and cruel young woman who has treated you as if you were beneath her notice whilst at the same time you are conjuring up visions of her rosy lips deferentially fixed about your manhood, then you cannot begin to understand the riotous images that filled my imagination and the shuddering impulsions which titillated all my nerves and sinews.

'After having poured tea and added cream and demerara sugar to my preference, I seated myself opposite her and fixed upon her the most intent and gracious look it was in my power to muster. An uneasy silence fell over us and then, after a ladylike switching and swishing of her skirt and petticoats, she fixed her dark eyes upon me and declared:

' "What chiefly brought me to agreeing to visit you, Richard, is the inexplicable part of your note to me. I cannot for the life of me understand how you could possess any kind of information about my future happiness, as you termed it, that would be of the least concern to me. Will you please explain your meaning?"

' "Certainly and gladly," I replied, as I put down my tea-cup with a *chink*. "Since we last met, I have developed psychic powers. You're interested in marrying a rich and powerful man, aren't you? Well, if you just close your eyes for a moment and hold out your hands, thinking of the spirit world all the while, I can forecast your future." She smiled slyly and, as if to humour me, closed her eyes and held out her hands. That was all I need to snap on the steel handcuffs; and my butler Robert quietly inserted a large lump of cotton wool within a mouth gaping with astonishment and gagged her with a pair of women's drawers. Her feet kicked out furiously but the two of us soon secured them with black leather thongs. She struggled and twitched to no avail as we carried her downstairs to the chamber I had prepared for the purpose of punishment.

'This chamber consisted of a bare room with an altar upon which reposed a marble statue of Priapus with red-tipped, erect phallus, with a tall white and a tall black candle on either side. Within the centre, there was a flogging-block, purchased from the firm which supplies these to Eton. As you probably know, it's a piece of stout furniture arranged like a low platform with a central "step". Patricia had to kneel on one end, bend across the step and have her hand-cuffs fastened at the other end so that her luscious bottom was elevated to precisely the correct angle. The attached restraining straps of brown leather secured her ankles. I then pulled away her skirt, threw up her petticoats and tore down her silken drawers to expose her pearly white, neat and naughty buttocks, twitching in furious affront and indignity. I removed her gag and she began to shriek and yell and howl.

' "I'll have the Law on you!" she screamed. "I'll ruin you!"

' "Oh, do be quiet; you've already tried to ruin me," I sighed wearily. "Your shouting does no good, Patricia." Now, the hobby of my butler Robert, whose forebears have been with the family for many a generation, happens to be photography. I'd hired a whore called Olivia that night, a pleasant black girl from Jamaica, and she inserted her fingers into Patricia's cunt and shoved her arse against Patricia's face as Robert took photographs.

' "You fucking bastard!" Patricia hissed. Robert and Olivia left the room silently.

' "Shut up, you silly bitch!" I snarled back. "You have endeavoured to blackmail me and now I'm going to do exactly the same thing to you. If there's the slightest sign of misbehaviour from you in the future, copies of the photographs just taken will be circulated among members of Society as proof of your decadent enjoyment of Satanism, black magic and perversion in some low-down Paddington brothel, leading to the ruination of all your marital prospects. And if you manage to find some wealthy pervert of a husband who is actually attracted to you on account of the fact, then they will be circulated as cheap and filthy post-cards for the sniggers of street-urchins."

' "I hate you!" She spat the words.

' "Good!" I exclaimed. "At last we've got something in common! Anyway, my advice to you is simply to submit to your chastisement for all the wrongs that you have done; and if you squawk too loudly, I'll simply double the number of strokes. Now be a good girl and raise your bottom obediently to suffer my just and punitive measures." She continued to writhe in a frenzy and fury and I must say that this made of her pearly white, curvaceous bottom a most appealing sight.

'Now, I decided to use a variety of instruments and there was indeed a method in my madness. As my friends know, I take a great deal of interest in these matters of flagellation. The reason for this lies in the essential natures of the three classes of punitive instrument: smack, cut and lash. To give but one example, a properly administered caning will leave prominent red and blue weals across the lady's stern. These marks last for days and are a necessary part of the terror of the cane but there is, in my view, no point in overdoing it. The answer is, surely, to inflict the second chastisement with another class of weapon, whose effects can safely and usefully be added to those already *in situ* because although it punishes the same target, it does so in a different way and with different emphasis. A bottom lacerated from a recent caning can therefore still be punished if necessary, provided that the second correction is inflicted with a birch, a tawse, a tapette or the palm of one's hand.

'Taking the same line of reasoning a little further, it is

therefore obviously possible to achieve still more variety and choice of disciplinary method when it is realized that two or more different instruments may be used, in succession, during a single chastisement. Instead of ten cane-strokes, do what I did to Patricia, which was to give her a sound spanking followed by three hard swishes of the cane. Let's face it, a bottom well reddened beforehand by a lusty encounter with a strong hand will be in even more sensitive condition to receive a few whippy strokes from a good, flexible cane.

'As it was, I could see that my loud and heavy spanking, each slap of which echoed throughout the chamber, ensured that her bottom was well-reddened and twitching, wearing thin my delinquent's reserves of energy and endurance and causing her to sob her apologies. As a result, the number of concluding stripes could be confined to a minimum for the sake of remembrance. I am not a cruel man; but I do enjoy attention to detail and an appreciation of nuance.

'When it comes to caning, I'm a great believer in "three-inch grooving". By that, I mean that the stripes should be confined to the three-inch zone at the centre of a woman's bottom, with one strip at each inch. Patricia howled and squealed as I lashed her twitching red bum at each one of them: ho! ho! Again she sobbed out her apologies for her shabby behaviour and promised that she would never conduct herself in such a shameful manner ever again. For my own part, I stepped back to enjoy the sight of her scarlet bottom, formerly so snow-white, trembling and wriggling and writhing on account of its weals and stripes whilst strapped helplessly to the flogging block. Oh, yes! There's a real pleasure in watching a flogged girl's bottom change its colours – better than watching a sunset.

302

'It's very erotic, so I took out my stiff prick and shoved it up a helpless cunt that had become wonderfully moist in the course of her chastisement. I took only a few thrusts and then I came quite gloriously. Yet when I stepped back and saw her glowing bottom changing colour, well, I just had the hots for her again. This time I shoved it right up her burning arse, I can tell you, and I groaned in the sheer ecstasy of my come as she squealed. Afterwards, I had my servants untie her, give her a bubble bath and send her on her way.'

'What happened to her?' I asked.

'Oh, she'd learned her lesson,' Sir Richard retorted. 'And she's since proceeded to marry a very rich, boring old fart.'

'Oh, Richard!' His wife Davina burst out laughing. 'Sometimes I just don't know whether you're a complete fool or the Devil himself!'

'If you're going to be a fool,' said Bellingham, 'make sure you spell it with a capital "F" and be a Great Fool.'

CHAPTER TWENTY-SEVEN

'You're obviously fond of games, Sir Richard,' Ram Singh said as the port came round. The ladies had withdrawn for coffee and liqueurs and probably also to get away from the men.

'Very much so,' Bellingham replied. 'And my favourite game is called "Jenkins." Every player gets a bottle of Scotch and has to drink it standing up in one go. The last one left standing up is Jenkins.'

'And what is the point of that?' Amin Shah enquired.

'What's the point of anything, my dear fellow?' Sir Richard retorted. 'I mean, what do you chaps do to enjoy yourselves?'

'I once gave quite an interesting dinner-party,' said Douglas. 'Electricity was wired to every seat of the eight snobs I had invited. Every time that any snob committed the slightest breach of dinner-party etiquette, he or she received an unpleasant and jolting electrical shock.'

'And how did your guests take it?' Ram Singh asked.

'They were all very shocked,' said Douglas.

'Serve them right,' Ram Singh as he seized the decanter of excellent vintage port, poured it out expertly with his right hand and passed it along to me. It was a perfect accompaniment to matured Stilton cheese with thin Captain's Biscuits, although, as Jerome K. Jerome has said, 'I mean the biscuits were thin, not the Captain.'

'Too many of the English people who come out to India are bloody fools,' said Captain Jack Rivers. 'I mean in the old days, it was actually the youngest sons of the gentry and the aristocracy trying to make their fortunes through trade. They had respect for the culture of India, which was a civilized society when us lot . . . hell's bells, we were just running around with blue woad on our faces yelling: "Wogga! Wogga! Wogga!" But the sons of our upper class understood that, which is why they often intermarried with the Indian upper class and came home sailing as enriched *nabobs* or *nobs*.' Ram Singh and Amin Shah nodded approvingly. 'The problem arose, in my opinion, with those bloody middle-class public schools and their bloody missionary Christianity.'

'Quite right, Captain,' Ram Singh responded. 'They had no respect at all for our culture, when they came out here. The missionaries tried to convert us to their wretched religion of sin and guilt. The only ones who went along with them were the Untouchables, the filth, slime and scum.'

'No one is an Untouchable in my religion,' Amin Shah declared, 'but there is no notion of sin or guilt in Islam. You bear your Fate with manly fortitude. We call it *kismet*. And,' he glanced approvingly at Ram Singh, 'the Hindus call it *karma*. It is essentially the same thing regarded from two different angles. Which apex of a triangle is the "correct" one? And who would choose to exchange this sense for Christian missionary nonsense?'

'No one,' Ram Singh answered, 'except a slave. Another mistake that's been made by the British Empire has been to send out their middle-class women. For a start, they cannot stand the climate. Nor can their husbands, who become impotent. The English women, meanwhile, who itch for sex, eventually allow themselves to be seduced by Bengali servants. In consequence, the entire mystique of the Great White Sahib vanishes altogether. The Bengali servant boasts of his conquests and the white man and woman become, not subjects of veneration, but objects of ridicule. Then the missionaries come and inform us that we should convert to their primitive, tribal beliefs. Frankly, Sir Richard, Lord Horby, Mr Douglas and Captain Jack Rivers, the average inhabitant of the Indian sub-continent much prefers your swaggering swashbuckling swankiness, which will leave him alone, to the mealy-mouthed moralizing of the mentally retarded missionary.'

We white men all raised our glasses to toast that.

'Please understand,' said Ram Singh, 'how you chaps came to conquer India: it *suited* us. India absorbs all its conquerors. You ruled a country of many millions with just your proverbial "thin red line". Many of us wanted that for we thought that we could learn certain things from you. And we did: your technology, for example. Your rule gave us efficient railways and civic transportation. You made the waters clean, cured disease and, insofar as you could, you made sure that the hungry might be fed. Your system of Justice could not be bribed, an unusual phenomenon for us, and although, of course, your courts always found in favour of an Englishman, which we expected, you nevertheless were utterly fair and impartial between our various castes in Hinduism, between Muslim and Sikh, between Parsee and Jain. This is why, when the British Raj ends, we will still like you and want to make friends.'

'Oh, steady on a minute,' Bellingham protested. 'I think you're quite wrong there, Ram. You're talking about the British Empire upon which the sun never sets, y'know.'

'It *will* set, sir,' Ram Singh answered, 'within roughly fifty years.'

'Bah! Humbug!' Bellingham snorted and tossed back his glass of port. 'Shall we join the ladies?' He followed that statement with a colossal sneeze into his scarlet silken handkerchief.

We all gave him a good 'Bless you!' and I must admit that at the time, I thought that Ram Singh, good chap though he was, was talking absolute bloody nonsense. Today, however, (1925), looking at the situation in India and reading about those curious fellows, Gandhi and Jinnah, and learning of all the agitation for independence, I have to admit that he may well have foreseen something which may be coming.

'Let us eat, drink, and be serious; hardly a recipe for a good time, is it?' I murmured as we joined the ladies – only to take a pace backwards in shocked surprise. Our eyes were greeted by a scene of sheer debauchery. Lady Alison had her head very much inside the voluminous skirts of Lady Jane, whose head lolled backwards with her pale cheeks flushing as she moaned softly in her rapture, twirling her high heel of her shining leather boot upon the back of Alison's white, satin blouse. They occupied a sofa. Rosemary and Claire had declined to take a love-seat and were sitting back-to-back. This looked perfectly proper until one realised that the left hand of each one was buried deeply within the other one's skirts and that they weren't sighing and groaning and panting on account of the beauties of the view. Emily had had her corset unlaced by Davina, who had released her full breasts and was licking and sucking at her nipples.

'Men sorting out the world can be such a bore . . .' Rosemary sighed as she came to orgasm.

'That's a statement that's all very well,' Douglas

responded coolly. 'Gentlemen, I have the feeling, some-how, that the ladies always find us a bore unless we have stiff pricks. And don't we find it a bore when we haven't?'

'Oh, well, I've got one,' Bellingham declared. 'Davina, d'you want to fuck with me or with some prick-less bitch?'

'Both . . .' Davina sighed dreamily, then melted into a warm and loving embrace in Emily's arms as her caresses brought off the latter.

'It seems to me,' Amin Shah remarked, 'that for these particular ladies, only the best will do.'

'YEAH!!!' they all screamed out with a ferocity some might have found to be positively frightening: but by this time I was used to the many moods and modes of Woman; and the sight before my eyes granted me much delight. I was about to approach Claire when the boat rocked and rolled so alarmingly that the ladies were all deposited sprawling upon the floor.

'Oh, hell,' said the Captain. 'I can sense a typhoon coming. If we're going to get through this one, I'll have to be at the helm. Kindly excuse me.'

The ship shuddered again and the women ceased their lascivious activities and looked alarmed. There was a howl of wind so loud that we were all aware of it within our chamber of pleasure and especially since a wave made all our bottles and glasses roll over and crash on the floor. I seized Claire in my arms, Bellingham grabbed Davina, Ram Singh and Amin Shah separated Jane and Alison; and Emily announced that she would be going to the assistance of the Captain.

'Oh, damnit!' Rosemary shouted as another big wave caused her glass to crash over and she fell into the arms of Douglas. 'We haven't got anything to drink!'

'No problem!' Bellingham cried out. 'I'll just get a

bottle from good old Mario in the bar!' Unfortunately, the next wave was so heavy that as Bellingham tried to walk, he missed his step and was flung across the room. 'Take more than that to knock me out,' he muttered through gritted teeth as he hauled himself to his feet and staggered forward on unsteady pins. 'Brandy!' he exclaimed defiantly, 'that's the way to get through a typhoon!'

The ship lurched as much as Bellingham as the man made his exit. I looked out of the window and saw a raging sea whose huge waves were washing up on deck and which were threatening to engulf and swallow our tiny ship.

'If the typhoon and the ocean are going to drown us all,' Jane declared in her plummy voice, 'why can't it be done now rather than keeping us all in suspense? Anyway, I'm going to go down fucking. You up to it, Ram Singh? Or is *Ram* a misnomer?'

'Not at all, my dear lady,' he answered. 'Let us fuck and die together.' Thereupon they fell down upon the floor, utterly oblivious to the stormy weather. Jane shrieked out her joy as he tore up her silken skirts with one hand, unbuttoned his fly with the other and then pronged her with his great big fucking whanger of a rod.

The boat tilted so sharply that I lost my balance and fell flat on my face. I was up in a trice, only for a heave of the mighty sea to send me flying into the arms of Claire. As I lay upon her breast, I saw Amin Shah sitting calmly in a chair with Alison on her knees before him sucking his stiff cock.

'Hmmm, rather like a lollipop, isn't it?' she mused in between sucks and licks. 'Oh, well, if I'm going to die at sea, I might as well die well.' Thence she returned eagerly to renewed cocksucking, her mouth and thin lips clinging on so hard to his prick that she was still hanging on for dear life when the next wave and the roll of the boat threw him out of his chair.

'Either we die or we don't,' Douglas was saying to Rosemary. He had pulled up her skirt and petticoats and pulled down her drawers; they were now fucking. 'Let's just move as the ocean takes us. If we die, it will be the *mors justi* – the death of the righteous in our noble act of fucking.'

'And if we don't die,' Rosemary returned as the boat rocked quite hideously, 'it will be the life of the righteous in the noble act of fucking.'

'Where *is* that bloody man of mine?!' Davina shrieked as the next wave made her chair tumble over, leaving her sprawling on the floor. At that moment, a member of the crew staggered into the room looking like a drowned rat.

'No one on deck!' shouted Able Seaman Higgins. 'Captain's orders!'

'D'you think we're all fools, same as you?' I asked.

'Oh, frigging in the rigging . . .' Davina sighed as she masturbated openly upon the floor as the ship swayed perilously. 'There's fuck all else to do.'

'Quite right, Madam,' I said; then knowing it could be the last fuck in my life, I hurled Claire down upon the floor, ripped down her drawers, buried my head inside her skirts and kissed, licked and sucked at her gorgeous, pouting cunny lips, with my tongue coming to tickle her clitoris. Thinking that if I were to suffer the dismal fate of being drowned at sea, I might as well go out with a bang, I prodded my rod into the gorgeous vagina of this girl, swiving her back and forth until death seemed really rather irrelevant. She gasped and sighed as I pounded her pudenda. I whirled my prick all the way around her cunt as the ship swayed, at one moment so violently that we were hurled against the room's wall. The winds screeched and the waves tossed us forth as we came together in sensational ecstasy.

A period of calm followed as we held one another close and tight. Was it the eye of the typhoon, in which case more would be coming that might be worse; or had we just sailed into one of its circles? None of us knew the upshot of the issue. We hoped to high heaven that nobody had been washed overboard as Able Seaman Higgins led us up to the forecastle. There we discovered Emily Ward-Bishop fiercely gripping the wheel as Captain Jack Rivers was giving it to her up the arse. None of us criticized him for his effective method of steering us through a storm: but where was Sir Richard Bellingham?

We all searched high and low, praying that the high seas hadn't taken him in a fit of absence of mind: and we eventually found him way below decks in a cabin that must once have been used to amuse the children of passengers. He had his dick in his hand and was singing softly to himself as he held a bottle of brandy in his other hand and swayed gently back and forth upon a rocking-horse.

CHAPTER TWENTY-EIGHT

It soon became evident that we had weathered the storm, owing to the Captain's unorthodox but excellent manner of steering the ship. Yet our perils were not yet over. On the following morning as we were all playing quoits on deck, suddenly a pirate ship appeared on the horizon.

'Piracy on the high seas?' I queried. 'In this day and age?'

'Oh, yes,' Captain Jack Rivers replied jovially, having just won money from Douglas at quoits. 'The South China Seas are still infested with pirate ships. It's less common in the Indian Ocean, but it happens. They see a passenger ship such as this one and they espy easy pickings.'

'And what do they do?' Alison enquired nervously.

'They ram the ship,' said Rivers, 'or else they board it via long-boats. Then they kill all the men and rape all the women, after which they throw 'em overboard down to Davey Jones's locker. If the ship's better than theirs, they take it over.' There was a pause while this information sank in. Everyone was trying very hard to keep calm.

'Could we simply out-speed them?' Rosemary enquired.

'Not as far as I can see,' the Captain replied. 'Here,' he held up a spy-glass. 'Take a look for yourself. It's hardly the colourful pantomime Jolly Roger.'

'How exciting!' Emily exclaimed. 'I do hope they'll be a good fuck.'

'Stop being such an idiot, Madam!' Captain Jack Rivers roared at her. 'Don't you realize that once they've fucked you they'll simply slit your throat? Meanwhile us men will have our balls cut off and stuffed in our mouths before they drown us.'

I took a look through the spy-glass and my blood ran cold. I don't think I have ever seen a more evil band of ill-intentioned cut-throats. I resolved to sell my life dearly.

'Any weapons aboard, Captain?' I asked.

'Pistols and cutlasses, that's what we need!' Bellingham declared. 'And we'll cane these savages yet!' The captain responded by having Able Seaman Higgins distribute precisely these weapons to all of us as the pirate ship drew nearer. I braced myself for the forthcoming conflict, resolved either to do or die.

'I admire your calm,' I said to the Captain. The women were visibly nervous. They knew that their men were no cowards and were resolved to fight until the last breath: but would we survive against a pack of professional pirates who vastly outnumbered us?

'You'll soon see why, Lord Horby,' Jack Rivers replied. At that moment, Able Seaman Higgins wheeled a cannon onto the deck and positioned it, peering through a gap. 'You see, I wouldn't sail these seas without one of these.' Actually it wasn't a cannon in the Nelson style: it was more the sort of field gun used in the Great War to come. The pirate ship fired a few shots which landed in loud splashes a few hundred yards away from us. Emily squealed, realizing that it wasn't a game any more. 'Bloody fools,' Jack Rivers muttered. 'They're way wide of the mark.' He lit his curved briar pipe. 'No idea of range at all.' He slightly adjusted the barrel of the gun. I

314

stared at the steam-ship heading toward us. 'They still can't hit us,' he murmured, 'but now's the time to hit *them*'. He fired the gun. The shell smacked straight into the engine room of the enemy and their ship blew up in a whirl of smoke and flame.

I don't know how many died at that moment or after, when the ship was sinking slowly, but the pirates were resourceful. Now it was their turn to do or die and they swiftly abandoned ship and piled into long-boats, brandishing pistols and cutlasses, rowing in a zig-zag pattern that made of their vessels an elusive set of targets. The Captain fired three times and missed, swearing heavy oaths and uttering imprecations. The women gripped their swords and pistols fiercely but grew more visibly nervous.

'No problem at all,' Douglas said coolly from behind us. We turned to see him carrying one of those (then) new-fangled machine guns. 'As the poet has it:

Whatever happens, we have got
The Gatling Gun, and they have not.'

Captain Jack Rivers helped him to set it up on the ship's rail. I watched with fascination as Douglas smoked a cigar and waited for the pirates' long boats to come closer, yawning like a lazy cat as their pistol shots failed to find us and plonked in the water, at least a hundred yards short of the distance. At a nod from Douglas, the Captain proceeded to turn the handle of this ingenious machine and the former pressed the trigger. A volley of bullets drilled holes in the pirate boats and killed a few more blood-bespattered victims.

'But now, and as I like to say, Ladies First!' Douglas declared and we could all see that the pirate boats were slowly sinking. One by one, Rosemary, Claire, Jane,

Alison, Davina and Emily stepped up to the Gatling and pressed the trigger as the Captain cranked the handle. It was really rather like going on a pheasant shoot. Anyway, the women bagged the whole bloody lot of them and afterwards hooted with delight. By the end, there was a ship slowly sinking and two long boats already sunk, with all men dead and spreading skeins of blood in the water.

'Splendid shooting, ladies!' Bellingham bellowed. 'As I've always maintained, *English* women are absolutely top-hole!'

It was a dark and stormy night indeed as we all sat down to dinner but a gale was considered a mere flurry following from the typhoon and the endeavours of the pirates who had been literally blown out of the water by superior Western technology, if that's the right term. I keep hearing it used more and more these days (1925). Marcel was on duty as chef and he gave us the delights of fish in the Indian Ocean as a *bouillabaisse*, a fish stew that was absolutely fabulous. We greedily chewed, licked and sucked meaty morsels of crab, lobster, crayfish, prawns and hefty slabs of sea-bass after which we slurped the soup.

The next course was *steak tartare*, raw minced fillet of beef with spices and capers and crowned with a raw egg, served with a multifarious variety of breads: dry toast, rye, granary, white, black, brown and so on. All of us relished the matter of feasting after a good kill. We then ate lambs' tongues and lambs' kidneys in an exquisitely delicious sauce of cream and brandy and herbs. The cheese board was tremendous: *always* have the cheese board, I say, *provided* that the chef is French. This was followed by a delicate apple tart with cream, which proved to be delicious.

We were all as happy over coffee and brandy as people

who have just fought off a pirate ship can be. Naturally, the matter had affected us: I saw that Ram Singh was going after the willowy, lisping Alison whereas Amin Shah now wanted the plummy-voiced, buxom Jane. Claire seemed to be besotted by the bravery of Captain Jack Rivers, who had steered us through two crises, and Emily was sucking up to me, so much so that she had unbuttoned my fly and was indeed sucking my stiff cock beneath the table. This was hardly bad etiquette at the Captain's table since Douglas had plunged his head beneath the skirts of Rosemary, who was sighing with pleasure as he licked her cunt and sucked her clit. Sir Richard and Lady Bellingham promptly fell down beneath the table yet again and commenced fucking like a pair of pigs. I therefore put Emily upon my lap, whipped up her skirt and petticoats to discover an ingenious slit within her silken knee-length knickers, and prodded my rod into her. As I came, the world seemed to explode before me; and as I came *to*, I noticed that Jack Rivers was exploding within the loins of Claire, whose own loins were astride him.

'I don't think we're doing too badly.' A sweaty Bellingham arose from beneath the table and helped himself to copious quantities of biscuits, butter, Stilton and port. Davina arose and brushed down her skirts demurely. 'Fighting and fucking! That's when two people come closest!' he declared. 'Mind you, I'd rather fight *with* a good man on the same side rather than *against* him: but when it comes to a good woman, I just want to fuck her!' Davina burst out laughing. 'D'you hear her?' he demanded. 'I do. And I tell you, if a man doesn't listen to his wife, he's just a bloody fool. If his reason for not doing so is that he claims that she's thick, why then, he's a *double* bloody fool for having married her in the first place.'

'Quite agree,' said Douglas. 'And that's why I think it's pointless to have separation of the male and the female at this table tonight. Let's all compose ourselves with all due decorum. We've heard stories told by Rosemary here and by Sir Richard; but Emily, my dear, surely it is your turn. How is the Society for the Promulgation of Petticoat Government?'

'It is *thriving*,' Emily replied. 'Why, just before I left England to enjoy this intriguing journey, I enjoyed the occasion of accompanying Mrs Joan Smythe on a visit to the marital home of two of her former pupils: Lady Charlotte and young Jeremy, her husband.'

'We were there!' Lady Jane chortled as Lady Alison smirked.

'Oh, indeed,' replied the Hon Emily Ward-Bishop, 'and your presence added greatly to my own joy. Well!' she continued animatedly, 'Jeremy and Charlotte have a stately home in Sussex. And that's just where we went. Jeremy's ancestral hall has become a shrine to Petticoat Rule. The four of us women were greeted by a maid and ushered into a drawing-room where Charlotte was seated. Behind her stood her husband Jeremy, looking *so* sweet in his skirt and *so* charming as he executed a perfect curtsey to us. We sat down to sip rare *fino* sherry and delighted in the sight of this formerly arrogant youth now reduced to petticoated servitude.

' "Jeremy has been a very naughty boy today," said Charlotte. "I was awaiting your arrival so as to punish him publicly. I really cannot *bear* his impertinence and insolence. Jeremy, you will bend over that chair, lift up your skirt and petticoats, lower your drawers and bare your bottom!" His bottom! I have long ago come to the conclusion that the cruellest part of the punishment of a man by a woman is that she invariably whips the bottom

and delights in it. It is so shameful for him, so ignomini-
ous, so utterly degrading, so *absolutely humiliating*. In
that, too, we ladies delight and glory. There are very few
women who do *not* delight in the idea of whipping; the
sense of complete power and the joy of acutely punishing
the animal nature of the male has to us an irresistible
attraction.' She laughed throatily. 'There are none who
have once wielded a birch against a man's arse who do not
consider it the most exquisite pleasure they can have, one
which they ever after perpetually love to enjoy. It is a
pleasure I regard as being essentially feminine.

' "Kneel down, Jeremy," Charlotte commanded, "Kiss
the birch that I have had pickled in my urine especially for
my attention to your bottom – isn't it neat and soft and
sweet, ladies? – and now kiss my hand." He had been
schooled into obedience and so this slim and delicate
young man trembled, obeyed and began to sob. "Now
say: 'Madam Charlotte, my darling lady wife, will you
favour me by birching my bare bottom for being naughty?
Please give me six of the best for that; and another six for
the audacity of having been under your petticoat." ' He
sobbed out the humiliating words as we girls just giggled.

' "What is the particular piece of insolence on account
of which you are punishing him?" I enquired.

' "He had the sheer impertinence," Charlotte replied
indignantly "to express the wish that he might some day
be 'emancipated' and *freed from the petticoat!*'

' "Shocking!" we all declared in chorus.

' "Precisely," said Charlotte. "His wickedness all arises
from his masculine garments. In consequence, I have
deprived him of them. My husband has to wear a skirt
before me. He is also subject to the regime of the corset
and the stay-lace." How we all tittered and how flushed
our faces became! Peradventure we might desire males

that we could put into petticoats.

' "Speaking of petticoats," Charlotte continued as her husband's small, tight bottom trembled at the thought of her impending wrath, "can anyone here lend me one?"

' "Oh, you darling girl!" Mrs Joan Smythe exclaimed. "I think you're probably my prize student. Oh yes, I can certainly spare one. I put on two this morning as it was so cold but they can be too much and I shall be glad to sacrifice one to productive usage."

'As it happened, Jane, Alison and I had also put on two petticoats that morning and now were only too pleased to take off and offer one to Charlotte. I'd forgotten to put on any knickers that day and so mine was soaked in my erotic juices and I strongly suspect that the same was the case for the other ladies present. Charlotte smiled graciously on receiving our four moistened petticoats, reeking with femininity, then slipped off one of her own. Mine was soft, white and silken; Joan's was of red flannel, trimmed with white lace; Alison's was of yellow satin; Jane's was of royal blue; and Charlotte's was of a stiffly starched white linen that crackled.

'Charlotte proceeded to make a bag out of them, warm and redolent with the juices of our femininity. She then slipped them over the head and face of Jeremy. There he knelt, this formerly arrogant and insolent young prick, his drawers around his ankles, his skirt and petticoat that he had to wear before his wife tucked up above his trembling bottom, cruelly exposed for the amusement and delectation of the ladies.

'Charlotte tapped his slender, firm bottom with her birch, commanding him to raise it higher. She proceeded to lash it in a way that made it smart and burn for our amusement. This wealthy, young and handsome young man twisted, writhed and howled before us with the petticoats, multi-coloured, of five women smothering his head, face and shoulders.

'This chastisement had the advantage of permitting me to observe closely the lovely forms of the fair disciplinarians and Charlotte's graceful movements as her birch rose and descended. I'm sure that the pain was very hard for Jeremy to bear and the worse it was, the more we tormentors smiled and enjoyed it. I held my breath. *Swish!* And the blow descended. The first few strokes were given with great precision and very scientifically from both sides, well over the whole of his bottom, which I'm sure was so thoroughly warmed that it felt on fire. Charlotte then asked Joan Smythe to pass her a fresh birch, which Joan smilingly supplied.'

'The sight of the weals rendered me quite furious with lust,' Lady Jane confessed as her ample bosom heaved.

'Oh,' said Lady Alison, 'I just kept frigging myself because I *so* like to see a man's pink bottom twitching beneath a lady's birch. The petticoats were then removed.'

'The succeeding strokes,' Emily went on excitedly, 'were divided into a particular punishing of each buttock; and the birch was very elastic – it had been well soaked and each one of the strokes made Jeremy's bottom jump. He sobbed out his apologies as his lady wife gave him permission to stand up and curtsey to the ladies. I noticed that his prick was upstanding, as if, despite the punishment, it still wanted to tear through the feminine frills which enshrouded it. The French maid, Hortense, looking rather dishy in her silken black dress with a white frilly apron, entered to present Jeremy's fishing rods to Charlotte.

' "A petticoated male," Charlotte snapped, "has no use for such things." She broke the beautiful, delicate rods across her knee and, striking her husband's cheeks with the fragments, ordered them to be used for firewood. "I have packed and sold your guns to a secondhand dealer," she declared sniffily. "In future, you will sit and sew and you will embroider my name, CHARLOTTE, the name of your wife, upon the petticoats that you will forever wear." '

'Oh, it was *such* a pretty piece of petticoating,' Alison sighed.

'And more, as you may well remember,' Emily said. 'Then Joan Smythe gave Jeremy a special present, with his wife's permission. Long, very tight suede gloves, twelve buttons each, were put by her upon her former pupil's hands and arms. A thread was wound around the buttons and sealed with a little gold seal, pinned to the wrist and bearing the coat of arms of her family.'

'And more than that!' Jane looked as though she were about to enjoy an orgasm. 'His corset and stay laces were secured by a small padlock, so that they could never be removed without his wife's explicit permission; and she wore the key on her pearl necklace, dangling just within the groove of her cleavage.'

'Lord Jeremy then had to go and stand in the corner,' Alison reminisced; 'face to the wall, knickers around his ankles, his gloved hands holding up his skirt and petticoats to reveal his scarlet glowing bottom, well whaled and wealed. We ladies took tea and admired the sight of this strong young male's firm buttocks changing colour. We gossiped and chatted and then agreed with his wife Charlotte that he should be given permission to pull up his drawers and lower his petticoats and skirt, provided that he crossed his hands behind his back and that our own petticoats were once more placed over his face as a token of female supremacy. Gosh! aren't we such bitches when we have a male cornered?!'

'Absolutely,' Jane declared firmly and approvingly. 'And as I recall it, Charlotte said: "Men are such pompous, vain creatures. But consider the shame of a man having the most animal part of him flogged by a girl!"'

'What degradation!' Emily laughed. 'But I think a husband should be perfectly helpless before his wife, turned up like a baby and spanked as she might choose in her good pleasure. It takes the conceit and nonsense out of a man. The worst part for a man of being whipped by a woman is clearly not the suffering; it is the power she thence derives over him by means of the exposure and by the experience of the pain she can inflict and the intimate relationship into which this places her, as she looks disdainfully at his abject condition. Why, she can never regard him as any sort of lord and master when she has made him twist and turn under the anguish of her lashes and when he knows that over his bottom, she can always brandish the rod.'

'What man,' Jane demanded, 'could hold his own with the woman who at any moment might say publicly: "Just wait until we get home and then I shall birch your bottom!"'

'The holy sceptre of the birch cannot be defied,' said Alison. 'And I recall Charlotte's words about her husband, young Lord Jeremy: "Sometimes, if it is my whim, he has to kiss my quim. For quite two hours I insist upon being pleased and amused thus. This is my construction of conjugal rights and the bondage is the most severe imaginable; there is no escape." Quite right, too!'

'Then,' Emily took up the thread of her tale, 'Jeremy was released from his corner. He had to curtsey to the ladies again and he did so with a huge, pulsating erection protesting as well as projecting through his skirt. Oooh!

what a sight! His face was as crimson as his bottom! then he was sent upstairs to dress for a vote at the House of Lords. Charlotte's maid attended to his *toilette*. He is always compelled to wear, underneath his male clothes, Charlotte's lingerie: long stockings and a tight corset; also a penis cage which permits erection and urination but which can only be unlocked for sexual purposes by his wife. This attire has a most subjugating effect upon him but it has made of him a complete dandy. We ladies love to flirt with a petticoated male and he is the envy of many men whose wives are always twitting them over being outshone by Jeremy.'

'The division-lists in the papers must be a perpetual nuisance to him,' Jane said maliciously. 'Charlotte always knows how he votes and he has to vote as Her Ladyship pleases. I was there on one occasion when he didn't. "You disobeyed!" Charlotte exclaimed, looking most uncommonly beautiful. "You disobeyed *me*! I don't care for Government whips or for any other whips except my own. Bend over *at once*! And Jane, kindly be my witness to this punishment." '

'Well, I've always been a good one for great games!' Bellingham exclaimed. 'And if the result is that my old chum, Lord Jeremy, consistently votes for more enlightened and libertarian measures, as he does, then so much the better for petticoat rule. Anyway, what's wrong with a good spot of fladge, eh? Let's all have some more brandy.'

Our revels were rudely interrupted by the abrupt intrusion of a stranger who was literally armed to the teeth, for he carried a dagger in his mouth, a pistol in one hand and a sword in the other. Clearly he was a pirate who had survived the battle.

'Good evening,' said Douglas. 'Why don't you just throw down your weapons and join us at our table for something good to eat and drink?'

This idiot responded by firing his pistol at Douglas but it misfired and went *phut*! Debate still rages among us as to who drew first and shot most accurately but no one denies that amidst this devil's Dozen, we all drew our guns, cocked their hammers and squeezed the triggers; and that there were twelve bullets in the body thrown unceremoniously overboard.

'The clitoris and the penis,' I observed as the ladies and gentlemen placed their smoking guns upon the dinner-table. 'Now: are we going to shoot each other or fuck instead?'

CHAPTER TWENTY-NINE

I have noticed that women love to swish their skirts and push out their bottoms after a particularly bloodthirsty triumph and this night was no exception. Some men tell me that they are frightened by both the manner and the matter: but to me it is simply an erotic sight that is worth seeing; and even worth going to see.

'Has anyone read the tales of Dauntless Dick?' Captain Jack Rivers demanded; and a number of us nodded for we had occasionally read of his exploits on purchasing the London *Evening News*. 'In one episode, Dauntless Dick is captured by the evil villain and hung by heels upside-down over a vat of sulphuric acid. His limbs are secured by chains as he hangs from a rope with a gas-jet flame burning through it. "Ha! ha!" the villain laughs. "Farewell, Dauntless Dick!" and the episode ends with the villain leaving the room and Dauntless Dick hanging by a thread over a vat of acid; and this thread is about to be burned through. Can anybody guess how the author solved the problem of getting Dauntless Dick out of this one?' We all shook our heads and waited for a relation of a masterpiece of writer's ingenuity. 'The next episode in the ensuing edition began,' said Jack Rivers; "With one mighty bound, Dauntless Dick was free!" Anyway, I've had enough of all this petticoat government!' And with one mighty bound, the Captain had seized Emily, thrown up her skirts and petticoats, pulled down her drawers and was noisily fucking her under the table.

'Ram Singh,' Douglas addressed him coolly, 'you're usually so silent; but do you have an erotic experience in your past with which you would like to regale us?'

'There was a most interesting one, Douglas,' Ram Singh replied as Jack humped Emily and she cried out her joys, 'On my last visit to London I entered a Circle Line carriage of the Metropolitan, District and Circle Line at Victoria Underground Railway Station, my destination being High Street Kensington. Unfortunately, the carriage was exceedingly crowded, and there were many women who could not find a seat. I found myself standing behind a most attractive and enticing Englishwoman. She was tall with a slender waist but a full figure, clad in a most delectable walking costume of black satin and wearing a black hat with a lace veil. Her gorgeous bottom threatened to split the skirt of her suit and her head was adorned by glossy blonde hair. The very sight of her gave me, I must confess, an instant erection.

'Now,' Ram Singh continued, 'normally I would never molest a woman, and I would certainly not make sexual advances to one I had never met before and who was simply standing in front of me in a crowded carriage on the Underground Railway. However, the train suddenly lurched, I was thrown back against the strut to which I was clinging and she lost her balance and it was she who fell back against me, her bottom inadvertently pressing itself upon my rampaging erection. I had expected her to jump away quickly but instead, she screwed the cleavage of her buttocks onto my erection with a slight wiggle. The wool of my trousers and the satin of her skirt were preventing full, fleshly contact, of course, yet she showed temporarily no desire to move. She moved away only when the train reached Sloane Square, but she did not leave the carriage.

'I stood up and, as the train moved on, the carriage being still as crowded as before, took the risk of allowing my stiff penis to brush against that gorgeous bottom, swathed so tightly in her smooth and shining satin skirt. She responded by pressing her arse against my rod all the way to South Kensington. On the journey to Gloucester Road, she softly rubbed her bottom against my prick. None of the other passengers had the slightest idea as to what was transpiring; and my impression of her face, which she kept turned away from me, was confined to its reflection in the glass windows of the carriage.

'The feeling of her gorgeous bottom rubbing against my trousered prick was quite exquisite and I came, endeavouring to disguise the matter with all due decorum; though I did emit a sigh. Seconds later, I distinctly heard *her* sigh and I felt her bottom, thighs and legs tremble. We left the carriage together at High Street Kensington, mounted the steps, handed in our tickets as though nothing untoward had transpired, and as we reached the street, she suddenly turned to face me. What a beautiful and voluptuous face she had! And she proceeded to astonish me by saying: "You're Ram Singh, aren't you, that chap whose come over here to lecture on Yoga? What a delightful man you are! You simply must come to tea." '

'Absolutely!' Lady Jane Fortescue hooted with laughter. 'That's just how we met! And I don't mind admitting that on the Underground Railway, the prick of Ram Singh was so bloody stiff that my cunt soaked my knickers all the way down to my knees. It was a delight to meet you, Ram, since I was *so* tired of my husband at the time. Husbands!' she snorted indignantly. 'They're never there when you need them and they're always there when you *don't* want them.'

'Jane, I had no idea that you were married,' I remarked.

'*Was* married, Horby,' she replied plummily, 'just the same as Alison heah. Oh, and we were Spanking Wives, weren't we, darling?'

'Certainly,' lisped Lady Alison Utterley. 'The only way to keep a husband in order is to make sure that his bottom is well-reddened before his daily kissing of one's arse.'

'And where are your husbands now?' asked Amin Shah.

'Oh, pushing up the daisies,' Douglas informed us casually. 'One went from malaria in the jungles of Bengal and the other one died on an expedition to the Arctic: frostbite, I think. Needless to say, they were encouraged to undertake these adventures of heat and cold by their wives. Quite right too: they were rich but quite ineffably boring. I call these ladies the Black Widow Spiders.' Jane and Alison did not exactly look displeased.

'It sounds as though the pair of you had American marriages,' Davina commented. When Jane and Alison looked puzzled, she proceeded to explain. 'It was either the wife of Morgan or Vanderbilt – or it could have been Rockefeller – who held a curious party in New York City about a year ago. Fifty couples were invited. There were two doors to the reception and one of them was headed: BOSS. Forty-nine married women walked through that door with their husbands walking through the other one. The fiftieth man swaggered boldly through the door headed BOSS with his wife walking humbly behind him. "How did you manage that?" the hostess enquired. He replied: "Wife's orders." '

'There doesn't seem to be much talk about love here,' Amin Shah observed with wry amusement.

'And what exactly *is* "Love"?' Jane demanded.

'You remind me, Madam,' Amin Shah returned, 'of the Cambridge professor who was lecturing his students and who said: "We all know what Electricity *does*. But can anyone tell me what Electricity *is*?" "Sir! Professor!" shouted some bright spark who'd jumped up at the back, "*I* know." "Then speak up, young man,' said the Professor. The student faltered and stuttered. At last he said: "Sorry, Professor, I *thought* I knew but I have forgotten." "Just my luck!" the Professor exclaimed; "There was only one man on this planet who could tell me what Electricity *is* – and he has forgotten." '

'Love?' A flushed Captain Jack Rivers arose from beneath the table and zipped up his trousers as Emily arranged her skirt and endeavoured to compose herself with all due decorum. 'Well, a man goes into a London pub, orders three triple whiskies, drinks them fast and bursts into tears. "Now, now," says the barman, "what's *your* trouble?" "I have spent a year of my life writing this beautiful love song," the man replies, "and I am a musician and poet of absolute integrity. *Not one word or note can be changed*. Unfortunately, whenever I have offered it in London, and I've been trying for another year now, if I'm not turned down flat, I have demands for changes. Being a man of total artistic integrity, I cannot agree. And so no one wants my beautiful and truthful song of Love." Whereupon he orders another triple whisky and bursts into tears again.

'Well,' Rivers continued in between gulps of cognac, 'the barman says: "There's a piano over there. Why don't you play us your love song and I'll give you my opinion?" So the man sits down and starts playing his love song; and, very slowly, people start listening. It's so haunting and beautiful that conversation dies in the saloon bar and the entire public bar comes over to hear it. People walking down the street are attracted by these haunting strains and the bar is packed out well over the limit. As the man reaches the climax of his love song, the hardest women are crying their eyes out and strong men are weeping unashamedly. As he finishes, there is a moment of reverent silence. Then they all burst into a frenzied bout of enthusiastic applause. "In my opinion," the barman declares, "that was absolutely fantastic. I just can't understand why anyone would turn it down or try to alter these marvellous lyrics or anything else. By the way, what did you say the title was?" The man replies: "*I love you so much, I could shit.*" '

'Ho! ho! ho!' Bellingham bellowed. 'Well,' he grinned broadly at Davina, 'that's not exactly the way in which I feel about you, my dear. Who cares what is love and whether or not I love you: here, now and at this moment, I *lust* you. In fact, I just can't wait to pull down your drawers, whip up your skirt and petticoats and plunge my tongue into your absolutely luscious cunt.'

'Oh, Richard . . .' Davina giggled, 'you do rather have your own way of putting it.'

'Always do what the Captain says,' Sir Richard responded, with a quick look at Rivers, accompanied by a wicked smile. With that, he seized his laughing wife and they both tumbled to the deep-piled carpet. Bellingham was as good as his word and lost no time in tearing down Davina's drawers, ripping their white silk in his urgency, and as she shrieked out in mock indignation and then billed and cooed with delight, he licked his lips greedily at the prospect and plunged his face eagerly into Davina's writhing vulva.

Captain Jack Rivers promptly seized Emily once again and they dropped beneath the dinner table to recommence their vigorous fucking, accompanied by loud yells and gasps. I looked up to see that Jane had stood up and that Ram Singh, who had previously been surreptitiously ogling her ostentatiously low bosom cleavage, had now embraced her from behind, taking her copious breasts within his palms, and pressing his rod against the writhing, generous bottom of Jane.

As Ram and Jane essayed their *frottage*, I noticed that Amin Shah had lain down upon the carpet with the back of his head resting comfortably upon the cushion of the sofa. Earlier I had seen him whisper into Alison's ear and her pale and haughty face had briefly flushed with pleasure.

'This is the best way to talk to you,' he said calmly, 'and anyway, you have a gorgeous and slender, twitchy bottom.' Alison preened herself, fluttered her fan, threw it down, swished her way over to Amin Shah, whipped up her skirt and petticoats to show that she wasn't wearing any knickers and, with a demure flutter of her blue-shadowed eyelids and a spiteful smirk, placed her bottom upon Amin Shah's face.

He groaned in an admixture of agony and ecstasy and Alison's bitchy face shone with sadistic pleasure. Her white teeth gleamed in a grin of glee. By and by, her expression changed, though, as her blue eyes became increasingly dreamy. She began to sigh and shiver and quiver, squealing as she squirmed out of control.

'How about a straight and very crude one?' Douglas said to Rosemary.

'I was thinking that you'd never ask me,' Rosemary responded; then arose to bend over a chair, throw down her fan and thrust out her derrière, beckoning Douglas to do the honours of unveiling her bottom, which quivered with anticipation. Douglas unbuttoned his fly to produce a stiff, thick member and without further ado, he rammed it right up inside Rosemary's arse. He roared like a lion as he did that and she shrieked out with the sheer unexpected ecstasy of it. He stuffed it in, back and forth, as she writhed and squealed.

Claire and I took one look at one another and at the scene around us and, with gasps of delighted astonishment, fell into one another's arms and tumbled down onto the carpet. She hitched up her skirt and petticoats to indicate that her white satin knickers had been deliberately sewn open so as to give her a slit of access. It was a joy to plunge my rampant rod right through this satin slit and on through another slit, the interior of which was silken. My palms grasped and caressed her beautiful bottom and my forefinger lovingly stroked and prodded the rosebud of her anus.

The boat rocked and rolled on the waves as we came together gently, having some improved idea of what love is.

CHAPTER THIRTY

Happy is he who rejoices over calm waters was a proverb with which both Amin Shah and Ram Singh concurred; and so did I when at length I saw this sight. The ocean seems to stretch for all eternity and yet one feels a unique calm of mind and a love coming back. I was very happy with Claire; indeed, everyone appeared happy with our pairing, however temporary. I seized the opportunity to take lessons in Yoga from Ram Singh and lessons in Sufism from Amin Shah; as well as lessons in shark-and swordfish-angling from Jack Rivers, finance from Douglas and boozing from Bellingham. After all, there's not much point in a long sea-voyage unless you learn things that you will never forget.

The lessons of Ram Singh were certainly physically productive. He proceeded, at my request, to teach me *Hatha* Yoga, which consists of mastering posture and breath control. *Ha-tha* refers to a union between the Sun and Moon, the male and the female in Nature, brought about in this system by use of the body. The theory holds that providing the posture is right – the first and most difficult step – the Sun and Moon can be mated within the human body via the action of breathing. It is held that breath through the right nostril – *Pingala* – affects a certain part of the central nervous system: and the same is allegedly true for the left nostril – *Ida*: as it is also for

335

breath between both nostrils – *Sushumma* – which affects the central spinal column, or so it is stated by the masters of Yoga.

Well, I don't know really, about the theory. The facts are that by practising Ram Singh's postures and breathing exercises, I became quite murderously randy and a much better performer in bed.

Claire was certainly pleased with the results and I was pleased too when it was her turn at the dinner table to tell an erotic tale a few days later. She began:

'Back in 1899, I recall a time in Oxford, sitting in front of the fireplace with a mug of tea, to which I had added a dash of spirits, and wondering where all the good men were as I stared into the flames of the hypnotic light burning and blazing within the inglenook; but matters would soon improve.

'Samuel Pepys said of Oxford in 1668, "a mighty fine place." I cannot disagree. I met such an interesting man there, William Richard Morris.'

'Ah, yes,' said Bellingham, 'he's done splendid work for arts and crafts, particularly in printing and book design: the Kelmscott Chaucer, for example. I quite like his poetry and his novel, *News from Nowhere* isn't bad at all. Mind you, and to be quite frank, although he's a charming chap in person, he does shout rather a lot and I simply can't stand his impassioned advocacy of his bloody Christian Socialism.'

'No, Sir Richard,' Claire retorted, 'I am not speaking of him. This is a *different* William Morris, one who attended a Church school in Cowley, leaving at the age of fourteen to repair bicycles, then gradually set up his own business and became the local cycling champion. When I met him, his exploits and his ingenious machines were becoming increasingly well known and he had just opened a shop in

Oxford's High Street. Oh! we had such a silly day together!

' "Let me take you to the River Isis," he urged. "It is the most beautiful river bank that I can envisage." Whenever I think of Isis, I am reminded of the Egyptian Goddess, the wife of Osiris and the mother or Horus in yet another story of the creation of the World. Isis? Is she not the Goddess of love, fertility, intuition, inspiration and secrets? She begins as a maiden, a virgin, finally coming to reach fulfilment of her sexuality in a growing and maturing love.

'This young man worked so hard to impress me. He lent me a bicycle to ride and to intrigue, absorb and claim my attention. He himself rode upon a Penny Farthing. I felt so intoxicated by the fresh air. The front of his bicycle supported a basket containing a hamper, including sandwiches, a variety of pastries, fresh fruit and cheeses and a bottle of mead that his mother had so kindly concocted. Home-made mead can be so intoxicating! and, given its honey base, also aphrodisiacal.

'It did not take us too long to arrive at our destination: and he had chosen a beautiful site by the riverbank. Cows mooed contentedly in the background while, upon the waterway, ducks swam, occasionally plunging their heads beneath the surface in the hope of finding fish. We spread out the picnic blanket and proceeded to feast upon the delicacies that had earlier been prepared. However, the mead was much more potent, intoxicating, temilent, than I had originally anticipated. Yet how we did guzzle this mead, fermented honey, the nectar of flowers and the sweetness of life! Gradually, William began to lose all his inhibitions, the restraints and discipline that too often can control and shackle a good man.

'When I kissed him upon the cheek, he reddened with

modesty, rather as though he were making a misguided attempt to maintain his fecundity through chastity.

' "Would you like to ride upon my Penny Farthing?" he asked me.

' "I would delight in this pleasure," I replied in a gracious and courteous manner. He assisted me in placing my bottom upon the saddle. What a hardened seat it was to my delicate posterior! And I found it virtually impossible to control this particular two-wheeled conveyance. Unexpectedly, the hem of my skirt was caught within the spokes and the machine began to wobble and I could no longer keep my balance; then I felt myself falling and hit my head upon a stone and then the world fell silent.

'I do not know how long I was in a state of unconsciousness, so defenceless and vulnerable. Slowly I climbed back into awareness to find that I was lying naked upon a picnic blanket with William Morris nibbling upon my breasts.

' "My darling," he said, "you looked so beautiful just then that I simply could not contain myself any more. My intrinsic and essential desires were so aroused that I found it so necessary to . . . to . . ."

' "To do what?" I enquired.

' "You appeared even more lovely and fair than The Sleeping Beauty," he answered. "My member began to pulsate and throb so hard!"

' "And what did you do then?"

' "I asked graciously for your permission to penetrate: unfortunately, you were not quite in a fit state to answer my question."

' "Would you like now to perform that action?" I asked.

' "Mademoiselle – or should I call you Milady, a much more appropriate term – I do not want to appear too vulgar yet I must confess and acknowledge that your cunt is absolutely beautiful, being sure that many a lover has compared it to a lotus flower. In my opinion, yours is more like that of a honeysuckle, often with a humming-bird hovering overhead, rapidly vibrating its eager wings."

' "They all want to reach the honey and acquire the nectar in the end," I replied. "Did you?"

' "I plunged my stiff rod into your beautiful cunny," he responded. "I had hoped that I could arouse you. Please do not feel too offended by my actions."

' "Not at all . . ." At that moment, I was still feeling a bit dazed. "Did you reach a climax?"

' "Why, yes, I did," he answered with great rapture. "My organ pulsated and throbbed within your most gorgeous quim and I felt like a fountain, a veritable geyser spouting out grand jets of spunk!"

' "Now that I am conscious again," I told him, "one finds it essential to repeat the process."

' "Milady, I am so willing."

' "Then let us do so." There is nothing more sensual in life than spontaneous orgasms. Our love-making on the river bank was better on the second time; and as for the third, I felt like Alice coming out of Wonderland!'

(Note, 1925: William Morris became one of Great Britain's leading industrialists and manufacturers of motor-cars: my chauffeur insists that a Morris Cowley is the most convenient for driving in London on informal occasions and I cannot disagree: The Author.) (Note: 1993: The Morris Minor and the Morris Mini-Minor have achieved legendary status as classic cars, with the latter being especially suitable for town driving: The Editor).

'Did anything else happen?' Douglas enquired.

'Oh, yes!' Claire exclaimed, her face flushing ever so gently. 'You see, when he had done, I could not help laughing. He asked me the cause of my merriment. "Nothing," I answered, "it just reminded me of something." Not wishing at any risk to cause him the least shade of vexation, I insisted that he lie by me and told him how I was led on to procure sweet pleasures for myself.'

' "Ah, darling!" he exclaimed. "What would I not have given to see you frig your delicious little cunt?" He asked me many more questions about my solitary habits and I went so far as to tell him that on the evening prior to his invitation, I was so full of thought of him that I had done it there and then.

' "By Jove!" he answered, "this is truly curious. Confidence in return for confidence, dear angel, to know that the same night and probably at the same hour, we were exchanging our souls in mutual spending! Once I had seen you, I went home madly in love with you. I could not believe that I should be happy enough to possess you but all my efforts tended towards that desired end. I went to bed and thought only of you. I was in a fearful state . . . you can guess how! I put out my light and conjuring up your image, covered your face with imaginary kisses. Then I did what you were doing and the pleasure was so great that I am sure we emitted at one and the same time . . ."

' "What!?" I exclaimed in mock horror and astonishment. "*Can* men frig themselves, as we do?"

' "Certainly. Why should this natural means of relief be denied to them? Your pretty hand and my ugly paw both perform for the purposes of solitary gratification."

' "But there should be *mutual* gratification," I whispered into his ear.

' "Oh, I pray you! Grant me this pleasure!" I responded by disclosing his instrument, which was sufficiently excited by our conversation to have shot up once more in its most splendid condition. I took his hand and placed it upon his throbbing member.

' "No, really . . ." he protested, "this is rank folly!"

' "No, sir!"

' "But I would sooner have *your* fingers or *your* beautiful bubbies, if you will only but lend them to me."

' "But me no buts!" I cried out. "I *command* you to make haste and do it to the very end, or I will no longer love you." My dear lover could refuse me nothing. He began, and leaning over him, I followed his convulsive shaking with a singular feeling of pleasurable curiosity. I soon took pity on him, however, and kneeling down on the river bank before him, made him finish between my breasts. Yet shortly after this caprice of mine, he began to caress and suck my nipples once more.

' "Now show me your little cunt," he sighed, "and frig yourself with your left hand." I obeyed his instructions, all the while wondering what was to come. I now wanted to spend again fearlessly. My lascivious instincts began to blaze yet again. The operation that I had begun jokingly to perform, on account of a bicycle accident and only to please him, had become serious in the extreme. There was William Morris, with his trousers down, insinuating his organ, rampant in a state of nature, under my right arm. The originality of this fantastical idea inflamed my imagination more than ever. I bent my head and avidly contemplated the beautiful tool, the tip of which appeared and disappeared at each stroke of my dear lover, who kept his own eyes fixed on my left hand, which was frigging away for dear life. Soon we mingled our rites, we warned each other that the end was nigh and our double discharge took place simultaneously.

'My next position was to place my body atop his face, my bottom reclining upon it and my legs stretched asunder as he began his adorable, lecherous licking. My eyes were closed and I was wrapped up in my enjoyment, tasting every one of the thousand delicious sensations that his tongue conjured up, when suddenly he drew away and motioned me to do the same. Instantly I saw why; for there was a boat coming along the river and both of us knew some of the passengers. And I was just about to spend in his mouth! Quick as lightning, we were on our feet at once, our dress arranged, and then seated at a proper distance. We waved casually to our acquaintances as they sailed by. I felt terribly giddy but nevertheless managed to collect my scattered senses.

'It was an interesting encounter,' Claire concluded her tale, 'but I then had to go upon my travels to sample many more.'

As soon as I decently could, I escorted Claire to my suite, leaving the others to smoke and drink and fuck, and tumbled her down upon the bed.

'Oh! You adorable girl . . .' I sighed. She clasped me in her arms and, as I slipped my hands beneath the silken skin of her gorgeous, rounded bottom, she took hold of my member and frigged it bountifully for some exquisite time and, when it was in a most glorious state of erection, she slid it into her slit.

I rammed my rod into her with a joyous abandon, pounding her pudenda, all the while regaled by her cries of lascivious delight. I roared like a lion as I came: and it was immediately afterwards, with my prick in her cunt, that I asked her to marry me and she accepted with a squeeze of her vagina that left the issue of her acceptance in no doubt.

CHAPTER THIRTY-ONE

It might well take another volume to describe our sea voyage back to England on the S.S. *Albion*, and our adventures at our various ports of call. The facts remain that the company was delighted with the news of my engagement to Claire and a good time was had by all during our return to dear old Blighty, which occurred in late December 1901.

Those of us who had been involved with the Hermetic Order of the Golden Dawn returned to find a scandal that was all uniquely frightful – and all over the headlines of the popular press. There I found allegations of the Satanism for which I had searched in vain in Paris. The Golden Dawn, of which Bellingham and I were still passive members, was receiving a great deal of unwelcome publicity on account of the trial for rape of one Theo Horos. His wife, Madame Horos, was charged with aiding and abetting the matter.

I took a great interest in this case, since the couple in the dock appeared to be blaspheming things which I had discovered to be holy. Mr and Mrs Horos were an unlikely looking couple: she was remarkably fat and he was remarkably thin. It came out in court that, in 1888, she had served six months' imprisonment for swindling a Mr Luther Marsh out of his Madison Avenue house and, a year later, she had served two years for larceny in the

State of Illinois. Her husband, whose real name was Frank Jackson, had been Treasurer of a 'spiritual' movement his wife had founded, 'The Koreshan Unity', but had had to resign from this position after meeting with some difficulties in attempting to balance his books.

(Editor's Note: 'Horby's' account is consistent with the evidence produced at the trial, save that he does not mention *The Flaming Star*: 'Official Organ of the Koreshan Unity movement': it is worth observing that the recent mass cult suicide and shoot-out with the FBI occurred in Waco, Texas; and that the cult leader was a David *Koresh*. Connections with the movement founded by Mrs Horos have yet to be thoroughly investigated).

According to the testimony given at the trial, Madame Horos said that she and her husband Theo had been appointed to do God's work, for Theo was a new incarnation of Jesus Christ while she, the Swami, was none other than the Mother of God, bent upon establishing the theology of 'a Theocratic Unity.' In late 1899, they had travelled to Paris to meet Mathers, Head of the Golden Dawn. Madame Horos, described by one witness as 'the slickest and most accomplished crook-swindler ever known,' nevertheless managed to convince Mathers that she was the real Anna Sprengel of Germany by repeating to him details of a private conversation he had enjoyed with Madame Blavatsky many years before. It was fortunately not long before Mathers realised the nature of the fraud and denounced it: but not before Madame Horos had stolen some of his property, thence decamping to London where she had carried out some peculiarly nasty pseudo-occult sexual rites in Gower Street in the name of the Golden Dawn.

Mr and Mrs Horos wanted to attract as many people into their orbit as possible, put these people through fake

Golden Dawn initiations based on the documents they had stolen from Mathers and obtain every penny and atom of sexual satisfaction they could from the idiots who believed them. Now, at that time, it was often difficult for men and women of the lower-middle classes, desirous of matrimony, to meet one another socially, and so advertisements were a common feature in the popular press. One Evaline Mary Maud Croysdale, commonly known as Vera, was lured to the Horos couple from her home in Hull. Theo Horos pretended that his wife was his mother and married her in a 'pagan' ceremony, climaxed by going to bed with her in order to confirm its consummation. Apparently Vera had her doubts as they essayed sexual intercourse but these were soon resolved by the presence in bed of Theo's saintly mother, the soul-reading Swami, who knew and approved of this action and sighed as they fucked. Vera was thence persuaded to 'lend' Theo some diamond ear rings, a diamond pendant and a golden brooch, all of which she never saw again.

It was not, however, for obtaining Vera's trinkets by means of a fraudulent promise of marriage that Theo was sentenced to fifteen years of penal servitude and his wife to a similar sentence of seven years: it was for the rape of a sixteen-year-old girl named Daisy Pollex Adams.

Daisy, later described in court as a 'pretty little thing' and who came from Birkenhead, had been invited to London with her fourteen-year-old brother 'in order to complete their education;' and their parents, a Master Mariner and a Police Court missionary, had met the Horos couple and given their consent. Daisy would be taught shorthand, typing, music, drawing and painting; while the boy would be taught singing at St Paul's Cathedral. This proposition turned out to be not as attractive as it initially appeared.

My heart sinks even today as I ponder her testimony; for I do not feel that she was lying. Theo told the naive Daisy that she had to spend the night in his bed. This was essential, he said, for him to expound privately certain secret teachings of the Golden Dawn to her. In due course they retired for the night where, after being informed by Theo that the Spirit of Christ was in him and that she was to be his 'little wife', Daisy was initiated into the practice of mutual masturbation. A few days later, full sexual intercourse took place with the consent of Daisy, who told the court that she thought that Theo was the Son of God and therefore could do no wrong.

Unfortunately, on August 27th, 1901, Daisy was 'initiated' into the bogus 'Golden Dawn', using Mathers's original rituals and thereby blaspheming their nature. The Horos couple continued to preach the virtues of vegetarianism to Daisy whilst themselves indulging in both beef and beer. Having fallen into arrears with their rent, they moved to Gloucester Crescent; and it is here that Daisy began to doubt the divinity of Theo and resisted his advances: so he raped her.

A newcomer to this unlikely menage, one Laura Falkner, brought in by a matrimonial advertisement published in *The People*, stated in court that she had been instructed to bring Daisy to the 'Swami's' bedroom; this she did, and subsequently heard the girl crying out: Oh! Theo, don't.' Later she saw Daisy leave the bedroom, her eyes swollen and red with weeping and said that, within the hour, Daisy had told her that she had been raped, saying: 'You don't know the treatment I received this morning. The Swami held me by the head.'

Despite this, Daisy was stupid enough to write a letter to Theo stating that she was very sorry that she had wronged him and 'would vow on her knees before God to remain true to him . . . even if . . . tortured to death.' The Horos couple were finally arrested as guests at the home of Daisy's mother, who had managed to cling to the purity of their ideals, surely a considerable tribute to the persuasive powers of Mr & Mrs Horos.

On 20th December 1902, Mr Justice Bigham was confronted with the statement of Mrs Horos that her husband was incapable of sexual intercourse. 'Bloody rubbish, Horby!' Aleister Crowley exclaimed to me in later years. 'I stayed with that pair of confidence tricksters once for a long weekend and he was always boring me by walking around naked with a rampaging erection.' Fortunately, Mr Justice Bigham was of the same opinion and after rightly stating that it was difficult to conceive of more revolting or abominable crimes, passed a stiff prison sentence on these two rather seedy sexual perverts and confidence tricksters. Myself, I applaud his action; but it was hardly good news for the Golden Dawn, whose Neophyte ritual had been (incorrectly) described by the Solicitor-General as being 'most blasphemous'. Even to this day, some who followed the case associate the Golden Dawn with the Horos perversions. Others view the members, not as the Great Adepts they considered themselves to be, but as a set of amiable lunatics. Bellingham and I saw no alternative other than to resign, as did so many other members of repute.

Since that time, one gathers that the Golden Dawn continues in its way despite schisms and much undignified squabbling. There are various groupings which purport to be *the* original Golden Dawn. Who knows? Who cares? I am inclined to agree with Amin Shah that if you faithfully follow the Golden Dawn theory and practice of the 1890s, it will make you an excellent individual of the 1890s: but that is of no use to me in 1925.

To my knowledge, Mathers carried on with his sincere beliefs until, after a severe quarrel with Crowley, he died in the Spanish Influenza epidemic of 1917-19. Crowley, of course, is still going, though who knows where *that* will lead. Yeats is in line for that thing they call the Nobel Prize; or possibly he's already won it. Myself, I feel that the Golden Dawn did much more good than harm.

As for Satanism, I had to tell British government agents that it doesn't exist, save among tiny and utterly insignificant groups of perverts. I'd rather like it if there were an international gang of Satanists bent upon wrecking civilization and seizing power, among all their other alleged perversions, since it would be such tremendously good fun to crusade against it. Alas! there is no such beastie.

I certainly needed a breath of fresh air after the court case and that is why I joined Claire to play tennis on the hard court that Douglas had recently established at a home he owned in Roehampton.

'I know it's supposed to be called *lawn* tennis,' he jested, 'but why can't we play it under other circumstances too?' Winter tennis in the open weather certainly gets the old muscles moving, and the blood, brain and sinews. Servants put out copious quantities of mulled wine, steaming softly as we played our games. The idea was that we all divided into teams for a tournament of Doubles, with penalties for the losers and rewards for the winners. Douglas and Rosemary appointed themselves to be impartial umpires, taking high chairs at each side of the net. Douglas wore a blue blazer and baggy white flannel trousers; Rosemary wore a white, tight, silken dress, and as she settled into her seat, her white-gloved hands opened up a white parasol.

The sun shone out of the arse of the Universe on this

cold, crisp, clear day as we drank our hot mulled wine, seized our tennis racquets and gathered before Douglas to hear the luck of the draw, gathered from slips of paper we had earlier tossed into his top hat held for him by Rosemary. He announced that the first match would be between Amin Shah and Jane Fortescue against Ram Singh and Alison Utterley, the reward being a thousand guineas each for the winners; and a public spanking followed by standing in the corner for the losers, the match to be best out of three sets. All concerned consented to the match.

Amin Shah wore very short shorts and a white shirt. Claire commented approvingly on his slender, wiry arms and strong, slim thighs. Jane wore a frilly but loose-fitting blouse with a long, white pleated skirt. As she grasped her racquet fiercely with her right hand, her left delicately whisked her voluminous skirt. Ram Singh wore a Cambridge pullover and immaculately creased white flannel trousers. Alison wore a frivolously frilly but loose dress of shocking pink.

The play in the first set was fiercely competitive. I soon enough had a rampaging erection on account of seeing beautiful female bottoms bent over to receive a service; and I suspect that Claire and Davina got similar joy from watching the men. Jane's service was so absolutely smashing that she won some of her games to love. By contrast, Amin Shah served a ball so slow that, on its bounce, it looked like a sitting duck. Alison missed its spin entirely the first time and the bold swipe of Ram Singh sailed way out of court. Ram Singh's own serve went straight like a bullet and almost as fast: its return was a set-up for his smash. Alison's serve came in a curve, spinning in a way to set up a defensive return.

Both men started to play on the ladies' lack of mobility

in their skirts, perceiving that when both women were positioned for the ball, they struck home and hard. The forehand of Jane was a devastating stroke; yet the spinning backhand of Alison more often than not resulted in a futile swipe of the ball into the net. Shah and Singh were all strength and scintillating agility, conducting brilliant volleys at the net. At 4-4 in the first set, I overheard Singh say 'Play on her backhand' to Alison; and Shah saying: 'Play on her forehand,' to Jane. However, as luck would have it, it was Shah's service to Alison, which played upon the weakness in defence, of her forehand drive to make it 5-4: then Alison's serve to Jane's backhand spun back as a lob in the air, Singh lobbed it back and Shah smashed it. This pattern of play took the game and the set 6-4.

Shah and Jane established a dominant pattern of play during the second set. Jane took the base-line, banging in solid shots of tremendous power and Amin was neat and nifty at the net. Ram Singh and Alison, trying to outplay them at mid-court, had no answer to these tactics and lost the second set 6-2. It was time for the punishment and leather stools had been thoughtfully provided. The losers of this particular game bent over them obediently.

Amin flicked up the skirt of Alison, pulled down her white drawers and commenced spanking her pale, slim bottom with his tennis racquet. Simultaneously, Jane bared the bottom of Ram Singh, attending with her racquet to the condition of his athletic buttocks with enormous enthusiasm. Six strokes each sang out as if the racquets were striking tennis balls: and two bottoms writhed, twitched and reddened. Once the punishment was over, Ram Singh and Alison Utterley, as agreed by forfeit, had to stand in diagonally opposite corners of the tennis court, hands behind backs and upon glowing bottoms, faces to the wire, thus unable to see the next match.

This was Bellingham and Davina against Claire and myself. Bellingham was wearing a white cricket shirt and long, baggy shorts. I wore a plain white shirt and old white flannels. Claire now astounded one and all by peeling away her long fox-fur coat to reveal a white, short-sleeved singlet with a knee-length, white pleated skirt that jiggered every time she twitched her bottom. By contrast, Davina was wearing a costume quite impossible for the playing of tennis. All that could be said in its favour is that it was white. The excruciatingly tight dress of shimmering satin rendered it impossible for her to take more than a six-inch step at a time; and, judging by the way in which her breasts jutted, her corset was so tight that any fast step taken would cause her to fall out of breath.

'I'm just hopeless at these things,' said Davina as Claire popped over an easy serve. It bounced before her, she essayed a faint stroke and she missed. Claire's second serve to Richard was much harder and faster. He swung mightily and missed. For all their many virtues and saving graces, Sir Richard and Lady Bellingham were not terribly good at tennis. Whenever she served, the ball was lobbed feebly into the net. Whenever he served, he hit the ball so hard that it was way out of court. Whenever Claire or I served, either she hit the ball into the net or he hit it out of court. This match went by very quickly, with Claire and I winning a point-less win of six-love, six-love; and Douglas and Rosemary both declaring it to be the worst game of tennis which they had ever seen. Now there was punishment to follow; and Douglas and Rosemary added to it by ordering Richard and Davina to drink a paper cup of orange squash each and to eat a dry and boring biscuit.

'Oh, do spank me,' Davina entreated me sweetly as she bent over.

'I can hardly wait,' Bellingham murmured as he bent

over. With one accord, Claire and I moved into action. She stripped Bellingham of his shorts and underpantaloons. I took my time in unfastening the garments of Davina but took delight in exposing her rounded bottom to the afternoon air. Soon the tennis racquets of Claire and I were whanging down on two red, writhing bottoms, the pale skin of which looked like neat lattice work. It was the corner for both of them as the final commenced.

We lost the first set 6-1, since we were completely outplayed. Whenever the ball was placed for Jane's forehand, it proved to be virtually unreturnable. Amin was putting so much spin on his balls that any return rendered one liable to a smash.

It was then that I saw something. Claire and I had been playing with her volleying at the net and I was driving the strokes in from the base-line. What would happen if we emulated Amin and Jane and proceeded to play it their way, only taking it further? And I recall Claire whispering to me: 'Just defend.'

This strategy confused our opponents, for they certainly were not expecting Claire's top-spin back-hand, fired from the base-line. As for the net play, I took my partner's advice and instead of trying to slam through the skilled defences of Amin Shah, I encouraged him in endeavours to slam through mine and concentrating upon returning every ball as if I were a rubber ball. We won the next set 6-2.

In the third and final set, Claire, in her short and fluttering skirt, took advantage of Jane's lack of mobility within her heavy pleats, and scored repeatedly with neatly placed shots. It was an erotic sight indeed to see Claire time that drop-shot perfectly, causing Jane to run in a flurry of skirt, just too late to reach the ball, yet forced to bend over and shove her bottom upwards as she reached.

I returned the most athletic of Ram Singh's skilful endeavours to take the deciding set six-love.

'Punishment now!' Douglas grinned wickedly and rubbed his hands with joy. Rosemary had dismounted from her umpire's chair and was walking towards us with an arrogant swish of her skirts and petticoats, as four penitents paid their forfeits by standing obediently in the corners of this wired cage.

'A good spanking, is it, Horby?'

'That depends,' I replied, 'upon what my partner, co-victor and affianced declares. After all, ladies first!'

'The penalty,' said Claire, 'is that Amin Shah will *not* bend over and expose his bottom to me, much as he may be dying to do so, for all I know.' Rosemary smiled broadly at her star girl pupil. 'No, no, I want him to bend over *backwards* for me!' She wriggled her young, athletic bottom within her short tennis skirt and the pleats appeared to flutter gleefully. 'Mr Shah, in payment of your agreed forfeit, I request kindly that you lay your back upon this leather clad stool here and expose your rampant rod for my delectation.'

'Your wish is my command, Madam,' Amin Shah responded graciously, rather as if he were a genie in some tales of *The Arabian Nights*. Obediently, he stretched back upon the stool, unbuttoned his shorts and produced a long, thick, stiff ramrod of a penis.

'Splendid!' Claire shouted with joy. She whipped off her drawers and in an impudent piece of cheek, she threw them at Douglas, who merely smiled. 'I'm going to ride you, Amin, as I would a stallion!' So staying, she plucked up her tennis skirt and with a hop, step and a jump, landed directly upon his stiff rod and sighed with the pleasure of the sensation. In no time at all, she was rocking back and forth and shrieking out her delight in it as the man beneath her whirling loins heaved his hips and sighed with pleasure.

I had my own penalty in mind for Lady Jane Fortescue. Although I rather liked her, she had always struck me as being quite unnecessarily haughty; as the lower classes say, she was 'a right bossy boots'. It was a pleasure, therefore, to have this typical Girls' Head Prefect at my mercy. I commanded her to bend over the leather stool and with her own hands to expose the gorgeous golden apples swathed by her skirts. It was such a pleasure to see her rounded bottom bared in the afternoon sunlight upon the tennis court and an even greater pleasure to thwack my tennis racquet upon the quivering flesh with a sound *ping!*

Her bottom jumped up and down in sportive fashion as I gave her a strong, overarm first service; a spinning second service that made her gasp as her rear twitched to the right; a sizzling forehand shot that made her jump; a slicing backhand which made her squeal; and a final, overhand spanking good smash which made her beautifully reddened behind shudder and quiver. As she surrendered utterly, I rammed my rod within her soaking quim, whipping it through her so swiftly that she screamed out and came at the instant that I did.

A gong sounded and the game was ended. Claire, who had just come all over the shaft of Shah, dismounted and smoothed down her skirt. Jane rearranged her dress as I endeavoured to observe all due propriety. Rosemary blew a whistle and, with all forfeits paid, Richard and Davina and Ram and Alison joined us joyfully for a glass of mulled wine.

We all enjoyed a very good dinner that night but I shall never forget Claire's words as we composed ourselves within a true four-poster bed around midnight:

'I feel so content now,' she sighed, 'knowing that I have experienced life to the fullest . . . my travels were most enjoyable. I would not say that I have been terribly promiscuous, no, never indiscriminate in my manner, though there is still a *wanderlust* within my soul.

'Life,' she said, 'is a pilgrimage, an exploration. One can gallivant around the World for so long before it becomes rather tedious. At the present time, it is so important that I can be here in England as I have been invited to a wedding and it is so essential that I should attend.

'I know the groom so well,' she murmured dreamily. 'What a handsome, intelligent man; with such charm and attraction and such powers of seduction! As for the bride, I know it will be the happiest day of her life – that slow walk down the aisle to the altar, accompanied by her father, she herself sequestered and camouflaged by a veil . . . to finally reveal herself before her husband!'

'Let's fuck,' I said.

CHAPTER THIRTY-TWO

I married the woman referred to in these Memoirs as the Hon Claire Woodrough shortly afterwards. (Editor's Note: Horby deliberately does not give the precise date; research is still being undertaken into the various couples who wed in December 1901 or January 1902). On account of our social position, we had to get married C. of E. style – at least the service is short – and then host a whole load of society bores.

The true wedding came a day after and was held at my country house. Claire and I just wanted a few special friends to be present. A long-forgotten ancestor of mine had constructed a network of caves beneath the property, although as Claire mentioned to me: 'I feel there an eeriness, spookiness, a frightening sensation, rather macabre and eldritch.' Well: this particular ancestor had been an associate of Sir Francis Dashwood, he of so-called Hell-Fire Club infamy. Much planning and consultation was devoted to the course of the ceremony. Eventually, we were all agreed.

When the moment came, I donned a black silk robe and gladly accepted a brandy in my study from Sir Richard Bellingham, a cigarette packed with hashish from Amin Shah, an opium pipe from Ram Singh, a Cuban cigar from Douglas and a tankard of mead from Captain Jack Rivers, all of whom congratulated me warmly on making a wise choice of wife. No doubt Claire was receiving similar encouragements from her lady friends.

'Since we're coming along during the Season of Yule,' said Bellingham, 'I shall tell a joke: did you know how the Fairy came atop the Christmas Tree?' None of us did. 'Well,' he explained, 'one Christmas Eve, Santa comes home rubbing his hands together and going: "Ho! ho! ho!" But Mrs Claus is sitting there with her arms folded and looking rather fed up. "I don't see what's quite so funny, Santa," she informs him. "I've hardly seen you over the past three months and whenever you do bother to come home, I find you to be quite scandalously drunk. Santa, I simply can't take it any more and I am leaving you," and she goes. So poor old Santa's wife leaves him on Christmas Eve and he has to cook all the Christmas dinners for the poor people himself. Well, he's not terribly good at cooking and he proceeds to cut himself and he burns himself a few times but finally he shoves all the dinners in the ovens.

'Then off he goes to the factory to make sure that the presents have all been wrapped. But the elves and dwarves and gnomes and goblins and imps and pixies are all sitting there with *their* arms folded and looking, quite frankly, rather pissed orf. No presents have been wrapped. Santa says: "Come on, what is this? It's Christmas Eve and we must surely wrap the presents." They reply: "Sorry, Santa, we want a wage increase." Santa says: "Look, I haven't got it. Business is bad and the Christmas spirit isn't what it used to be. Come along, chaps, have a heart and wrap the presents." They retort: "Sorry, Santa, it's a wage increase or nothing," and when he shakes his head, they go: "Right, lads! Everybody out!" So Santa has to wrap all the presents himself.

'Then Santa has to carry all the presents out to his sleigh

and load it up. Unfortunately, he's just finished doing that when a runner comes away. So Santa has to take all the presents off again, fetch his tool box and repair the sleigh – and he goes and smashes his thumb with a hammer. Finally he gets the job done, loads all the presents onto the sleigh again and thinks: "Better go and check the reindeer, I suppose." Well, Donner's suffering from rheumatism, Blitzen has a bad case of arthritis and Rudolph has a cold and so his nose isn't glowing. All in all, they're a very sorry crew.

'Santa goes back to his house. Now I did mention that he wasn't exactly terribly good when it came to cooking. The Christmas dinners are all burnt into a black, charred mess. Santa is just contemplating this string of disasters when there's a ring upon the doorbell. Santa opens the front door: and there is this exceptionally beautiful fairy smiling happily and saying: "Hallo, Santa! Merry Christmas! And I've brought you your Christmas Tree. What would you like me to do with it?"

'Well, what do *you* think Santa said?' Bellingham concluded. 'And that's how the Fairy got on top of the Christmas tree.'

Joviality reigned as the men escorted me underground and into the tunnels that led to the caves, eventually to reach an artificial river called the Styx, the channel of the dead. I paid Bellingham a golden guinea, since he was playing the part of Charon the Ferryman, and he punted us across.

Fires flared and candelabra flickered throughout the various chambers, causing a melting of the stalagmites and a dripping of the stalactites. Finally, there was the major chamber. I entered to see Claire lying naked upon a four-poster bed that had been transformed into an altar. Upon its wooden base was the sign of the Eye in the

Pyramid. Behind it, there was a quartet of statues: at the head, the androgynous goat-god, Baphomet; at one side Priapus with a red-tipped phallus; on the other side, Venus was caressing her cunt; and, nearest to the bed, Bacchus and Venus were entwined within a loving and lustful embrace.

Douglas as the High Priest and Rosemary as the High Priestess solemnly conducted me to the bed and altar as Claire twitched her thighs and moaned. Behind us was the Priest, Ram Singh, and the new Priestess, Emily Ward-Bishop.

Organ music resounded throughout this Temple as Douglas and Rosemary intoned solemnly:

Thou who art I, beyond all I am,
Who hast no nature, and no name,
Who art, when all but thou are gone,
Thou, centre and secret of the Sun,
Thou, hidden spring of all things known
And unknown, Thou aloof, alone,
Thou, the true fire within the reed
Brooding and breeding, source and seed,
Of life, love, liberty and light,
Thou beyond speech and beyond sight,
Kindling as my intents aspire.
Thee I invoke, abiding one,
Thee, centre and secret of the Sun,
And that most holy mystery
Of which the vehicle am I.
Appear, most awful and most mild,
As is lawful in thy child!

At that instant, I rammed my rampant rod right into Claire's gorgeous cunny and inhaled the sweet perfume of sandalwood as she squealed and squirmed in ecstasy. At that instant, they all started singing:

> For of the Father and the Son
> The Holy Spirit is the norm;
> Male-female, quintessential, one,
> Man-being veiled in woman-form.
> Glory and worship in the highest,
> Thou Dove, mankind that deifiest,
> Being that race most royally run,
> To spring sunshine through winter storm.
> Glory and worship be to thee,
> Sap of the world-ash, wonder-tree!

Thus inspired, I slammed into Claire, laughing happily as I caused her belly to writhe and squirm with pleasure.

'Glory to Thee from Gilded Tomb!' roared the men.

'Glory to thee from Waiting Womb . . .' the woman sang. Then, as we fucked joyously, they all joined in a chorus:

> Glory to Thee from earth unploughed!
> Glory to thee from virgin vowed!
> Glory to Thee, true Unity
> Of the Eternal Trinity!
> Glory to thee, thou sire and dam
> And Self of I am that I am!
> Glory to thee, beyond all term
> Thy spring of sperm, thy seed and germ!
> Glory to thee, eternal Sun,
> Thou One in Three, Thou Three in One!
> Glory and worship be to Thee,
> Sap of the world-ash, wonder tree!

A gong was struck and I came at that instant, fiercely and

firmly pumping all my juices into the luscious cunt of Claire, who was awash in her own floodings of lust and who came with me.

As we rested upon the bed that was our altar, the Priestess collected our mingled love-juices from the chalice that was my wife's vagina and, with a long silver spoon, placed them within a diamond-encrusted chalice of platinum. The contents were then mixed with mead, and offered to me. I indicated that Milady should drink of it first and she responded by graciously insisting that this chalice should first pass my lips. Having supped of this delicious delectation, I presented it to her and she relished her full swallow. The congregation then drank of it and subsequently smacked their lips with satisfaction.

Was there indeed a secret magical ingredient within this Love Potion? Certainly I felt myself spinning into a state of consciousness which was unlike any I had experienced before, entwined delightfully as I was within her writhing white limbs. It seemed somewhat to have dispelled the initial solemnity of the congregation.

'Yo! ho! ho! and a bottle of rum!' Sir Richard Bellingham was bellowing as he ripped her thin silk dress from Davina and proceeded to fuck his wife upon the floor.

I suddenly noticed that at the end of this chamber, there was a stake to which was attached an iron chain with hand-cuffs. Captain Jack Rivers must have noticed it too, for he had snapped the cuffs upon Emily, ignoring her status as a Priestess, pulled up her silken black robe and was now giving it to her up the arse with shouts of joy. Emily was shrieking with delight too.

Douglas and Rosemary had slid to the floor very softly and slowly but they were now fucking swiftly and slickly.

Jane was bent over the lap of Amin Shah, gasping out her pleasure as her rounded white bottom glowed and started to writhe on account of his solemnly administered spanking.

Alison was furiously riding the stiff prick of Ram Singh, who lay upon his back and gasped with satisfaction. So did this randy bitch soon enough.

I had been unable to resist inviting Mrs Joan Smythe, for she was now married to that awful poet, Wilfred Sedgewick: some member of his family had left him a fortune, allowing him to leave the Colonial Service for service of a somewhat different nature. Joan lay back in her chair, arrogantly tossed her long black satin skirt and petticoats over the head of her kneeling servant and sighed with deep satisfaction as, no doubt, his tongue licked her cunt. Personally, I think it was giving rather more pleasure doing that than spouting terrible poetry.

My penis was stiff. Claire's vagina was wet with the juices of her desire. I prodded my rod into her for an ecstatic union. At the instant of our orgasms, we saw the infinitely great in this vast and starry Universe and the infinitely small in the grain of life-giving pulsation within the atom: and from this conjunction between the infinitely great and the infinitely small come all things in an ecstasy of Creation. In an agonising shudder which shivered my timbers – yes! thus and not otherwise did I come to the Temple of the Holy Grail, to pour within it the very last drop of my life's blood.

'The male and the female,' Claire said. 'Energy! Energy!! Energy!!! THAT'S IT!'

We shall draw a veil over our honeymoon, for as I said to my wife, the rest is silence.

The Black Pearl Volume Four

EDITOR'S PREFACE
TO VOLUME III

Some words of explanation are in order for those unfortunate enough not to have read Volumes I and II of *The Black Pearl: Memoirs of a Victorian Sex-Magician.**

In Volume II, Horby continues to enjoy London life, seducing a suffragette he meets at a party hosted by Sydney and Beatrice Webb; attending the Rhymers' Club of Johnson, Davidson and Dowson; visiting brothels and exploring all sorts of occult societies. As a member of the Hermetic Order of the Golden Dawn, he supplies us with his own unique perspective on the quarrels between its leader, 'MacGregor' Mathers, William Butler Yeats and his curious friend, Aleister Crowley. With John Davidson, he visits the East End, smokes opium with The Smokers of the Sacred then returns to the West End to pass the evening at a strictly private club of flagellation confined to the nobility, the aristocracy, the gentry and all others who can pay its extortionate sums. He eats and drinks with Shaw, Wells, Chesterton, Belloc and Arthur Machen, recording their views on sex and society.

He visits New York twice. On the first occasion it is to witness the World Heavyweight Boxing Championship followed by a night with a secret society known as The Beautiful Female Flagellants of New York. On the second,

---

* Published in paperback by the New English Library.

his adventures include an evening with Butch Cassidy and the Sundance Kid, along with their 'Wild Bunch.' He continues to fornicate relentlessly. On his ocean crossing, he learns much about gambling from Arnold Rothstein, future banker to the New York Underworld.

Horby enjoys a wide variety of acquaintanceship. There is Robert Ross in Paris, Frank Harris in Monaco, James McNeill Whistler in Venice; and Prime Minister Lord Salisbury with his nephew and successor, Arthur Balfour, at an English country weekend where the issues of the day are decided. He becomes involved in espionage, epitomising the English ideal of the gentleman amateur, and in Berlin encounters the intriguing international spy 'Maria', whom he will later meet in both London and Paris. He is also initiated by German sex-magicians into the Ordo Templi Orientis (OTO) which practises sex for the enhancement of consciousness though the narrator already knows this from previous experience. Back in London, he sees the humiliation of a woman by a man; then hears of the humiliation of a man by a woman. He crosses to Paris for the wedding of his old friend, Sir Richard Bellingham, and finds the links of that occasion with secret societies which enshrine the act of sex to be quite astonishing.

Bellingham plays a prominent part in these *Memoirs*, though further research has still not elicited his true identity. Nor has diligent enquiry managed to discover the name of his bride, given in the text as Mrs Davina Price-Hughes, a wealthy widow apparently worth between one and ten million pounds sterling. Nor does the text make it clear whether Bellingham is merely a fortunately-born buffoon or a holy and divine Fool in an obscure English medieval tradition, as portrayed in Tudor times by Shakespeare when writing of Falstaff.

Other prominent characters continue to elude close scrutiny of their true identities. Horby's former governess, Rosemary, High Priestess of this secret cult, continues to write him explicit letters from Istanbul, Vienna, Venice and Paris, making love with him whenever there is an opportunity to meet independently; though some of her liaisons are outrageous. The same can be said of the Hon. Claire Woodrough, another pupil of Rosemary and Horby's first young love. She journeys to New York, New Orleans and San Francisco, encountering characters as diverse as Scott Joplin, Harry Houdini, William Randolph Hearst, Ambrose Bierce and Buffalo Bill, and learns more of the mysteries of Voodoo. She is a Priestess of this secret cult and joins Rosemary and Horby in Paris for Bellingham's astounding Wedding Reception.

The names of those who appear to witness Sir Richard Bellingham's Wedding Reception in a Paris Temple have obviously been put in a code understood only by the select few to which *The Black Pearl* would be distributed privately. An especially mysterious figure is the man Horby calls 'the Black Douglas', a fabulously wealthy international banker who has Rosemary as his mistress, among many other women; who dines with the Prime Minister of England to discuss international affairs; and who is also the High Priest of the cult of enlightenment via sexuality.

There are three more men of mystery: Ram Singh, a Priest at Bellingham's wedding, has invited Claire to his ashram. 'Pierre', a very strange figure who has witnessed the lesbian activities of Rosemary and Claire, plays the peculiar role of The Monk at Bellingham's reception-come-orgy. The unpleasant Viscount Maulerby arouses a repulsion that is justified fully in the foregoing.

The intriguing Mrs Joan Smythe continues to intrude upon the narrative as the Queen of flagellation and female domination, managing a variety of sado-masochistic schemes such as The Female Flagellants of New York, The Smythe Reform Academy and the Society for the Promulgation of Petticoat Government. One Miss Emily Ward-Bishop is enthused by these pursuits; although she also relishes the pleasures of receiving chastisement from a man and to judge by the text, would like to marry Horby, a fact angrily deplored by Claire Woodrough.

'The Black Douglas' is somewhat sadistic in his treatment of women, though they do not appear to object, and, from the text, he appears to be on excellent terms with four beautiful and unusual young ladies: Lady Alison Utley and Lady Jane Fortescue, mistresses to the wealthy and powerful who enjoy their own peculiar perversities: and Lady Candida Lauderdale and Miss Amelia Edwards, an actress, friends of Bellingham's bride, the former Mrs Davina Price-Hughes, former mistresses of Aleister Crowley – in common with their friend – and both of them ensnared by a desire for the decadent.

All these questions and issues are explored honestly, behind certain necessary 'blinds,' in the third volume of the *Memoirs*, which take the reader around the world in a bizarre travelogue of sexual adventure, education and experience. In common with its predecessors, this volume is hardly 'politically correct.' The narrator was possessed of many of the prejudices of his time, although he repudiates the vice of racism including anti-semitism and continually advocates an unrestricted love of women, coming all the while closer in his obsessive quest for the Holy Grail.

Some may see merely obscenity within this document, to which one can only retort that those who dwell within a conceptual sewer tend to notice very little other than their immediate surrounds. The more educated, however, may obtain invaluable insights into the sociology, history and psychology of the period, including perceptions deriving from world-wide travel, within these pages – pages of unique literary interest.

Geraldine Lamb PhD.,
University of California at Berkeley.

EDITOR'S PREFACE
TO VOLUME IV

For those who have not had the good fortune to read Volumes I–III of *The Black Pearl: The Memoirs of a Victorian Sex-Magician*, a few words of introductory explanation are essential.

In Volume III, Horby commences by investigating Satanism, Black Magic and the more sinister aspects of Roman Catholicism in Paris. His account of conversations with J–K Huysmans and Gabriele Jogand make for fascinating reading. Through his involvement with the extraordinary Maria, secret agent for every one of the Great Powers and Great Whore to Europe, he uncovers the sordid activities of the traitor to his country, Lord Maulerby.

As Horby continues to fornicate his way across Europe and then through Africa and Asia, he periodically receives letters from his former tutor Rosemary, herself fornicating in Montreal, across the Prairies by rail and in Calgary, Alberta; from the Hon. Claire Woodrough, doing the same in Highgate Cemetery, at a London dinner with the anarchist Prince Kropotkin and by the Taj Mahal with the Yogi and mystic, Ram Singh; and from Emily Ward-Bishop, writing of the fiercely dominant Joan Smythe and her Society for the Promulgation of Petticoat Government.

Proceeding to Munich, Horby meets the German magicians Guido von List and Lanz von Liebenfels, who would strike the modern reader as being precursors of Nazism and

Hitler. He then joins the mysterious multimillionaire Douglas for a Nile cruise followed by a period of wallowing in the fleshpots of Cairo. A mystical experience takes place at the Great Pyramid.

Horby sails to Ceylon, where he meets two old chums: Aleister Crowley, who has been practising Yoga under the tuition of Allan Bennett (who would later bring Theravada Buddhism to Great Britain) and the rakish Sir Richard Bellingham, on honeymoon with his wife Davina, whose wedding had made such an explosive end to Volume II. There is also the presence of the appalling poet, Wilfred Sedgewick.

On a steamboat to Madras, he meets the Sufi Amin Shah, seeing him again in that city and learning of international fraternities, sororities and magical groupings. The enigmatic Douglas is there to announce an extraordinary voyage. His ocean-going liner, the SS *Albion* under the captaincy of the beefy and hearty sea-dog Jack Rivers, will sail to England as a floating Abbey of Thelema on the principles enunciated by Rabelais in *Gargantua and Pantagruel*. The other passengers will be Sir Richard Bellingham and Davina; Rosemary; Claire; Emily; 'the willowy Lady Alison Utterley and the voluptuous Lady Jane Fortescue'; plus Amin Shah and 'the strange Ram Singh'.

Although they have to fight off pirates, the passengers have a wonderful time and it seems that whenever they are not having sex, they are telling tales of previous sexual encounters. Horby's description of this voyage is perhaps the most astonishing for the reader since the writings of Rabelais.

Upon arrival in England, Horby encounters the schisms and High Court scandal of the legendary Order of the Golden Dawn, of which he is a member. There is then a description of what must be the most bizarre game of tennis

ever played. This section of the manuscript closes with his
wedding to Claire where all participants rejoice in a general
orgy.

One wonders, of course, just who Horby was. Various other
documents have been published purporting to be by his
ancestors and descendants. Nor is it possible at present to
identify quite a number of the names of other characters
that he cites. Investigations are still proceeding.

In turning to Volume IV, we find an astonishing account
of the Edwardian and Georgian periods up to the First
World War. Once again, of course, Horby displays the
limitations and prejudices of his class and time: he is hardly
'politically correct'. Yet he surprises us in being quite
content to have 'an open marriage'. He gives us unique
insights into a variety of magical or other occult orders,
including the Golden Dawn, the Ordo Templi Orientis and
Aleister Crowley's A∴A∴: and also into the politicians
and other men and women in power who brought about the
Great War.

The narrator is, of course, obsessed with sex. He describes
graphically his many erotic encounters, as well as incidents
of observed lesbianism and many forms of sadomasochism.
There may be those who can discern nothing other than
pornography within this man's honest account of his astonishing life. One can only retort that those who see only
sewage tend themselves to be its creatures.

Horby is, in fact, utterly sincere in his search for his
personal Holy Grail and in his certainty that sex can be the
holiest act in the Universe. That is the honest and burning
conviction that shines through these pages of astounding
literary, historical, sociological and psychological interest.
One cannot help but feel that this work, however out-
rageously licentious it may at times seem to the contem-

porary reader, nevertheless somehow manages to enshrine some noble truths of the spirit.

Geraldine Lamb PhD.
Empson Professor of Literature
University of Moscow
Idaho

EDITOR'S NOTE

Since the first 'trade' publication of *The Black Pearl* (New English Library, 1995), a number of works have been published by the same imprint purporting to be by members of the Horby dynasty.

Some family history is given in *Unholy Passions* (London, 1997). Translated, edited and introduced by Marcus Ardonne PhD of the University of Cambridge, this work centres on a previous Lord Horby's account of his involvement with the 'Hell-Fire Club' of Sir Francis Dashwood, better named as 'The Monks of Medmenham' and/or 'The Friars of St Francis of Wycombe'.

More family history is given in *Vixens* by Alan Dale (London, 1997), evidently writing from interviews with a descendant who flourished in the 1950s.

Gothic Passions (London, 1998), again translated and edited by Marcus Ardonne but this time introduced by Gina Cravesit PhD of the University of Cambridge, is by the son of the author of *Unholy Passions* and provides further data.

Sexploited by Alan Dale (London, 1998) is based on interviews with one Victor Tory, a merchant of the 1980s, and mentions one 'Ackney 'Orby, a degenerate descendant. The same man figures in the Introductions by Dr Marcus Ardonne to *Arena of Lust* by Sextus Propertius (London, 1996), *The Secret Sutras of Sir Richard*

Burton (London, 1996) and *Unholy Passions* (London, 1997).

Wolverines by Alan Dale (London, 1998) is an account of 'Black Pearl' Horby's son's adventures as a British secret agent in Nazi Germany.

It is, in fact, possible to make a sort of sense of what initially seems to be a bewildering flood of data.

The Horby dynasty was founded, so to speak, by a tanner in the East End of London during the mid-seventeenth century: Dr Cravesit has informed me that he worked as a secret agent for King Charles II. In any event, 'Horby I' appears to have built up a nice little nest egg. It is unfortunate that he never wrote his memoirs.

'Horby II' used that nest egg to become a devastatingly successful man of business and made a fabulous killing on the South Sea Bubble Stock Exchange swindle of the early 1720s, enabling him to purchase his Viscountcy from his business associate, the Prime Minister, Sir Robert Walpole. He died a very rich man.

'Horby III' wrote his *Memoirs* in Latin, now translated into English and published as *Unholy Passions*.

'Horby IV' also wrote his *Memoirs* in Latin, now translated into English and published as *Gothic Passions*.

'Horby V' and 'Horby VI' appear to have been utterly undistinguished save in their hot pursuit of hunting, shooting, fishing and women, in that order.

'Horby VII' wrote *The Black Pearl*.

'Horby VIII' assisted Alan Dale in the writing of *Wolverines*.

'Horby IX' assisted Alan Dale in the writing of *Vixens*.

'Ackney 'Orby is an illegitimate descendant of Edmund Horby, a son of 'Horby VIII'.

The problem is that though all this data refers to a family that has played a substantial part in English culture and history, there is absolutely no reference to them in either *Burke* or *Debrett*.

Intensive research still continues.

G.L.

AUTHOR'S INTRODUCTION
TO VOLUME I

As I take up my pen to write of my life, I remain convinced that fighting and fucking are when two people come closest. You can grow close to a man either by fighting against him or by fighting with him on the same side as one slogs along through various battles. However, I am of the opinion that it is not possible to grow close to a woman unless one fucks her.

My personal view is that when fucking a woman, one should jolly well roger her brains out and give it some arse. I'm well aware that this view is thought unfashionable in our degenerate modern times. Female emancipation has indeed proceeded apace and I have never opposed it but the results have not been precisely what I wanted nor, one suspects, exactly the results desired by the fairer sex. It is indeed a delight to regard our modern young girls in their slim, short skirts but they lack the mystery and romanticism of the long, rustling white petticoats of yesteryear. These days, they all wear rosy red-leaf lip-stick and they all smoke and they pout sexily but despite all that delicious expanse of white thigh and ankle, they lack the eroticism of the women of my youth. These days one takes a girl for morning cocktails at 'The Apple Tree', goes on to luncheon at 'Pietro Le Fueno', proceeds to an afternoon session at 'Dolly's', where one's ears are deafened with jazz, takes afternoon tea at the Connaught, goes on to cocktails at the Ritz, sees the

27

latest play at the Theatre Royal, the Haymarket, has drinks and then dinner at The Savoy, and all the thanks you receive is 'Cheerio.'

Ah! It wasn't like that in the days of my golden, gilded youth! Women really were women in those spacious times! They certainly weren't boys with short bobs for hair, flat chests and thin skin and bone where the buttocks should have been. It is said that times have become increasingly sexually free. It is so and I welcome the development yet some inscrutable element has been lost. How is the matter best put? I am reminded of Lady Charlotte X, who always used to defend the institution of marriage on the grounds that it lent so much spice to the pleasures of adultery. Forbidden fruit does indeed taste so much sweeter. In a similar vein, one could advance the proposition that the very restrictions of my youth gave each forbidden encounter an exquisite charm that is wholly lacking in these present days that are so permissive and yet so cold.

Nevertheless, it is impossible for me to complain about a life indefatigably blessed by good fortune. I am hardly a rich man but even in these inflationary times it is just about possible to jog along on £100,000 a year. The only duties incumbent upon me are maintaining the lands, a job done most capably by the family stewards; and turning up at the House of Lords occasionally whenever there is a vital vote. My quiet position has enabled me to meet some of the most interesting men and women in the land and also to travel abroad to meet more.

Throughout my life, I have been a lover of Woman, in all her intriguing shapes and guises. Although I have enjoyed the good fortune of meeting with some of the strongest, most powerful and most intelligent men of my era, and although I have assuredly learned wisdom from their lips, I have received yet greater education from the labia of ladies.

This may be thought a peculiar view but I shall demonstrate my case.

Too many men of my acquaintanceship, however illustrious, have informed me that they regard the sexual act as being merely the prodding of a stiff rod between soft thighs into a soft and welcoming female orifice. Although their joy in this glorious matter can hardly be denied and although I take a deep share in their joy, knowing of it to my own good, I nevertheless insist that there is something more to the matter.

The sexual act, properly understood, is more than merely the delights of animal gratification, splendid though these are. It is more than the doing of a deed alleged to be 'dirty' and therefore somehow sinful, in consequence of which its execution imparts a sinister thrill, an added *frisson* of forbidden pleasure. It can be the holiest, most religious act in the World when a man and a woman come together and create energy between one another as a sacrament. It can elevate one's consciousness and enable one, if one dares say so, to evolve beyond the level of the apes who originally sired us.

During my life, I have been able to acquaint myself with a number of occult groups, from some of whom I learned much and from others of whom I learned nothing at all. Most of them have taught me techniques, nevertheless, which I have found to be useful. It is my willed intention to put down here all I know before I die so that possibly some others may benefit from the recounting of my experiences.

In the beginning, I knew nothing other than my rampant rod and of its lust for a slick, juicy cunt. By the end, I had discovered the Holy Grail. I shall begin, then, amidst the mist of ignorance, continue through a hard middle and, one trusts, finish with a flourish at the end.

AUTHOR'S INTRODUCTION
TO VOLUME II

As I commence dictation to my charming and beautiful secretary, whose name discretion forbids me to mention, and set forth the second volume of my *Memoirs*, a few more words of explanation are required if this work is not to receive more severe censure than that which it doubtless deserves.

'The proper study of mankind is Man,' wrote Alexander Pope and one trusts that his use of the generic term was inclusive of Woman. From an early age I have discerned the holy truth that the highest grace is conferred by the union of the male and the female in sexual congress. This perception was fully confirmed by my experience of a low mass at the castle of 'the Black Douglas', as I have referred to him, near Vienna. It is the purpose of this volume to explore my memory and retrieve from it the words and images of all encounters which have granted me understanding and wisdom, especially in terms of the practical application of my apperception.

O! how I sigh some mornings for those spacious days of the *fin de siècle* . . . ! We were all so young then and burning with lust for the World. If that be Decadence, then I loved every moment of it! Today (1925) it strikes me that so much Romance has gone out of the World. Take the recent postcard, for example, which I received this morning from my old friend, Frank Harris.

Hope you're still keeping it up, Horby! Why not come and visit me in Nice? Know the latest rhyme about the girls today?

*If the skirts get any shorter
Said the Flapper with a sob;
I'll have two more cheeks to powder
And a lot more hair to bob.
All the grimmest
Frank.*

I remain fond of the former lion of literary London, though he has been savaged by critics for the first volume of his autobiography, *My Life and Loves*, which I, for one, thoroughly enjoyed, both for its literary, political and social reminiscences and for its unabashed sexual candour. One gathers that he is presently subject to a wave of puritanical persecution. His mistake, in my view, was to cast pearls before swine in this increasingly narrow, moralistic climate of opinion, where even the United States of America, once boasting itself to be the 'home of the brave and the land of the free,' has had the stupid temerity to ban the imbibing of alcoholic beverages. Ah! how I savour the memory of those spacious days of my youth! I shall describe my visits to America in the course of this volume.

The mistake of Harris was to place his private life before the profane eyes of the riff-raff and one assumes that only the pressures of financial need persuaded him to embark on so inadvisable a course of action. I shall make no such error. This work is only for the eyes of my cultivated friends.

My morning post also brought a greetings card from H.G. Wells, thanking me for the dinner I gave him the other day. Wells has of course deservedly acquired world fame – and his amorous activities continue unabated. He is too sensible, though, to soil his reputation among the respectable by publishing publicly his reminiscences of his many encounters. 'If you don't like your life, you can change it,' he always used to say and the man was certainly a living example of practising what one preaches. In my case, however, I was too fortunate to have much desire to change my life and I do not regret anything that I have done. I regret only that which I *haven't* done.

It will readily be discerned by the reader that I received much benefit from my visit to Vienna and my witnessing of a 'low mass' of Sex-Magick. Allow me, then, to essay a narrative of my further exploration in my quest for the Holy Grail.

AUTHOR'S INTRODUCTION
TO VOLUME III

As I dictate these words of my Memoirs to my exquisitely efficient and charmingly pretty secretary, one cannot help remarking that some savour of the spacious days of my youth has gone out of the world. Personally, I blame the brutality of the Great War. Everything I knew seems to have become rather insane ever since the Armistice. I served my country in the Great War and I fought for freedom, justice and a better world for one and all, especially Great Britain. Where is it?

I don't enjoy seeing unemployed and disabled ex-soldiers on the streets, homeless and starving, especially since Lloyd George promised them 'homes fit for heroes.' I don't think it's right for the wages of the workers to be reduced by Government legislation. I freely admit that I am one of the lucky ones and that shrewd investments made by my assistants have made me richer now than I have ever been before. If I wanted to, even in this time of inflation, I could have a thirteen-year-old girl for the same price as in 1901: they're all out there whoring for their disabled fathers. It's just that unripe apples have never been of much sexual interest to me.

Take other aspects of modern life, for instance. Poetry? None of it rhymes or has scansion, rhythm or metre. Painting and sculpture? These 'Dada' chaps paint moustaches on a postcard of the Mona Lisa or else put their toe-nail clippings in a jam jar and have the nerve to call it Art! And some people are stupid enough to pay for it! Architecture? I see buildings being erected that look just like the Corn-Flakes packages of Dr Kellogg – and some poor people actually have to live in them. There's no grace any more and where will it all end?

Sex? These short dresses which expose lovely legs certainly arouse my carnal lusts – but why do the girls these days have to look as straight and flat in their figures as these new 'A' roads that our wretched Government is plastering everywhere across the landscape of our once beautiful countryside? The motor car, although it has its undeniable uses, farts forth fumes that poison our lungs. They'll be abolishing the railways next! Sometimes I really do feel like those old retired Colonels who write letters to *The Morning Post* signed 'Disgusted, Tunbridge Wells', for whilst I am certainly no Socialist, I'm damned if I know which aspects of the national heritage the Conservative Party is conserving.

Ah! It was rather different in the days of my youth when it seemed as though the world was my oyster and I travelled around the globe in search of its elusive black pearl. I invite you, gentle reader – as authors used to state a century ago – to join me in my exploration of the sacred mystery of Sex.

I had thought, after the adventures I described in my second volume, that there was precious little more for me to learn. How wrong I was! And I don't mind admitting it. There was still so much for me to discover as I journeyed around the world, witnessing all manners and mores and sexual customs, in my own singular quest for the Holy Grail.

AUTHOR'S INTRODUCTION TO VOLUME IV

I have pondered for a long time on whether or not it would be right to add to my *Memoirs*, since doing so might implicate the guilty and be seen as letting the side down. But, after much thought, here in 1926 I have resolved to consign any consequences to Hades and to dictate a further volume, covering the years 1902–1914, to my beautiful and delightful secretary, whose name discretion forbids me to mention.

In any event, these words will be read only by the privileged few. And that is just as well since, if those socialist and bolshie rabble-rousers were to get hold of my *Memoirs* of this period, it would hardly resound to the glory of the ruling class – of which I happen to be a member.

Ah! Those magnificent, spacious days before the Great War! How grand it all was! I was a mature and married man, madly in love with my wife (as these pages will make only too apparent) yet we acted in ways that today would be considered scandalous and that would be exposed by the yellow press. I can't quite believe the wave of puritanism that has come over this country, even though *our* class carries on in the way it always has done.

My old friend Aleister Crowley once told me that although he thought the Great War to be a bloody tragedy, he felt that it would nevertheless liberate people from old shibboleths. It has not done so and Crowley is and has been persecuted by the gutter press. Why, nowadays a man can't even take simple little pleasures such as hashish and cocaine – and in his own home! – without being guilty of a criminal offence.

Allow me to explain, courteous reader – as one would have written in a warmer and more civilized era – that quite a number of pursuits dominated my glorious years of 1902–1914. Firstly, there was my passion for Woman. This was principally enshrined in my love for my wife Claire: yet we had an open marriage. I did not see why our marital commitment should stop us from the riotous gaiety we had enjoyed prior to our wedding: and neither did she. In consequence, we were often apart and subsequently completely candid with one another, to our mutual satisfaction. We were both fortunate in knowing so many of the leading men and women of our era. Both of us relished the experience of being apart and then coming together with enticing tales to tell as, together and separately, we explored the fabulously wide range of sexual experience. By 1902, I had thought that I knew it all. I am happy to admit: how wrong I was!

The same words are true when we turn to Magick and my search, indeed my quest for the Holy Grail of Truth and Beauty. However, being now an Initiate of a Secret Order as opposed to the green innocent little boy I once was, I could tell the difference between the true and the false. What a ride it was, though!

My third interest was in Politics from behind the scenes. Here it is astonishing how wrong one can be sometimes. Despite my intimacy – shall we say? – with certain of the Suffragettes, I never thought that they would succeed in their objectives. At least I've been right about Adolf Hitler, a ghastly little Austrian would-be occultist whose bid for power in war-savaged Germany failed miserably and who, after far too little time in prison, has at least had the decency to vanish into a richly deserved obscurity.

However, I could not quite believe the incompetence of the men who were in control of Europe. It had always been thought that our class has a right to govern because it is very good at it. Having served in the Great War, I am not the only one having difficulties with sustaining that belief.

It was that same Great War that destroyed all our previous and automatic assumptions: it killed our whole world and endeavours to revive it have not been a success. The flower of our finest youth died in the trenches.

The Generals stank to high heaven but I shall, I hope, show you just how fine that flower of youth was.

CHAPTER ONE

Ah! What a fabulous honeymoon it was on the Riviera! Initially, Claire and I took a suite at the Hôtel de Paris in Monte Carlo. Everyone who works at that place, in whatever humble position, exudes a pride that proclaims the Hôtel to be superbly superior; and, actually, it is. The prices are as rich as the furnishings, but that hardly troubled Claire or myself. No expense would be spared on my honeymoon with my gorgeous wife. To this day I love her fine head of blonde curls, striking eyes flecked with blue and gold, small breasts like ripening apples, neat waist, pert bottom that thrust out and seemed to take a secret joy in every swish of her skirt, and lean lissom legs with well-turned ankles. Many fail to realize that one of the chief charms of the early days of marriage is precisely the sexuality we had earlier celebrated in magical rituals.

Of course, and as described, I'd been to Monte Carlo before with good old Frank Harris and his charming friend, Princess Alice of Monaco. That is why I wanted to show its delights to Claire. The dramatic heights of Monte Carlo give one a superb view. The town is named after Charles III, who opened the first casino in around 1865 to save himself from bankruptcy. This move was so successful that, five years later, he abolished taxation! Queen Victoria, who had occupied the same suite now in our temporary possession, thought that Monte Carlo was a den of iniquity. Bloody typical! The Prince of Wales, now King Edward VII, had always loved it.

So when Claire and I arrived in our suite, I flung her down upon our four-poster bed, pulled up her dress, tore down her knickers and proceeded to fuck her brains out. She screamed and she sighed and she cried as she came again and again. This was a good way to begin. I had already ensured that we had plenty of champagne and cognac and Armagnac, burgundy, Bordeaux and Beaune; so we refreshed ourselves before proceeding to the more subtle arts of love.

Claire smacked her lips as she snaked her long, slender fingers around my gigantic shaft and lustily fisted it up and down in her hand. Then, on the bed, she slid down on her knees to lick my knob, swirling her tongue over the wide uncapped helmet to my obvious delight. I threw my left arm around her waist. With my right hand, I fondled my wife's jutting bare breasts, topped by nut-brown nipples which I tweaked between my fingers.

'Suck my titties, darling . . .' she moaned and I complied eagerly, nibbling gently on one nipple and then the other as my own dear luscious bitch squirmed in delicious agony. Of course, rubbing a woman's titties is a prelude to the main event but Claire needed no further stimulation as, shaking all over, she spent with a happy yelp of ecstasy. 'Now it's your turn . . .' she murmured.

Holding my prick, which she gripped in both hands, she proceeded to wash her talented tongue all over my knob before closing her lips over my purple bell-end and sliding my thick shaft down her throat in one fluid gulp. Then she eased back, licking the underside of my shaft until she reached my balls, which she sucked into her mouth, swishing them around before releasing them to lick all the way back up to my knob. *This* really was an excellent sucking-off, since Claire now eased her lips over the head of my prick and slowly took my shaft into her pouting mouth while her hands busily circled themselves around my balls, gently caressing the wrinkly pink sac as her fair head began to bob up and down over my throbbing tool.

My own hand automatically shot out to caress her bottom as she gobbled more of my rigid cock into her throat. Her tongue darted along the sensitive underside and I jerked my hips upwards as she sensually sucked on my ramrod.

Thrilling spasms of pure delight swirled through my body until I yelled out that I was about to come. With her mouth still filled with my hot cock, Claire gently squeezed my balls as I shot a stream of creamy jism down her throat.

A wonderful, orgasmic wave of release swept through me once more as she swallowed every drop of my gushing emission, draining my shaft of its salty essence. Then Claire pulled my fast-shrinking shaft out of her mouth.

'Wasn't that nice, Horby?' she enquired as she licked her lips with satisfaction. 'Now, how would you like to fuck my little wet cunny?' She parted her thighs to give me a lovely view of her puffy pink love lips and that red chink of her cunny which stood out in the fair curly muff surrounding her dripping honeypot. Taking hold of my palpitating prick, my wife guided my knob between her yielding quim lips until her clingy sheath had totally enveloped my shaft and the hairs of our pubic bushes matted together.

Then she drummed the heels of her dainty feet against my bottom whilst my prick, renewed in vigour by her entrancing moves, slid in and out of her juicy cooze. A tidal wave of the most exquisite rapture washed over me and my eager cock once more stretched the walls of Claire's cunt to their limits.

She reached around my sides to grab my bum cheeks and

our movements quickened. Soon I began to shiver as I felt my impending ejaculation boiling up in my balls. So I slowed the pace of my thrusts until Claire's moans grew higher and higher and I judged that she was again ready to spend. At this point, I speeded up the fuck again, plunging my shaft in and out of her soft, wet crack until she arched up her back.

With a cry, she fell back as I shot a tremendous jet of jism inside her tunnel of love as we shuddered to a glorious simultaneous climax.

Both of us were hungry after that and so we took a carriage to Le Café de Paris, making a slight detour so as to see some of the sights of the place.

'Stunning,' said Claire as we admired the view of Monte Carlo from La Turbie, reached by a stretch of the Grand Corniche that crosses ravines through mountains. This charming old village still retains two medieval gateways and is scented with jasmine and bougainvillea. 'Stunning,' Claire said again as we viewed the Casino and Opera House, built by Charles Garnier, architect of the Paris Opera. 'Stunning,' Claire said once more as I pointed out the Salle Garnier, designed in 1878 and later the favourite performance venue of those brilliant at ballet, such as Diaghilev and Nijinsky.

'You know one difference between you and me?' I asked as the carriage clip-clopped forward to our destination. 'I'm a cunning stunt – and you're a stunning cunt!'

'Oh, Horby!' She burst out laughing. She would always call me Horby. She always had before. Why should marriage make any difference? On arrival at the Café de Paris, who did we see but King Edward VII – with whom we were both acquainted, naturally. He was sitting with an entourage of courtiers, as usual, but on seeing us he roared out in his throaty voice:

44

'Horby! You old bugger! And Claire! What a pleasure to see you, my dear! Join us!' How can one refuse the invitation of the King of England?

Actually, although I didn't know him *that* well, I had always rather liked him. He had come to the throne with a difficult task. He had to follow a much-loved and venerated sovereign – who, as his mother, had disliked and disapproved of him. She had firmly kept him out of public affairs so that, at almost sixty, he was taking over an important and complicated function for which he was utterly untrained. Yet he plunged into the work as eagerly as he plunged into his dinner.

And what a feast he ordered! It was just what Claire and I needed. There was bouillabaisse, a glorious fish stew, which included monkfish – I love it and call it 'poor man's lobster' – red mullet, snapper, conger eel and the essential ingredient, scorpion fish, with tomatoes, saffron and olive oil. The fish broth was served first with croutons spread with *rouille*, a spicy garlic mayonnaise, and grated cheese. The fish was eaten after the broth but the King had also ordered *Fruits de Mer*, the fruits of the sea: mussels, scallops, crawfish, oysters and giant prawns. To complete the dishes of fishes, there was sea bass grilled over a fire of fennel with aniseed-flavoured *pastis* flamed at our table. To add extra spice to the matter, there was *aioli*, a garlic mayonnaise served with salt cod, boiled eggs and snails; a *Salade Niçoise* of tuna, lettuce, olives, green beans, eggs, tomatoes, potatoes and anchovies . . . and then it was time for some meat.

The *Daube de boeuf*, beef in red wine and cooked in a pot-bellied casserole, proved delicious, as did the roasted *gigot*, tender lamb that was positively dripping with blood. *Ratatouille*, a hearty stew of onions, aubergines, courgettes, tomatoes and peppers, cooked with olive oil, herbs and garlic, proved to be an excellent accompaniment. Then the King said that he wasn't feeling particularly hungry this evening and he hoped that nobody minded if we proceeded to the cheese board. Fifty exquisite cheeses from which to choose were surely enough to satisfy anyone.

The English and the French still argue over whether there should be pudding before cheese or cheese before pudding . . . Myself, I think that every country has a right to its customs, so these days, whenever I am in France, I do what the French do. So did the King of England, for we now had *Tarte au citron*, a flan base of sweet pastry filled with an intensely tangy yet creamy lemon custard mixture. Cherries from Apt, citrus fruits from Menton, Cavaillon melon, figs from Marseilles, and the grapes of Provence appeared on our table. Then King Edward turned lovingly to the gorgeous girl seated next to him, whose name was Suzette, and he asked her what she wanted. She promptly asked for thin pancakes flamed in Cointreau and cognac. The King promptly requested these for everybody and they called the dish 'Crêpes Suzette' ever afterwards in honour of the pair of them. Actually, I have rarely eaten a dessert so delicious.

I found that our new King kept asking question after question, then he would interrupt answers with 'Yes, yes, yes;' give orders, scribble notes on bits of paper in his scarcely legible handwriting and then smoke one of his immense cigars, looking wonderfully like Henry VIII, only better-tempered. I had the impression of a man who, after long years of pent-up inaction, had suddenly been freed from restraint and now revelled in his liberty.

The faults of Edward were outweighed by his virtues. Yes, there was huffing and puffing and tantrums and prejudices, but he accomplished the adjustment of a monarchy into a democratic society remarkably well. He liked people and he had a talent for projecting his amiable qualities. He restored the State opening of Parliament, abandoned for forty years. He was hearty and affable with all, not standing on his dignity and so never losing it. Even the journalists loved him. (I was present in the last year of his reign when he was able to lead in his third Derby winner, Minoru, to deafening shouts of 'Good old Teddy!' from the assembled multitudes; quite a contrast to his mother, Queen Victoria, who was hissed at Ascot.)

'I am all for the British Empire,' he declared loudly over coffee, cognac and cigars. 'We can be the most powerful factor in world policy, advocating peace and harmony between the nations. But great heavens! How I detest my cousin the Kaiser. That bloody idiot will bring about a war if he's not careful! And none of the Great Powers want a Great War! Bloody stupid!'

No one could have called the King intellectual. His primary interests were drink, cigars, gargantuan meals and amorous affairs. Even so, he really did want to be a force for good in the World.

'Now we must go,' he rumbled as he put out his cigar. 'And let's not waste time, ladies and gentlemen. If there's one thing I simply can't bear, it is someone doing what I call a *Must Be Going*. Y'know, those wretched bores who say "Must be going" – so you are ready for their departure – and half an hour later, they're still bloody there! How's it possible for people to be so boring? Who's that fellow who wrote a book about vampires? Stoker or something. Yes, I think that these people suck one's energies away. If you're going, GO! And that's what we'll do now.'

It had been a very good evening and Claire and I returned to our hotel. How lovely it was to tumble her in a suite designed in a fashion later known as *La Belle Époque*! Claire had swiftly undone the buttons of her blouse and shrugged the garment off her shoulders. My shaft immediately swelled up when she tugged her chemise over her head and exposed her luscious bare breasts to my excited gaze, Then she licked her lips and sensually cupped the magnificent, snowy globes in her hands and pushed them into my face.

'How would you like to suck my titties?' she teased me, her mouth turning down at the corners in such a sensually sarcastic way.

'Definitely,' I answered. Then I reached out and rubbed my fingertips against the inviting, rubbery brown berries. I licked each one in turn, as a *sommelier* would taste a wine, and my tongue swirled around first one nipple and then the other as Claire drew back her head. Naked, we embraced as we rolled together on the bed, writhing around in each other's arms as Claire's tongue and lips hungrily sought after my body. I put my hand down between her thighs, so satin-smooth, and discovered that her knickers were already soaking wet with lubricating love-juice.

I pulled them off and ran my forefinger along the slippery groove of her sex. She moaned softly and spread her legs as my fingertip delicately explored the sensitive folds and my knuckle brushed against her erect clitty.

'Oooh, yes . . . *yes*!' she squealed as I rolled on top of her and my prick started to leap and dance about between her thighs, once more seeking an entrance in the glistening bush of hair through which her puffy pussy lips pouted so enticingly. My hands roved across her gorgeous breasts and I fingered her engorged thrusting titties as Claire clasped her hand around my pulsating prick and guided it into her dripping cunt. Sliding my cock in and out of her wet, warm cunny was quite heavenly and I moaned in sheer rapture as I jerked my hips to and fro, fucking my eager wife with unalloyed delight.

Our movements rapidly became more heated when I thrust forward hard, sending my shaft plunging deep into her squelchy slit. By heaven, how I enjoyed this magnificent fuck, slewing my willing shaft in and out of her juicy love channel! Claire yelped as she felt the tip of my knob touch the innermost walls of her cunt and she wrapped her legs around my waist to hold me firmly inside her as I continued to pound away, my prick driving in and out of the tender folds of her cunt from which her juices were liberally flowing.

She began to buck to and fro, her bum cheeks lifting themselves off the sheet as she closed her legs around me like a vice as I continued to pump in and out of her sopping sheath. How she screamed as she shuddered her way to a delicious orgasm!

As she slowed her pace, I set up another rhythm, fucking her with short, sharp jabs and she climaxed again whilst I panted out a warning that my own spend was near. Ah! My young bitch massaged the underside of my balls, and immediately this extra stimulation brought on my final surge. A hoarse cry erupted from my throat as I emptied myself into her, flooding her cunny with tremendous spurts of hot, sticky sperm.

She screamed with delight as the spunky gush sent shock after shock of erotic energy coursing through our veins. Next, she expertly milked my cock with repeated squeezes of her cunt muscles until I pulled out my deflated shaft and heaved myself off her.

We refreshed ourselves with champagne and brandy; then, being young and in love, we returned to the fray. Claire took hold of my renewed battering ram, rock-hard, and directed my purple-domed cock towards her pouting pussy lips.

'Now slide your cock forward . . .' she sighed, 'and you will see that the key will fit the lock.' With my first thrust, I pushed forward into her welcoming sheath; with the second, I was halfway home, for her cunt was so neat and small; and with the third, my entire pulsating prick was entirely esconced inside her juicy honeypot. Claire's tight little arse cheeks trembled with excitement.

I wanted to prolong this ecstatic experience and so I pushed in and out as slowly as I could. This seemed most pleasing to Claire, who responded with her own upward heaves to my downward thrusts. Her gorgeous bottom rolled violently as she clawed at my back – and I grasped her shoulders and began to ride her like a Wild West cowboy taming a bucking bronco.

Claire's legs straightened out and her heels drummed against the mattress as she arched her back, working her cunny muscles back and forth along the velvety length of my tumescent tool. With a hoarse cry of rapture, I thrust my cock so fully inside Claire's vagina that my balls fairly smacked against the tops of her thighs.

This so aroused my lascivious bitch of a wife – darling girl – that she rotated her hips wildly, lifting her lovely bottom to obtain the maximum contact with my cock. I groaned with lust as Claire's fingernails raked across my back.

'Yes!' she yelled out. '*Yes*! Ah . . .' she panted. 'Oh! So delectable! Now shoot your spunk and make me come, you horny bastard!' And then a primordial sound spilled out from deep within my gorgeous girl as an all-enveloping orgasm shivered through her body and, to our mutual delight, Claire reached her peak of pleasure just as the first convulsive shudders rippled through my body and my prick spurted out my tribute of sticky warm jism into her flooded love funnel.

That night I thought that there was definitely something to be said for married life.

CHAPTER TWO

'Married life? Yes! Love it!' Sir Richard Bellingham declared, 'and it can be even better when the wife is away . . .' We were sitting at Rules in Covent Garden, London's oldest restaurant dating from 1798. It's a place to go for solid traditionalist stuff and all the better for that. They don't know how to make soup there and their vegetables are usually overcooked but – by Gad! – their steak-and-kidney pudding is superlative. That was what I was having as Bellingham tucked into a mixed grill of rump steak – most appropriate for him – pork chop, lamb chump chop, pork sausage and a chicken leg. 'So how was the honeymoon?'

'*Excellent*! It was a real joy to explore the Riviera and some places in the interior of Provence.'

'Ah, yes!' he chuckled. 'Loved my honeymoon. After that? Y'know, Horby, the trouble with wives is that they can be a wretched, damn' nuisance if they're around the place the whole time. That's what I find with Davina. Sometimes I just can't wait for her to go out – so much so that when she makes some sort of stupid, artificial delay, I just want to take the arse of my dear lady wife and boot it right into the street – yet if she's away too long, I start to miss her.'

'I'm the same,' I replied as we toasted one another's health with an excellent Beaune. 'But, fortunately, Claire realizes the nature of my temperament. So here I am back in

London while she's still swanning about in France. How about Davina?'

'She's presently swanning about in Scotland. Ah!' He drank deeply of his glass and ordered another bottle. 'What a grand voyage we had, eh, Horby?! And it's worked out well for one and all of us. Douglas, a man I'll never understand – though he's really rather a damn' fine fellow – has gone and purchased an Earldom.'

'*Purchased* an Earldom? What, you mean it's like going into a shop?'

'I suppose it is, nowadays. The Tory Party is short of money. Anyway, he's bunked off to Spain for a bit with Rosemary.'

'Good for him and good for her. Hm.' I finished my course. 'Excellent. What's for pud?' I ordered jam sponge whilst Bellingham opted for treacle sponge with extra cream.

'Yes, Douglas is now the Earl of something or other,' Sir Richard continued. 'Good old Captain Jack Rivers is now employed by wealthy people to skipper their boats. He's sailing the seven seas, where he's happiest. Ram Singh and Amin Shah – both jolly good chaps, in my opinion – have gone to America and, in their separate ways, they are being paid a fortune to lecture on something called "spirituality". I wish them luck. Personally, I couldn't bear talking nonsense to halfwits.'

'And Alison and Jane . . . ?'

'Ah, yes!' Bellingham beamed broadly. 'Indeed, yes. Lady Jane and Lady Alison will be of the company later on tonight.'

'Excellent!' I declared enthusiastically, thinking of the voluptuous bottom of Lady Jane and the slender buttocks of Lady Alison. The combination of their sexy arses and their slim faces really was rather irresistible.

'So marriage hasn't deterred you from adultery?' he enquired as the Stilton was served – with a well-decanted bottle of vintage port, naturally.

'On the contrary. Adultery lends so much spice to marriage.'

'Good man!' Sir Richard roared with laughter. 'And I trust that Claire is of the same opinion . . . ?'

'Oh, indeed. I'm looking forward to more of her erotic letters.'

'Yes, I don't give a fuck if Davina has a fuck. I just don't want her emotionally involved.'

'That's how I feel. But tell me, Bellingham – I've been out of touch, what with my honeymoon and so on – what's the political situation?'

'Balfour's not a bad chap, as we both know, since we've often dined with him. You have to hand it to the man – perfect equilibrium, and an admirable temper and iron nerves. That fellow's got a fine brain. Always reading: in bed, in his bath, even as he shaves – science, philosophy, theology, detective stories, anything but the newspapers. We have quite a philosopher as our Prime Minister, Horby. Although, the other day, Davina and I attended a debate in the House of Commons. "How masterful, cool and collected he seems," she declared to me.

'Actually,' said Bellingham, 'he was asleep. The bugger never gets out of bed before midday. Then he dozes whenever he is bored. He dozes rather a lot at the House of Commons. Attending Parliament at all, Horby?'

'Not at present. No need. Why do so?'

'Oh, you're quite right there, old chap!' Bellingham laughed heartily and ordered more port, along with fruit and nuts. 'Why add to the boredom? Why have nothing to say and say it? It's just that I've got this unpleasant feeling that there are crises coming. There is something in England which I feel to be bubbling and boiling and threatening to change the country out of all recognition. What's this?!' he roared at the waiter, who had just served us with two small glasses of port.

'Your port, sir,' the young waiter replied.

'Oh, for heaven's sake!' Bellingham expostulated angrily, then checked himself. 'You're obviously new here and so you wouldn't know. My friend and I here *don't* drink dinky little glasses of port. *We drink bloody pints of port out of tankards like men*! So get them!' he roared in a voice of thunder. The young waiter shrank visibly and ran away to do Bellingham's bidding. 'Really! What is this place coming to? Ah!' he smiled happily as the pints of port were brought. 'That's better! Anyway, been following the boxing, Horby?'

'Been catching up.' I quaffed some port, which was excellent. 'The Heavyweight Championship of the World is still held by James J. Jeffries of America. I've seen him fight and they don't call him *The Iron Man* and *The Grizzly Bear* for nothing. He has destroyed every challenger, including the previous Champion, Gentleman Jim Corbett and my good friend, England's Bob Fitzsimmons. Fitz lost his title to him and challenged again. I read the reports. Fitz hit him with everything. It was even rumoured that he had plaster of Paris on his bandages beneath the gloves; and that Jeffries, hearing this, said: "Let him use it. I'll still knock him out." Well, good, old Fitz battered this giant, breaking his nose, cutting both cheeks to the bone, opening a cut over his right eye and closing his left until it seemed that the downpour of blood must compel the big fellow to surrender. Jeffries's seconds begged him to do so. "Nope," said Jeffries; and with a tremendous right to the body and left to the jaw, he stretched out our Fitz in the eighth round.'

'Bad news,' said Bellingham. 'I want an Englishman to be Heavyweight Champion of the World.'

'But there's some consolation. Something new called the World Light-Heavyweight Championship has been instituted – and at forty, our Bob Fitzsimmons has gone and won it!'

'Splendid!' Sir Richard exclaimed. 'I'll drink to that. But have we got nobody who can beat this American Jeffries?'

'No,' I replied. 'Unfortunately, that's the truth. I honestly think that he *is* the toughest man in the World. He seems to embody the spirit of an invincible and expanding America.'

'Humph!' said Bellingham. 'They'd better not touch the British Empire. Heard anything from your peculiar friend Crowley?'

'Yes. He's married now to one Rose Edith Kelly, a clergyman's daughter and sister of Gerald, an artist fellow I knew slightly at Cambridge. Crowley keeps sending me postcards from his honeymoon trip – Rome, Naples, Cairo and various places in India. Seemed to me at one point that he'd embraced Buddhism, since he sent me a postcard with the message: "Wishing you a speedy termination of existence".'

'Funny chap,' Bellingham remarked. 'I really don't know about all of this Magick stuff. I'm frankly completely disillusioned with the Golden Dawn. While you were away, quite rightly gallivanting about in Provence with Claire, I took a look at the situation. The Golden Dawn has split up into congeries of squabbling factions. I'm afraid I can't bear Yeats. Mind you, I don't care for Crowley either but I do agree with his nickname for Yeats: Weary Willie. So I want nothing to do with that group. Then I've tried the faction that's the "Holy" Order of the Golden Dawn under one Arthur Edward Waite.'

'Oh . . .'

'Dreadful! That frightful fellow has rewritten the rituals, lengthened them intolerably, removed the magical elements and bloody Christianized the fucking thing. No, thank you. I thought that I'd stay loyal to Mathers. At least I had some respect for the chap. Unfortunately, I don't care for his London deputy, Dr Berridge. I mean, all they do is sit around in circles imagining things and calling it astral travel. Bad news, old boy.' He finished his pint of port and so did I. 'Quick brandy, eh?' I nodded. 'How're *you* feeling about these things?'

'You must admit that you and I have witnessed some wonderful things, Bellingham.' He nodded. 'And whereas, earlier in my life, I was prepared to state that I didn't give a toss about any Holy Guardian Angel, I was wrong. Honestly mistaken. Ah! Cognac! Good! I truly *do* want a closer connection with this Holy Guardian Angel that Crowley is always on about and I *do* want more magical and mystical experiences. Frankly, from everything I know so far, the secret of Magick is Sex in a sacred context. That really *does* alter consciousness for the better.'

'Can't disagree with *that*,' Sir Richard returned as he paid the bill. 'So let's go and see Alison and Jane. They're now sharing some place in Primrose Hill.'

'How do we get there? I haven't brought a carriage. Too crowded in Central London. Frankly, I don't mind using the Underground Railway occasionally. Gives one a slice of life.'

'Quite agree,' said Bellingham, 'but you really must try *my* carriage. It's a *motor*-carriage.' We went out into the street and there it was, a rather elegant piece of machinery made by Daimler of Germany. Bellingham cranked up the engine which chundered into life. Then we climbed in and this ingenious mechanical contrivance went *put-put-put* and, dispensing utterly with horses and the horseshit all over the streets, we proceeded to move at a reasonable speed. Mind you, the machine did emit its own variety of foul and noxious odours.

'It's the future, Horby!' Bellingham bellowed. 'These things are going to go faster and faster.' Well, we got to Primrose Hill at a somewhat slower speed than two good horses could have taken a cabriolet but certainly faster than a horse-bus.

What a pleasure it was to see Lady Jane and Lady Alison again! They welcomed us with the finest Armagnac and good coffee. I was actually becoming a little concerned about them: I genuinely liked them and, if they did not make marriages within a couple of years, people might start to wonder.

But how sexy they were! If I had not married Claire, I might have thought of marrying either Lady Alison or Lady Jane. How they swished their tight skirts and petticoats! How they exposed a peeping ankle to one's delighted gaze! How they bent over, when serving drinks, to emphasize their arses!

Then, having served us fine brandy, Alison and Jane proceeded to amaze us, just as they had on our SS *Albion* voyage, by embracing one another and falling down upon this immense divan they had. Sir Richard and I looked on with delight at the display of their lascivious lusts as they slowly stripped one another of their clothes – and they really were enjoying being watched! Bellingham and I have seen too many extraordinarily erotic things to be easily shocked but we were still impressed by their slinky caresses.

Jane expressed further admiration of Alison's lithe body as she stroked her friend's proud, uplifted breasts before moving her hands down to the base of her flat dimpled belly and the thatch of brown curls that covered her Venus mound. Alison responded by smoothing her own palm over Jane's inviting moist bush of cunny hair. Who was going to make the most interesting moves?

'What a glorious little notch you have, darling!' Jane

breathed heavily as her left hand moved upwards to rub Alison's erect nipples. 'You must let me pay homage to its beauty.'

'Oooh! Jane! Stop it at once, darling, that's extremely naughty of you!' Alison exclaimed. But she made no attempt to move Jane's hand as the voluptuous girl pressed firmly on the fluffy fuzz of light brown cunny hair that shielded Alison's pouting pussy lips.

'Naughty but nice,' Jane returned as she pulled open Alison's quim lips and gently rubbed her knuckles back and forth across the entrance to her moistening slit. This insistent frigging of her sensitive quim soon made Alison purr with pleasure as she lay back on the pillow and let the trembling waves of ecstasy sweep through her trembling body.

'Oh, yes . . . please bring me off, you bitch . . .' she sighed and began wriggling with delight when Jane eased first one and then a further two fingers into her cunt, sliding them in and out of Alison's sticky honeypot at an increased rate of acceleration.

Jane gradually moved herself up over the writhing Alison, still keeping her busy fingers working relentlessly inside her sopping pussy as they exchanged impassioned, openmouthed kisses. My cock shot up to bursting point when Alison rolled over on her side and I saw her dimpled bottom tense as Jane toyed with her clitty.

'Oh! Ah! Aaaargh!' Alison shrieked out in blissful agony as she was brought to the very brink of coming by Jane's skilful finger-fucking. Her cries of delight were so loud and piercing that I wondered whether they might shatter our brandy glasses. It was all too much and so – rather like a peepshow on Brighton's Palace Pier – it was *Trousers Down Fast* for Bellingham and myself. Of course, that was exactly what these dear girls wanted. They rolled over onto the furry Afghan rug, the hugest I had ever seen, that covered the floor.

Both of them were *trembling* with lust. My quivering shaft stood sky-high, virtually slamming up against my belly as I jumped onto the rug next to the voluptuous Jane, who sat up and took hold of the throbbing tool that stood up so eagerly before her.

'Give him a good suck to begin with!' Alison laughed. Jane nodded as she bent forward and began licking my hairy scrotum, flicking the tip of her tongue around the pink-skinned ball-sac. I gurgled my appreciation when Jane opened her lips wide and crammed both my balls inside her mouth, gently sucking them as I gasped out my delighted excitement. Jane was obviously enjoying herself, although after a while she released me and then held the uncapped dome-crown of my prick in front of her face. She washed her tongue over the smooth surface of the bell-end before *stuffing* the rubicund helmet back between her lips.

Then she *gobbled* about half of my thick, blue-veined truncheon into her mouth and bobbed her head up and down my rod. I clutched her head within my hands as Jane slurped uninhibitedly on her fleshly lollipop.

'Bravo!' Bellingham shouted. Then this magnificent beast of a woman paused for a moment and, with her wide mouth filled with my pulsing prick, she looked up at me as if to enquire politely whether I was enjoying this splendid tonguing.

'Splendid! Splendid!' I cried out. 'Keep up the good work!' Jane withdrew, smiled, and wet her lips before resuming her work, running her tongue along my shaft as her head dipped back and forth. When my impending coming was obvious, she gripped the base of my cock and sucked and swallowed as she tickled me under my balls to speed the flow. Almost immediately, a stream of creamy spunk erupted into Jane's mouth and my prick bucked uncontrollably as she held my cock tightly between her lascivious lips.

Alison and Sir Richard looked on admiringly as Jane managed to gulp down every drop of my spunky ejaculation, lapping around the bulging knob and licking up the last salty drops from my shrinking shaft.

'Now fuck me,' Alison breathed to Bellingham. His prick was obviously in a state of avid, unbridled lust. Turning Alison over, he parted her pert bum cheeks with his hands to insert his bursting boner below them. As the tip of his rod touched her cunny lips, Alison turned her head and when their lips met in a burning kiss, she obviously drew his tongue into her mouth and cleverly wiggled her bottom so that he was able to embed his stiff cock deep inside her juicy cunt. With an impassioned jolt of their loins, his shaft was fully sheathed.

'You fucking bastard!' Alison cried out with glee as Sir Richard began to fuck her and their hips worked away in unison.

'AH! You fucking bitch!' he returned. 'I just love it, the way your sopping slit is clasping my cock. I glory in each tremendous thrust – ah! – and your love juices drip on my balls . . .' These were slapping against the backs of her thighs.

'Bastard!' she screamed.

'Bitch!' he roared.

And then they both came together and it was quite a sight to see. Both of them looked so *joyful*.

For a time, we all rested, entwined in embraces, but then the women were at it again. Jane rolled Alison onto her back and began to tongue her ear as she pressed her taut nipples between her fingers. Then she pressed her face quickly down to Alison's soft nest of flaxen pussy hair, exciting her almost beyond endurance.

'Ah!' Jane inhaled the heady aroma of Alison's aroused cunny. Then she began to lick out Alison's quim, forcing her tongue inside the quivering wet love-tunnel, sliding it up and down the slit, pushing and probing as Alison rubbed herself off against Jane's mouth.

This sight drove me crazy. As soon as the girls were done, I grabbed Jane and prodded my rod into her. Jane threw back her head in sheer rapture, tossing her mane of glossy blonde hair over her shoulders as she urged me to ram my rod harder and harder and deeper and deeper.

With her beautifully rounded bum cheeks cupped in my palms, she writhed quite savagely as my sinewy shaft rammed in and out of her dripping honeypot. She shrieked out her pleasure and I could feel the throbbing of her vaginal muscles. When she spent, with shuddering cries of release, within seconds great gouts of jism gushed out of my twitching tool and creamed every nook and cranny of Jane's clingy quim.

We collapsed down on the furry rug in front of the blazing fire. Both of us smiled as we saw that Bellingham's prick was standing to stiff attention and that he had moved round the rug to be behind Alison. In fact, Jane, discerning his intentions, passed him a nearby jar of double cream . . .

'Just what I need!' Sir Richard bellowed as he smeared it all over his rampant cock. He promptly proceeded to plunge his rampaging rod into the tiny rosette of Alison's rear dimple.

'Oh, Sir Richard . . .' she sighed. 'I didn't know that you were like that.'

'Bottoms up!' he roared. Alison responded by wriggling her arse until Bellingham's prick was deep inside her back passage. Taking a deep breath, Sir Richard threw his arms around Alison's waist and frigged her quim, simultaneously ramming his rod in and out of the now-widened rim of Alison's puckered little arsehole. This double stimulation made the darling girl squeal as she squirmed under the surging strokes of his shaft and she cried out with an exquisite, light-hearted gaiety.

'Aargh! Ah . . . I'm coming. Empty your balls in my backside, you randy rascal!' Alison's love juices appeared to flow freely as Bellingham flooded her bottom with a copious discharge of sticky seed and continued to work his way to and fro until, with a sound like the popping of a cork from a rare vintage wine, he unplugged his prick from Alison's bum-hole.

'Sex,' Jane commented, 'has to be the best spectator sport in the world! Although,' she added as an aside, 'personally, I prefer actually *doing* it.'

It might well have been a great joy to stay longer. But I had shot my load and so had Bellingham and I could see that he was moved by the same impulse as me: that desire to go home, be alone and rest content in one's own bed.

Of course, and as we knew, Jane and Alison were quite insatiable when it came to the romance of lust so they continued to play with one another. As Sir Richard and I put on our clothes, it was a delight to see Jane and Alison rubbing their pussies together. Earlier, I mentioned interesting moves. Jane had been dominant. But now, Alison climbed on top of Jane's back and brought herself off by frigging her clitty with her left thumb and forefinger and Jane's quim with the fingers of her right hand.

'I have always maintained,' Sir Richard proclaimed pompously, as he sometimes did, 'that the fellow who said that women were the weaker sex was a damned fool!' Jane and Alison burst out laughing. 'But what a splendid fuck! Thank you, ladies.'

'Yes, *thank* you, sweet ladies,' I said.

'Our pleasure,' they replied in chorus.

'Come again,' Alison smiled.

'Both your pricks,' Jane said, 'performed with distinction.'

CHAPTER THREE

As I compose these Memoirs, I can't include everything, obviously, so I have to be selective in picking the most interesting events. There's so much history packed into those twelve years from 1902–14, though it may fairly be said that for much of that time I was just living the life of an Edwardian gentleman of leisure. That sort of life has been described time and time again and the truth is that, wonderful though it is for a while, in the end one is wearied by it and yearns for something completely different.

I certainly received *that* when I accepted the invitation of Aleister Crowley to come and spend a week at his place in Boleskine, by Loch Ness. I was in need of a change and they do say that a change is as good as a rest. I arrived to find that Boleskine is a good, old-fashioned hunting lodge, having discovered on my way that, in the vicinity, Crowley was referred to in tones of awe and described as 'the laird'. Myself, I find his posturing as 'Sir Aleister MacGregor' and 'Lord Boleskine' to be perfectly *pre*posterous: but this sort of joking around doesn't really offend me, especially since he turned out to be a magnificent host.

He introduced me to his wife, born Rose Edith Kelly, daughter of a clergyman and sister of the painter, Gerald Kelly. (*Editor's Note*: Gerald Kelly eventually became President of the Royal Academy and received a knighthood.) I found the beauty of Rose to be dazzling. What a stunningly sexy bitch she was! What a magnificent beast of a woman! She was charming and delightful with it, too, though it struck me that she was drinking heavily even while pregnant. Still, it's no wonder that Crowley wrote such beautiful poetry to her and about her, his *Odes to the Rose*. 'Rose of the Earth!' 'Rose of Heaven!' 'Rose of Hell!' then 'A Fallen Rose'. I did not know then that their marriage would end in tears since, at the time, they seemed to be so happy together and it was a delight to witness the sight. Certainly Rose was also a most gracious hostess.

'Welcome!' Crowley boomed at me on my arrival, 'to the happiest house party in the Highlands!' Actually, it was. Crowley's kindly Aunt Annie, apparently the only female member of his family whom he could tolerate, ran the house admirably. The other guests were a mixed assemblage. There was the thickly black-bearded Dr Jacot Guillarmod, for instance, whom I found to be pleasant, indeed hearty company, who had accompanied Crowley and Oscar Eckenstein in their assault on K2, the world's second-highest mountain (Everest then being inaccessible to foreigners). Guillarmod's book *Six Mois dans l'Himalaya* had just been published in his native Switzerland. This remarkable first expedition ever on this mountain established a camp at 21,000 feet and Crowley had reached the altitude of 22,000 feet before abominable weather conditions, including a virtually interminable blizzard, forced them to turn back. The second expedition of the Duke of Abruzzi reached an altitude lower than that of the Eckenstein–Crowley expedition and was forced to turn back. This record has not been surpassed, nor that of spending sixty-eight days on the Baltoro glacier.

(*Editor's Note*: These records would eventually be surpassed after the date of this writing in the later 1920s but K2 was not conquered until the use of oxygen tanks in the early 1950s.)

The other male guest could not have been a greater contrast to the bearded, beefy, burly Dr Jacot Guillarmod if he'd tried. I refer to the thin and pale Lieutenant-Colonel Gormley. One night, over the port, he claimed to have been flagellated by over two thousand women.

'It seems a very large number,' Crowley commented. Gormley was obviously madly in love with Rose Crowley. I gazed at her with eyes of lust whilst he gazed at her with eyes of slavish adoration. Since he was an old India hand and could be rather witty, Crowley tolerated his attentions to his wife, who needed to be kept amused during her pregnancy. For her part, she appeared to treat him with a mixture of hellish laughter and dismissive contempt.

There was other interesting female company too during that particular week. Two friends of Rose were there: the willowy brunette, Lavinia Trevors; and the voluptuous and raven-haired Gertrude Silver. Both women were witty and socially accomplished. To complete the party, and to my delight, there was an old friend whom Gormley had brought: Emily Ward-Bishop, who had enthused to me about the delights of flagellation and petticoat government.

Well, we had a fine, high time of it. During the day, we men went hunting, shooting, fishing and climbing. In the evening we dined on freshly killed game and fish, accompanied by the finest wines from Crowley's cellar. What conversations we had around the dinner table! And what gay times we had after! – but more of that anon. How our host loved to hold forth! He was easily the best of us when it came to hunting, shooting, fishing and climbing; but he had many other tales to tell. He even mentioned golf; and St Andrews, the principal club in the lands of England, Scotland, Wales and Ireland had recognized his formidable handicap of four.

Anonymous

(*Editor's Note*: Author Ian Fleming gave his hero, James Bond, an eminently respectable handicap of eight.)

'After five years of folly and weakness, miscalled politeness, tact, discretion, care for the feelings of others, I am weary of it,' he declared after an excellent dinner. 'I say today: to hell with Christianity, Rationalism, Buddhism, all the lumber of the centuries. I bring you a positive and primeval fact, Magic by name; and with this I will build me a new Heaven and a new Earth. I want none of your faint approval or faint dispraise; I want blasphemy, murder, rape, revolution, anything, bad or good, but strong.'

And he proceeded to tell us an extraordinary tale. While in Cairo for the second time, returning after his honeymoon in India with his newly pregnant wife – I glanced at the heads of the tiger, the elephant, the water buffalo and the crocodile upon the wall – she had suddenly become 'like an oracle'. Now, I really don't recall the intricacies and how his wife managed to answer his questions on matters of which she had no knowledge at total odds of 21,168,000 to 1. Anyway, the essence of the matter was that, according to Crowley, the Gods had spoken through Rose, ordering him to be seated at a chair and a table in his Cairo flat between midday and one o'clock on the eight, ninth and tenth of April, with a pad of paper and a pen or pencil in his hand. So there he was, not knowing what on earth or in heaven to expect. Suddenly, there was a deafening thunderclap.

'Had! The manifestation of Nuit!' a deep voice with a musical timbre intoned. Crowley had turned to see a figure dressed as an Assyrian warrior, very darkly handsome. This figure dictated to him what the being called *The Book of the Law*. The next day between midday and one he dictated another chapter; and then another chapter on the following day.

'Is the resulting book any good, Crowley?' I enquired.

'Yes, it is,' he replied, 'but it is also very disturbing. It purports to be a communication from a praeterhuman Intelligence about the future of humanity. It predicts that all present social assumptions and political assumptions will be destroyed in blood and fire and in the cruellest possible ways. Everything that humanity has built up over centuries, especially modes of so-called civilized thought, will be cremated by the carnage that is coming.'

'And are there any ethical precepts in *The Book of the Law*?' I enquired.

'Yes,' Crowley replied, 'and I can summarize them and they make much sense to me. The first is DO WHAT THOU WILT SHALL BE THE WHOLE OF THE LAW. Obviously, if it comes, as alleged, from a praeter-human Intelligence, it cannot mean anything as fatuous as "Do what you want". It *must* mean: find out what you *really* want to do and then do it. The second commandment, so to speak, is LOVE IS THE LAW, LOVE UNDER WILL. I find it all splendid but, being a sceptic, although I swear that what I took down was dictated by some power or other, I could have hallucinated the whole bloody thing which was actually dictated by my unconscious . . . no, it just wasn't like that.'

'This is incredible!' I burst out. 'For what you have enunciated are precisely the principles that I have learned in certain Magical Orders.' I thought of my many adventures, especially those involving Rosemary and the mysterious Douglas.

'I don't know what to make of it,' Crowley returned. 'You see, I tried an experiment. *The Book of the Law* states in Part III:

' "23. For perfume mix meal and honey and thick leavings of red wine: then oil of Abramelin and olive oil, and afterward soften and smooth down with rich fresh blood.

' "24. The best blood is of the moon, monthly: then the fresh blood of a child, or dropping from the host of heaven: then of enemies; then of the priest or of the worshippers: last of some beast, no matter what.

' "25. This burn: of this make cakes and eat unto me. This hath also another use; let it be laid before me, and kept thick with perfumes of your orison: it shall become full of beetles as it were and creeping things sacred unto me.

' "26. These slay, naming your enemies; and they shall fall before you.

' "27. Also these shall breed lust and power of lust in you at the eating thereof."

'Well, I did that.' Crowley was holding the dinner table spellbound.

'Yes,' said Crowley, as more drinks were poured for everyone. 'And soon afterwards, I found a beetle on the bathroom floor. It measured one and a half inches in length and had a solitary horn that ended in its eyeball. During the two ensuing weeks, the whole house and garden were plagued with these insects . . . I sent one to the Natural History Museum in London for identification; it was politely returned with a note saying that the species was unknown. Mind you, this purported *Liber Legis* still remains an enigma to me. Even so, the slaying of the beetles appears to have worked.'

'Which enemies fell before you?' I asked.

'Ah . . .' Crowley lit a cigar. 'You see, I wrote to Mathers, our dear Head of the Golden Dawn, informing him of the *Liber Legis* revelation. He did not reply by letter in a civilized fashion. Hardly. He mounted a magical attack – my former mentor! – employing Abra-Melin demons. My pack of bloodhounds fell dead in their tracks! Rose! You're my witness.'

'That happened and I saw it,' this beautiful woman stated

calmly. 'And Aleister's servant Tom went mad and tried to kill me! But my brave husband smashed him with a salmon gaff and threw him into the cellar.' She smiled warmly at Crowley.

'Thank you.' He smiled back at her. 'Well, ladies and gentlemen, I responded to this outrageous assault by having the wretched imbecile led away by the police. But meanwhile there was a much more outrageous assault to cope with. The servant was merely a pawn in the evil game of Mathers. So I responded by invoking Goetic forces from *The Key of Solomon*. Having been attacked, I acted in self-defence by evoking Beelzebub and his forty-nine servitors to *blast* Mathers in Montmartre. I wanted to do to him all the harm he'd done to me, repaid with interest for launching an assault upon me in the first place. Rose saw the demons.'

'Oh, I did!' Rose cried out in the high, cultured voice of a clergyman's daughter.

'What did you see?' Dr Guillarmod demanded.

'Oh . . .' she sighed and leaned back as though she wanted her fine breasts to spill out of her low *décolletage*. 'I saw the demon servitors of Beelzebub pass before our eyes in the Temple. I recall Nimorup: he looked like a stunted dwarf with large head and ears. His lips were greeny-bronze and slobbery. And there was Nominon; a large, red, spongy jellyfish with one luminous, greenish spot, like a nasty mess. Of course I support my husband but I couldn't help feeling sorry for Mathers. Imagine,' she chortled, 'having *that* unleashed upon you!'

'As a final *coup de grâce*,' said Crowley, 'there was a ritual slaying of one of these peculiar beetles in our Temple while naming Mathers, just as *The Book of the Law* instructs. There's been nothing from him since.'

(*Editor's Note*: Mathers performed no major magical work thereafter and published nothing more of note.)

'So what are you engaged on now, Crowley?' Lieutenant-Colonel Gormley asked as he gazed with rapture at Rose.

'A number of things,' Crowley returned as fine old brandy, fruit and nuts were served. 'For a start, I'm now running a publishing company: The Society for the Propagation of Religious Truth. I'm engaged in the process of bringing out *The Collected Works of Aleister Crowley* in three volumes and these show the light of super-consciousness projected into the darkness of matter.'

'How can you do that?' Gormley demanded. 'You're only coming up to thirty.'

'Easily,' Crowley replied. 'I am prolific. Unfortunately, my darling wife,' he looked *so* lovingly at Rose, 'does not really care that much for my serious poetry so I am presently engaged upon writing a novel and a collection of naughty verses that are quite unashamedly erotic and obscene in order to amuse her during her pregnancy.' Rose smiled happily. 'It will be called *Snowdrops from a Curate's Garden* and it will be exceptionally pornographic . . .' – Rose laughed throatily – 'and it will contain delights such as my parody of Hamlet's extraordinary speech: *To Pee or Not to Pee*. The novel has Rabelais and de Sade as its predecessors as it relates the depravity of His Grace, an Archbishop. My first copy will, of course, go to my wife; thence, copies to my friends; and after that, I want the totally obscene *Snowdrops from a Curate's Garden* to go into bookshops where they may be bought by members of the Mothers' Institute or the Women's Institute in pursuit of edifying literature.'

'Splendid!' I declared. 'What other mischief have you been up to, Crowley?'

'Ah,' he smiled broadly. 'I wrote a letter to the local Society for the Suppression of Vice as follows:

' "Dear Sir,

"I find prostitution in this neighbourhood to be most unpleasantly conspicuous. Please do something to abate this nuisance which, day by day, grows for me more and more intolerable. I would willingly expend a considerable sum."

'Well,' Crowley laughed richly as he quaffed cognac, 'this wretched Society for the Suppression of Vice made a full investigation. Heaven knows how much it cost the buggers. Eventually they sent me a letter stating – much to their regret, no doubt – that they did *not* find prostitution in this neighbourhood to be *most unpleasantly conspicuous*. I sent them a postcard stating: "*Conspicuous by its absence, you fools!*" '

'Wonderful!' I exclaimed. 'Any other works in the pipeline?'

'Well,' he replied in a mock endeavour to look modest, 'I'll give you a copy of a work that's just come out, *Rodin in Rime*, lithographs of that marvellous man's sketches accompanied by my poems, inspired by his work. Ah!' he beamed fondly, 'those were fine days at Le Chat Blanc in Paris! Rodin! Surely the greatest sculptor of our age?! And there was your fine brother Gerald, Rose. He has the ability to become the greatest painter in England. My only worry is that he might consider something called *Being A Gentleman* to be more important. That's living death to an artist. I've told him to his face that I don't know one bad painter who isn't a gentleman.' Rose couldn't help shrieking with laughter.

'He's such a dreadful snob!' she cried out.

'Yes . . .' Crowley sighed, 'and a snob is not a gentleman. Still, he was marvellous company. Then there was Marcel Schwob, that brilliant critic and essayist, with his beautiful wife. Arnold Bennett sometimes attended. He's a charming man and he writes very well but I find that his eminently realistic novels lack *ecstasy*, the true test of fine Literature. Then there was this pleasant young doctor who used to hang around, one Willie Somerset Maugham. He said that he aspired to be an author but he seemed to have a rather commercial view of the matter.

' "Pity poetry doesn't sell, Mr Crowley," he said to me at one point.

' "Pity sales figures aren't poetry, Mr Maugham," I replied. I wonder. Will he, Willie, *ever* write a book?'

(*Editor's Note*: Somerset Maugham's second novel, *The Magician* (London, 1908) was based upon Crowley, casting him as the villain.)

'Crowley, I'm very happy about your literary success,' Dr Jacot Guillarmod stated solemnly. 'Indeed, only the other day, I read in a newspaper an article by one of my favourite English writers, G.K. Chesterton, about you and he declared: "Mr Aleister Crowley has always been, in my opinion, a good poet." Splendid, sir! I share your love of poetry though I cannot write it myself. But what are your plans for the hunting?'

'Tomorrow. You've only just arrived.'

'Yes,' Guillarmod grinned. 'Yet you did promise me some good hunting. I see here that you have the heads of the tiger, the water buffalo and the crocodile, among others. I have these too at my own home in Switzerland. It has been most enjoyable so far hunting the deer with you.' All the men nodded. Well-hung venison is so delicious if cooked rightly. 'But is there an animal in Scotland that is in the slightest degree dangerous?'

'There certainly is, my dear doctor,' Crowley responded gravely. 'There is a wild and dangerous beast, a ferocious ram that has accounted for the deaths of many intrepid hunters and which only the laird is allowed eventually to kill, providing that it can be done. You will have to be careful since this beast is as treacherous and potentially murderous as the Burmese water buffalo, which we have both hunted.' He paused as the Swiss doctor stared at him with rapt fascination. 'This fearsome creature is called: *The Haggis*.'

'Lead me to it, sir!' Dr Guillarmod yelled out proudly. 'The Haggis will not terrify me!'

'It has done for many a strong man,' Crowley returned solemnly. Everyone else was trying to conceal laughter and to keep a straight face. I think that Lieutenant-Colonel Gormley was tempted to rumble the joke; but Rose kicked him very hard under the table.

'Well, that's tomorrow sorted out,' Crowley declared heartily. 'What I propose now is that we all withdraw to more comfortable positions in another room and – no "sad stories of cabbages and kings" – let's just tell gorgeously erotic tales.'

CHAPTER FOUR

A great fire was crackling as we wandered into a room graced by comfortable and tastefully upholstered sofas. The floor was covered almost entirely by furry rugs from the skins of dead animals, presumably shot by Crowley. A servant gave us a choice of port, Madeira, cognac, Armagnac or Benedictine and we made our various selections. My Armagnac was superb and I noticed a similar satisfaction evinced upon the faces of of all the other guests.

'Dear Aunt Annie,' said our host, 'who is responsible for organizing this household, has retired early, so let's draw lots for our order of telling erotic tales.'

'Oh, Aleister!' Rose burst out laughing. It was such a rich, throaty laugh. 'Sometimes you're so ridiculous. Why talk when we can *do*?' Everyone looked interested. And when Crowley put the matter to a vote, we were all in favour. 'And I think that we should play by chance. I'm sitting with you,' she looked adoringly at her husband, 'and just look at the seating on the sofas!' Ah! The intuition of women! I was sitting with Emily, Gormley was sitting with Lavinia, Guillarmod was sitting with Gertie. 'Just pass out the cards for the order.' This matter was accomplished in a trice.

'Very well,' said Crowley, who had drawn the ace. 'Only too happy to oblige,' he smiled, 'but must be careful in view of . . .' He lovingly patted the growing tummy of his wife. I had never seen his face look so tender.

'Go for it, Aleister!' she cried out. 'I could do with some bloody pain relief!' Crowley promptly unbuttoned his trousers and lowered his silken pants to reveal a massive, throbbing tool. His wife cried out with joy at the sight and promptly whipped up her skirts and petticoats to reveal that she hadn't been wearing any knickers.

'You naughty girl!' Crowley roared. 'You deserve a good spanking!'

'Yes!' Rose exclaimed delightedly. '*When*?!'

Her husband responded by seizing her and placing her over his lap. She really did have a beautiful, snow-white bottom. Then the spanking came down hard, with Rose writhing and squealing at every stroke.

'Oh! . . . it hurts,' she squealed. 'It stings! Ouch!' And her gorgeous buttocks began to turn a pretty pink. 'Who are you?' Rose exclaimed at that point, 'Colonel Spanker?'

'Yes.' Crowley smiled grimly as the palm of his hand came down on his wife's quivering buttocks, turning them a bright crimson, a most delectable sight. 'Oh, what a lovely colour is crimson! Now, Rose, do you want me to turn your bottom from crimson to scarlet – or are you going to behave in the future? Pregnant or not, I'm not putting up with any of your shit. Say: "I shall behave, Master," or I'll tan your bottom scarlet and then maroon.'

'Oh! How it stings! Yes, I shall behave, Master.' It was so obvious that she was enjoying every minute of her exhibitionism before a select audience.

'Very well, I forgive you.' Crowley pulled her up and kissed her full lips. 'Now, roll over on your side . . .' I could have done with seeing more spanking, actually. The sight of a handsome husband taming his gorgeous wife through smacking her beautiful bottom is one I find highly erotic. But now Crowley and Rose lay side by side and the man was plunging his huge dick into his lady's cunny. I wish I could have caught a glimpse of that cunt, since it obviously aroused Crowley! He showed off his agility as, lying on his side, he managed extraordinary thrusts, at times making them very deep and very slow – and then suddenly working up to a quick, staccato rhythm that evoked joyous shrieks from Rose. Then it was back to the very slow thrusting as he caressed her voluptuous breasts and she sighed out her ecstasy. They came together as he roared and she screamed – and all of us spontaneously applauded.

Next it was the turn of Dr Jacot Guillarmod – who had drawn the jack – with Gertie Silver, that buxom, raven-haired beauty. As they stared at one another and wondered what to do, I thought of what Crowley had told me privately: *So far, my married life has been one long sexual debauch*. This was evidently true and I hope that it will be the lot of all married couples.

In this next scene, though, it was the woman who took the initiative. Standing up, Gertie stood in front of the fire and sensually divested herself of all her clothes to a ripple of appreciative applause before finally standing naked in the fire-light. Oh! Her haughty, high-cheekboned face and fine figure! My already sufficiently swollen cock started to twitch as I gazed at her splendidly firm breasts with their perky, berry-like nipples that stood out so firmly as she tweaked them up to erection between her long fingers.

The Swiss doctor was certainly up to the challenge. With a loud cry of joy, he tore off his clothes, revealing his powerful physique – though, for some reason, he approached Gertie with a huge erection ill-disguised by droopy cotton underpants. Meanwhile, my eyes were riveted on Gertie's snow-white tummy and dimpled navel below which lay a curly bush of chestnut pussy hair. I heard a collective drawing in of breath as Gertie ran her hand suggestively around Guillarmod's hairy chest before rolling down his absurd underpants to expose his enormous, thick prick. I could see it spring up and quiver stiffly against his belly before he strode behind her and slid his arms around her sides and fondled her bare breasts in his hands. Then he moved around and dropped to his knees between her parted slim, lissom legs.

Jacot Guillarmod pressed his face into Gertie's thatch of glossy pussy hair. She threw back her head and moaned with joy as his tongue found the crack of her quim. Then suddenly, he raised himself up to suck on Gertie's firm titties as he dipped his thick forefinger in and out of her moistening quim. She used both hands to hold his huge cock – which really was rather awesome in its girth.

Gertie's elongated nipples jutted out even more stiffly as her eager companion caressed each of her jiggling breasts in turn – and, suddenly and dramatically, Gertie moved back to the left wall, positioning herself just underneath the head of a leopard. Guillarmod stormed after her and his wide smile was met by the opening of her thighs.

She pulled his thick prick towards the waiting wet haven of her cunt, easing the purple knob between her pouting cunny lips and drawing it inch by inch into herself, until their pubic muffs were matted together. And now Guillarmod began fucking her up against the oak-panelled wall. She urged on the powerful strokes of his enormous todger by throwing her arms around his neck and clasping her legs together around his waist to force even more of his huge prick inside her pretty quim.

Guillarmod rapidly increased the pace of the poking, sliding his tool to and fro, faster and faster, as Gertie jerked wildly from side to side, panting with passion as she clung to him, thrusting her hips upwards to meet the violent pounding of the Swiss mountaineer's rampant rod.

He really did *give her one*, as the popular saying has it,

with his hairy chest shining with perspiration. He picked her up in his arms and carried her towards the fire, his prick still live within her. Then his body tensed and, setting her down, he slammed his shaft right into her, jetting his emission into her juicy pussy as Gertie sighed out her pleasure, wrapping and squeezing her thighs tightly around his and not releasing her grip until she had milked every drop of sticky seed from his spurting length. There was a positive *furore* of applause.

Guillarmod and Gertie, standing as naked as Adam and Eve, embraced softly, then kissed, and then held hands as they turned to us and bowed. Returning to their sofa, they noticed with joy the fact that a servant had placed robes for them, thus saving the necessity and bothersome duty of dressing again. Crowley and Rose certainly did like to make life easy for one.

Now it was the turn of Lieutenant-Colonel Gormley, who had drawn the ten of diamonds. This was appropriate, since his partner Lavinia was wearing one on her engagement finger. I thought that his notions of lovemaking left something to be desired since he turned boldly to Lavinia, smacked her in the mouth with a clumsy kiss and groped her right tit as though he were grasping an apple for firmness.

'You bastard!' she shouted. And, kicking his shins as she slapped his face, Lavinia sent Gormley sprawling onto the floor. 'Where are the servants to deal with this impudent rascal?' she demanded.

For a moment I thought that our joys had been temporarily spoiled by 'an incident'. But this was hardly the case: Rose and Lavinia were clearly good friends who had spoken previously about Gormley. Rose simply rang a bell and two strong men in kilts appeared, with one of them carrying a flogging block adorned with black leather straps.

As the first man placed the flogging block before the fire, the second man picked up Gormley as though he was a baby and flung him down across it. The straps were being tightened as Lavinia arose from the sofa and marched towards her victim with a fierce determination in her eyes and a smirk of triumph curling her mouth. The servants bowed briefly to Rose and Crowley and left the room as silently as they had arrived in it, while Lavinia took an obviously sadistic glee in unbuttoning the helpless man's trousers and pulling them down to his knees.

There were sudden hoots of laughter because he was revealed to be wearing a pair of ladies' *directoire* white silken knickers, with frills just above the knee.

'Mine!' Rose sang out; and Crowley looked amused.

'Well, Lieutenant-Colonel Gormley, your elegant ladies' knickers will just have to come down, won't they?' Rose promptly pulled them down to expose a pair of slim buttocks that had a tan and markings that indicated years of flagellation. Lavinia looked at Rose. That sexy bitch must have planned for this moment. She indicated a large bowl, placed in a corner, in which a birch was soaking.

Lavinia promptly fetched the birch rod and poised and switched it in the air as a happy smile adorned her pretty features.

'Well, Gormley,' Rose just *trilled* with merriment, 'as you know, Naughty Boys Wear Ladies' Knickers. I thought that would teach you a lesson – yet you have chosen to assault my dear friend Lavinia sexually. What an outrage! I *knew* that this was coming, that you could not control yourself. You must pay the penalty, you insolent child. The birch I commanded you to make on your previous visit has been pickled in my own pee. You deserve your just punishment. Take over, please, Lavinia.'

'Thank you, Rose,' that lady answered. 'Now, Gormley, you're going to get quite a flogging for your sexual mis-behaviour.' As her right hand wielded the birch rod, her left snaked under the belly of the man in bondage. 'Great Goddess!' she squealed. 'He's got a rampaging boner on him! What enticing insolence just before a birching!'

Everybody laughed happily as Lavinia took a sip of brandy, walked around the flogging block while composing her features into a stern expression, and suddenly unleashed her first stroke. There was a *whoosh* as her birch whistled through the air and struck Colonel Gormley 'right sore betwixt ye buttockes' as a seventeenth-century writer might put it. Gormley was silent but his bottom jerked up and twitched.

I have seen so many floggings that I count myself as among the connoisseurs in this esoteric matter. Yet, looking around me, I saw that I was evidently not alone. We all thought that it was a damn' good first stroke. But could Lavinia keep up this high standard? What was she chanting now as she was moving around the flogging block in a circle, with such dreamy eyes?

> *'Once around the glass*
> *And twice around the grass*
> *And thrice around the maple tree.'*

My darling tutor Rosemary had told me of this old Witch-craft chant from the West Country. I had no idea that Lavinia was a Witch and initiated into the Craft. She looked so conservative as she swished her skirts and petticoats; yet the genuine ones always do.

Having placed her glass of brandy before her bound victim, she circled him once and then whipped her birch again over Colonel Gormley's bottom. The twigs struck the upper region and he writhed. At that point, Gertie arose and placed a flowerpot containing just green leaves of grass beside the glass.

All of us agreed that the second stroke was an excellent one, although Gertie felt that the weals caused by the previous stroke were out of alignment with the pattern Lavinia had now set. I considered the matter and voiced my opinion that nobody was perfect.

'Anyway,' I said, 'there's several more strokes to go. Let's settle back and enjoy it.'

Lavinia now strode up to the bound man on the flogging block, tracing the birch softly across his whaled and wealed bottom. This man had fought Sikhs and other warriors out in India, yet here he was, bound over to the outraged Majesty of Womanhood.

'Do it first, Lavinia,' Crowley said, 'and we can always praise or criticize you afterwards. My wife agrees with my opinion that it's been jolly good so far.'

'Gormley,' Lavinia said, 'you haven't been punished enough. I see no signs of repentance.'

'I'm sorry, Madam,' Gormley gasped.

'Sorry?' Lavinia retorted in her prissy way. 'You've molested women without their consent and all you have to say is "Sorry"? Well, you're *going* to be sorry, well and truly sorry, my boy.'

With those remarks, Lavinia proceeded to give Gormley ten more strokes of the birch, with one falling every sixty seconds. She kept up a constant and delightful rhythm, for her right arm moved in *very* slow motion until it was two feet from its target, whereupon there was a sudden acceleration and the springy birch landed bang on target.

'She's doing it *so* well,' Emily remarked to me. 'Don't you see how she's turning his previously well-birched bum from a spring rose-pink to a summer rose-red? Oh! Look at that eleventh stroke! Marvellous! Oh! And the sweet dear is waving his bottom around as he squeals. What will happen, I wonder on the twelfth stroke?'

Lavinia stepped back several paces, rather as though she were a leopardess stalking her prey.

It was intriguing to watch her thrust her breasts forward and her bottom backward as her face flushed with sexual heat – and then she ran forward and took a wild swing at Gormley. The birch landed just under the centre and it was a good stroke.

'Maroon!' Rose shouted out joyfully. Maroon indeed; but there was also the interesting sight of Gormley's slim buttocks twitching north and south and east and west.

'Now, listen, Gormley,' Lavinia addressed him sternly. 'You're going to get a Devil's Dozen, which means another stroke. How strong I make it depends on what you admit. My friends tell me that you have been a wretched commander out in India. You have treated your soldiers like shit, sending them off to die without any need in pointless battles. You have been a wretched snob to your junior officers. *You're Colonel Gormless*! Say it!'

'Madam, I am Lieutenant-Colonel Gormless, but I swear that I shall improve.'

Lavinia responded by laying her birch softly upon his maroon, whaled and wealed and involuntarily twitching bottom.

'You know, my darling,' Crowley said as Lavinia undid the black leather straps, 'I'm reminded of a chapter I wrote earlier today and hoped to read to you as a bedtime story tonight in *Snowdrops from a Curate's Garden*. I thought that a flagellation chapter would be a good idea, since everybody seems to like it. So my flagellation chapter reads:

' "I am going to whip whip whip whip whip whip whip

whip whip whip whip whip whip—" ' His wife cut him short.

'Oh, do shut up Aleister. I really enjoyed the scene we saw before us. Didn't you?'

CHAPTER FIVE

Of course, I had spanked and fucked Emily Ward-Bishop on ever so many occasions; but I found her so delightful that it was a positive pleasure to be back with her again, playing what Shakespeare calls 'the two-backed beast'. Yet it seemed that this wasn't what was initially on her mind. Instead, she requested me to kneel in front of the fire, take down my trousers and under-pantaloons and expose my thick, rampant cock . . .

There were murmurs of respect from the ladies; then Emily knelt to pull my aching shaft towards her rich red lips. Suddenly, she raised her head and made me gasp when she slid those lips over my knob and took my prick into her soft, mobile mouth, swirling her tongue over the smooth mushroom dome of my tadger and sending shock waves of pleasure shooting through my entire body. I gasped as I placed my hands on Emily's blonde head and she quickened the movements of her tongue, washing my helmet as her right hand snaked down and began to frig her juicy cunt.

I closed my eyes and lost myself in the sheer ecstasy of the delicious sensation as Emily licked and lapped away, stroking her wicked tongue up and down the slippery length of my rod and pitching me into fresh paroxysms of delight. Then she squeezed her free hand around the base of my cock, sucking the sensitive underside harder and harder until I could feel the tingling power of the spunk rushing up inside my rampant rod from my tightened ballsack. Emily sensed that I would soon be spending, since she pulled my prick out of her mouth.

'I am going to swallow *some* of your spunk,' she announced primly, 'and then I want you to let the rest splash on my tits because I want to *feel* your cum as well as *taste* it.' With that, she replaced my cock in her mouth, rubbed her hand up and down my glistening wet shaft . . . and the first gush of spunk spurted into her mouth.

Her next move was to swing my prick downwards and aim my knob at her titties. Spurting strongly, I covered them with little white puddles of jism that Emily massaged into her skin with one hand, whilst with the other she diddled herself up to a second delectable spend.

I seized Emily in my arms and gave her a passionate kiss. Then my mouth slid lower and lower down her trembling body until it was pressed against her outer labia. I was hardly inexperienced at eating pussy so at first I licked her tentatively and tantalizingly, drawing the tip of my tongue along her sopping slit as I explored the manifold furrows of this exquisite flower that was opening out once again before me. Emily moaned in delight so then I started slurping with a fully uninhibited vigour on her moist quim.

She gasped as I inhaled the sensual bouquet of her deliciously aromatic cunt and darted my tongue between her quim lips to roam inside her juicy cunny.

'Go on, do it!' Emily cried out. *No submissive like a dominant*, I thought. 'Oooh, that's *so* nice! Yes, yes, tongue me out and *make me come*!' So I placed one hand underneath Emily's jouncey bum cheeks to press her cunny even closer to my mouth, which I opened wide to allow my tongue to probe her inner recesses; and in seconds I found myself licking the nub of her erect clitty.

After circling it rhythmically with the tip of my tongue, I

nibbled and sucked the hard little love button until she spent copiously all over my face. I swallowed up her sweet vaginal juice before I scrambled up and substituted my renewed rod in place of my lips at the entrance to her dripping tunnel of love. Emily responded by eagerly hauling up her hips as my stiff shaft shoved into her slippery crack.

Emily threw her legs across my back and heaved up and down in time with my robust thrusts as we enjoyed a most excellent fuck.

Despite the outpouring of her own cuntal juices, Emily's quim was exquisitely tight, holding me in the sweetest vice imaginable. Yet her juices were now flowing so freely, oiling the walls of her aromatic vagina so well, that my further thrusts were made even easier as my cock buried itself within the luscious folds of her slit. Emily cried out as I made one last lunge forward – causing her to spend again.

My balls were banging against her bottom as, with a hoarse cry of triumph, I shot a stream of hot, frothy spunk into her clingy cunt. I moved my prick inside her sated snatch whilst my seed continued to gush out of my knob in great jets as we writhed around on the rug, enjoying to the full this magnificent fuck.

At our end, we received a standing ovation! And then the insufferably randy Gertie leapt forward, shed her robe and knelt beside us in the nude. I withdrew my glistening wet cock from Emily's cunny. It was exciting to see my heavy, semi-erect shaft sliding out from between her swollen love lips. Gertie, meanwhile, seemed to be more interested in Emily's breasts than in my cock.

She began to kiss them, moving her mouth from one nipple to the other.

'Oh!' Emily cried out. 'Oh, darling Gertie! Please! Spank me. *Spank* me! Spank *me*!' Gertie gave her a flashing smile and sat up. Emily placed herself over her lap, exposing her tight, rounded bum cheeks to the lascivious gaze of one and all. And Gertie then began to smack the two beautiful white hemispheres of Emily's arse.

'This will teach you, young miss!' Smack! Smack! 'There! You naughty girl! Take that and that and that!' But she only slapped with a light touch and their naked bodies gleamed as Emily wriggled while Gertie's hand rose and fell, her large breasts capped with erect raspberry nipples trembling with each stroke.

'Oh, Emily . . .' Gertie cooed, 'I love the way your bum cheeks jiggle when I spank you. Your lovely arse is blushing so beautifully! It should always be this pinky shade, don't you agree, Horby?' Clearly, both girls were enjoying themselves and the question didn't really require an answer. Yet suddenly Emily reached up and grabbed hold of my thick, swollen shaft.

She requested me to kneel down beside her so that she could clamp her wide red lips around my rampant rod and she commenced bobbing her head up and down my twitching tool to the same rhythm of slaps that Gertie was administering to her tingling bottom. Emily lashed her tongue around my prick, which was now thudding away like a steam-hammer as I worked my hips backwards and forwards while her pliant tongue washed all over my bared penis.

I closed my eyes for a moment to wallow in the pleasure of this superb sucking-off. Then I heard Gertie whisper something and I opened my eyes to see that she was pushing Emily off her lap. This enabled Emily to kneel down in front of me and continue to suck my cock with undiminished relish. As she did so, Gertie raised herself up on her hands and knees and her glossy raven hair tumbled down over her elfin face as she lowered her pretty head and gently kissed the soft, ripe cheeks of Emily's bottom, now a pleasant, pretty pink.

Turning onto her back, Gertie slid her head between Emily's legs and, holding onto her thighs, began to worry her tongue around Emily's corn-coloured muff of pussy hair, which was already damp with the wonderful juices of her vagina. Emily gurgled as she gobbled furiously on my cock while Gertie teased the tip of her tongue between the lips of her pouting quim and then inserted her thumb into the dear girl's juicy snatch.

Suddenly, Gertie pulled her mouth away.

'Go behind and fuck my bum, Horby!' she gasped.

There was a very nonchalant expression on the face of Crowley as he passed me a small dish of olive oil, which I presume was kept for some of the lamps in the room. I knelt behind Gertie and directed my purple-domed rod into the crevice between her gorgeous buttocks. Emily's left hand helped to guide my tool towards the tiny rosebud entrance to Gertie's rear dimple. Meanwhile, Emily used her right hand to finger-fuck Gertie's cunt.

'Here we go, dirty Gertie!' I exclaimed. The oil of the olive had lubricated my prick very well and it was an easy matter to ensure that my prick was soon enough firmly esconced within the narrow canal of her back passage. For a brief moment, I rested content: and then slowly, very slowly, I began to thrust my prick in and out of Gertie's arsehole as I slid my arms under her shoulders. Then I squeezed her breasts as I rubbed her stiff, engorged tits.

Gertie began to shake all over at this double stimulation and at the feeling of Emily's tongue licking her clitty as the genteel girl drove her thumb and now two other fingers in and out of Gertie's wet quim. This delightfully lewd, three-way lovemaking was so arousing that I soon flooded Gertie's bottom with a copious deluge of jism,

Ah! What joy! There was an audible '*Pop!*' as I uncorked my knob from Gertie's bottom and she yelled out her own ecstasy in a frenzy of lustful glee as she shuddered to a climax and discharged a flood of vaginal juice over Emily's lapping tongue. We all collapsed in a heap on the soft rug before the fire as our audience applauded.

'*Mon Dieu!*' Guillarmod exclaimed.

'Well, my dear doctor,' Crowley came in instantly, 'I *did* tell you that this is "the happiest house party in the Highlands!" '

On the following morning, Crowley and Guillarmod were up early and keen for breakfast, which Aunt Annie ensured was served till midday. So was I, since I wanted to see stages in the execution of Crowley's joke. It was at this point that I became incredibly irritated with Dr Jacot Guillarmod, whom I had liked well enough until then. *The man had the gall to be brilliant at breakfast!* It was insufferable. Yet the breakfast was not. In fact, the porridge with which I started was the best I've ever had. Then, of course, there was bacon, eggs, sausage, kidney and black pudding: all jolly good. There was a delicious kedgeree too, using Arbroath Smokies – oh, that Finian haddock! – and mounds of toast with best Scottish Highland butter and marmalade. Although I couldn't bear Guillarmod's ceaseless nattering, I was in a good mood for I had spent a delightful night with Emily.

Suddenly our repast was abruptly interrupted by the loyal servant bursting into the room with disordered dress and wild eyes.

'There's a haggis on the hill, my lord!' he exploded breathlessly. Crowley and Guillarmod dashed to the gun case. Towards the end of last night, Crowley had described the fearsome haggis. It had been hard to keep a straight face. Guillarmod indeed knew the origin of the wild buffalo of Burma: when the British had destroyed the natives' villages, their cattle had escaped the bayonet and starvation by taking to the jungle, where they had become practically a new species. Crowley had therefore invented a Highland wild ram on the lines of the Burmese wild buffalo.

'I have dreamt all night,' said Guillarmod, 'of scaling a lonely and precipitous pinnacle and dragging a lordly haggis from his lair!' I'm sure that Crowley's rather fine 1852 Johannesburg port had aided those dreams. Myself, I shan't forget Crowley's enchanting descriptions of the rarity, the wariness and the ferocity of the haggis. However, he had asked me to stay out of the *practical* aspect of his joke so I simply watched with amusement and learned the rest from him.

'I trust to my skill,' said Crowley, as he armed himself with the .577 Double Express and gave Guillarmod the principal weapon of his battery, a ten-bore Paradox, with steel-core bullets. 'This,' he declared, 'is a reliable weapon. It will bring an elephant up short with a mere shock, even if he is not hit in a vital part. With such a firearm, my friend, you can advance fearlessly against the most *formidable* haggis in the Highlands!'

The ghillie, coincidentally named Hugh Gillies, tiptoed, crouching low, out of the front door and 'stalked' the fearsome beast across the Italianate gardens of Boleskine. Crowley and Guillarmod followed with their guns as I watched with amusement.

The icy rain must have chilled them to the bone before they reached the edge of the artificial trout lake. Crowley insisted on wading through this – up to the neck, guns held high – on the grounds that they would thus throw the haggis off their scent.

As they vanished from view, I went for a stroll in the grounds. What a curious sense of humour Crowley possessed! Guillarmod had missed the sign: THIS WAY TO

THE KOOLOOMOOLOOMAVLOCK (DOES NOT BITE), erected by the laird in the hope that some wayfarer might go and look for it. Crowley had told me that this animal created the greatest terror in the neighbourhood, the more so since it remained invisible. The hotel keeper of Foyers, determined to abate the nuisance, took his gun and tried to stalk it. Hugh Gillies had once seen him advancing by short rushes and in every way comporting himself as the military necessities of the situation demanded.

'She may no' bite,' said Gillies, 'but ah'm thinking she pu's legs.'

As I waited for the results of the hunting of the haggis, I walked to the shores of Loch Ness and smoked a pipe of straight, pure Virginia for a time. I don't know if what happened next was an hallucination or not. I recall Crowley mentioning something of this nature to me some years back. (*Editor's Note: The Black Pearl I.*) Well: what I saw was indeed a very strange beast. It was swimming swiftly and it had a very long neck. It came close enough for me to see that it had a small head, reptilian eyes and very sharp teeth. Then it vanished into the depths of the icy waters. I have studied some natural history and I am especially fascinated by the dinosaurs. What I saw looked exactly like a plesiosaur; though all scientific thinking has it that they were wiped out by – we don't know – *something*, sixty million years ago.

I returned to Boleskine and later I would hear more of the hunting of the haggis. Apparently, Crowley and Guillarmod emerged dripping from the lake and proceeded to climb a hill on all fours. Every time anyone breathed, they lay low for several minutes. Guillarmod soon reached the point where every bent twig looked to him like one of the horns of our haggis.

'I crawled and dripped and choked back my laughter,'

Crowley told me afterwards. 'The idiocy of the whole adventure was intensified by the physical discomfort and the impossibility of relieving one's feelings. That interminable crawl! The rain never let up for a single second; and the wind came in gusts wilder and more bitter with every yard of ascent. I explained to Guillarmod that if the wind should shift a few degrees, the haggis would infallibly get our scent and be off. I implored him to camouflage his posteriors, which arose in front of my balaclava, heaving like the hump of a dying camel.'

After an hour and a half, they reached the top of the hill, three hundred feet above the house, without hearing that hideous scream-whistle of alarm by which (as Crowley had carefully explained) the haggis announces that he has detected the presence of an alien enemy. Breathlessly, they crawled towards the area of grassy and heathery knolls that lay behind the huge rock buttress that towered above the garden and the lake.

The mist drove fiercely and wildly across the hillside towards them. It magnified every object to an enormous size. Suddenly, Gillies rolled stealthily over to the right and his finger pointed tremulously to where, amidst the unfurling wreaths of greyness, stood . . .

Guillarmod brought forward the ten-bore with infinite care. The haggis loomed gargantuan in the mist; it was barely fifty feet away. The brute was the size of a bear.

Guillarmod pressed both triggers. He shot well. Both bullets struck and expanded. He had completely blown away the entire rear section of Farmer McNab's prize ram – for which the canny farmer had earlier been paid, of course. They rushed forward, cheering frantically. Gillies had to be first in at the death; the remains of the supply of oats with which he had induced the newly acquired ram to feed in that spot all through the morning without moving might, if observed too closely, have detracted from the transcendent glory of that romantic scene.

That evening, at dinner, the atmosphere was positively Homeric. The haggis was brought in with the utmost ceremonial, and Hugh Gillies played the bagpipes as the goodly Swiss doctor sat back proudly. There was total hilarity and the utmost glee: the boastful Swiss doctor attributed our mirth and merriment entirely to our happy appreciation of his steadfast courage and shooting prowess.

Of course, haggis – essentially minced sheep's innards – is absolutely delicious, especially on a cold Autumn or Winter day. The only beverage that goes with it appropriately is Scotch whisky, so Crowley produced a crate of wonderful single malt that had been distilled by craftsmen in the Highland locality. We all became drunker and drunker – 'drunk enough to know we are immortal' as Crowley put it – and the joy of Guillarmod appeared to know no bounds.

Crowley solemnly presented him with the skull and horns; and we all shrieked out our congralutations as we applauded.

'I shall send the head of this dangerous wild haggis to be stuffed and mounted!' he proclaimed in his stentorian tones. 'A suitable inscription shall be engraved upon a plate of *massive* gold! I have vindicated the gallant Swiss once more!'

'I think,' Crowley returned, 'that the *Gazette de Lausanne* will literally foam at the mouth with your recital of so doughty an exploit.'

An exuberant and ebullient Guillarmod then announced his plans for another Himalyan expedition: Kangchenjunga, the third highest mountain in the world. A smiling Crowley agreed.

That is another story. Meanwhile, more than one big-game hunter has told me that, if you visit Dr Guillarmod's home, he will proudly show off his hunting trophies on his walls. And next to the tiger, the crocodile, the bear and the water buffalo, he has ostentatiously displayed that ferocious beast – the haggis.

CHAPTER SIX

Dear Horby,

And you are such a dear man to me. I am your wife and, honestly, I treasure you. I really enjoy our marriage between male and female rakes; and haven't I given you a good healthy son? I also love the way in which you say to me 'Do what thou wilt' as we saw in the magical rituals before and during our marriage. And now you tell me that Crowley has told you that he has received a Sacred Book from The Gods to this effect!

Well, well. Isn't it strange that I enjoy it when you tell me about your sexual exploits with other women? And isn't it strange when you tell me that you enjoy my descriptions of my own sexual exploits? Remember when we had a row last year and you told me to fuck off? Well, I did fuck off — and fucked around. After all, you do. But one of the things I really like about you is that you don't have double standards. Certainly, you gave me such a warm welcome when I came back to you that I have never forgotten it.

And now, here's you on some British Government mission to Germany and here's me in London, waiting and eager to hear from you; and there's you, demanding to hear from me in the meantime. And so you shall!

The social climate of this country seems to have changed in this year of 1906. It is as though, at the General Election, the country gave a massive heave and vomited out the Tories. What a Liberal landslide! It was more like an avalanche! And now there are also around thirty MPs of this minority Labour Party! Anyway, I was pleased to accept a dinner invitation which I received from the new President of the Board of Trade, David Lloyd George.

What a dynamic man he is! I wouldn't say that he's that handsome – but his Welsh voice is so mellifluous and he is so articulate that he might be able to persuade the ignorant that black is white. But let's 'get right down to the real nitty-gritty', as the Americans say. He seduced me after a splendid dinner in a private room upstairs at the Café Royale – you know, those rather splendid places where you tell me you take some of your floozies.

There I was on the bed, looking at him, and this fiery, passionate man gazed at me, let out a cry, seized me and, lifting me up in his strong arms, crushed me in a powerful embrace. I was totally engulfed in waves of idyllic bliss as our tongues slithered together and his hands moved to my breasts and caressed my firm, rounded globes. I let my own hand slide down to his lap and I drummed my fingers on the tubular bulge between his legs as he deftly unbuttoned my blouse and helped me discard the garment before sliding the straps of my corset off my shoulders. My naked nipples rose up like hard little tawny bullets to greet him as I unbuckled the belt around the waistband of his trousers.

His hand dived down. I giggled when David Lloyd George began to pull up my skirt, but I made no attempt to prevent him from pressing his palm against my pussy. I responded. I undid his fly buttons and he lifted his bottom to let me pull down his trousers and pants. My tongue passed hungrily over my lips since I thrilled at the sight of David's magnificent, beefy cock which rose majestically up from a curly black thicket of curls at the base of his belly.

I grasped hold of his palpitating, smooth-skinned shaft

and squeezed it for a moment or two before reluctantly releasing it so that I could take down my skirt and under-garments, allowing me to lie naked beside him. David gazed at my uptilted breasts and let out a sigh when I shamelessly smoothed my fingers over my pussy and diddled my fingertips inside my moistening quim. This was surely a clear enough signal that I wanted to be fucked.

'I'm ready for you now, David,' I whispered fiercely. 'Plunge that thick Celtic prick into my cunt and pump out all your frothy jism into my sticky honeypot.' I lay back and thought of England as I spread my legs apart to welcome a man who might yet be a prominent part of our island story.

Lloyd George rolled over on top of me and my whole body tingled with desire when he pressed his rod between my yielding love-lips, which opened like Aladdin's Cave to allow his stiff shaft to sheathe itself inside my welcoming cunny. Soon I had every inch of his cock lying snugly in my tingling snatch and then I worked my thighs upwards, wrapping my legs around his back as he started to piston his boner – oh! so fleshy, too! – in and out of my squelchy slit. How glorious it felt as his heavy balls slapped against my bum cheeks with each downward thrust and shivers of ecstasy ran through my body as, behind my closed eyes, I imagined how my hot, dripping quim was absorbing Da-vid's rampant rod as it slewed to and fro within my love funnel!

I was now so wet that I could feel my cuntal juices trickling down into my arsehole before seeping into the sheets. What a wonderfully energetic lover David Lloyd George turned out to be! He pounded away with such strength that he stretched my cunt to the limit with surging strokes of his thick throbbing tool.

Every nerve in my body thrilled with rapture during this

truly marvellous fuck, though these exquisite sensations were too delectable to last. All too soon I climaxed and his spend followed a few seconds later. I shrieked out as I thrashed around in the dizzy delirium of my orgasm.

After a quick series of ecstatic spasms, abundant jets of jism spurted out of David's prick and splattered against the walls of my cunt. Then he rolled over next to me – and to my great excitement, I could see that his lovely cock was still semi-erect and would shortly be capable of a repeat performance. I said as much to him and David smiled wolfishly.

'By all means, my darling Claire. Au Claire de la lune, indeed! I would love nothing better than to fuck you again – but just give me a couple of minutes to regain my strength. Tell me,' he poured the finest cognac for both of us, then glanced at the clock on the wall, *'would you be offended were I to introduce another man into the proceedings?'*

'Oh, you silly man!' I cried out. 'Of course not! The more the merrier! Just as long as he knows – as I trust you do – that my principal loyalty is to my husband who, for all I know, is probably fucking a couple of German bints right now! Anyway, who is this man whom you propose to introduce into the proceedings?'

'Have you heard of one F.E. Smith? He likes to be called simply Smith.'

'Of course I have! He is the most celebrated of barristers and a Tory MP. But what are you doing messing with him?'

'He may be a political opponent,' Lloyd George retorted; 'but I like him . . . and he could be very useful.' I lay back as he slid his fingers into the pool of moisture between my thighs and I closed my eyes to relive the excitement of our lovemaking as David's artful fingertips popped in and out of my sopping quim.

He frigged me so wonderfully that at first I did not notice the soft knocking upon the door.

'Come!' said Lloyd George. I did. Ah! I thought he was talking to me!

Well! F.E. Smith came in, adorned in evening dress — white tie and tails — looking as arrogant as I had seen him in the Punch *caricatures but frankly rather dishy.*

'Hallo,' I said as I began to fist my hand up and down David's burgeoning tadger. Hooray! I made this Smith, this impassive intellect, raise an eyebrow!

'Oh, do join in, old boy,' Lloyd George casually invited him.

'Yes, do. Do have a brandy and take those silly clothes off,' I said. 'Then come here and lie back on this bed.' I continued to frig David as I talked, sliding my hand up and down his slippery wet length.

Smith's eyes widened as I rose up and knelt between David's legs. I licked my lips and jammed down his foreskin as I leaned forward to kiss his cock, knowing full well that by deliberately arching my hips in this wanton manner, my pert bum cheeks would be jigging just a yard or so from Smith's flushed face, displaying my bottom and my pussy to this delighted yet flustered man who was slowly divesting himself of his clothes.

'You've now had a bird's-eye view of my cunt, Smith,' I called out, 'so you'd better let me take a good look at your cock.' I heard him gasp at my audacity. While he undressed, I busied myself by working over David's rock-hard cock, running my teeth up and down the blue-veined shaft, then sucking the glistening wet rod and flicking my wicked tongue over its slitted end as I cradled his hairy ballsack. There's no whore like the one who gives it away for free! 'Are you ready yet, Smith?' I exclaimed impatiently as I momentarily pulled David's cock out of my mouth.

Looking back, it was an unnecessary question. He had already pulled out a barrel-like cock-shaft that he was fondling and squeezing in his fist. I was so fired up by the sight of Smith's thick chopper that I wantonly wiggled my backside and pushed my firm white buttocks out even further towards him. Then I pulled my lips away from David's pulsating prick.

'What are you waiting for, you silly boy?' I taunted Smith. 'Or does Mr Lloyd George, your political opponent, have to give you a demonstration on how to fuck me from behind?' Smith smiled as he finally divested himself of his trousers and drawers.

'I hope, Madam,' he said, 'that I may feel free to slide my splendid staff into your clingy little quim . . . ?'

'Go for it!' I shouted. As he shuffled forward on his knees behind me and as I replaced my lips on David's moist, stiff shaft I reached out behind me.

Taking Smith's truncheon in my hand, I guided it into the cleft just beneath my bum cheeks until the tip of his knob touched my cunny lips. Then I started rocking back and forth between the two men.

I slurped on David's twitching tool as my bottom rose with every shove as Smith drove home. The contractions of my vaginal muscles soon sucked the jism from his cock, the slippery seed pumping out of its taut head as Smith heaved his throbbing tool in and out of my dripping cunt with all of his considerable strength. And, as Smith shot his load into my cunt, David gave a deep groan and his shaft began to tremble violently between my lips.

I realized that he could no longer hold on and so I pulled his cock out of my mouth until only the tip of the shaft was resting on my tongue. Then I gave one gentle tug on his tool and let him watch his seed spill out over my lips. When he had finished, I licked up all his salty spunk and gulped it down.

You see, Horby, I did that to show that, when it comes to fucking, the Tories such as Smith can indeed get it up and do it; but the Liberals such as Lloyd George are better.

Still, we had a very civilized time afterwards, though we had to dress to a moderate level of decency in order for the waiters to serve us more champagne and cognac and also Angels on Horseback – oysters wrapped in bacon on toast – and Devils on Horseback – prunes wrapped in bacon on toast. How the men talked then! Wasn't it Frank Harris who said to me:

'Claire, all women agree that there is nothing more interesting than male egotism – when a man has an ego!' True. And although F.E. Smith had initially struck me as being a pompous arse, how his wit had me laughing! You know of my encounter with Dr Sigmund Freud (Editor's Note: *Volume I); well, I agree with his theory that laughter is a sublimated orgasm.*

On his way to Parliament, Smith, a member of White's, is in the habit of dropping off at the Athenaeum for a pee. He's not in fact a member of that Club and of course it is considered exalted by some, but it is lower on the social scale than White's – or the House of Commons. Anyway, the fateful moment came when Smith was asked by an Athenaeum servant: 'Excuse me, sir. Are you a member?'

'Do you mean . . .' Smith retorted, 'that this,' *he looked around incredulously, 'is a club?'*

'He was,' Smith said of a man one day in the High Court, 'as drunk as a judge!'

'Surely you mean as drunk as a lord, Mr Smith?' the judge interposed with cutting asperity.

'Quite right, my Lord,' Smith returned.

Then I like the tale of when a judge interrupted Smith to state:

'Mr Smith: I have listened to you for an hour and I am still no wiser.'

'No wiser, perhaps, my Lord,' Smith shot back, 'but certainly better informed.'

'Ha! ha! Excellent!' David Lloyd George was roaring with laughter. 'But you know, Smith, I wasn't too keen on your wit on the day when some new Labour MP asked you for directions to what he called "the toilet". You said: "First on your right, second on your left, and you'll find a door marked Gentlemen. But don't let it bother you – just go straight in." ' I hooted with laughter but Lloyd George did not. His face was solemn as he said: 'Smith: that was cruel.'

And then, brushing aside Smith's clever excuses, David Lloyd George launched into an impassioned peroration in favour of the underprivileged in this country. How he spoke of Old Age Pensions and National Insurance and Unemployment Dole and relief of poverty and his vision of a National Health Service and of a society that was more just and was prosperous for all! Heavens above! Hearing this was almost more moving than his excellent fucking. Smith had moved me to laughter and now Lloyd George moved me to tears.

Both men will achieve great things in life but I know which man is going to be greater. Meanwhile I can't wait to see you again, Horby, oh! – my bloody darling husband! Hurry back into my snug cunt from Germany soon!

Loads of Love,
And Lust,
Claire

That was rather typical of the sort of letter I'd receive from my wife at the time, whenever I was away for more than a week. Smith, of course, became Lord Birkenhead. At the time I thought that Lloyd George was a radical firebrand but I shall describe what transpired. My feelings for my wife . . . well, they're expressed by the letter I wrote to her from Berlin.

CHAPTER SEVEN

All play and no work makes Jack a dull boy, is what I say; and that is why I sometimes do undercover work for dear old Blighty. Claire has done the same in her time and that is why I was able to be so frank with her, provided that my letter went via the British Embassy in Berlin.

Darling Claire,

It was so good to hear from you. I think that it was Aleister Crowley who said to me: 'The first duty of a husband is to find a lover for his wife: otherwise he'll never be able to get on with his work'. Well, I don't know what arrangements Crowley's made regarding Rose and his travels and expeditions in foreign parts but I'm certainly happy with our arrangement and glad that you are having a good time.

They've put me in a luxurious apartment overlooking the rather splendid Brandenburg Gate. My mission is to see Kaiser Wilhelm II as a Special Envoy and Plenipotentiary of the Kaiser's cousin, His Majesty the King. Moreover, I must visit him in the company of his adviser, the Englishman Houston Stewart Chamberlain who is mad about Germany, and ascertain the nature and extent of the latter's influence. I have wined and dined Chamberlain and convinced him that in addition to being a scholar and a gentleman and pro-German and anti-French, I am also an

*expert on the occult, for which the Kaiser has a particular
passion.*

(*Editor's Note:* After he fled from Germany to Holland in
1918, the ex-Kaiser passed much of the rest of his life in
studying occult literature).

*I'm seeing the Kaiser this evening and in the company of
Chamberlain; but more of this matter anon. Last night I
saw Maria von Huttendorf. Do you recall her? Sorry,
that's a redundant question. Who could forget her? She is
the Great Whore of Europe. I was the one who turned her
on to working for the British Empire. One knows of a
double agent and even a triple agent, but Maria . . . my
God! That damned girl is also a spy for the German
Empire, the Austro-Hungarian Empire, the Russian Empire, the Ottoman Empire, the French Third Republic and
the Kingdom of Italy. No one dares harm her because she
sleeps with everyone in high positions and is the most vital
conduit of essential information – or disinformation – in
Europe.*

(*Editor's Note:* Some varied activities of the spy, Maria von
Huttendorf, apparently the mother of the fabled Mata Hari,
are described in *The Black Pearl,* Volumes II and III.)

*It was a pleasure to see an old friend again and, needless to
say, I wined and dined this beautiful, voluptuous bitch quite
extravagantly at one of Berlin's grandest establishments.
She was extremely helpful in giving me information about
the Kaiser, his Generals, Chamberlain and, most important
of all, German naval estimates in the building up of the
Grand Fleet. After all, this is a serious threat to British
naval supremacy, which has gone unchallenged since Tra-*

*falgar, 101 years ago. There is also the disturbing fact that
the coal and steel production of the German Second Reich
is on course to surpass ours within five years.*

The Germans are disturbed by the Anglo-French Entente Cordiale, *which they regard as a betrayal of our
traditional policy of friendship with Prussia/Germany and
hostility towards France. As you know, France and Germany nearly went to war last year over Morocco. The
Entente Cordiale had given France a free hand there; yet
the Kaiser went there in his yacht, the* Hohenzollern, *and
made a rousing speech to the small German community
there, promising to do all he could to protect their interests.
Then he demanded an international conference to discuss
Moroccan affairs. When the French Foreign Minister
refused, German threats of war frightened the French
government so much that the Minister was pressured into
resigning – a great humiliation for France.*

*President Theodore Roosevelt intervened to calm down
hot passions, which is the first time the USA has ever
intervened in a European quarrel, and presently there is an
international conference at Algeciras. Anyway, enough of
that! I took Maria back to my apartment, gave her a
brandy and set about swiving her.*

*I slipped the straps of her brassière beneath the chemise
down her arms, having unbuttoned the former as we lay
together on the sofa. I was able now to cup her uptilted
bare breasts, pinching the nipples until they hardened
under my touch. Meanwhile, Maria's delicate hand had
strayed back to my lap as I helped her to unbutton my
trousers. My stiff naked cock sprang up to display itself
before her, vibrating with unslaked desire. It had been ages
since we had last fucked . . . all those years ago in Paris.*

*'My God, Horby!' Maria exclaimed as she wrapped her
fingers around my bulging prick. 'How your cock has*

grown since I last took it in my hand. Is this what married life has done for you?' I laughed as I threw up her skirt and slid my hand up her satin-smooth thigh. Maria gave a little jump when my probing fingers reached her pussy and she lifted her bottom to allow me to tug down her knickers.

Then the sultry Great Whore of Europe, whose hair might be any colour on any day, but which today was a flaming red, lay down along the sofa and parted her legs when I mounted her. Pushing her black skirt up around her waist, I carefully placed my prick between her yielding love lips and eased myself down to let my yearning shaft be slowly enveloped inside her squishy slit.

'Ahhh! How lovely! Come further into me . . .' she breathed as our lips merged together and her warm, wet tongue snaked a passage between my teeth and into my mouth. I pistoned my prick to and fro inside Maria's close-fitting honeypot as we kissed with an increasingly urgent passion.

Hers was one of the snuggest little cunts one could wish to fuck and I worked my way in until her neat little clitty was rubbing against my cock. When my prick was fully inside her and my balls were slapping against her bum, I paused for a moment to enjoy fully the delicious clinging tightness of her vaginal muscles around my shaft . . . and then I began to prod my rod in and out of her luscious cunt.

'Ai! Eeh! Ai!' She was panting hard. 'Oh! Horby! What have you been up to since I last felt you? Oh! What a joy it is to have your big, thick prick up my crack!' Naturally her compliment and her evident enthusiasm spurred me on to pump away even more fervently as Maria offered up her hard raspberry nipples for my delectation.

I sucked on each tit in turn and my hands slid underneath her to clasp those seductively rounded bum cheeks. We

114

were both content to fuck at a leisurely pace and glorious ripples of sheer delight ran through every fibre of my body as my prick slewed its way in and out of her juicy cunt. By now, her cunny was so well lubricated that my cock was sliding faster and faster up and down the length of her love funnel and soon I could feel the stirrings of an inevitable spend.

Yet I wanted to prolong this exquisite friction, so I deliberately slowed down the pace of the fuck and, from thrusting my shaft to and fro, all the way up and down, I switched to fucking her with a series of short jabs, pushing not much more than the empurpled head of my rampant tool into her sopping joxy. She was pleading with a note of anxiety in her soft voice for me not to come just yet.

I slowed down, almost to a standstill, continuing to let just the head of my prick probe quickly in and out of Maria's puffy quim lips. Happily, her rhythm had also slowed down and I was able to continue fucking her in time to her slow rhythm. I was able to relax and prolong the fuck at a slow and even pace, especially since – on this occasion, to my relief – she did not demand that we try and move ourselves into a more adventurous position.

Maria lay back along the plush upholstery and her hard, erect nipples rubbed sensually against my palms as my cock slid in and out of her pulsing pussy in time with the motions of her buttocks. Alas! All good things must finally come to an end.

When Maria finally felt the approach of her climax, she began to pant and jerk her hips. I responded by filling her cunt with my rampaging love truncheon – and she clutched at me, her fingers and her long nails digging into my back as I felt her body tremble with the first shuddering spasms of her orgasm. This whole scene was so sensually exciting that I just couldn't hold myself back any longer and I *flooded the depths of her cunny with a very fierce spurt of jism, filling her to the limit and beyond as her beautiful, voluptuous body writhed beneath my weight.*

'You gorgeous bitch!' I cried out.

'Oooh, what a gorgeous cum!' she exclaimed in return. 'Quick! Give my titties one last squeeze before you pull out your cock!' she squealed – and I duly obliged.

Afterwards we kissed, drank more brandy and then we dressed. There were some good Norwegian prawns in the kitchen so we ate those too. Perhaps unfortunately, it was then a case of back to business, but she knew that.

'Maria,' I said, 'it is known that you are working for every single one of the Seven Great Powers. But are you also working for my friend Douglas, who represents International *Capitalism?'*

'Really, Horby!' she burst into raucous laughter. 'For a man of your intelligence, you are sometimes surprisingly naive. Of course I am working for him. And you can tell your Masters that. Have you never read The Book of Revalations *in* The Bible? *The Apocalypse where there is a Beast with seven heads and ten horns? The seven heads are the seven Great Powers of Europe. The ten horns include Douglas and other forces of international capitalism – and also forces such as revolutionary Communism. Yes, I am the Great Whore, the conduit through which all powers pass. But I am using this to bring about Peace.'*

Well, darling, I must wrap this up and post it off. I'll write to you again tomorrow after my meeting. I send you all my love.

Horby

'Peace!' Maria had proclaimed. She was working for that. and I believed her! What a fool I was!

Darling Claire,

I'm back from the meeting and am writing this with a bottle of excellent German hock at my elbow. Typically, Houston Stewart Chamberlain, a fanatic for all things German, was determined to demonstrate the excellence of their railway system and so we travelled together by rail to the Hohenzollern Palace at Potsdam. In fact, their railway system is quite brilliantly efficient and we enjoyed good coffee and excellent Ansbacher brandy as we travelled.

Chamberlain is a tall, thin man with a correspondingly thin moustache and thin, greying hair. He dresses soberly in immaculate grey. This Englishman, born in 1855, went to live in Germany in 1882, obsessed by its history, its language, its mythology, its culture and its future. He has a Prussian wife; I haven't met her. Have you read his Foundations of the Nineteenth Century? *I doubt it. Very few English people have. This massive volume of twelve hundred pages, published in 1899, has sold over a quarter of a million copies in Germany and Austria-Hungary and made Chamberlain famous and influential and respected throughout the Second Reich.*

'Ever seen demons, Horby?' he asked me as our train sped through Prussia, faster than our fastest English express. 'No? Well, let me tell you, young man, demons, which I see, drive me on relentlessly to seek new fields of study and get on with my prodigous writings. One vision after another has forced me to change from biology to botany, to the fine arts, to music, to biography, to history.

'There is, you may notice,' he continued, 'a profound unity of inspiration in all my published works and they have a remarkable coherence. Yes! Jawohl! I feel goaded on by demons and my books, for instance, on Wagner, Goethe, Kant, Christianity and Race, were, I admit freely, written

in the grip of a terrible fever, a veritable trance, a state of intoxication . . . ah! so that I was often unable to recognize them as my own work because they surpassed my expectations. I trust I'm making sense to you.'

'Of course,' I smiled knowingly. I'd been told that Chamberlain was 'hypersensitive and neurotic and subject to frequent nervous breakdowns'. Looking at his twitching figure, his waving, claw-like hands and his manic blue eyes, this description made perfect sense.

'Oh . . .' he sighed heavily, 'once, in 1896, when I was returning from Italy, the presence of a demon became so forceful that I got off the train at Gardone, shut myself up in a hotel room and wrote feverishly on a biological thesis until I had the germ of the theme that since then has dominated all my works: Race and History.'

I felt depressed as I recalled my meeting in Munich years ago with those peculiar racist magicians, Guido von List and Lanz von Liebenfels, who in their occult absurdities appeared to venerate the Sign of the Swastika as a symbol of Aryan racial purity. (Editor's Note: see The Black Pearl, *Volume III.*) *But there was no stopping Houston Stewart Chamberlain now.*

'I,' he proclaimed proudly, 'have synthesized the views of Nietzsche and Wagner. I declare that the key to history is race! All civilization flows from the white race – and the Teutonic peoples are its purest representatives. The Jews? Why, they're the sworn enemies of the Aryans, bent on polluting our blood with interbreeding so as to induce a degeneracy that will allow the Jews to rule!'

'But I thought that Jesus Christ was a Jew,' I murmured mildly.

'That's another damned Jewish lie!' he shouted, his hands waving wildly. 'Have you not read my books and given them proper study!' he snorted indignantly. 'There I

118

prove beyond all possible doubt that Jesus Christ was not a Jew. He was an Aryan. My cogent, logical arguments are irrefutable!'

'So where do we go from here?' I asked earnestly, desperate to change the subject.

'To Potsdam to see the Kaiser, of course!' he cried out. 'And when we see him, I shall once again reiterate my essential points. We Aryans require a new religion, and Aryanized Christianity is not good enough. What is needed is a religion that will fit the needs of a German Master Race!'

'Specifically German?' I queried, biting my tongue for the sake of King and Country and the gathering of Intelligence, though the latter seemed in rather short supply at present.

'Yes,' he replied solemnly. His eyes blazed with mad, burning conviction. 'The British have abandoned their destiny. My former country is now lazy, sloppy and resting on its laurels. I mean, you've just gone and elected a Liberal Government that's in a stupid and fatal alliance with the Socialists. You are blind to the new values needed to assist the Germans in their triumphant evolution. It's a difficult problem, I admit, since though I see in mysticism the supreme expression of the Aryan spirit, I doubt whether this alone is suitable for the broad mass of German people. A new religion and a new god or gods are therefore urgently required since the German stands apart and waits for a god to descend from Heaven.'

Claire, my darling, as we left the train and ascended into the magnificent gleaming horse-drawn carriage that awaited us, I hoped that the Kaiser would not be too influenced by this ruddy maniac. I'll finish this section now and continue tomorrow.

Anonymous

I just can't forget how the Englishman, Houston Stewart Chamberlain, as the horses clip-clopped towards Kaiser Wilhelm II, roared out:
'God builds today upon the Germans alone!'

CHAPTER EIGHT

The Palace at Potsdam was certainly not what I had expected.
I suppose that I was thinking of the ornate, gilded and gaudy
Palaces of France and Austria: but Prussia is different. There
was wood everywhere, wood of high quality, fashioned out of
the fine timber that came from the states around the Baltic
Sea, revered as the finest by English timber merchants and
carpenters. There were floors, walls and ceilings made out of
wood. The wood was dark, as if to exemplify the origin of the
Prussians, and yet the Palace had a certain grandeur reminiscent of the finest English country houses. Yes, everything
was very wooden – and so was the Kaiser.

Kaiser Wilhelm II awaited Chamberlain and me in a
smallish wood-panelled chamber. There was a blazing fire
on the hearth, so it was warm enough. The ruler of the
Second Reich was wearing a smart, field grey Prussian
Officer's uniform, the insignia of which proclaimed him
to be a regimental Colonel. His spiked shiny helmet of
German steel lay beside him on his desk. Before him, he had
papers of state, some in an IN tray and more in an OUT
tray. I had heard that, whatever his faults, the Kaiser took
his role seriously and was a hard and conscientious worker,
just like his father before him.

Directly in front of his desk, so that he would see it
whenever he lifted his eyes from his desk, there was a
portrait of Frederick the Great, that extraordinary, cul-

tured enlightened despot and brilliant General, who had made of Prussia a Great Power. There was no portrait, however, of Otto von Bismarck, who had engineered the unification of Germany under Prussian leadership, smashed the power first of Austria and then of France in two swift wars and who had then created the Second Reich. Kaiser Wilhelm II had sacked him.

The Kaiser rose stiffly from his desk as soon as the Guards had loudly announced our arrival. Six men stood stiffly to attention, saluting and clicking their heels as Chamberlain and I strode one pace forward and stood to attention so as to present ourselves. The Kaiser had a pleasant expression on his thin face with its thick moustache as he walked towards us, reminding me of the wooden limbs of a child's toy in his bodily movements.

'Welcome!' he declared. 'Ah! My dear Chamberlain! The greatest intellectual of Europe! What a pleasure it is to see you again!' They shook hands warmly. 'And Lord Horby, Englishman of the Esoteric Arts, what a pleasure it is to meet you!' I'd never been publicly described in that way before, though I did not mind it, and I was pleased to shake hands with him, though I think his overly strong grip betrayed the inwardly weak man. 'Now, sirs – and just let's be informal and you call me *sire*, eh, Lord Horby?' For a moment, I thought I caught a glimpse of ponderous Teutonic humour in his eyes. 'Please be seated, gentleman.' We sat down on high wooden chairs that were, in fact, incredibly comfortable. 'I trust that a good German hock is acceptable to you . . . ?'

The three of us were served with the Kaiser's hock and, frankly, it was so fine that it beat French whites into a cocked hat! One glass of that – instantly replenished – was enough to make one dream of noble warriors and beautiful Rhine Maidens.

'Now, my dear sirs.' The Kaiser sat down behind his desk and drank hock with evident enjoyment. 'In my Palace we have nothing that is not German, as you will see over dinner. Well, Herr Chamberlain, have you had any more insights?'

'Indeed, sire,' Chamberlain replied. 'It is your onerous task to lead the German people to their destined World Supremacy! Make Germany strong! Ignore public opinion! Germany, first to invent the revolutionary motor carriage – thanks to Herr Benz and Herr Daimler – is now leading the world in technology!'

'Oh, indeed! *Wunderbar!*' For an instant, the Kaiser looked uncertain as to what technology was

'Sire, you must fulfil your divine mission whereby the German race comes to dominate and inspire the world! You, sire, are our modern Siegfried, the Saviour of your People! Don't worry about what happens at the Algeciras Conference as long as German strength is displayed. Germany can smash France any time it chooses and Europe, united, should be governed by the Hohenzollerns!' The Kaiser preened himself, fondled his helmet and tweaked his moustache.

'Herr Chamberlain,' he said earnestly, 'I honestly believe that it was God who sent your book to the German people and you, personally, to me. But you must see: I am *not* a warmonger. I desire Peace. And Justice! Justice for the Germans! You, Herr Chamberlain, you wield your pen. I shall wield my tongue – and also my broad sword. Herr Horby, you seem somewhat quiet and thoughtful.'

'Talk of a European war,' I answered, 'is enough to make anyone feel rather quiet and thoughtful. The foreign policy of Great Britain has always been and still is to contain by alliances any overtly aggressive Great Power on the Continent. We recognize Germany's sphere of influence in East

Africa and we don't interfere. We don't think that Germany should interfere in Morocco.'

'Nonsense!' Chamberlain shouted.

'Realism,' I returned.

After that, I only remember two sentences spoken by the Kaiser. One was: 'Do you like to eat?' Having enthusiastically agreed, we were conducted by the Guards into an ornate dining room built of wood where we were served with superb asparagus, a hearty leek-and-potato soup that the Kaiser ate with particular relish – so did I, actually – cracked and dressed lobster and crab from the Baltic Sea; a roasted suckling pig each, with roasted potatoes and fresh peas; then a delicious *Apfelmousse* – mashed apples with raisins and sultanas and double cream. Delicious! The hocks and Moselles served were heavenly although, as I discovered when a German red was served with the pork, German red wine just isn't a patch upon French – although German brandy comes a respectable third after French cognac and Armagnac.

'Do you like sex?' the Kaiser then enquired. Chamberlain and I said that we did. 'Good!' the Kaiser growled evenly. Our glasses were refilled and we followed the leader into a wooden gallery. There was a huge glass pane before us, giving us a view onto a small chamber furnished with chairs and a thick German carpet. A crackling fire blazed on the hearth. 'I need my recreation!' the Kaiser declared. 'Now! Watch first and enjoy later. But—' He turned just as he was about to leave. 'Lord Horby, what *is* this expertise of yours in occultism all about?'

'I will certainly answer that, sire!' I came back, wondering how I could translate what I had seen so as to make it acceptable to his severely limited mentality. 'During the Renaissance, Old Masters such as Cornelius Agrippa, Paracelsus and Doctor John Dee synthesized the work of the

Ancient World in giving us wisdom that explains the Universe as we know it – I hope for greater innovations – and gave us methods by which we can expand our consciousness and advance human evolution. There are groupings doing that at the present time and yes, I am a member of several. It is also true, sire, that one of the many ways of attaining consciousness of the Divine is through sex.'

'Good,' said the Kaiser, 'very good. Now watch this.' He went downstairs, entered the small room and checked a cupboard; then he rang a bell.

Two exceptionally attractive girls walked into the chamber of His Majesty. A Guard had whispered to us that our glass pane was also a mirror, seen from that room. How spicy these girls were! I am tempted to call them Spice A and Spice B but Salt and Pepper suits these ladies better.

Salt looked as though she had come from a traditional Prussian landowning family. Her nose was tilted high in haughty disdain. She had a rather willowy figure and long blonde Prussian hair. Pepper was black and had a full figure and long hair that curled in ringlets.

The Kaiser drew himself up in his fullest dignity.

'Now, then, you bad girls,' he declared, 'what have you got to say for yourselves? As Chairman of the Governors of a school I founded, I warned you only last week!' He snorted indignantly. 'Yes! I warned you about how I would punish you if you continued to chatter idly in class and be rude to your teachers.'

They looked very shamefaced and begged his pardon.

'I am a girl poor and passion-racked, Your Majesty,' said Salt, kneeling before him. 'My heart has always held sway over my head. I cry you mercy, my noble Lord!'

'Um . . . no,' said the Kaiser. 'It's too late to say you're sorry. I am going to give you both a good tanning. Now, who is going to be first?'

'I will, sir,' Pepper said meekly and the Kaiser licked his lips wolfishly as he put three chairs together in the centre of the room. Then he sternly ordered Pepper to lie down at full length across the seats of the chairs and pull up her skirt to receive her well-deserved punishment. As she lay obediently down on the chairs, I saw a bulge appear in the crotch of his trousers as he brought up a fourth chair upon which he would sit so that he could administer the smacks without having to stoop.

Then the Kaiser bared Pepper's bottom, smoothing his hand along the crevice of her buttocks prior to the commencement of the spanking. He rested his left hand on the small of her back and started to smack her with hard, firm slaps, but, I noticed, only on the right cheek, though the smacks still made her wince.

'My word!' the Kaiser exclaimed after only half a dozen smacks. 'What a contrast there is in the admixture of maroon and pink to the beautiful burnt sienna of your spanked right arse cheek. Still: I must not neglect my duty.' He set to work on Pepper's left cheek, giving it a series of sharp smacks which made it match the other in colour.

Pepper wiggled her smarting bottom. I turned my head momentarily to see that Chamberlain had both hands in the pockets of his trousers and also that he was breathing hard.

'Oh! Oh! Oh! No more, I have had enough, please!' Pepper cried out. 'My poor bottom is burning like fire!'

'No!' the Kaiser declared robustly. 'I think that you should have another round of three smacks on each bum cheek!' I saw that the bulge in his trousers was by now really rather noticeable. Pepper had obviously noticed it too: I saw her move her left arm up and she deliberately brushed her elbow against his stiff cock as she pretended to wipe a tear from her eye.

The Kaiser gave her three hard smacks on each cheek of her gorgeous buttocks. Pepper writhed and squealed,

'Dismiss!' the Kaiser roared. 'Go and sit over there!' His finger-flick indicated a sofa where Pepper could lie down. A servant brought her brandy. She drank it gratefully, though her bottom was still twitching. 'It's your turn now,' he barked as he turned to the blonde, who had such a fine, youthful figure. 'As I always say, everything in this Palace is *German.* The girl I have just spanked comes from East African *Germany!* But you,' he stared at the blonde, 'are pure *Prussian!* So you have no excuse. You have been even naughtier than your friend, so I am going to *birch* you.'

Salt nodded her pretty head and walked up to him.

'Good girl,' he growled. Then he walked over to the cabinet and took out a short and slender little birch-rod. Coming back and sitting down on his chair, he told Salt to take off her skirt and bend herself over his knees.

Silently, Salt unbuttoned her skirt and laid herself over the Kaiser's thighs. My heart began to beat faster when he exposed her perfectly proportioned white, rounded bottom. In the same way that he had held Pepper down, he placed his left hand on her back and, with an unusual smile on his face, he raised his right arm high in the air.

Then the rod hissed down and fell with a swish on Salt's plump white bottom, instantly marking her bum cheeks with red weals and making the girl cry out in pain. A second stroke of the rod made Salt throw back her lovely head with a jerk and toss her long blonde hair all over her face as she uttered a loud, shrill squeal.

The twigs raised another set of weals on her quivering bottom. I hadn't realized that a small birch could hurt so much, especially since the Kaiser had not flogged the girl *too* severely. Nevertheless, Salt wriggled and kicked her long, lissom legs in all directions as the rod swished down again.

'Ah!' Salt squealed. 'Ow! Ouch! Ohh! Yah! Stop! Enough! Oh, it stings! I can't take any more!' But he refused disdainfully to listen to her cries and he held her down firmly as he slowly counted up to six as he completed her punishment.

Chamberlain was pale, trembling and sweating. I had really enjoyed the show. *Surely he'll stop now*, I thought. But now, to my astonishment, I saw the Kaiser chuckling.

'One more for luck!' he proclaimed: and the rod flashed one final time across Salt's luscious young bum. She lay trembling across his knees, writhing from the smarting pain . . .

'Damn' good Hohenzollern entertainment,' Chamberlain murmured.

'Indeed,' I replied, while thinking: *So that's your Siegfried? So that's your future Great Leader of Europe? And what are the girls going to say?* I wondered. *Is it: Hooray! We've just been punished by the Kaiser?*

It was at that point that I saw the Kaiser scribble a note, ring for a servant and, when that servant instantly arrived, hand it to him. This note was then brought to us. It read, in the Kaiser's blunt manner: 'Come downstairs and enjoy some sex now!'

'Lead me to it,' I said.

CHAPTER NINE

The Kaiser sat back contentedly as Chamberlain and I entered to regard the girls I have described as Salt and Pepper. Chamberlain took a seat as I stood and we were both served with fine German brandy as the girls watched us. The Kaiser and the girls smiled benevolently. Chamberlain looked stiff in every way but the most vital one. I gazed thoughtfully at the huge mattress before the fire and then at the gorgeous girls, who responded by flinging themselves upon it and inviting me towards it.

Feeling fired up, I gladly obliged; and the three of us engaged in some splendid licentious embraces, pressing our lips together and waggling our tongues in each other's mouths in a delectably sensual way. Now, I have my own way of doing things.

'Salt,' I said, 'would you appreciate it if I were to lick out your cunt?'

'Oh, yes, that would be wonderful,' she sighed. There was a gleam in her big blue eyes as she laid herself flat on her back. Parting her thighs, she splayed open her gorgeous slit with her long fingers. 'My pussy is bursting for a spend.'

I began by rolling on top of her soft curves and drawing my body upwards until my tongue was level with her superb pointed nipples. I nibbled on them, sucking on their rubbery hardness until they were sticking out like two raspberry-coloured stalks: and then I let my tongue travel down the velvet skin of her tummy, pausing briefly to circle her belly button before sliding further down into the smooth golden hair that veiled her pussy. Just like a serpent, I slid myself down between her legs and gently parted her lightly scented pubic bush with my fingertips to reveal her swollen clitty.

As I pressed my mouth against the long gash of her cleft, I breathed in the appealing aroma of her cunt, a fragrance that I have always held to be exhilarating. Salt sighed with pleasure as I breathed deeply and then placed my lips directly over her clitty and sucked it into my mouth, where the tip of my tongue began to explore it from all directions.

I could feel it growing even larger as her legs started to twitch along the sides of my body and her heels began to beat a tattoo on the rug. I nibbled delicately on the fleshy morsel until I managed to send her off into an intense orgasm. She shivered all over as the exquisite force of her climax spread through her body. She breathed softly as I licked up the creamy cum from her cunt; and she murmured sweet nothings about a dreamy spend.

'That was,' Salt declared, 'almost as good as actually being poked by a real cock.' I took this remark as a compliment, even if it was somewhat backhanded. But Salt furthered my already formidable sexual education by going on to state that boys naturally prefer straightforward fucking since they always come sooner or later, but that girls always have to work to a greater or lesser degree to achieve a climax.

The Kaiser and Chamberlain chuckled. It seemed to me that they gained greater pleasure out of watching than out of participating. Good! I had these delightful girls to myself.

'Look at him,' Pepper commented. 'His prick is as hard as a rock. How thick and meaty!'

'Ladies,' I replied, 'I thank you for the compliment.'

'Sir,' they returned in chorus, 'you have seen nothing yet.' I wasn't going to argue so I settled down to enjoy the sensual feel of Salt's hands bringing relief to my aching muscles. Though my shaft was now aching for ejaculation, she teasingly kept her hands away from my frantic cock. But relief *was* soon at hand since, once she had completed the massage, Salt lowered her mane of silky blonde hair and planted a smacking kiss upon my lips. It was difficult to restrain myself as Pepper worked her tongue down my body, stopping briefly to circle my nipples before at last descending to my aching cock.

Pepper licked all around my empurpled head and then sucked in as much of my straining shaft as she could manage, stroking my balls with one hand and teasing my length with the other. Pepper's head bobbed up and down as she treated me to a most delightful gobble. Yet the instant that she had thoroughly anointed my pulsating prick, Salt burst out laughing and moved astride me.

'Lord Horby!' she cried out. 'I am now going to sit on your lovely thick prick and feel it glide into my wet little cunt!' As Pepper leaned back and Salt leaned forward, her jaunty red nipples brushed my chest. I slid my hands around them and rubbed her gorgeous titties between my fingers whilst she slowly impaled herself on my quivering chopper. This was to be a short, sharp fuck but memorable for its intensity.

Her cuntal muscles clung tenaciously to my cock as I jerked my hips up and down in order to slide it in and out of her tight but juicy sheath.

I thrilled to the feel of the clinging cunny wall, one hand clutching a quivering arse cheek as Salt bounced up and down upon my mighty tool. Then I felt a fresh electric stab of desire speed through my body as she took my tightening scrotum in her hand. The soft feel of Salt's fingers sent me over the top and I came – and how! – shooting my seed deep inside her cunt and flooding her love tunnel with a real torrent of sticky spunk. She kept gasping '*Wunderbar!*' and reached her climax as the jism pumped in torrents from my knob.

Salt milked my cock of the last drops of its copious emission.

'*Encore!*' the Kaiser shouted. I honestly wondered if I would be up to it: but I was up to just about anything in those days. As Salt rolled over, Pepper lay down upon the mattress and next to me. I stroked her glossy black hair, which tumbled so freely over her shoulders.

In a trice we were entwined in each other's arms and exchanging the most ardent of kisses as Pepper reached out to clutch my renewed and straining shaft. Her exquisite ministrations meant that it was soon standing up again like a thick telegraph pole between my thighs. And there was Pepper lying naked beside me!

I still stared in wonder at her lush, exquisitely proportioned uptilted breasts capped with their big, biteable nipples and her smooth black belly below which was displayed the prettiest pair of pouting quim lips imaginable. She slid an arm around my neck to cradle my head and we kissed again, our tongues meshing together as I let my hands drop onto the jouncy cheeks of her bottom, pressing her eager body against my rock-hard cock. We rolled from side to side until Pepper broke the embrace to grab one of the cushions and insert it under her back so that her thighs and cunt would be positioned at a perfect angle for my bursting prick, which she held tenderly in her hand.

I lay on top of her, nudging her knees a little further apart as she guided my shaft directly into her sopping crack. I was already so worked up that I pumped in and out of her juicy cunt at pretty high speed. Pepper moaned with delight as I slewed my sinewy shaft in and out of her tingling love channel.

'Oh, Horby! I've come!' she cried out as she writhed. 'You can shoot your load whenever you want to, you beautiful man!' I increased the pace until I was pistoning in and out of her squelchy quim at a great rate, my balls slapping against the lower curves of her buttocks as she wrapped her legs around me. She pressed up hard to meet me at every stroke.

I cupped her breasts, pinching the erect nipples between my forefinger and thumb as my cock thrust back and forth. We moved into the final stages of this voluptuous coupling. Pepper's lithe frame, oh! she of the long, lissom, lovely legs! – yes, her body twisted and bucked at the approach of my spend.

This came with my shooting of a powerful stream of spunk into her warm and welcoming vagina. Uniquely delicious warm feelings of delight spread out from my cock to every fibre of my body. We lay together, panting with exhaustion.

'Bravo!' the Kaiser shouted.

Salt and Pepper then gave him and Chamberlain an excellent cock-suck. After the girls had been dismissed, Chamberlain and I thanked the Kaiser for the excellence of his hospitality and he bade us Godspeed.

'I am a Man Of Peace!' he proclaimed for the umpteenth time. 'There should never be War between our two great Anglo-Saxon nations!' I don't think that the Kaiser is a warmonger. He is a sentimental and emotional man – none too bright – of grandiose ideas, with a gift for bombastic statements and tactless utterances. Impulsive and impetuous, his imagination a stage of Wagnerian dreams, he is increasingly identifying with the role that Chamberlain has thrust upon him, as a modern Siegfried, the saviour of his people. In my opinion, Chamberlain's advice will do no good.

> *Well, that's more than enough from me, my darling. Yes, German whores really are something special but English women are the best. KROWICH! – or, Knickers right off when I come home!*
> *All my love,*
> *Horby*

And now, all these years later (1926), I am looking through the copies I made of my letters as I munch a sandwich of rare roast beef at lunchtime and drink a glass or two of highly acceptable claret.

Houston Stewart Chamberlain certainly fulfilled one dream of his life in 1908, when he married Richard Wagner's daughter, Eva, and moved to Wagner's adopted town of Bayreuth.

This helped him to increase his influence upon the Kaiser. By 1912, Chamberlain was the monarch's closest adviser and was urging a war and a triumph of German military might. When the Great War did at last come, the Kaiser awarded Chamberlain the Iron Cross. The defeat of Germany and the collapse of the Second Reich for a time broke the spirit of Chamberlain.

No sympathy, I'm afraid. In due course, I shall write of my encounter with one Adolf Hitler. My work for British Intelligence throughout the years gives me access to certain information. Chamberlain welcomed Hitler to his home in Bayreuth in 1923. So deep was the impression made by this leader of a minor Bavarian political party – I think it's the National Socialist German Workers' Party, 'Nazi' for short – that he wrote Hitler a letter on the following day.

'You have mighty things to do. My faith in Germanism had not wavered an instant though my hope – I confess – was at a low ebb. With one stroke, you have transformed the state of my soul. That, in the hour of her deepest need, Germany gives birth to a Hitler proves her vitality; as do the influences that emanate from him; for these two things – personality and influence – belong together! May God protect you!'

And this to a stupid little jumped-up Austrian corporal who tried to create a national revolution in a Bavarian beer hall? Prison is the best place for this ghastly little fellow: and I continue to despise Houston Stewart Chamberlain.

(*Editor's Note*: Chamberlain joined the Nazi Party and occasionally wrote for its publications. One of his articles hailed Hitler as the saviour destined by God to lead the German people. The Nazis revered Chamberlain as a prophet and a sage. The *Voelkischer Beobachter* devoted much space to extolling Chamberlain's genius, and affirmed that his *Foundations of the Nineteenth Century* was 'the gospel of the Nazi movement'. When Chamberlain died in January 1927, he was convinced that Hitler would eventually fulfil the destiny he had foreseen.)

What *can* one say about the Kaiser? His sabre-rattling, encouraged always by Chamberlain, did no good. I like to think that my information assisted our side at the Algeciras International Conference. To be honest, the Germans had a good case, but the overly aggressive and arrogant tone in which they defended their rights offended us and fuelled the growing suspicion that Germany was a threat to world peace.

Great Britain backed the French. The outward result was

a draw. France was granted control of the Moroccan police, to be shared with Spain, whilst Germany obtained acceptance of her view that the problem of Morocco concerned all the powers. Yet the most important results had already taken place behind the scenes. Great Britain and France, formerly enemies but now in the *Entente Cordiale*, drew closer together on account of German aggression.

A party of senior British officers had even gone to Paris to discuss how the two nations could work together in the hypothetical event of a joint war against Germany. Germany's hope that the *Entente Cordiale* would soon shatter under pressure proved vain.

Of course, I was there when Great Britain doubled the stakes and launched HMS *Dreadnought*. This had taken a year and a day to build and had cost £1,750,000. It had ten twelve-inch guns – more than twice as many as were carried by any previous warship – and it ran on oil as well as coal. It made every other battleship in the world, including all the other British ones, obsolete. Of course, that fool the Kaiser responded by building up the German navy, which only made Britannia more belligerent. The new Liberal government might have ousted the Tories by a landslide but their strong defence policy was exactly the same.

Apropos that day of which I now write, I have a letter from 'Old Crow' in front of me. The expedition to Kangchenjunga did not go as well as he had hoped, owing to violent quarrels with Guillarmod. Crowley reached 22,000 feet, which was only surpassed recently. Then, after yet another quarrel, Guillarmod and his fellow mutineers left Crowley's camp and, as they were descending to the next camp, they were hit by an avalanche. Alex Pache and three unnamed coolies died. Crowley wrote to me that he was now about to pony trek across China with his wife and baby. Mentally, I wished him luck.

I'd given up on the Golden Dawn, disgusted by its squabbling factions. Little did I know how, in time, my life would be shaken up by the things that came from it.

CHAPTER TEN

'Guess what,' said Emily Ward-Bishop. 'I'm getting married!'

'Congratulations, Emily!' I exclaimed heartily. 'Here's to married life!' I was giving her lunch at Rules, which I rather like. It's London's oldest restaurant and it's been going since 1798. This establishment knows that *roasted* meat is not the same as *baked* meat and is one of the few places left where you can get the former. There is, of course, the upside and the downside, as there is with everything. Their ghastly soup is not worth having and the vegetables are grossly overcooked. However, no one can surpass the excellence of their roasted rare beef; and their roasted mutton is very good too. The baked potatoes are excellent and so is the utterly wonderful treacle pudding. 'Who is the lucky man, Emily?' I asked.

'His name is Christopher. I think you'd like him if you met him – and you *must* come to our wedding! He's a tall, slim fellow with lands in Somerset and he is something in the City. He is also a Conservative Member of Parliament.'

'Emily, I didn't know that there were any Tories left in Parliament after their massacre by the Liberals and the Labour Party.'

'He's a survivor, Horby. He thinks that, eventually, the present Government will so annoy everyone with its sanctimonious preaching that the people will want the Tories back again.'

'Has your marriage,' I asked over the port and nuts, 'got anything to do with Mrs Joan Smythe and her Society for the Promulgation of Petticoat Government?'

'Of course, Horby. It's got everything to do with it! I don't want a husband unless he's my slave. I've spent the past few months ensuring that. I don't suppose you know anything about the *breaking in* of a *fiancé*. No?' I shook my head but remained intrigued. 'I've done it in a series of stages. I feel, Horby, that I can tell you anything.' I smiled and nodded. 'Well, you see, I noticed that Christopher was highly attracted by my bottom and by my footwear. I therefore began by demanding that he come with me on a shopping expedition to Harrod's, there to choose various things that would be needed in the marital home.

'Christopher, by his own admission, is quite hopeless at shopping and I made sure that he had to walk behind me. Behind my behind, in fact. I knew how much he adores my arse and I knew that as I switched it from side to side, he was having a rampaging erection. I kept him on the boil throughout the day, walking behind my bum; and possibly about to come at any minute. We went back to his town house in Belgravia.

' "Do you *really* love me?" I asked. "I mean, if you don't we'd better just call it off."

' "No, my darling!" he responded fervently. "I truly love you. I will do anything you want."

' "Then show your love for me," I demanded. "Lie on the floor and kiss my boots!"

'He obeyed me and planted two kisses upon my shining black-leather high-heeled boots.

' "That's good, Christopher," I said. "You have the right idea. But, you see, you have to agree that one of us will be in charge of our marriage: and it will be me. I shall *not* be going to our wedding unless that is clearly understood." I then invited him to come to my home in Maida Vale a couple of days later. "Submission," I said. "That's the name of the game."

'I was pleased to see that he turned up,' Emily told me, 'and I had prepared the place for him. For a start, there was a flogging block, just like the one he'd had at Eton. There was also a birch, pickled in my own pee. I gave him champagne and prawns and sweet words to begin with. Then I spoke.

' "Christopher," I said, "you really must learn that your wife will take charge of your life. I demand that, before our wedding, you submit to a sound birching, just to let you know who is in charge."

' "Emily . . ." he began to reply.

' "It's Madam, actually, until we're married," I replied with cutting asperity.

' "Sorry, Madam . . ."

' "I should hope so. Take your trousers down this instant and lie over that flogging block!" He obeyed me, a good sign in a husband. He also has neat, tight white buttocks – and what a pleasure it is to birch them! I felt quite murderously randy as I poised and switched my birch in the air – and then I brought it down with a great big *swish*! How his bottom jumped! Hee! hee! I brought it down again with another mighty *swish*, concentrating this time upon the left buttock. The next stroke landed solidly on the right. It really was rather a joy to watch Christopher's bottom twitch and writhe as it did. I laid the fourth stroke dead centre. The fifth stroke followed fast on the upper regions and my sixth and final stroke was just above the thighs. What delight it was to watch his neat little bum twitching, all scarlet with pain and shame!

'*That*,' said Emily, 'was the moment that I *bound* him to the flogging block with leather straps. I took a high stool and, as I smoked a cigarette, I regarded him and told him that he was in bondage. Yes, and to *me*. But I wanted him to recover for the next stage. My white knickers were in fact sopping wet by this time. I released the straps and commanded Christopher to stand up. He did, his bottom burning brilliantly.

' "Christopher, my darling," I stated, waving the long, frilly white knickers in the air; "you will step into these. These are my knickers, soaked with my cunt juice. You will wear them. You will *always* wear my knickers underneath the trousers of your suit. They will persistently remind you that you are under female control. I shall give you my knickers every day and you will wear them as you speak in the House of Commons and as you preside over board – or bored – meetings. I really want my wet knickers to be nestling up against your prick." With that, I forced him to step into my knickers and it was a pleasure to see that the sight and feel of the thin, smooth satin had given him quite a monumental boner.'

'Did you take advantage of it and fuck him?' I enquired.

'No, no, Horby, I'm not a fool. Christopher will not get to fuck me until the day of our wedding!'

'Poor chap,' I murmured. 'But continue.'

' "I'm going to *petticoat* you," I told Christopher haughtily. "Come here!" I produced a gorgeous white petticoat of Irish linen trimmed with lace. "Now, step into your petticoat." He obeyed me and I smiled with pleasure. "Put this blouse on!" I commanded him: it was a frilly little white number. Again he obeyed me. It was *such* a positive pleasure to see him standing there in his petticoat. But I had another surprise for him. I smiled wickedly as I produced a long emerald green pleated skirt, lined with a slip of silk. I made him step into it and gleefully did up the buttons at the back.

' "What a good girlie you are!" I laughed as I regarded him standing humbly before me in his women's clothes. "Now go and stand in the corner as a sign of your submission to me as your future wife." He complied. "There! Hands behind your back! Face to the wall!" He submitted to my dictates. I let him stand there in his skirt for a while as I smoked another cigarette; but then I approached him, stroked his burning bottom and slipped my hand down underneath the belt of his skirt, behind his petticoat and knickers, to feel his luscious cock.

' "What a lovely prick you have, darling!" I declared as I fingered and teased his mighty tool. "But you *must* keep your face to the wall. Poor dear, your bottom must be burning. But I do enjoy stroking and tickling your prick . . ."

'Christopher sighed deeply and his cock shot his spunk into the palm of my red satin-gloved hand.

' "Oh, sweetie!" I exclaimed; "how charming! Well, you can stand in the corner for my delectation for twenty minutes longer. I shall have another drink and another cigarette as I watch your beautiful buttocks change colour." Actually, that's what I did, after I'd hitched his skirt up, along with his petticoat, and pulled down his knickers. I wanted to teach him a lesson. When I let him out of the corner, I could see that he was just *aching* to fuck me – but I smiled and said: "Not until we're married". And I made him curtsy to me.'

'Typical, Emily,' I said, 'absolutely bloody typical!'

'Horby, you always seem to be laughing at me.'

'Yes, Emily. Unless one is a dedicated masochist, how can one *not* do so?' She burst out laughing too. 'I wish you every success in your marriage to Christopher. Any news of Crowley and Rose at all?'

'Yes. After the Kangchenjunga expedition, which ended

in disaster – though it *did* set a record – Crowley hung around in Madras and waited for Rose to join him. Rose told me that, apparently, one night Crowley was attacked in an alley in Madras by some Indian Thugs. He pulled out his Webley and fired it. The newspapers subsequently reported that one bullet had gone through *two* Thugs. I don't quite know how that could be possible.'

(*Editor's Note:* According to the Warren Commission, it was easily possible for a bullet to pass through the late President John F. Kennedy and to continue on its merry way through the body of Governor Connally, who survived it.)

'I *like* Crowley,' Emily said. 'Though he does have his undeniable faults . . . But you know, when Rose finally arrived in Madras with the baby, he greeted her with the words: "Hello, darling! You're just in time to see me hanged!" Then they went off to China and pony trekked across it. Then he abandoned Rose in a port of Indo-China and completed another circuit of the world, this time in the opposite direction and via Shanghai.

'Unfortunately,' Emily continued, 'things aren't going that well for him right now. He arrived back in London to find that his wife was by now an incorrigible alcoholic and their baby was dead. He tells me that Rose was such a sloppy drunkard, she neglected to clean the nipple of the feeding bottle. He's heartbroken but he's stuffed her full with another kid. The marriage is very stormy. Rose is always drunk and shouting. Then there's Colonel Gormley, who is madly in love with Rose. He is a masochist just like Christopher. Apparently, he absolutely adores Rose as his ideal of female domination and he is *such* a masochist that he even relishes the fact that she openly despises him. Perhaps he gets sexual pleasure out of being the victim of her disdain. Crowley is tolerant since he wants some boys to keep his wife amused. But I tell you, Horby: he is *shattered* by the death of his baby daughter.' I was very sorry to hear that as I paid our bill and then took my carriage to Emily's place in Maida Vale.

And *who* do you think was there? There must have been some prior agreement, since within forty-five minutes, at the elegant house of Emily, as we were enjoying coffee and cognac, the butler announced Mr and Mrs Sedgewick.

Mrs Sedgewick was, of course, Joan Smythe; and her husband was Wilfred, that abominable poet. Mrs Smythe was there to congratulate Emily upon making a good marriage.

'And I know the truth about that!' Wilfred Sedgewick cried out. 'Listen:

'A propositional abstractional
Remain, that proposition may include
An indisputable as well exclude
Disputable, in sphere provisional
To stand immovable conditional.
Whence comprehension never to conclude
But ever know what thereto did intrude.
    Lest venturing become habitual:
    As in imaginary personage
Usurp the functionality bestowed
On creature by a providential hand,
    And rashly venturing themselves engage
    To journey through their lives without a road
That they can see or guide they can command'

'This is sublime art,' said Mrs Joan Smythe.

'Yes,' I murmured. 'Until the last five lines, one could almost see it beginning to make sense; and it seems to refer to the fear of Providence, lest venturing should become habitual. With one single line – "as in imaginary personage" – the whole idea is reduced to ruin. That line is a mammoth!'

'And I'm going to spank you, Wilfred, for writing such bad poetry,' Mrs Joan Smythe declared. She stripped her husband of his trousers and underpants and soon enough smacked his bottom a shocking pink.

Meanwhile, I made love to Emily prior to her marriage. I simply shoved my shaft inside her, worked it deep and slow for a while and then it was one quick short jab after another. Emily came when I really rammed it in.

CHAPTER ELEVEN

Every now and again, I like to go to a good brothel, in the same sort of way that a man likes to go to a good restaurant. I want a courteous welcome, I want pleasant service, I want something decent to drink; and, above all else, I want a good fuck, devoid of any emotional encumbrance, with a fine-looking woman. In those golden, gilded years, which I now recall so fondly as 'those spacious days', my wants and needs were amply supplied by the brothel of Mrs Arnold, just off The Strand.

Eat your hearts out today, young men! I know of nothing like it nowadays. Imagine: you ring a doorbell and, once admitted by a liveried servant, you enter a hall of gaudy splendour, all deep carpet, plush furniture and glimmering chandeliers. Then you are greeted warmly by Mrs Arnold, a plump, matronly and kindly woman. With gestures of respect, she ushers you into the bar. You take a comfortable arm-chair and order good champagne. Mr Arnold, a slim, handsome young man, will shuck you a dozen good Whitstable oysters if you'd fancy that to stimulate your appetite – and, on this occasion, I did.

There are other men in the bar, some sitting on stools, others in armchairs, and they are enjoying the ambiance as much as you are. There are plenty of beautiful girls around and, at a signal from your finger, one will come instantly to keep you company. If you decide, after a while, that she's not quite right for you, all you have to do is signal to Mr or Mrs Arnold; the girl will withdraw and another, if you so desire, will take her place.

On this occasion, as I slurped my oysters, I had my eye upon a slim young girl dressed in black and called Paula. Unfortunately, so did just about everyone else in the room. I sent a hand signal to Mrs Arnold to indicate that if Paula were the star turn, I would pay more for her than anyone else. I received jealous looks from all the other men and preened myself.

'You know,' Paula said as I served her some champagne, 'I am so glad that you want me.' This dark-haired girl with soulful eyes had a soft voice with a distinctive French accent. 'And when I saw you sitting here with an evident big hard-on between your legs, how I was hoping that I might be the one to ease this feeling!'

'Flattery will get you anywhere,' I murmured. The thought of fucking this pretty lady had made my cock swell up to bursting point. 'Yet you look so absolutely enticing!'

'Come with me,' she urged as her eyes lit up.

Now imagine that you are led upstairs by a slim, delicate and feminine hand. You have unbuttoned your flies in anticipation and as you enter a gorgeous and comfortable bedroom, you slam the door shut, then stand up against the bedroom wall with Paula. Her slender, warm body presses against you. She grinds her pussy against your stiff shaft.

'Ahhh!' she cries out, 'how exciting to feel a thick prick rubbing against me! Ooh! Lord Horby, too many men who come here do not have a proper erection – but *you* do! Oh! The very idea of having your cock slide into my cunt has made me all wet. Feel my quim and see for yourself.'

You run your hand up under her satin dress – and find that she is not wearing any knickers. There is no impediment to your fingers sliding into her damp pussy bush. Her body trembles when you begin to toy with her clitty.

'Oh! Oh! Oh!' she moans. 'Quickly now, take off your clothes and fuck me, you dear man!' Who could resist such a sweet command? While you tear off your trousers, she too undresses swiftly and, in no time at all, you are locked together in a naked embrace.

The underside of your stiff shaft throbs against her belly as your mouths mesh together and you fondle her apple breasts. She reaches out, grabbing your palpitating prick and guides you gently inside her. Your knob sinks between the delicate lips of her quim and well into the welcoming love channel beyond, the walls of which close deliciously over your cock, pulling you in deeper and deeper until your chopper is completely engulfed in her delectably squelchy vagina. You draw back and she squeals with joy as you thrust yourself into her again.

Then you lean back casually against the wall as the happy lady throws her arms around your neck and, with astonishing dexterity, wraps her legs around your waist, locking them behind you so that your prick is fully ensconced within her sopping cunt. Even so, you might, after a while, find this position to be a trifle uncomfortable.

So then you begin slowly to slide down the wall as she releases you from the scissor-like hold in which she has held your frame between her thighs. As you murmur sweet nothings, Paula steers you toward the four-poster bed and pushes you down there. She straddles you and lowers herself onto you, holding your straining cock-shaft lightly in her hand as it slowly disappears into her dripping cunt-shaft. The raunchy lady settles herself and then, sitting bolt upright, she arches her back so that her small, youthful breasts jut out proudly.

She purrs with pleasure as you reach up and squeeze her

tits in your hands. Then, putting both hands behind her swan-like neck, she shakes her head, tossing free her dark mane of hair before taking her weight on her arms.

She kisses you on the lips, moving her body upwards so that she is almost clear of your glistening cock. Then she lowers herself again onto your throbbing tool. Now it is *your* turn to gasp with delight as her puffy pussy lips brush the mushroom dome of your cock and she slips her luscious lust funnel down the stiff-standing length of your tool. You're panting hard as the slick, warm walls of her cunny close tightly around your swollen lust truncheon.

You quickly shunt your shaft up and down in swift, short jabs that bring you both to the very brink of ecstasy as you increase the pace to a near-frenzied speed. At your every thrust, Paula's gorgeous bum smacks against the top of your thighs. Her juicy quim seems to tighten its fleshy grip all the more, as if a suction pump has been applied to the bell-end of your rampant todger. Suddenly the massaging muscles of her juicy cunny tighten about you in a long, rippling seizure that runs from the base of your cock to the very tip of your knob.

This clutching spasm sends you to Lust's Elysium. A torrent of spunk bursts out of your cock-end and creams the inner crannies of her cunt. Gush after gush of milky jism jets out of your knob, spurting deep up inside her. She cries out in joy as she achieves a glorious climax. You both shout out your ecstasy together in a delirium of delight.

As you nevertheless continue to pump upwards, Paula grinds her pussy into your groin as she surrenders to the pleasures of her spend. She crushes her breasts against your chest as your fingers dig into the fleshy cheeks of her beautiful bottom, pulling her forward against you. And when the exquisite sensations finally subside, you pull her off your cock and reach down into her sopping sheath, dipping your fingers in the mingled juices of lust. Then you rub the pungent wetness over her succulent breasts, anointing her upstanding nipples.

For a time you lie in her arms. Then you look at her and smile and she knows that you want to go in due course. She smiles too and pats your thigh to signal that she actually enjoys your patronage. She rings a bell and a maid enters, bearing champagne and cognac. You take a glass of each together and smoke cigarettes while chatting pleasantly and laughing about a variety of inconsequential matters. Still smiling, for you feel genuinely happy, you dress, then you kiss her, give her a couple of gold sovereigns and take your leave.

'Come back soon,' she sighs, making you feel even better. You then go downstairs to a little room to see Mrs Arnold, who has made out your bill. You look at it. It is very expensive but you judge it to be worth every penny, so you pay gladly. You know full well that Paula will be giving herself to someone else after a half-hour break but you don't care. When you're in the mood, you'd like to have her again. Having paid, and as pleased as Punch, you stroll back into the bar where the girls salute you; and Mr Arnold, knowing how much you have spent – in both senses of the word! – welcomes you warmly as one man to another and gives you complimentary coffee and cognac on the house.

Then your cloak, hat and stick are brought to you and you feel joyous as you are bade fond farewells and go out into the night.

As I shall tell my son when he is old enough: 'Well, m'boy, that's how it was in those days.'

As it was, on this occasion, who should I bump into as I walked into The Strand but Arthur Machen! I hadn't seen him in years! We greeted one another warmly.

'Well met!' I declared. 'Still writing, I trust? Must say, I really liked your *Hieroglyphics*. What an excellent study of what constitutes true Literature! Ecstasy, you say. Yes, that's the key. And your recent *The House of Souls* was very fine, too. D'you know, *A Fragment of Life* and *The White People* are two of the finest things that you have ever done! But I also hear that you have been on the stage. A strolling player, eh?'

'Lord Horby,' he smiled gently, 'thank you for your kind words about my books. But I really did enjoy my time with Sir Frank Benson's Shakespeare Company.'

(*Editor's Note:* This was the forerunner of today's Royal Shakespeare Company.)

'Glad to hear it, Machen. Some months ago I heard good words spoken about you by Lady Benson. She told me: "I believe if I ever reach Heaven, I shall meet Arthur Machen there, and he will be the same, and look the same; he will wear no halo like the angels, and if he has wings, they will be concealed beneath a dusty old Inverness cape – but he will be the friend of Saints." '

'How good of her to say that.' Machen looked genuinely pleased.

'Come and dine with me!'

'Good of you to invite me, Lord Horby, but I am otherwise engaged to my club, The New Bohemians. In fact, why don't you come there with me? It's not far . . . just the Prince's Head in Buckinghamshire Street, nearby.' I accepted gladly. It was one of those soft November evenings when the leaves fall off the trees as you pass and there is mist in the air. As you walk, you feel as though anything strange could happen to you at any moment in this vast Labyrinth of London.

On our way there, Machen explained to me that he was a married man once again, his wife being an actress named

Purefoy. The book he considered to be his masterpiece, *The Hill Of Dreams*, would be published next year by Grant Richards, who had refused it ten years before. Machen was obviously pleased since it had taken him two years of agonizing toil to write it and, for all these years, publishers had flung it back in his face with insults.

(*Editor's Note:* When it finally appeared in 1907, *The Hill Of Dreams* was excoriated by critics, with one calling it: 'the most decadent book in English Literature'. In later years, Henry Miller declared that it was the finest novel that he had read.)

We reached the Prince's Head and went upstairs to an oak-panelled room where Machen was greeted warmly. There was a big barrel of excellent ale. Machen informed me that the old cigar box passed around was for contributions to the festivities. I was feeling in such a good mood that I dropped in ten guineas, much to the joy of the members.

'Thank you, Lord Horby,' Machen said quietly. 'Not one of us has money in any solid sense but some have – sometimes – a little more than others. This amicable arrangement is a simple and effective form of commonwealth.' He had told me that he was presently earning a precarious living from his books and from his sales of articles to various quality journals.

Machen introduced me to this motley crew. There was a journeyman tailor who could set the long table in a roar with stories of his tailor's shop and measurements of the inside leg. There was an Admiralty official, who struck me as being a steady, stout, good-humoured fellow. There was a city solicitor; three or four journalists; a Customs officer; a musician; an actor; a writer of lyrics for musical shows; and others whose occupations remained a secret. There was the poet, essayist and short-story writer, Richard Middleton, whose manner was sour and bitter. (I think that his *The Ghost Ship and Other Stories* is wonderful; but the poor man took his own life.) There was Edgar Jepson, noted for his novel *Number Nineteen*, a rather clever man with much charm. There was that noted wit, Cecil Chesterton, brother of G.K.C., but I found his squalid anti-semitism to be depressing. There was a young journalist called Arthur Ransome. (He later did jolly well with children's books such as *Swallows and Amazons*.)

'You know . . .' Machen said to me as *huge* plates of sandwiches were placed upon the table, 'we used to be a walking society for exploring London. Some walked well, most talked well, *all* drank well! Now we're all getting on in years. But believe me, Lord Horby, the pleasures of the vine and the tankard, as also of the table, partake of the sacred. That is why I declare in my *Hieroglyphics* that the greatest works of Literature are Homer's *The Odyssey*; *Gargantua and Pantagruel* by Rabelais; *Don Quixote* by Cervantes; and *The Pickwick Papers* by Charles Dickens! Now, try some of these sandwiches.' I did; and they were marvellous. What can be better than freshly baked and buttered cottage loaf and a choice of three fillings? There was rare roast beef with horseradish sauce; York ham, off the bone, with English mustard and lettuce; and mature Cheddar cheese with brown, home-made pickle. Great!'

Machen was Chairman that night and he proposed that we discuss the existence of demons.

'I don't believe in them,' the tailor said. 'They're just bogeymen to frighten children.'

'Don't agree!' Richard Middleton snarled. 'They are within us all the time.'

'Do you mean "demon" or "Daemon"?' I asked. 'After all, Socrates attributed all his intellectual gifts to the latter, which one might view as being an angel.'

'Can't be right,' the Admiralty official declared. 'Angels encourage Mankind to evolve and Demons encourage Mankind towards debasement.'

The City solicitor then treated us to a surprisingly learned discourse on Demonology and the Roman Catholic classification of the hierarchy of Hell. Cecil Chesterton expressed himself to be in full agreement.

'Are you really sure, sir?' Edgar Jepson adjusted his monocle. 'Have you been to Hell and conducted a survey?'

'You don't have the good fortune,' Cecil Chesterton squeaked angrily, 'to be within the Roman Catholic faith.'

'And thank God I don't!' Jepson exclaimed heartily.

'How I love it,' our Chairman, Arthur Machen, exclaimed, 'when we go at it hammer and tongs until the tankards go dry! More beer for everybody!' I reflected that his second wife must be doing him much good, since the shy introvert I once knew had metamorphosed into a garrulous extrovert. 'I believe,' he proclaimed, 'that there are Powers in this world beyond our ken. I have written about them. I am sure that there are angels on the side of God and Jesus Christ: and that there are demons, fallen angels, on the side of the Devil and that both sides struggle for the soul of Man.'

'Interesting,' I commented. 'Gentlemen, I don't believe in the Christian God. So how can I possibly believe in the Christian Devil?'

CHAPTER TWELVE

Barter's Oyster Bar really had grown since I had last been there. It was good to see that this was on account of the excellence of the food and the courtesy of the service, and there was, of course, the eminently reasonable nature of the price. There were now private rooms upstairs and my Memorandum 54321 informs me that I entertained the wild Sybil Pankhurst there in January 1909.

The intervening years had been pretty good to me. My marriage had continued well and I had fucked loads of other women, but I don't really have anything especially exciting to record. The reforming Liberal Government of Campbell-Bannerman was now the Liberal Government of Asquith, with Lloyd George as its principal figure. Unlike most of my peers in the House of Lords, I agreed with the reforming measures that were being taken.

Sybil Pankhurst was a charming girl. She had long blonde hair, a straight nose, a voluptuous mouth, a fine figure – and blue eyes just *blazing* with idealism. Having seen some of her paintings, I knew that she was also a very talented artist. She had genuine passion for the cause of the Emancipation of women, and she was allied to her mother Emmeline and her sister Christabel, but even they had found her radicalism to be a little too much. She was, nevertheless, campaigning hard for the newly formed Women's Social and Political Union. Her considerable artistic talents had been used for designing badges and banners.

'I feel I must help with whatever needs to be done,' she told me over the oysters. 'I used to be nervous of public speaking, so much so that my heart thumped terribly when I went to heckle that bastard Winston Churchill.' She tossed back a goblet of champagne. I ensured that her glass was replenished. 'He ignored my question. I persisted. Stewards tried to throw me out but some good men who like me prevented that. I seized the chance to mount the platform and make a short speech amidst the mounting uproar. Churchill *grabbed* me into a chair, telling me that I was to stay quiet. He then told the audience that nothing would induce him to give women the vote.

' "I am not going to be henpecked!" he cried out. Meanwhile, two stewards dragged me away to an ante-room, abusing and threatening me. I flung open the window and called down to the passers-by:

' "I want you to be witnesses of anything that takes place in this room!" They left me, but I escaped through a window. My blood was up. I held an impromptu meeting in the street and made a statement to the press.' This bold girl slurped another oyster. 'Now, I'd rather be an artist and carry on with my painting but I just can't stay out of the struggle. Three years ago, I was sent to prison for refusing to pay a fine of one pound. My dreadful crime was "obstruction". I was banged up in Holloway for two weeks.

'Conditions are grim there,' she continued as the oysters were removed. 'The bed was hard, the pillow like stone and, since the window of the cell did not open, the ventilation was exceedingly bad. The food was mainly oatmeal gruel, hard bread and, on some lucky days, either suet pudding or potatoes. The discipline is harsh there. We women were not addressed by name but by number. And I freely admit that as an active Suffragette, I have been in and out of prison ever since. So what? Fuck the bastards!

'Listen, Horby,' this intriguing woman stared at me hard as our scallops arrived. 'Since 1886, *four* bills have been introduced into Parliament to give women the vote. *Four* times they have passed the Second Reading – and *four* times they have got no further towards becoming law. Surely my exasperation is understandable? Now, tell me, sir, and tell me true, do *you* accept the notion of Votes for Women?'

'Yes,' I replied. 'It seems quite ridiculous to deny the vote to fifty per cent of the human race.'

'Thank Goddess you said that!' Sybil retorted, 'otherwise I'd tell you to take your scallops and shove 'em up your arse! Anyway, I don't want to eat any more. It was good, and thank you: but I've had enough. I see a bed behind you. You were obviously planning on that. Tell the waiters to go away and just fuck me!' I needed no second invitation. One of the good things about Barter's these days is that if you hire a private room, you're given the key and the waiters are instructed to try the door handle softly first. If it's locked, that means: Leave Us Alone.

We flung ourselves onto the bed and I stripped the thin silk from her to expose her lovely bare breasts, which jiggled so invitingly in front of me.

'Oooh! Lord Horby!' she squealed in mock anger, 'you are a disgrace! You naughty man! How would you like it if I squeezed your cock?'

'I'd love it,' I returned. Taking hold of her hand, I rubbed it against the bulge between my thighs. Sybil giggled and proceeded to unbutton my trousers and pull out my swollen shaft, which she cradled in her hands.

'My word!' this ardent feminist exclaimed. 'Your cock is so splendidly thick!' Holding my throbbing truncheon in her hand, this intriguing girl went down on her knees before me, wrapping her free arm around my waist as she ran her wet tongue slowly under my hairy ballsack.

This made me shiver all over as the beautiful young lady kissed my bollocks as she gently rubbed her soft hand up and down my palpitating prick. I groaned as, with one hand, Sybil grabbed my bottom and with the other held my cock and eased its crown between her generous red lips. I emitted a second groan as she sucked with uninhibited vigour on my stiff shaft which was now firmly jammed in her mouth.

What a joy it was to watch Sybil teasing my rubicund knob, running the tip of her tongue around the ridge of its head as she tenderly manipulated my balls through the pink skin of my scrotum! She purred with satisfaction when I began to jerk my hips and thrust my glistening wet chopper in and out of her mouth.

Sybil slurped away with unabashed delight on my cock and this exquisite sensation soon proved too much for me. I let out a moan of delight as I felt myself being swept inexorably up to the pinnacle of pleasure. I panted and murmured that I was about to shoot. When my blue-veined shaft began to tremble inside her mouth, Sybil realized that the moment of truth was only seconds away. So what did this independent artist and suffragette do? She jammed her lips tightly over my cock as the first spurts of salty spunk splashed into her mouth and my prick bucked uncontrollably as she held my rod lightly between her pearly white teeth.

I couldn't help the contortions of my face as further globs of jism hurtled out of my knob. Sybil gulped down my copious emission thirstily until I withdrew and lay back against the pillows, temporarily exhausted by this invigorating exercise.

'Ah!' Sybil smacked her lips. 'You naughty boy! You've

made me feel so randy!' she scolded me as she rolled over on her tummy to present me with a delicious view of her delectable rounded buttocks. 'As soon as you can, I want you to fuck my bottom.'

'I'd love to, Sybil,' I replied; 'though I'll need a little help to make my cock stiff again. Will you give me a helping hand?'

'Naturally,' she answered. 'Oh, good, there's still some butter on the table.' I complied with her request, dipping my fingers in liberally, then smearing it all over the crevice between Sylvia's voluptuous bum cheeks. Meanwhile, she took hold of my limp cock and flipped the flaccid organ up and down on her palm. 'This presently sad little cock really does look like a suitable case for treatment,' she murmured as she curled her long, slim, cool fingers around the shrunken shaft, and began to fist her hand up and down it, rubbing my prick at an increasingly brisk pace. 'Come on, my dear,' she muttered lewdly, 'I'm sure you can rise to the occasion if you put your mind to it. Hurry up now! I want to feel your good thick prick pushing its way between my bottom cheeks and then shooting a nice pressing of cock juice up my bum!' This lascivious frigging soon produced the desired effect.

My tool began to throb wildly as it rose up and swelled into its former sturdy state, jutting upward like an arrow ready to fly. Sybil gave my shaft a final squeeze and then adopted a new position on the bed, laying her arms flat and resting her head in her hands as she pushed her bottom up high in the air. I stroked my pulsating prick and then coated it with butter prior to taking up a new position, just behind her.

I proceeded to guide my glowing knob firmly into the cleft between her voluptuous bum cheeks, the opening of which was waiting to be invaded by my big cock. She panted when she felt me prong my rod against her puckered arse-hole and I pulled her buttocks outwards as I pushed my prick inwards.

I had no difficulty in easing my knob directly into the tight sheath of her back passage. Once my cock was fully ensconced inside her bottom, I began to work my tool in and out of her tightly clinging orifice, heaving my whole body backwards and forwards, making Sybil's beautiful buttocks slap sensually against my belly as we started to move lasciviously in a quickening rhythm.

As our motions became ever more frenzied, it seemed as though even my swinging balls were being sucked into the luscious depths of Sybil's delectable behind. We worked ourselves up to the summit of erotic delight – what a lusty pair we were! – and Sybil was shrieking out her own delight in a series of ear-piercing yells.

'Go on!' she shrieked. 'Fuck my bum! Oh, you big-cocked boy! Yes, that's right . . . don't stop thrusting! Faster, *faster*! I know you have a gallon of spunk boiling up in your balls for me!' she shouted as she wriggled to and fro, opening and closing her bum-hole as she clenched and unclenched her snowy-white buttocks.

I now leaned over her and fondled her lush breasts and firm titty-tips. From the way Sybil was waggling her bottom, there was no doubt that she was thoroughly enjoying the experience of having my stiff shaft slewing in and out of the tight sheath of her back passage. I continued to piston my prick in and out of her arse.

Suddenly, with a hoarse, choking cry of fulfilment, I flooded her rear dimple with a flood of sticky spunk and Sybil squealed with happiness as we shuddered to a glorious mutual climax, falling forwards in a heap of tangled limbs.

We lay together for a while and then she arose from the

bed and began to dress herself. I would have liked her to lie with me longer and I asked her where she was going.

'Horby, it's been great,' she replied with a genuine and dazzling smile. Then she poured brandies for both of us. As I drank mine, she completed her dressing. 'You really have inspired me. In your funny way, you're a good man.' She drank some brandy too. 'It's just that you have got my creative juices flowing. So I shall go home now and there I shall paint a picture based upon our encounter. If I don't go now, I shall lose it.'

'Oh. I was hoping soon enough to fuck your delectable cunt.'

'Ha! ha! What a compliment!' she laughed gaily. 'No, that's not on. You see, I'm still a pure vaginal virgin and I have taken a vow to remain so until Votes For Women is a measure finally passed. *No one*, not even a dear sweet man like you, gets to fuck *my* cunt until Women Have The Vote. And you make sure that you swing your weight behind that in the House of Lords. I would really like to remain friends with you. Thank you for a wonderful evening!'

Before I could recover my composure, Sybil Pankhurst had kissed me full upon the lips and departed. I smoked a cigarette and drank more cognac, feeling somewhat dazed by this extraordinary female. I've been called many things in my life but never 'a dear sweet man'. *I must be getting older*, I reflected as I dressed and then paid the bill.

I felt I could do with yet another cognac downstairs and so entered the bar to see a familiar figure haranguing a man who had obviously become his friend. Of course, I listened first before joining in.

'Captain Fuller,' he was saying, 'your book, *The Star in the West*, is the finest study of my works, my poetry and my philosophy that is ever likely to be written. And I assure you, sir, that this magnificent work has not been written in vain. No, no. In two thousand years' time, the world will be sitting in the sunset of Crowleyanity!'

I thought this an appropriate moment to approach the table. It seemed as though they'd drunk two magnums of champagne and were now engaged upon a third; and they'd had at least three dozen oysters each. Crowley greeted me warmly and introduced me to Captain J.F.C. Fuller: the initials stood for John Frederick Charles. He was a slim man but very fit and wiry and his blue eyes struck me as being perceptive and penetrating. He had good manners. I had heard that Crowley had been out in China and also in the Sahara: certainly he had matured. He now had an astonishingly magnetic presence.

'Do you realize, Lord Horby . . .' Fuller proclaimed. It was clear that he and Crowley were intoxicated; but so was I. 'Yes! Do you realize that it has taken 100,000,000 years to produce Aleister Crowley? The world has indeed laboured and has at last brought forth a man!'

'Too kind, sir, too kind!' Crowley laughed lightly. 'Though I still can't quite get over what you told me earlier. Remember *The Book of The Law* which I showed you years ago at Boleskine, Horby?' I nodded. 'Well, after ignoring it for years, I suddenly stumbled upon it again at Boleskine when I was looking in the attic for a pair of snowshoes. On rereading, it hit me like a thunderbolt. There is no doubt now in my mind that, like it or not, it was written by a praeterhuman Intelligence from another dimension. Of course, that sounds like real Cranks' Corner stuff. But I showed it to Fuller here anyway, fully expecting that he would dismiss me as a hopeless idiot.'

'I didn't,' Fuller stated calmly. 'The work is incredibly beautiful and I honestly think that it is a description of the way of future human evolution. It is positive proof that there *are* "Dominions and Thrones and Powers" beyond our conscious ken.'

I think that the three of us got jolly drunk that night. Today (1926) I discern that Fuller really is a remarkable man – as is Crowley. It was Colonel Fuller who pioneered the use of tanks in the Great War so as to win the great advance at Cambrai in 1917 – for the first time in years, church bells rang in London – and the even greater smashing of the German lines at the battle of Amiens. He also wrote jolly good books called *Yoga* and *Qabalah*, heavily influenced by Crowley.

(*Editor's Note*: After 1926, Fuller proved himself, as a Major-General, to be the leading military strategist of his era. In his books and lectures, he developed the notion of *Blitzkrieg* – 'Lightning War' – using massed formations of tanks and dive bombers and paratroopers behind the lines. The British dismissed his ideas; the Germans eagerly adopted them. He was one of the two Englishmen invited to Adolf Hitler's fiftieth birthday party. In later years, he distinguished himself further as an outstanding military historian.)

I will never forget how, on that night, Crowley, Fuller and I linked arms as we walked down the streets of London chanting: 'Do what thou wilt shall be the whole of the Law!' and 'Love is the Law, Love under Will!'

CHAPTER THIRTEEN

I was really rather pleased to receive a letter in fantastic handwriting, all curls and loops and flourishes in sepia ink, headed '44 Bedford Square' and with an elaborately decorative signature, 'Ottoline Morrell'. She would be 'At Home' on the next Thursday evening.

Well, I thought, as I sipped my mid-morning amontillado sherry, the Thursday evenings of the Duke of Portland's sister were indeed becoming a legend. I'd been told that you might meet anybody there, even the Prime Minister. Yet although her husband, Mr Philip Morrell, was an active Liberal MP, Lady Ottoline was not really one of the political hostesses like Margot Asquith. The guests she preferred were artists and authors, philosophers and critics. For a few moments, I wondered why on earth she had invited me.

I supposed it was because I had met her at an At Home of Margot Asquith. I thought that she had the head of a Medusa but she was very simple and innocent in spite of it and there was no doubt that she woshipped the Arts. I wondered, however, if there might be a hidden political agenda, since there was a right bloody crisis in progress. It was all due to David Lloyd George, who had been appointed the Chancellor of the Exchequer by Asquith. He was proposing 'The People's Budget' This would lead to Old Age Pensions, National Insurance and Unemployment

Benefit if passed. Of course, this meant higher taxes on the rich and landed and so the House of Lords was presently in an uproar against it. Why, there might even be *Death Duties* payable to the taxman on one's various estates.

Myself, I could not see why my peers in the Lords were getting their knickers into such a twist over the matter. I want to live in a civilized and humane Great Britain of which I am one of the most fortunate members. It struck me that the 'People's Budget' of Lloyd George, of whom Claire had spoken so well, would improve the lot of the working classes out of all measure compared to anything done previously, even by Disraeli. I was in favour since, after all, we aristocrats depend upon the workers. There are few men finer than the British worker, I firmly believe. Therefore, I really don't mind paying some more tax for the execution of what strikes me as being excellent, necessary and improving measures. I'm in the fortunate position of being so rich that I will barely notice the extra bite – yet my peers, who are nearly all in the same fortunate position, are squealing meanly like Hebrew misers.

Well: if the motive for inviting me was political, it wasn't actually necessary. Lloyd George and the Liberals could count on my vote. Anyway, I made my way there between nine and ten, passing between green double doors into a spacious hall. A parlourmaid ushered me up the gracefully curving staircase into the softly lit double drawing room, with its masses of golden chrysanthemums in great urns. Yellow taffeta curtains draped the tall sash windows, pictures – often startlingly modernistic – hung on the pale grey walls.

Guests stood talking in groups or sat on sofas heaped with silken cushions. Just about everybody was smoking cigarettes. I looked around with curiosity, searching for faces I knew personally or or from newspaper photographs and cartoons.

'Horby!' Lady Ottoline stepped forward to greet me warmly. She was wearing a robe of gold into which sparkling sequins had been sewn. '*So* glad you could come! There are *so* many interesting and talented people here tonight! Including and especially you! Champagne or champagne and brandy.' I asked for the latter and was brought a glass instantly by a maid. 'I suppose you think you've been invited here to discuss Politics. Not at all!' she declared with a flamboyant flourish of her left hand. 'My husband's up in Scotland, talking to the peers there. Whereas before, I was allowed by him to invite artists so as to leaven the political dough, tonight I have banished the political, professional bores. Give me Art any day!'

I laughed and looked hard at her, finding her face to be piquant rather than beautiful. Yet, somehow, she was terribly sexy. I knew that the Prime Minister, Asquith, had been having an affair with her. She'd also had an affair with the artist Augustus John; and also with the philospher and mathematician Bertrand Russell; and with many others. Her husband didn't seem to mind. As I looked at her, I recalled the words of Margot Asquith, the Prime Minister's wife:

'Oh, yes Ottoline. We all delight in her distinguished carriage, beautiful countenance and original clothes. In spite of an admirable sense of humour, I never heard her utter an unkind word – of how many clever women can we say the same?'

Yet opinion was somewhat divided. David Garnett said that she was 'extremely handsome: tall and lean, with a large head, masses of dark Venetian red hair, glacier blue-green eyes, a long straight nose, a proud mouth and a long, jutting-out chin made up her lovely, haggard face.' Myself, I felt that her face had a medieval strength, with its boldly baronial high-arched nose and deep mahogany-red hair contrasting with the pallor of her skin. From this strangely impressive mask proceeded a sonorous, nasal voice that drawled and rumbled and rustily hummed and hawed yet might subside, if she were amused or curious, to an insinuating, confidential murmur.

Mind you, there *were* murmurs about her, even at her own party.

'Oh, Ottoline's a character of Elizabethan extravagance and force,' Lord David Cecil muttered to me. 'At once mystical and possessive, quixotic and tempestuous.'

'I think that she's a rather oversize Infanta of Spain,' Osbert Sitwell whispered to me, somewhat ungraciously. There was a peculiar woman there called Virginia Woolf and I gathered that she proposed to hold her own Thursday Evenings of something called 'The Bloomsbury Group'. I spoke briefly with her and it was clear to me that she despised the workers. I found her to be a ghastly female and a wretched little snob.

'Ottoline,' Virginia Woolf said to me, 'is a mackerel swimming in an aquarium tank.'

'Does that make *you* a cod or a herring?' I returned. She turned her back and I went to talk to someone more interesting. The fact is that aside from Virginia Woolf and one or two other professional bores, Ottoline Morrell really had attracted an extraordinary company! Henry James, the novelist; W.B. Yeats, the Irish poet; Nijinsky, the legendary dancer; Lytton Strachey, that wonderfully and aptly cruel biographer of eminent Victorians; Max Beerbohm, whose sketching was as exquisite as his writing; new painters such as the visionary Stanley Spencer and the colourfully adventurous Duncan Grant; and an aspiring politician of the Labour Party called Ramsey MacDonald.

(*Editor's Note*: Ramsey MacDonald became Great Britain's first Labour Prime Minister after the First World War. And in those years, Aldous Huxley depicted Ottoline as Priscilla Wimbush in *Crome Yellow* and D.H. Lawrence caricatured her unkindly in his *Women in Love*, though he did admit: 'She is *really* nice – so generous – (though I don't like her parties).')

None of the statements I'd heard influenced me one way or the other. I just found her maddeningly sexy and wanted to fuck her. We touched each other with clandestine sensuality every time one of us crossed the room. Would the guests *never* go? I hid in the lavatory for a time as she pleasantly dismissed her last suitors. Then I marched forward, seized her in my arms, picked her up and demanded: 'Where?!'

'Why not here?' she replied. 'Just close the door very firmly. The maids know that it's a signal that I am not to be disturbed.' I complied with her request and returned to her. My prick had swollen up to its full majestic height. Suddenly Ottoline sprang upon me, pressed me down upon the carpet, unbuttoned my trousers and, greedily pulling down my underpants, clasped my cock between her hands. I could feel my scrotum tightening.

'Well, Horby . . .' she smiled. 'I must say that you do have a thick todger. Why, it looks good enough to eat, if you have no objection . . .' Ottoline's voice trailed off and, in a trice, her tousled head was between my legs. I let out a gasp of delight when she kissed my cock and washed its head with long, slow swirls of her pink, wet tongue.

This hot-blooded young minx looked up at me with a smile on her elfin face and then, bringing her mouth down over my rod, she ran the tip of her tongue along the length of my throbbing tool, sending electric shock waves throughout every fibre of my body. These erotic sensations were heightened as Ottoline continued to suck my cock with great relish, cleverly moving her mouth along my shaft so as to cover every inch of my palpitating prick.

Simultaneously, I hauled myself up and slid my hand between her bum cheeks to diddle her clitty as she lightly grazed the skin of my scrotum with her fingernails, smoothing her hand gently underneath my ballsack.

Soon enough, I began to tremble all over when I felt the approach of a searing wave which was building up to an ever-quickening pace inside me. My prick started to shiver uncontrollably as Ottoline's sweet wet tongue slid up and down the sensitive underside of my swollen shaft.

'Hold on, I'm coming!' I yelled hoarsely. 'I'm going to shoot all my sticky spunk down your throat, you ravishing little vixen!' This lewd warning seemed to make Ottoline suck even more frantically on my quivering cock and, within seconds, a fountain of creamy jism spurted out of my knobslit into her receptive mouth.

Ottoline smacked her lips as she gulped down every last drop of my tangy seed. Myself, I fell back on the floor before the fire, utterly exhausted from this wonderful ejaculation – or so I thought. I had reckoned without the formidable persuasive powers of Ottoline. She let me lie there on the fur rug for a while; and then she started to tease my prick once again. Oh yes, my cock began to stiffen. She grasped hold of my boner and smiled.

'Oh, you darling man!' she exclaimed, laying herself down on the rug and stuffing a cushion she'd grabbed under her bum to elevate her crotch. I seized the opportunity to bury my face between her thighs so as to chew and nibble upon her cunny lips. 'Oh, *do* lick my pussy now . . .' she sighed. I gladly resumed my tonguing of her sopping snatch. 'Ooh!' Ottoline squealed, threshing her body from side to side as I flicked the fleshy bud of her clitty until, with a high-pitched scream of delight, she achieved her climax and filled my mouth with a flood of salty cuntal juice. 'What a gorgeous spend!' she cried out. 'I *love* being brought off like that, but not many men can use their tongues as well as you can!'

Ottoline gasped huskily as she slid her hands beneath my shoulders and pulled me up over her.

'Now fuck me with your thick prick and fill my quim with jism!'

'What a joy . . .' I sighed as I substituted my pulsating thick cock for my mouth. Ottoline thrust her hips upwards as my throbbing tool thrust its way into her clingy wet crack. She threw her legs over my back and heaved her body in time with mine as we commenced a lively fuck.

Despite her juicy lubrication, Ottoline's ladylike cunt was still surprisingly tight, holding me in such a sweet vice that I could feel my foreskin being drawn backwards and forwards with each shove as my cock slid into the folds of her hairy slit.

'Go on! Go on!' she shrieked out when I paused for a moment to catch my breath. 'Fuck me harder, Horby! Slam in your cock! Aargh! That's it! I'm there! I'm there!' I lunged forward again. My balls slapped against her bum cheeks as, with a virile growl, I spurted a stream of spunk into her cunt.

I wriggled my bucking rod around inside her quim as the creamy jism gushed out of it, making Ottoline scream out joyfully as she achieved a second delicious spend. Our lively fuck had exhausted even this apparently insatiable girl. However, once she had recovered her composure she ran a hot bath, which we shared.

Ottoline and I have been friends ever since then. It's all very well to say, as some wit did the other day, that she was wearing a hat 'like a crimson tea cosy trimmed with hedgehogs.' It's true that recently she's been seen walking through

Bloomsbury with several Pekinese dogs attached by ribbons to a shepherd's crook. And she also had a taste, after sex, for bull's-eye peppermints, which she sucked and crunched somewhat noisily. Of course, it's not hard to poke fun at Lady Ottoline Morrell.

Yet, as I said, I remain her friend. I honestly think that her good influence spread far and that she really did make a lasting contribution to the literary and artistic history of our age.

CHAPTER FOURTEEN

What a heavy year 1910 was! One damn' thing after another! My speeches in the House of Lords in favour of the People's Budget of Lloyd George did no bloody good whatsoever. My peers, in their wisdom, refused to pass the Bill and caused a constitutional crisis. King Edward VII wisely advised Prime Minister Asquith that he should call a General Election to ascertain that there was a popular mandate for reform. This was held in January.

I don't know why, but the huge Liberal majority was substantially reduced. The Labour Party held to its position. The Conservatives recovered strongly. The Liberals still retained their position as the Party of Government but the matter was indeed precarious. *Who* governed this country? The House of Commons or the unelected House of Lords?

'Quite a problem, isn't it, old chap?' Sir Richard Bellingham said to me as we ate marinated mussels, accompanied by a vintage Krug, at the Café Royal. Bellingham was looking rather pleased with himself, since he had been elected to the House of Commons by some obscure shire that would vote for a pig if it were a Tory. 'Look, I'm not *against* the idea of the Government looking after the poor. But I do want the Liberals out and the Conservatives in. Furthermore,' he chewed a good mussel with evident enjoyment, 'I *do* want the House of Lords to retain its power.

It's our tradition. For heaven's sake, Horby, you're a member of the place. How can you possibly aquiesce in castrating the power of the House of Lords?'

'I want something better for everybody in England,' I replied. 'And I think that my peers are being totally unreasonable.'

'Oh, fuck it!' said Sir Richard. 'Don't you think that Politics is just such a ruddy bore? I have a better idea. Come back to my place. I have fine port and cognac and Armagnac there; and I've invited two rather pretty girls to come round later.'

'Sounds great,' I replied with a smile. 'Lead me to it!'

Bellingham certainly wasn't promising something he couldn't deliver. He now had a very pleasant town house in Mayfair where he provided the drinks he had earlier proffered: the vintage port he gave me was truly heavenly, like liquid velvet. As for the girls, the blonde Amelia and the raven-haired Sylvia, to describe them as being merely pretty was an understatement. They were both enough to make any healthy man randy and, in a trice, we were going at it.

Amelia knew just how to handle Sir Richard – literally. This gorgeous, ravishing blonde pounced upon him, unbuttoned his flies and, reaching in between them, produced his stiff prick and proceeded to fondle it with evident delight.

'Your prowess is amazing, Richard!' she cried out. She continued to rub her hand even more vigorously up and down his hot, hard shaft. I gazed with pleasure at this public tossing-off, though I thought it a pity that the miniature spunky fountain of white froth that jetted out of his bulbous knob in a looping arc fell directly into the bowl of peanuts before him.

'Richard!' Sylvia squealed, 'How good of you to flavour the nuts with your tangy jism. I am sure that they now taste quite delicious. Would you kindly give me some?' Her remark was greeted by roars of laughter from Bellingham and myself: now I *really* wanted to fuck this intriguing bitch. 'Richard,' Sylvia added, 'why don't you and Amelia entertain us properly with a *full* show of *l'art de faire l'amour?*'

'I don't see why not,' Bellingham retorted, grinning wickedly. 'I just hope that Amelia is willing to give me a helping hand again, so to speak.'

'All hands to the pump!' this wanton girl laughed as she gripped his mighty prick. She bent forward next and, peeling up the foreskin, lasciviously licked his knob. Then she took his shaft back firmly into her fist while he continued to undress. In no time at all, Amelia had cajoled his cock back up to its former majestic height. Sylvia now swiftly undressed.

My prick swelled up immediately at the sight of her naked charms. What exquisitely firm, uptilted breasts this girl possessed! It was no wonder that I immediately placed my hands on her pointy red nipples and tweaked them up to a fine state of erection. I took all the liberties I desired with this fair young damsel, kissing and sucking her lovely lips and then her firm tits as we sank down upon the Turkish rug that was all crimson and gold.

Meanwhile, Bellingham had knelt between Amelia's legs and rubbed the bulging tip of his rod along her pouting pussy lips as she moaned with erotic ecstasy. She grappled playfully with him so as so seize his thick shaft which she then wedged inside her juicy crack. I heard Amelia murmur that she wanted to be on top as she grabbed hold of his arms and rolled him over onto his back.

Then Amelia climbed on top of Bellingham's muscular frame and speared herself on his cock, which stood as stiff as a flagpole as she rode up and down upon it. As Amelia's tunnel of lust opened up to receive Bellingham's thrusting tool, her juices obviously began to flow. The sight of their vigorous mating, with its slick squishing, aroused me – and instants later Sylvia and I were locked even more tightly than before in one another's arms.

I caressed her breasts again as our mouths jammed together in an uninhibited open-mouthed kiss. At the same time, Bellingham was jerking his hips upwards and Amelia uttered a cry of satisfaction as his thick prick reamed out her tingling cunt. But he had not yet ended this lubricious fuck by any means, since he continued to slew his sturdy shaft in and out of her juicy snatch. Sylvia and I both watched with delight; and now her hand shot out to grab my stiff cock. Clamping her long, thin, satin-gloved fingers around my prick, this salacious young miss fisted her hand up and down my shaft. At the same time, Bellingham was closing his eyes and relaxing as Amelia bounced gaily up and down on his cock. With a great roar, he came – and so did she! It was a wonderful sight.

For my own part, I really lusted after Sylvia's arse. It was so white and neat. Yes, I had rolled her over and the crinkled entrance to her arsehole really had caught my eye. I truly wanted to bottom-fuck this lusty vixen and, having smeared my cock with the butter that Bellingham had conveniently left on the coffee table, I angled the prodding of my rod into the cleft of Sylvia's jouncy backside.

It was then that a really extraordinary thing happened. Amelia, who had dismounted from riding Bellingham, proceeded in a remarkably short space of time to manipulate his prick with her fingers back to its full strength yet again. Amelia then inserted her satin-gloved forefinger into *my* arse. I bucked and had little difficulty in inserting my cock into Syvia's back passage, fully and all the way – and we rolled onto our sides. This was when Bellingham plunged his freshly stiffened prick into her cunt.

Sylvia cried out in the excitement of erotic delirium as two cocks fucked her at once. How she visibly gloried in the sensation! Then she asked us to stay still for an instant, which we were happy to do. It was very strange, though, to feel my tool throbbing against Bellingham's shaft with only the thin membrane of Sylvia's anal canal between us. Then, at a cry of encouragement from Amelia, we both resumed moving our cocks.

What a spend we all had! Sylvia let out a high-pitched yelp of delight as she received two libations of hot, sticky jism simultaneously, one within her cunt and the other up her arse. Amelia broke into apparently spontaneous applause as we disentangled ourselves. Then she took our pricks in her hands and shook out the last drainings of spunk from our glistening shafts.

'Good God, girls!' Bellingham exclaimed as he gave us all generous measures of cognac, 'you've given me the finest two fucks I've had this year. Hasn't it been the best one for you too so far this year, Horby?'

'Certainly marvellous,' I replied – though, in fact, my best fuck had been with my wife on New Year's Eve. 'By heaven, 1910 is turning out to be one hell of a year!' At that moment I didn't realize just how unwittingly truthful I was being. 'Anyway, Bellingham, it's good to see that you are enjoying the privileges of the average Member of Parliament.'

'Oh, fuck off!' Bellingham shouted with laughter.

'I hope you voted for your friend,' Amelia said to me.

'No.'

'Why not?' Sylvia queried.

'Firstly, I don't live in his godforsaken constituency. Secondly, I don't support his political party. Thirdly, convicted prisoners, incarcerated lunatics and peers do not have a vote.'

'You're a wicked bugger, Horby,' Bellingham remarked.

'You're a one to talk,' I returned and the girls hooted with laughter.

'Oh, yes, I *am* a one to talk,' he replied. 'If I were an owl, I would hoot. If I were a dog, I would bark. If I were a cat, I would purr. As it is, I am a man, so I talk.' He quaffed his cognac and poured more for himself and for everybody else. As was customary *chez* Bellingham, the quality of the cognac was superb. 'Y'know, my idea of purgatory is being confined in a space with dull people where the rule is: "Let us eat, drink and be serious." Oh! If wine, women and song are too much for you, give up singing!'

Having said that, he seized hold of Sylvia, who yielded gracefully to him and, taking her on the Turkish carpet once again, he caressed the creamy globes of her pert tits. As they went at it, I stared with unabashed lust at the blonde Amelia's superb bare breasts, each one crowned by a tawny nipple set in a large rounded areola. While we had been drinking, she had put on a pair of tight white frilly knickers that served to increase my desire. I seized her and we too fell back on the Turkish rug, exchanging ardent kisses. My straining shaft was standing as stiff as a guardsman.

I shouted out my joy and, in fact, yelled wildly when Amelia encircled my rigid rod with her long fingers as her lovely head with its gorgeous mane of blonde hair plummeted down to my groin. She planted a welcoming kiss on my balls, which she was by now cradling in her hand.

Amelia's wet tongue fluttered out and tickled the tender crown of my cock before she opened her lips and slowly drew my shaft into her mouth. I prodded my rod to and fro in a frenzy of excitement. Amelia's tongue slithering up and down the sensitive underside of my shaft quickly brought me to the brink of an orgasm.

'I can't stop!' I yelled out. My cock was still sliding in and out of her rich red lips. 'I'm going to come!' Amelia bobbed her head up and down until, with a final juddering throb, I squirted my spunky tribute down her throat. Amelia swallowed my sticky emission with obvious joy.

We lay back and relaxed, watching Bellingham and the raven-haired Sylvia. He seemed to be quite obsessed with her breasts still, and his thick fingers were brushing the perky nipples as she raised her arms to unloosen the *coiffure* of her hair. This sensual movement lifted Sylvia's breasts even higher, heightening the colour of the flushed pink circles which framed these flagrantly erect little nipples. Heavens! I hadn't noticed before, but she too had slipped on lacy knickers, the purpose being to have them removed. The two lovely orbs of her ripe young breasts gently bumped together as she lowered her hands to wriggle out of her knickers.

Sylvia ran her fingertips through her fluffy dark triangle of pussy hair and licked her lips as she stared at Sir Richard's huge pulsating prick, which stood up so stiffly against his belly. Amelia and I watched with growing interest as Sylvia played with his chunky cock, sliding her hand up and down the throbbing blue-veined shaft. Then, rising on her knees, she kissed the empurpled head of his prick.

With a downward lunge, she plunged it far into her mouth and started to suck it with all her might. Bellingham sighed with delight and clutched her head in his hands as Sylvia crammed more and more of his thick prick between her lips. She must have felt the tip of his knob touch the back of her throat.

Bellingham bucked to and fro, obviously loving the

rapturous feel of Sylvia's wet lips slurping on his shaft. Waves of ecstasy appeared to ripple through his body. He inhaled a series of deep breaths before growling a hoarse warning that he was about to spend.

Sylvia gently squeezed his balls as he shot his load into her mouth – and, despite all her frenzied endeavours to swallow the whole gushing torrent of his creamy jism, a solitary trickle of spunk nonetheless escaped to roll down her chin and drip onto the Turkish rug.

Bellingham was uncharacteristically silent for a few minutes. Then he slowly roused himself and began to dress, a signal that we should all do so.

'Ah!' he declared. 'Splendid! Oh, you lovely girls! – eh, Horby?!' I smiled genuine acquiescence. Once we were all looking vaguely respectable, Belligham took two purses which I knew contained gold guineas and presented them to the girls. Later, he told me that they contained twice the sum originally agreed. As the girls thanked him, he thanked them, as did I – and then he rang a bell to summon his butler.

'Look, girls,' he said, 'I have to talk to my friend Horby here. It's been a splendid evening, quite wizard, actually, but I don't think that you've been eating enough recently.' He turned to his butler. 'Smithers, could you please conduct my guests here down to the scullery and give them bowls of the nourishing house soup . . . also there's a nice side of York ham there and, I think, a good pork pie. They can eat it all, if they want, and to drink with it, why, loads of good, strong English ale!'

'Very good, sir,' the butler returned impassively.

'Bless you, Sir Richard!' Amelia called out as they left the room.

'If we women had the vote, Sir Richard,' Sylvia said, 'then we would be voting Conservative!'

'That's my worry,' I said, though Bellingham was looking as pleased as Punch. In fact, he actually opened a box of Punch cigars from Havana and offered them to me. I selected one, as he did, and for a few moments of reflective silence, we both swam in the post-coital delight that is best accompanied by the imbibing of absolutely excellent tobacco. I later learned that Amelia and Sylvia had been so hungry that, after the soup, they had devoured the whole side of ham and the entire pie, not to mention two quarts of ale.

'Claire all right?' Bellingham enquired.

'Fine, thanks. Sends you her best wishes. She's in Paris at present. How's Davina?'

'Oh, she's jolly well, I'm glad to say. Presently enjoying Copenhagen. Look here, Horby,' he waved his cigar in the air, 'are you on for a spot of travel? They do say that a change is as good as a rest. Now you enjoy pugilism, don't you?' I nodded vigorously. 'Well, then, why don't we go and see The Fight of the Century?'

CHAPTER FIFTEEN

The Fight of the Century was being held on the Fourth of July at Reno, Nevada, a confluence of railway lines. It was to be between 'the greatest fighter that the white race has ever produced' and 'the greatest fighter that the black race has ever produced'. That meant that the undefeated white Champion, James J. Jeffries, known as 'the Iron Man' and also as 'the Grizzly Bear', would be coming out of the retirement he had announced in 1905 to face Jack Johnson, the first black World Heavyweight Champion, who had worn the crown since 1908, when he had slaughtered Tommy Burns before an incredulous crowd on Boxing Day in Sydney, Australia.

The promoter, Tex Rickard, who had had a stadium constructed for the occasion, was giving the gladiators quite incredible sums of money. Jeffries would get $158,000 if he lost and $667,000 if he won. Johnson, the black man, was getting a straight $100,000, win or lose. Word was put out to the gamblers that this contest would be strictly on the level, with Tex Rickard as referee, and that it would be a fight to the finish under the Queensberry Rules.

Many could not bear the thought of a black man being the Heavyweight Champion of the World. There had been a call and a cry for Jim Jeffries to come back and 'redeem the honour of the white race'. Both men had splendid ring records. This could indeed be what it claimed to be: The Fight of the Century.

As I think I've mentioned in earlier volumes, Bellingham was (and is) a fine travelling companion. We took the *Mauretania* to New York. It was a wonderful voyage and there were quite a number of delightful ladies on board. Our travel arrangements were in the hands of Thomas Cook and so we boarded our Pullman carriage at Grand Central Station. The Americans really had improved their services since we had last visited. It was a marvellous ride through unknown territory and, at times, through scenery that was truly spectacular and which we could view in the greatest possible comfort from the Observation Car. The food was bloody good, too. I'm sure that the chef in the principal dining car was French. If one wanted a change, there was a good bar where they served American delights such as hamburgers, hot dogs and pancakes with maple syrup, available at all hours. Sir Richard and I had separate compartments and we both remarked on the courtesy and efficient excellence of the black steward. To add to our delights, Bob Fitzsimmons joined the journey in Chicago and I was very pleased to see him again.

Bob Fitzsimmons of Cornwall has to be the greatest fighter that England has ever produced. As I have related, he won the Middleweight Championship of the World by knocking out the allegedly unbeatable 'Nonpareil' Jack Dempsey and then won the Heavyweight Championship of the World by knocking out the allegedly unbeatable 'Gentleman' Jim Corbett. The Great John L. Sullivan had called him 'a fighting machine on stilts'. Yes, this man was a physical freak. He had thin, spindly legs but the exceptionally muscular torso of a blacksmith – which had, indeed, earlier been his trade. There were freckles all over his face and his reddish hair straggled over his balding scalp in absurd tufts. But the boxers who ridiculed him soon stopped laughing when he hit them.

Fitz was among the hardest, most vicious punchers that the Ring has ever seen. Unfortunately, this was not enough when he faced his muscular giant of a challenger, James J. Jeffries. Fitz hit him with everything he had and the giant just grunted and took it. Then he knocked out Fitz in the eleventh round. Fitz then knocked out every top contender to qualify for another challenge. In this fight, he hit Jeffries mercilessly, breaking his nose, closing one eye, gashing cuts above the other and causing such a downpour of blood that the seconds begged Jeffries, a bloodied, semi-blinded hulk, to surrender. 'Nope,' the Champion replied and, in the eighth round, he flattened Fitz once more.

Fitz then went all out to get a new prize, the World Light-Heavyweight Championship, even though at thirty-seven he was an old man in boxer's years. His veteran's skills gave him an easy victory over young George Gardner and won him the title. Unfortunately, age caught up with him, as it eventually catches up with all of us, and two years later, in 1905, he was slaughtered in fourteen rounds by Philadelphia Jack O'Brien, a fighter adjudged, pound for pound, to be the fastest and most skilful boxer of our era.

(*Editor's Note*: The feat of Fitzsimmons in winning the World Middleweight, Heavyweight and Light-Heavyweight titles has never been repeated.)

'It's really good to see you again, Lord Horby,' Fitz said warmly, shaking my hand. I introduced him to Bellingham, who declared how much he applauded the athletic achievements of Fitz and ordered glasses and a bottle of Jack Daniels.

'Fine stuff, this!' Sir Richard proclaimed. 'One thing I like about America is their Kentucky bourbon. But *this* is their Tennessee sour mash whiskey – and I like it even more!'

'Quite agree, Sir Richard,' said Bob Fitzsimmons. 'Your health! Cheers!' It was pleasing and obvious that the two men had hit it off.

'What *I* want to know, Fitz,' said Bellingham, 'is this: who's going to win this sporting contest? I mean, I'm a betting man. I'm inclined, I admit, to back a white man against a black man, being white myself – though I *do* say: may the best man win! But you should know, really.'

'Yeah, I've fought both,' Fitz returned, 'and lost to both. Jeffries? I broke the bones in my 'ands 'itting 'im. Johnson? Well, I was well past my prime when I faced 'im but I really went for the bastard in the very first round. Unfortunately, I couldn't lay a glove on 'im. The man's a defensive genius. And he did absolutely nothing in return. One bugger of a reporter called that first round: "About as exciting as watching a crocheting match at an old ladies' home". In the second round, I went out there and the sod put me to sleep. I never saw it coming. I don't remember anything. Must've been a right peach of a punch. So you want to know who I think is going to win?'

'Well, yes,' said Bellingham, offering him a Punch corona which was gladly accepted.

'*If*,' Fitz declared, '*if* this fight had taken place in 1905, when Johnson first challenged Jeffries and was contemptuously ignored, I think that in a fight to the finish, Johnson would have broken *his* hands hitting Jeffries and, after fifteen rounds, he would have been way, way ahead. Jeffries would barely have touched him. But *then*, as the fight wore on, Jeffries would be wearing Johnson out. By the thirtieth round, 'e'd be murdering Johnson in the clinches, pounding 'is body, slowing 'im down. By the fortieth round, you take my word, Johnson would be on the floor.'

'But it's *not* 1905, though, is it, Fitz?' I came in. 'It's 1910. Jeffries hasn't been in the ring since 1904. He hasn't had so much as a tune-up contest. I heard that he's had to slim down from 300 pounds.'

'And *I've* heard,' the ex-Champion replied, 'that John L. Sullivan has recently left Jeffries's training camp, saying: "All I know, Jeff, is that all the world hates a quitter." I've also heard that Sam Langford floored Jeffries in training and was fired from the camp.'

Both Bellingham and I sat up alertly at that point. We had both seen the black Sam Langford fight at London's National Sporting Club. He had faced our national Champion, Iron Haig, who had tried and failed to land a solid punch on him for four rounds. At the commencement of the fifth, Langford had traced out a line in the centre of the ring with his feet and had then touched gloves with Haig. 'Oi! This ain't the last round!' Haig had protested. 'It is for you, baby', Langford had replied – and he had promptly flattened Haig on the precise line his feet had drawn. We also knew that Johnson had beaten Langford.

'You can get odds of five-to-one against Johnson,' Fitz said. 'It's all this white supremacy lark. Have I answered your question, gentlemen?' Bellingham and I smiled at him. 'Married man, are you, Sir Richard?' Bellingham nodded. 'But same as me and Lord Horby here, you don't mind a bit on the side . . . ?' Bellingham nodded *very* firmly. 'Well, there's some lovely ladies on this train. Interested?'

Bellingham and I could have kicked ourselves for not realizing what Bob Fitzsimmons now explained and which Thomas Cook had failed to tell us, too. At the front of this train, there were three carriages for the 'high rollers', and promoter Tex Rickard was taking his substantial percentage. Fitz led us through the first car, which was a gambling den, thick with cigar smoke and with a lot of high action going on. $100 was the minimum bet but many were playing for stakes of $5,000 or $10,000.

The second car was the brothel of Mrs Rita Lewis, a friendly, buxom blonde woman. Provided that you could pay her extortionate prices for the beautiful girls who swanned around you, you could make your choice, have a drink at the bar and then go to it in the third car. This had been divided into a section of private compartments and a section that was wide open. These areas were guarded by two men who looked like Wild West bandits, with revolvers prominently displayed in open holsters; and you had to book the spaces you wanted at various prices, with cash to be paid up front. The three of us agreed over Jim Beam bourbon that we would book the space that could accommodate several and then we would select our girls. I chose the dark, slender Juanita, since I had never enjoyed a Mexican whore before. Fitz chose the blonde from Kansas, Karen, who had a stunning figure – though, in fact, *all* the girls were showing off their gorgeous figures in the tight, clinging satin dresses they were wearing. Bellingham chose an equally voluptuous red-headed wench called Elizabeth.

'All on me!' he proclaimed in a manner that brooked no argument. 'It's such a pleasure to host two friends, particularly when one of them is Great Britain's greatest sporting hero!' The girls we had chosen all wore *gold* satin dresses. That meant that they were the most expensive. After that, it was silver; and then red; and finally black – but even black wasn't cheap. The six of us were conducted into a compartment containing four beds by Madam Rita Lewis herself. Then she left us to our own devices.

Instantly, Fitz threw Karen down on the bed nearest to the door. He whipped up her dress and petticoats and smiled when he saw that she wasn't wearing any drawers. She unbuttoned his fly to reveal his enormous erect tool and he plunged his rod within her. Bellingham and Elizabeth and Juanita and myself could not help looking on, fascinated. Fitz was pumping his hips very fast, the way a good boxer does, and Karen was panting with pleasure. At times he just jabbed the outer lips of her labia – though that made her sigh – at other moments he pronged his rod very deeply in and out of her – and she cried out – and at a certain moment, he just laid her back by the shoulders and slammed into her. She yelled out her pleasure and came.

Fitz held her very tight in his arms as she positively *screamed* with pleasure, as though no client of hers had ever given her anything like it. Karen cried out again as Fitz came. It looked as though he was pumping two bloody gallons of spunk into her. Then he sighed heavily and collapsed on top of her voluptuous body. About a minute passed, as though it were his rest period in between rounds of the boxing ring, and then he sat up and said:

'Thank you for the dance, Karen. It was lovely!'

'And I, too, thank you, Karen,' said Bellingham as he opened the champagne that Madam Rita Lewis had thoughtfully provided for us in an ice bucket, next to a bottle of something called Southern Comfort and another bottle of French cognac. Then, as he served the champagne to everyone, he proved to be quite astute. 'Fitz, I think you'd now like another woman, wouldn't you?' Fitz nodded. 'Anyone in particular?'

'The dark-haired one in the silver dress,' Fitz replied.

'Fine!' Bellingham exclaimed. 'Karen, go and tell Madam Rita to send her in.' He gave Karen a fifty dollar tip, for which she looked grateful, and the girl left the carriage. I now proceeded to undress Juanita upon the bed and Bellingham did the same with Elizabeth. We had only just begun our kisses and caresses when Lainy of Texas came in.

We couldn't resist stopping our own activities to see what would happen next.

I shall make a long story short. Bob Fitzsimmons turned her over and gave her a good rogering from the back – and I can't blame him since she had a beautiful bum. Bellingham and I indeed got on with our own fucking, as I shall describe, but that night, and at Bellingham's expense, Fitz just went and fucked one girl after another. I think it was something like eight girls – and he fucked them front and back and sideways and with the girl riding him and so on. That man was past his prime in the boxing ring – though he was still fighting and beating good contenders – but when it came to fucking, he could put much younger men to shame.

During all this erotic action, I had turned to Juanita. I had pulled her dress off her shoulders so that I could caress her apple-like breasts. Now I pulled it up and pulled down her white satin knickers. I traced my forefinger over her clitty and she sighed, so I did it again. Her long, manicured fingers with their scarlet talons reached out to caress my throbbing, stiff prick. Now it was my turn to sigh.

I could not wait any longer. I wanted her on her back so I could gaze at the beauty of her breasts, since she could not have been older than eighteen. I thrust my rod into her and she sighed again as I extended my expedition to its utmost depths. Then I started to fuck her very slowly. After a time, she began to moan – but with pleasure rather than pain. I could feel her little cunt gripping my cock tightly and in spasms. Every now and again, during this slow-moving rhythm, we had raised our heads to see what else was going on in this extraordinary railway compartment.

Fitz, of course, was fucking away again. Actually, I think I only looked once at Bellingham: Elizabeth was sighing as she sat on his face. I carried on fucking Juanita in slow motion and she carried on writhing, her hips eventually swivelling into a serpentine motion that made me rear up and then explode with a roar and a massive amount of cum right into her neat little cunny.

She came too and held me tight. After a time, I helped her to the drink she requested – a Southern Comfort, which I tried too: it proved to be splendid – and then we lay back, smoked cigarettes and watched everyone else. I think that Fitz was on his eighth and final fuck. Bellingham was banging his way into Elizabeth's arsehole.

'You British peeple are, I theenk, a beet crazy,' Juanita remarked. 'I do not understand you at all and nor do many of the Americans.'

I did not realize what she really meant at the time, only later. Juanita was a nice woman who was giving us a warning.

CHAPTER SIXTEEN

Juanita and I lay back on the bed. I was still blithely oblivious to what she had subtly told me. In fact, I was reflecting on how much I liked fucking in a railway train. There is something so enchanting about moving with the rhythm of the train as it travels; of sticking your prick into a warm, welcoming cunt to the beat of the *clackety-clack* as the locomotive goes along the railroad tracks. Then I looked at what Bellingham and Elizabeth were doing.

It was all quite enlivening. As she'd sat on his face with her voluptuous butt, this lascivious vixen had been leaning forward to suck his cock. Yet Bellingham now rose up in more ways than one and pushed the willing girl down on her back. He slid his hands under her thighs to fondle her delectable bum cheeks as he pressed his lips to her inviting cherry nipples, which he kissed and sucked in fine style. Then he pulled his hands away to part the thighs of Elizabeth and bent his head down to kiss the puffy pink lips that pouted out from her reddish fluffy bush of pussy hair. Although I could not actually see his tongue flash up and down her sopping slit, Sir Richard was clearly on tip-top form displaying his knowledge of how to palate a pussy, since Elizabeth was soon shuddering with pleasure.

I glanced at Fitz. Same as usual, he was banging away at some broad, only this time she was black and I think her name was Kristina.

'Enough! Enough!' Elizabeth was gasping. 'Please fuck me with your cock now!' Bellingham answered this heartfelt plea instantly by clambering up on her sumptuous curves. I noted with respect that Bellingham's cock seemed more huge than ever and was pulsing furiously in his hand as he guided it into the juicy cunt of Elizabeth. A loud moan from this lewd pair was the signal that his lusty cock had thrust into her cunny.

They kissed with an intense fervour as Elizabeth jerked her lovely bottom up and down to absorb as much of Bellingham's pulsating prick as possible. He began by pumping in and out of her squishy furrow with long, slow strokes.

When he changed the pace to one of swift short jabs, I distinctly heard his balls slapping against Elizabeth's wiggling bum cheeks as they thrashed away happily.

'Can you feel my cunny muscles gripping your prick as it slides in and out?' she demanded, panting.

'Uh.' He carried on fucking.

'What a gorgeous fat cock you have!' She twisted from side to side under his fierce onslaught. 'Oh, my God! Haven't you?'

'Uh.' He carried on fucking.

'Yes! YES! Push it deeper, that's the way! Oh, tell me, lover man, don't you just love it?'

'Uh.' He carried on fucking.

'I can't help feeling,' I remarked to Juanita as we drank good bourbon, 'that the female of the species is more articulate in these affairs than the male.' She burst out laughing.

'Do it to me!' Elizabeth was crying out.

'Uh.' Bellingham carried on fucking. Then suddenly he altered his rhythm, pushing his prick in much deeper.

'Ohhh . . .' Elizabeth sighed deeply as she clamped her

surprisingly dainty feet together behind him so as to keep every inch of his rampant rod inside her luscious quim.

'Aargh!' Bellingham cried out as she sensually rotated her hips and answered his powerful plunges with upward thrusts of her own.

'Oh . . . oh . . . OH!' Elizabeth shrieked. 'I'm coming! I'M COMING!' Bellingham's body tensed with a savage shudder as he pumped the first gush of sticky seed into her honeypot. While she clawed at his back, he discharged spurt after spurt of spunky jism into her love funnel. Juanita and I applauded the couple, who lay still for a few moments.

'Oh, *thank* you, Sir Richard!' Elizabeth exclaimed cheerfully as she sat up. 'That was a glorious fuck!' He thanked her with equal grace. Meanwhile, it seemed that Fitz and his gorgeous black whore couldn't seem to get enough of one another. And then a soft hand slithered across my waist from behind to stroke my own pulsating erection and Juanita's sweet voice whispered endearments into my ear.

'Oh . . .' she sighed, 'I can hardly wait to be fucked by your noble cock again, Lord Horby, after watching everyone else screw themselves silly!'

'Wonderful idea!' I responded; and I promptly hugged the delicious girl tightly. Juanita responded by raining eager kisses all over my face as I traced the circle of her mouth with my tongue, which slid between her lips. She slowly stroked my throbbing tool.

We fell back upon the soft feather bed as the landscape outside appeared to race past us and I let my hand move across her flat belly. My fingertips entangled themselves in the delicate nesting of chestnut curls that covered her delectable pussy mound. With a gentleness that was deliberate, I slid my hand all over the hairy muff of Juanita.

With my fingers pressed firmly on each side of her slit, I drew the yielding pussy lips apart. Oh! Those puffy love-lips! She squirmed from side to side when I jabbed my thumb directly inside her juicy honeypot. She moaned at the joy of it.

Now she wriggled with delight when I piloted two fingers into her dripping wet cunt. Yet it was my thumb that she made the principal instrument of pleasure, rubbing her fleshy clitoris against it until her juicy cumbud protruded out of her pussy like a tiny cock. Juanita was clearly enjoying being finger-fucked in this fashion so much that I stretched her cunny lips a little wider apart.

My fingers were instantly drawn deeper inside her quim as she drove me on to frig her with increasing urgency. I responded by moving my body downwards and she twisted her thighs around my head when I pressed my mouth to her lascivious quim. I imprinted a long, clinging kiss on the moist chink and rubbed my nose back and forth against her clitty, inhaling the pungent vaginal aroma.

Her body jerked in a frenzy of lust to meet my questing tongue as it probed her pussy, sending this sweet girl into paroxysms of delicious pleasure. I soon sent Juanita off into a series of heavenly spends by opening her folds and playfully biting her clitty, which sent fresh waves of ecstasy coursing throughout her body from the epicentre of erotic excitement between her thighs. The gorgeous girl shrieked out as she achieved an all-enveloping shuddering come that sent a deluge of her love juices flooding into my mouth.

'Now,' I murmured as I lifted my mouth from her sopping crack and she emitted a sigh of bliss, 'I shall fuck you with my cock.'

'Great idea.' Juanita reached down to hold my pulsating prick, positioning its empurpled head at the entrance to her juicy honeypot. I pushed forward and penetrated her tunnel of lust, not stopping until my throbbing rod was fully ensconced inside her lovely sheath. 'Mmm, that feels divine,' she murmured.

I began fucking her in a casually sinuous motion that ensured that my stiff cock caressed the slick walls of Juanita's cunny with every luxurious stroke. I reached underneath her trembling body, clasped her voluptuous arse cheeks with both hands and pressed the sublime young girl tightly against me as I embedded my shaft even deeper inside her sticky quim. Then I changed my rhythm and began to fuck her with long, powerful thrusts.

I shifted my hands up to her breasts, massaging the nipples until they stood up as hard, pointy peaks. I pumped away meanwhile, until I was on the verge of orgasm. Even so, I quickly realized that Juanita's heaving gasps indicated that she had also reached the brink.

I pistoned my prick into her wet, clingy cunt just three more times before we spent together. I bounced and bucked upon her curvy contours as I ejaculated my jism inside her.

'Well, chaps,' said Sir Richard Bellingham, who had seized the role of host, 'it's been a jolly good evening. Why don't we show our appreciation of the ladies here?'

'Good idea,' Fitz and I murmured simultaneously; and all three of us produced purses of English gold sovereigns, which were probably worth more in the West of America than in our own dear land. Anyway, each girl received ten as a tip. There would, of course, be the total bill to be settled up later. I wondered why Juanita gave me such a guilty look as the three nice whores left.

'You've heard of *Three Men In A Boat*,' Bellingham remarked. 'Well, can't help feeling that this is rather "Three Men On A Train". Anyway, drink up. I'm sure there're other people just dying to use this place and I can't say that I blame 'em.'

Fitz and I followed Sir Richard into the Reception Carriage.

'Magnificent, Madam Rita! Absolutely magnificent!' he cried out. 'Now – I'd like to settle up.'

'Glad you enjoyed it, Sir Richard. This way, please.' Madam Rita Lewis led us back into a smallish compartment, just off a corridor, and it was there that she handed him the bill.

'What's this!' Bellingham exclaimed indignantly as he looked at it. *'Twenty thousand dollars?! Why, that's . . . what? Four thousand pounds?!* This is an outrage!' It was.

'That is the bill for the services provided,' Madam Rita Lewis returned impassively. And only now did the penny drop for me regarding the warnings of Juanita.

'Well, I'm not paying *this!*' Bellingham declared. Madam Rita tinkled a little bell and the two gunmen we'd seen earlier came in to join us, staring at us hard and fingering their pistols in their open holsters. There was a silence so pregnant it was almost in labour. *Now* I realized what a crass error it had been for Bellingham and I to flash around the purses of gold sovereigns with which we had come to the Wild West of America. 'Now, look here, Madam Rita, or whatever your name actually is . . .' Bellingham was staying remarkably calm. Fitz and I were impassive. *'Here!'* Bellingham produced a purse that I knew contained five hundred golden guineas. 'This purse of gold is worth a minimum of two thousand, five hundred dollars. I am perfectly prepared to pay *that* for a splendid evening, so let's just settle for it, eh?'

(*Editor's Note:* Bellingham's offer was worth roughly twenty thousand pounds in today's terms.)

'No,' said Madam Rita. 'You're going to have to pay the full bill. I know you've got it on you,' she added impassively.

'Hm. Pity,' Bellingham murmured. This was the code word for moves we'd practised in London prior to venturing out here. In one fluid movement from each of us, the two cowboys were pinned up against the wall with our own revolvers pressing deep into their groins. I really enjoyed seeing the startled expressions on their horrible faces. 'I'd *love* to press the trigger and blow your balls away, you little fanny poo-poo,' said Bellingham, 'so don't move.' We took their guns and Madam Rita gasped like a fish on dry land.

'Mind if I do something, gentlemen?' Bob Fitzsimmons interposed. 'I see not,' for we had nodded assent while still looking puzzled. 'You see, I don't like my friends being threatened like this.' He moved even faster than we had and his blows shot out like lightning bolts. The man I was holding had his nose smashed utterly and so hard that he passed out; and Bellingham's prisoner received a body shot to the liver that made him collapse and moan in agony. 'The train's slowing down, gentlemen,' Fitz added.

Suddenly, Bellingham and I saw the point that Fitz was making. Realizing that he'd be watching the bitch, we hauled the ruffians to their feet, our guns pressed against their spines, and threw them out of the train doors. Heaven knows where and how they landed. Good riddance to bad rubbish! That's what I say!

'Madam Rita,' I said, 'are you going to call the police? And can you tell me one good reason why my friend Sir Richard here should now pay you a cent, a nickel or a dime?'

'Just pay me what you think is fair,' she sighed with quite incredible weariness. Bellingham took back his purse but from it placed one hundred guineas on the table . . .

Reno is a very primitive cowboy town. There are gaudy and tasteless luxury hotels there – Fitz, Bellingham and I were all staying at the Splendide – as well as gaudy and tasteless casinos and brothels, restaurants and bars. Even so, I have to admit that we all agreed after dinner that we'd had the finest T-bone steak, smothered in fried onions, that any of us had experienced. We were in cattle country, or rather, in a town that traded in cattle.

On the following day, we went to the stadium for our ringside seats. Men with rifles were guarding the place and, since feelings were running so high, one was frisked. Bellingham and I surrendered our revolvers whilst keeping our derringers up our sleeves. It was a blazing hot day and there were about 20,000 people there. All the sports of America were there, plus many crooks and journalists from all over the world. Of course, there were plenty of good-looking whores there, too. There was a small black contingent and they were all very well-dressed, just like their Champion.

I had put a lot of money on the Champion, Johnson. So had Bob Fitzsimmons, who now told me just how sly he could be.

'You see, Lord Horby,' he said to me, 'I'm telling all the papers that Jeffries is going to win. This keeps the odds at five-to-one. I'm not against Johnson on account of his colour. Being a Brit, I really don't like the way in which all the white Americans are against 'im.'

'Well, I've bet on Jeffries,' said Bellingham in his typically stubborn fashion. 'And I admit that, by that, I am declaring that a white, not a black, should be the Heavyweight Champion of the World. Jeffries has beaten all the best men – including you, Fitz, twice, with respect – and no one has ever come close to knocking him down, even. Although I do say, *may the best man win!*'

The sun was blazing overhead as the promoter, George Lewis 'Tex' Rickard, entered the ring wearing a ten-gallon hat to announce the arrival of Jack Johnson. Traditionally, the challenger must enter the ring first but many whites said that Jeffries had never been defeated and so *he* was the true Champion. What a boo there was from the crowd and so much hissing as Rickard welcomed Jack Johnson into the ring as the Heavyweight Champion of the World!

'Not for long!' some chanted. Johnson flashed the golden-toothed smile that had made white America hate him so much and, wrapped in his scarlet gown, sat down in his corner and rubbed a glove over his shaven head.

'And now!' Rickard shouted, 'another man whom some consider to be *the* Heavyweight Champion of the World – *James J. Jeffries!*' The crowd went wild. There was such cheering as I have never heard. As the Great White Hope stepped into the ring, wrapped in a plain white bath towel, the crowd went wild. Then his principal second, also a former Champion, the legendary 'Gentleman' Jim Corbett, whipped away the towel. The white 'Iron Man' stood before us and the crowd went wilder still. Bellingham was cheering too. At that instant, Jeffries looked as unbeatable now as he had been in the past.

I'd been reading articles about his training camp. It seemed that reporters had been reduced to remarking how friendly Jeffries might be if he weren't so unfriendly. I looked at Johnson. He was just sitting there and smiling. Then men touched gloves in the centre of the ring as Rickard told them the rules and then – with a *ding!* of the bell – The Fight of the Century began.

Jeffries charged out of his corner and straight at Johnson. The latter smothered all his mighty blows. Not one got through. In that first round, Jeffries swung punches that could have felled a tree, only he missed his opponent with every swipe. Puzzlingly enough, all Johnson did was retreat, duck, block, and flick out a couple of light jabs that landed on the forehead and chin of Jeffries. The second round was pretty much the same.

So far, Johnson had done next to nothing and Jeffries had done nothing to him. The bell rang for the third round. Suddenly, Johnson took command with a dramatic left-hand smash to Jeffries's jaw. It was all Johnson after that. Jeffries tried to stop him by wrestling him in clinches, yet Johnson astounded the crowd by proving to be the stronger man and shoving the 'Grizzly Bear' away from him. He then hit Jeffries how and when and where he liked and laughed away the latter's futile endeavours to harm him. Big Jeff was cruelly exposed as merely a tired old man.

'C'mon, Mr Jeffries,' Johnson was adding insult to injury with his verbal taunts. '*Do* somethin', man. Dis here fight's for de champ-een-ship . . .' Johnson prolonged the torture beneath the broiling desert sun and before the disbelieving eyes of a crowd who'd come to crow over the destruction of a black pretender. The Great White Hope did little other than paw the air, lurch, stumble and stagger like some hopelessly incorrigible drunkard. The mighty arms that had destroyed Bob Fitzsimmons, Jim Corbett and the ribs of Tom Sharkey now aroused only the mocking laughter of Johnson, paying back the white man for every humiliation ever visited upon him.

Jeffries – now the Great White Dope – stoically absorbed the punishment, just as he had done so many times before. He kept plodding, he persisted in pressing forward and he kept punching holes in the air. But, this time, there would be no miracle. He kept had nothing at all left to throw. He took to chewing gum. His mouth was cut, his nose was broken, his face was bloodied and his eyes were severely bruised. His blood flowed over Johnson's chest and back.

'How d'you feel, Jim?' Johnson asked him in the four-teenth round and hit him a few times more. 'How d'you like it?' He smacked him solidly in the face with three stiff right hands. 'Does it hurt, Jim?'

'They don't hurt,' Jeffries mumbled back. And it was in the fifteenth round of this 'fight to a finish' that Johnson decided to terminate the torture. A fusillade of blows sent Jeffries sprawling onto the canvas for the first time in his ring career. Johnson put his hands on his hips, grinned and posed for the motion-picture cameras. Jeffries somehow staggered to his feet and Johnson sent him tumbling once again.

'*Stop* it!' the crowd screeched. 'Don't let him be knocked out!' But Jeffries hauled his weary old body to its feet and Johnson slugged it to the canvas for the third and final time. It was over and a legend was dead. Johnson's victory sparked off race riots throughout the United States.

'Y'know, chaps,' Bellingham murmured quietly, 'I can't help feeling that the times, they are a-changing.'

CHAPTER SEVENTEEN

It was good to be back in London after a surprisingly pleasant journey from the West of America. The constitutional crisis was still going on, though, and it looked as if there would be another General Election in December. Meanwhile, Aleister Crowley was causing quite a stir and one heard rumours. I hadn't seen Crowley in quite a while and so I was pleased to receive an invitation to a magical ritual at his flat in Victoria Street. Yes, I would go there. I had read Captain Fuller's book *The Star In The West*, and, as far as I could see, this remarkable poet whom I'd known at Cambridge was trying to plant in English soil a form of Eastern Transcendental Hinduism/Buddhism/Sufism which attains to that altered state of super-consciousness that is called Samadhi – as I'd learned from Ram Singh and Amin Shah – under the guise of Ceremonial Magick.

I think that the average human being requires and desires ceremony. Anticipating such, it was a genuine pleasure to enter Crowley's flat and see him again. Everyone was enjoying champagne. Captain Fuller was there, as sharp and astute as ever. Crowley introduced me to the poet Victor Neuburg, a young man of great wit and much charm and with whom mine host appeared to be on intimate terms. There was an absolutely gorgeous woman there – Crowley's mistress, Leila Waddell. She was a Maori from New Zealand and she had beauty and grace. I shall never forget her glossy black hair that reached down to her waist.

A rather pretty, somewhat flighty elfin woman called Ethel Archer was there. (*Editor's Note*: In 1933, she published a rather truthful and delightful account of the Crowley–Neuburg relationship in her novel *The Hieroglyph*.) There was the enticing artist, Nina Hamnett. To my delighted surprise, also present were Emily Ward-Bishop, and Lavinia whom I'd met years ago up at Boleskine. There too was the delectable socialite, Gwendoline Otter. There was a Russian madman called George Raffalovitch who wrote short stories. There was a charming society palmist, one Count Louis Hamon, better known as 'Cheiro'. (*Editor's Note*: He was the author of the classic Western text on Palmistry.) A financial journalist from the *Sketch* had been invited, one Raymond Radclyffe, who openly professed his scepticism but declared that he had an open mind. Finally, there was a rather beautiful blonde, a Miss Florence Penny, who was virtually flinging herself at every man in the room.

'She must marry or go mad,' Crowley confided to me. Then: 'Brothers and Sisters of the A∴A∴' he declared in ringing tones. 'Welcome to another meeting. As you know, I have saturated myself with the magic of the East – a very real thing, in tune with the Eastern mind. I am well read in the modern metaphysicians, all of whom have attempted to explain the unexplainable. I abandon these! They appeal only to the brain and once their jargon is mastered they lead nowhere, least of all to *Ecstasy*! I hold with Ceremonial Magick because I think that it helps the mind to get outside itself. The fact is that if you repeat an Invocation solemnly and aloud, expectant of some great and mysterious result, you will experience, as most of us know, a deep sense of spiritual communion. Tonight, we shall be invoking Luna. Let us robe now: men in my study, women in Leila's studio.'

'Sorry, I don't have a robe,' said Raymond Radclyffe.

'Oh, that's quite all right,' Crowley returned. 'Just take your shoes off and make yourself comfortable.' I'd brought my old Golden Dawn robe. The next fifteen minutes were passed in getting ready. Various men vanished from the room. Eventually, a bell rang and a masked woman came to summon Raymond and myself to the Temple. Crowley had told me that he lived in a flat but we had to climb an almost interminable flight of stairs. We were received by a masked gentleman, robed in white – so he could have been any one of us – and bearing a drawn sword.

We were ushered into the Temple. The room was dark: only a dull red light shone upon the altar. The incense made a haze through which I saw a small white statue, illuminated by a tiny lamp hanging high on the cornice.

The masks were now removed. Captain Fuller, who had been the sentry of the Temple, proceeded to perform the lesser banishing ritual of the Pentagram impressively and in a manner duly earnest. Crowley commanded Cheiro to purify the Temple with Water. This was done. Then we witnessed the Consecration of the Temple with Fire and Crowley, now suddenly habited in black and accompanied by the brethren, led 'The Mystic Circumambulation'. They walked around the altar twice or thrice in a religious procession.

Gradually, one at a time, Radclyffe and I were beckoned into the circle. Crowley then requested Raffalovitch to 'bear the Cup of Libation'. Raffalovitch went around the room, offering each one of us a large golden bowl full of some pleasant-smelling drink. We drank in turn. I had no idea at the time that this drink contained peyote mushrooms from Mexico.

This over, Fuller strode into the centre and proclaimed 'The Twelvefold Certitude of God'. Artemis was then invoked by Cheiro, using the greater ritual of the Hexagram. There was another libation and then Crowley read us his *Song of Orpheus*. Following this song, we all drank our third Libation – and then the brothers led into the room a draped figure masked in that curious blue tint that we mentally associate with Hecate. This lady, the beautiful Leila, was enthroned on a seat high above Crowley himself.

By this time, the ceremony had grown weird and impressive and its influence was increased when Crowley recited Swinburne's 'When the Hounds of Spring are on Winter's Traces' as a further invocation of Artemis. Victor Neuburg – 'Frater Omnia Vincam' – was then commanded by Crowley to dance 'the dance of Syrinx and Pan in honour of our lady Artemis'.

This young poet, with whose superlative *The Triumph of Pan* I was familiar, astonished me with a graceful and beautiful dance which he continued until he fell exhausted in the middle of the room, where he lay until the end. Crowley then made supplication to the goddess in a beautiful poem of his that I hadn't heard or read before. A dead silence ensued.

After a long pause, the enthroned figure, Leila, took a violin and played – played with passion and feeling, like a master. We were thrilled to our very bones. Once again, Leila took the violin and played an *Abend Lied* so beautifully, so gracefully and with such intense feeling that in the very deed most of us experienced the Ecstasy that Crowley so earnestly seeks.

It wasn't over yet. The dancing began once again. Oh! How we danced around the altar, with hands linked and faces turned outwards! This dimly-lit Temple was thick with incense. Somehow the circle was broken yet we kept on dancing, each for himself or herself. Then we became aware of the presence of a stranger.

Some of us counted the people present and averred later that there was one too many. One of the weaker and more credulous brethren got scared or one of the stronger and more sceptical brethren remembered his duty to science – I don't know which – and switched on the light. No stranger was to be seen.

The lights were switched off again and there came a prolonged and intense silence after which Crowley proclaimed:

'By the Power in me vested, I declare the Temple closed.'

I agree completely with the article in the *Sketch* of 24 August 1910 by Raymond Radclyffe which ended:

'So ended a really beautiful ceremony – beautifully conceived and beautifully carried out. If there is any higher form of artistic expression than great verse and great music, I have yet to learn it. I do not pretend to understand the ritual that runs like a thread of magic through these meetings of the A∴A∴. I do not even know what the A∴A∴ is. But I do know that the whole ceremony was impressive, artistic, and produced in those present such a feeling as Crowley must have had when he wrote:

> "So that thou conquer Space and lastly climb
> The walls of Time;
> And by the golden path the great have trod
> Reach up to God!" '

Crowley was so encouraged by this that he decided to make matters public at Caxton Hall, Westminster, come October. This would have unfortunate consequences but I shall describe them in due course. On that particular night that I have described, we were all feeling sky-high.

It seemed that Crowley wanted to make up a foursome

with Leila, Victor Neuburg and Ethel Archer. After some good, stiff brandies, Fuller went away with Gwendoline Otter, Raffalovitch went away with Florence Penny, Count Louis Hamon – 'Cheiro' – went away with Lavinia, Radclyffe went away with Nina Hamnett and I went to Knightsbridge with Emily Ward-Bishop.

'My dear husband Christopher doesn't know anything about this place,' Emily told me. 'You see, Horby, I need a place where I can just get fucked by lovers.' It was certainly a luxurious flat, possibly even purchased with her husband's money. I wondered momentarily whether my wife Claire had done the same thing.

'So,' I said as Emily gave me a fine cognac and took one for herself, 'your husband Christopher remains the adoring slave you always wanted him to be, does he, Emily?'

'Oh, *of course* he does!' she exclaimed in return. 'Tell me, have you ever met my mother?'

'I don't think I've experienced that particular pleasure.'

'She's blonde with a good figure, same as me.' Emily let her breasts jut forward. 'In fact, one reason that I like my mother so much these days is that she reminds me so strongly of Joan Smythe. You recall that my father died in the Boer War?' I nodded. 'Well, Mummy went and married a filthy-rich banker called Michael about four years ago. Of course, she's got him around her little finger and under her thumb. These days, Mummy and I get on *so* well together. You see, Horby, once Christopher and I were married, he thought that the matters of our wedding dynamics were strictly between the two of us. Ha! ha! How wrong he was!

'There was a particular evening,' Emily continued animatedly, 'when I grew really, really quite cross with him. I mean, he'd done nothing all day! So I just went and slapped his face, turned around to switch my bottom to show who

212

was in charge and uttered the phrase that frightens him. That phrase is: "*Into Petticoats!*" My eyes are snapping as hard as my voice when I utter that.

'He knows that he has to obey. I give him half an hour. At the end of that period, I want him to present himself to me wearing knee-length silken white knickers, trimmed with lace, that I have left for him and that are wet with the moisture of my cuntal juices; a pretty white lacy bra; a suspender belt and black seamed stockings; a rather frilly white blouse with a brooch; a white petticoat trimmed with lace that I wore before our marriage; and an ankle-length soft green pleated skirt so that he's rustling as he takes every step – oh, and a pair of shiny black high-heeled leather shoes.

'He has to come into the drawing room once he's dressed, kneel down before me, then bend down and kiss and lick my boots of shiny leather – and then lick my high heels as he begs my pardon. Then I command him to stand up and drop me a pretty curtsy, which he does with delightful delicacy since I have trained him well.

'At this point, I usually order him to bend over, raising his skirt and petticoat. I pull down his knickers to expose his rather lovely small white bottom. Then I like to get a tapette from the cupboard and, as I swish my skirts, I poise and switch this device in the air. I have positioned Christopher opposite a big mirror so that he can see exactly what I am doing. And then the tapette comes down! *Thwack! Thwack! Thwack!* How his bottom writhes and twitches! It is *such* a pleasure . . .

'I take care in the way in which I redden his buttocks. My steady strokes initially turn his bottom pink – and then I lay it on thick and fast to turn his buttocks bright scarlet! Then Christopher has to get up, curtsy to me again and go and stand in the corner. I think I've told you before of the pleasure I get in fondling his stiff, thick prick as he stands there sighing with his face to the wall. Only this time it was going to be different in a way he had not expected.

'I had been shopping in various places and I now produced a pair of handcuffs and snapped them on his wrists. I also produced a pair of footcuffs and snapped them around his ankles. I smoked a cigarette and watched his spanked bottom twitch with anxiety.

'Soon enough, the chimes of the front-door bell sounded. It was Mummy. I had instructed the maid to conduct her to the door of the downstairs drawing room and had earlier ensured that everything we might need was present. By this I meant a splendid cold collation, with plenty to drink. It gave me much pleasure to greet my mother, usher her into the room and give her a seat and a glass of dry sherry.

' "There," I said, pointing at the petticoated male standing obediently in the corner with his handcuffed hands behind his back, "that's my husband." I could see that Christopher was just dying to run away – but the footcuffs meant that he couldn't.

' "Oh, you darling girl!" my mother Evangeline exclaimed. "That's exactly what I've done to break in Michael! What a charming sight. Do the maids know?"

' "Not yet."

' "The sooner the better," Mama replied. "*My* maids know. It's rather useful if you want help in getting your husband laced into a tight corset."

' "Turn around, Christopher!" I commanded. He obeyed me and stood there helplessly before us. His face? Oh! What a picture! It was as cherry red as his bottom.

' "What a pretty sight!" Mama hooted with delighted laughter. "You haven't punished him recently by any chance, have you?"

' "Well, I have, actually," I replied; then added: "Christopher! Turn around!" He obeyed me and I then lifted up his skirt and petticoat and pulled down his knickers so as to display his scarlet, glowing bottom to Mummy.

' "Keep his bottom glowing," she remarked, "it's the only way to control male misbehaviour. But why don't you get him to turn around again, so I can see his blushing face once more? Then unlock his handcuffs. I really would like to see whether he is capable of executing a pretty curtsy with his ankles shackled."

'I complied with her request. And so, my having unlocked the handcuffs, Christopher then had to hobble around and drop a pretty curtsy to me and to Mama as best he could.

' "Oh, Christopher!" she said warmly, "I never wish to see you in trousers ever again. On every occasion when I see you in the future you will wear a petticoat and a skirt for me."

'And that, Horby, is exactly what has happened. Christopher has to be dressed that way by the maids on every occasion that we go to see Mama at her place in Belgravia for Sunday luncheon and/or afternoon tea. You see, Christopher feels terribly embarrassed, arriving in his skirt, only to find that Michael has to wear a skirt too.

'Sometimes we allow the boys to change into trousers on condition that they behave themselves. On one occasion, we sent them out on some errand with strict instructions not to dare to drink. Of course, boys will be boys and, although they accomplished the errand, they both came back with beer on their breath – and so had to be punished. The first move was to deprive them of their trousers.

'Mama then produced a cane and asked me if I wanted one too. I said that I did and she gave me a thin, whippy one while switching the thick one that she had selected. The boys had to lower the frilly knickers we made them wear on all occasions – even to work – and bend over.

Anonymous

' "I will not tolerate disobedience!" Mama declared.

' "Neither will I," I added firmly. "Six of the best!" And mother and daughter proceeded to cane their husbands in unison. Those whippy strokes made a wondrous sound and it was a positive pleasure to see the men's bottoms jumping up and down. Obviously, and judging by the weals, we had different styles of caning. I wanted six weals neatly placed from the top to that sensitive area just above the thighs. By contrast, Mama wanted to lay on every stroke within what she called "the tropical zone". By the end, we had two well-punished and obedient husbands who had been ordered into petticoats.

'There was one final thing we did that gave Mummy and I the greatest of pleasure. We commanded our males to stand before us in their skirts and then lift them and their white petticoats while lowering their knickers to show us their rampant and stiffly erect penises. We then forced Christopher and Michael, whose buttocks were still blazing, to touch the tips of their pricks together in front of us.

'Well, Horby,' Emily Hawtree, as she now was, concluded her tale, 'you just can't imagine how good the sex was when – separately – we finally let the males loose on us that night!'

'A fascinating tale, Emily,' I answered, 'but I can't say I'd want to be your husband . . .'

'You'd be an impossible husband!'

'Quite. And from what you tell me, I don't think I'm missing out with regard to having your mother as my mother-in-law.'

'Oh, do shut up!'

'Certainly,' I assented as I ripped the thin silk from her nubile body. She sighed and then I threw her onto the floor before the fire and pronged my stiff rod into her.

I had to uphold the honour of the male. It was a joy to see her turn and twist and writhe.

'Aargh!' she shrieked, 'you're fucking my brains out!' – and then she came.

'Didn't know you had any,' I murmured; and then *I* came.

CHAPTER EIGHTEEN

I had a full English breakfast at home on the first of April 1911, as my Memorandum 5001 informs me. After the eggs, bacon, fried bread, sausage, tomato and – quite essential – kidneys, I lit an Egyptian oval cigarette and smoked it with enjoyment as I perused the paper with lots more tea, toast and marmalade to come.

The General Election of 2 December 1910 had left the Liberal Government clinging onto power quite narrowly. Bellingham had been returned to Parliament with a vastly increased majority. Sir Richard had really rather surprised me by working so hard to protect and advance the interests of his constituents. But the struggle between the Lords and the Commons continued. The matter was made even more complicated by the death of King Edward VII and the accession to the throne of his son, King George V.

I reflected that the world I knew was turning upside down. There was industrial strife, owing to the increasing power of the Trades Unions; sexual strife, owing to the increasing agitation of the Suffragettes; international strife, owing to our naval arms race with the German Empire; and constitutional strife, owing to the conflict between Commons and Lords.

It was therefore a relief to open a letter from my darling wife Claire:

Anonymous

Dear Horby,

My darling husband! I hope that you are well. I miss you. Wasn't it such a pleasure to meet up with Douglas and Rosemary in Paris? Ah! Paris in the Spring! There is nothing finer. I wish you could have stayed longer, but you said that you had to go back to London to support your strange friend Crowley in some libel case or other.

I'm writing this tonight in the bedroom we shared together at that beautiful house of Douglas's overlooking the Arc de Triomphe. I still love you. Oh! What thrills of sensual feeling sweep through my body as I recall the passion of our nights here, of lying naked on crushed and rumpled sheets and watching the early morning sunlight caress your body as you lay sleeping while I listened to the raucous sounds of the birds welcoming the dawn. Just thinking of your delicate features, your slender, hairy chest and your majestic member makes me tingle all over and I do so wish that you could be transported to my lonely bed! I can only console myself by remembering some of the wonderful moments we have shared together.

One that readily springs to mind is how we fell into one another's arms when the train from Brighton steamed into Victoria station. My train was late – I had been visiting an aunt – and you had been waiting impatiently on the platform to greet me. Darling, I shall treasure the memory of how your eyes lit up as you rushed towards me and engulfed me in an enormous bear hug. My lips spread into a wide smile as I felt the stiff pressure of your cock against my belly. Do you recall what I did next?

I pressed myself up against you as I slid my hand up the inside of your thigh and gently squeezed your erection, whispering my demand that you fuck me there and then.

'Darling, not here,' you said.

'What a prude you are!' I replied. 'It's just that I want

220

your cock inside my pussy so much that that I get carried away when I see you.' Luckily, you had brought the brougham. We clambered in and I snuggled up against you.

'Horby,' I said softly, 'I want to tell you something. It's been a warm day and so I haven't put on any knickers.' How I laughed when I saw your jaw drop! I took hold of your hand and trapped it between my thighs, feeling your fingertips against my warm crotch – and then your fingers traced the outline of my pussy lips. To encourage you further, I pulled my skirt up over my thighs and you slid your hands underneath the thin fabric.

I sighed with pleasure as you parted my pussy lips with your finger and teased the hooded nub out of my clitty. My breathing became ragged and my head tossed from side to side as I impaled myself on your stabbing finger. Do you remember how excited I became and how I clutched at your arm and urged you to fuck me without further delay?

Your defences began to crumble as soon as my hand stole across to your lap, squeezing and rubbing the straining bulge between your legs. I couldn't resist laughing softly as I watched your face contort with excitement and then – as I hoped – you threw caution to the winds and suddenly you were tearing off your trousers and pulling them down your legs.

'This is sheer madness,' you muttered as you rolled across me. I sank back and spread my thighs as I reached up and yanked down your drawers, catching my breath at the sight of your massive prick as it sprang into view. Then: 'Move up to me!' you commanded in an urgent whisper and, when I did, I grasped your hot, throbbing shaft and drew it down and forward until the swollen purple knob was rubbing against my yielding pussy lips.

'Yes . . . yes . . . YES!' I panted as I felt your width stretch my tight channel of lust. Then, with a low growl,

you started to drive your thick cock into my cunt, jerking me against the seat and lifting my bottom from the leather with the sheer ferocity of your thrusts. Your arms slid underneath me and you scooped up my bum cheeks in your hands.

'Oh, God!' you gasped. 'I have to come! I can't stop!'

'Shoot your load!' I yelled out in response. 'I want it all!' I cried out again as your jism drenched my cunny and my cunt convulsed into a series of pulsing spasms until I was left sighing with pleasure and exhaustion.

How good it was to be home! I know we have plenty of places but perhaps your town house is my favourite. You gave me some king prawns to eat and opened a bottle of fizz. It was Twelfth Night and I take the occasion as seriously as you do. There are really three major festivals during this period. Of course, there's Christmas Eve and Christmas Day and Boxing Day, as we English have it, though I prefer, as you know, to call the whole period Yuletide or Saturnalia, as you do, thank heavens. Well, we certainly had a good time, as usual.

Then there's New Year's Eve and New Year's Day – Hogmanay in Scotland – and once again it was excellent this time. Then there's a rather dead period, which was why I went to visit my aunt. But I was back for you on Twelfth Night. In Spain, this is the great feast of the Epiphany, of the Three Kings. In England during the eighteenth century this was celebrated with greater joy than Christmas Day. Their Twelfth Cake became the modern Christmas Cake. But we'd hardly seen that much of one another really during the festivities and tonight, on Twelfth Night, I only wanted to be with you.

'You're a very naughty girl!' you said sternly as your eyes gleamed. 'But let's undress while I decide what your punishment should be.' How your eyes gleamed as I

unhooked my skirt and began to unbutton my blouse! Darling Horby, I'm sure I don't have to remind you of what happened next.

When we were both naked, I gave a little squeal as you pulled me over your knees and I deliberately wiggled my bottom in anticipation as you pinched my bum.

'You've been a very naughty girl, haven't you, Claire?' you said sternly.

'I have,' I admitted.

'You know what happens to naughty girls, don't you?'

'They get their bottoms smacked . . .'

'Quite right!' you returned smartly. 'So brace yourself. I'm going to give you a sound spanking!' And with those words, you parted my bum cheeks and inserted the tip of the little finger of your right hand inside my pussy and slid it in and out for a few moments until my quim was dripping wet before pulling it out and beginning my punishment in earnest.

'Oh! Oh! OH!' I cried out as you started to slap my arse in a series of light, rapid strokes that made me wince as my bottom began to tingle.

'Quiet now, Claire!' you snapped. 'Your punishment isn't finished yet. I'm not letting you up until I see your bum cheeks turn pink!' Nevertheless, you didn't really hurt me and I felt so raunchy when you had finished smacking me and began to massage my wriggling backside: and I could hardly wait to be fucked when you hauled me up and threw me down on the Persian rug before the fire.

I parted my legs as you plunged your big stiff cock inside my soaking cunt and my hips moved with yours, picking up the rhythm as I wrapped my legs around your back as our lips met and my mouth was immediately filled by your tongue . . . Oh, darling Horby, wouldn't you love to be in bed with me now, pistoning your thick prick into my sopping slit and watching me lie back with a blissful smile on my face as you fondle my breasts and tweak up my perky red nipples between your fingers? Darling, I do so wish you were here, for my body is aching for you.

Alas! I am all alone in this room and can only play with my own pussy, sliding my thumb inside my cunny as I finish this letter and dream about your powerful shaft thrusting in and out of my juicy quim – and also I can think about the wonderful nights of passion we shall soon be enjoying together.

Loads of love and more,
Claire

Well! That was certainly a good start to the day! In fact, there really *is* something to be said for marriage, especially if, after years of it, your wife writes you letters like that! My wife was right, however, in stating that I had returned from Paris in order to assist Crowley.

I have described the excellence of what I saw at his flat in Victoria Street. I didn't especially want to join his Order but I had gone to see his public rites at Caxton Hall. For five guineas one received admission to seven rituals to invoke planetary energies: Saturn, Jupiter, Mars, Sol, Venus, Mercury and Luna. That meant seven evenings; though one could always go somewhere else afterwards.

I wasn't wasting my time. These rituals presented an extremely vivid, poetic picture, organized into a cosmic drama of seven acts. Man, unable to solve the riddle of existence, takes counsel of Saturn, extreme old age, and only receives, after much trouble, the despairing reply that there is no God. Jupiter, Mars, the Sun, Venus and Mercury are in turn invoked, but all are found wanting, because of their natures. At last the Virgin Moon appears, Madonna-like, throned and crowned, veiled and silent. She is Isis and

Mary, Ishtar and Bhavani, Artemis and Diana, but she is still barren of hope until the Great God Pan, the principle of fecundity, tears asunder the veil and reveals the hope of humanity in the Crowned and Conquering Child of the future – the hawk-headed God, Horus.

(*Editor's Note:* These Rites were again performed publicly at Conway Hall in 1995.)

I found these Rituals to be dignified in conception and to be executed in a stupendous way. In fact, they created the biggest sensation of the Autumn Season in London during that delightful October of 1910. Invitations were issued to the Press and to the Police. Long news stories were published, with photographs in most of the newspapers. I think that everyone who attended must also have enjoyed the 'libation bowl' consisting of hot spiced wine punch with buds of the Mexican peyote cactus. That, combined with the ritual, made me feel absolutely marvellous.

Unfortunately, Crowley had then been savaged by the gutter press. An unsavoury individual called De Wend Fenton at that time edited a smutty publication called *The Looking Glass*. After an unsuccessful attempt to blackmail Crowley, he had taken to vilifying him and everything he stood for in his foul rag. One vicious attack had followed another.

In fact, in 1913 De Wend Fenton was fined for sending indecent materials through the post.

But on the first of April 1911, I met Crowley and George Cecil Jones at Barter's Oyster Bar. Jones, whom I had known and liked back in the Golden Dawn days and whom Crowley had always praised to my ears as a great and wise Magician and who was certainly involved intimately in Crowley's A∴A∴ Order, was in a highly agitated condition. It was all to do with a passage in *The Looking Glass*, as follows:

'Two of Crowley's friends and introducers are still with him; one, the rascally sham Buddhist monk Allan Bennett; the other a person of the name of George Cecil Jones, who was for some time employed in Basingstoke in metallurgy but of late has had some sort of small merchant's business in the City. Crowley and Bennett lived together, and there were rumours of unmentionable immoralities which were carried on under their roof . . .'

As Crowley pointed out, this could hardly trouble the celibate Allan Bennett, meditating on the Clear Light in a Buddhist monastery thousands of miles away. But it *did* upset George Cecil Jones, who had a wife and two children and a position in the City to maintain. Jones urged Crowley to sue. Crowley declined. He argued that he was taken seriously by papers of quality – which was true – and that smutty tabloids were beneath his attention. For my own part, I urged Crowley not to go to court for he would have to justify his life in terms of the middle-class morality he despised.

I urged Jones too not to go to court. Unfortunately, he was a fiery Welshman who in appearance resembled the conventional representations of Jesus Christ. He was utterly determined to clear his name and absolutely nothing would stop him. What an obstinate Welsh cuss! I offered him the services of my lawyers but he declined them, saying that he preferred to stick with his usual solicitors – which proved to be a ghastly error. I offered my own services as a character witness for Crowley – I didn't really know Jones well enough for that. Although the oysters at Barter's were as excellent as ever, this meeting was a horrible failure.

The trial of *Jones v. The Looking Glass* came up in the High Court of Justice a few weeks later. As the judge remarked: 'This is like a trial out of *Alice in Wonderland*.' The whole case hinged on the character of Crowley. De Wend Fenton did not want to call Crowley as a witness since he would tell the court of the attempt to subject him to blackmail. Jones or his solicitor or barrister chose not to call Crowley because they feared that he might be too outspoken. Time and time again, the judge interrupted the trial.

'Surely the right person to tell us about this is Mr Crowley,' he kept saying. 'Why don't you call Mr Crowley?' Both sets of lawyers then promptly explained the absolute impossibility of discovering where Mr Crowley was – despite the obvious fact that he was there to be seen by all every day in the public gallery.

This grew 'curiouser and curiouser'. The defendants pleaded that they had not suggested that Mr Jones was a sodomite. They had not, and never had had any intention of suggesting that Mr Jones was a sodomite. Mr Jones explained elaborately and excitedly that he was not a sodomite. Captain Fuller came forward to swear that he had known Mr Jones since 1907 and that he was not a sodomite. The judge, summing up, said that, doubtful as the case might be on some points, one thing at least stood out sunclear, namely that Mr Jones was not a sodomite. It was also evident that the expressions that had offended the plaintiff were inoffensive; that nobody had ever suggested that Mr Jones was a sodomite.

The jury then retired. They were dazed by suppressed sexual excitement, I suppose. They thought that there was something curious about the evidence. All parties *breathed together* that Mr Jones was not a sodomite. The Latin for *breathe together* is *conspire*. That's what it was – a conspiracy! So they brought in the verdict that the article *was* a libel and that it was *justified!!!* – such verdict evidently implying that the defendants had perjured themselves, that the judge was a fool and that Mr Jones was a sodomite after all!

Sometimes I just despair of my fellow man!

CHAPTER NINETEEN

The consequences of the Jones trial for my friend Crowley were most unfortunate. Captain Fuller insisted that Crowley *had* to sue for libel now, as did Jones. When he refused, both men broke with him. In addition, he had broken up with his wife, his 'Rose of the World'. She had become a total dipsomaniac and she now entered a lunatic asylum, suffering from alcoholic dementia in the wake of the divorce. To Crowley's relief, she did recover; and to his grief, she then married Colonel Gormley, 'the eminent masochist' whom I had met all those years ago at Boleskine.

There were matters other than Crowley to occupy my mind that Summer of 1911. I had to attend the Coronation of King George V, which was done with all lengthy and due pomp and circumstance. Then there was the matter of the Parliament Act. This Bill would abolish the absolute veto of the House of Lords. Curiously enough, I was for it: and Bellingham, in the House of Commons, was against it. The new King agreed with Prime Minister Asquith to create 249 new Liberal Peers to give the Government a majority in the Upper House, if required. Opposition now collapsed as the Lords passed the Bill. Any British government now only needed a majority in the Commons for its measures to pass into law.

'Damnit, Horby!' Lord Curzon snapped at me. 'You've voted for a revolution greater than any since the Civil War!'

'You are a traitor to your class, sir!' I was told by all too many of my peers. The abuse annoyed me and so I decided to leave the country and go and travel for a while. My wife, who had supported my position, came with me.

Claire and I just wanted to get away from it all for a time. We agreed that we had both always wanted to visit Tangiers in Morocco. Consequently, we took the first boat out of Southampton, which happened to be the TSS *New York*. Unfortunately, it was somewhat lacking in the amenities that we had enjoyed on the SS *Albion* of Douglas, all those years ago.

(*Editor's Note:* Volume III of *The Black Pearl* has an enlivening description of this voyage.)

Nevertheless, we were reasonably comfortable aboard this ship. The voyage was not unpleasant, though it was good to disembark at Tangiers and establish ourselves in a suite at the Hotel Splendide. Here, everything was French and in the traditional manner. That meant that the food was excellent and that the waiters took genuine pride in their work.

The European quarter of Tangiers is all very well: but we wanted to explore the Arab part of town. Claire, in common with most women, liked shopping. In common with most men, I don't. Yet the haggling customs of North Africa altered my attitude and I grew to love haggling in the Casbah.

Haggling over prices, to a Moroccan, is a national sport. It arouses passion, requires practice and calls for sportsmanship. In a *souk*, the most important thing is that the bartering be done with a smile, not a scowl. I took to smoking a pipe, since this shows that one has plenty of time. Gradually, Claire and I evolved sensible rules. For a start, if you spot something that actually interests you, walk on by – at least twice. When Ali finally steered us into his emporium, we applied the second rule.

It is essential to know what you want. All we wanted on this occasion was a *pouf* for use by visiting children or as a footrest for adults. Both of us said that we wanted to look around, though. Alas! This didn't stop Ali from pressing all manner of useless objects on us. Claire, I know, was considering buying more than one item on the grounds that we might get a better price. But did I really want a dagger that, Ali swore, had previously belonged to a Sultan? I responded by praising his sales patter.

Of course, this showed that I was enjoying the game and flattered him. Claire added, regarding his asking price for the *pouf*, that he had to be joking. Having realized that we were not what the New Yorkers call 'plumb suckers', Ali called for hot mint tea and asked us to sit and take it with him. This is an essential feature of Moroccan social life, though it is designed to put the customer slightly in the merchant's debt.

Claire and I had agreed to operate in tandem and had worked out our rock-bottom price. We knew that the trader had calculated his with a one hundred per cent mark-up. We looked utterly aghast when he offered us his outrageous 'special price'. We'd both agreed earlier to pretend to quarrel but to operate by the principle of offering one third, being prepared to settle for half and to walk away if he only dropped by twenty per cent. So when he insisted on his original price, we smiled, shook our heads and started to leave.

'Wait!' Ali cried. He followed us to the door. We knew that if he did *that*, then he would eventually sell it to us. 'Tell me your best price,' he pleaded.

'Our best price would insult you,' Claire replied. There followed a few more minutes of haggling as I smoked my pipe and watched Ali offer to throw in the dagger for an all-inclusive price.

'Ha! ha! ha!' Suddenly Ali gave in. The price was agreed. 'Okay,' he said, 'but do you have something for me?' Claire must have known something, since she handed him an English keyring and a boiled sweet. His face evinced his delight. We left with our *pouf* and salutations on either side.

'Never enter a *souk*,' Claire said, 'without a supply of English trinkets that they can't get here.'

'I enjoyed that experience very much, darling,' I said, 'but it's taken us two hours to buy one *pouf* with a dagger thrown in for good measure. In future, I think I'll go to a normal English department store and buy the same thing for a similar price in five minutes.'

'Oh, Horby, you're so bloody old-fashioned!'

'Am I? Let's eat and drink here,' I liked the look of the humble place to which I led Claire. The locals were eating there and so were some people who were obviously French. While we were studying the menu, Claire fell into conversation with a Frenchman at the next table. This man was obviously enjoying his food.

'When a deal here is sealed with a handshake,' Claire declared to him, 'never try to reopen it.'

'Quite right, Madame,' the Frenchman replied. 'But having lived here in Morocco for twenty years, I say: if he completes a sale, it means he has won, whatever you may think. *Bon soir*.'

However, I had picked the right place. The wine of Morocco is hardly the finest in the world, but it is tasty, robust and full of the sun, tastes like the grape and is intoxicating. We began with a freshly caught red mullet that was just so sweet and tender; and then we proceeded to a freshly slaughtered grilled chicken, accompanied by *couscous* and a delicious casserole of vegetables. Delicate pastries, soaked in honey, were a fitting dessert.

As Claire and I walked back to our hotel, we observed

that wonderful North African sky that is so full of stars. I insisted on stopping at a bar so that we could sit outside and watch the stars and the moon. We drank coffee and cognac and smoked the thin pipes of hashish they brought to us at my request. We then walked on to our hotel in a delightful daze.

When we returned to our suite, we both lay down on the bed and Claire ruffled her fingers through my hair. Both of us undressed and smiled at one another. There is actually something quite uniquely erotic in fucking your own wife. She dropped her hands down to my waist and pulled me gently towards her.

She ground her belly against my pulsating prick and smiled. Then my wife leaned back and I drank in the proud thrust of her impudent, uptilted breasts crowned by their large raspberry nipples, which were already poutingly erect with desire. Sometimes one takes one's wife for granted. Yet now I caught my breath as I lowered my gaze down over her flat, snow-white stomach and to the crisp thatch of blonde hair nestling between her thighs. Then this voluptuous woman took hold of me and pressed her lips against mine, darting her tongue between my teeth as she slipped her hand down to squeeze my throbbing tool.

I shivered uncontrollably as she gently stroked my hot, smooth-skinned shaft with her cool fingers. Claire glanced down at my prick as she slowly frigged my twitching truncheon.

'You've still got a nice big cock for your age, that's for sure, Horby,' she laughed. 'But isn't it about time that it was put to better use?' She took my stiff cock within her fist and yanked it upward. Then we lay together on the bed and kissed wildly, our tongues deep in each other's mouths as Claire mashed her soft breasts against my chest.

She took hold of my hands and placed them on the

jouncy globes of her arse cheeks as she pressed herself against me, but after a short while, she broke the embrace in order to pull two soft cushions off the bed and throw them down upon the Moroccan rug that lay in front of it. Then she lay back, placing the last remaining cushion under her head with the other under her lovely bottom.

'Horby, you've been wasting your time with all those stupid females,' Claire murmured throatily as she spread her legs. 'Come and fuck me again!' She ran her hand invitingly between her legs, spreading her puffy pussy lips with her fingers to give me a glimpse of the red chink of her love channel. At last the moment of truth had arrived!

My heart began to pound as she reached out and clasped hold of my stiff cock, which leaped and bounded within her fist. Releasing my prick from the sweet prison of her hand, she now grasped my buttocks as I lowered myself down on her. In one powerful forward thrust, my bursting shaft sank directly into the tight wetness of her cunny, right to the root, until my balls slapped against her bottom.

For a short while, we just lay still, with my cock tightly engulfed inside Claire's channel of love. I almost swooned away with pleasure as I gloried in erotic ecstasy.

'I hope it's as nice as you thought it would be, my darling husband,' Claire whispered softly. 'How does it feel? As good as ever, I trust . . . now I want you to fuck me. Push your prick in and out of my pussy – and when the spunk rushes up from your balls – oh! – go shoot your seed right inside me!' Really, I needed no further urging. Claire lifted herself up eagerly to welcome my enthusiastic prick which was now thrusting in and out of her juicy cunt, clutching at my jerking bottom as she heaved herself upwards to pull me further inside her. She worked her hips in time with my thrusts and the stimulating caress of her cunny muscles around my cock made me buck up and down at an even more frenetic pace.

'Horby!' she squealed, 'slow down, slow down. I want to spend too, you know.' I responded to her request by indeed slowing down the pace of my frantic thrusts – and she looked down delightedly at my shaft, which glistened with its coating of Claire's cunny juice as it pumped in and out of her notch. I noticed how her love lips were clinging to my cock every time I pulled back – as if she were afraid of losing such a sweet stick of sugar cane. 'Now speed up again and fuck me as hard as you can!' she panted through tightly clenched teeth. 'Go on, Horby! Give me all you've got, you lovely big-cocked man!'

I slammed into my wife's squelchy snatch, fucking her as hard and as fast as I could. And now Claire was transformed into a raging wild animal, biting my shoulder as she writhed wildly beneath me until, with a long wail, she slumped backwards and her breasts and buttocks shook in a series of tiny spasms as she achieved a delicious orgasm.

This led to the muscles of her cunny squeezing my trembling tool even more tightly and this sent me speeding onward to my own climax. I could feel the sperm rising from my scrotum – and what a joy it was to spurt my emission deep within her and to hear her long-drawn-out sigh of satisfaction. My mind was in a whirl as I lay beside Claire, temporarily exhausted. My own wife had actually given me the best and most satisfying fuck that I had had in quite a while. We lay silent and close together.

'That was wonderful,' she said after a while and after some brandy. 'Now let me give you a lovely treat! Lie back and close your eyes while I give your lovely cock a nice big kiss!' Naturally, I was very happy to let Claire suck my cock again and a blissful smile spread over my face as she slipped down on her knees, directly in front of me. Holding my stiffening shaft in her hand, she squeezed it gently as she planted a delicate kiss upon the tip of my knob – and, in seconds, my prick thickened up to a rampant state of excitement. 'Your delicious big cock looks good enough to eat!' my wife said huskily.

She proceeded to wet her lips and gulp about half of my long, thick shaft into her mouth. I gasped as Claire washed my pricktip with her wet tongue and then, bobbing her head up and down, and in a slow, thorough tempo, she began to palate my cock with her sweet, suctioning mouth.

She now let go of my tool and grasped my buttocks with both hands to move me backwards and forwards as she eagerly sucked my tadger, suddenly releasing one hand from my bum to play with my balls as she swirled her tongue around my throbbing column. My frisky girl was clearly deriving great enjoyment from this sensual sucking, sliding her tongue up and down my throbbing tool, gently nipping, licking and kissing my delighted cock. Ecstatic stabs of desire crackled through my entire body as she sucked me off, tonguing my tip against the roof of her mouth so skilfully that I soon felt the surge of another powerful spend coursing up from my tightened ballsack.

'I'm coming, Claire!' I cried out. 'I'm coming! OH!' My hips were jerking faster and faster and then, with one final thrust I spurted a stream of sticky jism into my wife's mouth, every drop of which she eagerly gulped down . . .

That's really the story of our time in Tangiers. Claire and I shopped, ate, drank and fucked. However, as the old sayings have it, there can be too much of a good thing – and all good things must come to an end. I think that the secret of a successful marriage is when both husband and wife know the moment to get away from one another.

Claire decided to take a slow but luxurious cruise back to

England and I decided to visit Vienna. This involved a journey by boat to Rome and then a train. As I read the papers on both boat and train – I'd ignored them utterly for a time – it slowly dawned on me that I'd totally missed another international crisis, and that it had concerned Morocco.

The Germans had rashly sent a gunboat to Agadir to demand territorial compensation from the French. Once again, Kaiser Bill had been rattling his sabre. What a fool! This only served to bind Great Britain more closely to France. As I later learned, military leaders concluded secret plans for wartime cooperation. British troops would be sent to defend France, if necessary. The British fleet would defend the Atlantic and the North Sea while the French concentrated on the Mediterranean.

But, as I would find out in Vienna, there was something *very* strange brewing among the German-speaking peoples.

CHAPTER TWENTY

Darling Claire,

What an absolutely fabulous time we had in Tangiers! I hope and trust that you had a safe journey back and that I shall be home and with you next Saturday. No doubt you will be ready and willing to telling me enlivening tales of your erotic exploits. I look forward to them.

Presently, as you can see from the letter-heading, I am staying in the Imperial Hotel, Vienna, in the suite once occupied by the composer, Richard Wagner.

(*Editor's Note:* Adolf Hitler made it his headquarters after the *Anschluss* of 1938.)

I really am living in the lap of luxury. And what a pleasure it is to be in this City of Mozart and to contemplate the Blue Danube! I could go on forever about the palaces, the cathedrals and churches, the gardens, the history and the sheer civilization of this incredible Habsburg jewel in the crown of their Empire. What cultured people the Viennese are! I could write a book about the matter but since this is only a letter, I must mention just one thing.

I shall never forget the Stephansdom, bang in the centre of Vienna, which cathdral some have called the soul of the city itself. There was an earlier pagan shrine here on what is obviously a sacred spot and a Christian shrine has since stood here for over 800 years. All that remains of the original thirteenth-century Romanesque church are the Giants' Doorway and the Heathen Towers. The Gothic nave, choir boxes and side chapels are the result of a rebuilding programme in the fourteenth and fifteenth centuries, while the Lower Vestry is a Baroque addition. I was particularly impressed by The North Tower.

According to legend, this was never completed because its master builder, Hans Puchsbaum, broke a pact he had made with the Devil by pronouncing a holy name. The Devil then caused him to fall to his death. Yet what an unbelievable view of Vienna you have from the top of the North Tower! And guess who I met there . . .

Yes! It was my old friend, Maria von Huttendorf, spy for all the Great Powers and Great Whore of Europe. She too was staying at the Imperial. No offence to you, Claire, but we simply couldn't wait to fuck again. In common with all of us, she has grown older, and yet her beauty has ripened. In fact, when I started lapping up the juices from her cunt, they tasted rather like a vintage burgundy. We had lost no time in rushing back via horse and gleaming black carriage to my suite. Naturally I ensured that champagne and cognac were also present and correct. I could barely control my raging desire since Maria was wearing one of those fashionable hobble skirts in which a woman can only take small, mincing steps and so cannot help the fact that her bottom switches enticingly from side to side when she walks.

I stripped her of her clothes and then discarded mine. She gasped at the sight of my huge, rampaging cock, the tip of its knob pressed against the dimple of my belly button. Maria reached out for the empurpled head of my monster and it seemed as though her lips were drawn by an invisible magnet to its proud dome. She kissed this head and, when she swirled her tongue over the smooth skin, a tiny blob of 'pre-come' came out of its tiny 'eye'. She licked this up and swallowed it.

'Ah! It tastes so masculine with its delicious salty tang!' Maria gasped as she closed her lips tightly over my knob and circled the base of my thick boner with her fingers. Then she eased her face downwards to take in more of my throbbing tool inside her mouth and I sighed with delight as I gently pushed her head further down my shaft. But I didn't want to come just yet. Nor did she want me to come just yet. 'Why don't you play with my titties while I rub your cock . . . ?' she sighed.

I rushed her to the four-poster bed. Our mouths met in a burning kiss and I began to flick at her hard little nipples, exciting Maria even more as her hands slid over my erect cock and the balls beneath it. She cupped these and gently massaged them, then she grabbed my shaft in both hands, one on top of the other, and slid them up and down my hot truncheon. She pumped my glistening shaft so well that, in no time at all, my cock was jerking uncontrollably between her fingers.

A low sigh escaped from my lips as I squirted out jets of frothy white seed over her delicate hands.

It was time for Room Service. Thank heavens for the modern invention of the telephone! Thank heavens also for the old fashioned tradition of the four-poster bed with curtains. Maria and I drew these, smoked cigarettes, drank champagne cocktails and chatted. Eventually, the supper arrived and was placed on a table in my suite. I had gone by Maria's advice to order traditional food. We had both ordered a clear beef broth of two varieties. My Leber-knoedesuppe *was seasoned with parsley and marjoram and contained delicious small liver dumplings; the* Fritta-tensuppe *of Maria contained thin strips of lightly seasoned pancakes.*

I then had Tafelspitz mit G roeste, *since I'd heard that it was eaten every day by the Emperor of Austria-Hungary, Franz Joseph. I found that this consisted of thickly sliced top corner of silverside of beef, served with fried, grated potatoes and an apple and horseradish sauce. Maria had* Bauernschmaus: *a simple country platter of hot meats such as smoked ham, roast pork, frankfurters and a fried pork cutlet accompanied by sauerkraut with juniper and dumplings.*

'You know why I like eating varieties of pork so much?' *Maria asked me.*

'No . . . ?'

''Cos I'm a pig.' *Maria's teeth scrunched into her frankfurter. Indeed, for some minutes there was no sound apart from the satisfied sound of munching. We also dug into a superb mixed salad with* Eierschwammerl, *wild mushrooms that are picked in the Autumn. It is always a pleasure to eat good food but most pleasures pall in the end and we returned to the bed. Sex with this delightful and intriguing woman was once again a most exciting prospect.*

My cock was now restored to its full height. I pulled Maria to me and kissed her deeply, my tongue parting her lips and twisting inside her mouth. My strong hands were now on her bum cheeks which I pulled apart.

She uttered a yelp of surprise when I pushed the tip of my little finger into her arsehole. She sighed when she felt my cock beating stiffly against her belly. She twisted and writhed in my embrace as my free hand slid back from her bottom to my shaft which I rubbed sensually against her fast-moistening crack. I smiled, moved my head down and parted her legs before kissing her sopping slit.

The tip of my tongue tickled her clitty. Maria responded by twisting her thighs around my head as I sucked the pungent love juice that was now pouring out of her juicy cunny. Then I raised myself over her trembling body and pressed my cock against her yielding pussy lips.

I jiggled my rod between them, at first just inserting an inch or so, and after a pause I went right in there. Then I let my stiff cock rest inside her channel of lust for a few moments to give her time to feel how she liked having my rampant tool inside her.

'Wonderful . . .' Maria sighed lazily. 'My cunt is so well suited to hold your hot, hard prick inside me! Yes, I think I shall keep it there for a while.' I responded by pulling her love lips apart to ease the passage of my thick prick. 'Oh! This is a delicious sensation!' she cried out as my stiff shaft thrust into her sticky wet honeypot, in and out, in and out. 'Ooooh! This is wonderful!' Maria panted as she felt my balls slapping against her bum cheeks.

As I increased the pace, Maria begged me not to stop. I thrust faster and faster into her ripe pussy with every atom of energy that I could muster. Then, and with a loud shout, I spurted a fountain of creamy jism right within her joxy. We lay happily in one another's arms, then arose for brandy and cigarettes and realized that we hadn't had pudding yet. It was another case for Room Service.

This time I had Apfelstrudel, *apples and raisins encased in a light, flaky pastry dusted with icing sugar and served with a pool of thick double cream. Maria had* Palatschinken, *an Austrian pancake that is thicker than a French crêpe and filled with berries from the woods, curd cheese and chocolate sauce. Chocolate rather dominated this course since we had also ordered* Mohr im Hemd *to be shared between us. This is a steamed, rich chocolate pudding and is served with hot chocolate sauce. Chilled whipped cream, scented with vanilla sugar, had been added just prior to serving. This was all marvellous! – and then we went back to bed.*

My cock sprang up and bounced against the bridge of Maria's nose as she took hold of my throbbing tool and bent her head down to suck it. My eyes closed when Maria took hold of my shaft in her hand, gently stroking it as she licked my hairy bollocks. She pushed my shaft flush up against my belly as she tongued my scrotum, sucking on each ball in turn until her tickling tongue brought me to a fever pitch of delight.

I moaned with delight when she released my prick, lifted her head and ran her tongue up and down the sensitive underside of my shaft, before her mouth closed over my cock and transported me into another world. I gasped – and opened up my eyes to see Maria looking up at me, a wicked twinkle playing around her startling blue eyes.

She now swirled her tongue over my knob, gently playing with my tiny prick-end 'eye'. She bobbed her head up and down, taking almost all my length inside her mouth as I pushed gently back and forth, enjoying to the full the way in which my rock-hard chopper snaked down Maria's gullet with each slippery stroke.

I rotated my hips to increase the pressure of her soft lips on my shaft as she sucked greedily upon her fleshly sweetmeat. I could feel my lust truncheon tremble as I continued to fuck her mouth. I pulled her closer to me so that my pulsating prick absolutely spurted down her throat when I came and she gurgled her delight.

Of course, we had to have coffee and brandy then and we both talked about various things. Obviously she was feeding me information (or disinformation) to be passed on to the British government. I'll tell you more about that when I get home. Yet Maria claims also to have met and talked with you on the sea voyage from Tangiers to Southampton. Given our timings, I suppose that is possible, though it implies that she is on the move all the time. In fact, she told

*me that she had to leave for Berlin on the following
morning, and did so. But Claire, darling, was she on the
voyage with you? (I'll be here for another seven days and
so I really would appreciate a letter from you.)*

*After our coffee and brandy, we went back to bed and
John Thomas was I fear, misbehaving once more. This
time, I just thrust him into Maria's luscious cunt, slammed
him in and out and swived away until she cried out and tore
a cry from me too as I came.*

*I wish Maria, the Great Whore of Europe, every success
in her endeavours to keep the Peace. But I cannot help
having an increasing sensation of unease that this may no
longer be possible.*

*On the following day, Maria having gone, I simply wan-
dered around Vienna, eventually finding myself back in the
Stephansdom quarter and sitting in a coffee house called
the Hawelka, the atmosphere of which is warm and thea-
trical, for it is populated by artists, writers, patrons of the
arts and general bohemians. For coffee, I took a Phar-
isaoer, a strong black one with whipped cream on top,
served with a small glass of rum.*

*This establishment allowed any artist who bought a cup
of coffee to hawk his works around the cliente le. Thus it
came about that I was suddenly confronted by a most
curious individual who was trying to sell me postcards that
he had painted. Beneath his battered black bowler hat, he
had long dark greasy hair, a thin, pinched and pallid face
and a skinny body that made me think that he hadn't had a
decent meal in months . . . yet he did have incredibly
arresting pale eyes. He wore a shabby black overcoat that
had clearly seen better days and his black shoes seemed
about to fall to bits.*

I looked at the postcards he was proffering to me,

wondering whether he could actually often afford the price of a cup of coffee here. These paintings were mediocre, though they did have some technical competence. Either they portrayed massive and famous buildings in Vienna or else they showed cosy little houses in the villages and mountains of Austria. I was about to dismiss this man pleasantly when I saw a publication sticking out of his coat pocket. It was called Ostara.

You will, of course, recall that, about eleven years ago, I was in Munich to meet the magicians Guido von List and Lanz von Liebenfels – though neither was a 'von' at all – and how appalled I had been by their intolerance and virulent anti-semitism. Occasionally, my agents gave me reports in response to my curiosity about people I'd met: and I had learned that the ghastly Lanz von Liebenfels was living in Vienna, practising Ceremonial Magick, preaching German supremacy and anti-semitism – and publishing and editing a journal called Ostara *expressing his ideas I was feeling in a very good mood so I bought a few of this man's mediocre postcards, praised them – he looked visibly pleased – and invited him to join me for coffee and pastries. He looked delighted.*

'I see that we have something in common,' I said. 'You are reading the magazine edited and published by my old acquaintance, Lanz von Liebenfels. Allow me to introduce myself. I'm a visitor from England. Horby's the name.'

'Hitler. Adolf Hitler.'

'How d'you do, Mr Hitler! Which coffee?' Hitler ordered Schlagobers, *a strong black coffee with whipped cream. I plumped for* Kaisermelange, *a black coffee with an egg yolk and brandy added. 'Now, which cakes or pastries? I am a man of means, Herr Hitler, and a great believer in supporting the arts. So – have as many of whatever as you like!'*

He licked his lips greedily, like a small boy let loose in the village tuck shop. I simply had Dobostorte, *a slice of rich cake that alternates equal layers of sponge and chocolate butter cream and is glazed with caramel. Yet by the time I had finished speaking with this peculiar Adolf Hitler, he had eaten his way through* Linzertorte, Sachertorte, Mohnstrudel, Guglhupf, Rehruecken *and* Esterhazytorte. *I asked after Liebenfels.*

'He is a truly great man,' *Hitler replied in his deep, slightly hoarse voice. My German is not that good but I can tell certain accents, and his was that of the Austrian petty bourgeoisie.* 'Liebenfels is absolutely right!' *Adolf Hitler proclaimed.* 'The German-speaking peoples must unite to follow their inevitable world-historic Destiny, given to us by Providence, to take over Europe.'

'Great Britain won't be too pleased with that policy, Herr Hitler,' *I murmured mildly.* 'Why, that could lead to War.'

'I want a Great WAR!' *Hitler shouted, his fist bashing the table so hard that the sound rattled all the coffee cups in the place.* 'It will purify Europe through blood and put an end to the mongrelization and decadence and syphilitic degeneracy that presently constitutes the wretched so-called "Empire" of Austria-Hungary. Our future is with* Germany! Yes! The Second Reich! *But Great Britain has nothing to fear from us, Herr Horby. After all, the English and the Germans are both from the same Anglo-Saxon race. I can simplify the globe for you. The United States of America – degenerate mongrels though most of them are – takes and keeps to its own hemisphere. Japan, which has recently defeated those ridiculous subhuman Slavs, takes the Far East. Great Britain keeps its Empire and continues to rule the waves. And Germany takes Europe up to the Ural mountains.' He gave me a small smile, evidently very* *pleased with himself. I let him run on.* Pass the rope *is a very old English game.*

'*Should the Jews be allowed to pollute our noble Aryan culture?*' *this awful little man continued relentlessly.* '*No! A thousand times, no! Look at how they cunningly inter-breed by seducing our pure German maidens . . . and this is not the worst of it! I tell you what needs to be done. We need the Superman! As Nietzsche said . . . and my friend Liebenfels is right in saying that the Superman can be* bred. *Meanwhile, the rest of us, if we are of the Master Race and if we choose, can* evolve *into becoming Supermen by the practice of Ceremonial Magick.*'

'*And* you *have?*'

'*Yes, Herr Horby!*' *I have heard some preposterous claims in my time but hearing this weedy little runt claiming to be the Superman frankly took the biscuit.* '*I have been taught by Lanz von Liebenfels and in conse-quence I have experienced altered states of consciousness and contact with supernatural beings by means of Cere-monial Magick. I* know *that it is the destiny of Germany to conquer Europe, though not England. I trust that you agree with me.*'

'*Um . . . no,*' *I responded.*

'*Idiot!*' *he yelled at me.* '*Imbecile! Moron who does not understand the plain truths I have been trying to teach you! If all of England is like you, then heaven help her! We will* smash *you. The idea of treating wars as anything other than the harshest means of settling questions of very existence is ridiculous. Every war costs blood and the smell of blood arouses in Man all the instincts that have lain within us since the beginning of the world: deeds of violence, the intoxication of murder, and many other things. Everything else is empty babble.*'

'*I'm tired of you,*' *I returned.* '*You bore me. You really are the most pathetic little wanker that it's ever been my misfortune to meet. You're a waste of time. You're a waste of space. Adolf Hitler, you pitiful apology for a human being, just* fuck off!'

He rose to his feet, quivering with fury.

'I know what you are,' he hissed through his horrible yellow teeth. 'You're a Jew!' *I raised an eyebrow in return. I've been called many things in my life, but never that. Anyway, and on the whole, I like Jews.*

'Hitler, I'm not a Jew, actually,' I replied. 'Accident of birth has made of me an English Lord. But when I hear you, I would like to be a Jew, so just piss off and do something useful with your life, like swallowing a razor blade.'

I think that this awful Adolf Hitler is the worst man I've ever met, Claire, and his energy is so terrible that I'm still recovering from his projection of his hatred as I write this.

That's all for now. I love you.

Horby

Looking at that letter here and now in 1926, I find it quite incredible that Corporal Hitler won the Iron Cross First Class – comparable to our Victoria Cross – in the Great War and subsequently managed to lead a political party and mount an attempted coup against the Bavarian State Government. I hope fervently that he rots in hell but in the meantime I'm pretty sure that we have seen the last of this odious and obnoxious individual.

(*Editor's Note*: The experiences of Horby's son Robert on meeting Adolf Hitler when the latter was the Chancellor of Germany have been chronicled by Alan Dale in *Wolverines*, New English Library, 1998.)

CHAPTER TWENTY-ONE

My letter to Claire and her letter to me crossed in the post. Here is hers:

Darling Horby,

I had such an enjoyable voyage back to Southampton and dear old Blighty. And I met such an intriguing woman, Maria von Huttendorf, spy and Great Whore of Europe, whom you have often mentioned. She really does possess tremendous charm. In no time at all after our dinner together, we were lying on the bed in my cabin suite and drinking champagne and brandy. We both undid one another's corsets – just girls together – and we put on silken robes, blue in my case and scarlet in hers.

Suddenly, she passed her hands over her high pointed breasts which were topped by great tawny nipples which soon swelled up even larger as Maria played with them, twisting these rubbery bullets between her fingers. I became increasingly interested – and my eyes widened when Maria reached down to her valise beside the bed and extracted a leather belt that she strapped around her waist.

At the front, it sported a shiny rubber affair, coloured in pink and shaped exactly like a thick, stiff cock, complete with two carefully fashioned rubber-covered balls. I had never seen anything quite like it before – and then Maria pressed her soft, curvaceous body on top of me as she kissed me passionately on the lips.

'Relax, Claire,' she crooned to me. 'This ladies' comforter has been modelled on the prick of none other than young Winston Churchill. When I fucked with him after a party last year, I made, with his consent, a plaster cast of his cock and had my dildo fashioned to his measurements by Ein, Zwei und Drei, the famous Berlin manufacturers of saucy novelties!' So I parted my thighs to allow Maria to insert this imitation shaft between my pussy lips and I must say that this action had the desired effect!

I swung my legs around her waist and locked my ankles together behind her back. Then Maria leaned forward, the dildo starting to slide right into my sopping slit. I gasped with pleasure as Maria fucked me with this smooth rubber cock. Every time she thrust it forwards it rubbed against my clitty and at the end of each thrust, when the dildo was fully embedded inside me, it nudged itself into the deepest recesses of my dripping honeypot and sent electric sparks of ecstasy shooting through my body.

I slid my hand between Maria's thighs and worked my middle finger under the dildo so as to frig her cunt. The beaming smile on Maria's flushed face helped bring me to the boil very quickly. Maria and I climaxed together.

After a glass of champagne, a cigarette, a brandy and a giggle, we returned to it. Maria took off her belt and her dildo. I felt her finger slide along the crack of my backside. I had no idea of what was coming and my whole body shuddered involuntarily when I felt her manicured fingertip insert itself into the tight, puckered entrance to my arsehole and push relentlessly inwards until it had gained entrance up to her first knuckle.

She now dropped her head down between my thighs and started to lick my cunt. As for her finger, at first it was slightly painful as the nail rasped against my tender flesh but then the pain subsided into an incredibly erotic experience as she kept her forefinger jammed inside my bottom, rocking it slightly back and forth as she continued to lick and suck my clitty.

The sensations were so strong that very soon the walls of my vagina tightened and I came with a tremendous emission of love juice. Maria swallowed every last drop of my copious emission and I really loved her for that. For a while, I rested my head against her soft, bare breasts

We made love every night on that most memorable voyage. We talked much, too, though that's something I'll tell you about on your return. She is a fascinating woman and I must say that I like her very much. Yet I don't trust her, quite honestly. Call it female intuition, if you like. She is always carrying on about her love of Peace. I can't help wondering whether, in fact, her true Agenda is that of War.

Can't wait to see you again.

All my love,

Claire

I really didn't know whether Claire was right or wrong about Maria. In any event, it was good to come back to London and have a grand fuck with my wife again.

We both had a good time during 1912 though, on a personal level, it was a relatively uneventful year. The same could hardly be said for the state of the nation. It was a year of intensified industrial conflict, with a national coal strike in March and a London docks strike in May that culminated in a transport workers' strike in June and riots in July. The Suffragettes became increasingly violent in their agitation for Votes for Women: and the authorities became increasingly violent in their retaliation. Violence in Ireland was now worse than ever and it was hard to tell whether the Protestants or the Catholics were being more unreasonable. The nation was shaken when the greatest ocean liner ever built, the *Titanic*, hit an iceberg and sank on its maiden voyage. There were also the Balkan Wars, which some thought could provoke an international European conflict.

One event that left an impression on my mind was the November debate in the House of Commons regarding the use of the cat for procuring and for crimes against women and children. I sat in the Strangers' Gallery to hear that.

The Liberal, Mr George Greenwood, moved the omission of the clause which provided that *any* procurer convicted of a second or subsequent offence should be liable in the discretion of the court to be privately flogged. 'It's a return to the methods of barbarism!' Mr Greenwood said, amid pitying smiles.

Mr Arthur Lynch, a Nationalist from West Clare, who seconded the Amendment, described the horror of flogging. He spoke of an occasion he had witnessed and declared that the sight was 'an invariable nightmare' to him now. 'The man who did the flogging rejoiced in the work,' Mr Lynch told the House. 'He was an artist in it. He laid on the lash with such such vigour that at every stroke, the victim's whole frame quivered, his eyes rolled, his muscles stood out as though they would burst through his skin and his face turned livid. Even the hardened warders present, whose hearts had been inured, turned almost sick at the sight and were unable to face it.'

'Flogging is a deterrent for men whose instincts are animal instincts,' the Unionist Mr F.B. Mildmay proclaimed.

Mr McKenna, the Home Secretary, said: 'I am informed that in London, there are a number of young men, almost entirely of foreign origin, who live on young women even to the extent of fifteen or twenty pounds a week. These men accumulate fortunes in the trade. The police say that after the first conviction, if there is power to flog, there will be nobody to flog. London has become a dumping ground for this trade by men whom the police believe will be intimidated by the fear of flogging.'

'I would like to see,' the Conservative Sir Richard Bellingham had arisen, 'yes, see . . .' he swayed unsteadily, 'yes, *flogging* introduced in regard to all offences against women and children.'

'How many members,' asked Mr Leif Jones, 'would take the "cat" in their hands and administer the flogging?'

'I would,' Sir Richard replied.

'There's a lot of maudlin sentiment about all this,' said Mr Will Crooks, a Socialist. 'I'm glad these scoundrels have a skin that can be tanned.' Even the Tories cheered him. 'If the authorities want anybody to do the flogging, they can call on me.'

'When I was at school,' the Hon Edward Wood, a Unionist, declared, 'I was whipped three times before breakfast on one occasion and I'm none the worse for it! It had an extremely deterrent effect on me.'

The anti-flogging amendment was rejected by 297 to 44, a majority of 253 for flogging. Then the house went further and put in an amendment to flog for the *first* offence.

The Conservative Mr Austin Chamberlain rather summed up the feeling of the House of Commons that day when he said: 'The infliction of physical pain on a few men would be as nothing to the infinite misery which would be prevented.'

'Happy, Horby?' Bellingham asked as we wended our way to Rules after the debate.

'No,' I replied. 'I'm all for corporal punishment among

consenting adults in private; but I find judicial flogging to be barbaric.'

'Not for pimps!' he snorted disgustedly. 'We'll have to agree to disagree, old chap.'

'But *you* use pimps sometimes!'

'Yes, and I can't stand them. I'd rather deal direct with the girls. Look, Horby, this debate about flagellation has rather given me a yen for it. And I know just the place. A spot of supper first, sir! And then a spot of fladge!'

The dinner at Rule's was as good as ever. Bellingham hadn't told me but he'd gone and got himself a Rolls-Royce and so that was how we proceeded to a certain address in Maida Vale. There we were welcomed by the fat and friendly Mrs Weston and shown up into a luxurious room with a bar where several other men we knew – and who were as decadent as we were – were seated very comfortably in front of a two-way mirror. Bellingham took Benedictine and I took Armagnac.

The show began. A handsome middle-aged man with a handle-bar moustache, wearing evening dress, walked out proudly onto the stage below. The props consisted of an Eton flogging block and a table upon which lay a birch. He picked it up and poised and swished it in the air. All of us knew that he was Viscount Diddington, a Member of the House of Lords. As he stood there, he was nervously approached by an exceptionally pretty young girl who could not have been much older than nineteen. What brilliant blonde curls she had! She also had a fantastic figure. I wondered whether her tight dress of pink satin might rip spontaneously owing to the thrust of her breasts or else split in similar fashion due to the thrust of her bottom.

My query was answered by action soon enough. Diddington really did amaze me by pulling a big razor-sharp knife out of his inside breast pocket. The girl's face evinced terror.

'Welcome, Chantal!' He grinned at her wickedly. 'You really *have* been a *very* naughty girl, haven't you . . . ?' Chantal trembled and shrank back as Diddington approached her, knife in hand. 'Who was Jack the Ripper? *I* am Jack the Ripper!' His knife ripped through her dress, slicing it from top to toe and leaving it shimmering on the floor. Diddington then sliced through every item of Chantal's underwear and, having thus stripped her naked, he flung her down onto the flogging block, ignoring her loud and tearful protests, and bound her tightly with leather straps.

'Chantal, you have been deceiving men,' said Diddington, 'and therefore you must be punished.' He promptly gave her a couple of good strokes which made their red marks on her shapely rounded buttocks. 'It is right to suffuse the white flesh of your pretty bum with a rosy tint all over.

'Will you?' Diddington roared as the next stroke of the birch descended, '*will* you, you, you naughty girl, commit such deceitful wickedness ever again? There!' *Whack*! 'And there . . .' *Whack!* 'I can't swish hard enough to express my horror at the matter,' he exclaimed, striking every blow with great deliberation and force, until the writhing pert bottom of Chantal was covered with the raised weals customary with this kind of use of the Eton flogging block. Chantal's shriehs of agony and sobbing pleas for mercy echoed loudly around the small 'theatre'.

'Ah . . .' Diddington paused to walk around the block. 'I see that your face is a deep crimson. And your bottom . . . ?' The renewed sight of her gorgeous bum, just beginning to glow scarlet, evidently so excited him that his arms seemed to be strengthened at every *swish*, in order to give her a whippier one next time.

'Ah!' Chantal cried out. 'Oh! Oh! I will never do it again. How it burns into my flesh!' Chantal moaned as she was compelled to writhe and wriggle under the fearful cuts of Diddington. And the birching went on for about twenty minutes.

Now and then, Diddington had to slacken a little for want of breath. Yet the sighs and semi-suppressed cries of Chantal urged him on.

'This is giving me a most delicious sensation,' Bellingham commented.

'Ah, yes,' I replied. 'The idea of flogging a pretty young female has obviously fired up Diddington's blood so much more than if Chantal had been a boy.'

At last, as Chantal's scarlet bottom twitched most painfully, Diddington sank back on the sofa, quite exhausted from his exertions. Then he let out a great sigh and for some moments appeared to be in perfect ecstasy at the sight of the sufferings of Chantal. Then he made sure that she was released from her bondage – but at that point she had to kneel before him and kiss the birch that he proffered.

Never mind the ethics. Diddington and Chantal left the room to fuck. Bellingham and I were both rampant by this time and simply *had* to have *our* fucks with the many delectable girls on offer there.

On 29 November 1912, I attended the House of Lords debate on flogging.

'It would be an advantage if the power was given of inflicting corporal punishment for a first offence,' said the Lord Chancellor.

'I am willing to risk one innocent man being flogged in a generation,' the Archbishop of Canterbury averred.

'I do not think that anyone can doubt the influence of flogging as a deterrent,' the Lord Chief Justice asserted.

'I certainly favour flogging for a first offence, and I am willing to run the risk of being flogged in mistake', said Lord Willoughby de Broke.

'A punishment which may not unfairly be described as "brutalizing" is a proper punishment when we are dealing with men who are brutes,' was the considered opinion of Lord Lansdowne. Lords Crewe, Lytton and Russell dissented. So did I. My speech urging that corporal punishment was perfectly proper only for consenting adults in private was ill-received. The measure was passed.

Mild-mannered Mr Justice Darling was so impressed with the grim resolve of Parliament that he took the first opportunity in January 1913 to sentence one Timothy O'Connor, aged forty, to eighteen months' hard labour and thirty strokes of the cat-o'-nine-tails for procuring his wife for immoral purposes.

I could sense a growing barbarism in the air.

CHAPTER TWENTY-TWO

I was dying for a change in February 1913 and proceeded to experience one, though in a rather curious way. On 3 March, I learned that Aleister Crowley had turned impresario and that his show, 'The Ragged Ragtime Girls', was to open at the Old Tivoli in the Strand. This revival of old music hall songs and lascivious dances was an immediate success – I for one thoroughly enjoyed it – and as Crowley later told me: 'It relieved my mind of all preoccupations with wordly affairs'. A Russian impresario, one Boris Maskaya, was impressed and so 'The Ragged Ragtime Girls' were engaged for the Summer Season at The Aquarium in Moscow. Crowley asked me if I wanted to come for the ride. *Why not?* I thought.

I left Crowley and Boris Maskaya to make their own arrangements on the trains we had agreed to take. It was easy enough to get to Paris and we all travelled first-class but on the train to Moscow I arranged to have a carriage for myself. There were ten 'Ragged Ragtime Girls' on the train. Crowley's mistress, Leila Waddell, the Maori and violinist and such a beautiful woman, was the only one who kept a head on her shoulders. Of the other nine, three were dipsomaniacs, four were nymphomaniacs and there were two who were quite hysterically prudish and ineradicably convinced that outside England, everyone was a robber, ravisher and assassin.

The stocky and strong Boris Maskaya proved to be a rather good travelling companion and his thick waves of hair were quite a contrast to Crowley's recently shaven head. It was a pleasure to sit in the bar with him and with Crowley and to hear his stories.

'Ah, Grigoriev Yefimovitch Rasputin! I know him well,' Boris declared of that strange mystic monk who had somehow become the most powerful man in the Russian Empire after the Tsar. 'I come from Tomsk in Siberia, where the Maskayas are respected as a strong, land-owning, right-wing military family. The tradition is that it is always one son as an officer to the Russian Army and one to business. I am in this generation, the business one. Now, on occasion, I had business in Povroskoe, Siberia, and there is not much to do there in the evenings other than go to the tavern. And in this little tavern, I used quite regularly to meet with Rasputin, a local peasant. I always found his company to be enjoyable and his conversation to be stimulating. But I thought that he was a bit crazy and would never amount to anything.

'He then disappeared, some said on a pilgrimage to the Holy Places,' Boris continued as he slugged back more vodka. 'Well: you can picture my astonishment when I heard that he had become the principal adviser to the Tsar and Tsarina. I went to see him at the Winter Palace in St Petersburg and it was just the same as ever. I did some business with him and then we went out and ate and drank together and had ourselves a couple of pretty whores. He's a good fellow, is Rasputin. Don't hold with all this aristocratic hatred of him. They're simply jealous of him because this peasant is fucking their women.' Thinking of my duties to British Intelligence, I asked if I could be introduced to Rasputin. 'Of course, my friend, of course!' It was at that point that another man entered the bar. His head was shaven, just like Crowley's, but he also had a thick moustache.

He said that he was a travelling salesman and since he seemed to be quite interesting, I bought him a drink – I think he wanted strong plum brandy. He told us that his name was Gurdjieff.

'I'd buy more shares in the timber companies if I were you,' he told us as he extracted a Havana cigar from his inside breast pocket, lit it and smoked it with evident enjoyment. 'The build-up in the arms trade means a great demand for sawdust here in Russia.'

'Sawdust?' Boris queried. 'In the *arms* trade?'

'Of course,' Gurdjieff returned coolly. 'Big trade in that. It's what the Russian military put into the shells.'

'Just a moment,' I said impatiently. 'Sawdust is no good in shells. The shells will be useless.'

'Of course,' Gurdjieff returned in his deep, rumbling voice. 'But have you never heard of corruption? The manufacturers of arms are bribing the military, which is extorting money from the government and getting it via the payers of taxes. You are right, my dear sirs. The shells filled with sawdust are indeed quite useless. That is why Russia lost the war against Japan and will lose the next war against Germany. You see, men of business such as ourselves must take this into account.'

'Interesting,' Boris commented. 'But may I enquire into the exact nature of your business?'

'Profit,' Gurdjieff returned as the train drew up with a jolt in Warsaw. 'We profit from everything. Nothing can stop it. War or no war, it's always the same for us. We always profit.' He picked up his leather valise. 'Why should I care if millions of sleeping men soon kill millions of other sleeping men? The only serious business of life is to wake up.' With a shark-like grin, Gurdjieff bade us good day and left the train.

'Strange fellow,' Boris commented as the train moved off. At that moment, Aleister Crowley came into the bar, accompanied by his ten girls. I thought it was a pity that he hadn't met Gurdjieff. Meanwhile, a voluptuous blonde and member of the troupe called Sally kept wriggling her arse within her satin silver dress in a way I found to be utterly enticing. I bought her some brandy and then enticed her to come and take more with me in my carriage. After admiring it, she lay down on the bed and stretched back languidly in open invitation. I knelt down and massaged her lovely breasts as she purred with pleasure.

Taking hold of my hand and pressing it against her taut nipples, Sally encouraged me to suck the stalky darlings. I took all the liberties I desired with her, kissing her pretty breasts and frigging her wet pussy with my fingers. Sally stroked my cock and pulled me over her.

'Fuck my titties!' she cried out. With that, she tugged my chopper forward between her delectable breasts and I rubbed my shaft between the perfectly rounded globes while she cupped my balls in her hand. This was a delicious sensation but before I could spend, Sally moved my cock further upwards and brought the tip of my empurpled prick to her waiting lips. Having one's cock sucked is a delightful experience. 'Sucking his penis,' she sighed, 'is the deepest, most sensitive way in which a woman can pay tribute to her lover's masculinity'. With that, Sally gave me the most exquisite tonguing, working her lips around my shaft, licking and lapping all the while as she traced long, lasciviously wet kisses upon my quivering cock.

The tip of her magic tongue now encircled the head of my rod and was tickling and working its way around the tiny 'eye' on the top of the bulbous dome. Her teeth scraped the tender skin so delectably as Sally drew me in between her luscious lips. I gasped audibly when she lowered her head and ran her tongue along the sensitive underside of my throbbing tool, sending almost unbearable waves of ecstasy sweeping through my entire frame.

Yet every time this wicked girl sensed that I was on the verge of coming, she stopped her sensual sucking, thus prolonging our mutual enjoyment which for me was reaching new, previously unscaled heights of intensity. Sally's head bobbed up and down over my rigid tool until a huge shudder of pleasure shot through me and a fountain of spunk shot out of my cock and slithered down her throat.

Sally swallowed every drop and then flopped beside me on my bed for a while. As I have remarked before, I adore having sex on trains. Well, here we were going from Poland to Russia and I was rejoicing in the constant *clickety-click*. We took brandy together and in no time at all, it seemed, my prick was rising up again. I wrapped my arms around Sally.

We locked together in a passionate exploration of each other's bodies. She responded to my every move.

'I was thinking of taking my time . . .' she moaned, 'but my pussy is juicing so quickly . . .' Without further ado, she *straddled* herself over me and impaled herself on my cock. Then Sally rode me as if she were riding a bucking bronco, pounding the gorgeous, soft cheeks of her arse against my thighs as I gyrated my hips upwards and felt her cunny muscles grip my shaft as my rod pounded the depths of her clingy moist quim.

For at least five full minutes, we fucked without a pause until I could hold back no longer and, with a low, wordless growl, I flooded her cunt with a deluge of frothy jism. This fierce gush quickly brought on Sally's own climax and she shuddered to a thunderous orgasm as if an electric shock had crackled through her cunny.

With my hot, throbbing cock trapped inside her sweet

quim, Sally clenched her thighs together for one last ecstatic spend as I fell back exhausted. Again we drank cognac to recover. I had thoughtfully put by a case of Veuve Cliquot, so we opened a bottle and drank that too while chatting about things in general. I had also brought a hamper for emergencies and since I hadn't found the dining car to be that good – and neither had she – we opened some tins and packages and ate smoked foods: smoked oysters, tinned crab, smoked ham – and also German black bread with pickled herrings, Camembert and Brie with thin Captain's biscuits; and then some nice English biscuits with an orange filling that were covered with milk chocolate. This certainly revived us as the train steamed on its way.

Sally swung herself around so that she now faced the window and could see the flat plains of Poland go by. Then she leaned forward, pushing out the beautiful cheeks of her shapely bottom so that they were only inches away from my face as she closed her lascivious lips over the bulbous head of my shaft, which was still liberally coated with our mingled love juices. Sally's delicious sucking really did make my shaft stiffen properly again, and I gasped with pleasure at the enrapturing sensations caused by her warm, moist tongue as she gulped more of my cock further inside her mouth.

With the tip of her tongue, she began to strum the underside of my shaft, working her way wetly along its full twitching length. I closed my eyes and gasped with delight as, after just two or three swipes of her subtle tongue, my fully erect chopper was once again as hard as iron. At that instant, she pulled her mouth away.

'Mmm, what a tasty cock!' Sally declared. 'But I'd – rather than suck you off again – yes, I'd far rather you poked me doggie style.' With that, Sally leaned forward and impudently stuck her creamy bum cheeks in the air. 'Go on,

Horby!' she cried out. 'My nice wet tunnel of lust is ready and waiting for you!' Taking a deep breath, I guided my pulsating prick beneath her rolling buttocks, sighing with delight as my shaft thrust its way into her dripping quim.

Sally squealed happily as we fell into a fresh bout of wild fucking. She pushed her bottom back to force her cunny along the full length of my throbbing boner and I slewed my eager shaft in and out of Sally's exquisite cunt. My balls felt full to bursting and I could not delay the ultimate pleasure.

It came as no surprise to us when I suddenly exploded into a climactic release.

Sally was a nice girl. She was also intelligent enough to understand that what we'd enjoyed was simply a fuck between friends and nothing more. As our train steamed towards the heart of Russia, I had another girl called Jean. Crowley didn't call them 'The Ragged Ragtime Girls' for nothing. But Jean was not as memorable as Sally. With her I had a perfectly decent fuck, no more. Crowley was busy fucking with Leila and Boris Maskaya made a meal out of two girls called Roberta and Elaine. It was a very civilized journey on the whole – and in the holes.

I looked forward to meeting Rasputin, courtesy of Boris. And I couldn't help but think of that strange man Gurdjieff whom we had met on this train that was going from West to East.

In fact, I enjoyed my time in Moscow. 'The Ragged Ragtime Girls' caused a sensation and the house was packed every night.

'A success, Mr Crowley, a great success,' Boris Maskaya said to him. Unfortunately, Crowley had a quarrel with Leila and took up with a young Hungarian girl, one Anny Ringler. She was tall, tense and as lean as a starving leopardess, with wild, insatiable eyes and a long, straight thin mouth, a scarlet scar that seemed to ache with the anguish of hunger for some satisfaction beyond earth's power to supply.

'She can only feel through pain,' Crowley told me. 'My own means of making her happy is to inflict physical cruelties upon her as she directs me.' Eventually, the Summer Season came to an end. Boris Maskaya made money, so did Crowley and so did 'The Ragged Ragtime Girls'.

'The Ragged Ragtime Girls' went home to London. I decided to travel on to St Petersburg with Boris Maskaya and Crowley in order to meet Rasputin. Crowley told us that he had been inspired by Moscow to write what I regard as being his greatest poems: *Hymn To Pan*, *The Gnostic Mass*, *The City of God*, and *The Fun of the Fair*. I also agree with his remarks about Moscow:

'In Moscow,' said Boris Maskaya, 'in the summer months, day fades into night, night brightens into day with imperceptible subtlety, no?'

'Quite so, Mr Maskaya,' Crowley returned. 'I find that there is in the air itself a spiritual clarity which is indescribable. From time to time, the bells reinforce the silence with an unearthly music that never jars nor tires. The hours stream by so intoxicatingly that the idea of time itself disappears from consciousness.'

Yes.

CHAPTER TWENTY-THREE

It was an absolutely extraordinary occasion, that glorious Spring day in the Winter Palace of St Petersburg. There I was, having just finished a superb dinner hosted by Rasputin, at which Boris Maskaya, Aleister Crowley and the mysterious George Ivanovitch Gurdjieff were present; along with gorgeous girls of the court. There were Helena and Natasha from Russia, Sarah of England, Gloria of Italy and Sabrina of France. They dressed in tight, exquisite silk and their faces and their figures were quite dazzling. They all could have made a rather grand living as upper-class courtesans but in fact they came from good and wealthy families and gave their favours for free to men whom they liked. They were all clearly devoted to Rasputin.

I should explain how this came about. Boris Maskaya, pleased with his profits from Crowley's 'The Ragged Ragtime Girls', had promised to introduce me and also Crowley to Rasputin were we to travel to St Petersburg. Thus it was that we found ourselves passing through many magnificent chambers, attended by guards and footmen, and were finally ushered into the magnificent chamber where Rasputin sat, rather like Father Christmas at Yuletide in Selfridges. There was some numbering system that I didn't quite understand. What it meant was that Boris would see him first, then there would be this old, fat and ragged peasant woman, then I could approach the great man and after that it would be Crowley's turn.

Rasputin, a thin, short, wiry man with wild black hair and a wilder black beard, greeted Boris warmly, as an old friend. I think that Boris wanted to sell boots for the Army. Business without bribery was then impossible in Russia, so Boris handed to Rasputin a note of one thousand pounds sterling. Rasputin held it in his right hand.

'The deal is done, Mr Maskaya!' he exclaimed. 'It's always such a pleasure to see an old friend. Why don't you take a seat here, since I have a number of people to see prior to the excellent dinner I shall offer you?' Boris acquiesced. The servants of Rasputin promptly gave him champagne.

The old rag-bag of a peasant woman now approached Rasputin. She was a fellow villager from Povroskoe and had travelled all this way to see him because her daughter was desperately ill and required an operation to save her life which the old woman could not afford.

'Take this.' Rasputin promptly handed over the banknote for one thousand pounds sterling that Boris had given him. 'Should be more than enough. Andrei!' he shouted at one of his many servants. 'Ensure that Mrs Natasha Mikalovitch Nustankimkaya receives a fair exchange rate.' He turned back to the old peasant woman. 'This should be more than enough. Travel first-class back to Povroskoe.'

'Thank you, sir . . .' The old lady fell down on her knees and kissed the feet of Rasputin. He looked visibly embarrassed. Eventually she was escorted out of the room.

The interviews that I and Crowley had with this intriguing man were short. Both of us said that we wanted to speak with him about Magick in general and Sex-Magick in particular.

'*Ve-ry* good,' he growled. 'Come to dinner with my good

friend Boris!' And it was at this dinner that we met Gurdjieff once again. Rasputin introduced him as 'an old friend'.

The servants brought barrels into this magnificent dining-room. I thought that they might contain beer but Rasputin tore off the lids to reveal the finest black caviar, which he ladled out with a big soup spoon. After that there was a lobster and a crab, already cracked, on the plate for everybody. Rare prime rib of beef followed.

I noticed that in this large room with its roaring fire there were five beds. Suddenly, Rasputin grabbed the Countess Gloria, who had been sitting on his left, and positively hurled her onto one of these beds. Gloria appeared to be only too happy about the matter. This dark-haired beauty unbuttoned the trousers of Rasputin to bring out his enormous, rampaging cock.

'My, my!' Gloria exclaimed. 'What a hot shaft! And what a lovely big chopper! I'm going to have some grand fun with this monster lollipop!' This was obviously a sexual signal, so I grabbed the hand of Countess Helena and led this gay, willowy blonde bitch to another bed. Crowley had clearly developed a taste for Russian women, since he seized the Countess Natasha. Boris went for Lady Sarah of England.

'Well, my dear,' Gurdjieff gazed at the Marquise, Lady Sabrina of France. 'I think it's up to us.'

Helena slid her hand along my stiff, throbbing shaft. Then she delicately fingered the wide crown of my bulbous prick before she pulled it closer to her mouth so she could begin licking and lapping all around the empurpled dome.

I gave a throaty gurgle of delight as Helena circled her tongue all around the head of my prick and then I let out a yelp as she crammed as much of my thick tool as she could take into her mouth.

'Relax, my darling,' she said as she suddenly came up for

air. 'Lie back, enjoy my cock-suck and look at everybody else.' I sank back in bliss but took her advice.

Lady Sarah was sucking the thick cock of Boris with relish, varying the intensity and timing before she released it momentarily to look at his face. His eyes were closed and he was breathing heavily as Sarah returned to her sweet labours, giving his knob a long, swirling lick before plunging her mouth down to give the ridge a teasing nibble with her teeth.

Meanwhile, Crowley had been driven so wild by Grand Duchess Natasha that, with a hoarse cry, he wrenched his cock out of her mouth and tore off the rest of her clothes. Natasha laughed and climbed over him. Facing his feet, she lowered herself gently upon him with her hairy pussy directly over his mouth as she leaned forward to resume gobbling his quivering shaft. Crowley was clearly more than happy to repay the exquisite pleasure of her twirling tongue for he immediately parted Natasha's love-lips and pressed his mouth firmly against her moist pussy.

'Ah!' Sabrina cried out to Gurdjieff and anyone else who might be listening or watching. 'Warm waves of sheer ecstasy shimmy out from my cunt and I gasp with delight as I bend over you!'

'Darling Sabrina,' Gurdjieff responded, 'Ah! What a delight it is to roll my tongue all around your cunt as you bend over me, working your mouth up and down my blue-veined boner! Oh!' he exclaimed – and with good reason. Sabrina was running her teeth gently along the sensitive underside of his prick and then, sucking in his smooth, fleshy head, flicking her tongue teasingly over its slitted end.

Meanwhile, Rasputin, who had indulged in a spell of cunt-licking with Gloria, withdrew his mouth and slipped two fingers into her open wetness, sliding them in and out and visibly arousing both of them so much that it was clear from the expression on his face that he could only get satisfaction from a fully-blown fuck.

I felt exactly the same way . . . Helena seemed to share my feelings since she grasped my cock with both hands and rubbed it up to bursting point. Then she moved her soaking slit down over my thick shaft, sitting with her bum cheeks on my thighs as she rode up and down on my palpitating prick. I spurted my spunk into her and she shivered and shuddered with the rapture of it all. It was a wonderful fuck! But now we once more looked around the room to see what everyone else was doing.

Crowley had grasped the buttocks of Natasha and was squeezing them.

'Oh, your luscious tool!' Natasha was crying out. 'With your every thrust, you make my cunny muscles contract with your every downward thrust to our mutual ecstatic delight!'

'Why are Russian women so articulate?' Crowley murmured as he carried on slam-banging away.

'You wonderful man!' Helena shrieked out at Rasputin. 'Oh! that's too much!' she screeched as he reached down with his hand, obviously to invade her arsehole. Rasputin then began to force his strong shaft upwards in a fierce series of powerful jabs. 'Oh! Your prancing prick is trembling!' He gave a mighty heave upwards and it was obvious that he had spurted a stream of sticky jism into her cunt. 'My God!' Helena exclaimed. 'You have shot so much spunk into my quim that my pussy has overflowed and rivulets of your jism and my own cuntal juices have run over your quivering cock and are streaming down my thighs.'

Sarah, meanwhile, had pulled back from Boris in order to show him her forefinger sliding in between the pink pussy lips that protruded out of the flaxen hair between her thighs.

'Oh, what a copious ejaculation into my seething cunt!' Sabrina cried out to Gurdjieff. The prick of Boris was thick and stiff too as he rubbed his own forefinger up and down the cunt lips of Lady Sarah. The prick of Boris had clearly been further stiffened by the erotic sight of this pretty girl lewdly playing with her pussy. Now she was slicking her fist up and down his swollen shaft until it was visibly as hard as an iron bar.

Since I prefer doing to watching, I grabbed a bottle of cognac and poured a generous amount onto Helena's blonde bush, then rubbed my forefinger along her crack until she was begging me to fuck her properly with my big stiff cock. I licked and lapped up all the brandy prior to prodding my rod into my gorgeous girl with a mighty thrust. She gasped.

'Let's experiment now,' I said. She nodded as I withdrew my cock and asked her to sit on the bed with her legs dangling down and her feet on the floor.

'With pleasure,' Helena replied, cradling my throbbing cock in one hand as I rubbed her nipples up to erection. I moved between her legs and she took hold of my colossal chopper then gently placed its knob on the entrance to her cunny.

'And that's just what I'm going to give you!' I responded as I raised her legs a little higher so that Helena could rest her slim calves on my shoulders as I drove my thick prick into her willing wet cunt until my thatch of curly brown pubic hairs became entangled with Helena's blonde muff. Her yells of ecstasy were accompanied by the slap of my balls against her peachy bottom . . . WHAM! How I spurted into her! We hugged each other and lay together for a while, then we turned around to see that Gurdjieff and Sabrina, Crowley and Natasha, Boris and Sarah, and Rasputin and Gloria had all come to fucking and to orgasm. Rasputin then rose to his feet, thanked all the women for their attentions and informed them that: 'For the next two hours, it is the talk of men.'

The girls smiled and left the room. They were only some of the greatest ladies of several nations being ordered around by a peasant. Rasputin now produced a bottle of pepper vodka.

'What is your ultimate purpose, Mr Crowley?' he demanded as he poured out glasses for all of us once the ladies had left the room.

'Do what thou wilt shall be the whole of the Law,' Crowley answered in a sincere and solemn tone.

'I hope, Mr Crowley,' Gurdjieff came in, 'that you are not merely advocating self-indulgent nonsense.'

'Certainly not!' Crowley returned indignantly. '*Do what you want?* That's fatuous. All I'm saying is that you must find your true Will and do it. We must realize ourselves as animals before we can know ourselves as Gods. I say that you should find and do your True Will. This Law of Nature bids water to seek its level, sheep to eat grass and wolves to eat sheep.'

'This is all very well, Mr Crowley,' said Gurdjieff. 'Myself, I do not disagree. You are saying to humanity: "The truth shall make you free!" '

'Yes!' Crowley returned.

'But most human beings are asleep,' Gurdjieff objected. 'They do not *wish* to be free.'

'In that case,' Crowley replied, 'they are like farm animals and one hopes that they will breed well. One should simply be kind to them.'

'Will they be kind to *you*?' Rasputin asked.

'I am reminded,' Gurdjieff said, 'of the ancient Chinese curse: "May you live in interesting times".'

'No problem about that,' Crowley retorted. 'We do.'

The eyes of Crowley, Rasputin and Gurdjieff were so magnetic and blazing at that moment. But so were the eyes of Boris and myself.

'Well, I'm just a human being,' I declared. 'Just a man. And you three seem to me to be sitting here claiming some sort of superiority, as though you're superhuman. Maybe you are and maybe you aren't – but don't look down your noses at me. You can say that I am simply *homo sapiens*, a product of my genetics and environmental coditioning. Fine. But let me tell you that *homo sapiens* has evolved through our unique ability to see that, to evolve beyond it and to do this through Science and Art.'

'Well spoken, sir!' Boris declared heartily. 'Oh, yes, I have studied Evolution, so tell me, you three wise monkeys, on which planet in the skies has Evolution accelerated faster than on Earth?' Rasputin, Gurdjieff and Crowley looked at Boris and me with respect and then at one another.

'If only more men spoke as you two!' Rasputin exclaimed.

'And more women, possibly . . . ?' Crowley murmured.

'Given such splendid words, it is unfortunate,' Gurdjieff rumbled. 'The worst war of all time is coming.'

'No!' Rasputin shouted. 'I will use all my influence to prevent this complete disaster.'

'Sir Rasputin . . .' Crowley was shaking his head slowly and sadly. 'There is no alternative. A great war is coming whether you want it or not.'

'Whatever,' Rasputin returned. 'I live and die for peace, bread and land for my people and for the Romanov dynasty.'

'Well and good enough, sir!' Gurdjieff exclaimed. 'It's simply that you will die for it.'

'I am, in common with you, sir, a man of certainties,' Rasputin returned. 'I have declared my terms. I do not care to exist on any other. If you say that I am going to die, I laugh . . . shall we join the ladies?'

Remembering that scene now (1926), I recall how Prince Yussopov was the principal conspirator in the assassination of Rasputin. Completely contrary to all traditions of Russian hospitality, he invited him to a cellar in his home and gave him cakes and wine filled with enough cyanide to kill a room full of people. Rasputin ate and drank and asked for more. Yussopov pulled out his revolver and shot him six times. Rasputin fell over. Yussopov rushed upstairs yelling: 'I've killed Rasputin!' His fellow conspirators came down the stairs, only to see Rasputin crawling up them. So they all pulled out their revolvers and fired bullets until Rasputin lay still. Then they all picked him up but, as they were carrying him through the courtyard, the 'corpse' came to life again. They shot him some more and also clubbed him with their revolver butts. Then they carried him to the Little Nevka River, broke the ice and threw him in. No, he didn't drown. He died of exposure and suffocation while trying to break through the ice. The Russian Revolution followed soon after in that most terrible year of 1917.

I don't know what has happened to the genial Boris Maskaya. Crowley is presently under vicious attack from the gutter press. Gurdjieff is presently making a fortune in Fontainebleau where, at his 'spiritual' centre, he makes a fortune by insulting wealthy and idle people.

CHAPTER TWENTY-FOUR

I don't think that I shall ever forget the letter I received from my wife on 1 August 1914. She had gone to Paris ahead of me because Rosemary and Douglas were at last to be married there and Claire would be the Bridesmaid. I would follow later.

Darling Horby,

Everything is in order for the Wedding between Rosemary and Douglas, with whom we'll be staying, so please come as soon as you can. Meanwhile, what we've all been dreading has finally come to pass. As I understand it, on account of the assassination of the Austrian Archduke in Sarajevo, Bosnia by Serbian nationalists, Austria-Hungary has declared war on Serbia with full support from Germany. Russia, 'protector of the Slavs', has mobilized against both Austria-Hungary and Germany. Since France is locked in a close alliance with Russia, I feel that it's only a matter of time before Germany declares war on both Russia and France. And if the Germans decide to invade France, the easiest route is through neutral Belgium, the safety of which Great Britain has guaranteed under Treaty: and so the 'Splendid Isolation' of Lord Salisbury, with which we began the century, will be abolished in favour of a European war.

Mind you, everyone seems to be screaming out for War.

279

The crowds in Paris certainly are. I gather from the papers that more positive 'screaming out' for War is being done by crowds in Berlin, Vienna, Prague, Moscow, St Petersburg and London. I think that it is the end of civilization as we have known it.

Meanwhile, we're all trying to get on as best as we can. Do you remember Ram Singh and Amin Shah? They're both here in Paris for the Wedding and both men have weathered age gracefully. I decided to go to bed with Ram Singh. After a fine dinner, courtesy of Douglas and Rosemary, we retired to my room with cognac, Armagnac, burgundy and Beaune. We sat on the bed and Ram Singh leaned forward to kiss me. I responded immediately, sliding my tongue between his teeth as his tongue probed inside my open mouth.

It was good to know that I was still attractive to him. Had I enticed him by dancing down the stairs yesterday evening with my bare breasts bouncing up and down under my virtually transparent camisole as my bottom cheeks jiggled enticingly, covered only by my silky skin-tight knickers? Anyway, here and now, my senses began to reel when his expert hands moved under my camisole to fondle my naked breasts.

'Claire,' Ram Singh whispered in my ear, 'I've been willing this moment from the very first instant that I saw you again!' This randy artist slipped his hands onto my tits, pressing them together and showering them with noisy wet kisses.

Then Ram Singh buried his face in my soft, rounded spheres and lunged at my quivering nipples which instantly hardened under his lips. An erotic shiver sped through me when he nipped each one lightly between his teeth. Then he squeezed my breasts together, taking both nipples in his mouth simultaneously, flicking each engorged cherry with his tongue before sucking them in a strong, powerful rhythm that caused me to moan with delight. My blood was up now.

Climbing from the lap of Ram Singh, my breasts smeared with a mixture of perspiration and saliva, I tugged open the buttons of his fly – and out sprang his thick, stiff cockshaft. I held the huge pulsating tool in my hands and informed him that he could fuck me as long as we both undressed.

I wanted to enjoy the sight of his manly frame. As he rapidly undressed, I gazed with pleasure on his broad shoulders and deep chest, which was lightly covered with curly hair – though it was his thick cock that most attracted me as it stood majestically upright between his muscular thighs. Taking hold of his blue-veined boner, I fisted my hand at a great pace up and down his hot, smooth shaft as I planted a big wet kiss on that superb empurpled head.

I pressed his love truncheon into the cleft between my firm, jutting titties. I urged him to cream my titties with his spunky jism. I continued to wrap my fingers even more tightly around his cock as I continued to frig his pulsating prick. I don't exactly want to boast, darling, but, as you yourself will readily admit, no man worthy of the name has managed to hold back for more than a minute of this bosomy massage.

Sure enough, very soon Ram moaned as, in a tumultuous climax, he let fly a tremendous fountain of frothy seed and sprayed a white necklace of sticky spunk across my breasts. With one hand I jerked his quivering shaft from side to side and with the other I smeared his copious emission all over my rubbery nipples.

Then I pulled his prick upwards and sucked his knob so that he spurted the final gush of seed into my mouth. We *lay within one another's arms for a time: and then he astonished me by telling me that there was quite a queue for me.*

'Very well,' I said. 'Who's next?' Ram Singh made his exit . . . and enter Amin Shah! Our eyes locked together and we began to kiss. Yes, I kissed him passionately upon the lips. It had been so long! I then insisted that he too should divest himself of his clothes.

'Darling Claire . . .' he said softly before our mouths melded together again and my arms were once more wrapped around this gorgeous man. 'It is as if your soft, trembling body has been fashioned especially for my touch.'

I arched to it, sighing and gasping as I responded with my fingertips, my lips and my tongue. Caught up in an exquisite whirlpool of sensation, I flung myself on top of this man, whose cock was now pressing insistently between my thighs. Amin Shah responded by sliding his hands appreciatively down my curves, caressing my firm breasts and kissing my horned-up wine-red nipples, which now hardened so sensually under his nibbling. Down and down he went until his face was buried between my legs and his lips were only inches away from my thick fleece of curly pussy hair.

'Do kiss my cunny, darling,' I sighed softly as I pushed his head deeper into my crotch, opening my legs and then clamping my thighs around his head with a long, contented purr as Amin Shah began to lick my swollen pussy lips. His tongue swished around my quim, delving, probing and sliding from the top of my long crack to the base of my juicy slit, lapping up the fragrant love juices that were already dripping out of my honeypot. Amin Shah clearly delighted in muff-diving and had obviously acquired substantial skill at this noble art.

I moaned with joy and shivered all over when he stopped

licking my quim in order to pay homage to my clitty, which had hardened up like a tiny nut. He took my love-bud between his lips and nibbled its fat base with his teeth. When he began lashing my clitty with his tongue, my throbbings grew into twitches, the twitches into tremors and the tremors into convulsions until I shrieked out my delight as the delicious sensations of a shattering come swept through me.

I hauled myself up and clutched his pulsating erection in my hands. With a salacious giggle, I wound strands of my silky hair to make a web around the base of his shaft while stroking it slowly and feeling his tool throb under my gentle touch.

Then I moved my head forward and licked his wiry pubic bush. I moved my face slowly from side to side, enjoying to the full the voluptuous grazing of his rock-hard prick against my soft cheek. I looked up at Amin Shah and smiled as I moved my lips across the smooth, uncapped dome of his knob and kissed the tiny 'eye' out of which some drops of salty moisture had already started to ooze.

He let out a gasp as my tongue circled the empurpled head of his prick, savouring the taste of cock as I drew his shaft between my generous lips. Amin Shah cried out as my warm fingers fondled his balls as I sucked his shaft with intense verve.

He instinctively began to slew his prick in and out of my willing, wet mouth. I slurped happily on my fleshy lollipop.

'Claire!' Amin Shah roared suddenly. 'I feel that the sweet surge of seed is about to burst out of my cock!' Certainly he was panting hard. 'I can't hold back! I'm coming!' I did not attempt to pull away. I continued to suck his cock until, with a rasping growl, he shot his load and spurted a potent fountain of hot sticky jism down my throat.

'Good heavens!' I exclaimed, after I had greedily gulped it all down and licked and lapped his trembling tool until I had milked it dry. 'What an abundant spend, Amin!' I added, having pulled back my head and having released his now flaccid tool from its succulent prison. 'Oh, I do like sucking off a nice, thick prick like yours! I'm sure that I could happily gobble it for a full hour – but of course, this will never happen because all you men squirt off too quickly.'

Anyway, darling, do get here soon since I would much rather fuck with you than anyone else.

All my love,

Claire.

I arrived in Paris a few days later and the place was in a panic. Although I had a most intoxicating fuck with Claire and found it such a pleasure to see Douglas and Rosemary, Ram Singh and Amin Shah, Mrs Joan Smythe and (alas!) Wilfred Sedgewick again, there really was a most appalling crisis which was not alleviated by the otherwise welcome arrival of Emily Ward-Bishop and her nonentity of a husband, Jane and Alison with their pompous prats of husbands, Maria von Huttendorf with some nonentity of a husband in tow – and even the goodly Captain Jack Rivers with a nonentity of a wife and Sir Richard Bellingham with Davina.

Great Britain had declared war on Germany and Austria-Hungary, and we really weren't doing terribly well. The matter justified all my worst fears. Some months earlier, I had dined with Sir John French, Commander-in-Chief of the British Expeditionary Force, and his leading General, Sir Douglas Haig. This had been a deeply depressing experience since both men detested one another, which did not augur well. French had distinguished himself as a cavalry commander during the Boer War, lifting the siege of Kimberly, although he had all but destroyed the Cavalry Division in the process. He told me that any future war could be won by a good old-fashioned British cavalry charge.

Haig disagreed with him, arguing that any battle could be won by a good old-fashioned British infantry bayonet charge. I tentatively raised the issue of the American Civil War, which to my mind had demonstrated that modern technology had given the advantage to the defence, what with trenches and barbed wire and machine-guns.

'Nonsense!' French boomed.

'For once I agree with you, sir,' Haig rasped. 'Horby, listen to someone who *knows. The machine-gun is a vastly over-rated weapon.*'

These were the Generals in charge of the 100,000-strong British Expeditionary Force sent to defend Belgium against 1,000,000 Germans. From our point of view, absolutely everything went wrong. On 14 August, General Joffre, the French Commander-in-Chief, a man who had never commanded an army in action, who knew nothing of General Staff work and who neither wrote nor read memoranda, ordered an all-out assault on Alsace-Lorraine. For the Germans, this battle was like a turkey shoot since it was easy to spot the brightly coloured red-and-blue blue uniforms of the advancing French. The lances and sabres of the French cavalry and the bayonets of the infantry never came close to the enemy lines and they were mown down mercilessly by machine-gun and artillery fire. The flower of the French Army perished in Lorraine. We were told that there were 100,000 casualties: but I have since learned that it was more like 500,000.

Hindenburg and Ludendorff then smashed the attempted Russian invasion at the Masurian Lakes and Tannenberg on 27–30 August, clearing German soil of Russian troops and taking 30,000 wounded and 95,000 unwounded Russian prisoners.

Meanwhile, the German armies in the West had taken the crucial fortress of Liège on 16 August and were charging through Belgium to meet the heavily outnumbered British Expeditionary Force at Mons on 23–24 August. An extraordinary thing happened there, though. Arthur Machen was at this time working for the London *Evening News*. His editor requested a patriotic short story of the supernatural from him. Machen duly obliged and turned in some dismal piece of hack-work: in *The Bowmen*, St George and his Angels come to the rescue of the British Army at Mons.

There was an absolute *storm* of letters from the soldiers on the Western Front, claiming that Machen had invented nothing. They had with their own eyes *seen* the Angels coming to their rescue at Mons. Arthur Machen thought this most improbable but for a season was catapulted into a national fame which his finest works had failed to find. Time and time again, he insisted that he had written fiction but nobody believed him. *The Bowmen* sold over 100,000 copies when issued as a book. Unfortunately for Machen, the *Evening News* held the copyright and so he didn't make a penny out of it.

The whole matter is still a mystery. How *did* merely 100,000 British soldiers manage to hold off 1,000,000 German soldiers for two days at Mons?

But there was no time for any more fairy tales now. The British were forced into a fast retreat. By the beginning of September, the German military machine, in its full might, was coming down on Paris like a hammer on a nail.

'Looks rather serious, doesn't it, Ladies and Gentlemen?' the mysterious Douglas spoke up after giving us all a particularly excellent dinner. He was looking more cadaverous than ever; though my beloved ex-tutor, Rosemary, really had ripened into beauteous maturity. 'Our wedding will be tomorrow, 5th September. But there's more to it than that! Naturally there will be magical ceremonies. Naturally there will be sex. But this time, we've got to put the whole caboodle together with one central aim. Ladies and Gentlemen, kindly fuck in the cause of Western civilization!'

CHAPTER TWENTY-FIVE

The wedding of Douglas and Rosemary was held at a house owned by Douglas on the Champs Élysées. The venue of the ceremony was a Temple they had created together on the top floor and it was surrounded by glass, so that the visitor could look at the stars. We could also hear the booming of the big guns in the distance. The Germans had a giant cannon – Big Bertha – that was launching deadly shells from fifty miles away.

I don't know quite how Douglas did it, but certainly he was not looking a day older than when I had first met him way back in 1899. Rosemary *had* visibly aged but she had done so most graciously. She was approaching forty now and yet was more sexy than ever. I love that ripe maturity of a beautiful woman: it is rather like drinking a vintage burgundy.

Douglas announced that he and Rosemary had already been legally married in the Town Hall of Finsbury in London with Sir Richard Bellingham and Davina as witnesses.

'However,' he continued, '*this* is a *sacred* ceremony.' All of us were wearing robes as we had been told to do. Rosemary wore a silken robe of scarlet and Douglas a silken robe of black. Claire and I also wore silk, crimson in her case and royal blue in mine. 'My bride and I,' Douglas went on, 'will lie on this bed here, before the altar sacred unto Pan, and we shall fuck. I hope that you will also have a good fuck for yourselves and that you will wish us well. I also implore you to think very hard as you fuck on behalf of France in general and Paris in particular so as to prevent a conquest by the German Empire.'

With these words, he spreadeagled his bride before the tall black candles and the magnificent sculptured statue of Pan. Ripping the thin silk from her body, an action which made her sigh with unalloyed delight, he produced his thick prick from beneath his robe and thrust it deep into her.

Taking up the cue and noticing the many couches and beds, we all imitated his example. Claire and I, seizing a bed embarked upon a good, straight, old-fashioned fuck, just like our host and hostess. By contrast, Bellingham and Davina, who had also seized a bed, went at it in doggy fashion. Curiously enough, the willowy Alison and the voluptuous Jane had dumped their dull husbands for this occasion. The former was fucking with Ram Singh and the latter with Amin Shah. Captain Jack Rivers was having his massive cock sucked by his buxom wife. Emily Ward-Bishop was having her cunt licked by her husband and was visibly rejoicing in the matter. Mrs Joan Smythe was having her toes sucked by Wilfred Sedgewick. Maria von Huttendorf had dumped her husband and was masturbating on her own.

The heat of our sex was building up before the statue of Pan. I was reminded of the poem that Crowley had written in Moscow:

> I am thy mate, I am thy man,
> Goat of thy flock, I am gold, I am god,
> Flesh to thy bone, flower to thy rod.
> With hoofs of steel I race on the rocks
> Through solstice stubborn to equinox.

And I rave; and I rape and I rip and I rend,
Everlasting, world without end,
Mannikin, maiden, maenad, man,
In the might of Pan.
Io Pan! Io Pan Pan! Pan! Io Pan!

It was then that Douglas, in the midst of fucking Rosemary, demanded that all of us, in the midst of our relishing of sex, proceeded to chant in favour of Paris. We all went from 'Io Pan!' to 'Io Paris!'

Did our fucking and our chanting and our sucking actually do any good? Well, I only know the facts that followed.

We only learned after the Great War that the German Supreme Commander, Colonel-General of the German General Staff, Helmuth von Moltke, nephew of the legendary victor of the Austro-Prussian and Franco-Prussian wars, had a nervous breakdown within twenty-four hours of our ritual.

He had destroyed the attempted Russian invasion of East Prussia, he had destroyed the attempted French invasion of Lorraine, he had destroyed all the defences of Belgium, he had chased away the British Expeditionary Force and he had four Army Groups heading down to Paris. Victory for the Germans seemed to be virtually inevitable. Yet there was Moltke, 200 miles behind the battle front, demanding frantically: 'Where are the prisoners? Where are the captured guns?'

Again, we only learned this after the Great War . . . the Germans were operating to a Plan laid down by the late Count von Schlieffen in 1902. The idea was to knock out France in thirty days and then turn the resources of Germany against Russia. The dying words of von Schlieffen had been: 'Only make the right wing strong.' Moltke did not do this. He took divisions to reinforce German defences in Lorraine against a French attack. Such an attack did indeed occur but reinforcements were not needed.

He then went into a panic over the Russian invasion of East Prussia and transferred *more* divisions from the right wing to the Eastern Front. Again they were not needed.

On the night that we did our Sex-Magick ritual, Moltke failed to take advantage of British and French confusion in retreat. Instead, he allowed Colonel-General Alexander von Kluck, commanding the extreme right wing, to act upon his own initiative.

Kluck thought that he no longer had the strength to encircle Paris as planned and instead wheeled around south-eastwards in front of the city to attack the exposed flanks of the retreating French and English armies. On the night of our endeavour, the French and English counter-attacked in a last desperate attempt to save Paris – and that was when the battle of the River Marne commenced.

The stupid Sir John French had at least to cooperate with Joffre. Of the latter it can be said that the Great War was very nearly lost with him, but that it would almost certainly have been lost without him. As we fucked and sucked, a series of desperate assaults on the German lines and columns commenced, throwing Moltke into further anxiety and confusion.

Moltke sent a staff officer, one Colonel Hentsch, to the front, granting him complete authority. Hentsch, dismayed by the casualties and by the continuing Allied attacks, ordered a temporary retreat from the River Marne to the River Aisne in order to regroup. This was the final German error of the year and it made the Battle of the Marne, which ended on 11 September, one of the most decisive in world history.

The German advance was halted; Paris was saved; and

the French and British Armies now had time in which to recover their equilibrium. We didn't actually know that this would be the result as we were fucking and sucking away. Nor did we know that, after a race to the sea to outflank one another, ending in a dead heat, both sides would then dig trenches that stretched from the English Channel to Switzerland. Attempts to break this stalemate would be mercilessly stopped by machine-gun and artillery fire.

No, we didn't know that then: but we *did* want to have a good time. Claire and I looked around the Temple. The simple but effective mode of fucking used by Douglas was to pull his shaft completely out of Rosemary's cunt before driving it back in between her puffy pussy lips.

'I prefer a man to leave some cock inside my cunt on the outward stroke,' Claire commented.

'Why not?' I replied. 'Yet Rosemary does not appear to be unhappy on account of Douglas's total withdrawal of his tool before it comes plunging back inside her juicy crack.'

'Ah! And this is affecting me!' Claire exclaimed. 'Look at that mirror over there, Horby. Nudity always awakens my sensual passions and a delectable, liquid sensation is suffusing my pussy as I look at myself in the mirror with unashamed delight. With my eyes shining, I allow my tongue to emerge from side to side as I admire my elegant profile. Locks of my silky hair fall forward, the ends caressing my breasts and this sends further electric sparks shooting through my body and causing my rosy nipples to harden and rise.'

Glancing down at her heaving bosoms, I cupped the globular spheres in my hands, squeezing the soft, yielding flesh and tickling the hardening rubbery nipples.

Meanwhile, a wordless growl escaped from Bellingham's throat as he massaged the rounded cheeks of Davina's bottom and then brought his hands round to to her gently curving belly until he finally reached the fluffy thatch of curls between her thighs.

As for Douglas, the merest touch of his fingertips upon the outer cunny lips of Rosemary was enough to make her quiver with unslaked sensual lust: and a lightning flash of liquid fire shot through her entire body when his stray finger brushed the edge of her swollen clitty.

The eyes of Alison were blazing with passion as she looked at Ram Singh and, with her hips undulating in a lascivious rhythm, she pressed against him, crushing her breasts against his chest as she felt his steely stiffstander throbbing against her crotch. Her arms snaked around his shoulders, caressing the hard musculature at the back of his neck as his mouth opened to receive her darting tongue again.

The body of Amin Shah trembled all over as he took Jane's jiggling bum cheeks in his strong hands, kneading the jouncy globes as he pressed her cunt ever more firmly against his erection and made her gasp with excitement.

Yet, suddenly, everything stopped when Maria von Huttendorf threw her body onto the floor and started shouting.

'I am the Great Whore of Europe!' she roared like a lioness. 'And I have dedicated my life to bringing about this Great War. It will last for years and it will destroy all our known notions of civilization! So fuck on!'

'You bitch!' the husband of Emily Ward-Bishop shouted. From underneath a pile of clothing, he produced a revolver and shot her dead.

'You bastard!' Captain Jack Rivers roared as he produced a revolver from underneath *his* pile of clothing and shot dead this wretched man.

'Thank you,' said Emily. 'I only married him for his money, anyway.'